APRIL

APRIL
THE ULTIMATE CALL TO DUTY

REGINALD A. PHILPOTT

Published in the United States of America

ISBN: 978-1-64460-005-4 (*sc*)
       978-1-64460-004-7 (*e*)

Library of Congress Control Number: 2018957818

Published by Stonewall Press
4800 Hampden Lane, Suite 200, Bethesda, MD 20814 USA
1.888.334.0980 | www.stonewallpress.com
1. Fantasy (General)
2. Romance
3. Suspense and Drama
18.09.13

*I would like to dedicate this book to my wife Lyn, my Daughter
Elaine, and my Son James, for all their unwavering support, faith
and encouragement.*

Contents

Acknowledgments

I would like to thank my good friend, Alli Malone,
for her encouragement, her invaluable advice and expertise,
and for unselfishly giving her time to edit this novel for me.
Without her, this book would just still be a dream
on my hard drive.

After spending my life doing mainly manual work I suffered a few major health problems which left me unable to continue my usual lines of employment.

Frustrated and struggling to find a purpose in my life I remembered an ambition I was had but because of the pressures of work was forced to shelve. Many years previously I had read an article that turned out to be a fabricated lie, but I thought then, "what if."

The article told about a man who had vanished from his family home then reappeared sometime later as a different person. His excuse for the disappearance was he had been abducted and forced into what had happened.

I had started to write notes in long hand, pre P.C days, but shelved the project. So now the time had presented itself when I could re-erect my ambition.

Firstly I needed to create a character, then a reason why it might need to happen. But lastly, and most importantly, the way the person would react awaking up to finding that they were no longer the person they once were.

And so armed with this new goal I became another disabled person reborn into a new career. My second April book is close to finished and a third is half written.

In the opening chapter we find April seriously wounded and close to death as she is prepared to be shipped to hospital.

During her recovery April dreamt of how she'd been abducted from her beloved family, then turned into the untraceable killer she'd become. Or so that was how it was meant to be.

As her dream continued April recalled how the agents she had been partnered to stop the threat that was looming ever closer, had been killed, seriously wounded or defected along the way.

Each time April had become close to capturing or killing the powerful Drug Baron he had eluded her and fled.

With no care for her personal safety April continued on steadfastly with the task she had been set willing to die for the safety of others to make a safer world for others.

CHAPTER 1

Bass frantically dragged the lifeless body of Carlos De-Mundo off April as a medic reached her side. The battle hard soldier was moved to tears seeing the extent of her injuries as the medic searched frantically for a pulse.

"I have got a pulse, Sir. But it is an extremely weak one," he explained, as he professionally began to assess April's injuries.

"You must save her, soldier. She is a very special and courageous lady. I'll get you some help," he said, as he rang Field Marshal Sir Charles Hythe-Smith.

"April what's happening?" Charles started.

"It's Sergeant Bass Maloney here sir, I'm afraid I have got some very grave news for you," he began, fighting back the tears.

"What is it Sergeant? Has April been…?" Charles was unable to bring himself to finish the sentence.

"No, Sir, but she is very badly wounded, and her pulse is so weak we can only just detect it. She's holding on to life by a thread. My medic is doing all he can now. She is so damned courageous! We owe her so much," he said, choking back a sob.

"Get her to the hospital at NASA, and I will inform them to prepare for your imminent arrival. We're leaving immediately and will meet you there."

A helicopter started to load the prisoner from the surviving rabble. "Hold one of those choppers. We have a dire emergency here," Bass called, as the lead pilot approached him.

"What's the emergency sir?" he asked, as he looked at the medic working frantically to prepare April for the trip.

"This lady needs to be airlifted to the medical centre at NASA pronto. My medic will travel with you to attend to her." Bass urged the pilot. The young flying officer went to check whether he had sufficient fuel for the trip.

"I've just enough fuel so we can take her aboard. The rest of the prisoners are offering no resistance now. So if you can supervise their loading, sir?" The pilot asked Bass. The two men watched as April was loaded onto the helicopter as it was preparing for lift off, and the onward flight to the hospital at NASA, where April was to be treated.

The medic hastily hooked up the unconscious April to tubes. He then contacted Sir Charles asking for her blood type for the records. Then he connected her to a portable electrocardiograph.

Bringing the engines to life they started to lift from the ground and headed directly for the military hospital at NASA. The medic worked feverishly to stem the bleeding, stopping a number of times in order to resuscitate her.

Eventually landing at the NASA medical centre, they were met by two doctors, a team of paramedics, and a number of nurses. Hastily, but very carefully, they carried the unconscious agent from the helicopter, placing her onto a stretcher, and rushed inside as a second helicopter was touching down.

Sir Charles, who had been in Florida directing operations, and his medical team, poured from the second helicopter as they hurriedly unloaded their specialised equipment. They rushed into the theatre to attach April to the monitoring devices, and inserted the various tubes to help stabilise her life, before they were able to begin the long and arduous process of repairing the mutilated and broken body.

Spending a very long day in the theatre, eventually April's body was wheeled from it and into the recovery ward. The exhausted medical team retired to their quarters for a much earned and overdue rest. Charles left orders to notify him of any changes, no matter how slight they were. Then a fresh team of male and female nurses were appointed to attend at the patient's bedside.

The hours grew into days as April's condition very slowly, but steadily, improved. Charles remained at the complex and constantly received updates on April's condition. Three days had passed before her pulse returned to normal, as she slowly started to show signs of her impending awakening. Eventually April's eyes started to flicker, and then she opened her eyes fully as they grew accustomed to the strong lights in the ward.

Looking around at the unfamiliar surroundings, April's eyes eventually came to rest on Charles. "Hello again, Charles," she croaked as she smiled at him, "Fancy meeting you here."

"Hello, April. How are you feeling now? You've had us all worried sick about you."

"I feel like hell, I'm so stiff. Help me to sit up. Will you, please?" She asked.

Two nurses came forward to say, "We will make you more comfortable Miss Darling, but you are still far too weak to sit up. There's somebody very important here to see you—that's if you are up to visitors now?"

"Who is it, Mandy and the children?" April asked excitedly.

"No, I'm afraid not, but somebody equally as important I think you'll agree." Charles intervened and told the nurses to allow the guest to enter.

April waited patiently through the brief pause that followed. Eventually the doors swung open, two burly security men took up positions on either side of the doorway, allowing the well-dressed man with them to enter the room. April recognised him instantly as the President of the United Stated.

"Forgive me for not standing, Mr. President," she said to him as he approached the chair at the side of her bed and sat down, cupping her hands in his.

"Walter. Please call me, Walter, Miss Darling," the President insisted. "On one condition, if you will agree to call me, April, Mr. President."

"Very well, April, it's my pleasure and privilege to meet you at long last. I have been asking Charles here to introduce us for such a very long time you know, but he kept making excuses why it was not convenient. But now that we have you on our side of the globe, I insist that we have dinner together before you return to the UK. So that we can get to know each other a little better, and on that I do insist, even if it means me requesting the authorities detaining you as an illegal immigrant by withdrawing your passport. Then delivering you to the White House for further questioning," Walter laughed. "But I am determined that we have dinner together this time, April."

"I would be highly honoured, Walter. But why are you so interested in dining with me? I am just an ordinary person working for my country—a non-entity really."

"Well even though you are without any make-up, and in an unflattering hospital gown, you are still a very beautiful and classy lady, April. Besides, we owe you so much; you have helped rid us of that notorious drug baron, Carlos De-Mundo. When we rounded up and questioned the remainder of his henchmen, it led us to arrest another three of the world's most powerful, and dangerous drug lords, and all because of the information that they gave us. We are also at this very moment pursuing a further two. Not only are you very beautiful, and extremely sexy, if I might be so bold as to say that, you are also a very brave and courageous person, April. So we are all deeply indebted to you."

"I would very much like to dine with you, Walter, so let us drop the flattery now shall we? But on a more serious note though, I do need to talk to you about the attitude of a minority of your troops. I imagine you've heard about me shooting one of them in the leg?"

"Yes, but I've told him that he shouldn't have obstructed you in your duty, or tried to countermand your orders in any way. Then I presented him with an award, so he is happy about it all now."

"It's not only that, they can be far too bloody trigger happy at times, and they seem completely devoid of any humanity. But we can talk about that at a later date; over dinner perhaps? Also, there are other things like the deforestation of South America by world business men, Mr. President?" April finished, as the security men re-entered the room to remind him of another more pressing appointment.

"I look forward to our discussion. I will tell the doctors to notify me as to when you are well enough to be discharged, just so I will be able to arrange for our dinner date. But I do insist that it has to be before you return to the UK, April," Walter finished sternly, as the security men ushered him from the room.

Charles who had been sitting quietly amused at April's audacity in criticising some of the American armed forces. He rose to his feet and shook the President's hand, as the President left the room. Then he said to April, "Only you could have got away with those criticisms of some the American servicemen, but didn't I tell you how much he thought of you?"

"Sometimes they only need to be told to correct any problem that they have. As they say, ignorance is bliss. But when they are told about it they will act to correct it," she reminded Charles as the doctor entered.

She asked brightly, "Right, Doc. When can I get up?"

"Normally, it would take somebody four to six weeks to recover, but as your injuries were even more extensive than any I've ever witnessed before, it'll probably take you a little longer than that, Miss Darling."

"You don't know April as I do doctor. She has remarkable self-healing powers of her own. I suggest that we'll just have to wait and see, won't we? But does that stop her from sitting in a chair?"

"No, Sir Charles, not as long as she is careful with the tubes and wires attached to her. I will ask the nurses to see to that for you right away."

Two of the nurses made her more comfortable in a chair while Charles and the doctor were talking to each other out of her earshot. Eventually they approached her and Charles told April, "I've informed the doctor that I need to return to England. Now that he assures me that you are off the critical list, and on the mend, that is. But he has promised to keep me fully informed as to your progress on a daily basis. So, unless you need me to stay for any other reason, I must return home. After all, I do have wedding arrangements to finalise, and one that you need to officiate at."

"You go home to Mandy; I'm in safe hands here. And I can always ring you, can't I Charles?" April reminded him.

After everybody had left, the room became deathly silent as April began to think about how she'd been originally press-ganged into her present persona. In the quiet that encompassed the room, she soon drifted into a deep and natural sleep. Soon April was dreaming, remembering that fateful day when she was having a quiet drink with some friends at the local village public house. A stranger had appeared at the end of the bar, who, unbeknownst to April, was about to change her life beyond all recognition. He was coincidentally passing through her village at that precise moment in time on a mission, and all that had transpired since that first fortuitous meeting leading up to this present moment. The dream continued.

CHAPTER 2

George approached the bar and asked the barmaid, "The same again please, Joyce?"

As she poured the drinks, he noticed a man standing at the end of the bar out of the corner of his eye. He was looking towards him, but as George glanced towards him he quickly turned away, staring back into his pint of beer.

Unbeknownst to George, as the stranger toyed with his beer mat he was reflecting on how he had been chosen for this very unusual assignment. He was an ex-SBS officer, so he had very few true friends, and was used to working and living alone. In fact, the only other person in the department that he knew or spoke to was his immediate superior. The stranger thought that it seemed as though he would never find anybody to fit the criteria that had been laid down for him. He wondered if he was the only field agent to have been set this particularly unusual mission. Perhaps somebody else had completed the mission? He considered contacting the office, but he realised that if somebody had accomplished the task he would have been recalled immediately. So he returned to contemplating his monotonous task.

He looked up from his drink and turned his attention back to the assignment in hand. Again he turned his attention towards George.

He didn't know why, but there was something about him that drew his attention.

George took note of the appearance of this new stranger. He noticed that he was a man who was in his mid 30's, with rugged features. He stood 6ft-3 inches tall and was of slim built, and it was apparent just by looking at him that he took great pride in his personal appearance. It was also patently obvious that he spent much of his spare time working out in a gym. He had black short-cropped hair, and was very smartly dressed.

"Your change, George," Joyce interrupted his thoughts. "Is there something wrong? You seem to be preoccupied tonight."

"Not really," he replied. Picking up the drinks he returned to the table where his wife was waiting patiently.

"Something wrong, George?" Mandy asked. "You seem very worried about something this evening."

"Glance over towards the end of the bar. Can you see the tall man who is on his own? Is he looking towards us?"

"Yes! No! He's just looked away."

"What do you mean, Mandy? Yes! No! Is he looking, or isn't he?"

"He was looking this way, but when he saw me looking towards him he looked away quickly. Why? Is there something wrong with him?"

"Probably it's nothing, but he seems to keep staring at me for some unknown reason." Taking a long drink, and trying to change the subject, he said, "You look lovely tonight, angel." George's wife Mandy was attractive, although not super slim. She stood just over 5ft tall with a nice figure, dark eyes and long black shiny hair to match her eyes. She drew attention to her eyes with skilfully applied makeup.

"So are you, love. That man still keeps looking over at you, maybe he fancies you," she laughed. Then she added, "I know I do," squeezing George's hand affectionately. "Your new friend at the bar seems to be leaving now."

As George turned he saw him heading towards the gentleman's toilet. "No, I think he's just going to the toilet. I think I will go, too."

As he got up as Mandy joked laughingly, "Oh I didn't know you were like that, darling." Then her expression became more serious, she warned, "Be careful, George. He could very well be a pure nutcase."

"I will," he assured her as he left and headed towards the gents. Only being a smallish man, 5ft 6 tall, and weighing approximately eight & a half stone, and as he came from nearby Liverpool, often George spoke first, then put his brain into gear later.

When George entered the gent's toilets, he saw the stranger standing at the far end of the urinals. He glanced up briefly as George entered the room. There was an elderly gentleman about to leave, so George just walked towards the urinals and waited.

After the man had left he asked the stranger, "Do I know you from somewhere?"

"I don't think so," was the curt reply.

Realising by the southern accent that he was also a stranger to these parts, George carried on his inquisition. "It's just that you seem to be staring at me for some unknown reason."

The stranger began to look slightly embarrassed, but before he could answer the door opened and two people entered, deep in conversation.

The stranger looked relieved at this intervention, and he seized his opportunity to leave. "I have to go now I'll see you again sometime. Goodbye," he said as he hastily left.

George returned to where Mandy was sitting, who by now was in deep conversation with their two friends and close neighbours at the next table. As George sat down, she asked him, "Are you satisfied now, darling?"

"I suppose so. He's a stranger to these parts so he's probably just feeling lonely. I suppose he has to look somewhere, so I'm probably just being paranoid about it."

"I was just telling Joe, and Jill that you've clicked," Mandy laughed.

"You should have said something and I'd have come with you, George. Just in case there was any trouble that is," Joe remarked. Joe was an ex-rugby player, 6ft 6 inches tall with shoulders to match.

"No need, but thank you anyway, Joe. He seems harmless enough. Now can we change the subject, please?"

"George, somebody was asking about you, he said that he thought he knew you," remarked Sam, as he passed the table on his way to the bar.

"Who was that?"

"A bloke that was sitting by the end of the bar, but he's gone now, I told him your name and he said that you weren't the person he thought you were."

"He's probably only interested in your love life," Mandy teased with a devilish look on her face. "If he were to see you tomorrow night he really would fancy you. Perhaps I should stay at home in case he comes in here then?"

"Why, tomorrow?" asked Jill. Jill being Joe's wife; who, up until now had just been listening with intrigued amusement.

"The fancy dress evening, you are coming, aren't you. Jill?"

"Of course, we'd forgotten all about that, Mandy. Joe is going to be very adventurous and come in his Rugby strip. What are you coming as, George?" Mandy interrupted quickly. "That's a surprise you'll find well worth waiting for, I promise you. Although you should have found the time to have your haircut, George, it's resting on your shoulder now. Still, it will be helpful for tomorrow night. I'm coming as Cher, Jill. What about you?"

"Oh, Gypsy Rose Lee I thought. It should be a good laugh though. If nothing else, it will certainly liven up Riverlet."

Riverlet was the small country town that George and his family lived in. It was built on the original hamlet, and was so called after the small stream that passed through the centre of the village. There were about 2,000 houses, mostly privately owned, and it was built as an overspill town for Liverpool. Any social life was usually centred on, or around, one of the four public houses. There was a small shopping centre by the village green, and three churches of different faiths. It was fifteen miles to the east of Liverpool and, being very close to the motorways network, it made commuting to Liverpool and Manchester, very convenient for working, shopping and for any other needs.

The rest of the evening went off without any more mention of the stranger, who had returned to the guesthouse where he was staying.

He was giving his weekly report to his superior on his mobile phone.

"Are you any nearer to finding anybody suitable yet, Ron?" His superior asked.

"I'm not sure, Sir. Up until tonight I would have said 'no', but now I'm not too sure. There was somebody, who for some strange reason has taken my attention."

"Oh, and in what way?"

"I can't put my finger on it just yet, Sir, but there's something about him. He is only about 5ft 6ish tall and slimly built, but apparently he can turn his hand to doing just about anything. He's the local Mr. Fix-it, you might say, and he's also quite strong for his size apparently."

"Ok, when will you know more? We are running very short on time now."

"I'll see what I can find out tomorrow evening, Sir, and I'll call you back then. They're holding a fancy dress evening, so it could prove to be very useful."

"Make sure that you take your phone and ring cameras with you. You can then set up a live video link with me, just so that I can have him assessed for you. Also, take some bugging devices so that we can listen in on their conversations."

"Okay, Sir." Ron rang off and went down to the lounge where the only other guest was sitting watching the television.

"Had a good day, Mr., incidentally what is your name?" The lady asked.

"Marks Madam, Ron Marks. I hope so," he replied. Then he added, "If it all goes according to plan tomorrow evening my business up here should come to a satisfactory conclusion, and I'll be able to move on to somewhere else early next week."

"What type of business are you in exactly?" she asked, showing genuine interest.

"Personnel recruitment, Madam," he answered, taking a coffee off the small bar as he respectfully bade her, "Good night Madam," retiring to his room for the rest of the evening.

The following morning, Saturday, was spent as usual shopping during the morning. And after lunch George washed and vacuumed the car. Mandy did the ironing and cleaned the house. As it drew towards the evening meal, their children Pam and Andy began to get excited, because the fancy dress party was to be a family affair. At 7.30 PM, they began to prepare for the family's social evening out.

"Get ready kids," Mandy shouted up. "I've put everything on your beds. I'll finish it off for you when I've got myself ready."

George had just finished shaving as Mandy entered the bathroom. "Can't the children make less noise, Mandy?" he asked, as he walked through into the bedroom.

"You know our children. They're even noisy when they're asleep. Anyway George, it's time for you to get yourself ready, or have you chickened out?"

"No, I haven't," he answered, as he grabbed her playfully around the waist and pulled her onto the bed. "I love you, Mrs. Partridge," George whispered, wrapping his arms gently round her and giving her a long passionate kiss.

As their lips parted she gently pushed him away, telling him firmly, "There's no time for hanky-panky now. The children should be ready soon."

She had no sooner finished saying that than the door flew open and Andy said, "Mum, will you tell, Pam? She said I look sick."

"Pam, stop winding Andy up so we can all get ready, or we won't be going anywhere tonight," shouted George.

"Well, tell him! He keeps saying I look fat and stupid," retorted Pam.

"Wait until you see your father before you call anyone stupid!" Mandy joined in.

"Thanks a bunch," George snapped playfully as he watched Mandy completing her makeup.

"I've laid your clothes out," Mandy told him, as she re-entered the bedroom again after checking the children. "Do you need any help? I just can't wait," she giggled as she left the room again to finish getting the children ready.

George proceeded to get dressed in the outfit. He was going dressed as a temptress in a tight, slinky black dress with all the trimmings—black high heel shoes and stockings, etc. Mandy had even left him some padding for a bust, and long gold drop clip on earrings, with a long black wig to complete the transformation.

"Need any help with your make up, darling?" she shouted up the stairs. "I'll try it myself first," he replied.

After approximately 30 minutes, George descended tentatively down the stairs to be greeted by fits of laughter from his wife and children.

When they had all finally finished laughing, Mandy commented, "You can tell a man has put that make up on. Still, I suppose it goes with the image. Now, its half-past eight so we had better get a move on." Mandy then insisted, "You can walk to the pub like that tonight, darling."

"Ah pet, can't we take the car?" George tried to protest.

"No! The walk will be good for you," she insisted menacingly as she picked up her handbag. Then she handing George a handbag as she opened the front door and gestured with her head for the children, and him to leave. "Come on, chop, chop, I'm going to enjoy this evening," Mandy giggled childishly, "Me, making a fool of you for a change. Come on now."

As they stepped out of the front door there was a loud cheer from a small group of neighbours' that Mandy had arranged as a greeting committee. Amid the wolf whistles and catcalls they all started to walk slowly towards The Smithy, the local pub that was named after the forge that had stood on the original site.

"You're enjoying this, aren't you?" commented George. Whilst trying unsuccessfully to hide his extreme embarrassment.

"I told you when you forgot our anniversary that I'd make you pay for it," Mandy reminded him, with an enigmatic smile.

All the way to the pub there were constant wolf whistles and remarks. George's face was flushed with embarrassment during the slow 15-minute walk, which seemed like an eternity to him. But eventually they did reach The Smithy.

"At last," he said, breathing a sigh of relief.

The relief was short-lived as the bantering and heckling continued with his entrance. Mandy was encouraging the teasing as much as anybody, and George was powerless to do anything about it.

"I don't know why I let you talk me into this," he whispered.

"Because you love me darling, I'll bet you'll remember our anniversary next year though, and every other year after that, won't you?" she reminded him, whilst still giggling like an excited schoolgirl.

Because of the excitement, mixed with his sheer embarrassment, George hadn't noticed the stranger from the previous night, as he approached their table.

"You all seem to be enjoying yourselves this evening, do you mind if I take a photograph of you all?" the man asked, "Just so I can show my wife when I get home."

"No, not at all," volunteered Mandy, as she moved closer to George. "Move in kids, and you two as well?" she told Joe, and Jill, who were just joining them and beginning to soak up the party atmosphere.

"Let me introduce myself. I'm Ron, Ron Marks." He had used the assumed name to hide his real identity, which was actually Robert Montgomery.

As he leaned on their table, they were oblivious to the fact that he had placed a transparent disc on the underside of it with his fingertips. As he straightened up he pretended to stumble, placing his hand on George's back as if to steady himself, as he also attached another transparent disc onto his shoulder. Although it was completely transparent, and undetectable to the naked eye, it was in fact a new and highly sophisticated listening device. But it would dissolve after 24 hours exposed to the air, and leave no trace that they had ever existed.

"Would you like to join us, since you seem to be on your own?" Mandy invited.

"Thank you, but if you don't mind I won't this time. I have to leave early tomorrow morning so I must go and pack soon. I just thought I'd have a few pints in here first."

"Okay, Ron."

As Ron left to return to the bar, Joe said to George. "He seems to be ok, although he only came over when he saw you dressed like that. Don't go to the toilet on your own, will you? Unless it's to the ladies of course," he laughed.

As they all laughed at him hysterically, George told them, "You can all laugh, but there's something weird about that bloke, I'm telling you. You'll see that there is in time."

Joe stood up and went towards the gents' toilets. They were situated in the passageway that joined the lounge bar and the taproom, also allowing access to a rear exit door, which led directly onto the side street.

Five minutes later Joe emerged from the toilets with Ron. They were talking and laughing as they approached the table.

Joe said to him, "See you later, Ron." As he sat down, he told George, "He's recruiting for some big organisation, but he's leaving tomorrow. He says that he has just stopped off here for a short break, to recharge his batteries so to speak."

Mandy interrupted by nudging George, "You're wanted on the stage, Madam."

Arthur the compére was asking for George to join him on the small stage.

"What have you done now?" he asked hesitantly, with a worried look.

"You'll see, my darling," she replied, still grinning mischievously. "By the way, I've told them that you're going out name is April, just so that they won't know it's really you. Well, at least they shouldn't," she pretended to whisper.

By now most of the people near their table had joined in with the bantering, which was making him feel even more embarrassed. "You just wait, you will pay for all of this," George threatened Mandy as he walked towards the stage.

"I don't care. It will all be worth it," she shouted after him. Then she added, "I'm enjoying watching you squirm."

As he climbed onto the stage, amid the deafening wolf whistles and cheers, Arthur handed George a microphone. "You look very sexy tonight, April," he smirked. "What are your plans for later this evening?"

"What's with this 'April." George snapped back. By now he was almost rigid with embarrassment, as agitation was beginning to set in good-style.

"Mandy said that you're going out name was April, and that you would start the karaoke off for us tonight." Arthur told him, blowing George a kiss as he struggled to keep a serious expression.

"You all know that I can't sing," George tried to protest. But ignoring him, Arthur left the stage as the music to 'Lola' began.

He started nervously, "I'm not the world's most natural man, but I know what I am, I'm a man, I'm a man, but so is Lola." There was rapturous applause and laughter at the song that Mandy had chosen for him. As he continued, George began to relax so it didn't sound too bad. By the end of the song there was enthusiastic applause and catcalls, which were more because of the content of the song, than for the quality of the performance.

George had noticed that, all the time that he was singing, Ron had sat facing the stage resting his chin in his cupped hand, and with his index finger stretching upwards in front of his face. His mouth was moving as though he was in conversation, but he was sitting alone and apparently without a phone.

George was unaware of the fact that Ron was using a minute Bluetooth earpiece device, and had put his mobile phone on hands free so it was undetectable. He was in conversation with his superior, who in turn was directing the ring camera, so that he could record and document all that went on that evening.

"Is the bug effective, Sir?" asked Ron.

"Yes, the reception is good, but there are so many people talking that it's hard to single out George's voice pattern. But now that we have his voice pattern from the karaoke, we will be able to single it out." Then after a short pause, Sir Charles added, "You can pack up there now Ron. You have done a most excellent job for us. I'll be in touch with you again very soon."

During the rest of the evening the high spirits continued. Ron slipped away unnoticed as the evening drew towards its conclusion.

Mandy leaned towards her husband, and whispered, "You're not annoyed with me, are you darling?"

"No, of course I'm not. I have quite enjoyed it actually. But I'm still going to get you back though, but in the nicest possible way that is," he promised, kissing her lovingly on her lips.

"Come on children," she called, as they walked home with their arms around each other and their other arm around the children either side of them.

"Have you two enjoyed yourselves?" Mandy asked them.

"Yes," they answered enthusiastically, and told them everything that they, and the other children, had been up to.

After the children had finished a light supper, they were put to bed, and quickly drifted off to sleep due to the late hour. George picked up the remote control and searched for a late film to watch, as Mandy started to ascend the stairs.

"Are you going to get changed, Mr. Partridge, or are you intending to stay like that all night. Would you like to borrow a night-dress perhaps?"

"I'm very comfortable like this. Thank you very much. I can change when I go to bed," he suggested playfully.

"Suit yourself, or should that be, skirt yourself." Mandy giggled as she continued up the stairs, adding teasingly. "But I can see that I might have started something now."

Five minutes later she re-entered the lounge wearing a long black satin negligee. "The children are fast asleep; perhaps we should keep them out late more often. Well, if you want to look like the lady of the house I think you should at least make the supper for us." She was obviously still in a mischievously inebriated mood, as she snuggled down to watch the film.

Rising to the bait, George said to her jokingly, "You can't resist having a go at me, can you?" As he entered the kitchen he asked, "And what would madam like for her supper tonight?"

"Surprise me," was Mandy's casual response.

He eventually emerged from the kitchen with a tray containing a hearty supper of a mixture of bacon and sausage sandwiches. After they had finished eating the TV was turned off, as Mandy threw her arms around George. Kissing and hugging him passionately, she said, "I love you so much, Mr. Partridge. Let's go up to bed now."

"Even when I'm cross-dressed like a woman, you mean?"

"You're still my husband inside no matter what you're wearing; I'll always want just you, and nobody else. And you look absolutely gorgeous to me whatever you are wearing. I must admit though, you would make a gorgeous-looking lady."

Unbeknownst to Mandy and George, all of their slight remarks over the evening were being monitored and relayed by the bugging device.

The following two weeks passed uneventfully, and soon the memory of that eventful evening began to fade, as the day-to-day routines began to take over. There was no more thought or mention of the stranger Ron Marks. They had all dismissed him from their memory of that night, thinking of him as no more than he had described himself as, just passing stranger.

The following Saturday morning, George was busy doing his usual chores of cleaning and polishing the car, as the children with their friends, played in the front garden.

Suddenly Joe emerged from his house next door, followed by his wife Jill. "Can we have a word, George?" he said glumly, walking into their house through the open front door.

"Sure thing, Joe," agreed George, as he followed them into the lounge where Mandy was busy vacuuming. "Why the glum faces? Have you had some bad news?"

"You might say that George we have got to move from here," he told them. "For some strange, unknown reason, the powers that be have decided to end the contract up here. They tell me that if I wish to continue with the company they have a new vacancy for me at the North London branch."

"What are you going to do?" Mandy asked with concern.

"We don't have much of an option, do we?" Jill said regretfully. "We don't want to leave Riverlet, but if we don't take the offer we won't be able to keep up with our mortgage payments."

"They've offered us 15% above the market value for our house, a generous resettlement cheque of 20 grand, plus a promotion, with a large increase in my salary, and a company car." Joe explained solemnly. He confirmed, "It's an offer that we can't really refuse, but we will be leaving such good friends behind us."

Mandy and George sat back open-mouthed due to the sudden shock of the unexpected news. After a few moments, Mandy was the first to break the silence. "When are you thinking of leaving, Joe?"

"That's just it," he replied, with a distraught expression on his face. "We have to move by a week Monday. They'll arrange for the removal van and everything else for us apparently."

"All we have to do is to drive down there and they will do all the rest," Jill added. "They've even found us a nice house in Harlow. Joe apparently will be able to commute from there. We will have to go this afternoon to view the property, and then we'll travel back tomorrow afternoon."

"We'll be very sorry to see you both go," was Mandy's tearful response as she hugged Jill. "But we will come and visit you when you've settled in, I promise."

On the Sunday evening there was a knock on the door which was answered by Mandy. Re-entering the lounge she was followed in by Jill and Joe. Jill told them all about the new house, and the events that had transpired throughout the day.

Then Joe interrupted, "I was talking to Ken, whom I originally met Ken when we were both training together. We have kept in touch ever since. He was telling me, in the strictest of confidence of course, that this position I've been offered was only created last week. He also says that for some unknown reason the house is an important issue in our appointment, but he didn't know exactly why that was."

George asked, "What type of position is it, Joe?"

"They're calling it national coordinator. Apparently I'll be responsible for recording all of the staff's details nationally, and accessing the efficiency of each unit."

"Did he say why they want you, and what the urgency was?"

"That's just it. Ken can't see why they've created the position in the first place. In the past it has always been carried out automatically by computer, and the junior management has always had the responsibility of checking it as an important part of their managerial training. He reckons also, and it's just between us mind, the board isn't at all happy about it all, but somebody very important is behind it and are pulling all the strings. But nobody seems to know who it is, or why."

"That is very strange. And yet you're still taking the offer?"

"It seems I have no option." Then after a slight pause, Joe continued, "It brought back something that you said the other week, George."

"What was that?"

"Remember that bloke? What was his name Ron something? You thought that he was watching you, remember?"

"Oh yes, I remember. What about him?"

"He said he was in personnel recruitment. Maybe it was Jill and me that he was observing, and he could be behind this new appointment."

"And all this time Mandy thought it was my body he was after," George chuckled. Then he added seriously. "Well they must think that you're the right man for the job after going to so much trouble. Let us know if you find out anything more Joe, or whether I can help you in any way at all. What day are you moving or don't you know that yet?"

"It has to be next Friday or Saturday. Apparently the sale on the house can be completed within seven days as it's a cash sale, and your new neighbours are moving in within a week of us going."

"We must have a drink on Thursday evening then," Mandy insisted, as she sadly brushed a tear from her eyes. "I'll make us all a nice cup of coffee. We will be going on our hols in just over two weeks when the school finishes for the summer, so we won't see much of the new people at first."

Over the next few days they saw little of Jill, and Joe, as they were busy packing. On the Thursday evening Jill and Joe bid all their friends a tearful farewell when everyone gathered at The Smithy. They promised to return to Riverlet on a visit at the earliest possible opportunity.

When the new neighbours started to move in, Mandy noticed that, although the furniture was adequate, it was very sparse. It was as if they were newlyweds, setting up in their first home together.

As she was telling George this, Mandy added, "There were a lot of sealed boxes with what looked like computers, or C.D players, electrical stuff like that. His wife says hello, she seems friendly enough, but her husband seems to be older than she is, and seems a bit weird."

George had no reason to speak to them except for a, 'Good morning' or 'Good evening', in passing. While Mandy spent most of the following week preparing for the holidays. Then on the Friday she did her last minute checking, and seeing that they had all that was needed, Mandy packed the suitcases for the early flight on the following morning.

The whole family enjoyed a relaxing holiday in the Dominican Republic. The children enjoyed all their organised activities, while Mandy and George relaxed by the poolside, recharging the batteries, and working on their suntans. All too soon the holiday came to an abrupt end, and the time arrived for them to pack, and return to the humdrum reality of their everyday lives.

When the taxi drew to a halt outside their home, they started to unload the cases. George noticed the curtains move slightly in the new neighbours' window. "We're being spied on," he said to Mandy, nodding towards the partially open curtains. "And by the size of that bloody aerial he's put up, he has a two-way radio as well. I hope it doesn't interfere with our telly or I'll be round there to see him."

"Oh come in and I'll put the kettle on, they're probably harmless enough people," Mandy assured him. "It's teatime, and I'm not going to cook, so who's for a chippy meal?"

"Me, too," the children shouted in unison.

"We'll put the cases in and have a meal at The Smithy if you like." George suggested to her, as he picked up the remaining case and followed her inside. "Then you won't have to wash the dishes up either."

Mandy took the children up to the bathroom, and after making sure that they had washed properly, she told them to change while she got herself ready. George was the last to wash and change, but as he descended the stairs George noticed a bewildered look on his wife's face. "Is there something wrong, pet?"

"I don't really know, George," she paused, and then continued, "I just get the weirdest feeling that somebody's been in our house while we've been away, but I don't know why I feel that way."

"I'm scared mummy," Pamela cried, sensing the worry in her mother's voice.

"Your mother's imagining it all, Pammy," interrupted George quickly, as he tried to allay the children's fears as Andrew clung to him. "Nobody can get in here, it's like Fort Knox. I turned the alarm on and locked up, didn't I? So come on, let's go and eat, I'm starving!"

He avoided any more conversation regarding why Mandy felt so uneasy at home, or asking her what had made her suspicious about having intruders in their home. Reaching The Smithy, they gave their orders for their meals, then George left the bar carrying the drinks. He had no sooner sat down than Jeff, the landlord, approached.

"Had a good holiday folks?" he asked jovially.

"Great Jeff," replied Mandy. "Just what the doctor ordered. It was very relaxing."

He asked, "What do you make of your new neighbours then, George?"

"I haven't seen much of them, but I must say that they seem to be an odd pair. The curtains are always closed, and there's that big bloody aerial mast, which incidentally I don't think they'll have got planning permission for so quick. And then there's their van with blacked out windows and a TV aerial on the roof. Have you seen anything of the 'odd couple' Jeff?"

"Not really. Occasionally they come in for the odd meal. You can't have a proper conversation with them all you get back are one-syllable answers. He seems older than she is so maybe that's why," Jeff added thoughtfully. "You just see them at that table by the window and they talk among themselves, and they always stop talking if anybody goes within earshot of them."

"I felt as though somebody had been into our house," Mandy interrupted. "But as George's pointed out, the alarm's been on so it must be a figment of my imagination."

"I didn't say that exactly. I was just trying not to upset the children," George stressed.

"Talk of the devil," Jeff interrupted as he looked out of the window. "Their black van has just pulled into the car park."

"Well, we'd better change the subject quickly then," Mandy suggested.

"There's nobody getting out of it just yet. The aerial on the van roof is moving though. They must be watching the television in our car park, the cheeky sods. Don't they know that pubs are for drinking or eating, not for watching the television in vans in the car park?" Jeff laughed.

Although Jeff hadn't realised it, in fact it was a sophisticated tracking and listening devise, and was being tuned in to eaves drop on their every conversation.

"That's right, you tell them Jeff, and you can ask them who the hell they are while you're at it," suggested George.

Just then, Jeff's wife emerged from the kitchen with the meals, "Is there anything else I can get you folks?" she asked as she put the last plate on the table.

"No thank you, Carol," Mandy said to her. "It all looks very nice."

"Well enjoy your meals," Carol told them as she returned to the kitchen.

George was about to take his first mouthful of food when Jeff, who was still looking out of the window at the van, interrupted.

"They're getting out of the van and coming in. Well he is, but she's got into the back of van."

As they began eating their meals they gave little more than a slight glance at the man as he entered the lounge. The stranger ordered two drinks and then he left, carrying them back to his van. After the meals were finished, Carol came over to clear the table and asked if they'd enjoyed the meals, and if there was anything else that she could get them.

"No thank you, Carol. That was very nice, and it's saved Mandy having to cook. I'll get some more drinks from the bar though." George told her, standing up and moving towards the bar area. "Can we have the same again Jeff, please?"

"Did you see him in that long black coat he wears? Is he weird or what?" Jeff asked, as he assembled the drinks on a tray.

"Yes, I thought it was the grim reaper at first coming for me. Do they always dress like that?" George joked, as he picked up the tray of drinks.

"Every time I've seen him, but his wife, if they're married that is, she's a lot younger than him and quite good looking, I might add." Jeff explained as George returned to his family bearing the drinks.

After finishing up the drinks they shouted goodbye to the landlords, and left through the side doors to return home. George walked purposely passed the van and turned to Mandy as he remarked loudly. "You can't even see into this van, all of the windows are blacked out and the curtains in their house are kept closed. Either they've got something to hide, or they really are the world's weirdest couple." They then continued to walk home.

Reaching home, Mandy, and George, settled down to watch 'Songs of Praise,' while the children played on their PC's. After the programme had finished, Mandy got the children's clothes ready for the following day, then put the children to bed early. They were weary from the day's travelling. Meanwhile, George made two cups of coffee for Mandy and himself to enjoy while they unwound, and settled down to watch a late film. Reaching the foot of the stairs, Mandy dimmed the lights to make it more cosy and relaxing.

"I've never noticed that before, George." Mandy remarked as she cuddled into him.

"Noticed what? Or do I have to guess?"

"When you dim the lights the alarm sensor above the window has a slight glow."

George looked, and then he looked at the other sensor above the door leading into the kitchen. As he got up he said to Mandy, "The one opposite the window doesn't glow. I'll see if any of the kitchen sensors glow," as he disappeared into the other room. A few seconds later George re-appeared, and told her, "It's the same in the kitchen the sensor facing into the room from the outside walls reflect slightly, the other one doesn't."

"I told you somebody had been in here while we were away," she said looking very concerned.

He went into deep thought, then after three or four minutes asked her, "Have you or the children been into the dining room since we've arrived back?"

"No, we haven't. Why, George?"

"Well darling, I'm no detective, but as we live in a country town and its autumn, the fields are being ploughed, aren't they?" He led

Mandy into the dining room, switching on the lights as they went. "There should be a layer of dust around after two weeks."

He slid the fruit bowl from the centre of the dining table to one side. "Why aren't there any dusty marks around the fruit bowl?"

"I'm getting awfully scared, George!" Mandy exclaimed fearfully, gripping his arm tightly. "Why does somebody want to break into our house and take nothing, and be so careful to leave no trace that they'd ever been?"

"Too much trouble for comfort, I'd say. I'll make sure that the windows and doors are securely locked tonight," George reassured her. And then he promptly went from room to room locking all the windows, and bolting the outside doors. When he had finished, he sat back down alongside Mandy, placing a reassuring arm around her.

"I've just been thinking, George."

"Now that is a novelty," he jested, trying to make her feel at ease.

"I'm serious you buffoon," she rasped sharply. Still wearing a very worried frown, "There have been a lot of little things happening over the last couple of months."

"Like what, sweetheart?"

"Well there was that Ron what's his name? You know, when we had that fancy dress evening? Then Joe and Jill had a promotion offer out of the blue, one that they apparently, well according to Joe that is, were left with no alternative but to accept. He had to move quickly because, well again according to Joe's friend, somebody was anxious to move into the house next door to us. And now there's the odd couple next door, Morticia and Gomez."

"You're turning into a proper little Miss Marples, aren't you?" He tried to sound unconcerned.

But unbeknown to Mandy, George was also very disturbed by the way it seemed Jill and Joe had been forced into moving. So he suggested, "I think maybe I should ring to see how Joe's getting along."

Moving to pick the telephone up he stopped abruptly.

Mandy asked, "What's the matter, George?"

"Oh nothing," he told her. Then he turned to pick up his mobile. As he did so George touched his finger to his lips, signaling to her to keep off the reason for using his mobile in preference to the landline.

George dialled the number. After three or four rings, Joe answered. "Hello."

"Hi Joe, it's George, how is everything going down there? Have you settled in okay?"

"Not really George, we wish we were back up there with you guys. I don't even know why I've been sent down here; I sit round most of the day looking for something to do. How are you all doing up there? And how are your new neighbours?"

"That's why I'm ringing. Since you left, the people that have moved into your house never speak to anybody. They keep their curtains drawn night and day; even their van has blacked out windows."

"Weird or what, all I know George is they were anxious to move into Riverlet as soon as possible," Joe explained. "But I have no idea why it was so imperative to move into our house."

"The bloke that you know there, does he know anything about them, Joe?"

"I don't know, when we arrived here he'd gone and nobody seems to know where too, or why. He seems to have vanished into thin air." Then after a brief silence Joe suggested. "Maybe you should give them a knock, and asked them straight out whom the hell they are. If nothing else, it would put your mind at rest. You sound very worried, and I know that's not like you George."

"It's just little things that don't add up. Mandy thinks we've had an intruder while we were away on our holidays, but whoever it was has cleaned up after them, and I mean meticulously."

"Maybe she's just imagining it, George."

"No, Joe, you know how dusty the houses get here, particularly at this time of year. Yet there's not a single speck of dust on the polished dining table after two weeks."

"Do you wan—."

The line suddenly went dead. George tried to redial, but without any success. He then tried Jill's and Joe's mobile numbers, but again without any success. Finally, George called the operator and explained his reasons for concern, but she had no success in reconnecting him either.

"What's wrong, George?" asked a worried Mandy.

"I was speaking to Joe when the line suddenly went dead on me, but the operator thinks it may be a line fault, so she's going to report it to the engineers' tomorrow morning."

"Then why are you looking so worried?"

"Well, if it is only a line fault Mandy, then why can't I reach them on their mobiles?"

"You have to ring the police to see if they know anything," Mandy insisted. After phoning the Harlow police, who said that they'd had no reports of anything-untoward happening to date, but as George was very insistent that something was not right, they assured him that an officer would call round to check on them, and he would report back personally.

George left his number then he replaced the receiver. He told Mandy what was happening before going into the kitchen to make them a fresh cup of coffee each, to keep them awake and pass the time, whilst they waited for the police to report back.

An hour had passed before the front door bell rang. Mandy opened the door and walked back into the lounge followed by the local policeman, PC Martin Driver, who looked extremely serious.

"I'm sorry to have to call so late folks, but Harlow police have insisted that I call round and speak to you personally," he began.

"Has something happened to Jill, or to Joe?" Mandy asked him frantically.

"First of all sit down, won't you? It's both of them I'm afraid," he told them. "Apparently there was a gas cylinder in the house which exploded, fatally injuring both of them. They died on the way to hospital without ever regaining consciousness."

Mandy and George stared at each other open mouthed, a look of disbelief on their faces. After what seemed like an age had passed, George was the first one to break the silence. He asked Martin, "Did either of them suffer?"

"No, thank God, neither of them ever regained consciousness. They wouldn't have felt a thing," he reassured him.

"Why would Joe have a gas cylinder in the house, Martin? He didn't go caravanning or camping, and he didn't use it for his work.

Something doesn't quite sit right with me about this." George remarked thoughtfully, his voice a mixture of emotion and profound concern.

"What makes you say that, George?" Martin asked.

Mandy and George explained all that had happened to them, and voiced their personal fears for their own safety. PC Driver sat down and listened with intrigue to everything they told him. Then after they had finished he sat back, seemingly pondering it all.

Finally he admitted. "Before I joined the police force I was with the army's special service unit." As he spoke he walked round the room looking at the alarm sensors. Reaching up to one of them, he slid his hand over the reflective strip, and then with his thumbnail he teased up the corner of the strip before peeling it off.

After examining both sides of the strip, he then signaled, by touching his lips, that they kept quiet as he went round removing any remaining strips. He switched on the standard lamps as he looked carefully around them. Then he paused and looked carefully at the mirror showing them that someone had moved it slightly. He again turned his attention to the bulb in the main light and removed it, asking Mandy for a replacement bulb that he then fitted. Moving to the telephone he unscrewed the mouthpiece, and then removed a minute device from it.

Martin gestured for them to follow him into the kitchen, where he turned the radio and water taps full on. Standing closely, he whispered to them that somebody with influence was obviously very interested in what they did, and everything that was said. Martin then left with all of the evidence, promising that he would keep them fully informed about everything. But first he needed to ask forensics to examine the evidence.

"What's happening to us George?" a scared Mandy asked.

"I wish I knew, pet, but if I catch the bugger who's behind all of this," then raising his voice to a higher level shouted, "I can promise them that I'll make the bastards very, very, sorry." He turned back and took Mandy in his arms. "Darling, we have to promise each other that we won't lose hope if either one of us were to ever go missing."

Mandy hugged him, "Why do you say that? You know that I won't. Let's go to bed now. I'm very tired, and I just want you to hold me tight."

The next morning after taking the children to school, George and Mandy returned to find the police going in and out of the house next door. After parking the car in the driveway, Martin Driver approached. "Your suspicions seemed to have been correct about your new neighbours, George."

"Why is that, Martin?" Mandy asked anxiously.

"After what I found in your house I decided to ask for an emergency warrant, so that I could gain access into their house," he started to explain, gesturing to the neighbouring property before he continued. "But when we arrived at 0900 hours, the house was already empty. It looks like whoever it was, was so afraid of being exposed that they've decided to finish up whatever it was that they were doing here, and then vanished."

"What made you suspicious enough to ask for a search warrant, Martin? And I wonder when they went? Because I never heard a thing," George said with disbelief.

"The farmer saw two black vans speeding towards the motorway at around 0430 this morning. All that is left in there is the sparse bits of furnishings they had."

Then he continued, "The reflective strips on the alarm sensors aroused my suspicions of them. You see, just before I left special ops we were experimenting with them. We used them to bounce radio waves for listening devices, so as to give a better quality signal, and an all-round quadraphonic reception, by using the alarm sensors." Martin continued, "It seems that you have scotched whatever they were up to. So Mandy, you can sleep soundly at night from now on."

"Thank you, Martin," she said gratefully. Turning to George she muttered sorrowfully, "I suppose you'll have to go to work now that I don't need a protector. I was looking forward to a cosy day together."

"Just before you go George," interrupted Martin again, as if he had just remembered. "Somebody's left a note on my desk to suggest that you represent us all at the funeral for Jill and Joe. You seem to be the obvious choice as you were the best of friends. Also, you are a church-going family. So what do you think?"

"Well, yes. I would be going anyway. When is it to be, Martin?"

"I'll have to let you know. The autopsies are being done today, so I should know more by tomorrow at the latest."

"I will probably have to stay with the children, so will you be all right travelling that far on your own?" Mandy asked.

"Yes, of course I will. I can easily manage to drive there and back in the same day," George reassured his wife.

CHAPTER 3

As the morning of the day prior to the funeral dawned, the ringing of the telephone awakened George at five thirty.

"Hello," he said in a sleepy voice, looking at the time on the alarm clock.

"Sorry it's so early George, but I thought you'd be getting up very shortly anyway, and I will have to leave soon to appear as a witness in court," Martin apologised. "I have managed to wrangle some time off, so if you'd like me to come along with you tomorrow and share the driving, it would be my pleasure."

"I'll be glad of the company, thank you Martin. I was thinking that if we left here around seven in the morning, then we would arrive there in plenty of time for the funeral."

"Ok, I will see you about seven then, George. We'll use my car so that Mandy won't be without a car for taking the children to school, etc. Is that okay with you?"

George, thanked him before replacing the receiver, and then explained to Mandy, what would be happening the following day. Mandy admitted to George that she felt relieved that he will have company on the trip, especially as she realised how upset he might be feeling after the funeral was over. She added, "You know, Martin is turning into a real friend to us. He's not only averted whatever sinister deed was being planned for us, but he's taking the trouble to make your journey a much safer one." As she dressed she confessed. "I know it puts my mind at ease, just knowing that somebody's sharing the driving with you."

George finished off a porch that he was building for a customer. Then he visited the wholesalers on his way home to order the materials that were needed for Monday, when he would be starting his next job.

He showered, and retired to bed early to be fresh for the trip the following morning. Rising early, George showered again to wake himself up, and then descended the stairs as Mandy was placing his breakfast on the table.

"I thought you would need a hearty breakfast, just in case you don't get enough time to eat on your way down there, particularly if the traffic's bad." Mandy said to George, as she kissed him. "You really needed to have your hair cut; it is resting on your shoulders now. Still, the people will be too upset to notice I suppose."

"Thanks, pet. You're just too good to me. I just haven't had any time these last few months. Maybe tomorrow I'll find the time to get it cut." George told her, as he started to eat.

Hardly was the breakfast finished, when the sound of a car horn could be heard. Mandy looked out of the window, telling him. "Martin's here, George. Shall I let him in?"

"No, I'm ready now," George said as he picked up his coat and bag. "This is one journey I wish I didn't have to make though." George kissed her passionately before he left.

As he walked towards Martin's car, George noticed the back of the car was very low, as if there were some heavy object inside of the boot.

"What's in the boot, Martin? All you're worldly possessions by the look of the weight. Aren't you planning on coming back, or something?"

"It's for a stop I need to make on the way home," he explained as they started off. "You just relax and I'll drive as far as Birmingham. Then you can take it from there?"

"Fine by me, Martin." he agreed, relaxing back into the seat.

The journey was uneventful as the traffic was flowing freely. Martin had very little to say during the trip, but George presumed it was because of the sad and sombre occasion that they were attending. Making good time, and having plenty of time to spare, they stopped at the last service area to buy snacks and to freshen up before reaching Harlow.

After the funeral was over, George gave his condolences to the couple's relatives, adding their farewell before beginning the long trek back home. During the return journey, Martin seemed even less talkative than he had been on the outward trip. After they had travelled a short distance, Martin offered George a bottle of Coke. He explained, "I'm sorry, but I broke the seal by accident I haven't drunk any of it though, honestly," he jested.

"That's okay, Martin. I am a bit parched," George said as he accepted it gratefully. "After I've wet my mouth I'll ring Mandy to tell her we're on our way home, and how the funeral went."

As George started to drink he noticed Martin had a strange, even bordering-on-evil, smile. After taking long drink George got his mobile out to ring Mandy, but he seemed unable to co-ordinate his movements properly.

"Is there something wrong with you, George?" Martin asked, as he smiled ominously towards him.

George struggled to answer. He started slowly but with extreme difficulty, "I don't feeeel weeeell," George slurred out. "Ge e et m me t-t-to o a d do doct." Then he could not say anything more, and was unable to move a muscle. Only his eyes were responding as he glanced towards, Martin, who by now had pulled onto the hard shoulder.

Martin was making sure that George's seat belt was securely fastened. Saying as he commenced driving, "Don't panic George, you're not dying. The Coke was spiked. Yes, I will take you to a hospital, but you may wish, no, you will wish, that I hadn't." He paused as he negotiated a tricky intersection to leave the motorway. Then he resumed, "You know George, you were right this morning. I have got most of my worldly goods in the boot. The department have moved the rest of my things on ahead of us." He stopped and looked towards George, and he smiled a sickening smile. He then continued once again, "Of course I left no forwarding address so it's as if we just disappeared," he explained, shrugging his shoulders to show his lack of concern. Smiling smugly he added, "I'm still a member of the special services. You see, once you're a member of this elite group, you are always available to be recalled for a mission at any time. Robert, you know him as Ron of course, used to serve under me. When he recognised me and told his superiors, I was immediately re-enlisted." Martin stopped talking for a while as he seemed to struggle to remember the way. After one or two minutes, he resumed with, "I'm sorry if I misled you George, and of course you're very beautiful wife, who I've fancied like mad. When I pretended to uncover evidence, I was actually removing all the traces that we'd ever been there in the first place. So you see George, there's no proof to substantiate Mandy's story."

George could see that they were now heading towards the Cotswolds as the car began to climb a steep gradient. Martin slipped the car into a lower gear and pushed the accelerator pedal hard to the floor as the car began speeding up the hill. He continued, "We will soon be there George, then all will be revealed." With an evil laugh he added, "In more ways than one I might venture to add. Still, I believe you once said that you rather enjoyed it, so perhaps it may turn out that I have done you a big favour."

Martin remained mostly quiet for the remainder of the trip, which lasted around forty-five minutes. This pleased George, as he struggled to gather his thoughts, and make some sense out of what was happening to him. Like what did he mean perhaps he was doing George a big favour, and about him saying that he'd rather enjoyed it once, enjoyed what? It wasn't making any sense. He struggled silently to make some sense of what Martin had said, as he watched as the country lanes unwound in front of the car, with Martin negotiating the sharp bends skilfully, one after another. Although fastened securely in a seat belt, George was still being swung from side to side, unable to steady himself due to the paralytic-induced state he was in.

Finally, the car slowed down as it approached what looked like a private estate, with a very high wall surrounding it. Immediately behind the wall was a densely-treed area that ensured total privacy to the estate. This made it onerously unwelcoming to any would-be trespassers. Security cameras were in abundance to detect any encroachment upon its perimeter. The car drew to a halt in front of large iron gates, which were guarded by armed soldiers. A sign on the gate read, 'Private property of the Ministry of Defence. Keep out. Trespassers will be severely dealt with.' An armed guard approached the car, and another pointed his rifle towards the driver. Martin got out of the car and presented the guard with a document. After reading the contents of the document, Martin was allowed access, but was given an armed escorted up the long winding driveway. Finally the car came to a halt at the entrance to what could only be described as an extremely large, and very old, country manor. The access was up a flight of ten wide stone steps, which in turn lead to a pair of large oak double doors flanked on either side by armed sentries.

The doors swung open and four nurses came out, two male and two female, one of them was carrying a wheelchair. They were accompanied by a doctor, and a distinguished looking gentleman of around forty plus years of age, looking very official in his pin stripped suit. The car door swung open, and the nurses began to manoeuvre George silently into the wheelchair. As he was being strapped firmly into the chair, the distinguished gentleman began speaking.

"Welcome, George. There's no need to be afraid now," he tried unsuccessfully to reassure him. "We'll take very good care of you here," he continued, as the nurses completed strapping him firmly into the wheelchair. "I'm Field Marshall Sir Charles Hythe-Smith."

"What about me, Sir?" Martin interrupted. But he was soon to wish that he hadn't.

"You, Mr. Driver, are a very callous, sadistic, and extremely obnoxious person," retorted Sir Charles. "You have been monitored by a camera and microphone that we planted in your car. You took great pleasure in tormenting poor George here, even though he was already in a very confused state of distress." He signaled to the sentries to descend the steps, telling them. "Place him under armed guard; I will deal with him later."

Martin tried unsuccessfully to protest. They ignored his plea and he was led away by the sentries.

The nurses positioned themselves at each corner of the wheelchair, and then raising it, began to ascend the steps very carefully. Once they had reached the top of the steps, the chair was lowered to the ground, and then all but one of the nurses returned to their normal duties.

The remaining nurse pushed the chair through the doorway with Sir Charles walking alongside it. Going past a grand and winding staircase, the nurse continued on down the passageways silently, turning left, then right, until finally reaching the end of the long maze of corridors. Sir Charles opened a door and the chair was wheeled through into a round office.

"Here we are at last, George," said a relieved Sir Charles. He locked the doors before sitting behind his desk and making his introductions. "This is Nurse Jody Blackman, and she will be your personal nurse during your stay with us." Sir Charles programmed a predetermined code into his mobile phone and slid his hand under the desk to push a button. Shutters closed across the windows and George felt a moving sensation as the office began to revolve.

Nurse Jody noticed the look of fear on George's face. "Don't panic, it's all perfectly safe here. We're only going into another room," she explained as she tried to reassure him. The room stopped turning with a small jolt, and a door opened leading to a small ante room. Jody pushed the chair through into the adjoining room, followed closely by Sir Charles. He closed the doors which then triggered the new room to begin revolving. When it stopped, Sir Charles took a key from his pocket and opened a small panel adjacent to the door. Keying in a predetermined code, the room started to move again, but this time it began descending.

"I'm sorry about the theatrics, George," Sir Charles began to explain, "but this is a top secret establishment. I mean a very top-secret establishment like you have never seen before. From here we are able to perform all sorts of experiments and operations that the NHS can only dream about. The best thing is that we are not answerable here to anybody, so you can appreciate the need for all of this security."

The lift came to a stop then the doors opened silently. George was wheeled out into a brightly-lit private hospital corridor. As he was pushed along passageways, passing operating theatres, laboratories empty wards, and staff rooms, Sir Charles continued to speak jovially.

"I know you must find all this very daunting George, but let me assure you that we have assembled in here the finest medical team in the world. They are simply years ahead of any opposition. We can assure you of the finest medical treatment, and to you this will all be totally free." He paused while he told Jody to avoid the cleaners. Turning his attention back to George, he continued speaking. "When we have made you very comfortable, we will remove the paralysing drug from you. It's futile down here to try shouting, or escaping," he warned. Then wearing a more stern expression, continued, "We are over two-hundred feet below ground level. And this place is designed to withstand a nuclear attack. Also it's totally self-sufficient. We even boast our own air purifying unit that can keep purifying the air contained down here indefinitely."

The chair stopped at the doors to a private suite. As George was pushed through the doors he could see that it was fitted out in pure luxury. Jody wheeled the chair over to the bed and two male nurses appeared to transfer him onto it. They then left the room again without uttering a word.

Jody assisted Sir Charles in securing George's wrists and ankles to the cot sides. As they did so, Sir Charles explained that it was purely a temporary precaution for his own safely. Then he added with reflection, "Plus ours of course."

He felt a sharp pain in his arm when Jody administered the anti-paralytic injection. Then slowly, George could feel his mobility returning, as a tingling sensation crept over his entire body, starting moving upwards from his feet, until eventually he had movement in his entire body.

While moving only his head from side to side to release the stiffness, George was able to take in a fuller picture of the room. He could see by its fittings it had obviously been previously used by a female patient. The bed was made up with white satin sheets, and there was a dressing table on the right-hand side adorned with an assortment of jewelry and make up. Looking to his left, he noticed an easy chair next to the bed, and a comfortable settee bearing an assortment of silk covered scatter cushions.

There was a television, and a door behind it leading to an adjoining room. Then turning his head he noticed an open door behind him leading to the bathroom. George returned his stare to the front, asking, "Would somebody please explain to me what the bloody hell is going on?" He retorted sharply, while trying desperately to free his hands, "I'm not ill, and I haven't been in an accident. I was just drugged by that fucking maniac, Driver. So what the fucking hell is going on?" His voice was getting louder, as he grew more and more frustrated.

"Well," began Sir Charles, "to coin a corny old phrase, your country needs you. Our intelligence sources have revealed some very disturbing facts, and if they are correct, and we believe them to be so, the western world countries will become the third world countries, very, very soon, now."

"Yes, okay. But what has that got to do with me?" George snapped with growing frustration.

"I'm just coming to that. We have realised that sending one of our regular field operatives would simply not do, because we are well aware of each other's agents at a glance, and of their individual capabilities. The ones that we have sent have all disappeared."

"Ok. But what the fucking hell's that got to do with me?" George interrupted again, as he struggled to free his hands.

"If you'll stop interrupting me George, I'll get to that. Now what we'll need is to introduce somebody that they will not know, or be able to trace." Sir Charles, watching George struggling relentlessly, advised, "Save your energy George, the shackles are made of stainless steel. You haven't got a hope in hell of snapping them."

"Well release me," he demanded.

"Soon, I promise," assured Sir Charles. "Now where was I? Oh yes, while planning how we could best deal with the forthcoming threat, a master plan was hatched." Sir Charles paused while drawing his chair closer to George. "We obviously have a limited time in which to prepare, so we had to have a strategy. What we decided we needed firstly was, well it had to be a newcomer, somebody that is unknown to anybody outside of this unit. Secondly, what type of person? We needed somebody who is capable of working alone if necessary, using their own initiative. Then they must have adaptability, intelligence, and above all, a strong sense of loyalty and survival. But most importantly, they needed to have no traceable past. There are other points, but I have told you just the basics. So after a very lengthy and arduous search, Robert Montgomery came up with your name."

"Who the fucking hell is this Robert Montgomery nut?"

"I think you knew him as Ron Marks. Remember he was at The Smithy the night you had that fancy dress party? Well, he provided the means to enable us to observe you."

"I knew there was something sinister about that fucking slime bag," George snapped angrily.

"He was only following orders, George. He really is a very nice person when you get to know him. He's one of the best operatives we've got actually," Sir Charles explained. "Anyway, we observed you and agreed with Roberts's assessment of you. As we decided that we were running out of time, and other options, we needed to act very quickly."

George was thinking about all that Sir Charles was saying to him. Suddenly, his expression changed to one of anger. "It was you who killed Jill and Joe." George insisted, pulling violently at the cuffs again, trying desperately to free himself.

"No, believe me it was only a fortuitous accident. I do admit though, that we did turn it to our advantage."

George calmed down again and collapsed back onto the bed exhausted. Then he asked, "Okay, you have my attention, so what now?" After a few seconds he asked, "And what about Mandy, and the children?"

"Well," began Sir Charles. "Mandy has been told that you've only gone missing. We've paid a large sum of money into your joint bank account, just so that she'll be financially solvent for now. We will just have to take things as they come. And of course we will keep an eye on her for you."

After a short pause to assess George's reaction, Sir Charles then continued, "Don't worry George, your family will want for nothing."

"They'll want me." George said through clenched teeth. By now he was wearing a look of utter confusion and fear. Realising he was trapped, he added cautiously, "Well, I seem to have no option other than to go along with your sick little plan, do I? That is, at least for the time being."

"Good man, George," a relieved Sir Charles said as he stood to start removing the restraints. "Now perhaps we can remove these. Then I'll leave you in Jody's very capable hands."

"What's next?" George asked him.

"Well, Jody will spend the next couple of days administering the treatment you'll require, and then we'll have to take each step as it comes."

As Sir Charles left, Jody, who up until now had sat quietly in the corner, got up to commence her duties very efficiently.

Up until now, George had paid very little attention to Jody. But as she approached the bed he noticed that she was an attractive, slimly built, blond, who stood two or three inches taller than he did. She spoke in a soft West Country accent, and was dressed in a tailored white blouse and a black pencil skirt, which reached to just above her knees. The top two buttons of her blouse were open, revealing the plunging cleavage from her amply-sized breasts, and her shoulder-length wavy hair hung loosely, as it brushed against her cheeks. She looked to be approximately twenty-five years old, and a very beautiful young woman.

"Shall we get started, George?" she suggested cheerfully. Jody then moved his legs round to leave George sitting on the edge of the bed.

"I'll take your pulse, blood pressure, temperature, some samples, and do all of the usual boring medical checks first."

As she efficiently carried out her duties, she chatted generally and continuously. She asked George to undress and relax, and after a few hours had passed, she finally finished.

"That's the boring stuff out of the way. Now, how about some tea?" she suggested to him softly.

"That'd be very welcome," he replied with a hoarse voice. "It seems to have been such a long time since I've had anything pass my lips."

Jody picked up the telephone on the small table and asked for a meal to be served to them. As she turned back to face George, she saw that he had started to dress.

"Not in those clothes," she insisted, taking them from him. "Put these on," she told George firmly, as she handed him white silk pyjamas, and a silk dressing gown to match.

He looked at them and exclaimed, "These are women's clothing!"

"Yes, but nobody will see you. They're mine actually. Just put them on for the time being, until I can get you some new ones."

George tried in vain to protest, but Jody ignored him as she began to dress him in the pyjamas. Saying to him, "There, now that's not so bad now, is it?" as she finished doing up the buttons. "Now put the gown on," she ordered in a patronising, matronly manner.

Realising that it was futile to argue with her, he donned the gown as a trolley was wheeled in laden with a large variety of food. "Will there be anything else?" inquired the chef.

"No, that will be all. Thank you, Chef," Jody told him. "Can you give George's clothes to the laundry, please?"

The chef glanced at George and gave a wry smile, as he left the room.

Feeling very embarrassed, George blushed profusely. "Nobody will see me, you said. Who the hell was that then, Scotch mist? Now can you arrange for me to get my own clothes back please, seeing that you've had them removed?"

"They're being cleaned," Jody lied. "I spilt a drink over them."

"I never saw any sign of a drink being spilt," George said sternly, as he was growing more concerned as to the real reason for his incarceration. He found himself trapped in what could only be described as a secure and sinister, medical unit. And one that had a free license to do whatever it pleased. And they wouldn't be answerable to anybody; to use Sir Charles's own wording. "When will I know fully the reason why I'm here, and what exactly they're going to do to me? I'm not sick, so why have they got me here?"

"You know as much as I do, George. My job is only to see just how healthy you are," Jody explained apologetically. "What I do know is that you're going to be all right, and it is a matter of national security. That's why I'm only told what I need to know."

"What about these clothes I'm wearing. They're not yours, are they?"

"No. Well not really. I'm not sure about them either," she replied. Taking his hand as she sat next to him, she added, "But I promise you that I'll take very good care of you."

"I just wish I knew what's going to happen to me. I find all of this very foreboding," he explained fearfully. "And for how long must I wear these clothes?"

"Why, what's wrong with them really?" Jody asked, trying hard to allay his apprehensions. "You look very sexy in them, so try thinking of them as unisex pyjamas. Anyway, what does it matter which side they fasten on? And as all the staff here are aware of your importance to national security, then that's all that really matters, isn't it?"

He grunted his assent although unconvinced by Jody's explanations. "I suppose I don't have much of a choice in the matter anyway, but when can I see, or at least speak to, my wife, Mandy?"

"That's also something I haven't any answers for, but I will try to find that out for you," she told George reassuringly. "But for now just try to relax, you're perfectly safe here with me, so try to enjoy the rest." Jody suggested brightly as she left the room.

Jody went to her office. Sitting at her desk she picked up the telephone to report to Sir Charles voicing her concerns about her patient's state of mind. "He's having trouble accepting everything," Jody told Charles with concern. "You implied that he would settle down much more quickly, and said that eventually he'd accept things much more readily."

"We thought he would," replied a concerned Sir Charles. "Perhaps we should bring everything forward as quickly as possible. Then he won't have any other option but to comply, will he? And everything will be so different from then on."

"I'm not sure what you mean, Sir. I thought that there's to be a period to allow George to adjust to whatever it will be, mentally first, and then physically."

"I think we may have slightly misjudged your patient, Nurse Blackman," reflected Charles. "You will just have to keep him occupied until everything's prepared. That should be at least another four to five days' time."

"And how am I supposed to do that, Sir?" Jody asked abruptly.

"You're a woman aren't you? I'm sure you'll think of something. Remember that's why you are so highly paid by us."

Jody was annoyed by Charles's implications. Although she felt a certain sexual attraction towards George, Jody felt reluctant to go any further, fearing that he would spurn any sexual advances she made towards him. After all, he repeatedly expressed his concern over contacting his wife. Also, Jody was aware that every word and movement she made was being monitored.

After a few moments thought, she said to, Sir Charles. "I don't think he will have any interest in me sexually, so I don't really know what else I can do exactly. I've tried to reassure him, as you very well know."

"All I ask of you is for you to give it your best shot, Jody. I'm sure that you'll be able to use those womanly charms of yours to our best advantage."

"Ok, I'll try. But turn those bloody monitors off first. I will need to get something from the pharmacy to help me though," she insisted.

"Well done! Now I must go. Keep me informed won't you, Nurse Blackman?"

When she returned to where she had left George, she found the room to be empty. Her first reaction was one of sheer panic, but then she realised that he would never be able to find a way out. Asking a passing cleaner if she had seen a man leaving the room, Jody learned that George had walked down the corridor in the direction of the exit. But she was safe in the knowledge that the lift access was well and truly concealed, as she walked briskly after him.

Following the directions as he could best remember, George headed straight towards the lift shaft. When he reached where he thought it would be, he found himself confronted by what looked like a small office. He tried the door and found it to be locked. He looked through a window, but the office seemed empty except for a computer, a desk, and a chair. As he gazed into what seemed to be the window, something seemed artificial about it. Leaning against his hands to peer through, he thought 'it doesn't feel like glass.' Then George turned to look at the opposite wall and could see the sign, 'You are entering a high security area, trespassers will be shot on sight.' He looked up in the direction that they had pushed him, and could see the dispensary. So he knew without a doubt, that he had left the lift here where he was standing.

"There you are George," he heard Jody's relieved voice calling. "You shouldn't wander off alone without informing somebody, and that's namely me. Anyway, what're you doing here?"

"I was just stretching my legs. After all, you kept me immobilised for long enough," he explained, thinking it was better not to tell her the real truth, which she had probably already suspected anyway.

As they walked back together George chatted generally. Jody found this very infuriating. Every time she tried asking him more about why he was where she had found him, and what he was doing there, George avoided answering her by changing the subject. So she conceded that George wasn't going to give her a straight answer, and resorted to giving him a warning.

"Sir Charles will insist that I lock your door whenever you're left alone, George." So eventually he promised to let her know if he intended to have another wander round.

"Good" she said with relief. "Now why didn't you eat something? Wasn't it to your liking?"

"Yes it was. I just felt like a walk to stretch my legs first."

Reaching the room, Jody told him to go in while she ordered something fresh from the kitchen. George sat and watched some television, unaware that Jody had an ulterior motive for visiting the kitchen. On the way, she'd asked the pharmacist for a tasteless drug to add to George's food, so that it would make him more susceptible to her advances later that evening. The pharmacist was used to such unusual requests, so he didn't query why she wanted it.

Eventually the pharmacist emerged from the storeroom carrying a small phial. "This will do what you want, Jody. It's not like a date rape drug. Whoever it is will be fully aware of what they are doing, but unable to resist, and they will be able to perform for a much longer period of time than they would normally."

"Thanks. Will it have any side or after affects though?" Jody asked cautiously.

"No, just add a drop to the food or drink. It is completely tasteless and colourless, so it will not be detectable. It will stimulate the sexual prowess of whomever, and increase their sexual drive, as I've already explained."

"Ok, how long does it take to work, and how long will it last for?"

"It will work within fifteen minutes, and last for at least twelve hours," the pharmacist explained.

Jody left the pharmacy putting the small phial into her pocket, to keep it safe until later that evening. Collecting the trolley of food en-route, she rejoined George and they ate lunch together. This way, she could be sure that he ate his lunch, and didn't go on another exploratory walk about. As they chatted idly while eating, Jody suggested that she take him on a tour of the area later. This was something that Sir Charles had suggested, so that she could try to allay any burning curiosity he still held. This they did when the meal was finished.

While ambling round the area, Jody hugged his arm closely against her. She continually pulled it against her breast while trying to arouse some sexual feelings within him, hoping it would make it unnecessary for her to use any drugs. But any sexual feelings starting to swell within George, he kept well and truly hidden. After they eventually arrived back at the room, Jody asked. "Well, now you've seen everything George. How do you feel about it all?" She drew close to him and clasped her hands behind his neck.

Rejecting her advances, he pushing her gently away, he asked, "Where was the lift that we came down in? You haven't shown me that. Have you, Jody?"

"Oh, it's in one of those rooms down there," she said nonchalantly, gesturing with her head. "Why? You need a pass and a code to work the lift. Now why don't you just relax? Don't you like it here with me? Don't you like me? It will only be for a relatively short time, George."

"I find this place increasingly bloody threatening. So the sooner I get the hell out of here and return to my family, the better I'll feel about it all." With a deep sigh, he continued, "I just wish I knew why exactly I'm here, and what's being planned for me."

Jody sat on the bed ignoring the last remark as she picked up the remote control. She began flicking through the programs to find a film that she hadn't seen. Then she snuggled against George, suggesting that they relax and watch the film together.

As the evening drew on, the dinner was served and they ate it while watching the early evening news. Strangely, there was no reference to George's mysterious disappearance.

After they'd finishing their meal, Jody poured two drinks and handed one of them to George. But secretly she had added some of the drug that the pharmacist had given her.

"Here have a drink, George. It'll help you to relax." Jody suggested, with growing expectation, as she warmed to the challenge of seducing him. Although she was aware of his devotion to Mandy, this only served to add extra spice and excitement to her challenge. She doubted if it'd be possible without medical intervention. But the drug would make George's sexual desires override his profound love for his wife and family. Getting off the settee, she walked over and lay on the bed so she could observe any reaction to the cocktail, and the performance enhancing drug that she'd added to it, as she waited patiently for it to take its full effect.

George began to fidget, constantly crossing and uncrossing his legs. He was moving to one side then the other, while trying in vain to conceal his throbbing erection. But he found that it was impossible to hide it under the soft, loose-fitting satin pyjamas.

"Is something wrong?" asked Jody, pretending not to know the reason for his acute discomfort.

"No," George snapped abruptly, as he began to blush with embarrassment. "I'm just feeling a bit warm, that's all."

"Then why don't you take the dressing gown off? Then you can come and lay here beside me. It's much more comfortable."

Turning so that his back was towards her, George slipped the dressing gown off his shoulders and let it fall behind him. "I'm okay here," he insisted, continuing to try to hide the true reason for the discomfort, not realising that she was the cause of it. George had never felt like this before. What was the reason for it? He was so preoccupied trying to think of a reasonable explanation, that he hadn't notice Jody had now left the bed and was standing beside him.

"Come over here with me, George," Jody whispered in a husky, sexy, and inviting voice, letting the strong intoxicating aroma from her perfume wash over him. She took his hand and pulled him gently to his feet. He could only offer token resistance as she looked down to the erect penis pushing out his pyjamas. "Umm, we'll have to do something about that, George. Won't we?" Jody insisted, leading him reluctantly towards the bed.

"But I'm a married man," he protested weakly, "What about my Mandy?"

"I don't fancy her. Anyway, I won't tell anybody if you don't, George," she said in a teasingly seductive way, as she pushed him gently backwards onto the bed.

Kneeling astride him, she started unbuttoning her blouse, as she slowly moved her buttocks up and down inside of George's throbbing groin, as she slowly rubbed her fingers of the other hand across his nipples. He felt powerless to resist her sexual advances any longer. He began to respond as his hands moved up inside her blouse and bra, pushing them over her head. Slipping his hands behind her, he pulled her to him kissing her breasts, and teasing her nipples with his tongue. As his bulging penis penetrated her, she began to moan with extreme pleasure.

All thoughts of Mandy were fast disappearing as the growing anticipation in his groin took total precedence over all his other thoughts. Holding Jody to him, he rolled over until he was on top of her. They became locked in a passionate display of uninhibited love making, which continued long into the night. After they had finished he rolled onto his back exhausted, while Jody lay on her side observing any reactions.

Propping herself up on one arm she kissed George gently, saying to him, "Wow! That was something else, George. I've never made love before if that's lovemaking your way." Jody complemented him, laying her head on his chest. "Would you like me to get you a drink while you recover your breath?"

"Please?" He gasped breathlessly. "A coffee would be very welcome."

Going over to the mini bar she made two cups of coffee, slipping a mild sedative into the cup that she was going to give to George. Turning to carry the coffee over to him, she noticed that he was sitting on the side of the bed with his head bowed onto his clasped hands. Thinking George was feeling unwell, she asked him with an air of panic to her voice, "Are you ok, George? Can I get you something? Shall I fetch the doctor?"

After a couple of seconds, George raised his head to explain to her. "I'm fine. I was just saying my prayers, and asking God for his forgiveness."

This took Jody by surprise as she flopped heavily onto the bed beside him. She was totally lost for words, as a puzzled look replaced her usually jovial exterior. Eventually she asked, "Forgiveness? You asked for forgiveness for what, George?"

"For what I've just done Jody."

"But what's wrong with making love?" she asked, looking even more perplexed than ever.

"Nothing: Love's a wonderful gift from God, love for him and love for each other. But I'm a married man, so making physical love to you becomes wrong."

Jody lay back beside George. She was just lying silently, not knowing what to say. Five minutes elapsed before the silence was broken, by a still very confused Jody. "Well I enjoyed it very much. It didn't seem wrong to me," she confessed.

"I enjoyed it too, Jody," he told her, putting a consoling arm round her. "It's not a reflection on you personally. I think you're a very nice and beautiful woman. But I feel guilty because of my Mandy, and I pray each night because I'm a Christian."

"Ok, George. Now just finish your coffee and let's get some sleep. We'll sort this out tomorrow morning."

He finished first and climbed into bed. The sedative quickly took hold as he drifted into a deep and restful sleep.

Jody rang Sir Charles, who was not at all happy to be awakened at 3:00 am. She explained that she'd given George a sedative to prevent him from eavesdropping on her conversation. After she'd explained what had happened, and what George had said to her, Sir Charles advised her to keep administering the drug so he would lust for her constantly. He added that he knew of George's beliefs, but he didn't realise how strongly George felt about them.

"I feel so very guilty now, knowing how George feels" Jody started. "I haven't met this type of man before. He's a man with a conscience in his prick. It's a shame though, because I'm starting to really like him."

"Well I go to church, but I don't agree with all that George says. Sir Charles tried to stop Jody's feelings of guilt. "Just keep the pressure on him, he'll soon realise how wrong he is."

"Are you sure, Sir? I feel so sorry for him now."

"Do you want replacing, Nurse Blackman?" Charles asked her sternly.

"No, sir," she said cautiously, realising that he was growing impatient with her. "I'll be okay now that you've explained everything to me. I'm sorry I had to wake you at this late hour, Sir."

"Not at all, I'm glad you did now. It was something that I really needed to know about. We will speak in more detail about it tomorrow. Good night, Jody."

She wished him good night, and then rang off. Then she returned to where George was soundly sleeping. She slid into the bed beside him, and cuddled up. Soon she had also drifted into a deep sleep, feeling contented from their lovemaking.

When George moved to get out of the bed, it awakened Jody. Looking towards the clock she asked, "It's only 7 o'clock George. Where are you going now?"

"To get washed and a shaved, but you can go back to sleep if you want."

"It's okay," she yawned as she swung her bare legs out of the bed, revealing her total nakedness as she stretched. "But you don't need to get up so early now you know?" Jody protested.

"You go back to sleep then. By the way, I thought this was my bed?" Realising that he was still having a conscience problem, she decided to take Sir Charles's advice and keep him sexually aroused. She went to the mini bar to make two coffees, placing a dose of the drug into his drink. 'I will have to remember to ask Sir Charles to sanction further prescriptions at this rate,' Jody thought to herself.

When he returned from the bathroom, George's coffee was on the bedside table. Jody had left the room saying that she needed to visit her office to check up on the day's mail. But this was only an excuse, as the real reason was that she needed to speak to Sir Charles again, about prescribing her some more of the drug.

George drank the coffee and settled down to watch some early morning television, and again he began to get sexually aroused. "Why?" George asked himself, as he looked down at his erection while trying to conceal it. He thought, "I don't usually keep getting erections without a good reason."

His thoughts were interrupted by Jody returning. Noticing the worried frown on his face, she asked him, "What's wrong George? You seem bothered about something. What is it?"

Realising that he could not confide in his nurse, George thought quickly. He lied. "I was just thinking about Mandy and the children, that's all. Anyway, I think I'll have a soak in the bath now."

"Ok, but you look as though you might need a cold shower first," Jody suggested, looking down at his bulging pyjama trousers. "I'll get you some clean clothing."

"My clothes are back?" George said with an air of excitement.

"No, sorry George, I meant clean night clothes. Yours haven't been returned yet."

"Now how did I know that you'd say that," George remarked sarcastically as he walked into the bathroom to start filling the bath. As he soaked in the bath he tried to figure out why he kept getting an erection. Suddenly the realisation struck him, "Jody must be adding something to my food or drinks. That must be the reason for this."

Jody entered the bathroom to offer, "Would you like me to wash your back, George?"

"I can manage, thank you very much. Don't I get ANY privacy?" He said sharply, showing his extremely embarrassment.

"I'm afraid not. You're in a hospital, remember?" Jody replied as she ignored his objections and proceeded to wash him sensuously. "Why are you so hostile towards me? Don't you like me? After all I AM your very own private nurse."

"Yes I do like you very much, but I miss my family. How much longer will this all take?"

"Just be patient and try to relax, George," she said as she massaged his shoulders. "Stand up so I can dry you."

George found it hard to refuse her advances, and so they were soon back in bed, making passionate love once more. Later the lunch arrived, and as usual Jody started to pour out the coffee. George pretended to be doing up his pyjama buttons, positioning himself so that he could observe her. I was right! He thought, she has added something to my coffee. Thinking quickly, what can I do to distract her? George then slid the salt under the bed as Jody put the coffee down on the table.

"Is your dinner okay, George?"

"Yes, but they forgot to bring the salt," he complained.

"I'm sorry, I'll get you some more." Jody apologised as she left the room quickly.

Seizing his opportunity, he quickly switched the coffees. He was just in time Jody re-entered the room. "They send their apologies, but the chef was sure that he'd put the salt on the tray." She looked down, "It's there on the floor, George."

"Sorry, I must have knocked it as I sat down."

When lunch was finished the drug began to work on Jody, who by this time was becoming very amorous towards George. Eventually she locked the door and undressed, forcefully pushing a protesting George onto the bed and tearing off his pyjamas. Climbing on top of George, she became rampant as she took the initiative. She climaxed time after time, until George eventually found himself unable to continue. Guiding her onto her back, he resorted to helping her climax using his hands. When eventually she was satisfied, they both collapsed onto the bed exhausted. George was the first to move and dress. Then, watching Jody dress, he realised that he was becoming more and more attracted to her.

"You do have a very beautiful body, Jody," George complimented.

"Thank you George. You're not so bad yourself, you know. I don't know what came over me just then though; I just felt that I had to have you. Sorry." Jody apologised, her face red with embarrassment.

"What're you sorry for Jody? I enjoyed it, too."

Jody, feeling extremely embarrassed still, changed the subject quickly. "I will be back in a moment," she excused herself as she rushed from the room.

Puzzled at her embarrassment, George realised that it was because of the drug that she was adding to the drink. He thought to himself, "Now I need to decide how best to avoid taking any more of that drug. I can't just keep hiding the salt. I'll just have to think of a more permanent solution."

Meanwhile Jody was explaining to Sir Charles what had just happened. He confirmed what she'd already suspected, that the drinks must have been switched.

"That is unless you had inadvertently spiked the wrong cup?" Charles suggested.

"No, Sir. I'm very meticulous as to which side my cup or glass is put on when I go to make the coffee, or pour the drinks. So I couldn't have got them mixed up," she explained.

"Well, in that case, your patient is even more astute than we first gave him credit for. But that's not as bad as it might first seem. It might even prove to be more of a useful asset in time." Charles said thoughtfully, as if he was thinking aloud.

"Well I'm not sure what to do now, Sir," Jody muttered. "I have to be constantly on my guard with him."

"Just don't let George distract you from your duties. I'll arrange everything as quickly as I possibly can, so just try to wait another three days at the most. By the way, do you think you could shave him?" Sir Charles asked a surprised Jody.

"Where do you want me to shave him, Sir?"

"All over Jody, except for his head that is." Charles explained, as he added, "I thought you liked him, so just try to turn it into a sex game."

"I do like him; I like him very much. That's the trouble. I'll try to find a way to shave him though, but that's only if he'll let me. What operation have you scheduled for him?"

"Do not concern yourself about that, Jody. The less you know at this time, the better it will be for you. Well, you'd better get back to your patient now. I'll try to come and see you both tomorrow," Sir Charles promised. Then he abruptly rang off.

Jody was growing increasingly uncomfortable about it all, as it was the first time that she had become involved with the underhanded dealings of the department. To add to her predicament, she was beginning to grow more physically attracted towards George, and didn't want to see him hurt in any way at all.

When she returned to the room George was making himself a cup of coffee.

"I'll do that for you, George."

"That is okay, Jody. Would you like a drink?"

"A strong one," she muttered.

"What was that?"

"Yes please," she corrected herself. "Put a splash of brandy in it, a very large splash."

"Is there something wrong?"

"Not really, it's just been one of those days," Jody replied. "You know how it can get."

"Yes," George agreed, sitting beside her, and handing her the coffee. She cupped it in both hands as she sipped it. Nestling up against him, she confessed, "I'm sorry I spiked your drink George, but it seemed at the time to be the only way that I could get you to sleep with me. Can we call it a truce and just enjoy our little time together, just as if we were a real couple?" Jody pleaded hopefully.

"I don't know. It just doesn't seem right to me somehow."

"Don't you enjoy my company or something, George?"

"Yes, of course I do. But I'm married to Mandy whom I love very, very much. If I wasn't, then everything would be totally different. Besides, there's nothing else happening here, so why can't I just go home now?"

Putting her empty cup down, she swung her legs up onto the settee and lay her head on George's lap. Looking up at him longingly, she answered, "I know it seems that way to you. Sir Charles says that it'll take just a couple more days to get all of the tests results back." Hooking her arms around his neck she kissed him passionately before she continued. "Can't the rest just be our little secret? You don't seem to object to me that much, so I won't tell if you don't."

George, found it impossible to resist her as he held her close in a long and passionate embrace, and began fondling her voluptuous breasts. A few moments later Jody stood up, and then taking hold of his hand, she led George towards the bed. For an hour they enjoyed a natural uninhabited sex session, one that wasn't fuelled by the lust-inducing drug. When they had eventually finished, they laid back, exhausted. Jody was the first to speak, suggesting that they shared a bath. To this he readily agreed, and they slowly and sensuously washed each other's bodies.

Jody was starting to feel a stronger attraction towards George. Her pricking conscience wanted to warn him, and to tell him as much as she knew: about her involvement with the department, and of the future plans she thought the organisation had for him. But then she realised that it would be more than her life would be worth. After their bath, she asked George to lie naked on top of the bed, persuading him to allow her to shave the whole of his body, saying that he could shave her bikini line and legs afterwards. The day passed, and the mutual attraction between them grew stronger, leading them repeatedly back into bed to make love. The following days were spent much the same, but eventually they were interrupted in the evening as they were enjoying their evening meal by Jody's pager bleeping.

Jody left for her office to telephone the senior doctor.

He advised her, "You will be pleased to know that everything is set for tomorrow morning, Nurse Blackman."

Jody sat mortified. Although she knew that this day would some-day arrive, she had secretly hoped that it wouldn't, and that for some reason, it would eventually all be cancelled. There was a long silence. Eventually when she'd regained her composure and professionalism, Jody asked, "What is it that you want me to do, sir?"

"Firstly, when did the patient last eat?"

"It was about an hour ago, doctor."

"That might delay things a little, but maybe we can pump his stomach? I'll need to consult with the anaesthetist. Now, I believe you have been given a sedative and a syringe to keep until this moment arrived?" he asked.

"I have."

"Well, tonight put the sedative into his evening drink, and set your alarm for five am. Then administer the injection while he's still sleeping," the doctor instructed.

"Very well, doctor. What exactly are you going to do to him?"

"If you've not been made privy to that information, then I'm not authorised to tell you. You will have to ask Sir Charles. I have a lot to prepare before tomorrow, so goodbye Nurse Blackman, and thank you," he finished abruptly.

After asking Sir Charles, who would not tell Jody anything further, but he reminded her of her duties and of her position. Telling her that she knew all that she needed to know, and that all that remained was for her to follow her instructions.

Reluctantly she followed her orders. The following morning, George was taken while still unconscious, and wheeled through into the operating theatre.

CHAPTER 4

In the weeks that followed, three medical teams—from the surgeons to the orderlies'-worked in short shifts around the clock. The patient was then left heavily sedated and on heart monitors and drips. The face had been rebuilt with higher cheekbones, and almond-shaped eyes to create beauty. A womb was implanted, and voluptuous breasts were grafted onto to the patient, using a new, and completely innovational, method. The texture of the skin was then softened with chemicals. A rib was removed to reduce his waist size, and give him an hourglass figure, and then his penis was replaced by a vagina, leaving only the male dominant brain that was unable to be replaced. All of this transformation continued over a number of short periods of time, until eventually the project was completed. George was then returned to his room, but kept in a permanently semi-sedated state, until eventually all traces of what the patient had undergone had disappeared, thanks to the advanced technology used by the plastic surgeons.

It left no scaring or evidence that could ever relate to George's prior existence as a man.

Whilst still sedated, but in a semi-hypnotised state, psychiatrists and psychologists worked on the subconscious mind, trying to help the patient to adjust to the condition that had been forced upon him.

They attempted to erase everything that was in the memory prior to the enforced operation, and replace it by giving him a completely new persona: one that only existed from the time of the transformation. Hours had been spent in the gymnasium to attain peak fitness, and while the patient was sleeping, a variety of information was played into the subconscious mind. He was instructed in martial arts and foreign languages, and other relevant information that was now needed by the patient.

Because the patient had been kept in a drug induced semi-hypnotic state, and the memory had been cleared, learning was rapid, retaining information readily and without the need for it to be repetitive. Beauty consultants enhanced the personal appearance, while physical trainers sharpening reaction times to any possible danger that might arise. The patient became fluent in many languages, due to the development of the new experimental teaching techniques, which was fed into the subconscious memory during the hours of sleep, when it had been found that the mind was at its most receptive.

After months had passed the time came when they were to bring the patient slowly out of his/her drug-induced trance. Now they would witness just how successful their theories were when put into a more practical situation. Most of the techniques being used were purely speculative, and had only been tried out as a singular unit, so they were untried and untested in a complete transformation. The patient was aroused slowly into conscious awareness, and a natural state of sleep. They were then returned to what had become the familiar surroundings of their own suite.

Two male nurses, who had replaced Jody, and sat waiting for the patient to awaken both men being tall and muscular, one called Albert, and because of his huge frame was nicknamed Odd Job, whilst the other one, John, was slimmer but with a more athletic physique.

They sat reading while they waited for their patient to arouse from slumber. This gave the room an eerie silence; one which was only broken by the ticking off the clock.

John glanced at the time. "It's been nearly an hour now," he whispered. "How much longer do you think it'll take for her to wake up?"

"Very soon now, I should imagine," speculated Albert.

The talking seemed to disturb the patient. Her eyes began to flicker open. They both looked towards her in anticipation as she started to moan softly.

Then she opened her eyes fully, and blinked as if trying to adjust to the bright light.

"How do you feel?" John asked, as he stood up and moved to the bedside, while Albert took up a position on the opposite side.

"Ok." was the reply in a soft feminine voice. A strange expression crept over her face as she was heard her new voice for the first time. "What's wrong with my voice?"

"It's okay, it'll be the anaesthetics wearing off, I expect. Try to relax," John urged, trying to calm and reassure her.

The progress was being observed and monitored from behind a two-way mirror, by Sir Charles, along with most of the senior medical staff and two nameless men from the ministry. They were growing anxious as they observed the slow progress of their project.

"Call her by name," urged Mr Justin Jackson, the chief psychologist. He spoke into a microphone that in turn was connected to an earpiece in John's, and Albert's ears. They had decided to name her April, after the month that she had originally born as George.

"Would you like me to get you a drink, April?" Albert asked.

With this, her eyes widened. An expression of utter confusion was quickly replaced by one of sheer anger and frustration. April tore off the sheets and started to examine her newly acquired breasts. "I'VE GOT FUCKING TITS!" she shouted. Then as her hands moved downward to where a penis should have been, April discovered the newly acquired vagina. "WHAT'VE YOU DONE WITH MY PRICK, YOU FUCKING BASTARDS?"

"What do you mean, April?" asked John. "Don't get so agitated. It must be the anaesthetic wearing off. You've only been dreaming."

"My name's not April, and you fucking know it," she retorted. "Who is responsible for this? I'LL FUCKING KILL THE BASTARDS." April tried to get up, but John held her down on the bed.

"Just lie still. At least until you have calmed down, PLEASE?" John Insisted.

From behind the mirror one of the ministry men commented, "Obviously your experiment has failed. So you know what that will mean, don't you Charles?"

"Isn't it a little premature to be talking about failure, and what it will mean?" Sir Charles snapped at him sharply.

"That's your experiment in there, and it must never leave this building," the man insisted, in a very assertive and sinister tone of voice.

They turned their attention back towards the window just in time to witness April freeing herself from John's grip to make a bolt towards the door. It was locked. She turned back into the room just in time to see Albert lunging towards her. She rapidly sidestepped him as John then made a grab for her. Leaning back against the wall, she bent her leg up to her chest as John reached for her. Kicking her leg out straight she buried her heel into his stomach. This sent John hurtling backwards crashing into Albert, and the medical trolley, sending them both sprawling onto the floor.

Albert regained his senses first and made a fresh grab for April, but again she slipped his grasp. Realising that he was far too strong for her, she looked quickly round the room for inspiration. Seeing the television, April sprang towards it. Seizing it, as she then threw it at Albert. Albert, because of his size, was too slow in reacting, as the television caught him on his temple, once again sending him hurtling into a recovering John, who was just starting to rise to his feet. A loud snapping noise could be heard through the chaos. John cried out with pain, his leg twisted beneath Albert's bulk. Albert struggled to move off his now broken leg.

"Help us!" John yelled, looking towards the large mirror.

April realised that it must be a two-way mirror. Picking up a chair she threw it, watching as it bounced off the toughened glass.

"I'LL KILL YOU FUCKING BASTARDS," April screamed towards the mirror. She saw the reflection of Albert approaching her from behind. Turning, she kicked the other medical trolley towards him, sending him crashing to the floor again. The audience behind the mirror was forced to watch with terrorised amazement, as April continually alluded capture by the two highly trained, burley minders.

"Perhaps my assessment of her was a little premature, Charles?" The ministry man admitted, as they stood mesmerised, while they watched April defending herself. "She is certainly a force to be reckoned with. Perhaps we should see how the next few days pan out. That is, providing your men manage to eventually stop her."

April spun round as the door opened. She began to make her escape through it, but was stopped in her tracks as another four orderlies entered. She could see that the first to enter the room was armed with a syringe.

"COME TO JOIN THE FUCKING PARTY LADS? I must warn you, it is beginning to get a little crowded in here," she yelled. April backed towards the wall as she watched the approaching orderly on one side, and Albert with the limping John, approaching from the other. "COME ON YOU BASTARDS," her adrenaline was now running rampant.

As the orderly lunged towards her with the syringe, April stepped forwards and turned in one rapid movement. Grabbing the back of his overall, she used his weight to propel him into Albert.

Stretching out his hands to save himself, the orderly inadvertently plunged the needle into Albert's thigh rendering him unconscious. He fell onto John's broken leg, who again screamed out in excruciating pain.

April leapt over the bed giving her more room in which to defend herself. As she went she grabbed for a chair and sent it crashing over the head of another orderly, felling him unconscious at her feet. She then bent her knee up and released a vicious kick, burying her heels into the only orderly left standing, which sent him crashing to the floor.

Again she tried to open the door to leave, but without success. "LET ME OUT OF HERE YOU FUCKING SCUM BAGS!" She shouted. "I'LL FUCKING KILL THE FUCKING LOT OF YOU WHEN I GET MY FUCKING HANDS ON YOU."

Suddenly the door opened again. This time three armed security guards entered the room. The first one aimed his tranquilliser gun towards April. She kicked the door closed; jamming his outstretched arm and causing him to drop the gun. April quickly flung the door open wide. Leaping to grip the top of the door casing, she swung outwards and kicked the remaining two security guards in the face. She sent them sprawling backwards against the wall and landing in a stunned heap.

Landing as fleet as a cat, she moved swiftly towards the adjoining room, knowing that her captors were observing her from within it. Confronted by a locked door she tried to shoulder it open, but to no avail. April then turned her attention to the window alongside the door. Grabbing at a convenient fire extinguisher, April flung it through shattering the glass. The scene inside was one of sheer terror, as April made the onlookers vulnerable, and open to the full extent of her uncontrollable fury. As she reached in to unlock the door a sharp pain could be felt in her thigh. As she turned to retaliate her vision suddenly became blurred, as she slumped to the floor unconscious.

April woke to find her arms and legs shackled to a chair with tape across her mouth. Her head was bowed forward and her bedraggled shoulder length hair shrouded her face. April's head slowly began to clear as she jerked it upright, tossing her head back to remove the hair off her face.

Sir Charles was seated in a chair opposite her. "I'm sorry we had to restrain you, but it is as much for our protection as it is for your own safety," he explained cautiously. He watched as April tried in vain to struggle free. But she was unsuccessful, much to the relief of Sir Charles. "Just relax while I try to explain to you, PLEASE APRIL?" He paused while he waited for her to stop the futile struggling.

"Right, now that you've stopped struggling. The reason that we've done what we have, is a matter of national security. As we've already told you we came across you fortuitously when our operative paused for a rest in your home village. He was under orders to look for a suitable, but little known person. The reason we needed somebody new is because we know there has been a breach of our secret services website, so we realise that the identities of all our operatives have now been compromised." He paused again, growing increasingly uncomfortable under April's intense stare. "Look, you must realise that you can't escape from here, so if I make you more comfortable by removing the tape, will you co-operate, and at least hear me out? For the time being, will you just listen to what I have to say?"

April thought for a few moments, then, with reluctance nodded her head. Sir Charles signaled to one of the nurses, and the tape was removed from April's mouth. Again she continued to stare silently at Sir Charles, but kept to her agreement and remained silent, allowing him to continue without interruption.

"Thank you. As our men and women travelled the country, they'd been issued with a mandate of what to look for. And more importantly, what to do if they found a suitable person for the daunting task that lay ahead. What they didn't know was what our intentions for that person was, or as I should now say now is, what our plans for you were."

Then he asked, "Seeing that you have calmed down, will you stay calm if we take off the restraints?" April agreed, as it seemed futile to do otherwise.

"May I have a cup of coffee please?" she asked calmly and politely. Her new voice was husky, but in an extremely sexy way. "I can't get used to hearing myself speak with this new voice that you've given me."

"It must be very strange, but I assure you that you'll soon get used to it," Sir Charles affirmed. "If the personality transfer we'd given you had worked, you would have been spared all the trauma and pain that you must be feeling right now." Then as if he was thinking aloud, he added, "I wonder why it didn't work on you. It worked on all the other patients we had tried it on."

A distinguished-looking gentleman standing in the doorway suggested, "Perhaps she has too strong a willpower."

April looked up at the man inquisitively. Sir Charles noticed this and introduced the man as Mr. Jackson, pioneer of the personality transfer technique that they'd used on her. April, remaining tight-lipped stared at him, and then she returned her attention to Sir Charles.

———

"As I was explaining to you, we needed to find, or create, a new agent that would be untraceable on any database in the world. It needed to be somebody who was able to survive through their own initiatives. But we only had a limited time in which to work."

April impatiently broke her silence, "I don't care about your bloody priorities. What about me? I've lost MY wife, MY family, not to mention, MY manhood, in fact, MY whole life as it was." Tears filled her eyes as she reflected on the happy times that she'd spent with Mandy and the children. "Is there a reversal operation option for me, when whatever you have in mind is over? And what have you told Mandy and the children about me?"

Suddenly, her voice changed as she shouted, "IT WAS YOU WHO FORCED JILL AND JOE INTO MOVING, AND THEN YOU FUCKING KILLED THEM."

"No, April. We engineered the move but we didn't kill them. I admit it was a fortuitous accident that we turned to our advantage eventually, but we're not responsible for the death of your ex-neighbours."

She went into deep thought to consider this, and then nodded her acceptance of Charles' explanation.

Charles continued, "Regarding the reversal operation, I'm afraid not. You need to accept being the beautiful young woman that you have now become. Who knows, you may be happier like that in time. Just give it some time, April. Now regarding Mandy and the children, you have just been reported missing, and Martin's car was found abandoned at Margate. It has been left open like that, but we have led her to believe that you had a very large insurance policy, and it's paid out one million pounds to her. So you see; she will be financially secure for the rest of her life." Sir Charles paused while April digested it all. "We will of course need to make a final decision as to what to eventually tell Mandy, and when to tell her, but sometime in the future will do for that."

April looked very pensive as she digested it all. Her top priority was the well-being of Mandy and the children. "Sir Charles," she started, but was immediately interrupted.

"Drop the 'Sir', April, just call me plain Charles."

"Okay plain Charles. If I am to co-operate with you there has to be a precondition." April told him, as he gave a wry smile at her humorous retort.

"Anything you want, April. But within reason of course."

"That's rich," she sneered. "Is what you've done to me within reason? The condition is that you don't tell my family anything more than you already have. Well for the time being anyway, can we just leave it in abeyance?"

Charles reluctantly agreed to this before continuing. "Just now you gave us an account of yourself that was better than we could have expected. Five of our men required medical attention after their little encounter with you. John's leg is broken in four different places, and needed pinning. Now, I suggest that you get dressed, and then we will continue with your briefing. You will find there is a new wardrobe for you, and this nurse will assist you. When you are ready, I will meet you in the lounge at the far end of the corridor. Agreed?"

She nodded reluctantly again as everybody left the room, leaving the two women alone. At last she was eventually able to gather her thoughts, but that made her even more confused than ever. The main priority was, and always would be, Mandy and the children, so what should she do about them now? How, when, or even should, she ever make contact with them again? Even more importantly, how could she begin to explain away what had happened to her?

Before dressing she turned her attention to the two-way mirror, taking a sheet from the bed and draped it over, to stop any prying eyes. April then dressed with surprising ease, 'while thinking,' I've obviously been given some instructions whilst still under hypnosis.

Eventually April dressed in an elegant white tailored dress with plunging v-neckline, revealing much of her newly-acquired firm cleavage. She was then surprised at how easily she could walk in the four-inch stiletto heels. Her shoulder length blond hair shone as the lights reflected off it, and April bounced buoyantly, as she walked to the dressing table to apply her makeup.

As she was putting on her earrings, she thought again how natural it was feeling to be dressed as a woman. What became obvious to

April was that some of the preparation techniques they had used on her had worked. So at least they deserved to be congratulated for that much. The nurse sat quietly and without the need to intervene, so she was able to leave the room before April finished.

When April left the room she noticed that the door to the opposite room was slightly ajar. Very carefully she opened it to find the room was unoccupied with only a few sparse furnishings. On the desk there was a telephone, so she lifted the receiver and found that there was no outside line. She tried dialling nine, then she tried zero, all to no avail, so April decided that she would have to leave it until a later time. Just then, there was the noise of a door opening and closing, followed by footsteps getting increasingly louder, as they approached nearer and nearer to the office that she was in. She crouched down behind the desk, but found the tightness of the dress hindering her, so she slid the skirt partway up her thighs to facilitate ease of movement.

April smiled as she realised how much she still needed to alter her way of thinking, particularly while dressed in certain feminine attire.

She peered through the slightly open door as the figure of a man passed, then the footsteps stopped. There was the sound of a door opening, so April stood up and stealthily moved towards the door, and checked carefully to find the corridor was now empty. Sidling along the wall towards the open door she pressed herself back against the wall. When she glanced furtively into the office, she could see Mr. Jackson looking through a telephone directory. He stopped as he located his contact number and lifted the receiver, then he dialled seven five, followed by the number.

Silently April crept back to her room and sat at the dressing table pretending to be finishing off her makeup. A few moments passed and there was a light rapping on the door.

"Come in," April called, "it's open. They don't trust me with a key yet."

Opening the door, Mr. Jackson told her, "Charles has asked me to accompany you."

"I'll be about five minutes tell him. I've just chipped my nail varnish."

"Does that matter?" he snapped with frustration.

"You all contributed in turning me into a woman, so you can only expect me to act like one now. As I know, if my Mandy had chipped her nail polish, then she would have taken it all off and started over. Now, as I have already said, give me five more minutes."

"Ok, but be as quick as you can," he reluctantly agreed.

When he had left, April carefully crept across the corridor to the office opposite, leaving the door slightly ajar so she could hear if anybody else approached. Then with bated breath, April raised the telephone receiver once more. After taking a deep breath she dialled seven five and got an outside line. With her heart beating heavily and full of tentative anticipation, she keyed in the number to Mandy's mobile.

It began to ring, then after three or four rings Mandy answered. "Hello?" There was a long pause before April could not find herself able to respond whilst she was fighting back the tears. Again Mandy repeated, "Hello, can I help you?"

"Hello, I'm sorry to bother you," April started clumsily, searching hard to find words to explain what had happened to her.

"That's okay, now what can I do for you?" Mandy asked. "Is it about my George? Do you know where he is? Is he still alive?" she questioned anxiously.

"Yes, but you may find what's happened to him hard to accept. I don't have a lot of time to explain to you right now though." April was unsure of what to say next, but Mandy surprised her with what she asked.

"Are you going to tell me that you're with George, or that you are George?"

"What makes you say that?" asked April out of utter confusion.

"Oh, it's just a gut feeling I'm getting. There's something that's not quite right about your voice."

Falling silent momentarily, April then eventually said tearfully. "I had no say in what's been done to me, Mandy. I need to be quick before I'm found using this telephone. Martin Driver was working for them, and when we went to Joe's funeral he drugged me and brought me here. I have just re-entered the real world, and have found out the stark reality of what's been done to me."

April paused to gather her thoughts as Mandy interrupted, pleading; "I don't care what they've done to you. Just come home and we'll work something out, darling."

"I can't come home just yet as I've been enlisted to carry out an assignment for them first. But I needed you to know what's happened. Remember, you must not tell anybody or your lives could be in danger. Get my old phone and remove the SIM card in case the phone has been tampered with. Buy a new SIM free mobile telephone and put the card into it so I will know the number, but keep it with you at all times, and don't let it out of your sight. When you are asleep, put it under your pillow so that it can't ever be tampered with. And don't use it for any other calls. That way it can't ever be traced, so I can use it to ring you on."

"You make it all sound so terribly sinister. By the way, I didn't know that you had such a big insurance policy. What shall I do about that now?"

"Nothing, it's all yours. And it is serious, pet. Withdraw the money in cash and put it into a new bank account, one that only you will know about. But make sure that you're not followed when you do it. Then just wait for me to ring you again. It may take some time, even up to six months maybe, but I will eventually ring you again on your new phone."

"We all miss you, George. Please come home as soon as you can, love. We will work something out. I promise you, my darling."

A phone rang at the end of the corridor, April didn't know, but somebody had noticed that this telephone was being used on an outside line, and then informed Charles. Hearing a door open then close, and the approach of footsteps, April quickly told Mandy, "I'm sorry, I must go now; remember that I love you all!" Then she replaced the receiver hurriedly. Realising now that somebody might have traced this phone being used, April quickly dialled the speaking clock, putting the receiver only partly on so it was still connected.

Her eyes scanned the room searching for an escape route. She glanced towards the ceiling and recognised that it was a false ceiling.

'I wonder how much space there will be up there,' April thought. Removing her shoes she climbed onto the desk and lifted one of the ceiling tiles. It revealed a large, dimly lit working area for facilitating any maintenance that was needed. April hoisted herself up and took her shoes into the space with her. Then she slid the ceiling tile back over the hole.

"Nice of them to put emergency lighting up here," April thought to herself as she negotiated her way across, being careful to stand only on the framework supporting the tiles. She had travelled about ten metres to where wiring passed through a beam. It was where April calculated that the light was in her room. Lifting the tile next to it she found that it was directly over her bed.

Dropping her shoes onto the bed, April swung down, and then replaced the ceiling tile. Moving quickly to the wardrobe April removed the now dusty dress, along with the shoes, and put them away. She donned a low cut slinky black dress, and was just slipping into a pair of black stilettos when Charles opened the door.

"Have you just been into the room opposite, April?"

"I don't intrude on the other patient's privacy," she told him pretending not to know that it was only an office.

"It's just an empty office," he explained. "Somebody's been using the telephone in there."

"I heard two people while I was dressing if that helps you at all. Anyway, why would I be interested?"

"That's just the point the receiver hadn't been replaced properly. Whoever it was had just dialled Tim, the speaking clock."

"There you go then. Obviously they must have wanted to know the correct time." April offered the explanation as she stood up. "Will I do, Charles?"

April said buoyantly, as she twirled round, trying to change the subject.

"Yes, you look very nice." He was obviously preoccupied, still trying to resolve the telephone mystery. "Are you ready to join the others now, April?"

"Roger," she replied.

As they walked up the long corridor, Charles, who was still looking very perplexed, broke the silence. "You sound happier. What's happened to cause the change of heart?"

"I have now realised that you are right what's happened can't be reversed. So I might just as well except and enjoy the new experience. Besides, I'm starting to feel rather good as a woman. The clothes and the makeup are all feeling better and better on me. Maybe you should give it a try sometime."

"And you know nothing about the telephone?"

"Now who could I ring? And anyway, where would I start explaining all of this?" April explained, gesturing with her hands at the way she was dressed.

"I suppose it would be difficult," Charles agreed, as they reached the far end of the corridor. "Ladies first," he said teasingly as he tapped her bottom playfully.

"Oops, don't get too cheeky now," April joked, trying to conceal her true feelings. "Hello everybody, I'm sorry to have kept you all waiting, gentlemen." Then she turned her attention to the battered and bruised male nurses who were standing at the back. April apologised to them, saying, "I'm sorry about my temper fellas, but it was all quite a shock when I woke up like this. So you can well imagine how you would have felt."

Albert just nodded assent as April sat in the vacant chair. She crossed her legs, letting one leg swing to and fro, so as to draw attention to them.

"You have made a nice job of reducing my kneecaps," April remarked flippantly. "There's not even any scarring to be seen anywhere. How did you manage that?"

Ignoring April's remarks, an official-looking gentleman opened the meeting. "We have put a lot of time and money into making you what you are today, Miss. Outside of this room nobody knows of the true identity of who you are, or once were."

"EXCUUUSSSE ME," April said indignantly. "You speak as if you've done me an enormous favour. But did it ever cross your tiny little bloody minds what you were taking away from me? MY BLOODY PRICK," she snapped.

"I've explained that we chose you because of your other qualities," Sir Charles intervened. "So would you kindly let the Brigadier continue, PLEASE, April?"

"I'm sorry I spoke, but apparently nobody seems to care about MY feelings," she retorted morosely. "I suppose you think I should be grateful to you for all of this. But I don't feel that there's anything to be fucking grateful to you for." April sat back, "Sorry. Okay. Now I'm all ears… and tits."

"Thank you, Miss Darling," said the Brigadier. He continued, "We were expecting to have at least a further three months in which to prepare you. But with recent developments, and the information that has filtered through from our intelligence contacts, we will need to bring everything forward." He paused to sip some water before he continued. "We have reliable information that a world-wide network of sleepers has just been awakened, and that they've been called into immediate service. We're not sure what their intentions are exactly yet, but apparently only a few people are privy to that information. But what we do know is that it's a coordinated operation, and it is designed to bring about global devastation of epic proportions."

"In what way's that? We've lived with these insane threats for many years now, so what's so bloody special about this one? And what idiot's behind it all?"

"We don't have all of the facts before us yet. What we do know is that a new group has been recruited from within the Muslim communities worldwide. They are working independently of any traditional Muslim groups that we know of."

"As a Christian, I know that Muslims and Christians are very similar people in what our beliefs are, and the Muslim faith preaches total peace and love," remarked April.

"That is so Miss Darling, but this new group of radicals speak of a totally Muslim-dominated world. It says that it will rise from the ashes of a catastrophe just like the phoenix did." The Brigadier further explained, "The Taliban and traditional Muslims have distanced themselves from them. We're even enjoying the co-operation of Osama Bin Laden, Gaddafi, and people that opposed the western world on previous occasions. They're giving to us their full support and co-operation, just as long as we keep them fully informed as to our progress."

"And how do you plan to deal with this?" interrupted April impatiently. "Or don't you have that information for us yet either."

"From what we already understand, there will be a dual plan to operate simultaneously with each other. We think that one could be like a reserve plan, but we are unsure about that, if one was to fail or are foiled, then the other will still remain operational. That's purely speculative too. But what we do know is that a contingency plan is already operational and it will be implemented within a very short time now." The Brigadier stopped to take another sip of water and mop the perspiration from his brow. "Our fear is that they might use both plans, and that would bring about our Armageddon so to speak. You're a religious person, aren't you, Miss April?"

"Yes, but what has that got to do with all of this insanity?" she questioned, looking extremely puzzled.

"Does it not say somewhere in the New Testament about the joining of the north and south, and that will be a sign that points to the end being nigh?"

"Yes, but nobody seems to know exactly what it means. They purely speculate about it." April asked, "So what are you getting at?"

"It was in a message that we unscrambled. It read, 'We are to be united with Allah at the joining of the north and south.' We are unsure of what it means too, but we thought it might have some biblical connection. Maybe we're just clutching at straws there, but it's all we have to go." The Brigadier took another sip of water. "Now what we'll need is somebody who's not on our, or any other, known database. Someone that's capable of working off their own initiative, and to put it very crudely, can save the world as we now know it."

April glanced round the room. There were just twelve sombre-looking people including the nurses. She could tell by their gloomy expressions that this was not just a hoax or an exercise. Finally, April said, "It all seems very dangerous to me, and I don't see why you think it's within my capabilities." The Brigadier tried to interrupt, so April raised her voice slightly. "HOWEVER, I'm willing to try if you think that I can do something to help. But firstly, tell me exactly what I can expect to get out of this."

"What do you want, Miss Darling? I'm authorised to give you whatever you ask for, within reason," volunteered a small middle-aged man, who up until now had been sitting quietly ogling April's swinging leg.

"I will keep it simple then. When this is all finished I'll need to rebuild myself a whole new lifestyle, providing that I live through it all that is. So I'll need the financial security with which to do just that. As I hope this is only a one-off assignment, what one-off figure are you authorised to pay me?" Uncrossing her legs, April sat back and waited.

"How about ten thousand pounds?" the little man suggested.

As April stood up and moved towards the door, she snapped, "That's the charge for the way you've just been ogling my legs. And quite frankly gentlemen, it's an insult to my intelligence. So goodbye gentlemen, you can go and find yourselves another patsy, one that's desperate enough to accept your insulting offer." Opening the door April left the room.

"Why didn't you stop her?" the Brigadier asked Albert.

"Not after the last time we tried. She'd have wrecked this room and all of you with it. Is that what you wanted?" Albert asked. Shrinking back into the obscurity of the corner, he muttered, "Do you honestly think that I've got a bloody death wish or something?"

Sir Charles opened the door and asked April to return to the meeting.

Apologising for the little man's insult, he held the door open for her.

Noticing that the little man was still looking embarrassed, April asked him. "Are you still blushing, mate? I'm sorry if I embarrassed you with my bluntness. Now you can tell me this new, revised offer you've suddenly found for me."

"Money is not the issue here, so just name me a price. Quite frankly, time is fast running out for us!" Sir Charles urged.

"Ten million pounds," April didn't know why she'd said this amount, but she had just added three noughts to their offer. Plus it seemed like a good starting point from which to haggle.

To April's surprise Sir Charles agreed without a quibble. "How do you want it paid, April?"

"I'll need to open an account." Then she told him, "I'll need some new ID with which to do that of course."

"I will see to all of that later today. Now can we continue, April?" Sir Charles urged impatiently, nodding towards the Brigadier.

"If we are to protect the world as we know it, then we'll have to pull out all the stops. We have tried to pinpoint their position, but as yet without any success. What we do know is that it comes from somewhere within the African continent." The Brigadier paused to gather his thoughts before he continued once again. "Every time we get a fix on their location it changes, but of course a lot of the inhabitants there are nomadic, so that could be the reason why it's proving to be so difficult."

April interrupted, "Have you sent anybody out there to track them down in person?"

"Yes, but they have all disappeared too."

"Well where do I fit in then? If I try to locate them I'll probably disappear as they did. Or am I to be just a dispensable distraction to let somebody else get through?" April suggested.

The Brigadier, realising April had seen through his plans looked embarrassed. Trying to wriggle out of it, he explained, "That was our original plan Miss Darling, but we now think that you've much more potential than we'd first dared to expect. Maybe you and another agent posing as man and wife could remain anonymous." He sipped some more water as April was beginning to make him nervous again with her frankness. Eventually he asked, "Are you willing to take on this assignment, Miss Darling, or not?"

"Who will I be working with?"

"A Robert Montgomery," the Brigadier answered. "You won't know him of course."

"I think she might know him as Ron Marks," suggested Sir Charles.

"I've unfinished business with that fucking dirty toe rag." April threatened menacingly through clenched teeth.

"Remember he was only doing a job for us, April. In fact, he didn't know why we wanted you, or what happened to you after he had left. And I want it to stay that way, so there's no blame to be laid at his door, AGREED?" Sir Charles stressed insistently.

April thought for a few moments, and then agreed not to go down the revenge trail.

Sir Charles picked up the telephone and asked for Robert Montgomery to be shown into the room. A short time passed before the door swung open.

"Come in, Robert. I'd like to introduce you to Miss April Darling, your new partner for the revelations assignment"

"I can see that it's going to be a pure pleasure working with you, April," Robert commented, with a look of admiration, as he undressed her with his eyes.

"Down Romeo, this is purely a business relationship. DON'T you dare get any ideas above your station! I AM WARNING YOU!"

"It will still be all my pleasure," Robert repeated. It was obvious he had no recollection of her prior persona.

The next couple of days were spent briefing Robert, and April. They familiarised themselves with maps of the areas and its terrain. The time was fast approaching for them to leave for Africa, and whatever, or whoever; they encountered there.

CHAPTER 5

Before leaving for Africa April had secretly decided to move some of her money into alternative bank accounts, ones that were unknown to anybody else but herself and Mandy. She was now convinced that the bureau would attempt to retrieve the money as soon as she'd left the country, or in the event that she was killed.

As the agency began to trust April she was loaned a sports car for her personal use. She'd taken a few shopping trips, but was always aware that she was being followed. She realised that a plan now needed to be hatched. On one of her visits to the bank April had been purposely flirtatious with the young assistant bank manager, Arthur Aimsley. So much so, that he had left instructions with his staff that he, and only he, would handle Miss Darling's personal account. Having now gained Arthur's confidence, April told him that her money had come from a recent divorce settlement off her very wealthy, and highly influential, ex-husband.

Quietly sobbing, she told him, "I'm afraid that he'll use his influence to find the money, and take it back from me."

"Please, don't upset yourself. I will help you to hide it from him," Arthur offered, as he handed her a tissue to wipe away the crocodile tears.

"He will find it via the Internet using one of his computer experts Arthur. I know exactly how his mind works."

Arthur asked, showing genuine concern. "Well, what do you think we should do about it?"

After April had convincing him that some of the money needed to be moved in cash, but it would need to be put somewhere it would never be traced by anybody else? Arthur interrupted, telling her that on the following Monday he was to be transferred to a bank in London, where he would be given a full manager-ship.

"I'm delighted for you, but we must exchange telephone numbers for when I visit London," April suggested, pretending to appear excited. "So any plan's best implemented on, or before Friday."

"Oh yes," he answered sheepishly. He added, "I have a confession to make though, I'm a married man."

"I know; you wear a wedding ring." April then added reassuringly, "We can still keep in touch, can't we? Maybe you can be my personal financial adviser."

"Yes, that is a good idea. Here is my private mobile number," Arthur said eagerly, as he slid his business card towards her.

Putting it inside her purse, April lied, "I'm getting a new mobile phone soon so I'll text the new number to you.

"Now about your money, I've explained to my manager and he has reluctantly agreed to help you," explained Arthur. "Firstly, if you sign here to give me full authority, then we can start the ball rolling immediately. When do you need the money by?"

"Friday would by a good day, if that's at all possible, Arthur."

With Arthur's help four million pounds was set up in new accounts, a million for each of her children, then a million each for Mandy and April. Arthur set them up at his new post in London using bogus names, and then he transferred them into accounts in the names of the children. It was to lay in trust until their eighteenth birthdays, and then he set up two more accounts in the names of Mandy and April.

"I've broken the trail so it will be extremely difficult, if not impossible, to trace. I'm a computer buff in my spare time so I know exactly how to do these things," he boasted.

"How to do what things?" she teased, making him blush.

"Now you want four million in cash on Friday. That's an awful lot of money. Shall I arrange for security for you?" he asked, as he seemed genuinely concerned about her safety.

"No, I'll be okay, but there's something you can do for me though. Could you give me a letter of authority to introduce me to other banks? And could you hire me a fast car with a large boot to hold the four cases? Hire it in your name and put me down as the second driver. Then on Friday could you park the car behind the bank and put the money into suitcases in the boot? Would you do that for me please, Arthur?" she begged, taking hold of his hand. "This should cover any expenses that you might incur." April told him as she shoved an envelope towards him containing two thousand pounds in cash. "Now here are my driving license details for the hire car."

Opening the envelope he thanked her, and agreed to do exactly as she'd requested.

Unbeknown to those detailed to follow her, on one of the shopping trips, she purchased an extra complete change of clothing, a black curly wig, and sunglasses, also a complete set of underwear, accessories, and shoes, and left them behind the customer service desk to be collected on the Friday morning personally. She had also bought herself a new mobile phone and a laptop, and left them also with the customer service department.

On the Friday after an early morning workout in the gymnasium April showered, then as per usual informed Sir Charles that she was going out shopping again.

"You seem to be adapting to your new persona very quickly," remarked Charles.

"Well, I can't alter anything right now, can I Charles? So I might as well enjoy the fringe benefits that go with the new territory," she remarked casually.

"You might as well, my dear." Then his expression became serious as he added, "You do know that next week you'll be leaving for Africa, don't you?"

"Well I'd better make the most of what time I have left then," she said to him, "Because nobody expects me to return alive. Do they Charles?"

Charles felt embarrassed by her candid remark. He'd taken a personal liking to her, even though he knew that she was now actually a transsexual. He tried to hid his acute embarrassment by saying, "I hope and pray you can prove them all to be wrong, but for now just enjoy your shopping."

"I'd enjoy it much better if I didn't have a permanent entourage," she said to him as she started the car. Turning to a car with two men inside it, April called to them as she sped off. "Let's go shopping, you fat overweight baboons."

As they drew near to the town her thoughts turned to finding a way to lose her escorts. The traffic lights were on red as the cars drew to a gentle halt, and she could see that there was a long queue of crossing traffic waiting to go, as soon as they changed. While they were waiting to go, she glanced in the mirror and saw that a car had gotten between the escorts' car and hers. 'Good,' she thought. Leaning out of the window and asking the car behind her to reverse so that she could do a U-turn. The traffic lights turned to green as the lady behind duly obliged. April began reversing until she caused the car behind her to bump into, and hem in, the escorting car. The lady got out to apologise just as the lights turned back to red. April seized her opportunity and sped off ahead of the crossing traffic

Eventually pulling into a lay-by, she reversed her car slowly on a right lock until it hit up against a rubbish bin, so as to put a small dint and scratch onto the near side front wing. She continued on at speed until reaching the small town and pulled onto a garage forecourt.

"Yes lady, can I help you?" the mechanic asked as he approached her car. "I do hope so," she replied, as she got out of the car revealing as much of her shapely legs that she could get away with. "Can you repair the wing before my cantankerous husband kills me?" she pleaded, giving the mechanic the innocent little girl look.

"We'll book it in for you then. As you can see we are rather busy right now," explained the mechanic.

"I will pay you double in cash if you can squeeze me in now." April pleaded.

"I'm sorry, Miss. But it will still have to be next Thursday at the earliest," the mechanic told her firmly.

"I'll pay you an extra two hundred pounds in your hand," she bargained with him.

"Well, if you're that desperate lady, I suppose we can delay that car by saying we're still waiting for the parts," he said as he pointed to an old Morris Minor. "Let me see the damage then." As he inspected the damage he told her, "It's only superficial damage, Miss, so you can pick it up about lunch time. Will that do you?"

"There's one more tiny favour you could do for me. Can you keep the car hidden inside the garage? So if my husband passes through he won't see it?"

"Ok lady, but you seem to be absolutely terrified of him. Why don't you just leave the bastard if he's that cruel to you?"

"Because he's got plenty of money," April said as she was leaving. "Why else would I stay with the bastard?"

Walking swiftly towards the bank, while keeping alert for any sign of her pursuers, she smiled to herself as she envisaged them trapped between cars exchanging their details. Being a Friday morning, the bank was crowded. 'Good,' she thought, tapping gently on Arthur's door. 'I should be able to remain undiscovered.'

Arthur opened the door and she entered his office. Closing the door behind her, she explained, "I must rush, Arthur. I would imagine that you've a lot to do today yourself?"

"Yes, I hope to finish here about 2 o'clock. Will you be back before then?"

"If I get moving now I should. Is everything ready for me out the back?" she asked, as she took the keys from Arthur. April left the bank furtively with the security officers, and walked round to the rear of the bank to where the car Arthur had hired was parked. Then the security men put the four suitcases containing the money into the boot.

Starting the car and driving it a couple of blocks, she parked outside the department store. Then she approached the customer service desk to collect the parcels that had been deposited there previously. She took them into the changing rooms and completely stripped to remove any surveillance bugs that may have been planted onto her person, before redressing in the new outfit as quickly as she could.

She was now dressed in a smart tight-fitting black leather trouser suit and boots, and had donned the wig and sunglasses. Then she put her personal money and account numbers into the new handbag, leaving everything else behind the customer service desk to be collected on her return, except for the laptop and the mobile phone. She sped north, because she had calculated that they would probably search for her to the south, thinking that she had gone to the main town.

After thirty miles she pulled up outside a building society office in a small village and entered, requesting to see the manager.

A short time elapsed before a lady opened the door to one of the offices and invited her inside. After showing her the letter of introduction, she completed the business, depositing in the two accounts half of the money. After putting the account details in her handbag she drove to the next small town so that she could open the two remaining accounts to deposit the remainder of the money, which then concluded her business plan successfully.

Driving around on a circular route, deciding to take a further precaution and return to the town from the direction of the south. She pulled into a lay-by and activated the blue tooth on her new phone, and configured the laptop, connecting it to the Internet. She set up the four new accounts, putting all of the details of the new accounts onto an e-mail and sending them to a file, storing the new account details using the username wasaman, and the password dicgon2. How appropriate, April thought to herself. Before disconnecting from the Internet she decided to text Mandy, asking her to take her old phone into the garden, so as to avoid any listening devices that may have been planted inside the house.

She let minutes elapsed before summoning up the courage to dial Mandy's number. Eventually she heard her sweet voice answering, "George, I mean April, is that you, my darling?"

There was a short pause while she composed herself. Then fighting back the tears she answered, "Yes my love, and I'm missing you all so very, very much, my darlings."

"We all miss you too, April," was Mandy's tearful response, "when are you coming back home to us?"

"I wish I knew that. How are you and the children doing?"

"We're missing you so very much. I know what you said, but I decided to tell the children, and they can't wait for you to come home again."

Choking back the tears while explaining to Mandy, "I have to finish what I'm doing first. Now listen very carefully. I have opened four new accounts; there is one in each of our four names, but you must keep it a secret until I come home. If anything happens to me, and you don't hear from me for at least a year, then you can access the accounts, as you are a joint account holder on each of them. Open my old Internet account, you know, the first one that I ever had. Then go to email banking, username wasaman, all lower case, and the password is dicgon2. You will see my email with four bank/building society accounts in it. Regarding the account numbers, just take the first four digits as they are, but reverse the remainder of the numbers except for the last digit. Can you remember all that? I'll confirm it in an e-mail but put the email somewhere safe, and destroy it after you've memorised it."

"I think I can remember it okay, April, and I'll keep the e-mail safe, but not in the house."

"Good girl, I have to go now. I love you all. Kiss the children for me please." April turned off the phone quickly as she began to cry. After drying her tears, she touched up her makeup and composed herself, before proceeding with her plans.

Travelling up from the south towards the village, she then skirted the town. She was trying to decide how best to dispose of the evidence without leaving a trace to help anyone to retrieve the money. Stopping at traffic lights behind a truck loaded with scrap cars gave her an idea. If she followed the truck it might lead her to a scrap yard with a crushing machine. Well, she could only hope and pray that it would. Following the vehicle for ten minutes eventually led her to a scrap yard containing a crushing machine, and as she had hoped, it was operational.

Parking her car she carried the laptop and mobile phone in her hands and walked towards the crusher. She pretended to be looking for something in the line of parked cars that were waiting to be crushed. The man working the machine hadn't noticed her at first as she approached the car next in line to be crushed. Leaning in through the open window, April slid the laptop and mobile phone under the passenger seat. She turned and started to return to her car as the magnet began to lift the scrap car into the crusher.

"Lady, you'll get hurt walking round there. Tell me, what it is that you're looking for?" the man working the crusher shouted down as he dropped the car in, and it started to be crushed. She was now satisfied that the evidence was well and truly destroyed, so informed the man that she was okay, and left the scrap yard.

Driving fast she weaved skilfully through the country lanes. Eventually she got back to the bank and parked the car back behind it, and walked towards the shop for her original clothing. As she entered through the side door she noticed her escorts were there looking frantically for her.

As she'd expected, there was obviously a homing device in her belongings. Being a Friday the shop was very busy, so April was able to collect the parcels unnoticed, and quickly change. Packing the leather trouser suit into a carrier bag with the accessories, she left the changing rooms putting the wig in the rubbish bin, and then slipped unnoticed out of the shop via the side entrance.

Returning to the garage that had repaired the car, she settled the bill in cash and drove the car from the garage, taking care that she wasn't being followed. Driving down the main street back to base, April noticed that the other car had caught up with her. She waved to them as she accelerated and returned to her temporary home.

Parking the car, April got out just as the two men detailed to follow her came over to check her mileage. "You have done exactly the same mileage as we have," one of them remarked, "where the hell did you go then?"

"Does it really matter? The only thing that really matters is that I wanted some time alone, and without you two goons watching over me."

"Who are you calling goons? We looked everywhere for you and that bloody car," he said angrily. Then he insisted, "If you don't tell us we will have to report that you went AWOL."

"I've already told you I needed time alone, so I hid the car in a loading bay behind a Juggernaut. Then I just spent quality time shopping." April said flippantly. Then added, "Anyway, go on report it and admit that I lost you. You'll soon see just what that gets you, writing parking tickets I should expect." Then brushing past them April walked inside where Charles was waiting to greet her.

As April passed the open door of his office he called out. "Did you have a nice day, my dear?"

"Yes, thank you Charles. I've bought a leather trouser suit. Would you like to see it on me?" she asked him.

"Maybe later, but may I ask why you think we are treating you as an expendable person?"

"You all kept saying that you had transformed me so that I'd be a nonentity, an unknown to everybody outside of this department. I would be completely untraceable and without a past. You used the excuse that it was so that I'd have more freedom to travel unnoticed." She sat and removed her shoes. "That's better, my feet are throbbing. Now where was I? Oh yes, THEN, you want me to partner a well-known agent in the field of espionage, one that will probably be instantly recognised, so I'm probably being used as the decoy."

Charles looked surprised at just how astute she'd become. "You're very perceptible, aren't you my dear? I had hoped that you'd now become the key player in all of this."

"I thought I could never expect the truth, but what the hell does it really matter anyway?" April said as she sighed deeply.

"You seem unconcerned at the probable danger. May I ask you what the reason is for that?" The phone rang, interrupting them. Charles listened, and without saying a word replaced the receiver. "I hear that you lost the men we'd detailed to watch over you. It was for at least three or four hours, I believe. Do you mind my asking you where you went to?"

"I told you earlier that I wanted a little time on my own, so I hid the car and just kept avoiding those idiots."

"Well, they were two of our best men so it can't have been easy for you to avoid them for that length of time. Anyway April, I have convened a meeting to brief you and Robert at 1900 hours. That will give you three hours to shower, eat, rest, etc."

Just before seven o'clock April breezed into the operations room. Everybody else was already there patiently waiting for her impending arrival. Sitting in the empty seat next to Robert, April listened carefully while various people stood up in turn to give their reports. They proceeded to give them all the relevant information they'd been able to accumulate. Eventually, as the last person sat down, Sir Charles asked if either April, or Robert, wanted to ask any questions.

April shook her head, but Robert asked, "What, if any, back up can be relied on?"

"None I'm afraid. The fewer the people involved in this, the better your chances of survival. And if you don't succeed it won't really matter anyway. I believe that we will all be doomed," Charles said glumly.

"How much time do we have then, Sir?" Robert asked. "And will anywhere be safe if we do fail?"

The Brigadier, who had been sitting waiting patiently, explained to them, "We're not too sure on either point, but I will offer a calculated guess. We think it will be on or around the eleventh of next month, so as to coincide with past terrorist attacks. As for people's safety, we think the third world countries around five hundred miles either side of the equator, are possibly the safest zones."

April broke her silence. "Well, we had better start packing then. Where do we start from? Or don't you bloody know that either?" There was now an air of concern in April's voice.

"We'll fly into Gambia where I've a contact waiting for us. He'll pretend to be our guide while we're out there. He's a good man. He's somebody that I've worked with in the past," Robert informed April.

Turning to Charles, she asked, "Is there anyway Robert can use an alias? As his name is probably well known, a false name might buy us a little extra time at least."

"Yes that can be arranged, although with modern technology you shouldn't rely on it for very long. They'll most certainly soon find out his real identity, but it's worth a try." Turning to Robert, Charles suggested, "Ron Marks is one of your newer alias' I believe. We will have the necessary paperwork prepared for you. It just might buy you a little time, as April suggests."

Sir Charles, realising that April was glaring at him, turned and asked her, "Is there a problem?" Then suddenly he realised that Ron Marks was his alias when he first met April, while she was still George. He placed a hand sympathetically on April's knee. "I'm sorry my dear, I didn't think to ask you if you had any objection to that name."

Realising then that it was an unintentional and genuine mistake, she lifted his hand off her knee. "No, that's as good a name as any I suppose."

Excusing herself she visited the ladies room. When she was leaving it, April found Charles standing patiently waiting for her.

"I have a feeling you don't like Robert. Is it because he was instrumental in your selection?"

"Partly, I suppose Charles, but there's something about him. I just feel I can't trust the man for some reason. He's too secretive. How was he selected for this assignment anyway?"

"He volunteered for it. Do you think your mistrust of him is just because of past history between you? Is that what makes you suspicious of him, April?"

"No, I just feel I can't trust him as I've said. I get the feeling he knows a lot more than you've told him."

Charles put a reassuring arm around her. "Just be careful out there," he told April, trying to reassure her. "And make sure that you come back here safely, do you hear me?"

She pushed his arm away. "I'm sorry, but I don't feel womanly in that way yet. Don't you worry; I intend to keep a very close eye on him. Now we had better go back in before they send out a search party to look for us. Well, as long as it's not those two buffoons of yours they couldn't find the nose on their faces."

They joined the others as the briefing was concluding. "Robert will fill you in on what you have missed," the Brigadier told them as he gathered his notes before leaving the room.

The next two days were spent in preparation for the forthcoming trip. April had been given various devices concealed in her handbag, personal luggage. A compartment at the bottom of April's vanity case concealed a specially designed handgun, one that was completely undetectable to all known security checking equipment. The container with her makeup removal pads in it had a secret compartment at the bottom of it that contained surveillance pads. Another had pads that when primed exploded after a short delay.

Her mobile phone when activated had a built-in homing device, or it could be primed to explode if a certain number was fed into it first. Robert's mobile phone if accessed wrongly would explode, and if a certain code were fed into either of them, it would turn them into highly explosive hand grenades.

"Well, the time has come for you both to depart, all I can say is good luck and God speed, but most importantly, be very, very careful." He looked towards April as he finished. When he shook Roberts's hand, Charles told him, "Watch April's back won't you? She's become a very special person to me."

"I will sir," Robert answered. Then they left for the airport.

CHAPTER 6

They travelled under the guise of newlyweds who were going on their honeymoon. Before they left, Sir Charles had given her a number, one that would enable April to keep in contact with Charles from wherever she was at any time. He had expressly forbidden her to tell Robert about this for her own protection, since she felt him to be untrustworthy.

Robert, or to use his alias now, Ron, was dressed in a white shirt, casual grey trousers with a smart navy-blue blazer. April travelled in a white costume, white satin blouse, white stilettos and matching accessories.

"You look stunning, if you don't mind my saying so, April. I can see this is going to be a business trip where pleasure can mix in beautifully," Ron suggested.

"Get a cold shower Romeo. I've told you before that this is only a business trip as far as I'm concerned." April snapped at him as they alighted from the taxi. "You can get a trolley while I pay the taxi driver."

Whilst they waited for the luggage to be labeled at the first class check-in desk, Ron seemed unduly restless as he frequently looked around him. "Why are you so fidgety?" April asked, "Are you nervous about flying or something?"

"I'm always nervous about flying, until we take off that is," Ron's lied. "Have a nice flight," the check-in attendant said with a smile as April collected their boarding passes and walked towards the departure lounge. Ron glanced behind him again, and as though he recognised somebody he said. "I won't be long; I need to visit the gents."

Walking fast toward the toilets, he passed the first ones and continued on until he had reached the farthest one. April was watching carefully as he approached a man of African appearance. He then followed Ron into the toilet block. This made April feel uneasy, but she pretended not to notice while trying to act casual. Taking her phone from the handbag, she took the stranger picture as he left the toilet and sent it to Charles, adding a text message asking him to check the man out thoroughly.

When Ron eventually returned from the toilet, she asked, "Are you okay now?"

"Yes thank you, April, I'm sorry about that but when nature calls." Then changing the subject he suggested, "Shall we go straight through? We should be boarding in about twenty minutes." He offered April his arm reminding her. "We are supposed to be a newly married couple remember? So can we at least act like one in public?"

Reluctantly she took his arm as they walked through to the first class lounge. The flight was being announced so they went straight towards the departure gate. Within thirty minutes they found themselves being taxied towards the runway, and soon were en route for Gambia.

It was a pleasant flight. April pretended to sleep so as not to have to act as if they were newly married. She was becoming more and more uneasy by the involvement of Ron, and of his attitude towards her as his new bride.

Five hours later an announcement could be heard, 'Prepare for landing.' Then twenty minutes later the plane was touching down in Banjul Airport, Gambia.

Travelling first class they were first to disembark, and as they reached the carousel they found their luggage was already there waiting for collection. April put the cases onto a trolley and pushed the trolley towards the door to wait for Ron to arrive with the hire car. When he was putting the luggage into the boot, apologising for taking so long, April noticed that the other passengers had started to filter through. Among the first passengers to alight was the African gentleman that Ron had been talking to at the airport in London. He'd disembarked early and was only carrying hand luggage. Pretending to reapply her makeup, while sitting patiently in the passenger seat, April watched the man by using her makeup mirror. As he walked close to Ron, April saw him take an envelope from him, and put it into his inside jacket pocket.

April was already removing her coat and placing it carefully across the back seats. She suggested to him that he'd be more comfortable if he did the same. He removed his jacket, which April took from him, placing it carefully on top of hers, but purposely allowing the envelope to fall out onto the floor of the car. April quickly flicked it under her seat unseen by Ron, who was occupied starting the car and filtering out into the line of traffic that was leaving the airport, following the signs into Banjul. He stopped the car in a lay-by to look at the map for directions, before continuing on toward the hotel. When they'd finally reached it, the young porter showed them up to the honeymoon suite on the first floor, grinning broadly the whole time.

She asked Ron, "Why is he grinning at us like a Cheshire cat?"

The young boy, who up until now hadn't spoken to them, said. "You are just married lovely lady. You are a very lucky man sir, the lady is very beautiful." Ron agreed as they reached the room, tipping the boy generously as he thanked him.

"I think I'll get a shower, I feel dirty after all that travelling. Aren't you coming to wash my back, darling?"

"Make yours a cold one then. I'll have a shower *after you*," she answered, ignoring his feeble suggestion.

"Just my luck," he retorted mournfully.

"What's just your fucking luck?" asked April, as she tired at his childishness.

"Going on honeymoon with my lesbian wife," Ron commented as he gathered his clean clothes to change into.

This angered her. "If you knew more about me you'd stop this childish incessant pestering," she rasped sharply. "Anyway, we've a job to do, and THAT must take precedence."

He emptied his pockets onto the table and disappeared into the shower without saying another word. Seizing her opportunity, April picked up the car and room keys, and shouted through to him, "I won't be too long; I think I must have dropped my compact in the car." She picked up her compact to make it seem authentic when she returned, then she left the room rushing down to the underground garage.

When she walked from the lift, April disturbed a man who was near their car. The shadowy figure quickly scuttled off into a waiting car and sped away. Checking the car, which seemed to be untouched, and thinking that she'd only have disturbed an opportune thief, she quickly got the envelope from under the seat. 'Good, it's unsealed,' she thought.

Opening the envelope it revealed a map and what looked like instructions for something. Working as fast as possible April used the camera on her phone to copy the documents, placing them back into the envelope, and back behind the driving seat. No sooner had she locked the car door than Ron appeared.

"You've been a long time, April. Have you seen an envelope in the car at all?"

"I haven't looked for one," then glancing toward the car's rear seat she asked, "Is that it on the floor?"

As she opened the door to retrieve it, Ron snatched it from her grasp with a look of relief on his face. "Thank you, I thought I'd lost it for a moment."

April asked as they travelled back up in the lift, "Why, is the envelope important?"

"It's only important to me," he told her while trying to sound casual. "Are you going to shower now?"

"Yes, and I don't need you to wash my back before you ask," she retorted. "While you shower Miss High-and-Mighty, I think I'll try to find an English newspaper. Is there anything that you need?"

Shaking her head as the lift stopped she went into the room after watching Ron disappearing down towards the ground floor. Much as she was tempted to follow him, she was feeling far too exhausted and dirty from all of the travelling. So, after texting the photographs to Charles, she undressed and got into the shower.

She stood and just allowed the relaxing warm water to run over her tired and aching body. Soon her body started to relax, as the events of the day passed slowly through her tired mind.

Her tranquility was interrupted when she heard a bump in the next room. Stealthily stepping out of the shower and closing the curtain, as she took her pistol from the pocket of her robe. Trying to hold her breath as the water dripped off her naked body, April watched with bated breath as the door handle turned slowly and silently, and the door inched open. An arm brandishing a sub machine-guns pointed in towards the still-running shower.

Suddenly the shower curtain was rent apart by the spurt of automatic fire. She shot through the door and a dead body fell onto the shower room floor. After frisking it, she found no clue as to his identity, but noticed that he was Caucasian, and smartly dressed. Picking up his gun she walked through into the other room to place it by her bag, as the door opened suddenly. Taken by surprise, she was unable to return to the shower room to dress.

"Have you-" Ron started to say. Then he stopped suddenly with his mouth agape. He couldn't believe the sight that met him. "You've got no clothes on," he stuttered in disbelief.

"Well as you are continually reminding me we're supposed to be a honeymooning couple, remember?" April snapped sarcastically. "As you can see I was rudely interrupted so you can just close your mouth now. Anyone would think I was the first woman that you'd seen naked. You can move his body while I get dressed."

Seeing no point in hiding what he'd already seen, she started to put on her bra and briefs while explaining what had just happened. Walking through into the bedroom while continuing to dress, April noticed that Ron was still looking at her with a fixed stare. "Aren't you going to do anything but stare at me?" she asked, walking back into the living area wearing a skimpy top and a wraparound sarong. As she walked she pulled her hair tightly back into a ponytail.

Eventually Ron managed to speak, "I'm sorry. It's just that you really do have a very beautiful body, and finding you that way, well it took me rather by surprise, that's all." He put the body into the shower and closed the door. "I think that that room is out of bounds for the time being. I also think that maybe we should move on from here pronto, don't you?"

"Yes, but aren't you collecting some weaponry from somewhere near here?" she asked, as the adrenaline started to abate and she began to shake from head to foot.

Noticing this Ron put his arm round her, resting his other hand on her clasped hands as he tried to console her. He was surprised when April put her arms round his neck nestling her face into his shoulder. April sobbed uncontrollably for five or more minutes, while Ron just held her, saying nothing. He waited patiently for her to stop crying, and eventually she pushed him away gently.

"Sorry about that Ron, but don't worry it won't ever happen again."

"I'm not worried. Was that your first kill, April?"

"Yes," she replied, fixing her eye makeup. "It goes against my Christian beliefs really, although I know that sometimes it is necessary in the battles against evil."

"I didn't know that you were a believer. It won't endanger the operation, will it? Does Sir Charles know?" Suddenly his voice was filled with deep concern at these unanswered questions.

"Yes, Charles knows, and don't worry I'll do whatever I have to do," she assured him as she finished packing and closed the cases. "What excuse do we give for checking out so early?"

"We don't. We just leave. But first, as you've already said we need to collect the weaponry. I organised it when I went for the paper. Sorry I didn't trust you and tell you about it," he said apologetically. "If I go first you can lower the cases down from the side balcony. When I've put them in the boot of the car I'll drive round to the front and pick you up, as if we are going out for a sightseeing tour. With a bit of luck they won't find us missing for at least a couple of days. Oh, and don't forget to put the 'Do Not Disturb' sign on the door before you leave will you?" When April had passed the cases over the balcony she joined Ron in the car. "Ok now?" he asked, as they started to pull away.

"Yes, I'm fine now Ron, thank you. Is it far to our rendezvous with your contact?"

"About an hour on these roads I think. I expect the traffic will be pretty heavy at this time of day, too." he said as they headed towards a bridge crossing the river. "Try to sleep for a while, April. You look totally exhausted."

"What, with all this traffic noise? I'll rest my eyes for a while though," she agreed, snuggling down into the seat. April was now feeling very confused. Ron seemed a very concerned and caring person. He was not a bit like somebody about to assist in the destruction of mankind.

She must have fallen asleep out of sheer exhaustion, because the next thing that she knew the car was jerking to a halt. Sitting upright, April found that they were in a shantytown on the hillside. Looking down to her left she could see the river unwinding to the ocean from its source.

"Feeling better after your little nap?" asked Ron, as he opened the door inviting her to step out. "We're at my contacts place of work. So shall we see what he has on offer for us?"

They walked into an old dilapidated building. "Mind the oil patches. This place doubles as the local garage for its cover," Ron explained as he rapped on the office door. "Ladies first," he said, gesturing for her to enter first and then following into the gloomy office. Another door opened and the man Ron met at the airport walked in, and shook Ron by the hand.

"Nice to meet you at last, Ron. Can I get either of you a drink?" he offered, as he opened a drink cabinet.

Ron nodded towards April, "Ladies first."

"Make mine something strong if you have it," she told him with an air of trepidation. "I think I'm going to need it."

The man handed her a vodka, explaining. "Although we don't drink alcohol, I keep some here for my special customers."

She took the large vodka from him and gulped it down.

Ron looked at her inquisitively, "Is there something wrong, April?"

"No, I'm just a little confused, that's all. When you two met at the airport why didn't you introduce me then?"

"We weren't sure you could be trusted," the man explained. "I'm Abdullah," he introduced himself, bowing courteously. "And you are the lovely Miss April Darling that Ron has raved so much about. Your description of her was very inadequate Ron. She is far more beautiful than words alone could have ever described."

April found his flattery quaintly amusing as she smiled broadly, and thanked him. Then she suggested that they get down to the business at hand. Abdullah walked over to a table and removed the cloth draped across it. Pressing a button he opened the top revealing a large array of arms. "Do you know anything about guns, April?"

"Yes. They kill people." She then moved towards a hand-held rocket launcher that had been dismantled. Without saying a word she picked it up and assembled it, loaded it, and placing it back onto the table.

"Nine seconds flat, very impressive," Abdullah said as he applauded her. "Where did you get your knowledge of weapons?"

She joked, "It is just part of my misguided youth." Then she sat to finish her drink, oblivious to their conversation as Ron haggled for the best deal.

"He wants us to use his men as back up. What do you think, April?"

"You know him, Ron. I don't. Whatever you think is best. But remember the more vehicles that we use, the more open we will be to attack."

"If we change to a 4x4 Abdullah says that his men can travel in a seven-ton truck. That way we'll look like an ordinary hunting party," Ron explained. "That's if you agree. Anyway, what makes you think that we haven't just met?"

"He was at the airport and on the same plane. He passed you an envelope with a map in it. Do I really need to go any further?"

"You are extremely observant. I didn't tell you because I wasn't sure whether I could trust you or not. Again, I'm very sorry, April." he apologised profusely.

Saying that she needed some fresh air, she picked up her handbag and headed out of the front of the garage. Sitting in the car she put the air conditional on full, as she took the opportunity to check if there were any messages. She found that there was a voice message from Charles warning her to be careful. They knew Abdullah as a double agent, serving the highest bidder. He could not be trusted under any circumstances. Deleting the voice message, April reclined the seat so she could rest more comfortably.

Suddenly, April saw a glint of light from the rooftop opposite, as the sun reflected off something. Slowly April scanned the surrounding rooftops counting at least ten snipers. Thinking for a moment and pretending that she hadn't noticed them, April started the car and drove it round to the back of the building. Parking it, and returning to where Ron was still haggling.

"Feeling better now?" Ron asked.

"I'll feel better after we leave here," she told him, producing a pistol and pointing it at the head of Abdullah. "I see that your men have a reception committee waiting for us when we leave here." Ignoring his pleas that he had no knowledge of what was happening; April explained to Ron that it appeared they might have fallen into a trap.

Abdullah was still pleading his innocence when there was a noise at the front of the garage. "That should be my lieutenant, I told him to set up camp near the border for the men, and then to come back here to collect us."

Keeping her gun pointed at Abdullah, April stepped back into the shadows. Two men entered dressed in combat gear, "We've set up camp sir, and the men are ready for you to join them whenever you're ready," said the soldier. Then he noticed Ron and April as they stepped forward into the light. Seeing April's gun he started to raise his hands slowly.

"It's okay. You can put your hands down now." Ron told them as April replaced her pistol. "We just needed to be sure that's all. Now we've got to move quickly."

While April and Ron were discussing their escape, Abdullah explained to his men about being surrounded by guerrilla forces. April took control explaining to them, "That's good the truck is headed in the right direction, because we will need to leave by the back door. We will drive straight through the wall just about there, where it's the weakest point." She pointed to the loose boarding on the back wall of the clumsily built shack. "But firstly we must destroy anything and everything that we'll be leaving behind. Right Ron, we must be quick, they're probably only waiting to see if anybody else is coming before they attack. See those four props holding up the centre of the roof? Tape these grenades to the back of them about halfway up. Then run a cord from the pins to the back of the truck, but make sure it's long enough to pull the pins just as the truck breaks through the wall. I'll fasten grenades to that stack of ammunition and weapons, with a longer cord connecting them to the truck, so that as the roof collapses it will explode, and hopefully produce a huge fireball."

They worked feverishly, and when it was completed April asked if they had a spare car.

"Yes," said a confused Abdullah, with a puzzled expression as he handed her the keys. "But it's not very reliable. It's the blue car at the rear of the garage."

April thanked him as she removed some loose boarding in the back wall and squeezed out through the gap. She then drove the car round and parked it across the front entrance, but with the engine still running as if they were about to leave. She then placed a small remote controlled explosive device over the petrol tank before leaving it.

As she was returning inside April noticed some movement on the rooftops. "The guerrillas seem to be preparing to attack the building, so are you all nearly ready?" April urged them. "I don't think it will be much longer now before they start the attack."

"We're ready when you are," Ron confirmed as he fastened the final cord to the truck.

"Right, now start the truck. As soon as you hear me honking the horn go flat out through the back wall, and up the hill opposite without stopping, then turn left behind the shacks.

"We'll be following right behind you." explained Ron, as they left through the hole in the back wall. Ron started the engine as April prepared to detonate the explosive that she'd placed in the car at the front entrance.

"GO," she shouted, hearing the truck accelerate as it burst through the wall, as April pushed the button for the remote control. There was a loud explosion followed quickly by a second and third.

Following the truck up the hill, April glanced behind her. She could see a huge fireball as debris rained down on the scene of devastation. The smoke and dust masked them from the eyes of the guerrillas, as they had hoped. "Well, that party went off with a bang," she joked. "I wonder how long we have before they follow us."

"A couple of hours tops I'd say," Abdullah told her. "They're not very bright. As soon as it cools down and they can start sifting through the ashes, that's when they will realise that there are no bodies."

Even though they travelled as quickly as the truck would carry them, it still took an hour to cross the rough terrain of the open grasslands, until finally they reached the cover of the bush. They continued pressing on for several more arduous hours along the narrow winding trail, that at times seemed non-existent, eventually the bush opened up to where his men were camped in the small-concealed clearing overhung by the branches of the tall trees.

Abdullah explained that this was the rest of his party of mercenaries. They all ate what looked like a large stew, then April and Ron was shown to their tent, as Abdullah encouraged them to rest while they still had the chance.

Ron was soon snoring gently, but April tossed and turned restlessly. Eventually she abandoned all thoughts of trying to sleep. She decided instead to use the time to freshen up and put on some clean clothes.

While she was trying to gather her thoughts about the day's events, April suddenly heard shouting. Peering out through the flap of the tent she saw Abdullah and his men being held by rebel militia at gunpoint, who had crossed over from Senegal. Stealthily she crept to where Ron lay sleeping. Placing one hand over his mouth to prevent him from making a sound, April gestured for him to keep quiet and follow her. Before she could show Ron what was happening two armed men burst into their tent.

Reacting purely out of instinct, April lunged at one of the rebels' machine guns. Grasping it tightly she fell backwards bringing her feet up into his stomach as she threw him, keeping a tight grip on his gun. As he fell into the tent pole, his weight snapped it and caused the tent to collapse. April rolled out from under the tent and kept as low as possible, bolting towards the cover of the bush.

From this position she watched the two guards frog march Ron towards the rest of the prisoners, who were all gathered at the centre of the camp. April felt something brushing past her leg and froze. Moving only her eyes, she watched in sheer horror as a large python slid gracefully passed her.

Returning her attention once more to the scene in the camp, April saw two of the rebel's repeatedly beating Ron with the butts of their guns.

As she mentally ran through her options, she remembered an old film that she'd seen when she was younger. It was a cowboy film where an ammunition magazine was thrown onto a campfire to create a diversion. April took careful aim at the rebel leader who was standing over the fire, seeing that he had an ammunition belt slung over one of his shoulders. I'll only get one shot, she thought as she set the gun onto a single shot before taking aim and carefully squeezing the trigger. The man fell onto the fire and within seconds the ammunition on his shoulder began going off. It sounded as if the camp was surrounded, so the undisciplined rabble dropped their weapons and surrendered, holding their hands in the air.

From her cover April began picking off the rebels systematically. Using their utter confusion to the best of her advantage, she quickly disposed of the threat of the rebel forces.

Tentatively, April emerged from her cover. Abdullah and his men began gathering up their weaponry, as she quickly went to Ron's aide. He lay in a pool of his own blood, with one of Abdullah men working feverishly to stem the bleeding. Tears filled April's eyes as she gripped Ron's hand tightly. She asked, "He's going to be okay, isn't he?"

"Yes lady, now that I've stopped the bleeding he will be. Just let him sleep himself better now," the man told her as he lifted the unconscious Ron onto a make shift stretcher. "He'll have to travel with us on the truck, so that I can make sure that he's okay."

April thanked him, watching as Ron was carried towards the waiting truck. As they carried Ron past the prisoners one of them spat on him as he shouted. "DIE YOU INFIDEL DOG."

Seething with anger April swung her gun round and opened fire. "DIE YOU IGNORANT FUCKING BASTARDS." April yelled as she mowed down the startled rebels.

Eventually, when Abdullah had recovered from the shock of watching her temper, he reached out and lifted the barrel of her gun, pointing it upwards to safety. April snatched the gun from his grip then threw it down to the floor in anger.

"You have got a temper, haven't you April? What about the Geneva Convention? Besides, I want somebody left alive to question."

Sobbing uncontrollably, April yelled at him angrily, "FUCK THE GENEVA CONVENTION, DID THOSE BASTARDS OBSERVE IT? Besides, what were you going to do with them? If we take them with us it will only slow us down." she reminded him as she wiped the tears from her eyes.

"She has a point, sir," said Abdullah's lieutenant, who, up until now had stood silently waiting.

"Let's see who's still left alive, and what they know before we decide what to do with them. But I suggest that you try to get some rest now." Abdullah advised her, walking towards the remaining prisoners still left alive.

Reluctantly agreeing, she went to her freshly-erected tent. She lay on her bed and, because she was completely exhausted, she soon drifted into a deep, but restless sleep.

She opened her eyes to look at her watch and leapt from the bed, becoming aware of the stark reality that she'd slept for twelve hours solid. Emerging from her tent she was unable to see any prisoners.

"You must have been exhausted," Abdullah greeted her as he offered her a drink of water.

"Thank you," she said gratefully taking a long drink. "I needed that. Now how's Ron doing?"

"He's doing just fine, but I'm letting him sleep as much as possible," the lieutenant explained. "After you've freshened up we had better get moving."

Quickly she washed and freshened up as the troops decamped, and removed all signs that they'd ever been there. "How did you get on with the prisoners?" she asked Abdullah.

"They didn't know anything," he told her, "they just blindly follow orders."

"Where are they now?" she asked, glancing around the camp.

"They're tied up in their own truck with the rest of the corpses. So, are you ready to go now?"

"You killed them?"

"Not yet, but as you've pointed out, taking them along with us would only slow us down," he reminded her. He climbed into the 4x4 and waved the truck past, instructing his driver to follow it.

When passing the enemy's vehicle, Abdullah tossed in a live grenade as they drove off into the bush. A loud explosion was heard, and as April glanced behind her she witnessed flames high above the bush, as the remaining perpetrators were incinerated in the inferno. For hours the small convoy twisted and turned as it weaved its uneasy way east along the country track, avoiding any major traffic routes. April was oblivious to this, being lost in thought and silent prayer as she wrestled with her conscience over her part in the disposal of the rebels.

Eventually they drove into a small town stopping outside of an Internet café. April climbed out as Abdullah offered his arm to assist her.

"Thank you. You're a gentleman," she said gratefully, stepping down onto the dusty road. "I'm as stiff as a board now," April told him as she stretched her legs and rubbed her lower back. As they walked towards the truck parked behind she added, "I must see how Ron's doing."

April smiled broadly when she found Ron sitting up chatting to the other men. "Thank you," he said gratefully, "if you hadn't intervened when you did the bastards would certainly have beaten me to a pulp."

She told him jokingly, "I'm keeping that pleasure for myself," placing a reassuring hand on his shoulder, added, "glad to see you are feeling better though. Is there anything you need?"

Abdullah interrupted, "Let the doctor have a look at you now, Ron." Turning to April and asking. "Can we talk now?"

Walking slowly to and fro he told her that a large convoy of heavy trucks had passed through a few days earlier, adding that they were heading into Mali laden with electronic equipment, and what looked like large satellite dishes. "If Ron has to be hospitalised I'll arrange for somebody to stay here with him. He can follow us when he's feeling better. But we must continue to push on as quickly as possible," he insisted.

The English doctor came over to them, "A lesser man would be dead by now. As far as I can tell he seems to have a ruptured spleen, a damaged liver, and other internal injuries. It's hard for me to be sure of how much damage there is until the swelling subsides. I've suggested that he be moved into hospital, but he's refusing to go." Stopping to mop his brow he added, "I'd almost forgotten how pig-headed the English can be."

Ron struggled to join them supported by a man on either side. "I've told him that I can't, so just give me some bloody painkillers and let's get going. I'll visit a hospital later when it's more convenient," Ron insisted impatiently as he was helped into the car.

The doctor shook his head in exasperation as he gave April some tablets and pain killers. After thanking him and saying goodbye, the doctor returned to his ever-growing queue of patients at his makeshift surgery.

"How did they get all that equipment across the border undetected?" she asked. "Surely somebody would ask questions about what it was, and where they are heading?"

"You're forgetting this is Africa, April. The people here are so poor that if somebody gives them money to forget what they saw well, it's very hard to be an honest man out here when you're starving. But I think I know where they have crossed, so let's get going," Abdullah insisted, as he started the engine and headed out into the countryside.

"What about you? How do you remain honest?"

Abdullah smiled wryly. "I don't. I'm a mercenary, remember? But in this case we're all fighting for a common cause, survival." He eyed April up and down before he added, "Besides, I like the company." Looking in the mirror he told her, "Ron has fallen asleep; it's probably because of the painkillers. We will just let him sleep himself well."

"Where did you learn to speak such perfect English, Abdullah?" She asked, making polite conversation.

"I was at Oxford for six years reading politics," he proudly told her.

Moving as fast as the roads would allow them, they reached the checkpoint at dusk, as Ron woke up. Abdullah recognised one of the guards and walked over towards him and they both went into a small hut.

Fifteen minutes past. "I wonder if he's ok in there." Ron said with concern. "It's taking him an awful long time. Ah, at last, here he comes," he said with a sigh of relief as Abdullah emerged from the hut and returned to where they were waiting.

"Sorry it took so long. Apparently they headed through here two days ago," he started to explain. "Abe the guard has rung ahead for me, he is my brother, and he was here when they passed through. They told him that it was imperative to keep their whereabouts a secret; and they gave them a very handsome bribe, I believe. So I bribed them to tell us where they are now. Apparently they are just crossing at Sainsoutou, so we must go after them now."

Crossing into Senegal they pressed, on sharing the driving and attempting to sleep in between times. Avoiding stopping except for meals and fuel, they tried desperately to make up for the lost time, and catch up to the convoy before they could reach their base camp.

CHAPTER 7

The heat of the day was relentless as they trundled on through the barren savannah towards the border at Sainsoutou. Weaving between the sand dunes they edged towards the frontier crossing as the sound of helicopters could be heard growing louder. "Find us somewhere to stop Abdullah where we can't be seen. They may be looking for us," April urged.

It's probably just the army patrolling the border," said Ron.

"Maybe, but let's not take any chances," she suggested as the vehicles drew to a halt below a shallow ridge of sand. They hastily spread the camouflage nets just in time as two helicopter gun-ships skimmed slowly over the ridge.

"They're not a border control," he whispered. "It seems they are looking for somebody after all, and it's probably us."

"You said that you bribed them to keep our whereabouts secret. Besides, you told us that Abe was your brother." April said, as she opened the boot to access the arms.

"Abe's really my half-brother, different mothers, but we haven't met for at least three years now. I guess he took an even bigger bribe. What are you doing, April?"

"Listen," she said, pointing skywards. "Do you hear them going away?" Abdullah shook his head. "No," April continued. "They're not going anywhere, are they?"

Ron tried to stand, suggesting, "I'll help you, April." But then he collapsed backwards into an incapable heap.

"You just stay there quietly, Ron. You're in no fit state to go anywhere, and you'll only hinder me." April insisted as she loaded two hand-held rocket launchers. "I'll deal with this in my own inimitable way. You just stay well out of sight."

"Can I help at all?" Abdullah offered.

"No. But thanks for offering. I can move much faster on my own," insisted April putting her arms through the shoulder straps of the rocket launchers.

Then picking up a Magnum April tucked it into the back of her skirt saying, "Wish me luck."

Creeping out from under the camouflage net April moved cautiously between the peaks of the dunes, trying to avoid being spotted by the helicopters too soon as they circled slowly above. She then partly concealed one rocket launcher thirty yards from the ridge, and covered it with sand, but leaving just enough showing so it could be easily, and quickly, identified. Rolling over the crest of the dune, but still keeping as low as possible, April moved fifty metres further forward. Then she placed the other rocket launcher to the rear of the next dune, but still out of sight of the encircling helicopters. Peeping over the top of the dune, April saw one of the helicopters approaching very cautiously.

She ripped open her blouse and roughed up her hair so she would look disheveled, looking as though she had just been raped then left in the middle of the dessert to die.

April then stood up waving both her arms towards the approaching helicopter. "HELP," she shouted frantically. "WILL YOU PLEASE HELP ME?"

Seeing her slim, blonde, partially-clad figure, the helicopter approached sideways on. "Are you alone lady?" the soldier called to her as they moved closer towards her.

"Yes, they went that way," she told them pointing due east. "About two hours ago. There were two truckloads of them. Are you going to help me now?"

The soldier gave an evil smile as he pointed his gun towards April. Realising that he was about to shoot, she dived and rolled picking up the rocket launcher as she rolled over it. April rapidly fired it at the surprised soldier causing the helicopter to erupt in a ball of flames.

The other helicopter was fast approaching, its machine guns discharging rapidly. She sprinted in a zigzagging course to the other rocket launcher diving onto it. Grasping the butt and rolling April fired, sending a rocket into the open doors that exploded within the gun-ship. Within seconds the balls of flames had crashed onto the sand leaving no survivors. Retrieving the two rocket launchers April carried them back to where the party was waiting for her open mouthed, amazed at her sheer, but simple audacity.

"Let's go now," April ordered, placing the launchers back into their cases. Without speaking they brought the trucks roaring into life in readiness of continuing on towards the border. "I'm sure the explosions must have alerted the border guards. Can we cross any further north?" April asked, as she stood behind the open boot to change out of her ripped clothing.

"Yes April, just leave it to me." Abdullah willingly agreed as they resumed their journey. As they approached a fork, he veered left and followed the track north. Two hours passed by while April relaxed, and tried to catch up on her sleep. "We have crossed into Mali now," he announced proudly

Ron asked, "I didn't see the crossing. When did we cross over?"

"A couple of miles back," he explained. "They don't bother here because as you saw, the trail is almost non-existent. The slave traders used it originally, but most people don't even know it exists anymore. Those that do often get stuck because they slip off the trail, that was what all those abandoned vehicles were that we passed. I do need to reach Kayes by midday to meet up with a friend of mine. She's been trading with this madman, so hopefully she has some information for us."

"Hopefully," agreed April as she stretched trying to shake off her weariness. "Then perhaps we can get some shut eye before moving on. God knows we all need some proper rest." April reminded them, as she watched the sun rising over the River Senegal. "I'll drive and give you some rest now if you like," she volunteered.

Abdullah brought the convoy to a halt.

"Thank you. I'm feeling rather tired now. Well, more weary really. Just keep going due north-east until we reach Kayes," he yawned. "Excuse me. I must be even more tired than I thought," he said closing his eyes. Soon he was snoring loudly as they weaved and trundled their way onwards.

It was a barren country. The party passed through only the occasional sleepy village as they continued their journey. Making good time they reached Kayes by seven a.m. as the trucks ground to a halt outside of a small hotel.

Abdullah, suggested that April book a room while he went on ahead to meet his friend. "If I don't go alone she'll probably run off. But I'll be as quick as I can."

After booking a twin room on the ground floor April helped Ron to get into bed. As soon as she'd covered him with a mosquito net his eyes closed, and he fell fast asleep.

As she showered April reflected on the events that had passed during the last couple of days. But it had brought them no nearer to the source of the global threats. Stepping from the shower she could hear a strange noise in the next room. Quickly wrapping in a large towel, she rushed through into the bedroom where Ron lay sleeping, only to find that he was making a loud throaty rattle as he exhaled.

Racing to his side she felt his brow, and realised that he was running an extremely high fever. After taking his pulse she discovered that it was rapid and weak, and also seeing that he was sweating profusely and his skin was pallid. There was a large contusion where he had been beaten, which seemed to be slowly spreading across his forehead as she watched.

April contacted the reception desk to ask them if they'd bring up plenty of ice. This she then packed around Ron's body in an attempt to lower his body temperature. She placed an ice compress on his bruised forehead, and asked the porter if he'd fetch a doctor as quickly as he could.

She dressed as quickly as she could while she waited for the doctor or Abdullah to return. But seeing how seriously ill Ron had become, she went to urge the doctor to hurry personally.

On reaching the room the doctor examined Ron, and then working feverishly he connected a drip to his arm, and gave Ron various injections.

"Is he going to be all right, doctor?" April asked him as she assisted the doctor and explained how Ron had come by his injuries.

"Thankfully you packed him in ice or he would most certainly be dead by now. I will need an X-ray to confirm the extent of the injuries, and I'm sure he has a massive blood clot on the brain. I don't think he can survive being moved on these roads, but unless we can get him to hospital he'll die anyway. Are you his wife?"

She had to say yes because that was the guise that they were travelling under. "Would a helicopter help, doctor?"

"It's probably your best bet. But where the hell are you going to get a helicopter from?"

Ignoring the question April used her cell phone to contact Charles. Explaining to him Ron's condition, she stressed the need of an air ambulance so that they could move him to a hospital. Charles, pretending to be an embassy official, requested that the doctor stay with Ron until he could be shipped on to a hospital. He then informed them that a US convoy lay south of them off the coast of Accra. "A medical team is being dispatched as we speak and they will be there within a couple of hours. So, if the doctor agrees to stay with Ron, you should continue on, but only if you feel able to do so. However, it's far too late to get you a replacement for Ron. By the way, where is the person that did this?"

"I shot the bastard. In fact I shot the fucking lot of them," she told Charles, forgetting that the doctor was listening. "I'll be okay. Just make sure that Ron gets the best doctors to help him," April finished, and then rang off. Turning she saw the shocked look on the doctor's face. "I'm sorry, but you weren't supposed to hear that. Do you come from around here?" April asked, trying to make pleasant conversation, "because you speak such perfect English."

Eventually the doctor replied, "I'm of African descent, as you can see, but I grew up, and was educated in South London. I came out here because I wanted to give something back to my roots. Are you going to kill me, too?" he asked apprehensively. "I would like to know so that I can make my peace with my God."

April noticed his hand touching the dove badge on his lapel. "No, I had to shoot them in self-defense. I'm a Christian too, so I don't take lives lightly," April tried to reassure him. "So will you please take good care of Ron for me?"

Breathing a sigh of relief the doctor agreed, as Abdullah returned. "What's the matter with Ron, April?"

She explained briefly. Then after leaving Ron to the care of the doctor, she took him outside to find out what information he had gathered from his contact.

"You won't like what my friend has suggested," Abdullah told April hesitantly.

"Try me, because we're fast running out of time now."

"My contact is a woman by the name of Rebecca. She's part of a tribe of nomads that freely roam this area virtually unopposed. She knows that there is a large band of mercenaries being recruited by a Sheikh Mohammed Kahn, and at the moment he is camped inside of the Assil N'ajjer National Park. She also noticed a vast amount of electronic equipment being set up there, describing it as looking like a mobile NASA. Every time Rebecca's people pass through there, they're allowed into the camp to trade, and they even take orders for their next visit."

"Yes, but how will that help us?" interrupted April impatiently.

"I'm just getting to that now, April. According to what Rebecca has seen on her visits, anybody else who gets anywhere near to them is shot on sight, and without any exceptions. Nobody else can get close to them. If you are to get into their camp you'll certainly need Rebecca's help."

"Okay! And now what does she suggest?" April asked wearying at the amount of time he was taking to explain.

"She sees only two options. Either you join their train dressed in traditional Muslim dress, or she can pretend that they have captured you and they want to sell you to the Sheikh for his harem." He paused while waiting to see any reactions before continuing, "If you take the first option and they catch you, after abusing you, you will most certainly be put to death. What do you think, or have you any other suggestions?"

"I will travel as part of the train as normal. Then I can just play it by ear," April said firmly. "At least that way it would leave all the options open. Besides, I can conceal more weapons that way."

The next twenty-four hours where spent frantically preparing for the trip. Rebecca gave April a crash course in how a Muslim woman is expected to behave, while April busied herself concealing as much of her arsenal as she could comfortably get away with.

As the sun rose over the sand dunes, last minute preparations were being finalised as Rebecca entered the tent.

"I think you should wear these from now on April, so that you'll feel more comfortable in them when we arrive at the camp." Rebecca advised, as she handed her an Abaya and Niqab. "Make sure that you wear something cool underneath it though."

"I thought I'd wear my ordinary clothing under it, ready for a quick change if it's necessary."

"Maybe when we get closer to their camp April, but it'll be far too hot to travel in them. Now, when you're ready we'll be on our way."

April thanked Abdullah, who kissed her on both cheeks then hugged her tightly, wishing April good luck, and Godspeed. He then asked April to return to visit him when it was all over. Tearfully, she promised to return, and then mounted a camel to start the arduous trek to the rebel stronghold.

The party travelled onwards, breaking camp each day just before daybreak, then travelling until long after sunset, but resting under makeshift shelters in the hottest part of the day. They made good progress through Mali, and across Algeria, as the days past before they reached the Assili N'ajjer national park.

"We've made good progress, April," Rebecca confirmed. "We should reach where they are camped sometime tomorrow."

"I've been meaning to ask you, Rebecca, how is it that in a deeply Muslin country, that you, a mere woman, are accepted as a leader?"

"Because I've proved myself to them, April," Rebecca giggled, "everybody calls me Lara Croft around here. Now we will make camp shortly, and travel into their camp sometime tomorrow."

CHAPTER 8

When the dawn broke it found April mounting a camel for the final leg of the journey that would lead her straight into the heart of the rebel stronghold. "If you are ready April, we should reach their camp in about five hours." Rebecca announced.

"Yes, I'm ready. So let's go. These aren't the most comfortable form of transport I've travelled on. And the sooner we get there the better my arse will feel about it," April moaned. As the camels were brought to an upright position the train moved steadily off towards their destination.

As they travelled April was in a pensive mood, she was trying to anticipate what she would, or could, be meeting her. Shortly before noon her profound thoughts were interrupted by Rebecca.

"They're just over that hill April," she indicated with her hand. "Would you like to stop here for a short rest first?"

"No, let's go straight on into their bloody camp. They know that we're here, don't they?"

"So you've seen him too," Rebecca remarked, as she nodded towards the lone sentry at the crest of the hill. Rebecca instructed one of her men to travel on ahead, as she explained to April. "I've told him to announce our arrival so that we won't be fired on when we arrive at their camp."

Shortly afterwards the party found itself at the crest of a sand dune, looking down into the valley below. The scene was of a small army camped around an oasis. There was, in the centre of the camp, a large marquee that was supplying the electricity from the four mobile generators standing to the far left. Thick cabling protruded from each corner of the marquee, which in turn connected to an abundance of satellite dishes and aerials. Two heavily-armed sentries guarded a large canvas shelter to the right, which April assumed housed the Sheikh's harem. Adjacent to this was a lavishly adorned tent containing the Sheikh and his personal attendants.

Slowly they descended into the camp. They were told to set out the wares in a small clearing next to the water hole, so that the Sheikh would be able to view them at his earliest convenience.

Rebecca bowed her head in respect, as she moved her people to the designated area to prepare for trading. April sat with Rebecca patiently whilst the display was being prepared by Rebecca's people.

"I wish I could stay with you," Rebecca said hopefully. "You will need somebody to help you, and to watch your back for you."

"It's better if I do this alone. It could be a distraction having to watch out for somebody else's safety, particularly somebody that's become such a dear friend to me." Placing a consoling hand on Rebecca's clasped hands, April added, "I'll wait for my chance then slip away furtively. Maybe when this is all over I'll come back and tell you all about myself. And that, I promise will be a revelation to you."

With tears welling in her eyes, Rebecca threw her arms around April and hugged her as she sobbed. "You'd better come back to see me, Miss April Darling." Then without looking back she rejoined her people leaving her sitting quietly alone, trying desperately to clear her thoughts in readiness for the tasks that lay ahead of her.

At last the moment arrived when she must continue with her mission, but now she had to deal with it alone. It was a mission that had been assigned to her so very long ago, or that's the way it now seemed, because so much has happened in so short a time. Her thoughts turned to Ron, wondering how he was, then she realised that she must remain one hundred per cent focused or she could endanger everybody's lives. And so April returned her concentration to the realities of the present time. The faint whirling sound of helicopters in the distance broke her concentration. She listened to it growing ever louder as it neared the camp, and watched as the three Westland helicopter gun-ships came into view. They circled the camp then set down just beyond the marquee. A tower of a man alighted first; he was of Moroccan origin and stood close to seven feet tall. He stood proudly to attention as a number of official-looking gentlemen of various nationalities alighted from the helicopters, escorting them as they walked towards the Sheikh's tent.

Her attention was drawn to a white man who walked respectfully behind them. April didn't know why at first, but there was something strangely familiar about him. When he removed his sunglasses before entering the tent April gasped with shock, "Martin-fucking-Driver," she muttered to herself. "So that's how they knew our every move." April's thoughts were interrupted by Rebecca returning.

"Is everything ok, darling?" Rebecca asked as she sat cross-legged beside her. "You're looking very perturbed."

"I may have found our leak. An Englishman's just arrived who used to work for our special branch connected to the armed forces. I thought he was working for our government, but if so, what the hell is he doing out here now? Anyway, I have an old score to settle with him later."

"Don't jump to any conclusions, April. Check it out with London first," Rebecca urged. "He may be still working for you, but undercover."

"With all of this high tech electronics equipment contacting London will be a bit risky, won't it? Unless I just send a text, then they won't have time to trace it. At least I hope not." April then hastily composed a text to Sir Charles, asking, 'Martin Driver has just arrived at rebel camp. Can u confirm his status PRONTO?' Then she pressed send as she told Rebecca, "Now we'll just have to wait and see."

April did not have long to wait for a reply that told her, 'He is a traitor. He just vanished from here after trying 2 recruit personnel 2 go with him. Finish him at all costs.'

Showing Rebecca the message, April explained the need for more practical clothing to move round the camp after dark. After changing into looser fitting clothes, she waited with Rebecca for Martin Driver to reappear, so she could find an opportune moment to confront him. The time passed painfully slowly, but eventually the men started to emerge from their meeting.

April watched as Driver eventually emerged to be ushered to a smaller canvas shelter that he was to share with another man.

The sun was beginning to set as April said to Rebecca. "Soon it will be dark enough for me to separate Driver from his companion, *and his fucking breath.*"

"They will be given female attendants for their pleasure. If we change places with them it will be much easier for us to deal with the men," suggested Rebecca. "We need to get closer though, so as to be ready when the ladies appear." Then she added, "So you will have to take me with you after all. Won't you, April?"

They walked with their heads bowed respectfully as they crossed towards the tented area. The lady companions chosen to attend Martin Driver and his companion were about to enter their tent as Rebecca stopped them. Speaking to them in Arabic, she suggested they exchanged places with them. This they readily accepted, so they seized their opportunity and entered Driver's tent. "Come on in, ladies. Don't be shy. I'm Martin Driver, and this is Alan

Smith. Why don't you come over here and massage my aching limbs first?" he suggested. "I'm as stiff as a board because of the long journey without certain company," Driver laughed as he rubbed his crotch area. "What is up? You not speaky any English?" He scoffed as he pulled April towards him. "Well I'll give you a very quick lesson then." Martin added arrogantly as he pulled off April's Niqab. He became momentarily motionless, and speechless, as he revealed her face. April stared coldly into his eyes with a look that made him shudder. Eventually he managed to stutter, "Y-you are Eng-English!" He slumped back heavily onto the bed with an expression of surprise on his face. "What are you bloody doing out here?"

"The same as you are I expect, Martin."

"How do you know my name?"

"You introduced yourself when we came in here, remember? I'm April, and it's so nice to meet an English gentleman here in this god-forsaken hole."

"Oh yes. I did, didn't I? Sorry. How silly of me," he said, realising his mistake. The conversation was interrupted by a low thudding sound.

"What the hell was that?" Martin asked as he began to stand.

April pulled him back abruptly, "Let them enjoy themselves," she said, as she tried to regain his attention. "Besides, we met briefly in England once," April confessed as she slid her hand below her Abaya and grabbed hold of the dagger.

"I'm sure I would have remembered you," Martin said as he moved closer to her. "Unless you were wearing that bloody disguise, that is?" He laughed as he pointed toward the Niqab.

"Well I was sort of in disguise; I was in fancy dress you might say now." Lying back on the mattress April concealed the knife behind her back as she continued, "I've been told this will soon be the safest place on the planet, although I don't really know what they mean by that. After all, I'm only a simple woman in a Muslin world now. Well, at least at this present moment I am. But eventually I believe I'll be enlightened. Besides, the Sheikh has only entrusted a privy few with his plans."

With smug misplaced pride, Martin fell into the trap as he boasted, "I know."

"Oh, I don't think so, Martin. I can't see the Sheikh entrusting you, a mere infidel, with such privied information." April teased stretched and thrust forward her amply-sized, firm breasts.

Martin rolled up beside her, his arms playfully pinning her arms to the bed as he rose to the bait. "Well, let me tell you lady, that's just were you're wrong. He needs me. I've been training three thousand of his men in the dessert preparing them for the New World," he volunteered willingly as he began kissing her neck, while April tried to contain her feeling of severe nausea.

"What New fucking World? Has he gone back in time or something?" She laughed, as she tried to free her arms, but Martin held them too securely.

For the first time April realised how vulnerable and weak she had become in a petite female frame. This she found extremely daunting as Martin was now kneeling astride her, and under his weight she was unable to move as he pressed his lips to hers, and pushed his tongue inside her mouth. He pushed his legs straight, until his full body weight lay against her. April could feel his erect penis pressing hard against her, sandwiched between their stomachs. She was powerless, with no option but to go along with his amorous advances, at least temporarily. He released her arms as he moved his hands and began fondling April's breasts. His other hand slipped down and begun sliding her Abaya up to remove it, lifting his weight as he did so.

She quickly moved her knife under the sheet to conceal it. "Just a sec, Martin," April said breathlessly, trying to regain her composure. "Let me undress you while you tell me about this new future." He smiled, as April pushed him gently onto his back he willingly complied. Slowly and seductively she started to remove his trousers.

"Faster, here I'll help you," he said impatiently, starting to undo the buttons.

But April playfully slapped his hand away. "Pleasure should never be rushed, Martin. You'll find it well worth waiting for, I promise you." She began, "So you go on trying to convince me that the Sheikh has entrusted you, because I don't think so. He's probably just using you. You aren't that important to him really," April continued as she slipped off his shirt.

"Well, it won't hurt to tell you now I suppose." Between moans of pleasure he began. "In the big marquee there's a complexity of electronic equipment that's primed and ready for the final assault to wipe out western imperialism." Martin again moaned as April finally removed his trousers completely.

"Go on," urged April, "that proves nothing to me. I already knew that much."

He fell silent as she finished undressing him, then he asked in a serious tone of voice. "Why are you so fucking interested anyway?"

Thinking quickly, she lied, "Because I'm better when I sleep with an important man. So just convince me how important you really are to the Sheikh." April grasped his throbbing penis as he again moaned with delight. Closing his eyes he lay back writhing with sheer pleasure.

"Six months ago a sleeping virus was planted in all of the most important computers in the world. It's called Exodus. On the twenty-first, just seven days from now, it will be triggered from here to paralyse the whole of the western world's resources." He placed his hands each side of April's face pulling her onto his manhood. "Please?" he begged, as he guided her mouth onto his penis. Feeling sick, but realising that she had very few alternatives, April was forced through circumstances to comply. "That is very, very nice," Martin said as he held her head down on his penis.

"Go on," April struggled to say, with her mouth pulled firmly down onto him. "I find your importance a very, VERY, big turn on."

"Ok," Martin agreed reluctantly. "All of the world's computers will crash and the hard drives will burn up. Hence there will be no early warning systems, no banking, telephones, fresh water, gas, electricity, PC's et cetera, etcetera, nothing at all. Crime will run rampant, and total anarchy will prevail." He gasped as he ejected into her mouth, holding her head down firmly so she was unable to move off him.

She wanted to throw up, but knew she needed to keep up the pretence. Retching silently, April started gently caressing his testicles as she began moving her mouth up and down again, encouraging him to once more ejaculate. "What will that achieve? It won't take them very long to put things right again. Surely they must have backup systems?" April insisted, moving to lick his testicles.

Driver writhed uncontrollably as he struggled to continue. "While the world's rulers are preoccupied trying to restore some type of normality, and on or around the twenty-fifth, two massive nuclear explosions will occur at the north and south poles simultaneous. This'll cause massive tsunami that will engulf the northern and southern hemispheres and completely submerge them."

"But you will all be committing hara-kiri. What will be the point of that?" April snapped at him, sitting up as she began to pleasure him with her hands.

"Sheikh Mohammed Kahn has got the best eggheads in the world, who have worked out the size of the bombs that he would need, so that at least a thousand miles either side of the equator would remain totally untouched." He ejaculated again into April's hand. "You're very good, April," he complimented her, pushing April back against the bed. "But now it's your turn," he insisted, as he struggled to remove her under garments.

"NO!" she tried to protest, as he forced his penis inside her.

"You're nice and tight, you're just like a virgin really," he said joyfully. "It really is my lucky day."

She struggled in vain and was forced to eventually concede to his amorous advances. Unable to scream for help, April eventually relaxed and began to enjoy the very new and novel experience. "That's better, just you enjoy it." Martin encouraged as he ripped open her top, exposing April's breasts.

He pressed his lips hard against her as he began to fondle April's nipples. She surprised herself by reacting to his sexual advances, wrapping her arms and legs around him as she pulled Martin tightly to her, as April began to moan with the pleasure she was experiencing.

"Harder, harder," she shouted, and after two or three minutes past April climaxed, closely followed by Martin ejaculating. He rolled off her, lying back onto the bed panting, while April was busy trying to regain her composure. Then she noticed Rebecca's sad face peering through the drapes.

To Martin's surprise April produced the knife and pressed it against his throat. Warning him, "Don't you bloody move a muscle, and more importantly, don't make a single fucking sound." Then she turned her attention to Rebecca. "You can come in now, Becky. Is everything okay out there?"

"Yes, I've put him in bed so he looks as though he's sleeping." Then turning her attention towards Martin, she asked, "What about that bastard?"

Martin tried to speak but April pushed the blade harder against his throat. "Speak when you are spoken too only. You're just a bastard low-life traitor,"

She asked Rebecca, "Keep him covered while I dress, will you?" as she pushed Martin's gun towards her. She told Martin as she quickly put on the Abaya to cover her torn underclothing, "You're a gullible fool Driver, believing all that rubbish about a Muslim-dominated New World, and the ethnic cleansing of the remainder of our planet. From what I've heard he'll destroy you all, as well as himself in the process. He is just an insane fucking madman."

Martin again tried to speak as he cowered, while trying to cover his private parts with his hands. "Can I get dressed now, please? I'm sorry for what I've done, but I can help you. I'm actually still working undercover for London, you know."

"No you're fucking not, I've checked." (She couldn't resist embarrassing him further by ordering him.) "Put your hands on your fucking head, there's nothing worth covering there. We will tell you what to do, and when to do it. Remember you're a traitor working for the highest bidder. Now keep your hands on your head where I can see them, and tell me why we shouldn't kill you, right here and now? After all, you've just raped me, HAVEN'T you BASTARD?" April tried to convince herself.

Martin stuttered nervously trying to find the right words to explain. "I didn't really rape you; you seemed to be enjoying it too."

"That seemed true from where I was standing, April," Rebecca interrupted with an impish smile.

Blushing profusely, April told Rebecca, "I didn't ask you." She turned her attention back toward Martin, admitting, "Ok, I concede that point, but you're still a traitor to your own country."

He started to cry with fear. "Please don't kill me. Let me help you, PLEASE?"

She didn't know why, but April was starting to pity him. "Put some fucking clothes on. You look pathetically ridiculous. But no tricks or I warn you you're dead meat." Martin thanked April, dressing quickly. April continued, "Why did you do it, change sides I mean?"

"I used to be in the secret services, but because of an injury I was medically discharged. I then joined the police force as a village copper, but I was never happy there, so when the chance arrived for me to work for them again I jumped at it." He had finished dressing by now and was sitting on the edge of the bed.

"Working for them again, doing what?" insisted April, hiding the fact that she already knew.

"Delivering somebody to their base in the Cotswolds, George the poor sod. I don't know what they did to that poor bastard. Anyway, then they shit on me again, treating me like an errand boy, a gopher, so I got out again. The police force wouldn't have me back, a Sir Charles bloody Hythe-Smith made sure of that one. In fact, I was made completely unemployable in the UK because of that bastard. So, being desperate I used my S.A.S skills and volunteered to become a mercenary, and ended up training the Sheikh's army out here. What shall I do now? I've told you I can help you."

"You have told me everything I need to know," April reminded him, "so tell me why I shouldn't kill you now?"

"Not everything, there's a backup system in case for some reason this camp's destroyed."

Rebecca and April looked at each other in horrified shock. "What bloody backup system are you fucking talking about?" Rebecca asked him nervously. "You're just playing for time, aren't you?"

"There's an identical camp to this one in Zaire. It's in dormant mode at this time, but it can be fully functional within twelve hours. They only need to feed the computers with the right co-ordinances? Codes, etc., and it will start up automatically if this camp is ever attacked. Also, if there's a power failure, malfunction, or anything like that."

"And where's this camp?" Rebecca chipped in again.

"I can show you. It's about three hundred miles north west of Kisanga on the banks of the Congo River," Martin hastily added. "Are you going to let me live now that I've told you all about the Zairian camp as well?"

"Where's your cell phone?" April asked him.

"My cell phone, why? Here it is." He quickly passed it to her.

"Wait. I'll use our friend's in there first. I don't think he'll mind." April walked behind the dividing canvas and removed the mobile phone from the corpse. As she dialled the number for Sir Charles she paced to and fro, half listening in case they were surprised by a visit from one of the guards. Charles answered and April explained as fast as she could all about Martin Driver, and the revelation that a secondary twin camp existed in Zaire. She enlightened him of her plan to hijack a helicopter, and destroy this camp, which would give her a maximum of twelve hours to reach, and destroy, camp number two before the nuclear devices were activated.

"Just a minute," April said to him as she switched the phone off. Then she rang Charles on Martin's phone. "Sorry about that, they may have been trying to trace the call so I've switched phones. According to Driver, the helicopters have been adapted, removing any excess weight to allow for extra fuel tanks to be fitted. They now have a range of about four or five hundred miles more. When Driver needed to go to Zaire they refuelled at Agades, Yola, and Mbundaka. They used small airfields that are only used by charter firms and the flying doctors. Can you get us clearance to do the same thing, Charles?"

"Yes, but be careful of Driver's treachery, April. He's not to be trusted under at any circumstances."

"Will do, Charles, but now I must fly." April joked as she rang off. She was just in time, as two armed guards burst into the tent.

April hid her face with her hands.

"Are you okay, Miss?" one of the men asked in an American accent.

"He tried to rape me." April said pitifully, pointing toward Driver. "Can I kill him?" April begged as she advanced towards them. "It's my right remember?"

"I suppose it is," the American said as he handed her his pistol. "Here, use this one to do it with."

Taking the pistol April turned and pointed it towards Martin Driver, noticing that it wasn't loaded she pulled the trigger. Click, click. Turning back towards the smirking guards, April said to them. "But it's not loaded," sounding naive as she walked towards them.

By now the two guards were laughing uncontrollably so she seized her opportunity and grabbed one of the rifles, swinging it round, and hurtling the unsuspecting guard towards Rebecca. "This one's yours, Becky," April shouted as she lunged towards the startled American. "But you're mine, you big ape," April warned him as she pulled the

Abaya up so she could deliver a high kick to his throat. He dropped his rifle as he crumbled to the floor clutching at his throat while gasping for breath. April grabbed for his belt and removed his knife, burying it into his heart.

As she turned, April saw Rebecca and Martin tussling with the other guard.

Then April heard a loud snapping sound, as Driver broke the man's neck.

"I think it's time we disappeared, before the cavalry arrive," Rebecca suggested.

"I won't argue with that," Martin agreed, while April salvaged whatever weapons she could find on the dead bodies.

"What's that sound?" she asked, listening intensely as the sound of helicopters grew nearer. "It seems that we're having more company. Let's get out of here, and fast." April insisted as she moved towards the door. They sidled slowly out, but kept close to the tents as they moved furtively, heading towards where Rebecca's people were busily trading with the guards. As April watched, a helicopter landed and two gun-ships hovered overhead. Sheikh Mohammed Kahn was moving over towards it while she watched him; he clambered aboard with his favourite wives and personal guards. Then immediately the helicopter took to the air followed closely by the gun-ships, which escorted them south.

"Sod it! I wonder where they are going to." April asked with annoyance. "Do they know something we don't?"

There was a lot of activity in the camp as armed soldiers seemed to be conducting a tent-to-tent search. Suddenly, there was loud shouting as the three dead bodies were dragged from the tent.

"Two of my men are missing," Rebecca said angrily. Then looking down into the camp, she shouted, "They're down there. They're telling them what we're doing. Quickly April, get ready," she advised frantically. While April was removing the Abaya and dressing in her own clothing, Rebecca organised her people to draw their attention, and allow April to make good her escape.

"Spread out and open fire on them, we need to destroy this whole camp," Rebecca urged. Picking up a mobile rocket launcher she fired it into the marquee which erupted in flames, and set off a chain of explosions until the camp was turned into a flattened mass of smouldering ash. "I don't know what was in there, but it certainly helped," laughed Rebecca. She then watched the remainder of the Sheikh's men trying to escape the relentless accuracy of her troops. "I'm coming with you, and no more arguments this time," insisted Rebecca as she gathered up her arsenal. "Somebody has to watch your bloody back."

"But these remaining helicopters only have room for two people, Becky."

"If one of you can fly, I have a license. There are three choppers down there, so we can take two of them," Martin suggested.

"Sounds good to me, but will your people be all right, Rebecca? And do they know where to wait for you till all this is over?" April asked.

"Yes. Now let's get out of here. You're worrying like an old woman, April."

Keeping low, the three of them edged round to where the helicopters were standing. A group of six men had reached them first, trying to secure their escape. Martin signaled for them to take a helicopter each and dispose of its occupants. Rebecca and April nodded agreement as they each approached their chosen targets, and the unsuspecting men, from behind.

The noise of sporadic gunfire made it simpler as April swung open the door, pulling the pilot out and shooting the startled co-pilot. Then, turning the gun on the pilot, she shot him as he lunged towards her. Turning her attention then towards the others, April was just in time to witness Rebecca shooting the remaining man.

"Good work, Becky." she complemented her, adding as she opened the other door to remove the co-pilots body, "We will take this one. I'm sure I can fly it."

"What do you mean? You're sure you can fly it. Don't you bloody know?" Martin asked anxiously.

"I can fly most things, but I just haven't flown one of these before." April told him as she started the engines and put her helmet on. "Can everybody hear me?"

"Yes," they replied.

As they lifted off April told Rebecca. "Drop a grenade onto the remaining chopper so they can't follow."

Rebecca willingly obliged as they skimmed over the top of it.

Following Martin in a southerly direction, they passed over the camp. April could see it ablaze with the only survivors left standing seeming to be Rebecca's people. She watched them moving stealthily through the remainder of the camp, eradicating any survivors, and salvaging what weapons they could find.

CHAPTER 9

Rebecca was exhausted and took the opportunity to catch up on her sleep, while April and Martin headed due south towards Agades. It was during the very early hours of the morning they reached the first flying school to refuel.

"Have you seen Sheikh Mohammed Kahn and his guards?" April asked the man as he refuelled the helicopters.

"You've just missed them by a couple of hours. Are they friends of yours?"

"Hardly," she sneered. "The man's a purely evil bastard tyrant."

"I agree with that one, lady. We refuelled them, then when my friend gave them the bill one of them shot him in the back," he said sadly. "He's been rushed to the hospital, and they say that he'll live, but the bullet has severed his spinal cord so he will be permanently paralysed from the waist down. So if you catch up with them bastards, shoot them for my friend, will you?"

"We'll do that for you with pleasure. Now, you do take plastic I hope as that's all the currency that I've got on me?" April said hopefully, following him into his office.

"Not a problem, Miss," was his happy reply as he took the card to settle the bill. "You take very good care of yourself, lady. They're ruthless people that you're dealing with."

"Don't you worry about me, I intend to," she said to him as she left his office. "Worry about those bastards when I catch up with them. Let's go folks," April called to Martin as she started the blades twirling into life. Then she asked Rebecca, "Did you enjoy your little nap then, Rebecca?"

"Very much so, it's a pity that you can't have a short sleep too, April."

"There'll be plenty of time for that when this is all over," she told her as they pressed on. Crossing the Nigerian border as dawn broke, they headed down towards Yola.

"The flying doctors home's just to the west," Martin voice said over the radio. "Follow me if you please, ladies," he requested as he took over the lead into Yola. After about thirty minutes the helicopters were touching down on a small private airstrip.

A tall middle-aged man came striding out to meet them. "Hello folks," he said jovially as he offered his hand to shake. "You must be Miss April Darling? I've heard ever so much about you, so I'm very pleased to meet you in person at last." Then turning towards Rebecca, and Martin, he told them. "Go right on into the house and freshen up. My wife is preparing breakfast for you all."

The man was very cheerful and chatted constantly while refuelling the helicopters. Then, taking April by surprise, he asked, "How is Charles these days? He's well, I hope?"

"It seems that everybody has heard about me in advance, so much for secrecy. Yes he's very well. Do you know Charles?"

"Oh yes, we were up at Oxford together. He was a bit of a tearaway in those days, but don't tell him that I told you that," he added cautiously.

"I won't, but if you were at Oxford, then how did you end up out here.

Have you been a naughty boy or something?" April teased.

"No," he chuckled softly. "I was a prominent Harley Street surgeon but I became restless and got fed up with the rat race back home. So we decided to give God something back and so here we are. And we couldn't be happier, my dear. You know, Charles has told me all about you. It was quite a surprise when he called me though, as we haven't spoken for at least five years now. I wonder how he was able to trace us all the way out here."

"So you are Christians, I am too," she observed happily. "You must remember Charles has the means to trace anybody anywhere these days, believe me. He has an extremely influential job. Now tell me, what do I owe you?"

"Charles is going to settle the account." Then the doctor's expression became more serious. "Charles told me about your transformation. Are you comfortable with it now?"

"Let's just say that I'm getting used to it slowly, but I do miss my family like mad. You see, I didn't have any choice in all of this," she told him sadly. Then she added pensively, "It seems Charles is advertising my arrival in advance far too freely."

"We'll pray for you, April. Now about that breakfast shall we?" he invited, offering her his arm. "I'm sorry, I haven't introduced myself properly," he said to them as they sat down in front of a full English breakfast. I'm George, and this is my wife Mary," he announced proudly as he put an arm around his wife. "Now enjoy your meals."

After they had eaten and freshened up, April asked George for some medication to keep them awake for at least another twenty-four hours. Then bidding them farewell, April thanked them for their most welcome hospitality, before the three of them took to the skies once again, heading across the border into Cameroon.

They then continued on their journey down into Mbundaka for the last remaining refuelling stop before they entered the last stage into Kisangani.

"It's about two miles now. Would you like to lead us in, April?" Martin's voice broke the silence as he asked over the radio.

"I wonder why he wants us to go ahead," April pondered. "Will do Martin," she agreed as she took the lead. Rounding the next bend in the river the massive settlement came into full view. "Bloody hell, how many men are there out here?" April questioned aloud.

Martin's stern voice came over the radio. "Three thousand, I told you that the reserve camp was in the dessert. I just didn't tell you exactly where it was."

A warning light started flashing as he locked on to the heat of their exhaust. "So you're still with them are you?" April said to him, stalling for time while she was trying to think of a way of escaping his missiles.

"Of course I am. You are obviously blinded by your religion, so you can perish with all the other infidels. Unless I keep you for my personnel sex toy, that is. You were very good between the sheets. What do you think?" he suggested with a misplaced air of cockiness. "Would you like to be my little sex slave in return for your life?"

"Only in your dreams, you always were an arrogant bastard." April said as they banked to the right to cross the river again.

Martin followed closely while arguing. "You know nothing at all about me."

Rebecca was ready with a machine gun, and signaled that she wanted April to get him alongside if she could. April was trying desperately to shake Martin off as she thought, 'if only I could distract him for a moment'. She then said to him, "I've known you since you lived in Riverlet as a village copper. You were a pure bastard then, too." It worked as he fumbled for words.

"I can't remember you." Adding with some afterthought, "Nice try! You've obviously read it all in my file. That's how you know, isn't it?"

As their helicopter circled, followed closely by Martin's, Rebecca sat quietly waiting for her opportunity. "Do you remember George and Mandy, or Jill and Joe, or the funeral of Jill and Joe in Harlow?" Martin kept trying to interrupt as she ignored him. Continuing on, she asked, "Do you remember drugging poor George then delivering him to Sir Charles who was very annoyed with you?" April muted the radio while she asked Rebecca if she could get a clear shot yet.

"Not while were weaving. I think we'll have to land and take our chance, April."

"Not if I can help it." April was interrupted as a salvo of shots from Martin's machine guns hitting the engine. With smoke bellowing from it, April was left struggling with the controls as they started to lose height rapidly. "Gather what you can carry we're going down

Rebecca." Putting her arm through the straps April slung a Sten-gun and ammo belt over her shoulders, and then strapped a belt of grenades around her slim waist. "We are going to have to jump for it, Becky," April told her, as she struggled with the controls to try to keep some height.

Weaving and winding towards the camp with Martin in very close pursuit, the helicopters engine continued to splutter. April held the throttle fully open and heaved back on the joystick to clear the river again.

Martin's voice broke her concentration. "I'll let you live if you land now, you bitch."

"First we have to clear this river, Martin. Then we'll land. We seem to have no other alternative, do we?"

"Good girl. I'm glad you've realised your true place at last. But if you don't mind I'll stick close to you though, just to make sure that you don't try anything stupid."

"Stick as close as you like, Martin. In fact the closer the better I'd say." April encouraged him as she approached the campsite again. The soldiers began diving for cover as the threat of the copter crashing on top of them increased. April had an idea. Muting the radio she turned to Rebecca and told her, "Get a grenade ready to leave behind after we jump." Wrestling with the controls while trying desperately to keep their height for a little while longer, she continued, "As we pass over that marquee jump for it. It should act as an impromptu air bag and break our fall."

"Are you sure about that, April?" Rebecca asked hesitantly.

"We'll soon find out, won't we? Now you didn't hear what I'm about to say to that scumbag, but hopefully the shock will delay his reactions temporarily. Are you ready to jump, Rebecca?"

Rebecca nodded tentatively as April turned off the mute to talk to Driver again. "By the way shithead, *I'm* what they turned George into." Pressing the mute again she re-affirmed, "Ready, Rebecca? Pull that pin and jump, NOW."

They left the grenade behind and jumped, landing on the top of the marquee as the helicopter exploded. As April had anticipated,

Martin was flying far too close to manoeuvre clear, and flew directly into the fireball, his helicopter bursting instantly into flames.

April said callously, "GOOD BYE, DRIVER." Throwing grenades through the vent flaps she shouted to Rebecca, "LET'S GET OUT OF HERE," sliding down the apex followed closely by Rebecca.

They landed on an unsuspecting guard knocking him to the floor, then ran and dived for cover as the huge marquee was engulfed in flames as the camp was thrown into disarray. People were running aimlessly with nobody being sure of exactly what their responsibilities were in this scenario.

Using the utter confusion and heavy smoke to their best advantage, April shouted to Rebecca, "QUICK FOLLOW ME!" leading her towards the Sheikh's quarters. Drawing closer they saw Sheikh Mohammed Kahn being escorted into one of the nearby helicopters by his personal bodyguards.

"IT SEEMS THAT WE'RE TOO LATE APRIL." Rebecca shouted over the relentless noise. The fire had now spread to the fuel tanks and gas bottles, which began exploding. "We need to get to that helicopter before it explodes too."

April's only response was. "Can you give me some cover?" as she began to run towards the Sheikh's helicopters that were beginning to lift off.

Trying desperately to think of a way to stop them as she got within thirty feet, April stopped to take cover behind a truck when the Sheikh's bodyguards began shooting at her.

Noticing there was a coiled chain on the truck gave her an idea. Seizing it, April sprinted towards one of the rising aircraft and hurled the coiled chain into the rear rotor blades. There was a loud bang as the rotor snapped off, leaving them unable to control any direction. It spun aimlessly, before eventually crashing into the ammunition dump.

This added to the chain of explosions rapidly reducing the camp to smouldering ashes. The Sheikh's guards ran towards the blazing wreckage to check if there were any survivors. Taking full advantage of the confusion, they planned to make good their escape.

"REBECCA," April shouted. "This way while they're otherwise occupied saving their own skins." Reaching the remaining helicopter April took her pistol and shot the sole guard. "Get in quickly Becky," she urged, while climbing into the pilot seat and bringing the engine into life. In one smooth movement they took off. Rising quickly like a phoenix over the scene of blazing devastation, they left the campsite as it was rapidly being levelled into a pile of ashes.

April set a course for Kisanga then turned to Rebecca. "You've been very quiet. Is there something wrong, love?"

"No. Well not really. It just all seems such a criminal waste of lives, that's all," she said somberly. "Why are people so vulnerable?"

"I don't know, Becky. I guess it's because they're lonely and somebody like the Sheikh makes them feel important and wanted," April reflected. "It looks like the Zairian army is here to finish it all off for us. And look over there. Those gun boats are a bit late, too. It should be the SBS."

"SBS, who are they?" Rebecca asked as she smiled.

"That's better. It's nice to see you smile again. The Special Boat Squad is a very highly trained elite group of the armed forces, the best that there is in fact."

The conversation was interrupted by April's mobile phone ringing. "It's the boss. Hello Charles. You've just missed the fireworks display."

"I know. We've been watching you via a satellite link up. Are you okay?"

"Yes, we're okay. Have you located the bombs and the Sheikh yet?"

"Not the Sheikh, but we have located the explosive devices. There is a team of bomb disposal experts en route to each of them as we speak, and they should be arriving on site about now. When you reach Kisanga, head straight for the airport where I have left you a ticket at the B.A. desk for the flight home tomorrow. You'll have to change at Algiers I'm afraid, but then you'll fly straight into Heathrow. I'll have a car there to meet you."

"What about Rebecca, Charles? Without her help I couldn't have done it, and she'll need to return to her people in Gambia."

"Ok, I'll arrange a ticket for her as well. If she goes to the British Embassy in Gambia it will be there with a thank you present for her. Will a fat cheque help her cause?"

"I'm sure it will be very welcome. Thank you, Charles. I'm some miles from Kisanga and the fuel light is beginning to flash. We'll have to land and go the rest of the way on foot."

"Head for the river and I'll tell one of our boats to find you and take you in. I must go now; I'll keep you posted on the bombs." Charles said as he rang off abruptly.

April headed due south lowering her altitude till she was skimming fifty feet above the ground. "We should make the river on the reserve fuel tanks, but I don't remember James Bond ever running out of fuel like this, Rebecca."

"Who is this James Bond?" Rebecca asked.

"He's a fictional British agent, Becky. Oh don't mind me. It's a sick side of my humour. Look! There's the river." she pointed out as the engine started to splutter again. "Come on, baby, just another couple of miles." She said as she struggled to keep the engine alive. "It looks as though we'll have to walk the rest of the way Becky, so I'll have to put it down." April explained as she negotiated a bumpy landing just as the engine died completely. Grabbing what they could carry they set off in the direction of the river. It was no surprise when Rebecca took hold of her hand squeezing it gently.

"I love you April Darling, but I think you know that already, don't you?

Will you ever come back here to see me?"

"Of course I will Rebecca." April promised her as she stopped to give her a hug. "I could never forget all that you've done for me, now could I? Besides, I haven't left here yet, have I?"

A missile invaded the peaceful scene as it screeched through the air with a piercing high-pitched whistle, then exploded on the riverbank, very close to where the gunboat was moored.

"SHIT. Where did that come from?" April shouted as another missile flew over their heads. Turning, she could see a mobile rocket launcher and an armoured personnel carrier accompanying it. They were closing in fast on them and the rescue boats. There was still another half mile before the girls reached the river, but it was only a matter of time before the boat took a direct hit. April waved and called to the boat frantically, "GO ON! GET THE HELL OUT OF HERE."

The women lightened their load. Carrying only sufficient weapons to protect them then started running hard towards the river. "GO," April repeated to the boat.

"I WILL LEAVE YOU THIS TO FOLLOW US DOWN STREAM ON," somebody shouted back, as they lowered a Jet Ski into the water before racing off at high speed downstream.

"There is only another two hundred metres, Rebecca. We can make it." There was another burst from the machine gun. "Keep going," urged April as they began zigzagging to dodge the bullets, glancing behind to see how far they were still behind them. Although they were advancing on the girls fast, there was still at least a clear half mile between them as they reached the Jet Ski. April removed her backpack telling Rebecca, "I'll leave them a little present," as she set the device to detonate when it was tampered with.

"Please hurry April," Rebecca urged. "They're closing in on us faster now.
COME ON."

Closing the backpack, "That should surprise them," April told Rebecca as she mounted the Jet Ski. Starting it, they raced off after the gunboat.

Rebecca glanced behind and she saw the pursuing troops reaching the riverbank.

"Wait for it," April said to her as they slowed down to watch. 'BANG,' the backpack then erupted in flames, hurtling bodies and vehicles into the river. April said callously, "I think that's the end of them."

"We thought that before," Rebecca reminded her, as she clung tightly to April. "You know what I mean when I say that I love you, don't you darling?"

"I'm getting the message, Becky," she replied struggling to breathe under Rebecca's zealous grip. "There's the gun boat," April said to her with relief as Rebecca slackened her grip.

"I wish you would stay here with us April," she said mournfully as the Jet Ski drew alongside the gunboat.

"I'm sorry, but I do need to go back, Becks. I have some unfinished business in England I need to deal with. And remember, the Sheikh's still on the loose," she explained to Rebecca as they were helped aboard the gunboat. "Hello. Welcome aboard. I'm Lieutenant Edwards, James Edwards. I liked your entrance; just remind me never to upset either of you lovely ladies," the Lieutenant commented as he smiled broadly welcoming them aboard.

April saw that he was a muscularly built man in his mid-thirties, standing approximately six feet tall. "I have been ordered to take very special care of you both. But I must say, judging by what I have just witnessed you could take care of me better. Oh, and all of my crew as well, I should think."

"Hello James, it's nice to meet you too," April said as they stepped aboard the boat. "I'm April, and this is Rebecca."

"The pleasure is all mine and you are both very welcome guests aboard my ship."

After giving the crew their orders, James added, "If there's anything that you need at all, you only have to ask."

"What we could really use is a change of clean, dry clothes," April told him, "if that is at all possible."

"It will have to be regulation issue I'm afraid. If that's okay with you, I'll arrange for it straight away."

"As long as they're dry, and we can get out of these wet and smelly things, then it will do very nicely. Thank you, James."

A few minutes later a young naval rating passed them some dry clothing. After they had changed out of their wet things, April and Rebecca lay exhausted on top of their bunks. Because of their sheer fatigue, they had soon drifted into a very heavy sleep.

April was rudely awakened by a loud bang as the door was kicked open. Her eyes were slow to focus due to the lack of sleep, as she rubbed them trying to focus she felt the barrel of a gun prodding her in the stomach.

"Get up," she could hear a gruff voice ordering. April's eyes had cleared by now as she focused on the scruffy looking man armed with an automatic rifle standing over her. Blocking the doorway was an equally scruffy little man also training his gun towards them. Both of the men were dressed in dirty, smelly combat uniforms.

Quickly regained her senses, April bent her knees in towards her as if she was clearing the sheet covering her. Then suddenly she kicked out at the guard taking him by surprise, and propelling him into the other man. It sent them both sprawling through the open cabin door, and out onto the deck.

Before they could recover their senses April was on her feet and diving out towards them. Grabbing the tunic of one of the men she put her feet up into his stomach, then quickly turning onto her back April thrust with her legs, kicking him over the side of the boat, and splashing into the river Conga.

The speeding boat quickly left him behind as April turned to deal with the other soldier. Suddenly she felt a sharp crack on her head from a rifle butt, which knocked her out cold.

When she regained her senses, April became aware that her hands had been tied behind her back with her ankles bound together.

Rebecca stood in front with her with her hands on her head. "Are you all right love?"

Glancing round trying to assess the situation, April answered. "Yes I'm fine Becky, just a bloody headache. Now who the fucking hell hit me?"

"I did," April heard a familiar voice saying. A man stepped out from behind Rebecca with his face swathed in bandages, as he asked. "Don't you remember me? Well, that has hurt my feelings."

A cold chilling sensation ran down her spine as April recognised the voice. "How the fuck did you survive that crash, Driver?" she asked in a startled voice.

"The same way that you did, I jumped and landed on the opposite side of the marquee to you, and got burnt by the bloody grenades you dropped. I did think you would've seen me, but I guess you must have been otherwise occupied."

"You're just a lucky bastard. You didn't deserve to live," snapped April. "Tut, tut. Temper now, girls. I'd save it all for later because you will certainly need it when we reach the new improvised camp, and that is a threat." Driver warned, as he turned to speak to one of his men.

Using the distraction, April signal to Rebecca that she wanted her to escape over the side, but Rebecca shook her head.

When Driver turned his attention back, April asked, "What have you done with the crew of this boat?"

"Those who resisted me were shot. The rest either joined us or dived overboard," Driver boasted.

"Like that little scruffy, smelly man of yours. He was soon left behind us, but he needed the wash anyway," said April as she looked towards Rebecca.

Rebecca nodded as she realised what April was saying, that she would be more helpful to her if she were free. "Well, I'm nearly ready now." April announced loudly.

"Nearly ready for what?" a bemused Martin Driver asked.

"This," April replied as she launched a two-footed kick at Martin sending him hurtling into his men. "GO BECKY." She yelled to Rebecca, leaning to the side so Rebecca could dive over her, and over the side of the ship. As she did, April noticed James Edwards slide from under a tarpaulin, following Rebecca into the water.

Driver regained his composure as his eyes flashed angrily; he was embarrassed and furious at her sheer audacity, making him look a fool in front of his ill-disciplined men.

"You will regret that, you fucking bitch," he shouted as he delivering a hefty kick into April's leg. "Now you are completely alone, no friends, and definitely no witnesses." He grinned as he added threateningly, "Just you and us."

April's leg throbbed where Driver had kicked her, but she was reluctant to show any pain while anybody was watching her. Suffering silently, April wondered how she was ever going to get out of this predicament unscathed.

Eventually the boat started to slow down as it swung to the left, and moored alongside a jetty. Voices could be heard, so April presumed that the destination had been reached, and they were at the rebel's makeshift emergency camp.

"Come on. It's time for you to learn your fate, you bloody whore," Driver ordered with a misplaced air of complacency. "You won't escape me this time; I can assure you of that," he added, hauling April to her feet. "You carry her, I'm not going to untie her fucking legs," he ordered a reluctant soldier.

Without uttering a word the guard picked her up as if she were as light as a feather, placing April across his broad shoulders and following Martin ashore.

They wound through the large river-edged village, eventually reaching a large purpose built warehouse building. After entering it and descending down a flight of stone steps, they went into a very large well-lit basement.

The man dropped April heavily onto the stone floor.

"Careful with her," a kindly soft voice warned in broken English.

Turning April could see a small group of men. One of them she recognised as Sheikh Mohammed Kahn. "So we meet again. Are you surprised to see I'm still alive, my dear?"

"No, if this scum bag can survive it proves that the adage is correct."

"And what adage would that be, my dear?" asked the kindly Sheikh, smiling at her compassionately.

"That shit won't burn," April told him, wincing as Martin Driver kicked her again.

The smile left the Sheikh's face briefly to be replaced by a look of anger. Regaining his composure the smile returned, but now it was obviously a forced smile. "Place that man under house arrest. I told him that's no way to treat my guests," he ordered, pointing towards Martin Driver who was dragged away protesting. "If we untie you, will you refrain from any violence?" he asked April. "After all, it would only be a futile gesture on your part now, and expend unnecessary energy. Let me introduce you to my intelligence officer whom I think you already know?" the Sheikh suggested, as the Brigadier entered the room.

Trying not to look surprised, April answered. "At least give me the respect I deserve. You know that I will do all within my power to complete my mission."

He gave a deep sigh of despair, "Yes, I expected you would say something like that. But I'm afraid that it's far too late for you now. When you wiped out the other two camps it triggered the two explosive devices automatically, and they're on a twenty-four hour countdown. I'm afraid that the boffins that you've sent there cannot disarm them without these," the Sheikh told her as he pulled a string from around his neck. "You would need two keys for each device. But as I've already said, you can't stop them now. Soon, I will be the supreme ruler of the world."

For the very first time April noticed a hint of insanity in his eyes, and she now realised that time was of the essence. Looking round for some inspiration, April noticed one of the guards looking out of place. Staring towards him she recognised that it was Lieutenant Edwards.

April thought, "Perhaps he's still on the same side as me. He gives me no indication that he's James, but maybe he's just biding his time while waiting for his opportune moment. But how did he get here so fast?" She was perplexed, but she realised that time would soon tell her. April focused her attention back to her present dilemma again. How could she get the keys to the respective poles in time? Noticing that her ankles were bound with the knots to the back, a thought occurred to her. If she were kneeling then she might just be able to untie them.

"Could I please kneel? My legs are getting terrible cramp in them." April asked the Sheikh.

"Do not trust her, sir," advised the man she thought was James Edwards.

His treachery was puzzling April now, she thought he must have changed sides. "James, you traitor, so you have joined the loony party side," she rasped sharply.

"Who is this 'James'?" The Sheikh asked.

"Sir, she must know my twin brother. He's in the Middle East with the SBS."

"So that explains the physical likeness. But that's where it all ends. He's here, and you're not worthy to tie his fucking boot laces." April snapped sharply, showing her utter disdain.

He pointed his rifle towards April with the bayonet close to her chest, the Sheikh shouted for him to stop.

April pushed with her heels away from the gun until the gun was in line with her ankles. Without a thought for her personal safety, and in a brief instant, April lifted her legs quickly until they were above the gun, and brought them down onto the bayonet with her legs going either side of it as it severed the ropes.

"Good girl," she heard him say. "Now roll over so I can free your hands." He continued as he sprayed bullets into the guards. April rolled over as he freed her hands with a knife from his belt. "Now let's get out of here," he insisted as he handed her a pistol.

"Just a moment, there is one thing I must do first." April told him as the guards dropped like nine pins under his relentless accuracy. "The Sheikh's become a right pain in my bloody posterior." She leapt over towards the Sheikh ripping the keys from around his neck, as the Brigadier reached out for her gun. "No way, José." April said as she shot the Brigadier through the heart.

"It's too late, you can't change anything now," insisted the Sheikh, still clinging to his delusion.

"You're wrong about that. I can change one thing, mate."

"And what's that, dear? Join us?" the Sheikh, asked.

"No. This." She told him, shooting him between the eyes. "NOW let's go," April insisted as the gunfire stopped with the remaining men surrendering. Slinging an automatic rifle over her shoulder and holding a second one in her hands, April ordered, "All stay here for ten minutes, and then return to your homes and families. The party's now well and truly over." Starting up the stairs, she asked, "and what's your story James's twin brother?" as they reached ground level.

The news of the Sheikhs death had preceded them, and they were met with no resistance; the remaining dejected troops were oozing from the underground bunkers peacefully.

"I'm Winston," he introduced himself, offering April his hand, which she gladly shook.

"I'm April, April Darling. I must admit, you had me worried there for a moment, Winston." Admitted April as they reached the pad where the helicopters stood. "Have you got a phone, Winston?"

"I'm afraid not, April." He explained that it had broken so he'd thrown it away.

She took one from a dead soldier's body, "No matter Winston, I'll borrow one off him, I don't think he'll object."

Clutching the microphone of the helicopter she announced over the loud speaker. "You all have just fifteen minutes to clear this area and return home." The lethargic movements in the camp became a bustle of lively activity, reaching fever pitch as they clambered aboard anything, and everything, that moved.

Suddenly a shot rang out as April felt a sharp pain in her shoulder. Realising that she'd just been shot, April crouched down scanning the area for the perpetrator.

Winston took up a position to cover her, trying to shield April from any further attack.

"Are you okay, Miss Darling?" Winston asked as he saw the blood streaming down her arm. "Now where the hell did that shot come from?"

"Call me April, and yes I'll be okay. I can guess where it came from. I forgot about that bastard Driver. It must have been him." April looked towards the remaining vehicles but she couldn't see him, as the last vehicles left the camp ending the mass exodus. "DAMN IT! He's got away in the cover of the crowd," she snapped angrily.

Winston ripped April's shirt open to examine the wound. "The bullet's gone through clean, and I think it's missed your lungs and the bone luckily, April."

"Well, hurry and bind it up for me. We have to get moving."

"But I must stop this bleeding first, it seems as though it may pierced a major blood vessel." Winston explained as he applied pressure to the wound.

April winced with the pain, "Well hurry up and stop it, remember time isn't on our side." April explained with an air of urgency as she sat on an old oil drum. Then she noticed the worried look on the face of Winston. April asked him. "What's the problem? Just bind the fucker up tightly. I'll get it treated later."

"It needs cauterising April or the bleeding won't stop, then I'm afraid you might bleed to death."

"Well I don't see any medics, or field hospital, and we haven't got the luxury of time to go and look for one," she started wearily. "So, you'll just have to do your best. Won't you?"

"If you were a man there would be a way. But it's far too painful for a slender little lady like you," he told her as he continued to apply pressure to the wound.

April gave him a wry smile. "If only you knew the truth about that one, Winston."

"Knew what?" he asked, as he continued to apply pressure.

Now they were alone. Everybody that was still alive had left the makeshift camp.

"I'm afraid the bleeding isn't stopping so I'll need to do something," Winston agreed.

"Just get on with it you bloody chicken, anybody would think that it was you that was injured. JUST BLOODY DO WHATEVER NEEDS DOING WINSTON, AND DO IT QUICKLY."

She chattered nervously as Winston took bullets from his magazine and opened them, pouring the gunpowder from them onto a piece of cloth. The uneasy ambience was broken as a car drove up screeching to a halt. April held her gun ready, but it was Rebecca and James.

"What's happened?" Rebecca shouted, as she rushed towards April.

"She took a bullet in the shoulder which severed an artery." Winston explained, as he finished collecting the gunpowder. "I'm afraid this is going to hurt you, April. But it's the only way I know of stopping the bleeding."

James asked frantically "You're not going to cauterise it here like that, are you Winston?"

"If you have any better ideas I'd like to hear them now, James." Winston asked, again he turned his attention back to April. "I'm sorry about this, but please hold perfectly still and don't look?" he said sorrowfully as he poured the gunpowder into the open wound. He then made a torch of rolled up paper, which he lit. "Hold her perfectly still, will you?" he asked Rebecca and James.

April watched Winston nervously edging the flame slowly towards her shoulder. With her hands shaking uncontrollably she braced herself, gripping Winston by the arm April pulled it onto the wound to ignite the gunpowder inside her shoulder wound.

As the flame touched, April felt a searing pain, it was at least ten times worse than any pain that she'd suffered before, which culminated in a small explosion. Then April knew nothing as she passed out.

When she came to, April was aware of the noise of rotors. Opening her eyes she realised that she was aboard a helicopter. She tried to sit up, asking Rebecca, "How long have I been out for?"

"Not as long as we'd have expected you to be out, only about ten minutes," James replied. "We're just approaching the airport now."

"How are you feeling, April?" Winston asked. "I must say, you are one tough lady."

"I feel like hell," confirmed April as she moved her arm trying to get mobility back into it. "Ouch!" she yelled.

"Careful, you need to rest that arm until we can get you to a hospital." Rebecca advised as she tried to restrict April's movements. "You might start the wound bleeding again like that."

Pretending not to hear her, April asked, "Where is that bloody phone? Got it," she said as she proceeded to dial Charles' number.

"Is that you April?" Charles asked anxiously. "Yes, it's me Charles, the proverbial bad penny."

"Where have you been? I've been worrying about you. Are you all right, and where are you now?" Charles asked. "There's a change of plan. You will need to take one set of the keys, and James will take the other set. I've arranged for two Harriers to be at the airfield to transport you both onwards to respective Poles."

"We are just approaching the airport now Charles," April told him as they descended on the northern corner of the airfield. "There are two harriers. I believe we're to land alongside of them. Am I right?"

"Yes, there will be pilots and air crew to assist you both. Now is there anything else that you think you will need?"

"Yes, a locksmith, and a change of clean clothes," She told him as Winston landed the helicopter. "I have four keys, two are for each bomb, but I don't know which two are which. I'll need somebody to make me a duplicate set of the four keys, Charles."

"Just give me five minutes, April?"

When they landed Rebecca tried to assist April out from the helicopter, but she insisted that she was not incapable just yet. Then she made a fool of herself as she climbed out and collapsed onto the floor out of weakness.

"Be careful because you're still very weak through the loss of blood," explained Winston. "Here, stop being so pig-headed and let somebody help you until you get a bit stronger," he insisted forcibly as he helped April to her feet.

"I believe you need some keys cutting, Miss?" a voice interrupted. As they turned they saw a middle aged maintenance man in greasy overalls.

"Yes these," April waved the keys at him. "But they'll have to be very, very, accurate."

"Don't tell your grandma how to suck eggs, young lady," He joked. "Don't you worry about it. I think I know what I'm doing; it will just take me about five minutes. Over there are the washrooms where you will find a change of clothes for each of you ladies."

They thanked him then Rebecca and April headed towards the washroom. After a strip wash they dressed in the clean clothes. "Back into ladies clothing at last," Rebecca said gratefully, as April finished buttoning up her blouse. "There's some makeup over there darling, although you look stunning as you are."

Just smiling at her, April proceeded to skilfully apply her makeup. She had barely finished when James shouted in.

"The keys are ready, April."

"Ok, I'm ready now," she replied, as they emerged from the washrooms. "I hope those keys aren't mixed up now?"

"Do you think I'm an amateur—," the man stopped in mid-sentence as April came into full view. Realising that he was staring, the man continued, "By heck lass, you don't arf scrub up well," in a broad northern accent.

Taking the two sets of keys she kissed him on the cheek, replying jokingly in her native Liverpudlian, "So would those overalls lad, and thanks for the keys. Now let's get this show on the road people." April said to the others as she walked briskly towards the jets. Reaching the Harriers a crewman handed her a phone, informing her that it was Sir Charles calling again.

"Charles, we're ready to go now. Have you arranged for the refuelling stops?"

"You'll need to refuel in mid-flight so you can save time. Our American cousins have agreed to assist us with their Boeing KB-135 Stratotanker that's in the area. The pilots have been given the map references that they'll need. I thought if you go north in one plane, and Lieutenant Edwards goes south in the other, then you should make it. So good luck and God speed, April. There is only ten hours twenty-two minutes left and the clock's ticking, we have calculated that you should just make it with an hour to spare.

"Wouldn't it be faster in another more up-to-date type of jet, Charles?"

"Yes April, but because of the terrain the Harrier is your best bet of being able to land close to the site. Now you will have to get going, and may God go with you both."

"Thank you, Charles. I'll see you when I return." Ringing off she handed James one set of the sets of keys, explaining to him why there were four keys. Then turning to the pilot, April urged him, "Let's get going."

"You'll need to wear this flying suit, Miss," he insisted as he handed her the suit. "It's thermal, because it'll be very cold when we land."

Thanking him, she quickly put on the suit tucking her blond hair into the helmet. Then April asked him, "Will that do. NOW, can we get going?"

"That's fine," the pilot replied. Looking her up and down admiringly, he added, "It's a pity to cover up that heavenly frame though."

"Down boy, we haven't the time for frivolous shenanigans." April retorted laughingly, as she climbed aboard the jet.

CHAPTER 10

"Would you like me to help you get up, Miss?" offered the pilot. "I wouldn't want you to hurt yourself getting into my plane, now would I?"

April winced with pain as she tried to climb into the cockpit.

"I'm sorry, Miss. I didn't realise that you were hurt." he apologised as he carefully helped her into the plane.

"That's okay. You weren't to know, were you?" She thanked him. "My name's April, April Darling. And what's your handle?"

"George Harrison, Ma'am, I mean April," he introduced himself as he blushed slightly, "but I'm just plain George to my friends. Very pleased to meet you April," he told her as he took his seat and gave the thumbs up to the other jet, signaling that they were ready for takeoff. The other pilot then returned the signal. George closed the cockpit down and started the engines. "Are you ready, April?"

"I'm ready when you are, George." Then the Harrier began to lift off the tarmac.

Her shoulder was now becoming extremely painful. As she slipped her hand inside her tunic she felt wet blood. She realised that the strain of climbing aboard had opened up the wound, causing it to haemorrhage again. April tried to stem the bleeding by applying pressure with her hand and some tissues from her handbag.

"Are you okay back there, April?" George asked with concern, as he took the plane soaring up, into the clear blue sky.

"I'm fine, George. Just an old wound's started to bleed again, that's all.

It'll stop again soon. At least I hope it will."

"I hope so too because we haven't time to call at the hospital. Just you relax and enjoy the flight, April. Have you ever flown in one of these before?"

"No, only on a simulator, George," April informed him, finding that the bleeding seemed to have subsided again. "That's better; I've managed to stop it bleeding for now." April explained with relief, as George levelled out the plane at fifty thousand feet.

"We will keep it at this height and fly over water as much as we possibly can. It will give us a little more speed and saves on fuel." he explained, as the plane banked to the left, and then to the right before levelling off again. "Now I can switch on the auto pilot and relax for a little while myself, April."

"When do we refuel?" April tried to make polite conversation as she looked down to her right, watching the North African coastline giving way to the Med.

"It'll be in approximately four hours' time, and then one more hour before our final rendezvous. Why don't you try to get some shuteye, April? You look as though you're completely exhausted?" George suggested.

"I'm over tired. I'm afraid if I do fall asleep you won't be able to wake me up for days, George. So just keep talking to me, will you?"

The pain in April's shoulder was getting worse again, so she realised that she would not be able to sleep anyway. George wasn't aware of this and talked on incessantly. Except for telling her about his family, and the RAF, the rest of it was pure rhetoric. He only paused to check if April was still awake.

April looked at the Mediterranean Sea giving way the south coast of Portugal. "You're very quiet. Are you still awake back there?" George asked. He then continued, "If I'm boring you just tell me to shut up. Won't you, April?"

"No, you're doing fine George, real fine. I was just reflecting on the holidays I used to share with my family on the Med," April explained soulfully.

"You have a family. Do you have any children?"

Realising that her weariness had made her drop her guard, she quickly explained, "I meant when I was younger."

"Oh sorry, I misunderstood you. Have you been back there recently, then?"

"No, and it seems so very long ago now that it's hard to remember it, George. But I must holiday there again soon."

"Where in the Mediterranean is it that you want to revisit?" he continued to question.

"Southern Spain. It brings back such very happy memories for me there."

"You never know young lady. When this mission's over, surely then you can take a nostalgic holiday. Who knows? Maybe you'll meet somebody that could make you forget all about this. Or is there a special somebody already?"

"No, there isn't anybody George. And yes, maybe I will go back there again soon." She agreed, knowing that he couldn't possibly understand the emotional pain she was carrying. She wanting to return there with her beloved wife and children, but as she was, a husband and a father, not as she was now.

"Is there anything you need, April?"

"A stiff drink and some pain killers would be nice, George," she asked hopefully.

"Come on now, April, things aren't that bad surely. Or are they?" George asked April, showing that he'd completely misunderstood her meaning.

Laughing, she realised what he'd thought. April explained, "No, I only want two pain killers for the pain in my shoulder. The stiff drink, well, that's because I could use a stiff drink right now."

George chuckled to himself as he realised his blunder. "I'm sorry," he said finally. "I'm sorry I can't help with the stiff drink, April. But in this bag's a flask of cool water, and you should find a bottle containing painkillers in there somewhere as well." He handed a small first aid case back to, April, saying, "Remember, only two tablets," as he began to laugh again at his misunderstanding.

"Roger," April replied, as she rummaged through the first aid bag and finally found the bottle of Paracetamol. "Ah, there's only two in here anyway, so I can't top myself. Now can I?"

"What's wrong with your shoulder?"

"I stupidly used it to stop a bullet, George."

"You mean you've been shot, April. Have you seen a doctor?" he asked anxiously.

"I haven't had the time for such a luxury yet, George. But I will, just as soon as this is over," she reassured him. Changing the subject, she asked, "We must be nearing the first refuelling point about now, surely?"

"Yes, you're right. It'll be in about five minutes. Keep your eyes peeled for it, will you?"

They spoke very little as they approached the point where they were to refuel.

"There it is. It's right on cue," George told her, as he pointed towards a large plane cruising approximately three miles ahead of them. "Have you ever refuelled in mid-air before, April?"

"No, George." April answered as the small plane steadily drew closer to the larger one. "I wouldn't be able to get my car up here."

He laughed as told her, "Well just watch and learn then, young lady. I'll have to stop talking while I concentrate though."

George slowly edged towards the plane as it lowered the refuelling pipe. He then skilfully maneuvered a point on his wing towards the fuel pipe. There was a clanging sound as it locked on, which vibrated through the small jet. "We have locked on now, so you can start the refuelling." He confirmed over the radio. Turning his attention back to April, he told her, "This won't take very long love, and then we'll be on our merry little way again."

April sat quietly watching as they filled the fuel tanks. Eventually with the tanks full, George was able to release the pipe. Thanking the other pilot, he told them, "I'll see you on our return trip boys."

George banked hard and increased the speed, continuing on towards the North Pole.

"When is the next fuel stop, George?"

"In a couple of hours or so, I detect a slight scouse accent. Am I right, April?"

"Yes, I am afraid so, although it seems so deeply ingrained into my past. Anyway, my accent's not that broad now, surely. Or is it?" April snapped, with a slight hint of playful indignation.

"No, April. It's quite an attractive attribute in you." She teased, "Are you trying to flirt with me?"

"Er, no," he fumbled for his words.

"Don't worry, I'm only teasing you," she told him, apologising to try to relieve George's acute embarrassment. April sat quietly pensive, staring out at the ever-thickening clouds. While she was thinking of her beloved family at home in Riverlet her eyes welling up with tears as she remembered them. April's heart ached to hold Mandy in her arms, but it seemed it could never be as it was before. Her thoughts then drifted to the children as she realised that never again will they bounce on the bed to wake her. April was now realising just how lonely life had now become. Oh, how she missed them, and she expected that they missed her just as much.

As if to snap out of the sombrely melancholy state, and focus on the job in hand, she said to George. "The clouds are thickening now, above and below us it seems."

"Yes, and I believe at the Pole there's a blizzard blowing up, visibility is down to only ten yards in some places. I just hope that we can land this old crate safely. We normally wouldn't attempt such a feat in this kind of weather, April."

"What about the refuelling, will we be able to make that okay?"

"I don't know that either yet, but I hope so." George explained to April, as he struggled with the controls. The plane was being buffeted about violently, as the turbulence worsened. "We should know the answer to that in about fifteen minutes, April."

"Is it possible to climb above all of this, George?"

"I don't know love, they're checking on that right now for us. Just a minute, it's coming through now."

She sat quietly as George spoke to ground control. April was getting decidedly uncomfortable because the conditions were deteriorating so rapidly. "Sorry, April, but according to the met office we can't rise above or below it. We'll just have to do our best and ride it out. The consolation is that the storms here subside as quickly as they erupt."

"I'm sure that I'm safe in your hands, George," she reassured him. "But how will you manage to find the refuelling point in this?"

"We use a homing device. But it's whether we can couple up to it that's more important. Anyway, we'll soon know. There it is now," George said with relief.

"Right, I'll keep quiet while you concentrate again then." April confirmed as she watched anxiously while the pilots tried time and time again to couple up.

"The conditions are too bad. I can't line her up to it, and even if I do the turbulence might rip us apart causing us to explode in mid-air and destroying both planes."

"How much fuel do we have left, George?"

"About two and a half hours. Why do you ask?"

"Well can he stay in the area and wait for are return trip. We can only hope this weather will subside a little by then, George."

"He's already suggested that, but if it doesn't abate by then we'll be history."

"Do you think you will be able to land in this though? We're now entering the final hour."

"What happens if we can't make it, April?" he asked, as he descended cautiously through the blizzard.

"We'll all be history. So you see it's all down to you now, George." she encouraged him as she stared into the white wall of snow, looking for a suitable landing area.

"Are you serious? I was only told that it was urgent, and to do my best. I was not told that it was bloody imperative!" George continued, with an air of panic in his voice.

Lights began to pierce the white wall of the blizzard. "There's the camp site now," he said with relief. "Now all we have to do is to land this bloody old crate."

As they cautiously descended George wrestled with the controls. He was trying to keep the small plane steady as it was tossed about in the swirling winds, as if it were a feather. "I'm not sure that we can land in this! The wind's far too strong."

"We must George, we must. Maybe if you get as low as possible I can jump for it. But by whatever means I can, I must get down there, and right now."

"I'm trying my best, but what will happen if I can't? I mean if we crash land or the likes," George said to April as they descended to within twenty feet, "because it's bloody murder trying to hold her steady enough to land."

"You've heard of Armageddon? Well, this will be ours. Anyway, I have faith in you." April tried to encourage him as she glanced at her watch. Forty-five minutes left. April knew that she couldn't panic George or they might end up crash landing. Then there would be absolutely no hope left for humanity as we know it.

"If I can get down behind that snow mound over there it might act as a wind breaker for the final ten feet of our descent." He pointed towards a high snow covered mound. "It seems like our best bet at the moment."

"Go for it, George. You underestimate yourself. I know you can do it." April tried to boost his confidence, quietly watching him preparing for the final ten feet of his vertical descent.

"Brace yourself April. I'm going straight for it. But it will be a bumpy landing. If you believe in a God, now is the time to pray to him."

"I do, and I will. So don't you worry we're in safe hands. You'll do just fine, George."

"I hope you're right, April. Because here goes nothing," George told her as the wind carried them towards the mountain of snow. As he brought the plane closer to the ground the small mountain of snow gave the plane some protection from the wind, as he had hoped. He was now able to land quickly and safely. He closed down the engines and quickly opened the canopy. "Be very careful climbing down, April. There will be ice covering the wings and the fuselage."

"Thanks for the warning." April said as she wearily climbed out. Then she slipped as she stepped onto the ice-covered surface. "Ouch!" April cried out as she landed on her injured shoulder. The wound opened up and once again the blood began to flow even more profusely than before.

"Are you all right, Miss?" she heard a friendly voice asking, feeling a hand offering to help her up. "Here, let me help," a man said as he guided April to a sled. "It's only fifty meters Miss, so we'll soon be there." he informed her as he drove the sled through the icy blizzard. "Joe will bring the pilot, but we must hurry. We're here now, Miss." he told her as eventually the sled stopped at a canvass structure, and he helped April into the shelter.

Weak from loss of blood, April struggled to find the energy to stand up. She hadn't spoken to anybody, trying desperately to conserve her final ounce of strength. "Hello, I'm Richard. I believe you have some keys for us, Miss?" the man asked as he guided her to a seat.

Finally April replied wearily, "Yes here they are, but I don't know which two are which. You may need to try them all." April was beginning to feel faint now as she passed him the keys.

"Thank God you got here in time, Miss." Realising that she was unwell, he added with concern, "Are you all right, Miss?"

"Yes. Now just stop that bloody bomb, will you?" April insisted anxiously as she watched from where she was sitting as they tried one key after another. True to form it was the final key that fitted the first lock. "Now use the other key on the same ring," April urged, knowing that she'd kept each pair of keys together.

They tried, but without any success.

"It goes in but it won't turn fully," said a voice shrilled with panic. April mustered her remaining strength. "Here let me have a try."

"It's no good Miss, we're all doomed," a young fresh-faced lad shouted hysterically.

Reaching the bomb April noticing that there was only five minutes left on the clock. She tried to turn the key, but it only turned half way. "There must be a bloody burr on this key. Have you got a small file, and something that will act as marking blue? Oh, and have you preferable got somebody with engineering skills to help me?"

"We haven't got the luxury of an engineer, but there are a few tools here, Miss," the man offered hopefully. "Are they any use to you?"

Noticing there was a small file and pair of vice grips in the toolbox, April assured him that they would suffice.

"Is there anything in my make-up set that will act as marking blue?" said a lady, as she passed April her purse.

Nodding, April confirmed that they should. Thanking her, April coated the key with lipstick, while the young lad shouted hysterically.

"Can somebody shut that poor fucking bastard kid up before I shoot him?" she insisted irritably. Then April inserted the key and turned it until it stopped. Removing the key she could see the mark where it wanted filing.

The young hysterical lad had now been moved to another tent to be sedated.

"That's better. Now I can hear myself think," muttered April, as she held the key in the grips and began filing the offending part. "That should do it." April said as she took the key out of the grips, and inserted it in the lock, "EUREKA," she cried as the key turned fully.

A hand reached over her shoulder and pressed a red button. "Twenty eight seconds to spare," a voice said with relief, "Well done, my dear."

April looked into the face of the elderly gentleman, realising that she hadn't been aware of the time because of her fatigue. "Thank you," she said gratefully. "I had clean forgotten about the red bloody button. Have you got a phone and a doctor here?"

"Here, use my phone, but I'm afraid we don't have the luxury of a doctor. Why? Are you hurt?" asked the elderly gentleman, as April unzipped her flying suit to reveal her blood-soaked shoulder. "My God, you are hurt. What has happened to you?" he gasped, as he saw the extent of her injuries.

"It was my own fault; I was stupid enough to stand in the way of a bullet." April joked, trying to make light of it and mask just how much pain she was actually in. Lethargically she dialled Charles's number.

"Hello." She heard him say. Everything now was becoming very distant and vague.

"Charles we've disarmed it. Has James managed to disarm his yet?"

"Yes, April," he answered triumphantly. "Have you had any problems, and are you all right?"

"Just about, you can tell our friend in Africa. You know; the one that cut the keys for me that I had to file a burr off for it to work. So his granny does need to be taught how to suck eggs after all." By now all of her energy was fast leaving her body. "And tell Rebec—." She slumped to the floor unconscious dropping the phone.

"April! APRIL!" Sir Charles' could be heard shouting.

The elderly gentleman picked up the phone. "She has fallen into unconsciousness, sir," he said sadly. "She looks very ill to me. She's lost a lot of blood, and she's totally exhausted," he informed Charles, with a concerned expression. "We owe the lady so much too."

"I need to get her back here urgently. Is the pilot still with you?" Charles asked.

After a short pause the pilot said to Charles. "Flight Lieutenant George Harrison here, Sir."

"This is Field Martial Sir Charles Hythe-Smith, and I need to get Miss April Darling back here urgently. Can you help me?"

"Yes Sir, if we can get her into the cockpit that is. The weather here has just abated temporarily," George said with relief. "Miss Darling is something special, isn't she?"

"You will never know just how right you are George. Now, how soon can you be airborne?"

George asked the man administering first aid.

"Five more minutes tops. I've stopped the bleeding for now, but for how long I don't know. She needs to be moved to a hospital with extreme urgency because she needs a blood transfusion, and the wounds need addressing," he told George.

Returning his attention to the phone, George asked Sir Charles, "Did you get all of that, Sir? Five minutes tops. Then ten minutes to get her to and into the plane. We should be airborne within twenty minutes." He confirmed, "Where shall I take her, Brize Norton?"

"No here, I'll send you the map references. Now please hurry," Sir Charles urged.

When the man had finished dressing the wounds, a lady helped George to put April's flying suit on her, preparing April for the flight home.

After taking her swiftly to the plane, George said, "She's deteriorating fast, I do hope I can make it. She deserves a break after risking her life to save us all."

Soon, they were winging their way towards the first refuelling point, then onwards towards the second.

Nearly seven hours later the plane landed in the grounds of the department headquarters in the Cotswolds.

CHAPTER 11

Close to death, April was hastily taken down to the medial unit from whence she had originally emerged as April Darling. Amid the flurry of feverish activity, she was attached to machines that monitored every progress, or setback, twenty-four hours a day. A saline drip was attached into one arm; whilst in the other arm a variety of injections were administered.

Jody, April's original nurse, had been reassigned to her. She sat quietly at the bedside, and constantly monitored April's temperature, blood pressure, respiration, etc., every thirty minutes. The doctors waited patiently for her condition to improve, so that she would be strong enough to undergo the operation, having the monitors relayed to them in the lounge area where they sat relaxing as they waited patiently for her to sufficiently improve.

Twenty-four hours passed before a slight improvement could be noted, but it was still insufficient for them to be able to go ahead with the operation on the damaged shoulder. Thirty-six hours passed as April still very steadily improved. It would be very soon now when the patient would be strong enough for the doctors to repair her shoulder. The orderlies were told to begin preparing the theatre, while the medical staff scrubbed up, and donning their gowns and caps, in readiness for the delicate operation to come.

"Sir Charles, who was pacing impatiently up and down the corridors, had moved his office down to be closer to his prodigy. Secretly his affection for her was becoming more than that of a business relationship. As a result, he made constant enquiries of Jody as to April's condition.

Finally, after forty hours had passed, it was decided that the patient was sufficiently strong to undergo the operation. April was wheeled once more into the theatre.

The surgeons skilfully reopened the wound. They then cleaned the residue from the injury, and started repairing the damaged blood vessels and sinews. Finally they closed up the wound using their revolutionary laser techniques so as to leave no hint of scaring on April.

"There, it's all done. You can tell Sir Charles that she's going to be okay."

Then with afterthought the head surgeon reflected, "I think the old dog's fallen for her." Realising that he'd spoken out aloud, he hastily added, "But don't tell him that I said that, will you?"

There was a flurry of laughter from the other members of staff. This being the first sign that the tension gripping them had finally lifted.

April was returned to her room to recover. Because of her physical exhaustion this took rather longer than was normally expected. Twenty hours passed, before she finally began to stir.

"Sir Charles," Jody called. "I think that April's about to wake up."

Sir Charles, who had left instructions to be called immediately when April awoke, burst into the room.

"Is she okay?" he asked anxiously as he entered the room

"She's going to be fine, Sir Charles." Jody reassured him. She was busily registering April's temperature, pulse, and blood pressure. "Shall I fetch you a cup of coffee now, Sir?" Jody offered. She was aware that he had hardly eaten or slept since the news of April's near fatal injuries had reached him.

"Thank you, Jody. That would be much appreciated. A sandwich would not go amiss either, if that would not be too much trouble." he added.

Jody returned after ten minutes carrying a silver platter. It bore three cups of coffee, a plate of plain biscuits, and an assortment of sandwiches. "I've brought an extra cup for when April wakes up, Sir."

"A good idea Jody," Sir Charles answered her instinctively, seeming preoccupied with April's state of unconsciousness. He stared intensely at her closed eyes, willing them to open. "It's been almost three days now. She must have been totally exhausted, poor thing." His comments broke the eerie silence in her room.

They seemed to disturb the patient as she raised her arms above her head to stretch. April's eyes then flickered and opened, as they adjusted to the strong lighting. Eventually she turned her attentions towards Jody and Charles. Smiling at them, April asked, "Hi there. Where am I?" Recognising the familiar surroundings, she added, "I see I'm back here in Dracula's castle? Have I been asleep for long?" As Jody handed her a cup of coffee, she remarked, "I can see that my shoulder's now healed. I must have slept for at least a month."

Charles moved to her side and gazed down at April's smiling face. His eyes were reddened and filled with tears of relief. Kissing her cheek, he explained, "It's been days now. You were totally exhausted. After we had repaired your shoulder we just let you sleep yourself well. George flew you back here, and just in time too, I might add. A few hours longer and you wouldn't have been strong enough to pull through the operation."

"So I have George to thank, do I? I hope he's to receive some recognition for his part in all of this, Charles?"

"Don't worry about that, I've already seen to it April." Changing the subject, he asked. "Would you like some more coffee?"

"Please, Charles." April said, as she handing him her empty cup. "Did you manage to stop the computer virus by the way?"

"Yes, we got a lucky break there. We found that one of our top men was heavily involved in it. So he was very keen to co-operate in return for a reduced sentence." Charles explained. "He removed the virus for us, and we for our part promised not to prosecute him."

"YOU LET HIM GO!" April shouted, "What's to prevent him from reloading the virus."

"Don't panic, April. We know exactly where he is at any given time. He had a bad laceration on his leg. While it was being treated by the surgeon, who incidentally was one of our chaps, we implanted a minute homing device into his leg. So you see, we thought it all out, and we are able to keep tabs on him from a safe distance. He's at this present time in a flat in Chelsea that is owned by a renowned terrorist. We've been watching them, and we know that he has bought a ticket to Singapore. My guess is that he plans to travel on from there to where he intends to go next. But just as soon as he's sure he's not being followed. Anyway, you just concentrate on getting well, my dear. That's what the most important thing is to me right now."

"I've laid here long enough, Charles." April said impatiently as she threw back the bedclothes. Sitting on the edge of the bed, she asked Jody, "Now where are my clothes?"

Jody looked towards Charles, who, after a short pause nodded his consent. Then Jody helped April into an adjoining ante room, and assisted her to get dressed.

She dressed in a red loose skirt, white blouse, and black boots. After applying a minimal amount of make-up, April emerged back to where Charles was still waiting for her. "Will I do Charles?" she asked him buoyantly.

"Radiant as ever, my dear," he complimented her, as he stood and crossed the room to where she was. Again Charles kissed her on the cheek. He asked,

"Would you do me a very great honour, and permit me to buy you dinner tonight?"

"Of course, I would expect nothing less from you, Charles. I'm famished, and I can't remember when I last ate."

"There's just one condition though. No shop talk. Is it a deal?"

"It's a deal, Charles. But afterwards we need to decide how to handle our virus friend." April reminded him, "Because I couldn't go through that hell again."

"And I would not want, or expect you to my dear. So we will discuss it tomorrow," he promised. He offered his arm as he asked, "Now shall we go, April?"

———

After thanking Jody for what she'd done to help them, they left the medical unit, and returned home to prepare for their evening out.

The evening passed as they dined at Charles' favourite club. Every time April tried to approach the subjects of security, and the imposing threat that still might exist, Charles skilfully steered the conversation away from it.

Finally, when the meal was over, April was feeling quite tipsy. This was because to the mixture of medicated drugs she'd been treated with, the wine, and the fatigue due of the lack of natural sleep.

Charles summoned his chauffeur, and asked the driver to take them to his apartment.

Arriving at the apartment, April teased, "Aren't you going to seduce me, Charles?" giggled April.

"I think you've had a little too much to drink tonight, April." Charles told her in a low, embarrassed voice.

"Go on. Why don't you admit it, Charlie boy? You want to fuck me, don't you?" she continued to tease. She wrapped her arms around his neck, trying to pull him onto the bed.

"You're very drunk, April," he told her blushing profusely. "Maybe you need a cold shower?"

This only gave her more ammunition with which to tease him with, as April started sobering up. "A very good idea, we'll have a cold shower together first." She started to remove her boots. "Then you can fuck me."

"No April. I meant you have a cold shower." He suddenly realised that April was sobering up so he smiled broadly. "You're winding me up, aren't you, April?"

Her expression became more serious now. "I'm not sure, Charles. All of my feelings and hormones are very mixed up right now."

"Well, let us take everything very slowly then." Charles suggested as he kissed her. But this time it was on the lips, which only added to April's confusion as he drew away. He told her, "Have a good night's sleep." Then he reluctantly left the bedroom.

Waking at six am the next morning, April showered and dressed before walking into the morning room. "You're an early riser, Charles." April said when she saw him eating his breakfast.

"Good morning, April. Sit down, and Maria will serve you your breakfast." He invited, as a Filipina lady entered from the kitchen. "Maria, meet April. April, this is my trusty housekeeper, and a dear friend, Maria." The ladies exchanged greetings before April sat and ate her breakfast.

After she'd finished, April followed Charles into the lounge where he was finishing reading the newspaper. "Now, can you explain what's happening to our computer maniac?"

"Certainly my dear," he began, "as I've already told you, we're tracking his every movement. As I've told you, we needed to give him an anaesthetic to repair his tendons, so while he was out we also fitted a minute camera and microphone into his forehead. We have also fitted a small remote explosive devise inside his chest cavity; so that we will have the means to detonate him at any given time. That is, should it ever become necessary to do it?"

"And who is following his movements?" April continued with concern. "Do I know them?"

"It's a small team I assembled myself. I have put an old friend of yours in charge of it though, Martin Driver, he—."

"WHAT!" April interrupted, shouting as she sprang to her feet. "You have put that bloody fucking low life toe rag in charge! Didn't you get my messages about him, Charles?"

"What messages? Martin told us how he'd saved your life by pulling you free from the burning helicopter, just before it exploded."

"SHIT!" she shouted again, banging her fist down on the coffee table. "He's the leak you've been looking for, and he's tried to kill me on more than one occasion. I sent you a text to warn you about him. Didn't you read my messages?"

"I'm sorry, it never reached me. His face was all burnt and he explained it happened when he was pulling you clear from the blazing wreckage. That's what made his story seem all the more plausible." Charles tried desperately to justify his mistake.

"I hope you know where the fucking rat is now. That's all I hope, Charles." April told him, her voiced laced with sarcasm. "And I also hope that he doesn't know about the devises you've planted in that computer fellow?"

"No, thank goodness," Charles sighed with relief.

"Well that's something I suppose. But I'm afraid he has to be interrogated. And either you lock up him in a high security unit and throw away the keys or I take him out completely. And the latter would be a much cheaper and safer option. He was also the toe rag who put the bullet in my shoulder." April rasped through clenched teeth.

"Well, we'd better get to work then." Charles suggested, refolding his newspaper neatly before walking through into his bedroom. "I'll get my car sent round to the front door in about ten minutes, April."

She said nothing. After brushing her hair April put on her coat, and picked up her purse and mobile phone. "I'm ready when you are, Charles," she called. She found Charles was already waiting for her in the lounge.

"Right, my dear, let's go then," he invited, as he held the door open for her.

Then after picking up his brief case, he followed April out of the door.

While the chauffeur drove to Charles' office, April tried to wrestle with the events that had transpired over the last three or four days. She asked, "Has anybody else had access to your mobile phone, Charles?"

"Only when I slept, April, I give it to Michael Waterford. But he's one of my top security men. He's worked for me for at least five years now, and I'd trust him with my life."

"You may have done that, Charles. Can we have your phone rechecked without his knowledge? Although the messages will have been deleted, they will still be in the memory somewhere."

"Of course, if it makes you feel happier and clears Michael's name," agreed Charles, as his phone rang. Answering it, she heard him say, "Hello Michael." Then his expression became serious as he listened intently. Without speaking he ended the call. "They've lost track of Martin Driver. We're watching all the ports and airports, in case he tries to leave the country. Apparently he went into a paper shop, as he usually does each morning, but he never emerged again. He must have left via a rear door."

"I hope they've arrested the shop keeper. He must have been the one that allowed the scum bag to leave by the rear entrance," April's voice became harder as she grew more increasingly frustrated. "Who the hell was watching him anyway?"

"A team from the lower ranks was following Driver. It seemed to be just a routine operation. Ah, we are here at last thank God. You know, you've far exceeded our original expectations of you, don't you, April?"

"Don't give me all of that flannel, Charles. I've thought long and hard about what's happened to me," April started, as they walked towards his office, "I was created so that I'd be expendable, a scapegoat, or a ready-made diversion. You can call it what you like, but it was so as to allow the other operatives to escape. Of course, if I was captured I would not be traceable. Remember, I've no past to trace. Stop me when I'm going wrong, Charles, won't you? Only it backfired when Ron was injured. Didn't it? How am I doing so far?" Charles was looking decidedly uncomfortable by now. "And now I've emerged as your best, no, probably your only, bloody hope." April finished, as she sat alongside Charles at his desk. "Right, now that I've said my piece. Firstly, will you have your phone checked, and on that I must insist."

He called one of the other technicians who within minutes entered his office and took the mobile phone, but only after Charles had explained what he required him to do with it, and Charles impressed on him that it must be covertly.

"Now, can we meet with this bloody shop keeper, Charles?" April said insistently as she headed for the door.

"Not so fast, April," Charles intervened. "Special Branch is the expert in these matters. So we should let them deal with him."

"Experts my fucking arse. We don't have the luxury of the time that they will take. Anyway, I just need to know how they are getting on, that's all. Also, if they have found out anything about him yet that will be useful to us." April reassured Charles, inviting him to leave with her. "Are you coming, or do I have to go alone?"

"I suppose so. But just to ask them what they've found out, April." Charles insisted reluctantly. "And no interfering, agreed?"

"Now would I," April jested coyly. "We just need to re-enforce the urgency to them. That's all."

Driving through the country lanes they chatted idly. Eventually, after approximately thirty minutes, the car stopped at the gates of a long driveway, which lead to a large Manor House. They both produced their authorisation, and were escorted to the old house. Upon entering, they were led along a maze of passageways, and down a flight of stone steps. Then they entered a large cellular office.

The man behind the desk got up and approached, "Charles, you old dog. What an unexpected pleasure. And this lovely lady is-?" he asked flirtatiously.

"This is one of my best operatives, or should I say, probably my best agent now. Meet Miss April Darling," he introduced her. "But be careful George, I must warn you that she has a very venomous bite," he added with a smile.

"Pleased to meet you," April greeted him.

"I can assure you that the pleasure is all mine, of that I can certainly assure you. Can I call you, April? And you can bite me anytime, and anywhere, you like." George pretended to whisper, as he guided April to a seat. "As you know I'm George. Now what can I do for the lovely lady?"

"Another George, they seem to be coming out of the woodwork nowadays. I knew a George once," April sighed. "But it all seems so very long ago. And then the pilot was called George," she remarked, glaring towards Charles, who had sat in a seat opposite her. He looked sheepish because of her cutting remarks, as he fidgeted with his collar, so April changed the subject quickly. "We have come to check if you have made any progress with our shopkeeper man? Remember it's pretty urgent, George," April urged, as he cupped her hands in his.

"Don't you worry your pretty little head about him? Just you leave it all to us. We know exactly what to do in these matters, April. I can assure you about that," he tried to convince her.

"I told her that, George. But she insisted that we came down here to see for ourselves," Charles explained. "I must add though, she is normally right about this type of thing."

"Well I can tell you that he's a tough nut to crack, April. But, we will get there eventually. And of that, I can assure you."

"Can we just see him?" April asked assertively but impatiently. "It's not a pretty site for a lovely lady too-," George started.

April stopped him in mid-sentence saying firmly, "Don't worry on my account, George. I've seen things that would probably make even you queasy."

Without another word, George led them through a door and into an anteroom, where they would be able to observe the interrogation via a two-way mirror.

After watching the torturous interrogation methods for some thirty minutes, the prisoner was bloodied, and barely conscious. But still, they had no success in extracting any information from him.

"Your so-called experts are just wasting their time here." April snapped out of frustration. "Charles, where is your professor of the tricky toys brigade? Get him on the phone for me will you. I've an idea to discuss with him."

"Why? What have you got in mind?" George asked, with a puzzled look on his face.

"Just let me talk to him and you'll see, George," April insisted.

Charles took out his phone and dialled the number. After introducing April, he handed her the phone.

April then asked everybody to give her some privacy.

When she was alone she began, "Could you make a very special gun for me, please professor?"

"Certainly, what type of weapon would you like?"

"Well, it must look like a normal gun, but with very special bullets. I don't want the bullets to fire normally; instead I want a small dart to leave the chamber. When the dart hits the target, I need the victim to immediately fall to the floor unconscious, but giving anybody watching the impression that they're dead."

"Yes, that would not be too difficult. Will that be all, Miss?"

"Well, when the dart hits the skin can a small capsule on the tip be made to burst, so it will look like a bullet wound?" she added, crossing her fingers in hope.

"You're asking a lot, aren't you, Miss?" The professor thought for a moment. "Yes, I should be able to put a small tip on the dart so it will burst on impact. How long is the victim to remain lifeless for?"

"Ten minutes should be long enough, professor. How long will it take to make them?"

He went quiet again while he made a few calculations. "About a week should be sufficient I would think, Miss."

"Try a day or two, please, Professor."

"Impossible Madam," the professor said indignantly. "Do you think I can just buy what I need at the nearest supermarket? I have to craft what I invent wi-."

"Whoa Professor, I didn't mean to offend you. I do know that you're the best in your field; Sir Charles has already assured me of that. But we don't have the luxury of time on our side at the moment. If we could get you more man power, would that be of any help to you?"

There was another long silence while he pondered the task. "Maybe if I had four, or five, good people that I handpicked myself. Then, I should be able to craft it in forty-eight hours, for you. But that's only contingent upon my having all the resources at hand, Miss."

"Of course, anything, but be as fast as you can, please, Professor." April stressed again.

"I'll need verification from the Minister. Also, I will need air transport to fetch one of the men that I'll need. He incidentally is skiing in the Alps with his family, and he'll not be amused at being disturbed. Now can I speak to Sir Charles?"

April called Charles in and handed him the phone. "He wants to speak to you AND the Minister."

"Professor, I'll have the Minister call you with all the clearance that you need forthwith." Charles explained. Then he listened for a short time before confirming. "Yes, April can be very demanding can't she? But that's one of her strongest attributes. That's what makes her so very special to us," He listened again, and gave a short laugh before ringing off.

"Right, that's done. What now?" Charles asked. "Shall we get George in so you can bring us both up to speed?"

"Okay" April said flicking off her shoes. "My feet are killing me Charles. I seem to have been on them for days," she digressed.

"Perhaps I should give your feet a massage." Charles suggested, as he opened the door to beckon George in.

"That's very kind of you Sir, but I think I'll pass for now." George said with a cheeky grin. "I've far too much work to do at the moment."

"Not you, you blithering idiot. I meant April."

Giving her an admiring look, he said, "By far the better choice I would say, Charles. Now I must get back to business, if you'll both excuse me?" as he began to open the door to leave.

"Not so fast. There's been a change of tactic. April thinks that she may have found an alternative plan to speed things up with. Tell him, April," Charles urged, as he massaged her aching feet.

"Obviously he's been trained in interrogation techniques, and so is oblivious to all the pain. You and your team will probably end up killing him without extracting any information from him at all, George."

"I was forming that opinion myself. He's certainly proving to be a tough old nut, that's for sure."

"Precisely, that's why I'm having some very special toys made. If you just continue with your methods for a short while, but don't bloody kill him will you? I'll come in and interrupt you. Then you just take your cue from what I have to say." April finished and put her shoes back on.

While admiring April's legs, he agreed and returned to his task. Saying, "Right, let's get back to business."

After three or four minute April stood up. "Right, just follow me Charles." She told him, as she left the room and proceeded towards the interrogation room next door, with Charles following closely behind her.

April said to him, "Now to instil some confusion and false security into this man's tiny little mind." She opened the door and swept into the room authoritatively.

"What the fucking hell's going on down here? Do you want this man to think that we're all barbarians down here?" she shouted. "Untie this man at once, and fetch him a warm drink." She lifted the prisoner's head gently and looked into his swollen blood splattered face.

Removing a tissue from her shoulder bag, April began to tenderly dab the blood from round his face.

"I'm terribly sorry, sir. If I'd known how you were being treated, then I'd have come down here much sooner." Trying to console him, she continued, "It would have been much easier on you to have told them whatever they wanted to know, but I can see that you're a very proud and brave man." The man tried to speak, but the words wouldn't leave his bloodied, swollen mouth. "Don't try to speak now sir. Just you rest."

Then turning to the confused George, she ordered. "Get this man a doctor, and a change of clothing. When he looks something like respectable, then you can let his wife and children come to see that he's okay." April turned smartly and left the room closely followed by a protesting George and Sir Charles.

Once the door had closed behind them, and they were out of earshot of the prisoner, April explained. "It's only to gain the confidence of his family. Explain to him that it may take a couple of days to complete the paper work, but then he should be free to go home again. However, in the meantime he can have anything that he wants, within reason. And his family can have unlimited access to him."

Looking very confused, he asked, "For how long do we need to keep up this pretence, April?"

"I'm not too sure yet. But hopefully it'll only be for a couple of days, George."

"And what will we do then, April?"

"It will have a far better affect if you don't know that, George. And, it will be much more dramatic and believable." she told him as she fastened her coat. "I'll let you know when as soon as I can." Charles and April brushed past the open mouthed George, and left the interrogation unit.

She dined with Charles, and slept in his spare room, as she'd done on the previous nights. But she was awakened early the next morning by the ringing of the telephone. "It's for you, April." Charles called in to her. "The professor would like a word with you."

By this time April had entered the lounge, fastening her gown as she walked. "Hello Professor. And what can I do for you this fine morning?"

"I need to know what size gun you will need, and how many bullets, Miss Darling?"

"Oh, a small hand gun that will fit inside my pocket or my purse will suffice, and approximately three to six bullets."

"Three bullets and a small hand gun you can have first thing tomorrow morning," he explained. "I have all the necessary materials at hand to do them. Any more would take me a few days longer, Miss Darling."

"Three will have to do me then, and thank you, Professor. Have you been working since the early hours?"

"My team assembled yesterday at eighteen hundred hours, and we've been hard at work ever since then, Miss Darling."

"Call me, April. Everybody else does. Do you mean that you've worked right through the night! Well, I'd better let you finish then so that you can all get some well-earned shut eye, professor," said April before replacing the receiver.

"I hope you appreciate that man, Charles. He's a very conscientious person, you know? Anyway, I'm going to shower, and dress." April said, as she closed the bedroom door behind her.

"We do appreciate the professor. He was knighted in last New Year's honours list." Charles called through the closed door. Adding, "I've some work to do at the local office. What are your plans for today, April?"

"I thought I'd waste a day browsing round the shops." April suggested, as she walked from the bedroom towelling her wet hair. "It's something I haven't had much time to do properly. Well, not since you messed round with my hormones that is, and everything else as well I might add." April smiled broadly at Charles.

"You look stunning when you smile, April."

"Why, I thank you kindly, Sir," mocked April playfully, as Charles pulled back her chair at the breakfast table. "That also sounded like a change the subject time to me."

"Maybe, will you be calling at my London office later, April? And would you like my driver for the day?"

"No thank you, Charles. It'll be much easier for me if I use a taxi. After all, your car would only be standing idle for most of the day while I shopped. I will ring you when I'm finished if you like and then YOU can pick ME up personally." April was trying to remove the worried look off Charles's face. "Now go on or you'll be late. I'll be just fine on my own."

Charles bent over and kissed her on the cheek. "I know April. But old habits do die hard you know. And I can't help feeling protective towards you."

April laughed. "You know I can protect myself probably better than you can."

Charles just nodded his agreement, and left for his office.

Alone at last, April thought, as she ate breakfast. What Charles didn't realise was her longing to speak to Mandy and the children again. She was feeling tormented within her heart. She felt torn between the deep love that she felt for her family, and her patriotic loyalty to her beloved country. April knew that she must see the assignment through to its bitter end, no matter what the cost was to her personally. Only then would she be able to consider seeing her beloved family again.

But for now, she felt an overwhelming desire to at least speak to Mandy. So after finishing breakfast, April left Maria to her daily tasks, and left to hail a taxi to go to the local shopping area.

Browsing around the shops, she took careful note as to whether she was being followed. She noticed that at each shop she visited, the same two ladies were there too. April thought, 'Right, I'll soon lose you two bitches.'

She found it was proving to be more difficult than she'd first anticipated.

The more April tried to lose them, the more vigilant they became.

Finally she realised that she'd need to revert to dirty tactics. Seeing that one of them was at the jewellery counter, April moved closer to her. Then, unbeknown to the woman, slipped an expensive gold chain into her handbag, ensuring that she had chosen one with the security tag still attached to it.

'That's one trapped,' she thought to herself. Then looking around she noticed that the other lady was standing opposite her, looking at dresses. April headed straight towards the ladies toilet.

The second lady took the bait and followed her inside. As she entered the toilets, April was hiding behind the door to one of the cubicles. Springing out, she took the woman completely by surprise, wrestling her into an empty cubicle. Holding her down with one hand, April dragged off her tights with her free hand. She used the tights to bind her arms and legs together, completely ignoring the woman's futile pleas. Then she ripped a sleeve from her dress and stuffed it into her mouth, preventing the woman from shouting for help.

Jamming the door to the cubicle closed with a handy sweeping brush, she left the woman helpless, but unharmed, with, April's mobile phone, minus the sim card, in her pocket.

This she'd done as a precautionary measure, in case an electronic tag had been attached to it. As she walked from the toilets, April placed the sign, 'Do not use, cleaning in progress,' in front of the door.

Re-entering onto the shop floor, April saw that the other agent was watching. Her face was a look of a mixture of uncertainty and bewilderment. Realising that she was about to head straight into the toilets to see what was delaying her colleague; April rushed towards the exit door, certain that she'd follow.

April was reflecting on how tiresome it was all becoming, having to lose the surveillance officers each time she went out alone. She thought, "Doesn't Charles realise that I'd always complete the assignment, whatever the cost was to me personally."

Reaching the glass doors, which opened automatically, she saw the reflection in the glass of the lady agent getting closer and closer to her. Stepping through the open door, April stopped abruptly and stepped back into the store.

The lady following her was in nowhere land, and had no alternative but to continue through the open doors. The alarm was triggered instantly, and the doorman hastily stopped the lady. Then a team of security officers appeared and encircled her.

"Thank goodness for that. I thought I'd triggered the alarm off for a second." April said with relief, as she approached the small crowd.

"No lady. Just move along now. We've caught the culprit red handed," explained one of the security men, as he held up the gold chain that she had planted on her.

"Thank you." April said gratefully, as she got into the taxi parked at the kerb side. She asked the taxi driver to go round the corner and stop. Paying the driver, and giving him a generous tip to forget he'd ever seen her, she walked swiftly through the side streets towards the railway station.

Going to a public telephone, one that was not easily viewed from the roadside, April proceeded to dial Mandy's number. But only after she was sure that it was safe to do so.

After three or four rings Mandy was heard answering, "Hello. Can I help you?"

After hesitating for a moment, she eventually answered. "Hello sweetheart, it's me George, I mean, April."

"Hi April, how are you?" Mandy began cheerfully. "Don't be ashamed of calling yourself April, we know that it was all forced onto you. By the way, I have explained what has happened to the children."

"How have they taken the news?"

"Surprisingly well I thought. They're very excited about seeing you again. They're always asking when you are coming home. Anyway, when will you be coming home, darling?"

"Soon, I hope Mandy. But I still haven't finished what I need to do for them yet."

"And what's that, April?"

"I can't tell you that I'm afraid, it's all a matter of national security. You know, top secret, and all that stuff. Anyway, it'd put you and the children in grave danger if I told you." There was a long pause before she could continue. "I miss you all so very, very, much," April choked out, as she fought back the tears. Changing the subject before it became a full flood of tears, she asked, "Is the house still being watched, Mandy?"

"Not really, I spoke to the men, and invited them in for a coffee."

"You didn't Mandy. Did you really?"

"I did. We had a nice little chat. I told them that I was aware of their presence, and asked them why they're watching us. So after telephoning their boss they explained that they're making sure we're not in any danger. They said it was because you disappeared in mysterious circumstances. Anyway, we've come to an understanding. Now I give them tea or coffee when they need it. I even let them come in to watch the television, and use the loo. But I've promised to inform them if I ever need to go anywhere." Mandy boasted, being proud at having taken control of the situation.

"And where are they now, pet?"

"Having a pub lunch, April. Don't worry though, as you've told me, I always keep this mobile hidden. It's only you and I that know about its existence. But I always answer it cautiously, just in case it's a wrong number."

"Good girl, Mandy. Let's keep it that way too. Now how are the children? Are they there?"

"They're at school, but they'll be sad about not being here to speak to you. If you tell me when you'll call again, I can have them here for you to speak to them."

"I don't always know that, there are some loose ends that need tying up first, maybe in a couple of weeks." Then with hesitation, she added, "You do realise that if I'm ever to come home we'd have to move house, and that we can only ever be just friends."

"But good friends though."

"Yes, very good friends, darling. But our marriage as it was will be over forever," she had to admit painfully.

"Yes, we do have such a lot of things to talk about, don't we?" Mandy agreed. To lighten the mood, Mandy suggested, "Just think sweetheart, we can have girlie nights out together. That will be fun, but only after we've adjusted to both of us being female of course, just so there'll be no jealousy between us. Who knows? You may eventually be able to get a reversal operation in the fullness of time, and that mightn't be so very far in the future either."

"No, it shouldn't be too far away, I hope. I'll call you again very soon from an Internet Cafe. One with a web cam, then I can send you some pictures of myself, so you can all get used to seeing me as I am now." April was starting to feel very downhearted by now. With an aching heart, she added. "I miss you all so very much, and I can't wait to come home again." Her eyes started welling up with tears as she fell silent, while trying desperately to compose herself. Finally, she said to Mandy, "I must go now, pet. I'll phone you again soon though, I promise. Always remember that I love and miss you all so very much."

"We love you too, April," Was Mandy's sympathetic response, as she realised that it was becoming upsetting for her. "We'll see you soon, very soon," Mandy added, as she rang off.

It was a few moments before April was able to compose herself. Finally, replacing the receiver, April walked towards the shopping area. The rest of the day she spent shopping, buying a new mobile phone, and an array of clothing and jewellery. Then, April returned to the store from whence she had first started.

Approaching the front entrance, she could see that the two female agents who were being subjected to a severe berating. It was by who seemed to be their boss.

"Don't be too hard on them mate. Remember I've been trained by the very best." April interrupted, trying to defuse the situation. Then she handed the man her bags, continuing, "Here, you can carry these. And I've told you to stop bullying these poor girls. Now who's going to give me a lift home?"

The man reluctantly agreed. After placing the parcels in the boot of his car, they travelled silently back towards Sir Charles's home.

April broke the silence. "My, my, we are in an unforgiving mood today, *aren't we?*"

"It's not funny, Miss," the man snapped, as he drew the car to a halt outside Charles's home.

Becoming very annoyed at his persistently bad attitude, April grabbed him in a headlock. "Now you just listen to me, you scumbag. You couldn't have followed me, without my losing you. Now stop giving the girls such a hard fucking time about it."

There was a tapping on the window as she released one hand to open it. "WHAT?"

"April, is there a problem here?" She heard Charles asking in his kindly voice.

"Tell this crazy woman to let go of me, Sir!" the man struggled to say because of the tight grip she had round his throat.

"Tell this scumbag to lay off these girls before I throttle him, just because I fooled them, and lost them. And that reminds me. You and I need to have a very serious talk about all of this."

"You had better do as she says," Charles advised the man.

April noticed the girls grinning upon seeing their bullying boss humiliated.

"Okay," he conceded. "I'll lighten up on them. But they should never have lost her."

"As I've told you before, don't expect them to fucking do what you couldn't fucking do yourself!" April snarled at him impatiently, as she got out of the car. "You girls let me know if he bullies you anymore. THEN, I'll rip his bloody head off completely."

After he removed her parcels from the boot and handed them to Charles, the surveillance officer sped off at high speed.

"He wants sacking, Charles," urged April, as she watched the car disappearing round a corner. "That man's a pure chauvinistic pig."

"It's all in the pipe line, April. We've been observing him for some time now. I'll organise his demise as soon as we get in." he promised, holding open the front door for April to enter.

"Anyway, you bugger. Why don't you trust me, *yet?*"

"But we do trust you, April," he retorted, surprised at what she'd said. "Then why did you have me followed YET AGAIN?"

"It was all simply an innocent misunderstanding my dear, I promise you, and by that stupid imbecile." Charles explained as he lifted the telephone receiver

April then listened to Charles telling somebody to organise the replacement of the surveillance boss. "Send him into the field." He paused to listen. He then added, "I don't know or care. See if we can use him in South America, or somewhere equally remote. And stop the surveillance on Miss April Darling, like as per yesterday, so to speak." He rang off abruptly. "Now that that's done are you happy my dear?"

"Yes, Charles. Thank you." April answered, kicking off her shoes and stretching out on the settee. "So tell me, what brings you home so early-y-yish."

"The professor rang to say that he has finished the project early. So when do you want to collect them from him? And what are you planning to do then?"

"All in good time, Charles," answered April as she took a coffee from Maria. Thanking her, she then turned her attention back to Charles. "Tell the professor I'll collect them from him first thing tomorrow morning, will you, Oh, and thank him for me too please."

"Okay." Charles said, as he returned to the telephone. When he'd finished, he told April that it'd all be ready and waiting for her early the next morning.

Then he disappeared into the shower room.

She was so comfortable that she fell asleep, only to be awakened by Charles returning, "I'm sorry. Did I wake you, April?"

"It's okay, Charles, I need to have a shower anyway. But I'll show you what I've bought before I do," she suggested, allowing herself time to wake up properly.

After showing Charles the results of her laborious shopping, she headed into the shower room. "Are we eating in or out tonight, Charles? Just so I'll know what to wear." She called through, as she turned on the shower.

"Out, April. I've booked us a table for four, at seven thirty."

"A table for four people. Who else will be joining us?"

"Some dear old friends of mine, I hoped you wouldn't mind. They're a nice couple. You'll like them, April."

After showering, April dressed in a short red cocktail dress. Then the evening was spent in the pleasant company of Charles's friends.

As the evening drew to a close, Martha, the wife of Charles's school friend, remarked how attractive April was. She added how lucky Charles was to have such a charming and intelligent fiancée.

Glancing towards a very embarrassed Charles, she decided not to embarrass him further. April smiled coyly placing her hand on top of his. "No Martha, I'm the lucky one." She answered, much to the relief of Charles. "But we must make time to choose the ring soon, Charles."

"He never talks about anything else. He seems completely besotted by you, April. Of course, now that I've met you at last, I can fully understand why. When's the engagement to be announced formally?" Martha continued to probe.

"We haven't set a date for that yet, either. We'll need to sort out a few problems at the office first," April explained, feeling strangely self-confidant about it all.

After leaving the restaurant, Charles remained very quiet as he still felt embarrassed by Martha's forthright tongue. Linking his arm and snuggling up to him, she finally asked, "You're very quiet tonight, Charles. Has the cat got your tongue or something?"

He smiled. "I haven't heard that saying for years. No, I'm just a little bit embarrassed at Martha's loose tongue, that's all. But she means well, April."

"Well, I found it strangely flattering. It seems to have completed the mental side of my womanly guise, in a rather strange sort of way." April explained to Charles while resting her head on his shoulder. "I know I'm getting mixed feeling inside right now, but before I make any decisions about us, I really must talk with Mandy and the children first."

"They may not wish to speak to you, April. Or they might even find your story totally unbelievable."

"Oh but they do. I've kept in touch with them, Charles."

"How, I mean when, I-."

"Shush, Charles." April stopped him, placing her polished and well-manicured finger to his lips. "I knew that you would probably be listening in on my mobile. So at every opportunity I bought a new one. I spoke to them, and then disposed of them immediately."

"You crafty, bloody mare!" a shocked Charles shouted.

She was staring open-mouthed at him. "Charles! That's not like you at all." April was startled at Charles's reply. Then as she snuggled up to him once again, she added solemnly. "I still need to look after them you know Charles, and to visit and help them whenever it's possible, or necessary, to do so. I still love them very much. Nothing will ever change that fact. Even though I know Mandy and I have no future together as man and wife."

Charles put a consoling arm around her. "That's all right, darling. Whatever makes you happy is just fine by me." He drew her tighter to him as she gazed into his eyes. Hooking an arm around his neck, April, pulled his head towards her and kissed him. It was a long and meaningful kiss, full of passion. "Is it the effects of the alcohol?" she thought to herself. I am feeling extremely sexy tonight.

April's thoughts were interrupted by the car drawing to a halt outside Charles' apartment. "I'll need the car at 0630 tomorrow," he instructed the chauffeur as he closed the car door.

He led April through the lounge and into the bedroom and then drew her close, kissing her and caressed her gently.

Gently, she pushed him away. "We shouldn't. We've a very big day tommo-."

Charles stopped her in mid-sentence as he began kissing her again. "We'll worry about that tomorrow," Charles reassured her. They then made tender passionate love, which went well into the early hours.

April was surprised at how gentle, yet passionate, Charles could be. Eventually, they drifted off to sleep, feeling very content. April was securely entwined in his strong arms.

She was the first to rise. After showering, she dressed in the spare bedroom, to avoid waking him. She was reading when Charles emerged at 0530.

"Good morning April, have you been up for long?" he asked, as he greeted her with a kiss on the cheek.

"About an hour Charles. Maria is just about to serve breakfast." April told him, taking her seat at the table opposite. "I hope you've slept well?"

"Very well thank you, as you well and truly know already. But, I'm afraid we have a busy day ahead of us. So if there's anything at all I should know, April?"

"Not really, Charles. I'm relying solely on the element of surprise. I'll only say this to you, no matter what happens today, or what I seem to be doing, just don't over react. That goes for everybody else as well. Remember things aren't always what they seem to be at first." she reminded him, as they finished breakfast.

"You've lost me, darling," said a bewildered Charles. "Now I'm even more confused than I was before I asked."

April just smiled at him without saying another word. The sound of the car horn could be heard, as Charles's chauffeur drew to a halt outside the front door. "It's time to go to work," he said, as he helped April on with her coat. They set off on their way to the office, chatting idly to each other as they journeyed, and avoiding any further mention of what was to come.

When they reached the office, April went directly to the laboratory to collect the gun and ammunition from the professor. She loaded the gun and placed it in her coat pocket. "Thank you, professor, and thank your team for me, won't you? Oh, and enjoy your well-earned vacation," April said gratefully. "Incidentally, where are you going? Or am I asking a rather personal question?"

"No, my dear, I'm going to visit my daughter in Miami," he said proudly, opening the door for them to leave. "Be careful won't you, Miss Darling?" he warned with a serious tone to his voice. "And remember, always shoot at the body. It's a much larger target."

"I will, professor. Don't worry about me; you just go and enjoy your time with your daughter. Give her my love, won't you? And tell her she's a very lucky girl to have somebody as caring as you for a father."

The professor's warning had unsettled her a little, but she knew instinctively that it was important to stay focused, and deal with any danger as it came. Reaching Charles's office, April asked him to notify her when the prisoner's family arrived then went straight to her old quarters.

It was mid-morning when Charles opened the door to find April kneeling in silent prayer. He stood and waited patiently until she'd finished, and had risen to her feet.

She asked him if the prisoner's family had arrived yet.

Charles, ignoring the question, asked her why she felt the need to pray. "Well, why not?" she asked him. "Is there any set time when I should talk with my creator?"

"I didn't mean it in that way, April. I just meant is there a particular reason why you felt the need to pray at this moment?"

"Well, firstly I have neglected to talk with God over the past couple of nights. Secondly, I'll need his guidance for what I'm about to do. Now, has the family arrived yet?"

"Yes, they're in the waiting room with the man now."

"Good, let's go and see them then. Remember what I've warned you about though, and DON'T interfere. As I've said to you, things won't necessarily be what they seem to be."

Charles's mobile phone rang. "Yes," he answered. Then his expression became serious. "Find him," he snapped as he rang off. "It looks like you may have been right about leaks in this department yet again, April. Michael Waterford's now gone AWOL. Nobody's seen him since he rushed from the office at lunchtime yesterday. It seems he's also cleared out his office, and his apartment, he was last seen by a neighbour early yesterday afternoon when he was carrying two suitcases out." Charles banged his clenched fist against the wall. "Why didn't I check when you first voiced your concerns about him?"

"It's far too late for recriminations now, Charles. At least we now know for certain who was leaking the information. Anyway, we'll have to deal with him in due course."

"The best thing is I put him in charge of watching Martin Driver. Guess who he was last seen leaving with?"

They both said in unison, "Martin Driver."

"Let's deal with one thing at a time. As I've said, first our friend in here," she told Charles as they reached the interview room.

George was already there waiting impatiently for them.

"Right, let's get them in from the waiting area. At least we can get this over with. He should be able to tell us where Waterford and Driver are heading."

"That's if he'll talk to you. He hasn't said anything up until now, no matter what we've tried, April." Charles reminded her.

"Oh he'll talk to me. I promise you that, Charles."

"I like you're optimism, April. But, I'm afraid if my men had no luck with him, then I don't see how you'll make him talk," George interrupted.

"Watch and take notes, George. I'll show you just how it's done the Darling way using a third party," she told him as she swept into the room.

The man and his family where directed into the room. They were happy because they were under the misapprehension that they were about to all leave together. The man beamed broadly, "Good morning, Madam. Thank you for your very timely intervention the other day. So can we all go home now?" he asked cheerfully.

Pointing for him to sit opposite her, April then asked his wife and two children to sit either side of the table.

"There are still a few unanswered questions to clear up first, sir. Now firstly, I must tell you that I don't believe in the systematic beating ways of your previous interrogators."

The man relaxed back in the chair at what he thought was good, and welcome, news.

April warned him sternly, "But believe me, Sir, YOU WILL co-operate with me. And of that I can assure you. So, are you going to co-operate freely and tell us what we want to know?"

"I've already told you all that I don't know anything, Miss," the man said smugly.

"Oh I think you do, sir. Now once more, and for the final time before I get annoyed with you, tell me, where are Martin Driver and Michael Waterford heading?"

"Martin, Michael? Who are they? Okay, you've got two names but I don't know anybody by either name, Miss. Or is it Ms.?" he repeated sarcastically.

"Would you risk the lives of your wife and children by continually lying to me? It's all over now. So you might as well tell us what we need to know, NOW," she demanded loudly, banging her fist on the table.

"How can I? I've told you that I don't know anything." His answers were becoming cockier which was frustrating to April. "Who're this Martin and Michael? What are their full names?"

"Please tell them so that we can all leave together!" his wife interrupted.

But he just folded his arms and sat back. "And what are you going to do if I don't say anything. I've already proved that I can take your pathetic beatings."

April was becoming exasperated with the arrogance of the man, "How about your wife and your children?" April produced the gun from her pocket, "Which one of them would you wish to send to Allah first?" she threatened, waving the gun menacingly towards each member of his family.

The man sat up abruptly. He said tentatively. "You wouldn't dare, Miss."

"Ok, I'll choose for you then. Now this is your very last chance to avoid bloodshed. WHERE'S DRIVER HEADED FOR?" April demanded, pointing the gun towards his wife.

"You're just bluffing, Madam," the terrorist said, pretending to relax as he reclined in the chair.

A look of horror spread on his wife's face as April pulled the trigger. A shot rang out, and his wife's body slumped to the floor.

Sheer shock came over Charles's and George's faces. They tried to speak, but April prevented them from doing so. "NOW, which one of the children is to be the next to join your wife, SIR?"

The man screamed. "YOU MAD FUCKING ENGLISH BITCH." He tried to reach his wife's body, but was prevented from doing so by the security guard.

Again April demanded, "Now which child is to be next?" The youngsters where mortified into a state of terrorised horror.

"Okay. I'll tell you everything you want to know. Just don't hurt my children, please?" pleaded the man.

Turning towards Charles and George, April asked them to have the prisoner escorted into an adjoining ante room, and to interview him as quickly as possible.

The man had barely left the room when his wife began to stir. "She's still alive!" a shocked Charles and George said in unison.

"Quickly, call the paramedics." George called to one of his men.

"Stop panicking George. She's not harmed in any way. Did you really think that I'd shoot her DEAD, just because of a crummy scumbag like that? Did you really?" she asked, while helping the lady into a chair, apologising profusely to her for the little hoax.

"It seemed realistic enough to me." Charles admitted, as April gave the lady a glass of water. "But I suppose it had to be really."

"Well I have certainly learnt something about interrogation from you today, April. Charles was right about you, you are some very special lady. Unorthodox definitely, but very effective I could certainly use you on my team," he confessed.

"Yes, okay, enough of the flattery." Then April apologised to the lady again before she was ushered out of the room.

The man told them everything that they needed to know. About a small new campsite on the Brecon Beacons, and the remaining five hundred men assembling there who were trying to resurrect the Sheikh's dream.

Michael and Martin had set themselves up as self-appointed leader, vowing to continue the work of the late Sheikh, but they were now funded by a drugs baron, but he didn't know the name of the drug baron. He did however confirm that they would definitely be en-route to the camp within the next couple of days.

When the statement was complete, and Sir Charles and George were completely satisfied that the man had told them all he knew, April then informed him of her little hoax, and told him that his wife and family were all safe and well.

He was then allowed to see his family briefly, before being taken to prison to await trial for terrorism.

After putting the pistol and remaining special bullets safely into her handbag, as a back-up should she need it, they returned to Charles' office.

CHAPTER 12

The following days were spent relaxing, while waiting for news of the whereabouts of Driver and Waterford. Taking long drives in the country and spending hours shopping, April was able to expand on her wardrobe, and relax.

To her surprise, Charles kept his word not to have her followed. So on a convenient day, April took advantage of her freedom and pulled into a lay-by on one of the country lanes.

She then rang Mandy. "Hello, April my darling," she heard Mandy's soft voice answering. "Is anybody there?" Mandy continued after the long silence.

"It's so good to hear your voice again," April eventually managed to say to her. "How are you all keeping, my love?"

"We're all fine. More importantly, how are you? Where are you now?"

"I'm okay, but I'm still in the South Midlands working. I should have some time-off very soon now, so I'd like to come and see you and the children, if I may?"

"Of course you can come to see us anytime you want to. Haven't I told you that it's as much your home as it is ours?" Then after a short pause her voice became serious. "You realise that it's been a very long time, and that I thought we'd never see you again."

April cut in. "Are you trying to tell me that there's somebody else?"

"Would you mind very much if there was?" Mandy, asked tearfully.

"Of course not, pet. We could never be a proper man and wife again. Anyway, I have no past now, remember?" April thought that she'd prepared herself for this day, but she felt as though a large hole had just appeared in her life. Trying to conceal the deep pain she continued, trying hard to sound happy for Mandy. "Is he anybody that I know?"

"No, I don't think so. He moved here about a month after you disappeared, and the children get on well with him." There was an uncomfortable silence before she added nervously. "I've told him everything about you. I hope you don't mind, April? He was very concerned and understanding. He said he didn't think anything like that went on, well not in this day and age, and he feels so sorry for you. He's even offered to move away from here if it'll make things easier for us."

"Tell him that there's no need for him to worry. Well not unless he ever hurts one of you that is," April warned sternly. "But I don't think that's going to happen, he sounds like a really nice person to me."

"How about you, looking at you're photographs you look absolutely stunning? Is anybody showing any interest in you at all?"

"Yes, a few. Mainly my boss is getting ideas above his station, if you get my drift. But first and foremost I have an assignment to finish. Maybe then we'll see. Perhaps we can all have dinner together sometime?"

"Yes, I'd like that darling. Just let me know when and where." Mandy said, sounding very relieved.

"Soon, but as I've said, there's something I must do first. What does your new fellow do for a living by the way? Does he work for himself, or who does he work for?" April asked, worrying whether the department had placed him there to keep a watchful eye on Mandy and the children.

"He's a plumber, a central heating engineer or something like that. You can ask him all you want when you meet him. But don't steal him for yourself. Will you, April?"

"I won't. I must go now, Mandy. Give my love to the children? I'll ring you as soon as I have a bit more time."

"Good bye, my darling. Remember that we all still love and miss you very much." Mandy ended as April rang off.

Still reeling from the shock, April stopped at a village café for lunch. She decided to ring Charles.

"Hello darling. What can I do for you?" Charles asked cheerfully.

"You can tell me why you didn't inform me about Mandy's new man, Charles."

"I did not want to see you hurt, April," Charles explained. "I'd hoped if I gave it sufficient time, then it would make it easier for you to eventually accept it."

"Is he out of your bunch of misfits, Charles? And tell me the truth."

"No he definitely is not. You can set your mind at ease about that."

"Good, because if anything ever happens to Mandy or the children, well you'll find out just exactly what you've created in me," she warned him.

"I've already realised that, and I promise you that Mandy will never get as much as a parking ticket." Then switching the conversation, he said sombrely, "We have just located Waterford. He was trying to hire a private light aircraft and pilot for Friday. We now know where they're lodging too, and we're watching the house very closely."

"But discretely I hope. Remember, Waterford was trained by you lot. He'll spot anybody watching the house, from a mile away."

"I know, but it's proving difficult. Do you have any suggestions that might help us?"

"I haven't seen the bloody place, have I? Is there anywhere round there that you can plant a web cam, just so that you can watch them at a distance, Charles?"

"There's a phone box that they use right opposite the flat actually. I'll get somebody on it straight away. Are you on your way back now? I'm about to convene a meeting about this."

"I'll be there in thirty about minutes." April confirmed as she rang off. Forty-five minutes later, April rushed into the room apologising for being late.

Charles had begun convening the meeting of official-looking gentlemen. "These gentlemen represent all sections of our armed forces, and the government," he explained. "I have gathered them here today so that we can dispense with any, and all, bureaucratic red tape. We can then commission whatever back up you will need. I have already explained to them that we need to apprehend the remaining group with some urgency, and to deal with them as it is found to be appropriate. Gentlemen, permit me to introduce, Miss April Darling," he announced proudly. "She will be handling the final assignment: which is to eradicate any remaining threats that are still found to exist."

"Good morning, gentlemen," April began. "I'm not going to bore you going over what's been said beforehand. I am sure Sir Charles has covered the most important details most thoroughly. Also, I'm led to believe it's all covered in the notes that you have before you. So are there any questions, gentlemen?" April paused as she looked around the table at the assembly shaking their heads. "Good. Now on Friday I will want an identical aircraft to theirs. I want it fuelled and ready for takeoff, with parachutes on board. Also an army helicopter to follow me at a discrete distance, to back me up, just in case I need to jump out that is. I plan to be flying as a novice pilot taking a flying lesson, but I'll need two highly trained pilots to act as my instructors."

She paused to allow the tea trolley to be pushed into the room. "The rest gentlemen, well I can only inform you about that after my return."

"Why?" A voice called from the far end of the table. "Is it highly classified information, or something? Because everybody here is covered by the official secrets act, as you well know."

"Yes. I'm well aware of that," assured April. "But, well I can't tell you because I don't really know until I see what's happening on the day. Then, I'll have to play it by ear."

"You mean you have no plan of attack so to speak, Miss Darling?" the man persisted.

Charles tried to come to April's aid, but she prevented him from doing so. "It's hard to plan your attack when you do not have all the facts." April told him firmly. "Unlike you, I'm not always given the luxury of forehand information. I need to deal with whatever happens, when it happens."

"I'm sorry, Miss Darling. I didn't mean to question your methods. Or your preparations." the man apologised. "So what can we do to help?"

"Well, as I've already said, an identical aircraft, parachutes, and two top pilots at the controls," she repeated. "Also, we need some type of backup system ready to move in and destroy their camp or to help to capture and repatriate the entire camp. Well, as soon as we have extracted all the information we need."

"It is in a very rough terrain. How do you intend to execute the operation?" a military man questioned.

"I suggest with air power. A fleet of helicopters will suffice I should think." she answered sarcastically.

As the other remainder of the assembly laughed, the man explained. "I know that, Miss. What I meant was how do you intend to execute the operation? So we can position the task force as close as possible to you in readiness, but far enough away to be undetectable. So we'll be able to spring into action at very short notice."

"I know, and I'm sorry about the sarcasm. So please, all accept my apology. I'm sure Sir Charles will furnish you with all of the relevant details," she finished.

Then moving towards the tea trolley, she poured herself a coffee and reclined in a lounge chair, remaining oblivious to the plan that Sir Charles and the assembled men were attempting to formulate.

"You are fully aware, gentlemen, that this fragmented group is about as volatile as you will ever get. I'd suggest that when you create an exercise as near as is safe to do so, that you will need to commence it over the next day or so. But be careful you don't create any suspicion and alarm them. And don't make a move prematurely. We must be very patient." April insisted, as she started to walk from the room. She called back, "I'll be in the gymnasium if you need me, Sir Charles."

April knew she must rid her mind of her beloved Mandy and the children so she could see the assignment through to its bitter end.

April was conscious of the fact that any distraction would definitely cost her, her life.

Remembering her trainer's words she worked out hard, clearing her mind, and toning her body. 'He was right. Strenuous exercise does help to clear your mind for you,' she thought.

Over the next couple of days April waited patiently. She prepared herself with daily runs and visits to the gymnasium, and prepared her mind through prayer and meditation.

Some days later, and after having dinning with Charles, April bade him good night, and retired to bed.

She was awakened by the ringing of the telephone. "Driver has just ordered the plane to be ready for takeoff at first light," a voice told her. "I'm on my way to pick you up now, Miss Darling."

After thanking the person, April, looked at the clock. "Two a.m.," she muttered to herself.

She phoned Charles, then showered and dressed, choosing to wear a black leather trouser suit over thermal undergarments that could double up as a jump suit if it was necessary. April put the tranquilliser pistol inside her shoulder holster, and tucked a backup pistol into the back of her belt. April then hid a smaller pistol in one of her boots.

She was just finishing a coffee when the doorbell rang. It was the man chosen to masquerade as one of her instructors. So collecting her handbag, and double locking the apartment, they then proceeded up to the Liverpool flying school. To be ready for a dawn take off.

Chapter 13

"Good morning, Ms. Darling. My name's Joe. I'm your chauffeur, and one of your pilots," the smiling young man greeted her. "It's going to take us about four hours to drive up to Liverpool, so we'll need to get moving if we're to take off at daybreak."

"Three and a half at this time of night, and incidentally, call me April."

"The beautiful lady talks as well," Joe mocked, "A little light conversation, and such attractive company to boot. That will certainly help to pass the time much more pleasantly."

"Yes, okay Joe. Would you like me to drive? I know the way there like the back of my hand."

"No, it's okay." Joe reassured her. During the long drive they chatted idly to break the monotony. Eventually they arrived in South Liverpool, the home of the Liverpool Flying School. After presenting his passes to the security guards, Joe drove through the gates, and on towards their plane. "We're here," he said to April, holding open the car door. "The other pilot's already aboard. He's a good man, one of us, if you get my meaning."

Once aboard, Joe introduced her to the other pilot, Glen. Then he secured the door in readiness for takeoff. After a short wait, Joe answered his phone. "Shall we get going? They've just taking off from a private aerodrome, and are headed this way."

The plane climbed to fifteen thousand feet before April took over the controls, posing as the trainee pilot.

"They should be coming into view pretty soon now," Joe advised. Peering through the side windows, he told April, "I think I can just see them coming."

"Time to play the novice then," She started the plane acting unsteadily.

"Can you tune in to their radio, Joe?"

After Joe had found their frequency, they could hear Martin Driver's comments. "Ah up, Michael. It looks like we have ourselves a learner ahead. Just look at that. They're going to stall if they're not careful. We'd better give them a wide birth, Michael. Flying like that they could bring us both down.

What the hell is the instructor doing not correcting them?" he questioned, as they came closer.

"Let me know when they get level, Joe?" April asked, as she continued with her charade.

"They are a few hundred feet behind us at present. They're coming up to your port side fast though, April."

As they drew level to tease what they believed was a novice aviator, they were stunned to find April waving at them, as she brought the plane under control. Turning the radio to send, April greeted them. "Hello boys. Fancy meeting you two scum bags up here, as if the air wasn't polluted enough."

Pulling back on the joystick and opened the throttle fully, April put the plane into a steep climb taking it into a full somersault, and finishing in a position directly behind, and slightly above them.

"Where the fuck's she gone?" she could hear Martin Driver shout, as the radio was put on mute. "You take the controls and keep it steady." April instructed Glen, as she climbed out of her seat. "Pass over them, but keep slightly above them."

Turning to Joe, April asked, "Has the helicopter taken up a position just behind us yet?"

"Yes, April. They're just coming into position now" he answered, as April moved towards the door. "Why, what are you planning on doing?" Joe asked nervously as April slid open the door.

The wind was exceptionally cold as they started to cross the snow-capped mountains on the way to the Brecon Beacons. "I don't know exactly yet, I guess I'll just have to play it by ear as per usual." She said as she put on her thermally lined jump suit, and wrapped a long rope, with a hook at either end, round her waist.

"What shall I do?" Joe continued to question.

"Don't worry Joe. I'll tell you if there's anything you can do to help me.

By the way, have you ever done any skydiving?"

"Yes, sure I have April, plenty. Why, what makes you ask that?"

"I believe it's a bit like swimming. Is that right?"

"It is a bit I suppose," he agreed. "If you spread your body flat, then it slows you down. If you go head or feet first, it speeds up your descent, etc. What do you want to know that for?"

"How can you change direction, Joe?"

"Well, just like swimming really. You just point your body in the direction you want to go, and providing the wind isn't too strong, that's the way you'll go." By now the worried expression on Joe's face resembled panic. "Whatever you're planning on doing, wouldn't it be more advisable for me to do it?"

"Unfortunately not," April assured him as she fastened her helmet.

"Just keep above them and go a bit more in advance of them, will you?" April shouted to Glen. "And ask the helicopter to start moving closer to us. But tell them to stay well below, Joe," April instructed them, as she watched their plane start to advance ahead of Martin Driver's.

"The helicopter's moving up now." Joe told her as he replaced his mobile phone. "Here, put this chute on," he suggested, handing April a parachute

"No. It may hamper me, Joe. We seem to be about the right distance now. Don't you agree?" she asked, as she saw the helicopter below them drawing ever closer. "What was it that they used to shout as they jumped out? Oh yes. 'JERONIMOOoooo,' April shouted, as she checked her tranquilliser gun was in her side pocket, and dived out of the plane.

She had the sensation of floating as she followed Joe's advice, moving round towards the open door of Martin Driver's plane. By now, their hired pilot had taken over the controls from them.

As April approached the open door, Driver and Waterford were watching open-mouthed, their guns at the ready in their hands. Taking the tranquilliser gun in her hand, April then passed over them as she fired a dart into Martin Driver's leg.

He plummeted headlong from the open door. Michael Waterford lunged forward, trying to grab a hold of him. April discharged the remaining dart into his leg, and sending headlong from the plane after Driver.

Quickly she went into a dive pursuing them, as she gained on them rapidly. The adrenaline rush made her oblivious to any danger, as she didn't realise the height from which they were rapidly descending.

Catching hold of Driver's leather jacket, she removed the rope from round her body with her free hand and secured one end, clipping it to his parachute harness. Floating over towards Michael Waterford, April then fastened the other end of the rope onto his harness, and held up the centre of the rope for the approaching helicopter to hook up to.

As the cable swung towards them she grabbed for it, placing the rope onto the hook then held on to it, as she signalled that they were ready to be winched aboard. The crew began to winch them up.

Suddenly Driver began to recover, as he struggled frantically to release the rope. Realising it was a futile struggle on his part he began to kick out at April. This caused her to lose her grip she had on the rope.

She went plummeting towards the fast approaching terra firma. "Oh God, please help me?" she prayed.

The remarkable stories she'd heard of survival started flashing through her mind. There's always a chance. The fat lady hasn't sung yet." April tried to convince herself. "If the snow is soft and deep enough, it could break my fall." She was still trying to convince herself as she surveyed the rapidly approaching scene below.

"There's a skiing school. I wonder if that could be of some assistance to me." April muttered to herself. The ground by now was drawing dangerously close. "There's also a ski jump. If I can hit the slope just at the right angle, then it should deflect my fall. The deep snow on it will also act as a brake."

April's thoughts were interrupted by the sound of the approaching helicopter. She glanced up at it. "It will never reach me in time."

Turning her attention back to the dilemma facing her, she directed her body towards the ski slope. Thinking, "It's touch and go whether I'll reach it in time," as she struggled to move her body weight to line up with the approaching slope, "Only seconds to go and I'll know if I've guessed correctly," she thought, as she approached the edge of the ski jump.

She slid down the ramp of thick snow with the elegance of a competent surfer, and as she had anticipated, the thick snow helped to slow her down. Leaning backwards to keep balanced, April slid gracefully, as the snow drifted before her.

The members of the ski club could only look on agog at April's antics.

Slipping off the end of the ramp at speed, and in a slightly upward direction, it propelled her towards the large mound of soft snow that had obviously been made previously, from the snow being cleared off the ski slope.

While holding her arms outstretched in front of her for protection, she was catapulted into the mound of snow at full speed. April hit it so hard that she left a deep imprint of her body in the snow, which was at least a foot deep, as the force of the impact knocked her out cold. Regaining consciousness, she lay on her back, waiting for her head to clear, and regaining her thoughts.

"Are you all right?" was the faint sound April could hear the man asking her in a deep Welsh accent.

Her head cleared more as she became aware that a large crowd was surrounding her. "Are you all right, Miss?" the man persisted.

"Yes, I'm fine." She eventually regained enough of her senses to reply. "What happened? And how long was I unconscious for?"

"Only a couple of minutes Miss. What happened? Where the hell did you come from?" were the questions from the perplexed man.

They were interrupted by the sound of the approaching helicopter. "Lay still, Miss. We have sent for a doctor for you," a lady told April.

"I haven't got the time for that, I'm afraid. I just slipped and fell. Now help me up, will you please? I'll be okay." April insisted, as she struggled to her feet. "I'm just a little bit stiff and bruised. That's all," she explained, as the helicopter landed.

"Thank you for your help, but now I must fly." April told them, running towards the waiting helicopter.

"Are you okay Miss?" asked the airman, as he approached April. "That was such a lucky break."

"Don't I look as if I'm okay? Now let's get the fuck out of here," snapped April clamouring aboard.

"Are you Miss April Darling?" the pilot called back, as he took off. "There's a call for you."

"Hello, who is this?" April snapped, as she plugged in the head set. "Charles. Are you okay, April? I heard about your fall."

"Yes, Charles. God was on my side luckily. Is that all you wanted? Because I'm a bit tied up at the present time," she reminded him. Seeing that Martin Driver was edging slowly towards her, she shouted, "TIE THAT BASTARD TO THAT HOOK, BEFORE I HANG HIM FROM IT BY HIS BALLS," as she pointed to a hook near the door.

"MI 16, have just intercepted an Internet message to, Driver. It was urging him to recruit more men urgently and to keep the dream of Sheikh Mohammed Kahn on track."

"Did the message get through, and where did it come from?"

"Yes, the message got through to Driver. That's why he's en route to that makeshift camp. I'm sure he's under the misguided impression that he'll be the new Sheikh in all this. The message came from Carlos De-Mundo of Columbia. He's the most powerful of all the drugs Barons"

"And where is he now, Charles?"

"Columbia. There's a detachment of Special Forces from England and the U.S. They're on their way there to eliminate him and destroy his business, as we speak. So you just concentrate on completely destroying that camp." Then he added, "There's something else that you need to know, April. Michael Waterford is working for us, but undercover. So watch his back, won't you?"

"I'll keep that in mind. I must say that I'm not sure if you're right, Charles.

Anyway, why didn't you tell me that sooner?"

"I thought the fewer people who knew about it the better it would serve our purpose."

"WELL THANK YOU FOR THE FUCKING TRUST." April shouted, as she ripped off her head set.

"We are just approaching their camp site now, Miss Darling," the pilot informed her. "We should see it when we cross the next ridge."

"It seems your boss doesn't trust his little bed mate." Sneered Driver sarcastically. "Perhaps there's somebody else-A REAL WOMAN."

Ignoring his remarks, April thanked the pilot. She stood by the open door and watched as they crossed the peak, and the campsite came into full view. "Where are the other helicopters?" she asked the pilot.

"They're coming over that ridge over there." He pointed to a fleet of helicopter gun-ships and personnel carriers, just coming into view. April watched as they went into formation and circled the camp. Armed troops stood in the open doorways, their guns trained on the disorganised rabble of men below them, who were meandering around aimlessly.

Sitting near the open door, oblivious to the cold wind that howled in, April was preoccupied pondering the lack of trust Charles was showing in her. Suddenly, Martin Driver broke free. He lunged towards her, trying to bundle April through the open door, and to certain death.

Seeing his reflection in a Marine's visor, she quickly stooped down. Driver's momentum carried him over her, and out through the open fuselage door. She tried desperately to hold onto his jacket, so he could face standing trial. But hearing the jacket ripping, she was forced to watch helplessly as Martin Driver slipped from her grasp.

"AH——Ah," he screamed, as April listened to him falling. Peering down she saw his bloodied body impaled prostrate on one of the tent poles, his body lying twisted and disfigured.

A U.S. Marine, also watching, remarked. "I think that's the last we'll see of him. Are you okay, Miss Darling?"

"Yes, thank you. He was only a poor, disillusioned, misguided fool." April remarked mournfully. "He lived by the sword, so he died by the sword. He lived in a fanciful world, dreaming of a pure utopia that could never, ever have existed."

"You're fucking next." April heard a voice from behind her threatening.

She spun round just in time to see Michael Waterford aiming a sub machine gun at her. "Charles told me you were working undercover. It's all over now. You don't have to pretend any longer, Michael. You can stop the charade, Martin Driver's dead now," stuttered April, as she sidled further into the helicopter, urging, "Put the gun down now, Michael."

Out of the corner of her eye she saw a young marine edging round behind Waterford. April avoided looking directly at him, so as not to alert Waterford of the young marine's intentions. She continued to try to hold Waterford's attention. "So you even fooled Sir Charles, did you?"

"That fucking old fart," Waterford started. "It wasn't hard for me to dupe him. The fool lives in cloud cuckoo land. But now it's your turn, Miss April fucking Darling," he said menacingly, waving the gun towards the door. "Are you going to jump? Or do I have to physically throw you fucking out?"

"A big strong man like you, I wouldn't stand a chance. Now would I?" April said, using an air of inferiority whilst playing for time. She could see the marine was edging closer, ready to seize Waterford.

"I'm glad you know your place, bitch. NOW FUCKING JUMP OUT."

Climbing laboriously to her feet, April moved slowly towards the open door. The helicopter was still slowly encircling the camp in a gradual descent. "Okay," She said to Michael. "I suppose if I must, I must." She placed a hand either side of the door.

"JUMP, YOU STUPID BASTARD." Michael yelled at her, nudging April in her back with the butt of his gun.

He was now close enough so April brought her heel up behind her, delivering a mule kick, which caught Waterford squarely in his testicles. He winced with pain, as April swung around and grabbed the bar above the door. She delivered a karate blow to the chest, causing him to stumble backward towards the door on the opposite side.

A young soldier quickly swung the door open; leaving Waterford teetering on the threshold. As he struggled for a grip so he could pull himself back into the helicopter, the young Marine seized his opportunity, hitting him squarely on the jaw with a well-placed right hook.

"Now you fucking jump," he insisted. Waterford lost the fight to hang on, falling backwards out of the helicopter. He was sent plummeting backwards towards the ground, breaking his back as he landed. He was begging those round him to finish him off, pleading, he could not face life as a cripple.

The helicopter descended and finally landed on the blood soaked snow, as se alighted April, issued a stark warning. "I will personally permanently cripple anybody who fulfils Waterford's wish."

Hearing this, the small crowd that had gathered round Michael Waterford dispersed, as the helicopter finally came to rest.

April stepped from it with the kind help of the young marine. "Thank you," she said gratefully, as she alighted from the aircraft. "And what's your name, my chivalrous young friend? Just for my records, you understand."

"Brad, Ma'am. Sergeant Brad Willis," he answered courteously. "May I have the honour of escorting you until the area is declared a safe zone?"

"Thank you. That would be a pleasure." April readily agreed.

They made their way towards the body of Michael Waterford, and found the paramedics already treating him. April asked, "Is he going to be okay, Doc?"

"Who are you, Miss?" the senior medic asked.

"This is Miss April Darling. She's the agent in charge of this operation," Brad introduced her.

"Sorry Miss. He'll live, but at a high cost," he said. "He will be paralysed for life from the waist down. I'm Doctor Adams, by the way," he introduced himself as he shook April's hand.

"Pleased to meet you, doctor." April told him. She then told him, "He'll need to be interrogated by special branch as soon as it's humanly possible."

"That's some handshake you have. It's almost like a man's handshake. But I can see that you're definitely not a man." The doctor commented. He stood to his feet giving April his card. "This is my mobile phone number. Ask somebody to ring me about him. Will you?"

"Thank you doctor and thanks for comparing me to a man." April added mockingly. "You'll never know the irony of what you've just said to me. I'll get this number to my boss."

Just then her phone began to ring. Answering the phone she said to the doctor, "Speak of the devil."

"Hello, Sir Charles. I have a Dr. Adams with me. He would like to speak to you. Incidentally you were wrong about, Waterford. He's just tried to bloody kill me." April said, as she handed the doctor the phone.

After the doctor finished he handed the phone back to her. "He wants to speak to you."

Thanking the doctor. April asked, "Right, Charles. What is it now?"

"Your work is now completed there, and you've done far better than we could have ever anticipated," he started, "so I'm sending a helicopter to collect you. Then we can discuss your future, well, both our futures I hope, and your future with the department."

"I need a little time to relax before I'm ready to discuss my future, or make any commitment. After all, you wouldn't want to rush me into giving you the wrong answer would you?"

"No, of course I wouldn't. How would it be if we took a short holiday together?"

"Maybe, but first I will need to see Mandy and the children. Then we will see, Charles."

As April continued to encircle the makeshift camp, surveying the scene of dejection and devastation, she told Charles. "Whoever you appoint to interrogate these poor devils, tell them to go easy on them will you? You should see the sad look of despair on their poor dejected faces."

Just then two ageing people crossed in front of them arguing. So intense were they in disputing each other's roll of importance, that they seemed oblivious to the activities which surrounded them.

"Who the hell are they?" April asked.

"He's Colonel John McManus of the U.S. Marines. The other is Brigadier Sir Alfred Winstanley of the British armed forces." Brad explained as they walked past Michael Waterford, who was being loaded aboard the air ambulance. "Rumour has it that they're actually related, Cousins I believe. They never stop arguing tactics. They just try to score points over each other; the army should have pensioned them off, years ago. Anyway, they're an embarrassment to both our countries now. The sooner they're given the order of the boot, the better."

He paused as they came back into earshot, then he continued. "I think that they keep sending them into situations like this hoping somebody will shoot them," Brad joked.

Returning to the phone, April apologised. "I'm sorry, Charles. I forgot about you for a minute. Now, as I was saying. They're just poor misguided fools who have no aim or purpose in life. They seemed to have been just drifting through life until the Sheikh, or somebody like him, came along and sold them a dream. They're actually harmlessly, following him like sheep. Maybe our politicians have a lesson they could learn from all this."

"If only, April, if only," Charles reflected. "But I'm sure that they're heads will stay firmly stuck in the sand as per usual. Anyway, I'll see you when you get back here, April. My helicopter should be with you at any moment now."

Looking up at the hive of activity above, she saw a fleet of helicopters flying to and fro. They were ferrying the injured to hospital and the captives to their designated destinations.

Within, April was experiencing mixed feeling of excitement and trepidation. She was looking forward to her first meeting with her beloved family, since she had been abducted and transformed.

"Well, Brad. I guess it's time for me to move on. So thank you. You take care now. It's been a pure pleasure meeting you. And thank you for your courteous, and so pleasant, protective company." April said to him, as she boarded the helicopter to return to Charles's office.

"The pleasure was all mine Miss April," the young marine shouted after her.

As she tried to relax, her head was full of confusion packed full with unanswered questions about her family and the future. Thoughts like how would Mandy and the children receive her in her present persona? What could the future really hold now? But most importantly, will she ever find a doctor who was able, and willing to return her to being plain, George Partridge again? These; and many more unanswered questions, she would have to address now. Now that this mission seemed as though it was finally all over, and she had the time to do it.

Again, April phoned Charles. When he answered, April told him. "Don't say anything. Just listen to me, Charles. Now that it's all over, and there's time to ponder my present and future. Tell me, Charles. Why is it that I'm fitting into my new persona so comfortably? And why can't a doctor find any clues as to who, or what, I once was?"

There was a very long silence. Eventually, Charles started too explained. "Okay, I now know that you can handle the truth. But don't get complacent about this assignment being over, April. Remember, we haven't had verification that this De-Mundo character, has been taken out yet. You know only too well that vermin like that take some eradicating. Remember, the threat still may not be fully over. Well, not yet. Anyway, as I've already told you, the operation you underwent was a very new and revolutionary pioneering operation. Unlike the normal transsexual operations, we actually removed all of your male dominant body organs from you. Then we transplanted female body organs from young donors to replace them. You actually have female organs inside you; a uterus and ovaries; even breasts have been grafted onto you, etcetera. You may even start having periods in the fullness of time, or even have a child sometime in the future. The complexities of it I don't fully understand yet. They are still in the early stages of development, and the new technique that the plastic surgeons used left no traces of scaring."

Then there followed a long and uncomfortable silence. "Are you still there, April?" he asked.

"Yes, I'm still here, Charles. So that's why it cannot be reversed. Also, it's why there are no tell-tale signs of what you've done to me. Or of whom I once was?"

"I'm afraid so. But that's not such a bad thing, is it, April?" he asked, hopefully.

"I need some 'me time' to digest all of this, and all that has happened to me. I will ring you in a couple of days, Charles." April said sadly, as she rang off. She now knew that all of the possibilities of returning to being plain old George were fast disappearing, and the reality of a future being permanently as April Darling was fast hitting home.

April redirected the pilot as to where she wished to go, so she could gather her thoughts in solitude.

Because she was so perplexed, she still hadn't considered any possibility that they may have implanted minute surveillance censors inside of her.

She settled back and closed her eyes. The tensions of the recent events slowly left her with a feeling of total confusion, and anticlimax. April was left wondering if each new assignment would end up in the same way—successfully, and yet leaving her feeling totally and completely inadequate. And would they ever capture, Carlos De-Mundo? Or would this nightmare still live on?

Eventually, when she was feeling rested and relaxed, April decided the time was right for her to return home to face the realities that needed to be addressed.

CHAPTER 14

As the morning dawned to reveal a crisp, but sunny day, April woke-up in her apartment alone. She took a long and relaxing shower because she had been far too fatigued in the early hours of the morning, when she returned home from the self-imposed retreat, to do so. She stood under the shower and allowed the warm water to wash over her soft, silky-smooth skin.

April now realised that she may have to finally accept that there was little chance of returning to her former self. So she was finally able to totally relax for the first time, and accept being the attractive woman that she had now become.

With her restful holiday over, her thoughts now rapidly turned towards her beloved family again. How should she now think of them? After all, Mandy wasn't her wife anymore, nor could she ever be again it seemed, except maybe in a civil partnership. Would it still be fair if she thought of the children as her own? After all, she could no longer expect to be treated as a father.

These, and many more problems, were running through her mind. The ringing of the telephone interrupted her thoughts. Wrapping herself in a towelling robe, April walked through to the lounge and picked up the receiver.

"Hello."

"Good morning, my dear." Charles greeting her cheerfully, "I haven't woken you, have I?"

"No Charles. I was just taking a relaxing shower. Trying to wash away the recent days, and clear my thoughts."

"Could I buy you breakfast this morning April? After all, we do have rather a lot to discuss."

"Yes, I suppose we do, Charles. However, I will need to dress first or I'll get arrested. Shall we say about ten thirty?"

"Ten thirty it will be. I will pick you up at your apartment," he told her as he rang off.

Before dressing, April dialled her Swiss banker. "A very good morning to you," April replied to his warm greeting. "I was wondering if you could do me a very special favour."

"Of course, I will, Miss Darling. You know I'll help you in any way I can."

"Well, we know that the organisation I work for is still searching and trying to retrieve some of the money that they've already paid to me."

"And I will see to it that they do not find it," he interrupted.

"I know you will, and I thank you for that. No, the reason I'm ringing is regarding protecting any future payments I receive. They'll always pay me up front, well until I've completed an assignment. But then they will try to recover some of it at a later date, and blame it on hackers."

"I know their type. But as I have already said, I'll do all within my power to protect you and your assets. So, what more have you got in mind, Miss Darling?"

"Just call me, April, Well could I set up other accounts that I could transfer into? Accounts that can be set up to electronically withdraw any money automatically, immediately that they pay it in. But can it give the impression that I've withdrawn it all in cash. Then, if you put forty percent of it in each of my other two private accounts and twenty percent into my security box in the vault in cash. If they do manage to find the accounts, they will be under the impression that I've withdrawn all of the money in cash, and deposited it elsewhere."

"Very crafty, I can see that you've given it a lot of thought and worked it all out. Well, that shouldn't be too much of a problem. I will set the accounts up and email you the account numbers, but leaving out the letters that I will put in a separate email. Now just give me a moment?" he said, as he placed the call on hold. Eventually returning, he continued, "I've used the other names that you gave me as user names. Read the middle part of the number I send you in reverse, as usual. The first and last two numbers read straight except transfer them over. Can you remember that?"

"Yes thank you. You are an angel. I must buy you dinner the next time you're in London, or I'm in Geneva of course. So Email the numbers to me under 'laundry,' will you?"

"Isn't that a bit obvious, April?"

"It's too bloody obvious. That's why they'll probably miss it." April told him confidently. "Now I must go and dress. Thank you for everything you've done for me."

"Thank you for your business, and I look forward to meeting you again soon, Ms. Darling. I mean, April. Goodbye." he finished.

April dressed herself in a tightly fitting red dress with matching accessories. At precisely ten thirty on the dot her doorbell rang.

Asking over the intercom, "Hello, is that you, Charles?"

"Yes, my dear. Are you ready? I thought we'd eat at my club."

"I'm coming right down, Charles." April slung a coat over her slender shoulders. Picking up her purse and keys, April locked the door to her apartment, proceeding down to where Charles was patiently waiting.

"Beautiful as ever, you look positively radiant. Now shall we go and eat?" he suggested as he held the car door open.

"Thank you, Charles. But after we've eaten we must have a serious talk about the future of my children."

They dined amongst ideal chatter. When they'd finishing their meal they retired to the club lounge. "Shall we sit in the corner so that we will not be disturbed?" she suggested.

They talked for nearly an hour. Mainly it was April doing the talking. Charles patiently listened sympathetically to all her concerns, and about the causes of the mental anguish that she was still experiencing. When she'd finished, he used his handkerchief to dab away April's tears.

Finally, Charles gently cupped her hands in his. He suggested, "Well, I have listened very carefully to you. I think the only way we can start healing the mental, and emotional scars, is to face up to them." He paused while the waiter brought them fresh coffee, "So, my darling. I suggest that we buy lots of presents, and go up to Riverlet to get the healing process under way. But remember, it'll be just as hard for Mandy and the children, as it will be for you."

"Yes, I know that Charles, and you are quite right as usual. So shall we go shopping, or do you have to work today?"

"No. Thanks to you I have some time for us, as long as I keep my mobile phone turned on at all times, that is. You must remember that they haven't found De-Mundo's body, yet."

Removing her mobile from her handbag, April started to dial Mandy's number. This pleased Charles as he now realised that April was starting to trust him sufficiently to speak to her beloved Mandy while still in his presence.

"Hello, Pet. It's me, April." Was April's reply to Mandy's welcoming voice, "The time has finally arrived when we'll be able to all meet up. When will it be convenient for you?"

"I've told you that this is still your home, and you will always be welcome in it anytime you choose to visit, my love." Mandy then added with afterthought. "I suppose it'll be strange at first, especially for you darling. But we'll soon all be bezzie mates again, won't we?" Mandy said cheerfully.

"Charles and I were thinking we'd travel up there tomorrow evening. We'll stay in a local hotel overnight. Then meet up on the Saturday morning?"

"That would be super. But why not stay here, April?"

"One step at a time, it's going to be hard enough for us remember. Will that be okay with your new fellow by the way? And will he be there when we come on Saturday morning?"

"As long as you don't mind, because he's longing to meet you from what I've told him about you."

"Well, I hope he's not disappointed then. I'll see you on Saturday morning, love."

After putting the phone down April turned to a patiently waiting Charles, "I'd sooner go through the experience, and the hell, of the last few weeks again, than face Saturday, now that it's finally arrived."

"You're going to be just fine, my love. And remember, I'll be there for all the moral support that you might need. Now let's hit the shops as they say?" Charles joked, trying to cheer her up.

"I know you'll be there for me. I thank you for all your support, Charles. But I'm still very nervous about it all, you know. I can't help that. Now let's get some presents to take for them." April finished, as Charles draped her coat over her shoulders.

The afternoon was spent searching painstakingly for suitable gifts to take up to Riverlet. Then April had them professionally wrapped by the Harrods gift department. They spent the evening at the theatre relaxing. Then they retired to bed early, in preparation of the long journey to come.

Rising early, April breakfasted before visiting the hair salon. Returning home she packed a suitcase before dressing in her new outfit, the one that she'd purchased especially for such an occasion.

Charles gave his chauffeur the weekend off. Then they set out on the arduous trek north, so April could finally meet up with her beloved family again.

Stopping for lunch en-route, April and Charles arrived in Riverlet during the early evening, and decided to have drinks in the hotel bar. Dressed in a gold figure hugging dress, April adorned herself with jewellery. With her white artificial three-quarter length fur coat draped over her shoulders, she attracted admiring glances from the passing clientele and staff alike.

"Something seems to be amusing you, April?" Charles remarked.

"I remember most of the staff and some of the guests here too. I was just wondering if I'd get the same admiring glances if they knew exactly who I originally was."

"Oh I see. Now that would be interesting to know. Wouldn't it?" he agreed.

Just then April's expression changed. Charles asked, "Is there something wrong my dear? You look as if you have just seen a ghost."

Before April could answer a ladies voice interrupted. "Hello, April my love. It's so nice to meet you again, at long last."

The glass slipped from April's hand as she embraced her former wife. With tears filling their eyes, April asked. "What are you doing here? Oh who cares? It's so wonderful to see you again." After which, April apologised to the bar staff for breaking the glass.

Mandy explained, "Well, you said you would stay the night at a hotel. So we thought that it could be this one."

"I'm sorry. Please excuse my manners. Charles, this is Mandy. Mandy, this is Sir Charles." April reached towards the man standing behind Mandy and added. "And you must be, Victor. I'm April and this is Sir Charles. We've heard so much about you from Mandy. I feel we already know each other."

"Can we get one thing straight before we go any further?" Charles interrupted, leaving April looking momentarily perplexed. "Drop the Sir. I'm just plain Charles to my friends, and I'm very pleased to meet you both." He kissed Mandy on the cheek before shaking Victor's hand.

"And we're very pleased to meet you, Charles." Mandy and Victor said in unison, which caused April to take a fit of the giggles.

"Don't mind me." April eventually apologised. "Now what would you both like to drink?"

"Vodka neat and lager for Victor, and I'll have a large vodka and lime, no ice," Mandy said.

They ordered a round of drinks and took them to a secluded table to give them privacy.

As they sat at the table, Mandy placed her chair close to April. "I can't get over you, darling. You look absolutely gorgeous! In fact, breathtakingly stunning I'd say, wouldn't you, Vic? There's not a man in this bar that doesn't keep glancing over at you."

"So people tell me," April said modestly, as she watched Victor swallowing his vodka in one gulp. "Your coming here unannounced has rather taken the wind from my sails though. Anyway, how's Pammy and Andy? And why are they not with you?"

"I've left them with a babysitter. Do you want us to go and get them love?" Mandy volunteered excitedly.

Victor returned with another round of drinks. He swallowed the Vodka again in one gulp, just as he'd done previously.

"Shall Charles and I go and collect the children while you girls get acquainted?" Victor suggested. He remained standing, waiting for Mandy answer. "It won't take us very long, and I know they're dying to meet you again, April. In fact, they can hardly contain their excitement, just knowing that you're coming up here today."

"Do they still allow children in the Smithy?" April asked Mandy, with a devilish twinkle in her eye. Mandy confirmed that they still did. "Well, when you two have finished your drinks go and collect the children. Then WEEE'LL all meet up at the Smithy."

Mandy asked with genuine concern, "Are you sure about the Smithy, darling? It must hold such terribly painful memories for you in there."

"Yes, I'm fine with it all now. Aren't I, Charles?" Charles had been sitting, quietly listening.

"Yes, my dear. I think you can handle just about anything you need to now."

"Right, then that's settled." April said as she finished her drink. "I'll settle the bill. You two collect the children." She told Charles and Victor as she walked towards the bar.

Reaching the bar April found Victor standing beside her. "I hope you don't mind if I pay the bill, April. Only I do need to get some cash back."

"Be my guest, Victor." April stood to one side as Victor asked to settle the bill, and for some cash back, handing the bar man his credit card. "I'm very pleased to meet you at long last, April. Mandy talks about you constantly, and I can fully understand why now that I've met you in person. Maybe now that she's met you, but as you are now of course, she'll finally accept it all."

The barman asked Victor to sign the credit card receipt. "Blast! I've done it again." Victor muttered as he corrected the r in his name that he'd written backwards, needing to initial the correction. "I must say, you're a very beautiful lady. Maybe Mandy should be jealous of me talking to you alone." Victor joked, trying to draw attention away from his error.

Smiling broadly, April said to him, "I can see I'll have to get used to all of these flattering compliments," as they were returning to where Mandy was sharing a joke with Charles. "Shall we go now?" asked April, as she excitedly linked Mandy's arm.

"Come with me, Charles. We'll follow the girls after we've collected the children." Victor suggested, as he led Charles away. "We'll be right behind you, so get the drinks in?" Victor called back, as they disappeared through the front door.

"Good night, ladies." The barman shouted over. "If the men have been stupid enough to stand you two girls up, well I'm free later, you know?"

"You're working, so you're out of luck. Good night." April said as they left.

Once outside, Mandy linked April's arm. "How do you really feel now, my love?"

"Don't look so worried, Mandy. I'm fine about it all now. I feel better now than I'd ever have expected to feel. Although, I'll never stop trying to reverse all of this," April told Mandy as they walked towards the door of the Smithy. "How are you and Victor?"

"Fine, but we don't see a lot of each other. Victor works out of town most of the time. Why do you ask, darling?"

She told Mandy thoughtfully, "Oh, it's nothing really. I'm just being nosey."

"Come on, April. I know you better than you know yourself, remember? Why all the interest in Victor? I know you don't fancy him. So what is it my love?" insisted Mandy.

"It's just a gut feeling I've got. It's probably nothing more than my protective instincts towards you and the children. Can we please change the subject now that we've arrived at the, Smithy?" April asked, as she breezed through the door that a man hastily held open for them.

"Thank you. You're ever so kind." April said, as she led Mandy into the Smithy lounge.

"I can assure you that the pleasure was all mine, ladies." the man assured them. "Who's your delectable young friend, Mandy?"

"You'd be surprised if you knew, Paul. Perhaps one day I'll be able to tell you." Mandy told him as she swept through the doors, followed by the perplexed Paul.

They had hardly placed the drinks on the table when Charles and Victor arrived with the children.

Pamela could hardly contain her excitement. She shouted, "Daddy!" running to hug April as tightly as she possibly could. Andrew stood behind Pamela unsure of what to do next. So April offered him her hand to shake, which he grabbed eagerly, and clung on to it tearfully.

"Hello, Darlings." April greeted them. "My, haven't you both grown up."

After noticing the puzzled looks of astonishment on the other people in the bar, April advised them. "I think you'd better call me April from now on, kids."

The children tried to object, reminding her that as far as they were concerned she's still, and always would be, their dad.

Mandy came to the rescue, "Perhaps we can compromise and call her Auntie April. Would that be better?"

They both agreed reluctantly as they pushed in to sit on either side of April. "I can't get over how much you've both grown." April said as she wrapped her arms around them. "Andy, you'll be starting at the big school after the summer holidays, won't you?"

The Smithy manager, Jeff, interrupted. "I hope you don't mind my asking you something, Mandy?"

"No not at all, Jeff. What is it?"

"Well, I've been elected by the odd bunch of misfits at the bar," he started, as he gestured towards the bar. "We couldn't help overhearing the children call this lovely lady 'Daddy'. George was their dad, and George this beautiful specimen of the fairer sex certainly is not."

Mandy and April looked towards each other as they both broke into a fit of laughter, until eventually Mandy was the first to compose herself.

"This is, Miss April Darling. What can I tell them about her, Sir Charles?"

Charles shrugged his shoulders as he turned to April. "The cat is out of the bag now, so the ball is squarely in your court, my love. We think that the assignment is now all but over with. So, I'll stand by whatever decision you feel comfortable with."

Jeff looked on perplexed as April turned back to Mandy. "There's nothing to stop you from telling him the truth now that it seems to be all over. That's if that's what you really want to do?"

Mandy burst into another fit of the giggles. She eventually managed to splutter to the patiently waiting Jeff. "I'm sorry about the laughing, Jeff. Anyway, April here was George. He, or should I now say she, was forced against his, or her, will, to become, Miss April Darling." Mandy paused as Jeff stared open-mouthed towards April. Trying to digest what Mandy had just told him.

"When you've stopped your bloody gawking and drooling Jeff, I'll continue." Mandy insisted, as Jeff stopped staring at April, and turned his attention back to Mandy. "George was originally abducted from here as part of a top secret experiment, and this is the first time we've clapped eyes on each other since then. And this is Field Marshal Sir Charles Hythe-Smith. He works at the Ministry with April."

"Well fuck me sideways!" Jeff exclaimed. Then he suddenly remembered the company he was in and apologised. "I'm very sorry. Please excuse my language, children. It just sort of slipped out. She is absolutely gorgeous, Mandy. Hey, Carol! Come over here, will you?" he called to his wife, who quickly obliged. "Meet George, or April, as he, or she, is now known."

"George who, don't you mean Georgina?" the puzzled Carol suggested to him.

"No you moppet, you remember George, Mandy's ex-husband who disappeared." Jeff clumsily tried to explain, still reeling from the shocked news himself. "Well, George is now, Miss April Darling."

"Well I'll be," Carol muttered. "I wish somebody could make me look that bloody good. You're absolutely stunning, George. Err, I mean, April."

She then called over towards the bar. "Hey, you lot. Do you remember Mandy's husband George that disappeared? Well meet George." Carol shouted excitedly, pointing towards April. "He's now known as Miss April Darling. What are you all drinking? It's on the house," Carol asked. Adding, "I think I need a stiff drink myself, Jeff," as she headed back behind the bar.

Carol brought the drinks over. "I'll just finish up in the kitchen, and then I'll join you if I may. You can fill me in on all of the gory details, April?" Carol suggested, before disappearing back into the kitchen.

The evening passed as the children chatted incessantly to April: wanting to know all about her new persona, and repeatedly asking when she'd be coming home to stay. Mandy, Charles, Carol and Victor, could only look on in amusement until the evening drew to a close.

"Are you sleeping in our house tonight?" Pamela asked.

"We've booked into a hotel for tonight, darling. But next time I'll stay with you." April promised a mournful Pamela. "But I'll see you both in the morning. What time shall I come round?" April tried to cheer up the children.

"Seven o'clock." Andrew suggested eagerly. "We'll get up very early."

"Shall we say ten o'clock so I can have my breakfast first?" April said kissing them both good night. The children reluctantly agreed, as Mandy and Victor kissed Charles and April good night. Then they went on their separate ways.

"I sense that there's something wrong, April. What is it?"

"I'm not sure, Charles. There's something weird about Victor that doesn't quite sit right with me." April told him, as they strolled towards the hotel arm in arm.

"In what way is that? I must say he seems okay to me. He's a little quiet maybe. But okay. So what's giving you all of this concern?"

"Did you check him out when you found out about him and Mandy, Charles?"

"Well in a way we did, briefly. But we didn't see the need for a thorough investigation. Why? What's the problem?" Charles asked April again, as they reached the hotel. "We'll have a night cap in the lounge before we retire. That way, you can tell me about it in some more detail," suggested Charles, as April's phone rang.

"Okay, make mine a Bacardi and coke." April agreed. She put the phone to her ear. "Hello sweetheart." She greeted Mandy. Then April just listened. A look of shock covered her face. "How often has he been here?"

After listening carefully again April rang off, confirming that they'd meet up and talk about it the next morning.

"Was that Mandy, April?"

"Yes, Charles. You're not going to believe what she's just told me. She says that Ron Marks has visited here on a number of occasions just lately to see Victor."

"You mean our Ron Marks. Robert Montgomery? I wonder what he wanted here." Charles said thoughtfully. Adding, "Of course he doesn't work for the department anymore. His injuries were so horrific that we had no alternative but to medically retire him. Does Mandy have any idea what he wanted?"

"No. But she said she'll come round early tomorrow morning on her own. We'll just have to wait until then to hear what Mandy has to say," April told Charles as she emptied her glass. "Anyway, I'm off too bed now. I feel totally exhausted after all that's happened here today, and the travelling of course. Are you coming, Charles?"

"Yes. As you say we'll just have to see what tomorrow has to offer." Charles agreed, as he followed April into the lift.

They went straight to bed. Because of their fatigue from the day's events, mixed with the alcohol that they'd just consumed, they soon drifted off into a deep and restful sleep.

The ringing of the telephone awakened April. "Yes." April said to the desk attendant, glancing at the time and noticing that it was only six a.m.

"I have a call for you, Miss Darling. It's from a Mrs. Mandy Partridge. Will you accept the call?"

"Yes, of course I will. Put her through, will you?"

"I'm sorry to wake you so early darling, but Victor has just received another early morning phone call, and he says he has to go out of town again to do another job. I answered the phone, and I'm pretty sure that it was that Ron Marks."

"When's he going, Mandy. Did he say?"

"This afternoon, pet. Vic says it's a long drive and he needs to be there to start the job tomorrow morning. He says that he'll mind the children though while we go shopping." Then Mandy asked. "So what time shall we meet?"

"We'll come and pick you up so that I can give the children their presents." April suggested. "I'll call about nine o'clock if that's not too early. By the way Mandy, what type of van does Victor drive?"

"He hasn't got a van, only a car. A Jaguar I think. Why?"

"Oh, I'm just being nosy, that's all. We'll see you soon, Mandy," Said April as she replaced the receiver. After telling Charles about the conversation, April insisted that he had Victor thoroughly checked out, and with extreme urgency.

"There's something about his voice too. I can't quite place it but I detect a very slight accent. And I've never known a plumber without a van before. How the hell does he pick up his materials?" April explained as she finished dressing. "We'll need to have him followed until we're sure about him. Will you arrange for that, Charles?"

"Of course I will, if you really think it's necessary. What do you think he's up to, April?" Charles asked, as he held the door open for them to go down for an early breakfast.

"I need to get a tracking device out of our car. I'll activate it, and attach it to Victor's car, Charles."

"A good idea love, it'll save us follow him too closely. I hope it will prove you to be wrong this time though, I quite like the fellow personally." Charles finished as they reached the dining room. Taking his mobile from his pocket, Charles said to April, "I'll just put the wheels in motion for a surveillance team, if only to put your mind at ease."

"Ask them to check out Robert Montgomery's movements while they're at it, Charles."

"Certainly," agreed Charles, as he proceeded to instruct his surveillance officers. "Right, that's all sorted out. Now for breakfast my dear. I'm absolutely famished."

After breakfast they both returned to their room to freshen up, before driving round to Mandy's house. "Don't leave Victor alone with the children until we get back, will you Charles? It's just a gut feeling I'm having about Victor and Robert Montgomery."

"Of course I won't. But do try not to be too long, won't you?"

"No, I won't be, Charles. But I must get Mandy to tell me more about Victor." April continued to explain as they reached Mandy's front gate.

The children rushed out to hug her. "Auntie April, can we come with you?

Can we please, pretty please?" Pamela begged.

"If mummy says that it's okay, then of course you can both come with us." Mandy agreed, so April suggested that Charles could go along with them too. He distracted Mandy and the children by putting them into his car while April seized the opportunity to attach a tracking device beneath the wing of Victor's car, which was parked in Mandy's driveway. With that done, they all set out towards the shops in Charles' car, leaving Victor at home alone to prepare for his forth-coming trip.

April avoided speaking to Mandy regarding Victor. She waited for a more opportune moment in which to do so. After lavishing the children with more gifts and clothing, the opportunity eventually presented itself. Mandy needed to try on some new outfits.

"I'll come with you if you like?" suggested April, "You kids wait with Uncle Charles."

Once inside the cubicle, she asked Mandy. "How much do you really know about Victor's past, before he came to Riverlet, that is?"

"Nothing, Victor won't talk about his past. He says he wants to forget it and start a new life here with us. Why the interest? Is there something wrong with him?" Mandy said casually as she twirled round. "How do I look, darling?" she asked casually, seeming unconcerned about the interest in Victor.

"You look beautiful as ever, Mandy. So as far as you're concerned, Victor has got no past before you?"

Mandy thought deeply for a short time. "Come to think of it, no." She answered as she put on another outfit. Turning around, she asked, "Will you zip me up please? All he ever says about his past is that he wasn't allowed to have a childhood."

"And that's all you know about his past! The sum total of Victor's life is he didn't have a childhood!" April exclaimed with alarm.

"Well, yes. Every time I tried to ask him anything else he changes the subject. Why?" Mandy did another twirl, asking, "Which dress is the nicest?" as she admired herself in the mirror. "That's when I see him of course. The phone keeps interrupting us, and then all Victor says is that he must go. He rushes off then to do another job somewhere else."

"They're both beautiful on you, pet," agreed April. She was lost in thought. "You might show me some enthusiasm!" Mandy snapped mockingly.

"Who are you most interested in, Victor or me?"

"I'm sorry love. Was I that obvious? You look great in them both, so I'll buy them for you." April offered, trying to make amends for her obvious lack of interest. "It's just that I worry about you all."

"I know you do, and I'm only teasing you. Thanks for your concern, but we're ok, honestly." Mandy apologised as she kissed April on the cheek.

Little more was said about Victor as they continued with the shopping expedition, with April continuing to buy gifts and clothing for Mandy and the children.

"We must not forget to take something back for Victor so what does he need, Mandy?"

"I know he needs a watch. He lost his other one."

At last a stroke of luck, April thought to herself. Amongst the surveillance equipment she'd brought with her was a specially adapted wristwatch. It was fitted with minute sensors that would allow headquarters to track the movements of the wearer, and to monitor their conversations. If it were checked or X-rayed by any known bugging detectors, it would just appear to be a normal wristwatch.

"I have a beautiful watch in the car that is brand new. It's a very expensive one, so I think I'll give Victor it as a peace offering."

Mandy said to April. "Haven't you bought it for somebody else, April?

Anyway, I got the impression that you didn't like Victor very much."

"I'm only being cautious Mandy, trying to protect you all. Now come on kids, let's go and pay for all these goodies."

To everyone's surprise Andrew volunteered, "I don't like Victor that much either. That's who you're talking about, isn't it?"

"Yes darling. But why don't you like him? You haven't said anything before about him," Mandy asked, placing a consoling arm around him. "I thought you liked him. What's he done to upset you?"

"Nothing really, he's just dead creepy. That's all," said Andrew sadly. "He's always texting with his phone if you go out of the room. And once when he was in the toilet I looked at his messages, and they were all funny. I couldn't understand any of them."

"How do you mean funny, Andy?" interrupted April, as she became more deeply concerned.

"You know, French or something. I didn't understand them."

Glancing up at Charles, April noticed he was becoming more intrigued by the conversation too.

"Here's the car so let's get in and you can tell us all about it," Charles suggested. He then started the car and turned out into the traffic, starting back towards Riverlet. April was seated in the back with the children either side of her, and Mandy sat in the front seat beside Charles.

"Is there anything else weird you can think of, Andy?" persisted April. He shook his head.

Pamela prompted, "Andy, tell them about when we went round to his house. You know. It was when he was putting stuff in the boot of his car."

April asked in a soft and gentle voice. "What was all that about, darlings?"

"We went to tell him that Mummy wanted him. But he shouted at us for going round to his house without asking him. I wish you were our dad still. You would fix it all for us." Andrew continued sadly.

"So do I darlings, but I'll still fix it for you, you'll see." April promised as she placed her arms round the children's shoulders. "I can see that we'll have to live much closer to each other now. We all have to talk about it." Then April asked. "By the way, what was Victor putting into the boot of his car. Did you see?"

"Yes. There was some guns and stuff," Pamela spoke up. "Guns, and what stuff?" April asked.

Andrew explained, "You know, stuff. Big tin boxes with handles on the sides, like Army boxes. Some wooden boxes as well."

"Have you any ideas, Charles?" Mandy asked, becoming more and more concerned for the children's safety.

"It sounds like arms and ammunition boxes. But we'll have to make certain somehow before we can ask him about them." Charles called back to April.

"That's just what I was thinking, Charles. We'll need a stop and search unit here, and pronto. See if you can organise one will you, Charles?" But he was already dialling the number. "And tell them they must wear their body armour."

"I'm ahead of you for a change," he gloated. Then he continued to issue instructions to the person on the other end of the phone. Instructing them what type of backup was needed, he urged, "Hurry, he's leaving for some type of assignment."

They stopped at Victor's house on the way home to give him the present of the watch, inviting him to dine with them later. Then they continued to Mandy's house.

"I should have seen the signs coming. But I didn't know," sobbed Mandy, as they arrived home. She asked fearfully, "What are we going to do now?"

April assured her. "I'm not sure yet, but try not to worry, Pet. You and the children just stay out of it all. Please."

"Don't you worry we intend to, don't we kids?" Mandy said nervously, while the children just nodded, also looking profoundly afraid. "But I can see that you have lost none of your ability to take care of us."

"You will be careful, won't you, Auntie April?" Pamela pleaded, as she gripped her arm tight. "We don't want to lose you, again."

"Don't you worry about me sweetheart, you can't get rid of me again that easily." April tried to console them. "I may not be able to be a proper husband and father anymore, but I'm still your guardian and very best friend. Aren't I, children?"

The two children clung to her. "Our very, very, very best, bestest friend." Pamela confirmed.

There was a knock on the front door that Mandy answered. Re-entering the lounge she told them, "That was John next door. He said that immediately after we left Victor started moving his possessions out of the house. John says that he was quite some time in here so is everything ok? I told him that it was, but I wonder why it took him so long. He never kept that much here." Mandy added thoughtfully. "And I wonder why he chose now to do it?"

"You probably spooked him last night. You know, telling him about who April was, and introducing me as a Ministry man."

"Yes, I never thought about that. How stupid of me, Charles"

"No, you're not stupid, my dear." Charles tried to comfort Mandy as he placed an arm around her. "He seemed to be a perfectly nice ordinary gentleman to me as well, only April has developed a sixth sense about these matters. Now, where the hell is that bloody armed response unit?"

"It would have been better to have stopped and searched him en-route, some distance away from here, Charles. To make it look like just a routine check."

"It may have to be, April," he rasped, as his impatience grew.

Andrew was looking mournfully out of the window when he shouted. "There's Uncle Victor, now."

Springing to her feet, April quickly moved towards the window, "Where, darling?"

"He's gone now. He was going very fast up that way." Andrew explained as he pointed towards the motorway. "Will he be coming back here?"

"We'll see. This might all have a perfectly innocent explanation. Who knows, he might just be going on a proper plumbing job like he's said, and the boxes may just be full of his tools."

Charles was busy on his phone trying to redirect the armed response units. "I don't know which bloody way he's gone. Activate the tracking devise we planted." He continued to order impatiently. "What do you mean you can't track him?" Turning to April, he said, "The incompetent fools seem to have lost him. Ah, they've got the devise working now. Where is he? IDIOTS," Charles yelled, turning the phone off. "You'll never guess what's happened now, April?"

"He hasn't taken his watch with him."

"Got it in one, that's unless Victor's doubled back and is back at home, they've surrounded the house, and want to know what to do next. Shall we go there now and supervise them?"

Putting on her coat, April warned Charles. "Tell them to keep out of sight as the house may be booby trapped." She had just finished giving the warning when a loud bang shook the house. "SHIT." She yelled. "It seems like we're too late." Rushing from the house followed closely by Charles, they left Mandy and the children huddled together on the settee.

As April and Charles approached Victor's house they witnessed a further series of explosions, blowing out the windows. The house then collapsed like a pack of cards, and was reduced to a pile of rubble.

"Victor must be an explosives expert. He certainly knew what he was doing when he booby-trapped this house, and leaving the others either side untouched. It's going to take our forensic experts forever to sift through those ashes." Charles commented.

Suddenly, April was filled with fear as she kicked off her shoes. Holding them in her hands she sprinted stocking footed back towards Mandy's house.

"Where are you going now?" he called after her.

But ignoring him she rounded the corner into the avenue.

Pushing open their front door, April grabbed the children's hands and pulled them outside. "Come on, Mandy. Quickly, follow me." April shouted assertively. They rushed down the garden path and into Charles's waiting car. Charles had eventually realised April's concerns, and why she was suddenly filled with panic. They then raced from the scene just in time, as

Mandy's detached house erupted in a huge fireball.

"What alerted you?" Charles asked, stopping the car at a safe distance from the house.

"When you said that Victor must be an explosives expert the way he'd set the explosives. And John next door telling us he was a long time in the house, I just thought he might try to buy himself some time by blowing up Mandy's house as well. He knew just how deeply I still felt about the children and Mandy."

April suddenly realised that she was frightening the children. She turned to Mandy, "I'm sorry we're neglecting you all. Now is anybody hurt?"

"No." Mandy finally found her voice to say. "What's happening to us, April? Why does he want to kill us?"

"It's not personal, darling. He probably thought that we'd still be out shopping, and he's trying to buy himself some time. It's my guess that Robert Montgomery's involved in whatever's going on here. When he found that I'd gone, he knew that you would then all be vulnerable. Knowing Rivulet was a sleepy little hamlet he told Victor about you, If, Victor is his real name, then, Victor moved in here and befriended you."

"But we could've all been killed! He doesn't know that we got out in time, does he?" Mandy argued. "If these are the type of people you have to deal with, I-I-I don't know how you remain sane. Is this the type of world that you now belong to?"

"It's not easy I can assure you," interrupted Charles. "But you would be surprised at just how professional April has become. She's the best there is in this particular field right now. Now, as April has said herself, we must now get you all to safety immediately."

"Can you organise that, Charles? Then I can go ahead after these maniacs," she urged, "If you all travel in Mandy's car, I can go in your much faster car and prepare myself."

Kissing them all goodbye, April sped off. She promised to wait for them to arrive before going after Victor and Montgomery. On the long drive alone she tussled mentally with the problems that lay before her. Like where could she now start looking? How could she pick up their trail?

Travelling at speeds in excess of a hundred mph, April soon reached Spaghetti Junction. Skirting it she continued eastbound. It wasn't long before she was drawing close to the M.1, then towards London.

Slowing down, to negotiate the intersection which would allow her to head southward, suddenly April was recklessly overtaken by a speeding car.

"Those are the bastards now. They must have stopped somewhere to eat." April muttered to herself as she recognised the occupants. "Montgomery and Henderson together, but who's the third man?" she wondered as she swung the car back onto the motorway, travelling in pursuit of them.

Due to the sudden change of direction, April caused the cars behind her to swerve violently, as they crashed into each other trying to avoid her car. April glanced in the rear view mirror at the sheer havoc the sudden change of direction had caused.

"Whoops! Sorry about that." April said apologetically, as if the occupants of the crashing cars could hear her. Speeding off after her quarry, April called Charles on the voice-activated car phone.

"We are about twenty miles north of—." Charles started to say.

"Just listen to me, Charles." April interrupted firmly. "I'm chasing after the bastards right now."

"Chasing after whom, Henderson and Montgomery?"

"Yes, Charles. And there's a third man with them. Can you have them tracked by satellite? Just in case I lose them that is?" April asked as she skidded round the tight bends.

"Yes. Where are you now?"

"On the A 14 heading south towards the Cambridge area. I've just pasted through a small sleepy village. They're driving like bloody lunatics, so you'd better tell PC Plod to try to clear the roads ahead of us. Do it quickly before somebody gets killed. Oh, and get somebody to sort the mess out at the intersection of the M.6, and M.1. Swerving to follow these bloody idiots I caused one hell of a pile up there."

"I will do at once, April. I'm just putting you on hold while I sort it all out." Charles said, as he made a series of phone calls. Then he eventually returned to tell April. "That's all done. They have picked you out and are following you. Please be careful," he implored her.

"Don't you worry, that is my sole intention," she reassured him as she rang off.

Continuing at speed Montgomery, who was driving, realised that they were not going to shake April off. So they resorted to their guns, as Victor leaned out off his window and shot wildly towards her car.

Weaving the car to avoid being hit by the bullets, April opened her window to return fire, aiming at their tyres to attempt to make them stop. This failed because of the constant swerving of their cars, but April noticed that a stray bullet had punctured their petrol tank causing their car to lose its fuel.

"They'll eventually have to stop now." April said to herself, as she patiently waited for them to run out of petrol. They travelled on southward, pressing on fast, on the now clear roads. April could see they were approaching a racecourse, noticing that a light aircraft was circling above it, descending in gradual circles.

Suddenly, as they neared the gates they swerved sharply and crashed through them, as the small aircraft landed and was taxiing towards the approaching car. April was travelling too fast, and was far too close to them to follow immediately as she slammed on the brakes, and skidded to a halt with smoke bellowing from her tyres. Slamming the car into reverse, April returned to the spot where they'd crashed through, and quickly continued the chase after them, but was just in time to watch their plane picking up speed for takeoff, as a large explosion ripped the air when their car exploded.

Forced to watch helplessly as the light aircraft soared up into the cloudy skies; April picked up her phone and explained to Charles what had just happened, asking him to have the progress of the plane kept under surveillance by a satellite tracking system. Particularly noting where they finally ended up.

Unable to give pursuit at this time, April continued driving towards London. As she drove, she accessed the car phone and use the opportunity to seek independent advice regarding reversing her gender. "Could I have a consultation today, please?"

"I'm sorry Miss, I'm afraid there's not a single appointment available until Monday," the lady receptionist told her. "Shall I pencil you in for then?"

"I'm afraid that will not do, I have to go out of the country on business, and I'm not sure exactly when I shall be returning. Could the doctor make an exception for me?"

The receptionist asked. "Might I ask who recommended us to you, Madam?"

This question took April by surprise as she fumbled for an answer. She said out of desperation, "Field Martial Sir Charles Hythe Smith." Then she realised that she should never have brought his name into it.

"Ah yes. We know Sir Charles very well. Just one moment please, Miss?" She said, before April could retract Charles as a reference.

"Hello. You are a friend of Charles I believe. How is the old dog doing these days?" the doctor opened the conversation jovially.

Thinking quickly, April answered. "He's doing fine, engrossed in his work as per usual. But he did find the time to give me your number, so that must say something, I suppose." April lied. She'd acquired the number from the phone file on his desk without his knowledge.

"Well what can I do for you, young lady?"

"I'm Miss April Darling. Could we have a quiet word in confidence please, doctor?" April asked, while negotiating the slip road off the M 25.

"Could you be here within the hour, Miss?"

"Will twenty five minutes be okay? I have to pass you on the way to Charles' apartment." Then April added. "Don't tell Charles about my ringing you, will you? I would like to tell him myself."

"You know that I'm bound by the 'Hippocratic Oath,' to keep patients confidentiality. So don't you worry about that, I'll see you soon then, Miss Darling?" he finished, ringing off.

CHAPTER 15

Breezing into the clinic April asked the receptionist to inform the doctor of her arrival. Eventually the surgery door opened and a kindly looking, middle-aged gentleman invited her into his surgery.

"Now my dear, what is it that you need to see me about so urgently?"

April then gave him a brief description of everything that had happened to her.

The doctor just sat and listened to her very intensely. When she'd finished April was looking downward, as though in shame or embarrassment.

"Well," began the Doctor, "Firstly my dear, you can hold your head up high, you have no reason to feel any shame. In fact, you are an extremely attractive young lady. I have of course heard rumblings about this experimental surgery being revolutionary. But only that it was still in the infancy of development, and that it was definitely not ready for human participation, and not by a long chalk. Now, I would firstly need to give you a CAT scan. Then I'd need to examine you, if that is okay?" April nodded her assent. "Good," the doctor said as he stood up. "Now you go into the changing room and put on a gown for me, will you?"

"It won't take very long will it, doctor? Only it is imperative I get to our apartment before Sir Charles arrives home. That should be in approximately two hours from now."

"It shouldn't do. I promise I will be as quick as I possibly can. Now go and get ready will you, please?" the doctor urged.

After giving her a CAT scan and then examining every inch of April, the doctor then told April to dress and return back into his surgery when she was ready.

"Well, my dear. I don't know quite where to begin. Firstly, I can't find a single shred of evidence to re-enforce your claims that you have ever been anything other than the very beautiful lady that you have now become. Usually, there are certain physical characteristics that cannot be altered, although I do admit to knowing about the technology that they're experimenting with. It seems that you have now become the perfect woman in every way, and leaving no tell-tale signs at all to substantiate your claim."

He stopped as if to gather his thoughts. "The problem is April, may I call you April?" she nodded. "When your body goes through such a dramatic transformation as yours must have done, and it must have been a very dramatic one, it takes a lot of preparation, both mentally, as well as physically, drugs, counselling etcetera. All before your body can undergo the transformation physically. Undergoing it twice could, no would, prove to be fatal at best. Or it could leave you permanently insane at the very worst." He relaxed back before continuing. "I am sorry I cannot be more hopeful, April. I can't imagine the anguish you must be experiencing. All I can suggest is that you give yourself a little more time to adjust to it."

"I'm sorry to have wasted your time. Now how much do I owe you, Doctor?"

"No, my dear, I truly am sorry I can't help you. Regarding the bill, well it's gratis to you. And anytime you feel the need to see me, or maybe even just to talk, my door will always be open to you," the doctor told her very sympathetically.

As April left the clinic she was feeling downcast, dejected, and disappointed as she drove towards Kensington, and Charles's apartment. Suddenly a thought occurred to her. 'The doctor seemed to know a lot about my operation. Supposing that he was in cahoots with Charles? He would then have to say that it was impossible. I can see that I'll have to get an independent opinion on this.' April told herself, as she raced to reach the apartment first.

Arriving at the apartment, April switched on the computer, and contacted Bert. She asked him to download all the relevant details he had uncovered, and send it to her computer. After finishing packing she was pouring herself a drink when there was a knock at the door. When she opened it, Charles, Mandy, and the children all laughingly greeted her, obviously sharing a joke together.

"You took your time getting here, Charles. Have you had any feedback regarding their whereabouts, yet?"

"No, not yet, April." Charles replied, as he and Mandy began to giggle again.

Indignantly, April remarked, "You all seem to be getting along very well together."

"Do I detect a hint of jealousy, April?" Charles teased. "Now where are you up to?"

Ignoring his remark, April continued, "I've taken the liberty of asking Bert Williams to pipe his consul through to ours, so that we can see where they're up too."

"You're not annoyed with us, are you?" Mandy asked with concern.

"No, of course I'm not. I'm just very busy at the moment. That's all." Then returning to the PC, April asked Bert. "Where are they headed for?"

"Due south to France, or maybe even Algeria," he suggested.

"Keep following them. Just a sec, WHO THE HELL ARE THEY?" April shouted with shocked disbelief, as a number of similar aircraft appeared from nowhere, and began to bunch into a formation. "Where are they now, Bert?"

"They're half way across the channel, April."

"No, I meant which one is Henderson's plane." April clarified, as the formation entered into the clouds.

"Sorry, I misunderstood you. It's hard to say which one is their plane; we'll have to hope that they all land together, wherever they're headed. Ah, here they come now. It now looks like they're heading back here, April."

"Something's not quite right about this, Bert. Just a minute, how many planes entered the clouds?"

After a few seconds had passed, Bert confirmed, "Ten, why?"

"There are only nine now, so the scumbags are still hidden in there somewhere. Is there any way at all that you can find them?"

"I'll see if we can use heat sensors to pick up their exhaust. We may be lucky, who knows? I'll call you back if we have any luck, April."

"Okay, Bert. Can you also detail somebody to watch where the rest of them land?"

"I've already asked Gina to do that for me. Speak to you very soon, April," Then turning to Charles, April asked him, "Will you detail a group to apprehend these pilots? They'll probably land in the same aerodrome they left from. And have you managed to find anything out about Victor Henderson yet?"

Charles rang his office. After a lengthy conversation he returned his attention to April. "Victor was born in the Ukraine but grew up in Russia. He studied law at Oxford, which is where he learnt to speak such near perfect English. While he was there he got sucked into an extremist group that call themselves, The Combaos. It stands for Communism by authoritative Order Society. It's a radical group of Red fundamentalists. He then disappeared for a few years, and then he emerged on Mandy's doorstep, so to speak. Apart from that we know very little else about the man."

Mandy interrupted, "What alerted you to him, sweetheart?"

"As I've already explained he has a very slight accent. Also, when he signed the cheque at the hotel he wrote his r backwards."

"He said that he was dyslexic. That's why he gets his r, n, and e back to front."

"Well, that's what made me suspicious of him, Mandy."

Then she turned her attention back to Charles. She asked him, "Anyway, if they knew that much about him, tell me why the hell they didn't keep better tabs on him?" she snapped with annoyance.

"It seems somebody somehow may have slipped up. But don't you worry, when I get to the bottom of all of this somebody is in very serious trouble, April."

Bert interrupted. "Are you still there, April?"

Returning to the computer, she answered, "Yes, we're still here, Bert."

"I have now picked up their trail again. If they keep on the flight path that they're on now they're heading towards Poland, or Belorussia. The cloud cover should break very soon, and then it's clear skies all the way. Then it will be easier to follow them." He paused momentarily. "There's something else that you should know about, an intercontinental missile has just landed in Wembley Stadium."

April asked anxiously. "Bloody hell, how many casualties is there, Bert?"

"That's just it, April, there are none, April. The warheads hadn't been armed, and we don't know where it came from either. It's my guess that it's some kind of warning, but I'll keep you posted on it as I find out more facts about it. Now I'll get back to following this bloody plane."

"Keep on top of them, and inform us of any new developments, Bert. No matter how trivial it may seem to you." April asked, leaving the line open. Turning back to Charles, she suggested. "You should send some of your men out there, so that they will be ready to pounce. Well, when we find out what they're up to, of course."

"I was thinking that you would be the best person to send, April," he suggested.

April's concerned expression was replaced by one of extreme anger. "ME!" She shouted. "Haven't I bloody done enough for you lot?"

"You're the only name the department has suggested to me. Remember, you have now proven yourself to be our finest agent. Besides which, have you checked your bank account lately? You are the highest paid operative that we've got, or ever had. So that makes you eligible to be called into service at any given time."

"BOLLOCKS, all your talk about our future. You've just been using me.

YOU'RE NOTHING BUT A FUCKING BASTARD."

"No, April. Don't think that." Charles tried to explain, placing a consoling arm round her shoulders.

"Yes, my love, no, my love, three bags fucking full, my fucking love!" April continued to shout tearfully, pushing his arm off her shoulders. "All I've been to you is an experiment, and somebody to shag, so, PISS OFF!" April cried, storming into the bedroom and slamming the door behind her.

She lay across the bed sobbing and was oblivious to the door opening.

"Are you okay?" April heard Mandy's soft voice asking with concern. "Don't upset yourself, please pet. It's not worth giving them the satisfaction."

"I'm sorry. I forgot you and the children were still here for a moment. You should not have seen, or heard, any of this," April explained, dabbing her tear filled eyes. "I'm okay. Now we must go back and make sure that the children are all right," April told Mandy, as she moved towards the door.

As they re-entered the lounge April apologised to the children as she passed them. Then she returned to the computer, as Bert was bringing Charles up to speed, while Mandy and the children went to freshen up.

"Ah, feeling better now?" Charles asked tentatively. "I've got to be, HAVEN'T I?" she snapped.

Bert butted in. "Sir Charles is right, everybody's suggested you for this assignment, April."

"Don't you fucking start, Bert. So I'm an open topic for conversation now, am I?"

"No. You left the line open during your tyrannical rant. Bert, and whoever else, could hear you." Charles tried to explain to her.

"Let's just forget it. I'm sorry that you had to witness that little outburst, Bert. Now what's happening?" April asked, returning to the job in hand.

"It's okay. I understand I'm a married man. Now we're still tracking them, and if they stay on their present course they seem to be heading towards Warsaw. But they seem to be a little bit confused as to where they're headed for, they have frequently altered their course," Bert explained.

"Any luck with the identity of the third man?" she asked him, trying to ignore the fact that Charles was present.

Bert tried to steer him back into the conversation, "I think you have that information, don't you, Sir Charles?"

Charles explained, "Yes. It's a Flight Commander Glen McDougal. He works at a top secret R.A.F base in Scotland, just outside Aberdeen, and I mean high security like you've never seen it before, April. He went on a long weekend leave last week, but he never returned, and it seems that some vital documents may have also gone astray with him. We have put out a worldwide alert for him."

April said impatiently, "I can tell them where he is, he's in that bloody plane. What did he do in Aberdeen?"

"He was in charge of a military unit that does highly classified work." Charles started.

But again April interrupted, "I mean was he doing anything specific just before he absconded? Is the base strategically important in any way, shape or form?"

You had better come to the point, Sir Charles," suggested Bert.

"Yes, I suppose I should. It seems he was put in charge of a project to develop a new prototype plane for the military. It will revolutionise tactical warfare as we now know it." Charles stopped, realising Mandy and the children were returning.

"Sorry to interrupt, I just need my handbag. I thought we'd be wise to take a little stroll round the area to familiarise ourselves with it. Well, seeing we'll have to spend some time down here. Which will be the nearest school for the children to attend?" Mandy asked.

"Go left out of the front door, then take the third right, then the first on the left. I know it's a fee-paying school, but you can just send me all of the bills. The P.M. sends his children there, so it must be a pretty good school with a high level of security." April emphasised. "Now all of you give me a kiss. It looks as though I may be gone when you arrive back. Charles will look after you." Then, with afterthought, April glared at him as she added through clenched teeth. "At least he'd better do, if he knows what's good for his health."

"You know I will. It goes without saying that I'll take them all to meet the headmaster as soon as I get the time," he reassured April, as Mandy closed the door and left.

Bert asked, "They seem to be very nice people. Is she related to you, April?"

"Yes, in a funny sort of way that is, Bert."

"How do you mean?"

Charles could see how Bert's persistence was upsetting her. "Can we stick to the task in hand, Bert," he insisted. "April can tell you her life story when she's got more time to spare."

"I'm sorry, Sir. It's just that it seems they're such nice people that I wondered why this Victor Henderson tried to kill them?" he explained.

"I don't think it was personal. He was probably just trying to cause a diversion to allow himself time to get away," explained Charles.

"Maybe, maybe not," Bert ventured. "Or maybe there's something he doesn't want them to tell you."

April was in deep thought when the doorbell rang. "Maria will answer it," Charles asked, as Bert continued to seek a motive for the apparent attempted annihilation of Mandy and the children.

They were interrupted by, Maria. She announced that Mandy had just returned with the children.

"Ask them to come in here for a moment, will you?" Charles asked.

"We have found the school," Mandy started, but was interrupted by April. "Good, now can we leave that for a moment? We need you and the children to think very hard and carefully. Is there anything, no matter how insignificant it may seem to you, that Victor has ever let slip?"

A confused Mandy asked. "Like what?"

"Anything at all," urged Charles. "For instance, who did he call?"

"I can honestly say I never knew him to ever make a call to anybody," explained Mandy. "He received plenty of calls, but them he explained were for his work. But he never made any calls that we know of." Then as if she was talking to herself, Mandy added. "The funny thing is I never realised that until now."

"How about emails or texting," Bert chipped in, "do you know who he texted?"

"Not really." Mandy said thoughtfully, shaking her head.

"How about asking the children?" Bert's voice interrupted again. "No, sir," they answered in unison.

"Andrew, when you saw those phone numbers on his phone, do you remember who it was too?" April took over as she held his hand. "Don't be afraid. I'll protect you now. You know that you can tell me, so did it say who it was to?"

"James Bond."

"James Bond. Did it say his name was, James Bond?" April asked. "No, don't be silly. It was his number," Pamela joined in.

"What do you mean his number?" April was now becoming very confused, yet intrigued.

"That's all I can remember, the number started with 007," Andrew explained. "Then there were more numbers. But I can't remember any more of them."

"That's ok darlings, you've done very well. It will be a great help to me," she assured him. Returning to Charles and Bert, she told them, "I don't think he'll remember much more than that."

"What network begins with, 007?" Charles, asked Bert.

April reminded him, "It's not a network, and it's a country. Russian numbers begin with 007 remember,"

"Of course, that is right April. They're probably headed for somewhere inside Russia," Bert speculated. "I'll just check how far their plane would take them if their tanks were full of fuel."

Turning to Charles, April asked, "Are there any of our operatives anyway near that area?"

"Yes, April. There are also two working alongside of us, a French and American operative. They're trying to foil an assassination attempt on President Blodinski."

"And where are they now?"

"Minsk, in Belorussia, and the other two were in Latvia the last I heard of them. Why do you ask, April?"

"I think I know where they're heading," Bert's voice interrupted. "Kaliningrad. There's to be a large anti-government rally held there on Sunday. It's my guess that's where they're heading for. To disrupt it, and stir up a riot."

"Where is Kaliningrad? And what's so important about it?" April continued to probe.

"There's a hard core of fundamentalists there that supports the old regime. They are fighting for independence so that they can return to a more oppressive type of rule," explained Charles.

She questioned, "Surely the Russian government can just move in there and crush it, Charles. After all, that's what they have done so successfully in the past."

"Yes, but they are anxious to show the world how much they've changed. That's why they've asked us to work alongside them to help to crush this threat." Charles continued, "But we aren't sure if the demonstration is just a decoy. It could easily be used just as a distraction for some other devious purpose."

"For what purpose would they need to do that, Charles?" she continued to question.

"We're not too sure about that yet, but this Glen McDougal is a very devious character. Apparently he caused a diversion by blowing up his own car, and with his closest friend still inside it. He's not a very nice person to know at all."

"He doesn't sound it." April added with a shiver. "What does he do for an encore sell his wife and kids into slavery?"

"He probably would if he were married. Just a minute, can you see that plane? Close in on it, will you Bert. They obviously know that they're being watched, and are trying to confuse us," explained Charles. "Now they've altered their course again. If they keep that heading they must land at Kaliningrad as we first predicted."

"Remind me, where is this Kaliningrad?"

"It's a small piece of headland sandwiched between Poland, Lithuania, and the Baltic Sea, April. Kaliningrad's a strategically important sea port on the Baltic," Charles explained.

"Well, as it's now Thursday, and the rally is on Sunday, that doesn't leave a lot of time, does it?" she reminded him.

Charles asked her tentatively, "Will you go? Please, April?"

"Do I have any choice?" she snapped at him. "It seems you've not only taken away my life, you've also made me into your personal puppet that allows you to pull the strings, and manipulate me to dance to your tune, or to do whatever other devious thing you so wish me to do, and whenever the urge takes you."

"No my love, don't think of me like that, I—" Charles started.

"Don't you use that 'my love' bit on me again. You know that I'm right, Charles," she snapped at him. Returning to the PC she apologized to Bert, "I'm sorry you have to witness this stifling atmosphere again. Now is there anything else, Bert?"

"It's okay. I know how you feel, April. I'll keep tabs on them, and keep you fully informed." Bert said, breaking his link with their computer.

Mandy re-entered the lounge from the bedroom. "Do you have to go away again, love?"

"I'm afraid so, pet. There's no rest for the wicked. You know, I must be a purely evil bitch the rest time that I miss," she hugged Mandy and the children.

"You're our Dad," Andrew half shouted as he clung tightly to her. It had seemed a long time since she had heard Andrew call her Dad. "You're the best dad in the whole world, even though you are now a very beautiful lady."

"Thank you, Andy," she replied tearfully. "That's the nicest thing anyone's ever said to me." Brushing a tear from her eye, April gently stepped back, telling them. "I must go and prepare now," as she closed the bedroom door behind her.

CHAPTER 16

Five minutes elapsed before April emerged from the bedroom. She was dressed in a smart trouser suit, and carrying a suitcase and vanity case.

"Has Bert got back to us yet, Charles?"

"Yes, my love. As we thought they have landed at Kaliningrad and headed straight towards the harbour area." Adding sheepishly, as his voice tailed off. "Then we lost them."

"What was that, Charles? Speak up now. Don't be so coy, you said that you lost them, AGAIN." April added sarcastically, "Well, surprise, surprise. Now that's a turn up for the books, isn't it? Or it would be if them incompetent oafs you employ ever did their jobs properly." April rasped as she put on her coat. "And how did they lose them this time. Oh I know, with lots of practice?"

"They walked into a violent demonstration of a hundred or more protesters, so we couldn't follow them any further," Charles explained. "Do you know what you'll need?"

"I rang the professor from my mobile, and he'll get everything ready. He's going to send them to me here. What about the transport for me?"

"We thought maybe a yacht, April. You'll be able to slip into the harbour at night, if need be." He paused to see if April reacted, but she just kept a bland expression. "The American and French agents will be there to meet you. Our English operatives are finishing up in Latvia. They'll then join up with you."

The doorbell rang. After a moment Maria showed a dispatch driver into the lounge. "He insists that only you can sign for this parcel, Miss April."

"Thank you, Maria." April said as she signed to take delivery of the parcel. "Now would you be kind enough to show the gentleman out, please?"

Without another word Maria dutifully did what she had asked, as April examined the parcel. She packed its contents into her luggage, and tucked a pistol into the back of her belt.

"Right, hopefully that's all my tools packed. So I'll be off now." April told them, as she hugged Mandy and the children goodbye. After gathering her luggage together she said to them, "Charles will take you to my apartment. Just make it your own. My car is in the basement car park for you also to use." Reaching Charles's car, she asked. "And where do I collect this yacht from, Charles?"

"Folkestone, we'll drive to the heliport, and then I've arranged for you to be flown on from there," he explained, as the driver turned the ignition key and fired the engine into life.

During the short trip Charles brought April up to date on what they presumed was happening. He also promised to download to her mobile phone, any more information that came to light.

Transferring to the helicopter, they took the short flight and landed at the quayside.

April heard a familiar voice calling, "Nice to see that you've recovered so well, April. How are you?"

Spinning round, April yelled excitedly. "James!" Throwing her arms round him, she asked. "What the hell are you doing here?"

"I volunteered for this mission as soon as I realised it was you." James explained as he hugged her. "Now, we're due to set sail in ten minutes. If you are ready we'll climb aboard?"

"Aye, aye, skipper." April mocked, saluting playfully. Adding, "I'm ready when you are mate," as she clambered aboard the yacht. "Now where do I stow my gear, skip?"

James smiled broadly at her jovial antics as he detailed a rating to escort April to her cabin. "I'll see you at dinner, April," he told her, before starting the procedure to cast off.

The weather was fair leading to a pleasant crossing. This pleased April, because she had a tendency to suffer from slight seasickness.

As April walked into the mess hall that evening, James stood up to greet her.

"A vision of beauty as always, April," he kissed her on the cheek, "This is my No1 and he'll be joining us for dinner. That's if you don't object?" James asked, gently pushing her chair closer into the table.

"Of course I don't, James. I'm very pleased to meet you, Mr. No1."

"I'm First officer Johnston Ma'am, Bill Johnston," he announced proudly in an American accent, as the steward began to serve the starter course.

"Now what have you been up to?" James asked eagerly. "Tell me everything. I want to know it all."

Explaining about the trip to the Arctic, and her fight back from the clutches of death, April continued, "Charles led me to believe that we had a future together, but I guess that he was just using me, as usual. ANYWAY, they say that you learn from your mistakes, so here I am. Now what have you been up to, James?"

They reminisced about what they had been through together. Laughing at all the funny moments they had shared. Then James explained to Bill how they'd had to cauterise April's shoulder.

"I can imagine the pain that you must have endured, April." Wilber flinched; he screwed his face up as he envisaged it. "Many a man would not have been able to endure that, let alone a slender lady, as we well know. Don't we, James?"

James nodded his agreement, and then his face became serious. He asked, "What are you going to Kaliningrad for. Nothing too serious or dangerous, I hope?"

"No," April, not being sure whether she was able to fully trust Johnson, reassured James, "No, I just need to retrieve some papers. Now, how did you come to be on this boat?"

"Boat, Madam." James interrupted with playful indignation. "You mean this ship, Madam. Boats have oars I'll have you know."

She giggled at this explanation, "I haven't heard that saying for years. It was my late father's favourite reply."

Bill tried to join in, "Was he an ex-naval man?"

"Yes, he was ex-merchant navy. Anyway, can we please change the subject now?" insisted April, dabbing a tear from her eyes as she fondly remembered her beloved father with affection. Changing the subject, April told James, "I visited a prominent Harley Street surgeon about a reversal, James."

"That would be a pure criminal waste, let alone downright sinful." James remarked, eyeing her up and down appreciatively.

"Reversal for what?" a bemused Bill asked.

James and April broke into a fit of laughter. She assured him, "You're wiser not asking that question, Bill. Believe me; you simply wouldn't believe the answer looking at me as I am now."

"That's right, No1, you just simply would not believe it," echoed James. "I heard rumours that a Harley Street physician was instrumental in your operation, April. I hope it wasn't the same person."

"It probably was. I stupidly took the number from Charles' phone file. Anyway, it seems that all may not be lost though." Then after a few moments thought, she added, "When I get back I think maybe I should get a second opinion."

They completed lunch among the chatter. Then April asked James, "When do we arrive at Kaliningrad?"

"I thought we'd time our arrival for dusk, April. So that you can gain an extra advantage for whatever you are up too."

"A good idea, so I ought to be able to get some shuteye, then."

She was awakened by a fever of activity and noise. Emerging onto the deck to witnessed James and Bill being held at gunpoint.

"WHAT'S GOING ON HERE?" April yelled at the large middle-aged officer.

"Ah, you must be, Ms. Darling," he said courteously. "I was just asking for you but they refused to co-operate with me. Now I am sorry but you can put your hands down now that we've found this very beautiful lady. I'm, Captain Boris Lewinsky, of the Red Guard." he announced proudly as he clicked his heels together. "I'm here to offer you my assistance and protection while you're in my country."

"On whose authority, may I ask?" interrupted James.

"You must remember that you're in my country now. Anyway, call your superiors if you want verification," suggested Boris.

April proceeded to ring Charles. When he answered she told him of Boris's intervention.

"Where are you now?" he asked.

"About two miles off shore, I think. There's a pilot boat that's brought Captain Lewinsky out, and it's leading us into the harbour as we speak."

"Russia has offered us the assistance of Boris. They have made it quite clear that we have no choice in the matter, well not if we are to expect full co-operation from them in return. Is it okay with you?"

"I suppose it is, Charles. He could prove to be quite useful. He's so big."

"What do you mean, April? How big is he?"

"Well, let's put it this way, he would make that nurse of yours odd job look like a midget." She explained before hanging up.

"Right, Boris. You're in. But you take your orders from me. Is that quite clear?" she insisted.

Boris readily and meekly agreed. "If that's what the lovely lady wants, then it will be my honour to serve under her." Boris confirmed.

April just gave a wry smile.

Watching silently from the bridge, the ship drew ever closer to the impressive sea wall that sheltered the bay. The yacht then followed the pilot boat into the harbour.

Boris was proudly telling April, "That city we are passing is Baljijsk. It's a very beautiful and historic city with fine imposing architecture. Now we are entering into the bay leading to Kaliningrad. It is another very beautiful old city," Boris continued proudly.

"Okay Boris, I get the picture. I won't have much time for sightseeing while I'm here." she told him, showing signs of exasperation.

"Then you must come back to see our beautiful country. Yes no?" Boris persisted.

"Yes, okay I will, when I have a lot more time to enjoy it properly." Changing the subject, she turned to James, "It was a very pleasant crossing, James. How long are you allowed to stay here for?"

"We have a twenty-four hour pass for shore leave. After that I'm afraid we have to return to old Blighty." He said as he watched the coxswain guiding the ship into its designated mooring position. "Weigh anchor, No1." James instructed, as he informed April that she'd be ferried ashore by the motor launch. "Can we meet up later for dinner before we go, April?"

"That would be very nice, James. Will about 1900 hrs do? Where shall we all eat, Boris?"

"I'll see you on the quayside at 1900 hrs and take you there personally," Boris concluded. He then boarded the launch accompanied by Bill, as the launch travelled over to the dockside.

Boris and April disembarked, followed closely by No 1. "Where do you think you're going?" April asked with surprise. "Return to your ship, No1. Inform Lieutenant Edwards I'll join him later, for dinner."

"I will accompany you to ensure your safety, Madam," Bill explained as the launch sped back towards the ship.

Beginning to feel uneasy about it all, April gathered up her belongings. "Come this way. I have arranged transport for you." Boris led them towards an official black limousine.

"When did you arrange it? I never saw you making any calls." April said nervously. "Bill, perhaps it will be best if you do follow us after all?" suggested April, as they reaching the car. Boris held the door open for her as she tentatively climbed inside it followed by Boris and No1.

"I'll travel with you Miss Darling in the same car. If you don't mind that is? Well, it doesn't really matter if you do mind." No1 insisted, as his tone of voice became sinister. Boris spoke to him in Russian and, to April's dismay, Bill answered him fluently in the same mother tongue.

"What's going on here?" April demanded firmly, pretending that she couldn't understand them. "And where are we going?" But the question was ignored as they continued to speak casually in their native tongue.

Finally Bill, who was sitting on the opposite side of April to Boris, spoke. "Speak, when you are spoken to, you English bitch."

A surprised Boris told him sharply. "That's no way to talk to a lady."

The car drew silently to a halt as the chauffeur leaned over the seat and produced a gun. He pointed it threateningly towards Boris, who cautiously raised his hands. "What's happening here?" he demanded nervously.

"Now it's your turn to shut up." No1 gloated, as he opened the car door. "So out you get, Boris," he insisted, nodding towards the chauffeur.

Boris carefully stepped out of Bill's side of the car. As he passed Bill he made a lunge towards him, but he mustered all of his strength to propel Boris through the open door, as the chauffeur fired two shots and Boris collapsed into a lifeless heap.

April grabbed at the door handle frantically trying to escape, but was foiled when the door wouldn't open.

"Do you think we're that stupid, Miss. The child locks are activated." the chauffeur said smugly as the car sped off.

April was now becoming more and more fearful for her safety. "Where are we headed, Bill?" she asked, as she searched desperately for a means of escaping. But he ignored her as the car began to wind up the mountain road, and out of Kaliningrad. Thinking logically, April realised that the door beyond him had no child lock applied. 'I must find a way to reach that door,' she told herself, as the driver skilfully negotiated the hazardous mountain bends at speed. She also knew that she should stay vigilant for any opportunity that arose, so she could make her escape quickly. Sitting back, she patiently waited for an opportune moment to manifest itself.

Bill was becoming complacent by April's apparent inability to escape. He was of the impression that she was only a mere slender and defenceless lady, as he chatted relentlessly with the chauffeur, and was not paying attention to April. She noticed that there was no verge on his side of the road now, only a sheer drop. As they climbed higher up the mountain road, she knew that now was the time for her to make her move.

Fidgeting as if uncomfortable, eventually she ended up sitting diagonally with her back resting against her side of the car. Suddenly, as the car sped around a tight bend he was forced to grab at the door armrest so he could steady himself. April realised that it had to be now or never. Throwing all of her weight against him she smashed his face against the window, causing him to drop his gun.

He lent forwards clutching at his heavily bleeding face. "YOU BITCH!" He yelled.

April reached past him and pulled at the door handle and, as she'd anticipated, the door swung open. The chauffeur struggled without success to help No1.

"Goodbye to bad rubbish," shouted April. She placed both of her feet into the small of his back and pushed him out. "Aaaarggghhhh." April heard, as his body went through the door and hurtling over the edge of the cliff to meet his most certain demise.

She was trying to escape herself as the car rocked when it swung into a right hand bend, causing the door to swing shut. There was a loud click when the chauffeur activated the child lock. At the same time a transparent bullet proofed screen closed between them, cocooning April into the rear of the car. "That should restrain you," the driver's voice said. Then he switched off the car's tannoy.

April now was truly alone and trapped, retrieving Wilber's gun April concealing it in her belt before relaxing back into the plush seat. Watching, as the mountain road became a highway. Then the car sped on towards the town sign-posted Baljijsk. A misty dawn was breaking, when the limousine drew into the harbour area and drove along the sea wall. Eventually, the driver brought the car to a halt as he peered out into the morning mist, which had now descended over the harbour, giving it a very sinister appearance.

April's knocking on the glass screen was ignored, much to her annoyance. Thirty minutes passed before the chauffeur's voice spoke over the speakers again.

"It looks as though your lift's just arrived, madam."

"What lift?" April asked, as the screen opened slightly. "You'll soon see."

April tried to activate her phone but without success. She still couldn't get a signal. 'I hope they can trace me if I leave the batteries in.' April thought to herself, as she watched a dinghy coming up to the harbour steps. Four heavily armed men ascended the steps, and spoke briefly to the driver.

"COME!" one of them demanded. As she stepped from the car he prodded her in the small of her back with his rifle. He ordered, "You go first into that dinghy," prodding her with the rifle again.

Growing afraid, but also very angry, April warned. "Prod me again you bastard and I'll cure your constipation by shoving that gun right up your jacksey, and then I'll pull the trigger."

He prodded her defiantly again as he smirked. Within a split second she'd turned to face him, and grabbed his rifle in both hands. Then falling onto her back she threw him head-long toward the remaining men, while they stood looking on aghast and riveted to the spot, as their Captain was hurled headlong into them.

The force carried the Captain off the edge of the pier, and into the water. He struck the stone steps as he fell down into the icy cold depths below. The three remaining men quickly regained their composure. Then three simultaneous loud clicks could be heard as the bullets where brought into the breach positions.

"Okay. But I did warn him," she conceded, raising her hands in surrender.

They hadn't noticed that during the scuffle April had moved round, placing them between the jetty and herself. Two of the men peered down into the water searching for any sign of life, leaving only one man to watch over her.

She noticed that in their enthusiasm to locate their Captain's body, they had become very closely gathered together. 'If I can distract them for a moment, I'm sure I'll be able to take them out.' she thought to herself, as they continued their searching. April was staring at the guard then moving her eyes to his left looked over his shoulder, she then returned her stare towards him. Keeping repeating this eventually the guard became curious.

"What the fucking hell are you looking at?" he asked, turning to look for himself.

This was the chance she had been waiting for. Springing towards them, April jumped high in the air. She curled her legs closely against her body and unleashed a forceful two-footed drop-kick, sending two of the men crashing from the quayside. Landing gracefully and spinning, she kicked the shocked remaining man across the jaw, sending him sprawling onto the floor. Then April rolled the unconscious man's body over the edge, and sent him crashing down the stony jetty steps too.

Turning towards the limousine for a means of escaping, she saw the chauffeur dashing away as she approached his vehicle. Stopping, April suddenly realised the possibility that the limo could have been booby-trapped. She tentatively released the bonnet catch and ran her fingers round it, searching for any trip wires. Reassuring herself that it was safe to do so, she raised the hood to reveal an explosive device taped to the exhaust manifold, and ticking.

Yelling, "SHIT!" As she saw that the clock only had four minutes left to run. Returning to the cab, after checking that the devise had not been wired to the ignition, quickly she removed her belongings then started the car. She jockeyed the car into position, and while standing beside it reached in and shifted the automatic lever into drive. The car quickly picked up speed as it approached the dockside.

The bloodied head of a recovering sailor appeared above the sea wall. But the car was upon him before he could avoid it. He screamed as the car carried him over the edge once again, exploding as it plunged into the cold and foreboding water. Walking to the steps, April peered down at the scene of devastation below. She could see the remains of an inflatable dinghy sinking slowly beneath the waves, carrying with it the mutilated body of one of the men, deep into the watery depths of the bay. Seeing that there was no sign of life, April shuddered as the realisation of it being a very cold and murky morning, suddenly struck home.

Now her mobile had a signal and she was able to use the phone, so she rang Charles.

"I've been waiting for you to ring. We've been tracking your signal. Are you okay, April?"

"Yes," She answered tearfully as she began to cry uncontrollably. "I felt so scared and alone, Charles." April eventually blubbered.

Charles was overcome with concern; he had never observed any sign of fear in April before. "Are you alright? I'll send some help out to you immediately, April. Haven't the agents managed to contact you, yet?"

"No, but I will be okay now. It was just the feeling I had of being trapped, alone, and helpless." Suddenly they were interrupted by police sirens, as police cars screeched to a halt. "I'll have to call you back, Charles. The police have just arrived," she said as she turned off her phone.

A thickset man strolled towards her. "What happened here, and are you alright, Miss?"

"Yes, thank you. But I don't know who they were. They just abducted me and brought me out here; it must have been a case of mistaken identity."

"I know who you are, Miss, and why you're here. Is there anything I can do to assist you?" the policeman offered.

Bursts of gunfire pierced the mist from three rubber dinghies that were coming fast up to the Jetty.

The police fell like nine pins as they desperately reach for their own weapons. April dived for cover behind a dockside warehouse, as the police cars exploded under the relentless gunfire.

The dinghies moored up against the pier. Armed men jumped from the dinghies mounting the steps, while gunning down the remaining police officers.

The firing had now stopped as the men hurried towards where April was taking refuge, executing any survivors as they passed between them.

Holding her breath, April prepared herself to be executed along with the policemen. She had her pistol at the ready, prepared to take as many of the men with her as she possible could. But suddenly the steel butt of a pistol pressed hard against the nape of her neck.

"Don't move a muscle," a gruff voice ordered. "I have her here," he called to the other men. April felt a sharp pain in her arm as her knees became weak as they buckled. Darkness crept over her, as she crumpled to the floor unconscious.

Her eyes were heavy and still closed when she became aware of the presence of the throbbing of engines. Her head slowly cleared as she opened her eyes to the realisation that she was in a cabin, aboard a ship, but it was a cabin without portholes. Hearing the sound of water she decided that the cabin must be below the water line, and that would be the reason that there wasn't any portholes. Her head ached violently as she came to her feet and tried to open the cabin door. It was to no avail she found it firmly locked. She was trapped so she returned to the bunk and sat on the edge of it, waiting patiently for somebody to come and unlock the cabin door.

Thirty minutes passed before she heard the door being unlocked. Sidling to hide behind the door ready to pounce on who entered, April stopped in her tracks when she was confronted by the imposing figure of Boris.

"Hello again, April. I must apologise for my little charade, and of course for this temporary confinement. But now that we are at sea you are free to move round. After all, there's nowhere for you to go, is there?"

"So you are with the traitor brigade after all." She remarked sarcastically. "And how do you know that I won't attempt to jump ship?"

Boris smiled enigmatically. "You can hardly jump ship from a submerged submarine. Now can you? And yes, I thought it was about time for me to earn a little extra money for my retirement. Now if you're ready, I'll give you a guided tour of the sub."

"I suppose I don't really have any other options at this very moment. I was going to ask you for something for my headache, but all of a sudden it seems to have disappeared. It must have gone with of the shock of seeing you. I do warn you, you will eventually pay for this."

Boris gave a smug smile as he offered her his arm. April ignored the gesture as she swept past him.

"Right, now where do we start?" she asked him anxiously, wanting to familiarise herself with the plans of the submarine.

"We'll start his way. You know you shouldn't be so hostile, April. You and I would make a very formidable team," he told her as he led the way round the sub, explaining its various functions. "And this is the galley where we eat. Come to think of it, you must be famished, Miss Darling." Boris then instructed the chef to prepare her a snack.

"Thank you. I am feeling hungry. Now do I have the freedom to roam the ship, or am I still confined to my quarters, Boris?"

"Of course you can. There's little damage you can do down here that won't harm you as well as the sub."

"Okay. I'll roam round the sub just for the exercise. Is it alright if I go on deck for some fresh air?" April joked, as Boris sat opposite her. "What side are you on anyway, Boris?" she asked candidly.

"My side of course, I'm considering myself this time, I've put enough time into serving my country. But don't misunderstand me I still love my country very much. But now I have to think of the fact that I'm getting no younger, and what do I have to show for it all?"

"I'm sorry, but you won't get my vote on that one, Boris. AND, I'll do all within my powers to stop you doing whatever, or with whomever, you are involved with."

"Well that's your prerogative, April. However, right here and now you're totally helpless. So enjoy your snack, I'll see you in the control room after you've eaten," Boris finished, leaving her to her meal.

Alone, April had the time to gather her thoughts. Why had Charles not been alert to what was happening? More importantly at this very moment, where are they heading for? These were her biggest unanswered questions.

The steward interrupted April's thoughts, "Your soup, Miss Darling," he announced as he served the starter. Then he looked nervously round to check that they were alone. He whispered, "May we talk please, Miss?"

"Yes, fetch your coffee over here and sit down. You can keep me company while I eat."

Again he frantically looked round him. "My name is Jeff. I'm the chief steward, Jeffrey Charmers. I work for the KGB, and I've been following Boris Blodinski for months now. We know that he's a traitor, but not for whom he's working. So I have infiltrated this little group to follow him to whoever he's working for." He stopped to mop his perspiring brow. "Can we work together and share information?"

She was now feeling glad that there was at least one friendly face aboard. "Yes we can, Jeff. I'll be very glad of some help. Tell me, what do you already know? More importantly, tell me where the hell you think we are going?"

"I don't know a lot, but apparently we are heading out into the Atlantic to rendezvous with another sub. But who and why I still need to find out. However, I think it has something to do with a drug baron."

"Thanks for the meal, and the company." April cut him short in a loud voice, warning Jeff to change the subject.

Before he could speak a voice behind him told April. "You're presence is requested in the control room, Miss. I've been detailed to escort you there."

Jeff started busying himself clearing away the dishes, as the man escorted April towards the control room.

"Ah, there you are. Did you enjoy your meal, April?"

"Yes Boris, but that's not why you've sent for me, IS IT?"

"Lighten up as you say in your country. I've been given very strict orders to keep you alive until our rendezvous. The boss seems very anxious to make your acquaintance, personally."

They were interrupted by a familiar voice. It threatened, "Then he just wants to fuck you, and use you as his sex toy." as April spun round.

"Robert Montgomery, and Victor Henderson, a pair of murderous bastards together, I'll kill the both of you now," April told them, as a burly officer restrained her.

"Because I was fucking your precious Mandy," Victor taunted, "She was just good shag, but that was all she was to me. She's just a common slut really," he continued to goad.

April saw red as she broke free from the grip of the burly officer, and made a grab for Henderson's throat. While holding him in a vice like grip, he struggled to breathe. She grabbed for a pencil off the chart table, and forced the point between his ribs piecing his heart.

His lifeless body crumbled to the floor before a startled Boris could speak. April then moved for Montgomery, stopping suddenly as she heard the clicking of a gun.

"Hold it right there, Madam." Boris warned firmly. April slowly raised her arms. "My, my, you are a wild cat, aren't you? It seems the rumours about you don't even begin to do you justice. Now, Robert. I would suggest that you go to your cabin and keep out of the little lady's way." Boris insisted, as two sailors carried Victor's body from the control room.

Beating a hasty retreat, Robert scuttled away under April's relentless glare. Only after he had gone did Boris order his men to release her.

"Now lady, do I need to confine you to your cabin too?"

"If you mean will I leave Montgomery alone? I'll kill the bastard the first moment I get." April threatened through clenched teeth.

Boris gave orders for an armed guard to protect Robert. "Thank God we only have another three days to keep you apart from him," commented Boris, with a deep sigh.

"Why thank God. Obviously you don't believe in him," retorted April sarcastically.

"I used to, my dear. I used to. Perhaps deep down inside I still do," Boris reflected.

"Well, if I'm wrong about that I'm sorry," she said earnestly starting towards her cabin, followed at a safe distance by an armed guard. April told them, "I know the way sailor. Don't be so nervous, you haven't upset me, YET."

"It's just a precaution to ensure that you get there." Boris explained. "We wouldn't want you doing a detour on the way. Now would we?"

Ignoring his comments April stepped through the doorway and headed straight towards her cabin. Lying on the bunk amid the deathly silence, except for the rhythmic throbbing of the engines giving some semblance of life, April, began to sob uncontrollably. Despite her outward appearance, inwardly she was petrified of travelling by submarine.

She must have cried herself to sleep because a knock on the cabin door awakened her.

Hastily composing herself, April called, "Come in."

As the door swung open Jeff entered bearing a tray. "Your lunch, Madam," he closed the door behind him, "You've been crying. What's wrong?" he asked with concern.

"I've always had a fear of these things, and this one seems to be leaking water at every seam, Jeff."

"Don't worry, April. I know this is an old tub but it is perfectly safe. Whoever Boris Lewinsky is working for has retrieved and restored it at great personal expense."

"But why has he? Wouldn't it be easier in this day and age to just get on a plane?" April asked, while eating her lunch.

"It seems it's all to do with some drug baron. A comrade infiltrated the De-Mundo organisation before he was brutally tortured and killed. That's why I volunteered for this assignment, so I can avenge my friend's death."

April interrupted, "De-Mundo. Do you mean, Carlos De-Mundo?"

"Yes. Do you know of him, April?"

"I know of him all right, Jeff. There was a task force dispatched to destroy him."

"Yes, well it seems he was warned about it in advance so he went underground. Anyway, he's back with a vengeance and threatening to infect food, medicines, reservoirs, and everything that he can think of, with his cocaine shit. Just so he can turn us all into dependant junkies."

"I suppose that's where I will come in to it, Jeff."

"Yes. Well, being a woman you should be able to get closer to him than anyone else." Jeff looked into April's expressionless face. "That thought doesn't seem to faze you at all?"

"No. Somehow I could see what was coming. So I'm supposed to do what the combined British and American Elite Forces failed to do, am I? I don't think so. If they couldn't get to him, what makes them think that I can?" April demanded.

"After all that I have heard about you? You are an extremely resourceful woman, and if I may be so bold, stunning with it." He waited for her reaction again before continuing. But she still remained emotionless. "Anyway, the drug enforcement agencies are getting too good, so I believe he's now transporting his shit via submarines."

"How many of these subs has he got?" she asked, as she became more interested by it all.

"Nobody knows exactly. Two or three would be my guess. Anyway, I must go before I'm missed. I'll fetch you your lunch at eight bells. Sorry, I mean dinnertime to you. You're free to move around because the guard has gone now. Just keep away from Montgomery for the time being, will you, so that you can remain fully focused on the task in hand?"

As she needed a few moments to herself, she locked the door to avoid any interruptions. She leant against the door for a few moments, drawing a few sharp breaths to help steel her nerves. She made her way to the en-suite to wash away the feelings of despair, only emerging when some of the weight of it had been removed from her shoulders. April was about to take a stroll round the sub when there was a knock on the cabin door. Opening it, April was handed a note by a young rating inviting her to dine with the Captain.

"Tell Boris I'll be there at eight o'clock sharp," she replied to the young rating as he scuttled away nervously. Making her way towards the galley, April found Jeff was not alone; Robert Montgomery was sitting at a table eating his meal. He looked up in shock as April entered the galley.

"Don't worry, Mr. Montgomery. I'll let you enjoy your last meal; you'll keep for the time being. After all, a condemned man is allowed a last meal isn't he?" remarked April ominously, as she walked passed him. She requested a cup of coffee from the steward.

She sipped her hot coffee slowly, all the while staring fixedly at Montgomery. Feeling uncomfortable with this undue attention, he pushed himself away and from the table and hastily returned to the safety of his own quarters. April ate the remainder of her lunch, watching as Jeff began clearing nearby tables.

As he cleared the tables nearby Jeff chatted idly to, April. While he was cleaning the adjacent table he whispered, "I'm to be transferred to another sub."

"Why? And more importantly when?"

"Tomorrow, that's when they'll be transferring you, April."

"Have you any idea when and how?"

"Twenty two hundred hours tomorrow, I believe."

April was going into deep thought as the sub started to vibrate. "What the hell's happening?" Her knuckles were white as she gripped the table tightly.

Jeff began to laugh. "It's alright. It's only the captain blowing the bilge tanks."

"And what the hell are they?" she continued nervously.

"The bilge tanks are what keep us submerged, April, and it gives us our trim and stability. It seems we are about to surface."

"Listen, I haven't very much time. Can you make me a bomb to explode in the galley here, Jeff?"

"Well yes. I can put something in the microwave to explode, but why?" he asked, becoming nervously curious.

"I want you out of it when the time comes, can you just tell me how I can set it off?"

"Well, if you think that's best I'll leave it in that top cupboard in a red bowl for you. Just put it in the microwave on three minutes, and then run like fuck," he urged. "It'll crack open that seam across the bulkhead effectively breaking the old tub in two halves. Of course, the doors will all automatically seal off the galley so it can still limp home."

"Can it now. Well Jeff, how many of the crew are worth saving, do you think?"

Jeff confirmed, "None that I know of. They're all just mercenaries, so they're only in it for the money. They would even shop their own mothers for a couple of roubles."

"Well then. Now where can I find some really fast-setting glue?"

"There are two tubes of it in the top drawer. I use it to repair all sorts of things, sticks like shit to a blanket. Why, what do you want it for April?"

Boris entered the room to interrupt them. "There you are, April. I see that you are looking after Miss Darling, Mr. Charmers. That's very commendable of you. Mr. De-Mundo wants her delivered to him unscathed. Now, if you please Miss Darling-."

"Ms., not Miss, Mr. Lewinsky," April corrected him.

"Ms. Darling, and its Captain Lewinsky to you on board this boat," Boris corrected her. "Now I'm afraid I must confine you to your quarters for a short while."

April asked indignantly. "Why? What am I supposed to have done now?"

"Besides murdering Henderson, you mean, and threatening to kill Montgomery of course? Not very much. Now we're about to surface for a short while, that's all."

"So why do I have to stay in my cabin? Can't I get a breath of fresh air too? Anyway, where are we now?"

He thought for a short time. "Only with an armed escorting, you can. That's if you must visit the bridge. We need to surface for a short while to bury Henderson, and to recharge our batteries. Of course we need to take on some fresh air as well. Be careful though, the sea is very rough and we are two hundred miles south-west of Ireland, if any of that means anything to you. Now are there any more stupid questions?" He asked her impatiently, as a call requesting that he returned to the control room was announced over the tannoy. "Stay down here and I'll send somebody to get you." he ordered as he left for the control room.

Alone again she turned her attention back to Jeff, the galley steward.

"I think he fancies you," Jeff said with a smile. "You smile at him and he lets you get away with blue bloody murder, and I mean that literally."

"Well I don't fancy him. Now, can we get on with planning what we're going to do? You say that there's nobody worth saving, so let's set out a plan of action to scuttle this old tub, and put it to bed permanently. If you can just leave the explosive handy for me, I now have the glue so I'll do the rest."

"Are you sure you wouldn't rather me do whatever for you?"

"No. It is better if you keep well out of it from now on. I'll see you later, Jeff." April left and returned to her cabin to dress in warmer clothing.

After the submarine had surfaced April was allowed to go aloft briefly, but decided to return to the relative safety of her cabin because of the adverse weather conditions. Eventually, with the batteries charged and Henderson buried, April could feel the sub steady as it descended below the tempestuous waves. She spent the remainder of the day alone in her cabin with the exception of visits to serve her with her meals, and of course, Boris, who used every opportunity to check on April's well-being.

The time grew ominously nearer to the time of their rendezvous, as April was now feeling fearful as the time approached when she was to be transferred to another sub.

She visited Boris in the control room to ask, "What time are we due to surface?"

"Who said we are going to surface, April?"

"I thought you said we were rendezvousing with another vessel?" she explained, looking very perplexed.

"We are. But I didn't tell you that so I don't know how you found out. Anyway, we will be, but from down here," Boris started. "Thanks to Mr. De-Mundo's influence and money, he has developed a unique way of transferring people and goods underwater. Away from those prying eyes of the do good Samaritans, the customs and excise offices, etc."

"What do you mean, aren't you going to take anything on board?" April continued to pry.

A wry smile covered Boris's face. "What do you think we're here for, a picnic?" Boris snapped. "Don't worry about us; you'll be occupied in Mr. De-Mundo's private quarters, and in more ways than one." he sniggered as his face grew harder. "I should get well rewarded for delivering you safely to him. Now go and get your stuff together. We'll be there in about thirty minutes."

April now knew why Boris hadn't tried making a pass at her. 'Gosh, was I that predictable when I was a bloke.' she thought to herself, as she gathered her belongings together quickly.

Removing an empty drawer, April punched out its plywood bottom. Then she snapped it into half inch wide slivers, an inches long. She then placed them with the tubes of glue into her handbag, and very carefully opened her cabin door to check the gangway was clear.

She thought to herself as she sidled out, heading in the direction of the stern of the sub. "Good, there's nobody about. They're all occupied elsewhere." As April passed through each bulkhead door she glued a sliver on the lock receiver, so that it wouldn't be able to seal shut properly. Reaching the stern, April then moved towards the bow, repeating the procedure as she went. Occasionally she stopped while a seaman passed her until she eventually reached the torpedo room at the bow of the sub. Returning quickly, she went into the galley, just as Jeff was about to leave.

"What can I do to help?" he asked anxiously.

"Nothing, I've explained why to you. Now just go and tell them that I'm just finishing off a coffee, and I'll follow you post-haste."

"The bowls in that cupboard up there for you," said Jeff as he started to walk from the galley. Stopping, he added, "Oh, just leave those full plastic containers each side of the microwave will you? They'll create a huge fireball when the microwave explodes, frying anybody left alive. Then the fuel tanks should finish the job off." He continued through the open hatchway without another word.

Working feverishly, April loaded the microwave and set the timer on three minutes. Pressing the start button, she rushed towards the power isolation switch over the door and tripped it off, plunging the galley into total darkness, before quickly continued forwards towards the torpedo room, to be transferred to the other submarine.

"Ah, there you are. I was just coming to look for you." Boris started. "Now be a good little tart and board your love tub. Your belongings are already stowed aboard for you." Boris sneered as he gently guided April into the small tunnel.

She was in a steel telescopic construction that connected the two submarines together. It was a totally and revolutionary new innovation, which been designed and built by Carlos De-Mundo's boffins.

April moved tentatively, but quickly, into the tunnel. A loud clanging noise behind told her that the sub she had just left had sealed its door. Continuing through the tunnel, April was aware of the danger of the tunnel rupturing, or an underwater current ripping the subs apart, thus signalling her end.

She was also conscious that somebody could enter the galley at any time to reconnect the power supply. It would cause the old sub to explode, and that would also signal her demise. She thanked God when she reached the other sub in safety.

"Hurry, we must be on our way quickly!" April heard a husky voice urging, as the hatch clunked to a close behind her. A sailor signalled the sister sub that they were ready, and a whirling of electric motors could be heard as the tunnel was retracted.

"Right, let us be on our way." The husky voice commanded, as April turned to face the tall, handsome Colombian. "I'm sorry my dear, let me introduce myself." He started as the submarine rocked violently. "What the fucking hell was that?" He demanded.

"It seems that the other submarine has suddenly exploded, sir," a rating informed him.

"Can we pick up any survivors?"

"I'm afraid not at this depth, Sir. It seems all hands will be lost." The lad explained, as he looked towards April, who was smiling smugly.

Following the boy's stare, the handsome gentleman asked. "And what do you know about all this, Miss?"

"Me. I was here with you, wasn't I?" April told him with mock innocence.

"Will you escort Ms. Darling to her quarters and confine her there. Your belongings have already been stowed, so make yourself at home while I decide what I'm going to do with you. It seems that what I've been told about you doesn't even start to do you justice. You're an extremely attractive vixen. But I'll tame you can mark my words Miss Darling, I WILL TAME YOU. Now take her away." he ordered the rating.

"Aye, Aye, Mr. De-Mundo, sir." the young lad answered respectfully.

"So that's the infamous Carlos De-Mundo?" she asked the rating as she was escorted to her quarters. "I'm not impressed. Anyway, I see that this is a very different type of sub to the other old tub I was on. You know the one that just vamoosed." April continued to chatter nervously.

The escorting rating looked at April with disdain. "This is a nuclear submarine, Madam. Mr. De-Mundo has had it built secretly at his own personnel expense. It's unique in many of its features, as you have already experienced. Now this is your cabin, 'STAY IN THERE UNTIL SOMEBODY SENDS FOR YOU!'" he shouted, as he slammed the door closed.

CHAPTER 17

April heard the sailor sliding the door lock firmly into place. She looked at the time, 'Twenty-one thirty, there's no realisation of time down here, she thought, as she slowly and purposely looked around the cabin. It gave the appearance of a stateroom with its en-suite shower, king-sized bed and plush furnishings.

Gradually the realisation that this must be Carlos's private room dawned on her. "SHIT!" she shouted. Realising all too clearly why she had been incarcerated inside this particular cabin. Frantically fumbling for a way to secure the door, April then realised that it would only be a futile gesture that she could never win. Carlos would only force her to relent, in exchange for her food.

"SHIT AND DOUBLE SHIT!" April shouted again. Again she was reduced to tears by the fear that gripped her. Feeling helpless, vulnerable, alone, and isolated. April wept bitterly. Once again she tried her phone but without success. "No phone or help. I don't even know if Jeff Charmers is alive or dead," April muttered to herself. "It seems that I've no choice open to me other than to play ball with this Carlos De-Mundo character. Or at least for the time being until I find out what his intentions are. After all, I'll be of no use to anybody dead," April convinced herself. She sat back on the bunk reapplying her makeup, to cover up the blotching she'd got from crying. April's thoughts were interrupted by a quiet tapping on the door.

Composing herself April shouted, "Come in. The door isn't locked."

The young rating had returned bearing a silver platter. "Your supper, Ma'am," he said as he placed it beside her on the bed. "Is there anything else I can get for you?" he respectfully asked. "Mr. De-Mundo has assigned me to be your personnel steward. My name is John, but everyone round here calls me Ben," he continued chattering as he poured a mug of coffee.

"How do people get from John to Ben?" April questioned.

"Because I've got a pinched face Miss, they say that I look like a rat. If I can help you with anything in any way, you only need to ask me."

"Thank you, John. It's so nice for somebody to be civil to me for once. Do you know how long I must stay cooped up in this cabin?"

"Just try to be a little patient until Mr. De-Mundo sends for you, Miss. Then he will explain where you can and can't go," the boy told her. As he started to leave he hesitated, then he finally said to April, "Mr. Charmers said he will come to see you as soon as he has the time."

"You know Jeff. I mean, Mr. Charmers?"

"Yes Ma'am, He-,"

She interrupted, "Call me April. You can keep Ma'am for the Queen, or somebody older. Unless you think I look old, that is?"

"Oh no, Ma'am, I mean, Miss April. You're a very beautiful woman. You're pretty enough to be the queen. Anyway, Jeffrey Charmers is my boss. I suggested that Mr. De-Mundo transfer him here when the other chief steward died."

"Oh, I am sorry to hear that. What did he die of?"

Again the boy hesitated. Then acting on the information that Jeff had given him, he decided he could trust April. "Asphyxia, Ma'am, I mean Miss April. Somebody suffocated him."

Staring at the boy for a long time, April saw the fear that was in his eyes as he waited uneasily for her to respond. Finally, April remarked, "Well that was fortuitous for us then, wasn't it? Don't worry about me. Anything you say stays with me, and only with me."

Suddenly the door opened and Carlos De-Mundo stepped inside. "Haven't you ever heard of knocking?" April snapped abruptly.

"This is my boat." Carlos explained in his thick Spanish accent. She shouted back at him, "And this is my cabin."

"Our cabin," Carlos corrected. "Haven't you got any work to do?" He snapped at the startled young lad.

April shouted indignantly to an equally startled Carlos, "And don't you take it out on him, either. What do you mean, OUR CABIN?"

Eventually, Carlos gathered his composure. "I'm sorry, Miss Darling. Can we start over again, please? Turning to the boy he said to him politely, "I'm sorry to you too, son. Thank you for looking after Ms. Darling. Now will you please excuse us?" The young boy looked apprehensively towards April.

"You go now, and thank you. I'll be alright, so go on," she repeated, as the lad reluctantly left.

"That boy wants teaching to use some manners," Carlos muttered, forgetting momentarily about April.

"Let me make one thing crystal clear to you. He's only a young boy trying to look after me. After all, isn't that what you told him to do?"

"Yes, I suppose I did." Carlos reluctantly agreed as he sat down beside her. "Well, if you or any of your crew hurt him, I will personally make you pay for it," stressed April as the door opened again. A tall muscular Colombian entered the cabin.

"And who the fucking hell are you? You do not come in here without my say so. SAVVY?" April yelled.

"Hang on a minute. This is MY cabin as well," Carlos corrected her.

"Well then, I'd better leave. Now, where are my alternative quarters?" she started to assemble her belongings together.

Carlos started to laugh as he stood up. "You're going anywhere lady without my say so. Do I make myself clear?"

"And who is going to stop me, HIM? I don't think so." April asked calmly, pointing towards the grinning man.

"I warn you not to push him, or you will most certainly regret it."

"You will get no co-operation from me with empty threats of violence, Carlos," she told him as she started to leave the cabin.

The big man put his arm on April's shoulder to try to stop her.

She spun round to face him grasping the Colombians arm, forcing it over her shoulder then twisting it up behind him.

"I'll tell you this only once more my friend. You keep your dirty fucking hands off me," warned April, as she released her grip. Then she turned to pick up her belongings while Carlos watched silently.

He nodded consent to the man, who grabbed at April, slapping her across her face with the back of his large hand. Blood began to run profusely from her nostrils, as she reeled backwards under the sheer power of the crushing blow. April crashed hard against the steel bulkhead and slid down the wall, landing in a stunned and mangled heap.

He looked down at April grinning portentously, as he thought that he had rendered her unconscious. But to his and Carlos' surprise, April sprang up like a cat, grabbing the Colombians lapels. She twisted him across her thigh and slammed him to the floor. Grabbing him round his trachea she raised his head, as she grabbed for her stiletto with her free hand, and buried the heel in his temple, dropping the lifeless body on to the floor.

April turned towards Carlos, he was quickly moving for a drawer containing his gun. She was on her feet by now as she kicked out at the drawer trapping his hand, Carlos sank backwards onto the bed screaming with the pain.

"Okay, you win. Now calm down and let's talk about this," he pleaded. "Start talking. And you can start by telling me why I shouldn't finish you off, too?"

"I'm sorry. I seem to have made a very bad mistake with you. Can we start again, PLEASE?" Carlos continued to plead as he nursed his damaged hand.

April relented, as she looked at his pathetic face, and couldn't help feeling compassionate towards him. "Here, let me see to your hand, Carlos," she offered, gently taking his hand in hers and very carefully and tenderly examining it. She explained, "I don't think it's broken, but you might have dislocated the middle finger. I'll check it again when the swelling's subsided a little."

"Can it be strapped up till we reach land?" Carlos asked hopefully.

Looking towards the Colombian, he added, "I'll need to bury his body."

Carlos piped the Master at Arms. "Can you send a detachment for Rafael's body? It seems he has just met with a fatal accident."

"When we reach land?" probed April.

"No, we can bury him at sea so that there are no awkward questions to answer," he started. "We'll need to do it via the air lock in the torpedo room."

"What air lock? Is it for your divers?" April continued to appear interested as she bound up his hand.

"No. That air lock's aft. I mean the one that launches the mini two man sub. It's bigger to allow for his bulk. Anyway, don't you go getting any ideas; it has to be operated by at least two people."

"I was wondering why you were so willing to tell me about it. It's because I won't be able to operate it, isn't it? There, your hand is done. Now how does it feel?"

"Much better thank you," he answered, as there was a knock at the door. "Come in," he called. Four men entered carrying a large body bag. After manhandling the heavy corpse into the bag, they swiftly left. Carlos asked April, "Could you please pass me that packet; it's just to help to ease my pain."

As she passed the packet over, April told him. "You fool, Carlos, taking your own shit. Haven't you seen the devastation your death dealing's done to other people?"

"I was going to ask you if you wanted a snort, but you've just answered that question for me. Anyway, I'm not dependent on it you know."

"That's what they all say. But I warn you Carlos, IF EVER, you try to give me anything like that, in ANY shape or form, well that's the day that you'll die of an overdose," April threatened, very, very firmly.

He looked perplexed, "How do you know that?"

"I'll be the one that's pouring the rest of your shit down your fucking throat."

"Ok," he said, refraining from taking his drugs, "I get the picture. You know, I can't work you out, Miss April Darling."

She asked, as she put away the bandages, "And why's that, Mr. Carlos De-Mundo?"

"You're as hard and ruthless as any man I know. The ultimate lethal weapon I believe. And yet you can be so tender and caring like the beautiful woman that you are. The way you dealt with Rafael, compared with the tender way you examined my hand. It just doesn't make any sense," Carlos explained. "How's your nose now, by the way?"

"I'll live. Now what about these sleeping arrangements, have you come up with any better suggestions, Carlos? And just call me, April."

"I'm afraid not. There's either in here with me. Or there's in the crew's quarters with the men."

"Well Carlos, why don't I sleep in here alone, and you kip in with your men?"

"That wouldn't do much to boost morale, now would it, April? Maybe we can work something out in here?"

April knew exactly what he was working towards. After all, even a blithering idiot could deduce what he really had in mind. She looked deeply into his eyes and she could see a much gentler man than she had first expected. He was coming across to her that he could be a very kind and considerate person, but only when he wished to.

"You know if you weren't a drug baron I would be flattered by your attention. But you are, and that side of you I find extremely ugly and hideous. I'm sorry to have to say that, Carlos."

"So if it wasn't for my chosen profession you would consider my offer?" Carlos said. "Well, that's a start I suppose."

"Right Carlos, how about escorting me round your ship, or boat, or whatever you want to call it?"

"A boat and it will be my pleasure, April. Can we at least be friends for now?"

"I suppose we can, at least for now. You're not as bad as I had first been led to believe you were," she said, as she refitted her shoe after wiping the blood from the heel. "Now, let's go and inspect your little boat." April agreed, linking his arm. She realised that she had to shelve any personnel feelings for the man, and his empire, and concentrate on the task in hand.

Carlos took April's arm readily as he walked proudly round the sub. He boasted about the many extras he had had installed. Finally, they entered the torpedo room. "Now this is my ultimate defence system in here," he bragged.

April asked with burning curiosity, "In what way is that, Carlos?"

"Do you see those crates being opened over there? They're normal torpedoes we use for defending ourselves against coast guards, shipping, etc., etc. Now those in the black crates are intercontinental missiles. Each one of them can deploy thirty nuclear war heads at a time, and they can all be controlled by this single panel over here."

She questioned, "Why are you telling me all of this?"

He warned in a stern voice, "Because my dear, you are watched very carefully by me at all times. So you're powerless to interfere with any of my plans."

"But why are you showing me your vast arsenal of devastation?" she continued to press.

Carlos became even more serious. "You can see the damage I can inflict from down here, and we're virtually undetectable to most satellite tracking systems. I could, if I so wished to do so, wipe out the Northern Hemisphere as you now know it."

"Then why haven't you?"

"It is purely a case of simple economics, my dear."

She interrupted again, "Oh I get the picture. It's because they're your most lucrative markets?"

"Got it in one, But make no mistake, I'll use them if I have to. I've already sent them a warning shot. An unarmed missile landed at your Wembley Stadium I believe?"

"So that was you? What is it that you want?"

Carlos leaned against a crate. "That is simple, Miss April Darling." He paused to observe any reactions, "YOU."

Shocked and stunned, by Carlos's revelation, April was at a loss for words. Sitting on the revolving chair by the panel she looked contemptuously at Carlos. Eventually, after much thought she said to him, "And just when I was beginning to think you weren't as bad as you first seemed. Then you had to crawl out from under your slimy stone again, didn't you? Why me? You can have any tart or whore that you want, so why me?" She retorted bitterly.

"That again is very simple my dear, because it's you. You must be just about the most delectable woman on the planet, April. You're beautiful, with a stunning figure, intelligent, sexy, and physically capable of just about anything. You're beyond explanation. Words alone are insufficient to adequately describe you." He stopped again to observe any reaction.

She asked him calmly, realising her vulnerability, "And what choice do I have?"

"None, I'm afraid." Carlos told her as she started to stand.

"And if I resist?" April persisted. Carlos pointed behind her as she heard the click of a rifle. Again, April sat and held her hands up. "Okay. You win. I admit you have the upper hand at this time."

"Not convincing enough. Perhaps you need a little time on your own to consider your predicament. Take her to the brig house," Carlos instructed the two guards watching over her.

As she attempted to stand the men pulled her back into the seat again, as Carlos produced a syringe. "Hold her arm steady, will you? I'll give her something to make her sleep."

He neared April who stared intensely at the clock, trying in vain to resist the drug. '0130hrs,' she thought as he gripped her firmly.

"It seems you must learn the hard way, Miss Darling." Carlos told her as he injected the drug into her upper arm. "Give it a few moments to work," he ordered his men, as April's body became limp. "Sleep well my love. You'll soon be completely dependent on me. Just wait and you'll see." Carlos kissed her on the cheek. "Now take her down to the brig house, and take very good care of her."

April was awakened by the noise of somebody talking. Her head was pounding as she tried to sit up, but she was prevented from doing so by Carlos' hands, that were pressing down firmly against her chest. "No you don't my pretty little minx. Just you lie still," insisted Carlos, as April's head began to slowly clear.

Her eyes started to focus, as she became aware of the presence of two other men. 'They look strangely familiar,' April thought, as she slowly fixed her eyes on them. One man began to speak with a Scottish accent.

"McDougal and Montgomery, I thought I'd seen the last of you two murderous bastard traitors," April said in a weak voice.

"I'm sorry to disappoint you then. I transferred here just before you did. It was while you were setting the explosives, I presume. It was you, wasn't it? Glen here was already aboard," Robert boasted.

"Forgive me if I don't look happy to see you're both still alive," April snidely remarked as she started coughing. "Do you think I can have a drink and two painkillers, please Carlos?" she asked meekly.

"Of course you can, my dear," Carlos agreed willingly, asking the steward to fetch a drink for her. It was Jeff Charmers. At least I know that he's still alive, she thought.

Again she tried unsuccessfully to sit up. "Why must I stay lying down, Carlos?"

"Just until your temper subsides a little bit more," he told her, as Jeff returned with a cup of tea.

"Well I can't drink lying down, can I?"

"Just a moment then," Carlos told her as he bound her legs together. Insisting, "Now just sit there, and sit still." He sat opposite, aiming his pistol threateningly towards her.

She drank rapidly to quench the seemingly unquenchable thirst. "May I have another cup, please?"

Her brow was beaded with sweat, and her skin was pallid. April said in panic, "I'm terribly cold and I feel sick too." She began to balk; "Quick, I'm going to be sick."

Carlos freed April's legs quickly. "Hurry up then. Go to the toilet," he ordered, as Montgomery and McDougal shrunk back away from her.

She vomited uncontrollably. After she'd finished, she swilled her face in cold water. She thought, "That's better," as she re-entered the cabin April glanced at her watch. 'It's only seven A.M. What are they up to?' she wondered, but she didn't need to wait very long to be answered.

"Feeling better now? Back on the bed so I can watch you," Carlos insisted. April complied readily because she was feeling far too ill to resist.

"Now give me your arm, my sweet," ordered Carlos, as he produced yet another syringe.

"NO! Please Carlos?" April tried in vain to protest as she struggled to free herself. "I'll do whatever you want. But not this way, please. NO Carlos."

Carlos ignored her plea as he pumped her arm with even more of his concoction of drugs. Soon April had drifted back into an erotically dreamy state.

As soon as he had witnessed the results of his heinous act, Carlos told them all. "Right, we will let her sleep again." He shepherded McDougal and Montgomery from the cabin, but left two of his men on guard in case any emergency should arise. Again she was awakened by the presence of Carlos, "Come on my little sweetie. It's time for your medicine again."

When she attempted to raise herself up by pushing against the bunk, April felt a sharp pain in her hand. Glancing down so as not to alert Carlos, April could see the sharp point of a broken mattress spring, 'That might come in very handy,' she thought to herself. Then she hauled her tired aching body to the toilet once again to vomit.

Looking at herself in the mirror, April was appalled at the sight that looked back at her. Thick black rings encircled sunken eyes. Her pale skin was covered in beads of sweat. Her dull hair was knotted and bedraggled, and her underclothes felt damp and sticky.

She thought, 'Gosh I look and feel awful. Please God, help me through this dark and evil time. Please help me find a way out of this mess,' she prayed silently, while returning to where Carlos was waiting.

She asked, "May I change my underclothes, please?"

"I suppose so, is there any particular reason why?" Carlos asked casually. "They are in that top draw over there."

"I feel all damp and sticky. I don't know why."

No more drugs please Carlos," pleaded April as she returned from the shower room after putting on clean panties.

"It's noon, so would you like some lunch?" he asked, ignoring her request. "Just a sandwich and a cup of coffee would be very nice." April asked courteously, realising that she must keep up her strength.

Carlos sat quietly while April ate lunch, dismissing all the other people from the room. Eventually when she had finished, he called the steward to remove the tray.

"Now lie down my sweet little treasure," he insisted, still brandishing his pistol.

"No. Please Carlos, no," April tried to protest. But it was futile as Carlos again plunged the needle into her arm.

This time he was unaware that she was pressing her hand down hard onto the sharp point of the broken spring. Rolling her eyes up before closing them, April, feigned a drug induced sleep. She felt Carlos kissing her tenderly then she heard the door closing behind him.

Opening her eyes a little to confirm that the room was now empty. April decided they should remain closed in case of a surprise visit from somebody. So she used this time to talk with God in prayer. It was something that she'd neglected to do of late, because of the drugs that she'd been forced to take.

Opening her eyes slightly, April noticed that only an hour had past. And she was now starting to feel drowsier, so April pressed harder onto the spring. Feeling a searing pain as the point penetrated to a bone, and blood began to trickle onto the mattress. This made April grow fearful that her little secret might be discovered.

The door opening interrupted her thoughts. As she opened her eyes very slightly, April could see two men staring down at her seemingly unconscious frame.

"She should be in a deep enough sleep by now," April heard one of the men saying. But she had to remain motionless and pretend to be unconscious. "Let's fuck her again, nobody will ever know."

Feeling sick to her stomach, April daren't move a muscle without being discovered. 'I'll have no choice but to brace myself and endure whatever they do to me.'

First she felt her blouse being unbuttoned, followed by the unclipping of her bra to reveal her firm breasts. One of them started fondling and kissing at her nipples, while she could feel the other man sliding up her clothes.

'How I'd love to kill these bastards. But, I'll need to remain perfectly still,' she thought to herself as a hand started toying with her vagina. 'These bastards disgust me,' she was forced to endure their horrific abuse. Suddenly, April felt the weight of a body on top of her as a penis penetrated her. Her body felt numb as he pumped and pumped until he ejaculated.

"Your turn now," he told the other man as they changed places. Feeling them toying with her breasts as the other guard pushed his throbbing penis inside of her, and pumping until he had also ejaculated.

Her body now was completely numb with shock, as she was humiliated time and time again. She felt that they'd sunk as deep into depravity as they could possibly reach. But soon she was to realise how wrong she was, hearing one of them suggesting that they finished off by masturbating onto her. April knew that she still must endure it, whatever they intend to do to her. April felt their two penises brushing across her lips as she could sense them masturbating.

"I'm coming." April heard one of them shouting out excitedly. "I'm coming."

"So am I, quick open her mouth," said one of them, as April felt a penis ejaculate into her mouth, followed immediately by the other man ejaculating also into her mouth.

"That was so good. We've been so long at sea without a woman and then this heaven." One of them could be heard saying as the sound of the door suddenly opening disturbed them.

"WHAT THE FUCK ARE YOU TWO BASTARDS DOING?" she could hear the voice of Carlos shouting, as the scene of utter disgust and debauchery greeted him. Carlos saw her bare breasts and the semen that was running from the sides of her vagina, and mouth.

As he looked he saw it still dripping from their penises. He called the Master at Arms, as he covered April with a sheet.

"My poor darling, I assure you, I never meant for this to happen to you," he said with genuine concern, keeping his gun aimed towards the culprits until two armed men entered the cabin.

He ordered, as the men begged for mercy, "Take these two fucking deviants away and cut off their balls, and their pricks. They will have to piss like a woman from now on, and then see how they like it."

"They showed no compassion towards, Ms., Darling," he retorted. "Now you have your orders. Show them no mercy, or you'll be the next ones to suffer the same fate," he reaffirmed to the Master at Arms. "NOW JUST DO AS I'VE TOLD YOU."

The two men were escorted away protesting, but April had to keep up her pretence of being in a drug-induced sleep. Carlos washed her, and again she was surprised by his tenderness.

"Please forgive me for allowing this debauchery. I thought I could trust my men." Carlos apologised; thinking April was still in a very deep sleep.

Wanting to cringe when he began washing around her vagina, she knew she must still remain emotionless, needing to still keep up the pretence of being drugged. Eventually Carlos removed the remainder of her clothing to facilitate the completion of the blanket bath.

She needed to think fast as he began to wash her left arm. When he went into the bathroom for clean water, April clenched her right fist. She dug her fingernail into where it was bleeding from, so that he'd not discover her little ruse. April was just in time as Carlos returned to complete his task, eventually starting to clean her hands.

"My poor angel, you've dug your nails into your hand." He said soulfully, as he completed his task. Then he covered April with a bed sheet, and before he left the room he told her, "Sleep tight, my lovely little angel; you should awaken in the next hour or so," before closing the door behind him.

Continuing with the deception she lay motionless, although she felt the effect of the drug had long since worn off. There was no need to self-inflict pain on herself to ward off the effects the drug brought about. Thirty minutes passed before April calculated it would be safe for her to rise from her pretend slumber.

Grabbing for a robe, she took it into the shower. April stood just allowing the water run over her naked body, as she frantically scrubbed at her skin, trying to remove the filth that she'd had to endure.

Sobbing uncontrollably, April realised only too clearly that there'd be no escaping the memory of what she'd just been forced to endure. Losing control of time as she immersed herself in self-pity, until she was suddenly brought back to the reality of the here and now, when a light knocking on the cabin door interrupted her thoughts.

"I'm getting a shower," she called out.

Jeff Charmers called back inquiring as to whether she was alright?

"I'm okay now, Jeff. Would you fetch me a cup of coffee in about ten, fifteen minutes, please?" April then heard Jeff's footsteps walking away as she thought, 'I'm all alone and unprotected from such filthy degenerative acts.'

Sitting on the edge of the bunk she began to cry and shake uncontrollably. "Those bloody drugs," she muttered to herself. "I must fight them and go cold turkey, and I must suppress all outward signs so that nobody will suspect. Oh God. Please help me. Death itself would seem like a merciful escape at this present moment in time. Please give to me your strength to draw upon, so that I can see this assignment through to its bitter end. Who can I trust, O Lord? Is there anybody down here that I can trust? Is Jeff Charmers all that he says he is? Or am I truly alone except for your loving presence, Dear Father? You O, lord, are with me always. Please give to me a sign if I do have a friend aboard this submarine."

A knock at the cabin door interrupted, "Your coffee, Miss." April heard Jeff's voice calling.

Unlocking the door she let him enter. "Would you place it on the dressing table, Jeff?"

He noticed the damp and bloodstained bedding. "What's happened in here?" he gasped. He looked up into April's bedraggled face. "And you, April, if you'll forgive my saying so look like shit. What's been happening to you?"

"I'll tell you later, but not right now, Jeff." She promised, proceeding to skilfully apply her makeup. She thought to herself, "This is one advantage of being a woman; the make-up will hide a multitude of sins."

"I don't know what's happened to you but I'll pray for your safety," Jeff began, "may I make your bed up with some clean linen?"

She asked, "Do you really believe in God, Jeff, You're not just saying that?"

"Fervently April," Jeff boasted. He made a bundle of the soiled bed linen before asking. "Don't you?"

"Oh yes Jeff, I do. I was praying when you brought my coffee and that's an answer to my prayers, just knowing that I can trust you."

"I told you who I was."

"Yes, I know. But I've learnt just how fickle people are with their loyalties. I would like another hot cup of coffee when you've the time, please?" she asked, continuing to apply her makeup.

"I'll fetch it as soon as I've replaced this bedding," promised Jeff. He picked up the bundle of dirty bedclothes. To April's surprise, he whispered, "If you need to call anybody, just let me know."

"That's some remarkable transformation April," remarked Jeff. "You are back to your old radiant self."

"Why, I thank you kindly, sir," mocked April playfully. She scribbled a telephone number and a message onto a piece of paper, handing it to him furtively.

"You don't look so bad yourself, Jeff," replied April, she then lowered her voice to a whisper. "Tell Charles that I'm ok, but I could use some more help."

Jeff assured her that there was no need to whisper, so April began to talk in a normal voice. "Have you any idea where we're heading?"

"We're going to somewhere in the Caribbean. My guess would be Haiti. That's where Mr. De-Mundo transferred his operations to when the Brits and Yanks got too close. I believe he grows a lot of his dope out there now."

The door opened and Carlos De-Mundo entered, as Jeff continued to clean the cabin.

"Thank you, Mr. Charmers. I can see you have been looking after, Ms. Darling for me. Perhaps I should promote you to be her personnel steward. Now will you leave us alone, please?" he said forcibly, as Jeff reluctantly finished up and left.

Carlos asked how she was feeling, then invited April to have lunch with him. Then they walked arm in arm to the galley. As they ate,

Carlos talked about everything, except his future plans for April. But she was happy just to sit and listen to him, taking the opportunity to rest and build up her strength. Eventually, he escorted April back to the cabin.

She tried not to act surprised when he followed her into the cabin, deciding it would be wiser to succumb to his advances, allowing Carlos to seductively undress her, while kissing her on nape of her neck passionately. He continued kissing round April's neck, and down to her breasts. April responded apathetically at first, feeling sexually scared by the debauchery that she'd been forced to endure earlier. Slowly and passionately, he made love to April long into the night, until eventually falling back onto the pillow beside her. Placing his arms round her, while gently caressing her hair, he eventually ventured to ask.

"You didn't resist me, April. May I ask, why?"

"Why should I, Carlos? A woman has her needs too. You know?"

"Good," he replied. He rolled towards her gently taking April back into his arms. "I can see that we're going to get along just fine from now on." Carlos told her, as he slipped into a very contented sleep.

Unable to sleep, feeling very unsettled and perplexed, April was surprised that she felt comfort in holding Carlos as he slept. Strangely April felt safe and secure in his arms, even though she knew that he was capable of being very ruthless and extremely volatile. Also at the earliest opportunity, she knew that she must kill him.

While pondering the situation that she was trapped in, April wondered whether she'd ever escape from this alive. Carlos interrupted April's thoughts, as he began talking in his sleep. She smiled with amusement, thinking to herself, 'It could be his undoing, talking in his sleep, giving away all of his little idiosyncrasies.' Then April grew more attentive to what he was saying when she heard him mention the name of Jeffrey Charmers.

"I've found out that he's a KGB spy, so he must never reach dry land alive. See to it so that we bury him at sea, with no witnesses," Carlos ordered whoever he imagined he was talking to. She tried to hear more, but Carlos just rambled on. So April rolled Carlos onto his side to stop him talking. Now she was armed with the knowledge that she must now warn and try to save Jeffery Charmers, but how? April was thinking about it as she drifted into a deep sleep herself.

Waking earlier than Carlos, she decided to take an early shower. She was dressed only in her white silk underwear when she walked back through into the bedroom.

Carlos was awake by now as he propped himself up onto one elbow, watching appreciatively as April dressed. "Have you enjoyed the show?" she teased.

"Yes, very much so, you're a very beautiful lady you know, and with a dream of a body." Carlos complimented, as he walked into the ensuite to take a shower as well.

"I'm going on ahead to the galley. I need a coffee," she called in to him. Carlos shouted over the sound of the running water, "I'll follow you when I'm dressed."

Walking briskly to the galley, April discovered, as she'd hoped, that Jeff was serving breakfast.

"What can I get for you, Miss Darling?" Jeff asked politely, guiding her to an empty table.

"Just listen to me, I haven't got much time before Carlos arrives. He knows that you're, KGB, and he plans to have you killed. I'll delay him as much as I can, but we must get you off this sub somehow."

"But how can we do that? We're two thousand metres below the surface. If we can force them to surface, a Russian ship, which is disguised as an Albanian freighter, is only fifty miles away and heading towards us. I believe that your SBS is with them. But first we have to surface, and there's a fat chance of that happening."

"Let me think about it while you cook my breakfast. I'll have a traditional English breakfast if I may, Jeff."

While he was preparing breakfast, April was concentrating on Jeff's dilemma. For some odd reason that was unknown to her, April's thoughts kept turning back to the two-man sub in the bow section. "Lord," she said quietly. "Is that the way for Jeff to escape to safety?"

As Jeff began to serve breakfast, April asked if he'd be able to navigate the two-man submarine.

"I think so. Why? What do you have in mind?"

"Our God seems to be guiding my thoughts towards it as your only means of escape. So be prepared to go at a moment's notice." April told him, as Carlos entered the galley.

"I see that you're taking good care of my guest again. That's excellent." Carlos said to Jeff. "I will have my usual."

"Please?" April finished for Carlos.

A confused Carlos asked, "What do you mean?"

She told him. "I said please for you because you forgot to say it. Remember manners cost you nothing, as my mother used to say to me."

"Please, Mr. Charmers." Carlos reluctantly conceded. While they ate Carlos chatted idly, as he just enjoyed April's unopposed company.

"You haven't told me where we're heading, Carlos. Or is that a secret too?" probed April, as she playfully started to feed him the remainder of his breakfast. "Or are we heading for your native Colombia?"

"You'll soon see. You know, I've only known you for a short time, and you make me blissfully happy. How do you feel about me?"

"Safe and contented, Carlos, as if I've found my true soul mate," she lied, smiling broadly at Carlos.

"Good. We're going to make a formidable team, you and I. Now I've some work to do."

"Am I still confined, or can I freely roam the sub to exercise my legs?"

Carlos kissed April. "Of course you're free to do whatever pleases you. So if you want to exercise those beautiful legs of yours, you are most welcome to do so." Carlos told April as he left the galley and headed towards the control room.

After he'd left, Jeff said to April, "It takes two people to launch the mini sub, and if we're in the sub, then who'll seal the inner door?"

"I won't be coming with you. I will do it for you, Jeff."

"But if Carlos ever finds out that you helped me he'll kill you for sure, April!" Jeff reminded her on the verge of panic.

"Let me worry about that one. So just you make sure that you're ready. By the way, when does your shift end?"

"I have three hours from thirteen hundred hours when I have a siesta in my cabin. Why do you ask?"

"I'm not sure yet, but it might be a useful time for me to use," she remarked, as she left the galley heading towards the bow section. Sauntering, as though just idling away time, she was in fact purposely working her way toward the bow. April eventually reached the torpedo room, going straight to the escape hatch.

A seaman called over. "Can I help you, Madam?"

"I'm just looking. Well, being nosy really. What's this?" April asked as she pointed towards the mini sub, pretending not to know.

"It's the two-man probe, Madam. It's loaded into that chamber ready to be launched, that's if Mr. De-Mundo needs to escape here post-haste. But somebody has to seal it from in here, so you won't be able to go for a little ride in it." The man sarcastically remarked, smiling at April patronisingly. "Now if there's nothing else Miss? I have to leave now."

"No. Thank you, you have been most helpful." April assured him as she idly ambled slowly around the deck waiting for him to leave. Eventually she was alone, and able to examine the escape hatch more thoroughly.

Seeing the door could be jammed from within by inserting a steel pin into a hole that would prevent it from opening, April searched for a suitable pin. 'Ah this should do very nicely,' she thought, selecting a suitably sized drill bit, and placing it on the inside of the doorframe, "I'll not be here to release the sub so I'll need a timing devise to activate it. If I was to suspend a cord above it with a weight dangling from it like this," April searched and found a thin rope which she suspended from a beam with a heavy metal drift on the end of it. 'That should do it. Now I'll need a small remote charge to sever the cord, which is something that I'll have to make up and bring with me later. Now for those damn warheads," muttered April, as she began to examine the nuclear missiles.

"They're all from different countries, England, France, U.S.A. etc., the crafty bastard, just so that they'll blame each other for it."

Clipping off the inspection panels in turn, April was able to cut the orange coloured wires to make them all malfunction. She then replaced the last panel before heading aft-wards.

She stopped at the galley and told Jeff, "I think I've sorted it all out for you. Instead of having your siesta, go to the torpedo room after you've finish the lunch. I'll meet you there." April then continued on to the control room to join Carlos.

April wondered round casually. She asked Carlos questions incessantly, about the controls, and the variety of navigational devices.

"I'll have to go and change now. Shall we meet in the galley about noon?" April suggested to Carlos, kissing him on the lips. "We'll have to have an early night again tonight, won't we?" she whispered, trying to remove any suspicions from his mind that he might have been still holding.

He tapped her playfully on the bottom. April pretended to scream like a little schoolgirl as she ran away. "I'll see you at lunch, you naughty boy." April called back, as she disappeared down the gangway towards her cabin.

Quickly opening the underside of her vanity case, April removed a simple, but minute, timing devise and small glass tube. Then she glued a hook on either end. April set the timer to explode at fourteen hundred hours, before putting the small assembly into her purse. Then April dressed in an extremely short and low-cut dress. "That should keep his attention," she thought to herself, looking at herself appreciably in the mirror before leaving for the galley.

Carlos was already eating his lunch when April gracefully entered the galley. When he saw her he stopped eating, his mouth half open as he started to drool. Eventually he managed to mutter. "You look fucking gorgeous." She smiled as she sat opposite him at the table. He continued. "I swear you are the most beautiful creature I've ever seen."

"Well, I thank you. Shall we eat now that the flattery is over with?" suggested April, as Jeff began to serve her lunch.

Carlos chatted incessantly, like a child who had just discovered a new toy. Finishing his lunch first, he had to respond to a request to return to the control room.

He asked politely, "Will you join me when you've finished, darling?"

"You know I will, darling. I'll come after I've finished shopping." Carlos looked perplexed. "Pardon, April. What do you mean?"

"I'm being facetious," she explained. "Of course I'll come to the control room. Where else would I go?" April assured him, tenderly squeezing his hand. "I'll be about ten, fifteen minutes, finishing my lunch."

Waiting for Carlos to get out of earshot, April returned to eating her meal. As soon as he'd left, April discarded her meal, and led Jeff hastily towards the torpedo room.

"Tell the guards that Carlos' told you to serve them lunch here." Then she advised Jeff, "Add some of this to their lunch to knock them out cold," as she handed over a small flask. "Quick, we must hurry."

Reaching the torpedo room, April waited for the guards to go into a deep sleep before joining Jeff, to avoid seeming to be implicated. She set up the explosive device to make it drop the heavy drift onto the mushroomed launch button, and coated the cord with gunpowder she'd obtained from a bullet to make it burn up and leave no ashes behind, then it would remove all the evidence of the method that had been used.

"Now get into the launching tube while I close it for you. Put that pin into that hole, and it'll jam the lock handle."

"I don't know how to thank you, April." Jeff said, kissing her on both cheeks. "But will you really be okay?"

"Yes. I'll be just fine. Now get the hell out of here, now. I've set the charge for fourteen hundred hours, so just be patient. And make sure that you're ready with the hatch sealed down." April explained, as she tried to appear unconcerned about her own personal safety.

"Good bye, my dear friend. God will watch over and protect you." April said to him, as she closed and sealed the hatch door. She watched as Jeff inserted the pin and climbed into the mini Sub, sealing it closed.

She was now truly alone, and afraid. But she realised that she would have to hide her true feelings, or she was in no doubt that she'd be the next in line to be killed.

Returning to the control room April flirted constantly with Carlos, realising that it's her only hope of survival, to remove any suspicion that he still held of her. Nearly an hour passed. She looked up at the clock, 'Only five more minutes,' April thought.

"Come and sit on my knee," Carlos invited. April willingly obliged. "God, you are so gorgeous," he hugged her. "I'm such a very lucky man."

"No Carlos. I'm the one that's lucky." April contradicted, as the submarine vibrated. "What the hell was that?" she pretended to be startled.

"What exactly is happening, No1?" demanded Carlos. "Somebody has just launched the mini sub, sir."

"Well, get after it and see who it is before you kill them," he ordered.

"We can't at this speed because by the time we slow down and turn round they will be long gone." No1 explained, as he looked towards April.

"Don't look at me like that! I was in here, remember? Anyway, you'd better do a roll call and see who has gone missing."

"That's right. She has been here with me for at least an hour or more, No1," Carlos reminded him.

"Of course sir, I'm very sorry, Madam. Will you please forgive me? I'll check the crew list now." No1 confirmed, as he left the control room.

Returning ten minutes later he told Carlos that it was Jeffrey Charmers. "Well I hope he drowns, because he's a long way from any land," Carlos snarled. Then turning to April, he added, "Well my dear, you'll need a new steward now. Maybe young Ben would do you. Did Charmers give you any inclinations what he was up to?"

"No. Why should he? He did seem to be in a rush serving dinner though. Anyway, I would've tried to talk him out of it." April tried to seem unconcerned. "It's sheer suicide all the way out here. Was he alone?"

"It seems so, Madam. But somebody had to have helped him. We must find out who that was," No1 explained.

"Why?"

"It takes somebody on the inside to help to work the airlock, and to launch the sub." Carlos explained. "I wonder just who'd be stupid enough to have help him?"

"Are McDougal and Montgomery still here? I haven't seen those treacherous bastards anywhere, Carlos."

"Yes April. I've confined them to their cabin for their own safety. Why do you ask?"

"Well, we know that they'll work either side of the fence if the price is right. It's only one thought. Remember that they're freelance mercenaries really." April tried to plant a seed of suspicion in his mind.

"How do we know that you're not working against us?" Carlos' No1 asked. "I admit I am. But not on this particular occasion." April explained, leaving them both at a loss for words.

"Well, you were here with me this time. Maybe we'd better keep a close watch on those other two bastards," Carlos instructed his number one, as they continued on their journey.

CHAPTER 18

Resigning herself to being trapped and alone, April was left with no alternative other than to play along as Carlos' willing mistress. That is if she was to survive from the present situation she found herself in. 'I can't depend on Ben to help me he's far too young and timid.' April was mulling it over as she dressed in a pair of tight denim jeans and a white revealing blouse. 'If I were to involve Ben it could endanger both our lives,' she thought as she walked towards the galley for breakfast.

"Good morning." April greeted Carlos, as Ben was starting to serve him breakfast.

"Good morning, madam." Ben fumbled as he drew a seat back for her. "What would you like for breakfast?"

"I'll have my usual bacon and eggs. But firstly may I have a cup of coffee to start the day off, please?"

"Certainly, Ms. Darling," Ben confirmed as he scurried off to get the coffee. The galley door swung open as McDougal and Montgomery, began to enter. They immediately turned to leave when they saw that April's was there.

"Don't leave on my account shit houses. I'm biding my time for you two scumbags."

Changing their minds they scurried in, sitting as far from April as they possible could get, and trying to avoid having any eye contact with her.

April was preoccupied with Carlos. She asked him, "How's your hand now that the swelling has subsided?"

"Yes, it has. But it's still very painful."

"Here, let me take a closer look at it for you?" she offered. April gently started to remove the strapping, "As I thought, it is dislocated." She confirmed, as she examined it. Without warning, April gripped Carlos' wrist, and with the other hand pulled his finger sharply, slipping the joint back into its socket. Instinctively she ducked, as Carlos cried out with the pain lashing out with his other fist.

Then she said as she sat up, "You missed me, Carlos. Tell me how it feels now?"

"It's ok," he said as he moved his fingers, saying gratefully, "Thank you," as he leaned over the breakfast table to kiss her. "I'm sorry I lashed out at you, but it was purely an instinctive reaction. Luckily you were quick enough to duck."

"Well I knew what was coming," she confirmed. April noticed Robert Montgomery smirking. "I'll wipe that bloody smirk from your face if I come over there, you lumps of dumb shit." April threatened, making Montgomery cough nervously.

She added, as she stood up to leave, "That's right, choke you fucking bastard it will save me the job of killing you."

"You haven't finished your breakfast, April."

"Suddenly I've lost my appetite, Carlos." She answered as she past behind Montgomery.

April waited a few seconds before she re-entering the galley furtively, "BOO!" she shouted as Robert Montgomery was about to sip his hot coffee.

With the shock he dropped the cup of hot coffee into his lap and cried out with pain. He clutched at his trousers trying to hold them off his penis. Bolting from the galley he screamed out, "YOU'RE A FUCKING MAD BITCH."

"It must have been something I said." She glibly remarked, smiling as she left the galley and returned to her cabin, leaving a stunned Carlos, and McDougal, in a state of total bemused shock.

Carlos eventually joined April in their cabin, having recovered from the shock of witnessing her odious display. He commented, "That was a bit naughty of you wasn't it?"

"It couldn't have happened to a nicer bloke." she replied sarcastically, as she freshened up her lipstick. Then smiling with amusement, April added, "He's still alive isn't he. Although I must admit, his dick will be a bit sensitive for a while."

"God, you have got an evil streak in you. Remind me never to upset you."

April thought to herself, 'You have it to come, I warned you about not giving me any of your shitty drugs.'

"You have the smile of an angel, my darling." Then becoming more serious he told her. "Montgomery I don't really need, but I have an important job for McDougal. So don't harm him April?"

"I'll keep that in mind, Carlos. Now can we change the subject? It's getting a little bit boring. Tell me Carlos, when are we going to surface?"

"We should be docking sometime this evening. Why? Are you feeling claustrophobic?"

"I'll admit that it's not the most scenic way I've travelled," she remarked as she refitted her earrings. "Now what surprises do you have in store for me today? A trip to Harrods maybe?"

"I will take you on a shopping trip that will blow your mind away. But after I have concluded my business of course, then I'll cover you from head to foot in furs and diamonds, so as to enhance your natural beauty." He promised April as he took her hand in his.

Reluctantly, April responded, as she was becoming more and more aware of her vulnerability.

Mid afternoon was approaching as April was returning to her cabin from the control room. Suddenly, a glancing blow struck her head from behind.

"Die, you fucking bitch, die." April heard Robert Montgomery shouting as she spun round to face him. "I'll kill you, you evil fucking cunt." He continued his tirade of abusive expletives like a raving lunatic.

Falling headlong onto the floor under the second blow, April instinctively went into a forward roll. Montgomery dived at April, missing her and falling hard against the metal decking. Recovering quickly, she sprang to her feet and drop kicked Robert Montgomery as he stood up, catching him full force in his stomach.

"You'll never learn will you, you stupid bastard?" she shouted at him, while pulling him to his feet by his hair. April faced the pathetic dishevelled figure, and told him, "I should have finished you off earlier."

"Help me to finish her?" Montgomery asked a terrified McDougal. "Not me, Robert." He said, and then he fled from the scene.

Carlos and the crew gathered and watched the spectacle unfold.

"I'll kill you myself then," Montgomery yelled, lunging for the fire extinguisher.

Spinning on one leg, April used the other leg to kick him across the head. He reeled under the blows as she repeated it kicking him aft, as he tried desperately to escape April's deadly accuracy.

Montgomery lunged towards the stern, trying to seal the door closed behind him.

But April was too fast and jammed the fire extinguisher in the doorway.

Montgomery swung his clenched fist to punch her face, as she evaded him, causing him to punch the steel bulkhead.

"You heartless bloody cow. But I'll stop this." Robert yelled as he produced a pistol.

Not allowing him the time to aim it April grabbed at his arm, and using all of her weight she thrust him face first into the half open door, as the gun to fall from his hand.

Seizing his opportunity, he rushed towards the airlock, locking himself inside it. His bloodied face peering smugly through the reinforced glass window at April.

"What are you going to fucking do now, you clever fucking cow?" Montgomery shouted, pushing a two fingered sign up against the glass window.

April looked round at the smirking faces of the crewmembers, as they witnessed her frustration. She then looked back towards the gloating Montgomery's face. "I will not let him escape me this time," April promised herself. She broke off a chair leg and jammed the airlock hatch closed, then smiled back at a bemused Montgomery. April waved him goodbye as she pulled down the lever to flood the airlock.

The spectators were frozen silently to the spot with the shock of April's callousness, as they witnessed her pulling the lever that opened the outer doors and sent Montgomery to a watery grave.

"That's washed the smirk off his stupid face," she mumbled. Pushing past the stunned Carlos and crewmembers, she told them, "I told him not to call me a bitch again, but would he listen to me?"

When the adrenaline started to subside April became aware that blood was dripping from a wound to her head. "The bastard's cut me," she snapped, as she continued toward her cabin.

She was cleaning her blood-splattered face as Carlos entered the cabin, "Are you okay, April?"

"I will be Carlos after I've changed out of these bloodied clothes."

"That was a bit naughty of you. Wasn't it, April?"

"I've owed him that for a very long time, believe me. He kept just reappearing."

"I don't think he'll come back this time," Carlos smiled nervously. "Just remind me never to get on the wrong side of you."

"How do you know that you haven't already?" April asked, as she turned, asking him to zip up her clean dress.

"Have I? I haven't meant to if I have. You'll tell me if I do, won't you?"

"A girl must have her little secrets. You'll just have to watch your P's, and Q's, from now on Carlos?" April said firmly. "There, that should hide the scratches. Shall we have our dinner now in peace?"

Carlos escorted April to the galley in silence. April could now sense a tension developing between them.

Carlos was first to break the silence, "You know, we haven't been on board for a week yet April, and you've killed two of my men."

"Is that all? I must be slipping," she joked as they dined. "Now can we change the subject, please? This one is getting very boring."

"We should be docking at about midnight," Carlos told her, in an attempt to calm her down.

Glancing up at the clock April remarked, "About four hours from now. So now you can tell me where we are going?" April asked, as she took advantage of his fear.

"Les Cayes. Do you know it?"

"It's in Haiti I believe." April tried to pretend that she was surprised.

"You know your geography, April. So can I trust you not to try to get away from me?"

"And why should I want to do that? She wrapped her arms round his neck attempting to convince him that she was now accepting him readily.

"Good," he said as he kissed April passionately, "it makes things so much more pleasant for us."

The remainder of the time April spent accompanying Carlos wherever he went.

As they were approaching the island, Carlos was explaining to April that they would not be docking in the main harbour. "We enter through an underwater tunnel, then surface on the inside of the mountain in a huge cavern," he boasted, "that way it makes it that much harder to track us via any satellite surveillance systems. Now I must concentrate while we navigate the tunnel," Carlos told her, as his Captain began barking out orders.

Finally the order to blow the ballast tanks was heard, followed by the sub bobbling as it surfaced.

"All hands on deck," the Captain ordered, as the hatch was opened.

"Ah, Terra Firmer at last," she said with relief. A gust of fresh air was filled the submarine. Picking up her purse April asked Carlos, "Do I have to follow orders too?"

"The men have gone ahead to form you a guard of honour, April."

"How nice of them," she smiled. "McDougal, does he get an escorted as well?"

"We're not doing it because we don't trust you. The men respect you for the way that you dealt with Montgomery. Apparently, they didn't like him either." He explained as they reached the top deck.

The droning of generators filled the air, drowning out the sound of the feverish activity that met them.

"These people work for me down here in this network of grottos. I employ whole families paying them four or five times what the national average is." Carlos proudly boasted.

"And then you get it all back because they've become addicts breathing in this opium polluted air day, and night," April suggested scornfully. McDougal was following closely behind, as April turned to ask him, "And what about you Glen, do you swim?"

"Aye, I do that. Like a fish, Madam. Don't you? Or are you relying on Mr. De-Mundo to save you?" he replied sarcastically.

Carlos was now preoccupied talking with his Captain.

"Prove you can swim then?" she asked, pushing him from the wharf and sending him splashing headlong between the submarine and quayside. "Ups, I'm awfully sorry about that." She apologised insincerely.

"You bloody cow. What was that for?" he questioned, spitting the water out that he had swallowed due of the shock of the sudden attack.

Carlos was quickly at April's side, "What happened here? Did he slip?"

"Sort of, he boasted he could swim so I asked him to prove it," she told him with a look of innocence. The Master at Arms was finding it very difficult to conceal his amusement.

Turning to him Carlos demanded, "And what do you find so amusing. Did you see what happened?"

"Yes Sir, Mr. De-Mundo. Mr. McDougal was goading, Ms. Darling. So," he was having difficulty talking while he was still laughing hysterically. "Then Ms. Darling pushed him into the dock."

Carlos was finding it hard to keep a straight face himself now. "So I shouldn't blame, Ms. Darling then?"

"No Sir," he continued to laugh.

The saturated McDougal walked up to them, "I'm glad you lot find it so fucking funny. But I'll have the last fucking laugh. You'll see if I don't." McDougal threatened as he lunged towards April.

April side stepped, and again caused him to fall headlong back into the dock. Everybody, including Carlos, became helpless with laughter as McDougal again floundered in the water.

"I'll kill you, you vindictive fucking bitch," McDougal yelled.

"I keep telling him not to call me a bitch because I don't like it. Remember Montgomery? Well he called me a bitch." She said, smiling innocently as they proceeded to walk along the dockside.

April's head was beginning to spin as she was forced to inhale the heroine-filled air. Psychedelic lights starting flashing before her eyes, so she walked briskly up the stairway and out into the fresher air. She took in deep breaths to clear her head.

Carlos finally joined her as he struggled to regain his breath. He asked April, "What was the hurry?" As a small shore party was hastily formed to accompany them.

"I needed some fresh air. I've been breathing that stale air for days," she fumbled to find an excuse.

"The air conditioning is the finest you can buy," he argued.

"I was still breathing everybody else's stale air. Now can we go, please?" April asked him anxiously, changing the subject as she began to shake. "I must be getting summer flu," she remarked, covering up the real reason for her discomfort.

Carlos offered "Shall I get you to a doctor?"

"No. I'll be ok." She told him as McDougal finally joined them. "Have you stopped pissing about now mate? Dry yourself off so we can go?" April goaded him further.

They preceded a hundred metres down to a small clearing where an assortment of vehicles had been parked.

"We'll travel in this open top jeep," Carlos told April. "The rest of you men can travel in the truck down to the town. But remember, to be back here by noon on Wednesday." Then he cautiously threaded his way down the mountainside as April tried to relax, letting her long hair blow freely in the warm night air.

CHAPTER 19

As the sun rose on the subtropical morning, the feeling of fresh air against her face felt good to April. She took in deep breaths while allowing her long hair to blow freely in the wind. Wrestling mentally trying to understand why she was here. 'I must find some seclusion so that I can speak to Charles,' she thought, as they neared the flat plains that panned out from the mountains to the sea.

April sat up abruptly at the sight that lay before her. There were large factory buildings which were surrounded by well-cultivated land that stretched out as far as the eye could see. Crops of opium, cannabis, and every type of drug known to man that could be farmed. They all cumulated in a kaleidoscope of colours that stocked the fields. Driving through between the fields of workers, April could see their dull lifeless expressionless faces as they worked industriously like robots to gather in the seeds.

"How unhappy they seem to be," April remarked.

"Why? They should feel honoured too work for me," Carlos insisted arrogantly.

"Why should they feel honoured because it's you? You're just another employer to them. One that they're totally dependent on I'll admit, and in more ways than one I should add."

"NO. I'M NOT JUST ANOTHER EMPLOYER. IT'S ME, CARLOS DE-MONDO. THEY ALL REVERE ME OUT HERE," he shouted at April angrily.

April began to laugh. But suddenly she realised by his expression that he was being deadly serious. "You really believe in what you're saying. Don't you, Carlos?"

"Why shouldn't I? It's true is it not? I'm extremely rich, handsome, debonair, and desirable. So yes, it is a great honour to work for me."

"You're just another narcissistic person at heart, Carlos. I like you, but you won't get any hero worship from me. I can definitely assure you of that. You're just turning all of your employees into addicts. That's why they're so faithful to you. They are totally dependent on you."

Then April realised this was a serious mistake, as she watched his expression change to one of extreme rage. Suddenly he lashed out bloodying April's nose and threatening that she'd pay for such a loose remark. April's first instinct was to strike out in defence. But she resisted the desire to attack, or kill him, at this particular time. Instead, April apologised to him meekly.

"I'm sorry, Carlos. I shouldn't have said that. Of course you're right, you do pay them very good wages to work for you."

His anger subsided into a smug smile, convinced that she was in accord with him.

April was becoming very heady in the pollen-infested atmosphere of the crops, as Carlos eventually drew to a halt outside of a large villa. She followed him, as he entered the building amid respectful bows and curtsied from his staff, which only fuelled his over inflated ego.

"See how they all respect me," he said, as he approached a beautiful dark and sultry lady. "Meet my wife, Maria." He announced proudly, as she kissed him passionately.

"I've missed you so very much my darling. And who is this ugly bitch, MY SLAVE?"

"Meet, Miss April Darling. You'll both be sharing me as I wish from now on." He told them haughtily, as Maria tried in vain to protest. "No buts. I Carlos De Mundo have spoken!"

Ignoring Maria's icy glare, April meticulously surveyed the room. She asked, "Do you mind if I freshen up?"

He snatched her handbag and searched it. "Good, there's no mobile or weapon in it. Maria will show you to the bathroom, AND NO BITCHING."

When the ladies entered the spacious bathroom Maria locked the door. She grabbed April's hair from behind and pulled her head back sharply. "Listen to me. NOBODY'S TAKING CARLOS AWAY FROM ME. Not now. Not ever. I'll kill anybody who tries it. Now is that clear to you, bitch?"

"Perfectly, now let go of my hair. And don't call me a bitch, I don't like it." She warned Maria in a calm voice.

"Don't tell me what to do, bitch. I'll tell you," Maria, tried to correct, April.

Growing tired of her pathetic attempts at bullying, April in the blink of an eye had reversed the roll that ended up with Maria in a very firm headlock. "I'm fed up with all this. Now it's your turn to listen to me. I've no designs on, Carlos. I'm just doing what I have to at the moment so I can survive. Carlos abducted me in Kaliningrad, and I'd gladly leave here right now if I could. And as I have warned you, DO NOT CALL ME A BITCH AGAIN." April told her firmly as she cautiously released her grip. "Now can we at least be friendly enemies?" she suggested, offering Maria a hand of friendship.

Maria shook her hand. "I'm sorry. I thought you were just another floozy he'd brought back with him. Perhaps I can help you to get away, April?"

Thinking hard and long as she looked deep into Maria's eyes, April could see an air of ingenuousness and profound sadness about her. Deciding that she needed at least one friend, April cautiously said to her. "I'll manage that when the time is right. But first, I have things to do here. How about you? You don't seem like Carlos's type somehow."

Maria sat on the rim of the bath. "You're here to kill him. Aren't you?" She whispered.

"What makes you think that?" April asked, as she began swilling her face. "I can recognise another agent when I meet one," Maria said confidently. "Maybe you're right, but then again, maybe you're wrong. So tell me, who are you working for?"

"The American's F, B, I, and you're for the Brits I suppose, judging by your accent?"

"Yes. Well something like that anyway," she was avoiding admitting to anything. She suggested to Maria, "We should pool our resources don't you think. You could start by tell me what your orders are?"

"When we have more time April, but not right now. Right now we'd better get back in there." Maria told her, as she opened the bathroom door. Carlos was snoring merrily as the two girls crept past him to sit on the veranda.

As she carried out some refreshments April began to shake violently. "Do you need a fix, April?" asked Maria, noticing her extreme discomfort.

"NO. I'll be ok in a moment."

Maria, showing genuine concern, said, "You're going cold turkey, aren't you April?"

"Yes, all because that bastard in there kept pumping me with heroine. But he'll eventually pay for this, my God, he will regret what he did to me." She vowed, as the shaking began to subside.

"Now I'm going to be sick," April panicked, picking up her handbag she rushed stealthily past the snoring Carlos and into the bathroom.

Vomiting violently until her abdomen was sore; April sat on the edge of the bath to recover. She decided she should use this convenient and private time in which to try to contact Charles. Taking hold of her bag, and removing one of the pivot pins in the hinge, April opened the false base that contained among other small items, a mobile phone. Quickly turning it on, she opened countless text messages from Charles inquiring as to her present whereabouts. 'Good, I have a signal at last,' April thought as she accessed his number.

"Hello, Charles. It's me," April began as she started to sob. "I'm going to kill this obnoxious fucking, bastard."

"What's wrong, April? Where are you? We have been out of our minds with worry thinking something may have happened to you.

But you must stick with it while we find out just what's happening. But I'll try to get you some help out soon."

"You keep saying that. Well you'd better pay the same as last time into my account immediately, or I will finish him off, right here and right now." She threatened.

"Okay! We knew that this was to be a high-risk operation so the money will be no problem. I'll have it paid into your account immediately. Now don't do anything rash will you?" he urged.

Composing herself, April started, "Okay. Just listen very carefully I haven't got very much time. Carlos De-Mundo brought me from Kaliningrad to Haiti, via his private submarine. That's why you can't always track him by the way. I'm on his farm just outsides Les Cayes, which is apparently where his main operations were transferred to. Also, will you check out his wife, Maria? She says that she works for the F. B. I. I must go now, I can hear somebody coming," April said quickly, returning the phone to the secret compartment.

Maria called softly, "Are you okay in there, April?"

"Yes. I'm coming now." April said, as she unbolted the door to leave.

Telling Maria, "Now I'd like a very long cool drink on the veranda."

They chatted idly while sipping their drinks. Eventually they were interrupted by Carlos calling. Maria dutifully went to his side; five minutes past before April could hear raised voices. Then Maria reappeared.

"He wants you," she snapped snottily, "I can't see why though," beginning the odious attitude once again, while winking at April.

"Yes, Carlos. What can I do for you?" she reluctantly asked.

"Unfortunately that will have to wait, my gorgeous little vixen," He said, patting April's bottom while rubbing his bulging trousers with his free hand. "But it will be well worth your waiting for, and that I can assure you. Now, Glen McDougal's on his way here so I want you to behave yourself. I need you to be extra nice to him. Extra especially nice," he said, sliding his hand up April's thigh as he smiled. "You know what I mean. Don't you?"

She was totally unprepared for his amorous advances, and suggestions. Steeling herself, she smiled enigmatically while he was toying with her vagina. "No. I won't sleep with him. I thought YOU loved me."

"I do darling. But this will be a very special favour for me." He insisted, as April faked an orgasm, pretending to go weak at the knees.

"Do I have any choice?" she asked, as McDougal appeared in the doorway. "Now go on. Apologise to Glen, and show him that you really mean it?" he told her, gently pushing April towards McDougal. He patted her breasts as he said. "Hasn't she got nice tits, Glen?" inviting, "feel just how firm they are?"

April smiled enigmatically again as McDougal enthusiastically grabbed at her bosom. "Oh yes. They're very firm. And if I might add, they're amply proportioned too." McDougal was taking as much time as he possibly could.

"Well. Don't mind me, Glen. Take her in that spare bedroom and give her a good fucking, she's hot for it. It will be doing me a big favour; I've got to keep Maria happy."

Glen McDougal eagerly responded. "Well, if you put it that way Carlos, I'll be glad to help you out. Come on bitch, you can see what a real man can do for you?" McDougal said enthusiastically. He grabbed her arm pulling her into the bedroom.

After closing the door, McDougal ordered her, "Strip off and let me see that heavenly body you're hiding under those clothes, and do it seductively facing me. So that I can watch you're every sexy move."

April was trapped. There was no help that she could rely on. She was even unsure of Maria's sincerity. So with no other alternative, she had to perform this odious and obnoxious request.

Glen McDougal watched enthusiastically as he drooled with every article of clothing April removed, as his penis bulged in his grimy ill-fitting trousers. Eventually, April reluctantly stood before him stark naked. Then he started caressing her naked body. She could smell the heavy stench of his body odour and his repugnant breath as he pulled her onto the bed, proceeding to explore every inch of her with boyish enthusiasm.

"Aren't you going to undress, Glen?"

"No. It's only you that needs to be starker's. So that I can see what I'm fucking," he said arrogantly, laying his full weight on top of her.

Ridged with shock, April just stared at a fixed point on the ceiling. McDougal was oblivious to April's feeling as he was selfishly preoccupied with fulfilling his own perverted desires. April fought back the tears as she was subjected to his sexually perverted needs again and again. April was unable to resist without making him, and Carlos De-Mundo, suspicious. She was left without any immediate alternative but to comply with the odious wishes of, Carlos De-Mundo.

Eventually he rolled off her onto his back. "That was good my feisty little wench, very good in fact. I think I'll ask Carlos to make you part of our little deal," he said breathlessly as he gripped the back of April's hair. "You don't talk much do you? I like that in a woman. So you can use your laughing gear for this," he insisted, as he thrust her face against his penis. "Now see if there's anything left in the tank?"

Reluctantly, April took hold of his limp penis.

"Not with your hands you stupid bitch, stick your laughing gear round it."

April, had to fight back the urge to vomit as she took his penis into her mouth, as reluctantly she moved her head slowly up and down on him.

"That's better. Just keep fucking going like that," he insisted, as April unwillingly complied with his perverted demands. He encompassed her with his legs and held April's face between his hands moaning with desire. She could feel his penis swelling with passion as he grew closer, and closer, to his ejaculation point.

He shouted at her, "SUCK HARDER, YOU BLOODY COW," as he reached his climax holding her head firmly as he ejaculated into April's mouth. She tried unsuccessfully to struggle free as he ordered, "SWALLOW IT, YOU BLOODY COW."

April began to balk as he pinched her nose closed.

"Swallow it I said. You owe me that much for pushing me into that bloody dock," he continued to insist. April was struggling to breathe as she was forced to gulp down his obnoxious sperm. "That's better, you bitch. Do what you're told like the good little whore that you are now. Now that you've been well and truly fucked, you can get dressed." He told April arrogantly as he zipped up his trousers. McDougal added, "Maybe we can have a repeat performance later?" he laughed loudly as he left the bedroom.

Alone and helpless April buried her head in the duvet and wept bitterly.

She was totally unaware that Carlos had entered the bedroom until he placed his hand on her shoulder.

"Come now. It wasn't that bad. Surely you've had other men before me." He tried to raise April's head but she resisted strongly. "I said pull yourself together and get used to it. Why else would I need to keep you alive, if not as a carrot for my clients? So deal with it, and get used to it. That's if you want to continue living." He reminded her, and left the room.

This made her extremely angry as she fought back the urge to cry more. Grabbing for her robe, April dashed into the bathroom and securely locked the door, propping a chair under the handle to ensure that she got some privacy: while she attempted to wash the stench of McDougal from her body. She finally started to relax as she searched for a way to get rid of these venomous people. Eventually she got hardened to her task, she resolved to make McDougal, and De-Mundo, rue this very day. So April finished showering, dressed, and returned to the lounge.

"Ah, so you've decided to join us at last, have you?" Carlos commented, as he handed April his empty glass. Demanding, "You can make yourself useful. Now fill this up for me."

April silently obeyed.

Maria was quick to come to her side, "Are you okay love?"

"No. But I'll get even with them. You'll see. I'll make them pay," April vowed resolutely to her. She returned their full glasses to them, and asked Carlos, "Do you mind if a take a walk?"

"No. There's nowhere you can go that isn't my land. Who knows, you might even come to your fucking senses and realise that a women has only one purpose in life, and that's for the pleasure of men," he snarled, as April walked out into the fields, oblivious of his misplaced arrogance.

Maria offered as she linked April's arm. "Can I keep you company while we get some fresh air together? Let me show you around," she suggested, as they walked out into the fields. "I'm sorry I wasn't able to help you, but I didn't see it coming. You see, Carlos and his business associates will see you as an extremely attractive, and lucrative, asset. You're very, very attractive, and they know that you're an ex British agent too."

They walked silently for a few moments before Maria added. "There's something about to happen though, but I'm not sure what it is yet. It's something to do with the nuclear missiles, and Glen McDougal."

April asked casually. "You mean a large drug consignment?"

"No. Well, I don't think so. Carlos is hell bent on exacting revenge for what they did to his Colombian homestead." They walked near to a large storehouse as Maria explained, "This is where they manufacture the vast variety of drugs. That building behind it is a laboratory where they experiment for any new drugs, etc. Now the biggest building here, well just you take a look for yourself, April." Maria invited, as she opened a side door. The site that met them astounded April. It was an extremely large hanger housing a vast array of aircraft, helicopters, crop dusters, private jets, and more towards the rear of the hanger, "Bloody hell the wages of sin."

"You can say that again. I overheard him whispering to McDougal about a new aircraft coming soon, but that's all I've heard. I don't know the what, the where, the how, or the when," Maria finished thoughtfully. "Now, we'd better get back," she advised, as she slowly started back towards the house. "Are you coming, April?"

"You go on ahead. I need just a few more minutes to get my head round what is happening here," She told her as she watched Maria walking into the villa.

Alone, April sought refuge behind a car. This gave her a sheltered vantage-point from where she could secretly access her phone and ring, Charles.

When he answered, April proceeded to tell him what Carlos had subjected her to, and what she feared his future plans were for her.

"I'll kill that bastard, McDougal before he touches me again," she vowed. "Not so hasty April, remember we need to know just what they're up to,"

Charles warned her. "Then you can do whatever you wish to them."

"But what about me, don't you ca—," April broke off in mid-sentence, "You don't care what happens to me, DO YOU? There's somebody else, ISN'T THEIR?"

"No my love," he fumbled.

"There is. Who is she? And how long has it been going on?" April asked angrily.

"Don't get so angry, April. First and foremost you are England's No 1 agent. You must concentrate on your assignment. We'll talk about it when you get home." Charles tried to pacify her.

"DON'T GET FUCKING ANGRY. NOW WHO THE FUCK IS SHE?" she insisted even louder.

After a short silence, Charles admitted in a quiet, whispery voice. "Mandy and I are to be married." He then waited through a very long, and uncomfortable, silent pause for her retort.

Seething with anger, in her mind she called him every expletive she could think of. Finally, she composed herself. "I hope that you'll both be very happy. I also hope Mandy knows just how lucky she is in finding such a, how shall I put it?"

"Gentleman," Charles suggested.

"No. I was thinking more along the lines of, TWO-FACED, COWARDLY, FUCKING LYING, BASTARD!" April shouted, as she fought back the tears. "Well if you want me to endure this debaucherous treatment until you get your information, and while you're sowing your wild oats with my Mandy, it's going to cost you twice as much. Now pay it into my Swiss bank account NOW, or I'll sort out these bastards once and for all. And it doesn't matter what you have to say about it, because then I'll just disappear."

"What if the ministry won't pay?" he tried to stall.

"No more funny jokes, Charles. I'm definitely not in the mood for them. We both know that you have limitless resources, so just send me a text when you've done it so I can double-check it. And do it NOW. Or I warn you that I won't endure this sick, debauchery treatment, any longer." April warned him firmly, as she noticed Maria looking for her.

Telling Charles sharply, "I must go now so just sort it all out."

"I'm over here, Maria." She called to her, hastily replacing the phone into its compartment.

Walking back to the house, April explained that she was resigning herself to the plans that Carlos had for her. She detected there was a bleeps from her phone, so once inside the house she headed straight to the bathroom. Locking the door, she checked her two messages. One was from Charles, confirming that the money had been paid into her account. The other text was from the bank, telling April that they'd cleared the money as she'd previously arranged for them to do. Confidant that the money could not now be retrieved she deleted the messages, and turned off the phone, returning it to its safe place.

Going back into the lounge, she was now feeling alone, and rejected. April thought to herself that death itself would be a welcome escape from all of this. But she was reluctant to commit suicide because of her strong Christian beliefs, which forbade her to take this option as any escape.

Betrayed by the only people she'd ever loved, and feeling trapped and alone, April knew that at the present time there was only one option open to her. She would have to become a submissive to these depraved and degenerate people. Just to survive, and finish off her assignment.

"Ah! I see the whore has finally decided to grace us with her presence," Remarked McDougal. "I was beginning to think that she was too good for our company. You know, like the high class hooker that she is."

April now realised that she must extract the necessary information post-haste, if she was to spare herself having to endure McDougal's lecherous depravity any longer than was necessary.

"Tell your associate, if he calls me a whore, hooker, or bitch, once more, then I'll personally separate him from his puny little prick. Then I'll force feed him with it."

"You'd better take notice of her. Remember, Montgomery?" Carlos reminded Glen.

"Yes. But you're here to protect me. Aren't you?"

"If you carry on goading her it will be on your own head, Glen," Carlos warned. "I'm sorry about his mouth, but what I've said still stands, April. Unless you comply with my wishes, and the wishes of my clients, I'll have no alternative but to use drugs on you again. Now do I make myself clear?"

"As crystal," April said as she sat beside Maria, wondering what she needed to do to extract the necessary information.

"Can we at least be friends and start again?" McDougal suggested, as though he could read April's thoughts.

"Let's start again then," reluctantly April agreed. "Now can I get anybody a refill while I'm getting Maria and myself, a drink?" She asked chirpily, as she opened the drink cabinet. "You know my father was a seaman, he used to call the drinks cabinet a fog locker."

Glen McDougal, anxious to make amends, remarked, "Yes, I've heard sailors call it that, April. I'll have rum and black if I may?"

Continuing serving the drinks until way beyond dusk, they all chatted idly. "That's the most you've spoken to me all day," Carlos remarked to April as everybody reclined on the balcony.

The ringing of the telephone interrupted the party atmosphere as Carlos went to answer it. After returning he informed Glen McDougal that the arrangements were now in place. April avoided commenting on this, knowing that she'd be enlightened about it all in due course.

"When do we go?" McDougal asked.

"I haven't received the intricate details yet, but very soon I think."

"When do the other pilots arrive here, Carlos?"

"When I get the okay I'll tell you, and then you can meet up with them. It will be much safer that way. Now can we change the subject?" Carlos insisted impatiently as Maria refilled his glass. Glen McDougal drank so much that he passed out, much to April's delight. Allowing her to rise early while he, and Carlos, where still snoring away merrily.

She sat trying to formulate a contingency plan to escape when the time was right. 'What's going on though? Why are other pilots needed?" She wrestled mentally with the conundrum that was slowly formulating. "I must find out more somehow, and quickly. But how, I'm missing so many vital pieces to this puzzle.'

Her thoughts were interrupted by the emergence of, Maria. "There you are, April. Have you been up for long?"

"About an hour or two, I couldn't sleep. Did you sleep okay, Maria?"

"Like a baby. Carlos was so drunk that he just passed out. What about, Glen?"

Giggling to herself, April confirmed, "He passed out too thank God."

"God, in this forsaken cesspool of a land April, can you believe in a God out here?"

"God is everywhere. He's even here, Maria. Don't you believe in him?"

"It's hard to believe in anything like that in this dump. Why would a God allow this suffering to happen?"

"The suffering, along with evil, comes from Satan, the Devil. And the struggle between good and evil will continue until the end of time, judgment day. God gives us the free choice whether to follow him, or to follow Satan?"

What she had to say left Maria looking pensive. Eventually, changing the subject, she asked, "What are your orders? Have you any plans, yet?"

"I've no specific instructions. I've been told to just play it as it comes. As regards to my plans, I don't really have any of them yet either. What about you, Maria?"

Maria looked round nervously to check that Carlos was still sleeping. She then lowered her voice to a whisper, "I was recruited by the American secret services while I was still in Colombia. It was me who pinpointed where they were to bomb. Then Carlos took us on his private jet, and we escaped to here. Since then I've not been in touch with them because Carlos is becoming suspicious."

Surprised, April asked, "Let me get this straight, you were willing to die as well?"

"Look at me, April. I've become a hopeless drug addict now. So tell me what's left for me to live for?"

Placing a consoling arm around her, April vowed, "If we get out of this, I will personally see to it that you get the finest medical help that money can buy. So you must not give up hope, Maria."

Maria sobbed at her show of kindness and concern as they hugged. Eventually drying her eyes, she promised. "I'll help you in any way that I can to eradicate this evil, heartless, bastard. Just tell me what you want me to do?"

Heartened by Maria's renew resolve, April reassured her that when the time was right she'd bring her up to speed with what plan she had made.

A half-drunken McDougal shouted from his bedroom, so April went to see what was wrong with him. He playfully pulled her back into the bed but found that he was unable to get an erection.

"You must have used it all up last night, Glen?" she lied, knowing that he'd been far to intoxicated to remember a thing about the previous evening.

"Oh yes. I was good wasn't I," he pretended to remember, "That must be it."

"I'll get you a drink while you get dressed if you'd like?" April offered as she left the bedroom. She was still unsure of Maria's full commitment, so she played her cards close to her chest, waiting to find out which way she'd jump if made to choose, particularly, if she was in need of a fix at the same time.

Over the next couple of days the girls relaxed and talked. While McDougal drank until he reached a state of oblivion, allowing Carlos the time to complete his business transactions.

April's little ruse was working; Carlos began to think that she was accepting the situation, and was settling for the lifestyle that he'd put on offer.

"Tomorrow the other pilots will be available shortly after dawn, Glen. You should be en-route for Scotland by lunchtime at the latest. Leave the drink and drugs alone from now on. IS THAT CLEAR?"

"Okay, you're the boss. It'll be good to tread on Scottish soil once again, even though it will be briefly." Then he reflected sadly, "And probably for the last time."

"You made your choice and decided to accept the money that I'm paying you," Carlos reminded him. As April sat bemused, trying to work out what they were up to. Fighting back the urge to ask, she decided to appeal to McDougal's over inflated ego as soon as she was able. So she just sat and waited until Carlos had finished making the final plans.

CHAPTER 20

"Let you and me retire for a siesta?" McDougal suggested, taking April's hand and leading her into the bedroom.

'That saves me looking for an excuse,' she thought, this time going willingly into the bedroom with him.

"What, no resistance this time?" he remarked with surprise.

"Not now that I know you're such an important person to, Carlos." April feigned her admiration. "I absolutely adore important and powerful, men," she said, as she appealed to his misplaced self-importance.

"Oh, yes. I'm very important to, Mr. De-Mundo. He needs me to help him with his future plans."

"What plans are they, or hasn't he made you privy to that information?" April teased, as she seductively removed her top and pushed McDougal backwards onto the bed.

"He tells me everything," he boasted. April was slowly unbuttoning his shirt while straddling his body. "The power game does really turn you on. Doesn't it?" he said as she ripped off his shirt.

"Oh yes," April lied again in a huskily and sexy voice. Saying as she unzipped his trousers, "Now let's see that enormous cock of yours." She flattered grasping it, and starting to masturbate him.

McDougal started to moan with pleasure, but April stopped just before he could ejaculate. She moved her hands to massage his chest, while moving her buttocks up and down within his groin.

"It's not very dangerous what you're doing for Carlos though, is it?" April tried to sound disappointed, as she continued to probe.

"Yes, it is very dangerous. Don't you believe me?" Glen asked, as he pushed her hands back onto his penis. "I have to steal two very important and secret military aircraft. They're so unique that they're the only two prototypes in existence. I know, because I'm the one who helped to design them, and they're at my old factory in Aberdeen. They have been fitted with the most advanced stealth technology, which makes them hard to detect, and they have an arsenal of weaponry that is so advanced even we couldn't defend ourselves against them." He bragged to April as he ejaculated into her hands. "They also have an increased fuel capacity which will enable them to fly one and a half time the circumference of the planet. Now fuck me till I'm dry?" He begged, as he fondled April's large breasts.

Removing the rest of her clothing, April straddled him once again as he told her. "You nearly upset the party by killing Montgomery he was the one that I'd trained up to be my second pilot. So we had to delay things while other pilots were recruited and trained." McDougal bragged, as he continued fondling her breasts, toying with the nipples with his tongue.

She was moving slowly up and down on him as he moaned uncontrollably. April was aware of what pleased a man, and how to tease him so that she could extract any relevant information. She was drawing on her earlier experiences as a man herself, which is why she'd become so good.

"That's so good. You certainly know how to please me," he admitted, as April slid off him to toy with his testicles.

"What a pity you have to leave tomorrow. When do you expect to be back here, Glen?"

"If there are no hitches, it will be in five to seven days," McDougal confirmed, as he expended his final sperm and started to dress. "I'm finished now, so you can get dressed too," he coldly told her as he turned to leave the room.

'What selfish prig's men are? I hope I had more consideration for a ladies needs when the role was reversed.' She had just finished dressing when Carlos entered the bedroom.

"Maria will keep you company while we drive into the village for the pilots." He then told her as he started to leave the bedroom, "And have a good shower, we will be partying tonight."

This frightened April, 'What does he mean by a party?' She was wondering as she returned to the lounge to join Maria. "What's all this about a party? And with whom will it be?"

"Party, its one enormous orgy, I hate them. You have to willingly succumb to whoever wants or grabs for you. The last time I had to endure sex with six different men while the others looked on goading and cheering." Maria remarked with utter disdain in her voice. "I really hate the way they treat us out here. We're just like unpaid prostitutes to them really. And it's all just to satisfy their lustful fantasies." She continued sadly, as she suggested, "I usually get totally pissed so that I'm oblivious to what they're doing to me. You'd be better if you did the same thing, April?"

"Unfortunately I'll need to keep alert, so I'll just have to endure it all. BUT, remember that revenge is sweet my dear friend, they'll all pay for this one day, and that should be very soon, that much I can promise you," April swore to Maria, as she placed a comforting arm around her.

"When you go you will take me with you, won't you, April?" Maria asked, as she clung tightly to her.

"Of course I will, darling," she promised, kissing her on her forehead. "It shouldn't be very long now, so make sure that you're ready when I give you the signal. Now shall we go and get some fresh air?" she continued as they strolled out into the blazing sun. "It's so hot out here, I need a cool drink."

"I'll fetch us some fruit juice," Maria willingly volunteered.

Watching her walking away, April took the phone from her purse and dialled Charles' number. She was greeted by a tired, "Hello."

"I hope I've disturbed your sleep. Or better still, disturbed you in mid sex." April bitched bitterly.

"The sarcasm doesn't become you, April," Charles started. "You need to stay focused on the assignment in hand. That is if you want to live through it. You can't afford to get distracted."

"Oh don't you worry about me, I intend to come back and sort all my affairs out." Sensing the uncomfortable tone in Charles's voice, she stopped him from answering. "Just listen to me. McDougal and some other pilots are leaving for Scotland tomorrow. As far as I can ascertain, they are going to steal the two-prototype, stealth jets. The one's that he was working on in Aberdeen. What they want them for I don't know yet, unless Carlos has a buyer lined up for them, of course. Make sure that you move them to a secure place, and do it now, Charles. By the way, did you check out Maria yet?"

"I'll see to it that security is put on high alert around the planes, just until they can be moved. And yes, Maria is kosher. But remember, she's a drug addict now, so she can be volatile and unpredictable. Her thirst for revenge is her only goal in life now. Apparently De-Mundo wiped out her entire family, husband, children, parents, and siblings. She really does carry a lot of hate for him."

April was so shocked at what Charles was saying that she didn't notice Maria returning.

She asked April, "Where have you kept that hidden?"

Jumping with the shock, she asked, Charles, "Maria has just returned, can I come clean with her?"

"Yes, you'll need some help, and she's your best bet at this precise time. Maybe, she's you're only hope, although we do have a small contingent of marines just over the border on exercise. And the S.B.S has men out there somewhere, not sure where but there're holding them in readiness until you give us the okay."

"Good. I'll ring you again soon." Returning the phone to its compartment, April insisted to, Maria. "This is our only life line right now. Keep stum about it, won't you?"

"You know that I will, April. Have you been checking up on me then?"

"Yes, I had to make sure about you. But you are sincere. I'm sorry about what happened to your family though."

Maria's facial expression became hardened, "I want to be the one to kill that bastard when the time comes. I was wondering if you were for real, but now I know that you are. Now what is our next move?"

"I'm afraid we'll need to stay patient for a little while longer. Now we need a plan of action for tonight. Tell me everything you know, Maria?" April listening intently as Maria graphically described the horrific details of what April could expect.

Asking her, "What part has voodoo and witchcraft got in all of this?"

"A very big part April, you must remember these people grew up with its fears, and superstitions. They firmly believe in all that the witchdoctors tell them."

"Well, if you keep close to me then I'll try to find us a way out of this." April explained, growing more and more afraid for their personnel safely.

"I must shower and dress before the boss returns," April told her as she walked into the bathroom. Standing with her eyes closed, just letting the hot shower wash over her naked body, April concentrated her thoughts on the evening that was to come. She tried to imagine every possible scenario that could possibly be expected to arise, and how she could deal with each one if it did.

Suddenly the shower curtains opened as the naked Maria stepped inside. "I hope you don't mind sharing. Don't look so worried because unfortunately I'm not making a pass at you. But we do need to talk," she whispered, "and the running water will cover any bugging devises Carlos may have planted."

"No, I don't mind. There's plenty of room for two of us in here. So what shall we talk about?" April joked, as she tried to hide her acute embarrassment. Her old male instincts were stirring deep within her, as she brushed up against Maria's naked body. She thought to herself, 'Thank God I no longer have a dick, or it would become patently obvious just how I still feel about a woman.'

Maria interrupted her thoughts, "Pass the soap while I wash your back?" April willingly agreed to let her.

"Why are you so tense? Anybody would think that you really did fancy me." Then with a serious tone to her voice, she asked, "or do you?"

"Do I what?" pretending not to understand.

"Fancy me? Only it's okay if you do," Maria explained hopefully. "I would welcome a little tenderness after enduring these selfish, sweaty, pigs."

April turned to face her with her nipples standing out hard and stiff, "I do fancy you. But not as you imagine I do, and certainly not right now." April tried to explain to Maria as she gently took the soap from her. "Someday I'll explain to you though, and then you'll understand. It's to do with who I used to be before I became an agent."

"I don't care about your past. It's the here and now that interests me. Not tomorrow, or yesterday. Who knows, we might not even survive tonight." Maria argued as she fought back her tears. "I just want somebody to love me again. I mean, really love me for who I am," sobbing as she hugged April.

April noticed Maria's shear lonely desperation for the very first time, as she gently stroked her soft, jet-black hair. "Would you settle for a big hug and a promise that I'll keep us safe. No matter what happens tonight. Then when this is all over, well who knows what will happen?"

"Yes, but I don't know how to tell you this, April. Carlos has special plans for you tonight, and you aren't expected to survive them. I'm not sure what they are, so please be very careful."

"Don't you worry your pretty little head about me, Maria, as the song says, I WILL SURVIVE, and, I definitely do not believe in all of this mumbo jumbo stuff? I only believe in the powers of my Almighty God. Now go on, spoil me," she suggested handing Maria the shower gel.

Maria's face lit up at this show of kindness, as she tenderly and passionately, washed April from head to toe. Returning the compliment, April then bathed Maria as she squirmed and giggled, rubbing her naked body against April at every conceivable opportunity. Eventually, the water began to run cold.

"Come on, get dressed Maria?" she urged, playfully smacking her bottom.

Again Maria hugged her.

"You'll never know how happy you've made me feel today," she said gratefully, kissing April on the lips.

"Good. Now what do you suggest I wear tonight?" April chirpily asked. Trying to suppress her personal fears, "I want to knock them all dead, LITERALLY."

"Here, borrow this." Maria smiled as she handed over a red taffeta dress. It had a tight figure-hugging bodice, built in half cups, and a plunging neckline. With a full flowing skirt that reached to just above the knees.

"Thank you. This is absolutely gorgeous. But what're you going to wear?" April asked, as Maria produced an identical dress in white. "Oh, I see, so we're going to be twins for tonight. Are we?"

Maria smiled as she passed over a matching pair of strappy shoes with a four-inch stiletto heel. "These should fit you, I hope," said Maria, as she zipped up her dress. "They're a size thirty nine."

"Thank you. They're just my size. Now I need some sort of back up?" April confirmed, as she opened her trolley case.

Maria watched with intrigue as she dismantled it into parts. Removing the trolley handle to form the butt of the gun, then unscrewed a small section of the tubing and attaching it to the butt, forming the barrel. Turning the case over April removed the wheels, and out of the axle she took a small rod. "This is the firing pin, Maria," she explained. Unclipping the centres out of the wheels, April clipped it all together to form the trigger mechanism. Then April clipped it into the butt and fired the empty chamber, click. "Good, it works." Removing the remainder of the axle hubs and fitting it in place, April complete the bullet chamber. "See, a lightweight gun as you can see, and it all works too."

"But what will you do about the bullet, April? It's all in vein without the bullets."

"Don't fret, Maria. I have them too," she assured her. Then April proceeded to unzip the suitcase lining to access a small hole in the beaded hem, she held the hem between her forefinger and thumb, and pulled the lining to extrude bullets from within the hem.

"See, Maria. I've come prepared like a proper girl Scout," laughed April as she loaded the gun, placing the remaining bullets in the compartment at the bottom of her bag. "And now for a holster," April pondered as Maria looked on. "I can't strap it to my thigh, so can I alter this dress a little?" Maria nodded to her enthusiastically. Putting a small tear high up in the lining, April poking the gun barrel through it, then secured it with a toothpick, "Now how do I look, and is there any tell-tale signs?" April asked, as she performed a twirl.

"You're just amazing, April Darling!" Maria announced as she hugged her. "No. I wouldn't have known that you had a gun under there at all."

Laughing loudly, April said, "I bet you say that to all your boyfriends."

When Maria realised what she'd said, she collapse onto the bed in an uncontrollable bout of laughter, dragging April with her.

"I wish you had that type of gun, April," she managed to say eventually. "Oh, how I wish you did," Maria repeated again as she clung tightly to her.

"Cheer up. You never know, I might turn out to be a transsexual," she half joked.

Maria asked enthusiastically, "Are you?"

"You'll have to wait and see for yourself. Wont you?" teased April, gently pushing Maria away and telling her, "Now we must finish getting ready."

They had just finished as a car pulled up in front of the house and blew its horn.

"To war, and now the fun will begin." April said as she slung her bag diagonally across her shoulder, and got into the open top car, as the night was rapidly engulfing the cloudless sky. They drove up the mountainside heading towards the growing number of beacon fires at the summit on the hill.

"The driver's very quiet. Hey, has the cat got your tongue, mate?" April teased. The man turned to face them and April instantly recognised him. "Winston! What the hell are you doing out here?" she asked with delighted surprised.

"The boss thought you might need some extra help so I volunteered," he explained. "James has just crossed the border, and is standing by with a small detachment near Port Au Prince. He's just waiting for my signal then he'll move in."

"Do you two know each other?" a surprised Maria butted in.

"Yes, we certainly do. This lovely lady was my African Queen, so to speak," Winston joked. "Is?" he stopped, and nodded towards Maria.

"Don't worry. I've had her checked out and she's kosher. She's working for the F.B.I, and has a personnel vendetta of her own to settle." April told him, as she smiled towards Maria. "Are you on your own, Winston?"

"There are three of us who have infiltrated De-Mundo's organisation."

"Well, I don't want any of you to blow your cover on my account, no matter what happens to me. And I've told Maria the same thing. Keep well out of it, SAVVY?"

"Yes, but I don't like it April. Carlos knows that you're still a British agent, so he'll do all within his power to belittle and demean you. Then they'll most certainly ceremoniously kill you. And they'll do it as painfully, and slowly, as they possibly can," confirmed Maria.

Winston argued, "That's all the more reason why we're here as your back up."

"Your time will come, but not tonight Josephine. Now is that perfectly clear to both of you. I WILL, look after MYSELF."

"You're the boss, I suppose," Winston reluctantly agreed. By now they'd reached the party which was just coming into full swing. "What if?" he started to say, but was cut off in mid-sentence as they were met with the whole chaotic scene.

The complete area was festooned with the tools of witchcraft hanging from each and every tree, eerily illuminated by the array of campfires that lit up the clear night sky. Around the fires danced half-naked men and women, intoxicated by the drug-laden air that they were being forced to inhale.

"No ifs or buts. You don't blow your cover no matter what happens to me.

Now is that perfectly clear, Winston?" April reiterated firmly.

"Patently," Winston reluctantly agreed. "You're right as usual," he admitted reluctantly as they reached Carlos who was sitting cross-legged at a campfire.

CHAPTER 21

"There you are. At last you've got here," Carlos greeted them. "Come and sit down each side of me and have a little drinkies. NOW the fun is about to begin."

"Of course my darling," Maria readily complied, as she took two tumblers of rum from a tray and handed April one of them.

Carlos's face became distorted with anger, as he shouted, "HAVEN'T YOU GOT ANYTHING TO CONFESS TO ME, MY DELECTABLE BRITISH SPY?" grabbing at April's throat he pushed her back until she lay flat on the ground. "I know that you think you're too good for us, and certainly above taking any of my medicine," he said menacingly as he shook a bag of white powder in her face, "but I can promise you, Miss April fucking Darling, that tonight you will wish you had. JUST SO THAT YOU WOULD BE STONED OUT OF YOUR TINY FUCKING BRITISH MIND, and be completely oblivious of what I've got in store for you tonight, MISS APRIL FUCKING DARLING." Carlos continued to threaten, as he gave a sinister laugh and released his grip on her throat.

She was feeling giddy because of the heavy smoke, and the drug filled atmosphere, as the relentless pounding of the jungle drums fuelled the dancers into a frenzied activity. April just looked on silently. She was watching for any opportunity in which she could escape.

Feeling the worse for his drinking, Carlos staggered towards a bush to empty his bladder, which allowing Maria the chance to edge closer to April.

"This is what I hate, the witchdoctors and their bloody sorcery. Are you sure you're going to be okay love?" she whispered.

"Yes, Maria. Don't worry about me. As I've said, I don't believe in all of this mumbo jumbo."

"I'm afraid I didn't, but I do now. After tonight I can assure you, that you will too. So please, can I help you to escape before it's too late?"

"No, thank you. You must not get involved or Carlos will certainly kill us both. I have a mission that I need to complete, and no matter what happens to me you must not try to help me, Maria. Careful now, the drunken bums staggering back," April laughed, trying to hide her true inner fears.

"Have I missed something?" asked a much-relieved Carlos.

"No. It's just a girlie joke." Maria explained, as Carlos resumed his position between them.

While Carlos was preoccupied, exposing and fondling Maria's voluptuous breasts, April used the time to survey the scene of lecherous depravity. Amid the steady crescendo of the rhythmic drums, she could see that the witchdoctors were dancing themselves into a frenzied trance around the fire, and were perilously close to the cliff edge.

Across to the left three men huddled around one of the fires smoking and drinking. One of them looked towards, April. It was Winston and his colleagues. Winston signalled that they were ready, but April shook her head and returned her stare towards the ground. April now turned her thoughts to the only help that she could always rely on as she began to silently pray.

"Most gracious and heavenly Father, yet again I need to call upon you in my hour of need. Allow me to draw upon your unyielding strength to help me through this dark and dangerous hour. Keep Maria, Winston, and his colleagues, all safe. Help them to refrain from intervening and risking their own lives in order to save me. No matter what befalls me, it will be your will, Oh Father. I place myself in your hands my Lord. For I ask you in the precious name of the, Lord Jesus Christ. Amen."

Hardly had she the time to open her eyes than she was grabbed by both arms and hoisted to her feet. Two burly men then carried her over toward the witchdoctors, who were at their beacon fire.

Placing April between the fire and the cliff edge, she stood facing the formidable figures of the tall painted witchdoctors from across the flickering flames. This made them look even more sinister, while they were chanting and waving their spears threateningly toward her.

She seemed trapped, and with no obvious means of escaping. April felt compelled to watch their evil stare, which made things even more ominous, with the reflections of the fire continuing, as the fire continued to flicker and crackle. This only added to the relentless noise that was rapidly filling the air, growing louder and louder in an unending crescendo.

Her legs where now becoming heavy and sluggish as she tried in vain to elude the spell that they were beginning to weave on her. Eventually turning his back on April, the head witchdoctor raised his arms aloft. A ghostly silence instantly engulfed the camp, as the air became still and stagnant. It was as if they were all frozen within an instance of time.

The hoard of followers sat silently with baited breath. They were transfixed to the spot by the magical occasion as they waited with anticipation for their cue to continue.

The brief moment that passed seemed like an eternity. April was unable to move a solitary muscle as she had been rooted there waiting to hear her fate.

Although, still keeping his back towards her she was still compelled to watch, unable to turn away. Watching in total horror as his head began to spin round slowly through one and a half revolution, coming to rest facing her. While his back remained facing towards her, as he stared with his blood red piercing eyes the eyes began to grow larger, as his face distorted. Suddenly, two Tigers sprang at her from within his pupils, popping like soap bubbles when they reached April's face, evaporating into the night air as suddenly as they had appeared.

Still felt compelled to stare into his eyes without blinking; April's eyes became dry and sore. She was transfixed in their presence, being bound to the spot by their pure unadulterated evil. Then once again his head began to spin, but this time it spiralled upwards like a corkscrew, coming to rest looking at her from three feet above on a giraffe like neck.

She grew more and more afraid, but remained unable to move a solitary muscle voluntarily, as the events of her life began to flash before her. The evil face that confronted her began to smile ominously, with a knowing smirk, as if he was able to read April's every innermost thought.

His head began to grow blocking out the bright moonlight, as April was deafened by his loud foreboding laughter as it reached its peak, then his head shrunk back to his normal size.

The dark and evil figure reached out his hands towards her. His torso then revolved through half a revolution, coming to rest in its normal position. Facing April, with his arms still outstretched. Slowly he opened his clenched fists then out of one of his palms he blew a multicoloured dust into her face.

She was powerless to avoid it, as she felt the wind from his breath blowing so hard that her hair and skirt billowed out behind her in the strenuous wind of his breath. It felt as though he was blowing a force ten gales into her face, as she still remained firmly rooted to the edge of the cliff.

After he'd stopped blowing, April could then feel her body changing. It now began to feel weightless, and yet, she still could not escape the evil trap that she was now in. Her every movement remained firmly bound to the control of the sinister evil of the witchdoctor. While her thoughts and senses remained a free spirit, allowing her to experience their every fearful and evil unspoken threat.

Pointing his forefingers towards her hands he slowly mover them up, as she were forced to follow his every sinister silent direction, until her arms extended into the cruciform position. Moving his hands and pointing upwards, her now weightless body followed until it hovered horizontally above his head, looking down toward him. She was determined that she wasn't going to die here, and that she must suppress her innermost thoughts and fears, so her intense training kicked into emergency mode. All of her expressions and thoughts became totally bland, and completely fearless.

"Are you still a British Agent, April Darling?" The witchdoctor broke the sinister silence with his deep booming voice. He found her silent very poignant as she refused to answer. Angry at this audacity, he told her sternly, "Very well, but you will regret your misguided disobedience, April Darling." Directing her with his index finger her horizontal body moved slowly away from him until it hovered unsupported but facing downward, moving slowly out beyond the edge of the cliff. The moon was shining brightly now as it lit up the scene below. April could see that she was suspended and unsupported a hundred and fifty feet above the canyon. Gripped with fear, she instinctively knew that if the spell was broken now it would most certainly lead in her instant death.

Again, he repeated, "Are you still a British Agent, April Darling?" this time he added, "And is Maria helping you?"

In spite of her present predicament April found the courage to shout, "No, you bastards. I'm not. And if I was I wouldn't ask that drugged up bitch to help me." Whilst she still stared at the sheer drop below her, she could see that over to the left there was a ledge twenty feet below. A small river cascaded from it, and formed a spectacular waterfall dropping over a hundred feet into the perilous rapids below. The rapids formed into white water as it washed over the jagged rocks, which hastily ran out to the Pacific Ocean. Instinctively realising that although escaping via this canyon would be an extremely hazardous and foolhardy undertaking, it was not an impossible one that could be dismissed readily.

Because April avoided thinking about her employment, or about Maria, the witchdoctor was unable to read the answers he required from her mind. This left him feeling extremely angry and frustrated.

Out of desperation he closed his eyes, releasing his hold momentarily on April, as he tried desperately to break her concentration.

But still April continued not to be drawn into thoughts about her mission. She could see from here that there were tree branches, periodically growing out from cracks in the precipitous rock face.

"You are either an extremely brave lady, or a very foolhardy one. So for the last time before you die, are you still a British Agent, April Darling?" he demanded sternly, as he grew more and more intolerant of April's strong willed resolve.

"I have already told you, so if you won't believe me you will just have to go and fuck yourself, WONT YOU? What're you waiting for you ugly fucking bastards?" she retorted angrily as she tried desperately to call his bluff.

"Very well on your own head be it," he warned. April began to fall while remaining in the prone position as she saw the jagged rocks and rapids fast approaching. Suddenly, she came to an abrupt halt just ten feet from eternity. Then slowly her body ascended until she was looking down on the evil gathering once more. April slowly returned to the ground at the original spot on the edge of the cliff where she stood originally.

Carlos's voice interrupting, "Enough of this, you'll obviously never break her this way. We'll have to resort to violence after all." He told the witchdoctors firmly, "Strip her and bring me a bullwhip?"

April searched desperately for inspiration. The only open route was still the cliff she thought to herself. Watching as Carlos's henchmen approached from either side. "These witchdoctors need eradicating, and it'll also buy me some time." Feigning a faint and falling to her feet, she quickly accessed the gun in the lining in the dress and shot the startled witchdoctors through their foreheads in quick succession. Carlos and his henchmen fell to the ground with shock, reaching for their own weapons.

"Not so fast," warned April, as she sprang to her feet as lithe as a cat, pointing the gun directly at Carlos's head. "Tell your lackeys too slowly and carefully place their weapons on the ground then back away. If you don't, I'll shoot you. First I'll shoot your diminutive, ugly cock off. Then I'll blow your fucking ugly head off. Get the picture, Carlos?"

He urged them to comply with her demands. As they retreated, he warned, "You can't escape me. Give me your gun and I'll let you live?"

"Oh yea, right, just as if," April laughed as she picked up another pistol. "I think I'll take my chances if you don't mind. Now get over there with the rest of your disorderly shit." April gestured towards where his men were sitting with their hands raised. "Pronto," she ordered as she fired a warning shot near his feet.

Tempted to finish him here and now April realised that she was hopelessly outnumbered if she missed, and would then be at the mercy of the drug fuelled mob.

Carlos scuttled towards his men as April quickly moved over to the cliff edge, taking full advantage of everybody's temporary shock. Placing the guns into her shoulder bag, she then suddenly dived off the cliff.

Descending parallel to the face, April launched herself towards a protruding tree that was twenty-feet below, and ten feet closer to the cascading cataract.

Catching hold of the branch, April swung up onto it, then using the strength of her legs she thrust off toward the next protruding tree only just grasped hold of it in time to save herself. Her arms now felt as though they were leaving their sockets so she paused momentarily to rest them.

Spears, bullets, and inanimate objects, began reigning down from the top of the cliff, so April was forced to immediately continue despite the pain that she was suffering in her shoulders.

"Twenty feet from the falls I'll be able to fall into, and with, them. The water should have worn a deep reservoir in the rock over the centuries where I will land. Here goes nothing I'll just have to take my chances." April persuaded herself putting her feet on the rock face and pushed herself off and into a vertical dive.

Plummeting towards the base of the falls, amid the hail of bullets and spears that were still raining from above, April knew that she had only a small area in which to land. Trusting that it would be deep enough for her to enter the water safely, she realised that she could most certainly be diving to her death if she'd miscalculated.

Her body entered into the deep water and she was thankful that her calculations had been correct, and that she'd landed in a very large deep sump of water. Resurfacing out of sight of the cliff top, and between the cascading cataract and the precipitous moss covered rock face behind it. She trod water while resting and giving her time to gather her thoughts, and to recover her strength.

Clinging to a jagged protruding piece of rock, she could see that the moss-covered crag would be extremely slippery for her to climb. But it did seem to be her only means of escaping to a place of solitude where she'd be able to rest, a place from where she could plan her means of survival. In the dim flickering moonlight that filtered through the gushing waters, April was able to make out what looked like the entrance to a cave about ten feet above.

"If I can reach that cave I'll be able to rest," April thought to herself, while searching for a solid foothold on the rock. Slowly and laboriously, she ascended towards the cave. Her feet kept slipping on the treacherous surface, but eventually she reached the cave entrance. April could hear the voices of the marauding hoard now, as they searched for her body. It became obvious that Carlos had promised to reward anybody handsomely that found her, whether dead or alive.

Taking refuge inside the cave while she waited for the search to be abandoned, she was now alone, wet, and totally exhausted. April sat on the floor of the dark cavern resting her head on a convenient rock. Dishevelled, and trapped, she began to weep bitterly, until eventually through sheer exhaustion, she cried herself to sleep.

April was awakened abruptly by the presence of something touching her legs. Cautiously peeking, she could see a large snake slithering across her, as it slithered towards the entrance. Aware that Haiti had no poisonous snakes, she waited patiently until it had passed over her. The cave was well lit now, as the bright sunlight of the morning filtered through the cascading waters to form a spectrum of colours, deflecting into multicoloured rays that lit up the front of the spacious grotto. Although there were a number of harmless snakes around, that were mainly lying dormant about the floor, there were also a large number of venomous insects. Tentatively rising to her feet, avoiding the tarantula by her leg, April sidled closer to the entrance. She stopped suddenly as she heard loud voices over the sound of the gushing waters.

"Search meticulously for any sign of that English bitch. Or bring me her dead body. I don't care which. But I want her, or proof that she died in the fall." April could hear Carlos ordering his men frantically. "I'll pay 1 million gourde to the person that brings me her body." he offered, out of sheer desperation.

While pondering her problem she searched for a means of escaping. She suddenly had the profound feeling that she was being watched. Slowly, April scanned the cave as she peered back into the darkness at the rear of the grotto. "It seems that I'm alone," she thought. She then turned her concentration to her present and dire situation. Carefully she continued edging towards the entrance, trying to discern what was happening above the noise of the thunderous waters.

Stopping in her tracks at the sound of rattling, "That sounds like a rattle snake, but they aren't native to, Haiti," April thought as she took her phone out of her bag and turned on the torch attachment. She shuddered as the torch shone on a nest of dormant rattlers.

"Fucking hell, I'm glad I missed you lot last night." She whispered to herself, noticing that they were nesting on an old board. Again, April had a strong feeling of being watched, as she spun round quickly and shone the torch into the depth of the cave, as a number of small people quickly dived for cover behind the rocks.

"Children, where did you lot come from? You can come out. I won't hurt you."

Tentatively they revealed themselves to her. "We are not all children," a voice called out from the darkness as a three-foot tall man emerged to confront her.

"I'm sorry, but I have to ask you, are you midgets?" she questioned, watching open mouthed as twenty or more of them manifested themselves.

"We're all that's left of our race of small people. You're not going to disclose our secret cave to anybody are you?"

"No, your secret's safe with me. Besides, I have enough problems of my own right now, without taking on any of yours. My name's April, April Darling," she introduced herself, as she offered to shake their hands.

"I'm very pleased to meet you April, my names, Adam. Why's Mr. De-Mundo, trying to kill you?"

"It's a very long story, Adam. Why, are you a friend of Carlos De-Mundo?"

"Hardly, he killed my wife and children. He probably thinks that we're all dead by now, too," Adam told her sadly. Then he added, "We thought they were going to kill you, but if you stay here you'll be perfectly safe. They think that this cave's haunted by demons so they won't enter it," Adam explained. "As you've found out, they're a very superstitious group of people."

"Yes, well that would be nice. But I'm afraid that there's something I must do first. Is there another way out of here? I must get a change of clothing without anybody seeing me."

He told her, "We can go for your clothes if you tell us what you want, and where it is." One of the little people whispered to him, "Joe says that a number of men have just left the Villa, they're going towards the harbour, or the airport. Shall we stop them for you?"

"No. I need to know where they're going exactly," April, explained to Adam. "How can you get my clothes?" she asked him with a burning curiosity.

"We have our ways, and Maria helps us of course. You do know, Maria.

Don't you, April?"

"Yes, we're good friends. Can you bring her with you?" April asked him out of concern for Maria's safety, "Only Carlos will eventually kill her if you don't."

"We've tried before but she says she has unfinished business with him first," Adam sadly told her, then added, "She's so caring towards us. We worry for her safety as well."

"Has Carlos gone wherever with them?" shivering as she watched a tarantula walking across her foot.

"Don't be afraid of them, they'll not harm you unless you threaten them. The insects with the most fatal stings we've disposed of, and the rattle snakes we brought with us from America and we manage to keep them dormant," Adam assured her. "Yes. Carlos' gone off to the harbour, or airport, with them. But he'll be back in a couple of hours. He's left armed men outside the Villa on the off chance that you might return I imagine."

"Okay. Well I won't disappoint him then, but we'll have to hurry," urged April. She removed her phone from the handbag and dialled Maria's number.

"Hello," Maria answered tentatively. "It's me love. Are you alone?"

"Yes. You're still alive. Are you okay, April?"

"Yes, I'm fine. Now just listen. We need to get you out of there and fast."

"Not until I've dealt with Carlos, April."

"We'll deal with him together, Maria. But you must get out of there before I can destroy him, and his empire."

"Where are you now? And how are you going to destroy him?"

All the questions were making April feel uncomfortable. "Don't you worry about that I have it all planned. I'll explain it all to you as we go along. Now can you get all of my belongings together? And yours too of course."

"I've said that I'm not coming with you until I can see this shit bag dead," she insisted. "And then I MIGHT come with you."

"I've promised you that we'll kill him together but if you stay there I can't destroy him, Maria."

"Okay, but you will have to hurry," Maria urged. "It'll only take me five minutes to gather together all that we'll need."

"I'm on my way so I'll see you soon," April ended, as she rang off. Turning to Adam, she told him. "She sounds very strange," while loading her small gun. "Now tell me, how do I get down to the Villa?"

"We'll show you the way. But that gun is far too small, we have got some AKA rifles stashed away just for such an occasion. Shall we get them for you? Then we'll show you our secret entrance and route down to the Villa. Although, because you're taller than us you'll be much easier for them to spot," Adam remarked, as he led her to an arsenal of weaponry.

"This small gun as you call it is much more powerful than it looks," April corrected him, returning it back into the lining of her dress, "I killed the three witchdoctors with it. But I'll take an AKA with me as well, if you don't mind." April agreed as she examined and loaded a rifle. "Right, lead the way boss. Let's go and kick some ass, and teach Carlos De-Mundo a lesson he won't forget in a hurry. I hope we can get out this way or we will need a shovel, and pick axe." she joked, as they wound their way along dimly lit passageways and emerged at the edge of Carlos's estate.

"Are you sure this isn't a trap?" Adam asked her. He could see the land completely devoid of any workers.

"I'm not sure of anything, Adam. Will you all stay here and watch my back for me?"

"They can stay, but I'll be coming with you. And you haven't got the time to argue about it, April," Adam smiled. "So if you circle from the right, and I circle from the left, we can watch each other's backs." He insisted as he started to creep between the crops in the fields.

Keeping as low as possible, April began circling towards the rear of the villa, being extra vigilance as she passed through clearings in the crops. Furtively, they drew closer to the villa.

April's foot kicked against an inanimate object. Looking down, she discovered it was a half-full bottle of coke a worker must have stuck into the ground. This inspired a brain wave, as April emptied the bottle, and forced it over the muzzle to act as a crude silencer. 'That should stifle the gun shots a little, and help us to buy a little time.' April thought to herself as she got closer to the house.

"Got you, you little squirt." she heard the gruff voice of one of Carlos's men saying. "Come and look. I've caught myself a little sprat," he called to the other man, laughing and jeering to belittle, him.

"Let me go, you fucking bully." April could hear Adam protesting, as she crept up closer to them.

The man held Adam at arm's length as they continued to deride him. "Right you little shit-house, tell us who's with you and I'll let you go."

Supporting herself on one knee, April took careful aim at the man holding Adam. The shot then was hampered by Maria joined them, obscuring her view.

"Move out of the way, Maria." April muttered to herself, while willing her to move. She remained obscuring the view, stopping April from getting a clear shot. Quickly turning her phone on, April rang the villa.

"At last," mumbled April as Maria went to answer the telephone. In the same instance she discharged a single muffled shot, shooting the man in his head as simultaneously he dropped Adam to the floor.

Maria reappeared. "That was, April Darling. Where's that bloody English bitch?" she heard Maria shouting in panic. "WHERE'S THAT BASTARD BITCH?" She yelled at a surprised Adam, violently shaking him.

The other guard turned slowly trying to locate April's whereabouts, as she fired again and killed him. A third big Colombian emerged from the villa and dropped his weapon, raising his arms. "Don't shoot me," he pleaded, as he held his hands above his head.

"YOU FUCKING COWARD," Maria screamed at him as she picked up his gun and shot him in the back. "Now show yourself, you bitch," she called out.

April crept up behind her unnoticed. "I'm here!" she said as she confronted Maria. "Now drop that gun and tell me what the hell's going on."

"Go to hell." Maria spat in April's face. "I was just playing you for the gullible fool you are."

"Why?" April asked, as the change in her attitude was puzzling her.

"So that I could watch you die. Carlos gives me everything I ask for. He loves me. You're just his English whore."

"But you said that he wiped out all of your family?"

"Those pigs, I was glad to get rid of them. Carlos saved me because I despised them all. All they used to do is abuse me, and treat me like their personnel slave. They made me prostitute to get money for them."

"What about your children, Maria?"

"I had no children I just said that to gain the F.B.I's confidence. All I had was an abusive father, a drunken bitch of a mother, who didn't care anything about me at all, and a pimp of a husband. So Carlos was a Saint compared to what I had before. Now fuck off back to England, you cow. You were supposed to have died at the party last night," she stopped abruptly.

"Go on Maria, just how was I supposed to die?"

"We were going to watch the men take it in turns to fuck you until it nearly killed you," Maria gloated.

April was finding it hard to control her anger, "And what then?"

"The witchdoctors would bleed you, and then drink your blood for its magical powers. Then they were going to toss what was left of you off the cliff." Maria gloated as she took advantage of April's mental distraction, kicking the rifle from April's hands as she dived for the pistol. April quickly recovered from the shock and fell back, causing Maria to miss with her first shot. April reached into her dress, grabbing at her pistol, and shot through her dress, hitting Maria through her heart.

This saddened her as she'd looked on Maria as a trusted friend. "I must be slipping not to have seen through her. She was just setting me up." She thought to herself while retrieving her rifle.

"I thought she was on our side," she heard a shocked Adam remarking. "It's a good job you are an accurate marksman, I mean markswoman, April. And your little gun did come in handy after all. Didn't it?"

"Just lucky I guess. Now I must go into the hanger. You can return to the safely of your own people now, Adam, just until I'm finished here. But firstly, I must get my things, and a few of Maria's, because I don't think she'll need them anymore." April remarked apathetically, as she entered the house to hastily pack a haversack.

Adam asked, "What are you going to do now?"

"I'm going to wipe out his profits." she explained while walking towards the hanger, "I intend to torch all of his crops. But I must hurry now that we know that the lackeys will be on their way back soon."

He volunteered, "Well I'll help you, April?"

"How, Adam. Can you fly one of these?"

"Er, no, can you, April? But I must be able to help in some other way." He persisted.

"Okay, I give up. Maybe you can just help me to fuel up the plane. But then you'll have to go home. Do you promise me?"

"Okay. I promise," he reluctantly agreed.

April began to drain the crop spraying tanks as he asked, "What're you doing that for?"

"If you turn on the petrol pump, then start refuelling the plane through this hole here. Then we'll fill the spray tanks with petrol instead of fertiliser so we can have the biggest bonfire that you're ever likely to see." She told him as she emptied a five-gallon drum of fertiliser. "And yes, I can fly these old rust buckets, Adam."

Working feverishly until soon the plane was ready. April, then asked, Adam, "You can fill these empty cans and we'll strap them into the rear seat. They'll explode on impact like an incendiary bomb."

Adam started to fill the empty drums, after he'd filled the drums he stood on the wing as April passed the fuel up to him. He then stacked them carefully into the rear seat of the plane.

"I wish you'd take me with you," he repeated, trying to evoke her into feeling pity for him.

"Good, I've found a parachute and a rope," April proceeded to strap on the chute. After securing the cans using the rope, she explained. "You can't come because I'll have to bail out, and there's only one chute. Now will you open the hanger doors for me? Then wait for me at the caves, Adam." She jammed the fuel pump nozzle open to allow the petrol to continue spewing out onto the ground of the hanger, and eventually spreading to the surrounding buildings.

He pressed the button and the doors began to open to reveal a dust trail fast approaching as Carlos was returning with his thugs. "Fuck, the bastard's on his way back," yelled April, bringing the engine into life.

"I can't get back!" Adam panicked. "What am I going to do now?"

As the plane started from the hanger, April grabbed at Adams shirt scooping him up into the cockpit. Jokingly saying to him, "You'll do anything to get your own way. Now you'll have to squeeze in and sit on my knee. But sit perfectly still." She said firmly as the plane began taxiing towards the approaching cars.

"We're going the wrong way, April!" He screamed, pressing his foot on a non-existent brake.

"It's not a car with a brake there," she laughed, "we need to turn for takeoff so just hang on and be patient." She swung the plane round amid a hail of bullets from the approaching convoy.

Pulling back on the throttle, the plane started to pick up speed as the cars began to draw level with it. "Come on baby," April said to the plane as it picked up speed. Then gradually the plane pulled ahead of the pursuing cars. Soon she was pulling back on the joystick, and taking the plane soaring up into the clear blue skies.

Banking hard and sweeping low, they began to spray the petrol round the perimeter of the estate, working in ever decreasing circles towards the Villa at the centre.

April continued this until both her tanks were completely empty. "We very nearly had enough fuel to finish the job off, but it should still all burn." She shouted to Adam over the noisy engine as she swept low towards the villa.

"Hold the joy stick steady for me, Adam? But be very careful not to move it." April held a drum of petrol over the side of the open cockpit as they neared the villa. "That's it, just keep it steady now?" she released the drum directly over the house, "BINGO!" She shouted, watching the drum crash through the roof and causing it to burst open, drenching the house with its inflammable liquid contents.

"Quick. They're driving away." Adam panicked again as he watched the convoy turning, and streaming back up the long driveway.

April could see Carlos driving furiously ahead of the convoy, dashing for the safety of the hills.

Swooping low above his head, she caused him to brake viciously, as the trailing cars crashed into him. April climbed steeply to three thousand feet and put the plane into a steep dive, aiming it straight towards the villa.

Taking the rope from the drums to firmly secure the joystick, and keep it on target, as she unclipped the seat harness. "Time for us to go," she told a sickly looking Adam. Asking, "What's up with you, are you feeling airsick?" To which he could only nod. "Never mind, we'll soon be on terra firma. Now here comes the tricky bit," she explained grabbing him firmly round the waist, and hooking her other arm through the parachute handles. Using only her legs, April kicked clear of the fast descending plane.

Adam was holding April firmly round her neck, clinging to her so tightly that she could barely breathe or move. Eventually she managed to yank at the rip cord, releasing the chute as it jerked, slowing down their decent. Then they began to float gently down towards the earth, well clear of the blazing fields.

Watching as the plane hit the house, erupting into a large ball of fire, which spread rapidly throughout the estate. The narcotic fumes filtered up with the heat, making a kaleidoscope of colours as the sun rays filtered through it like a prism. Then it eventually evaporated into the upper atmosphere.

As the flames accelerated up the runway it ignited the convoy of vehicles, causing them to explode. One by one they cart wheeled, the occupants being flung into the air as if they were toys. The buildings then started to rupture as the flames billowed towards them and into the hanger, as the rolling cloud of heavy smoke slowly engulfing the land.

The light planes were thrust from the hanger, flipping over like cardboard cut outs. They ended up undercarriage uppermost, with one of them ending up on the penultimate car, with the tail-end truck ploughing into it, swallowing it up in the conflagration.

Watching the mayhem of horror as the aviation fuel tanks exploded with the heat, and sprayed out jets of burning fuel onto the remainder of Carlos's private army, like a gigantic flame-thrower.

"Look, Adam. That bastard Carlos, and a truck load of his henchmen, are escaping. They're heading towards the border with the Dominican Republic I presume," April shouted over the noise, as they finally floated to the ground, landing harder than usual, due to the increased weight of the two of them being in tandem.

She quickly turned on her mobile phone and called Charles. "We've been worried about you here, are you okay, April?" he started.

"What do you care," she retorted, still feeling extremely bitter, "just listen to me?" She then quickly described all that had transpired. Finished with, "De-Mundo has escaped the bastard; he seems to have a charmed life. Anyway, I think he'll head towards, Jacmel. My guess is that he'll keep close to the coast, cross into the Dominican Republic at Pedemales where it is quiet. Then I think he'll probably drive to the port of Barahona, to hire a speedboat. He will probably cross the bay into Santo Domingo harbour."

"Why do you think he'll head to, Santo Domingo? He won't get past the border guards. Or will he?" Charles interrupted

"Remember they're very poor and mostly corrupt out here, so he probably has some of them in his pocket, I've destroyed his crops and aircraft, and he probably expects us to be watching for him at Port-au-Prince. So the next best choice has to be Santo Domingo. Alert James, Winston, and co, to try to intercept him," she told him as she gathered up her belongings. "Tell them that I'll catch up to them as soon as I possibly can. Oh! Can you send a team out here so they can relocate some friend of mine? Better still a-team of workers to help them to build their homes, I couldn't have managed this without their help. They're what are left of an ancient tribe of small people."

Adam stood proud as he heard April praising them.

"Tribe of small people, I thought they'd all become extinct a long time ago?" said a surprised, Charles.

"Well there's a small tribe of approximately twenty-five here living in a cave, and I believe that there's another small tribe of their cousins, about the same number living in remote areas of the Amazon," April informed him. "Now I intend to get some rest, so I'll be here for at least another twelve to twenty four hours. Then I'll contact you." April finished as she rung off. Leaving the phone turned on, to recharge the solar batteries.

CHAPTER 22

It was becoming dusk as they trudged towards the caves. "I think I'll sleep under the stars tonight," she told, Adam.

"Why? Is there something wrong with us? Do we smell, snore, or something like that?" A confused Adam asked indignantly.

"No, not at all," she insisted, placing a consoling arm around his shoulders and kissing him on his forehead. "I need a good rest before continuing on and I won't get it with all of those insects crawling all over me, Adam. Anyway, it's now time for you all to move out of the caves and built yourselves proper houses. You can reclaim Carlos' land, because I can assure you that he won't be back here, so he won't need this land anymore."

"But April, we'll need to transfer the land ownership to us. You must also remember that we're not builders, so where the hell do we start?"

"You heard me telling my boss to send a team of people out here to help you, and I'll give you my mobile number in case you need more help or advise from me. You'll all be just fine. I'd do it all for you if I had the time, but Carlos has to be caught and dealt with. So I need to go after him, like yesterday."

"I know you're a very plucky Lady, but that's far too dangerous for a slender lady like you. Let somebody else go after him, can't you?"

Adam pleaded. "I know that you're very resourceful, you've proven how you can survive against all the odds, but Carlos De-Mundo is so very dangerous."

"It's now time for you to worry about your own people, not me. I promise I'll be okay." April kissed him again on his forehead as they reached the small settlement.

A makeshift canvas shelter containing a Lillo was quickly erected. "Is this private enough for you, Miss April?" A young man asked enthusiastically, mopping the sweat from his fevered brow.

"Yes, it will do very nicely. Thank you all so very much. Now I think I should lie down before I fall down."

"Firstly, will you have some supper with us, please?" requested Adam.

"After all, you are our guest of honour."

"I'd be honoured to share in your supper, but you must share the credit too, Adam. It wasn't all my doing remember. You did have a very big part to play in it."

The ringing of her mobile phone interrupted. "Damn and blast. I knew I should have turned the damn thing off. Yes, Charles. What is it you want this time?" She snapped impatiently.

"I thought you'd want to know that it seems you were right. There has been a shootout at the border control at Pedemales. They've killed at least six people, and severely wounding a number of others."

"Is it De-Mundo, Charles? And were any of our men amongst the dead?"

"Yes, it was Carlos De-Mundo and his men, and yes, two of our men are among the dead."

April could sense the sadness in Charles' voice. "What are you not telling me? Who was it that was killed?"

"I'm sorry to be the one to have to tell you this, but there's not any easier way of putting it." He took a deep breath before explaining. "Captain Winston Edwards was among the fatalities, and Lieutenant James Edwards is still missing."

He waited with baited breath through the long silence that followed, tears flooded from her eyes as she sobbed bitterly.

Eventually Charles intervened. "You have to pull yourself together my dear, and carry on. That's what Captain Edwards would have expected you to do. You know, he was very proud of you. When he heard that this was to be your assignment he insisted on being part of the team."

Again there was a long silence while April struggled to control her feelings. Eventually, dabbing the tears from her eyes, April sobbed. "I know, but he was such a dear, dear friend to me. If you'd have let me deal with Carlos De-Mundo when I had him in my sights Winston would still be alive today, and James would not be missing."

"It's this dirty business we're in. Winston understood that, AND SO MUST YOU," Charles told her firmly. "Now, I'm sorry but you mustn't let them escape you this time. Go after them, and get them this time."

"Yes, I suppose you're right. Can you get me a chopper and clear me with the border guards?" she asked as she began preparing herself.

"The chopper is en-route, and the embassy is getting you clearance as we speak. So just be very, very careful. And remember, no matter what clearance we get, money will always speak louder than words in the poorer countries. So good luck and God speed. Do we need a team to clean up the corpses out there?"

"No. I've cremated them, Charles." April said sarcastically, as she heard the chopper approaching. "Don't worry about me, worry about that fucking bastard when I eventually catch up with him, AGAIN. How would you like his head Charles? Would you like it on a stake as a trophy to decorate the trophy cabinet? Or maybe on a platter, like what happened to John the Baptist?"

"Preferably still on his body. We still need to extract certain information about his distribution network, and finances. He should also undergo the indignity of standing trial for his crimes."

"Yeah right, then you can lock him up in a nice comfy cell. Okay, I'll take extra special care of him just for you. I'll rap him up in white cotton wool, and then tie a blue ribbon round him. Just think of the cost of a trial, then a life term in prison. I thought we'd agreed I could finish him. I could save you all that. And remember, he'll always be able to use his money to continue his death dealing from prison. Anyway I must go now, my taxi is just landing," April finished her rant, as she ended the call abruptly.

She watched as a gargantuan man alighted from the helicopter. The man stood at least seven feet tall, and had a muscular physic to match his size. "Are you, Miss April Darling?" he asked politely, in his soft American drawl. "Yes, that's me. But you must be the biggest taxi driver I've ever seen!" She said playfully with a broad smile whilst gathering her sparse belongings. "Did your mother stand you in a bucket of manure when you were a kid to make you grow, like you would a tall oak tree? Just for the record, exactly how tall are you?"

"No she breast fed me until I went to high school," Was his witty retort. "I'm seven foot three inches tall, ma'am. Now let me stow your belongings for you?" He insisted, reddening with embarrassment at her candid humour.

"I'm sorry. I didn't mean to embarrass you," she apologised, as she saw his obvious embarrassment, "now tell me what our orders are"

"Field Martial Sir Charles Hythe-Smith is waiting to speak to you. I must say that you're not quite what I'd been led to expect. From the way that they'd described you and your capabilities, well, I expected somebody with the physic of a male iron curtain, hammer thrower. I certainly never expected a petite little filly like you, Ma'am." He explained sheepishly.

"Very well and tactfully put. Now I'm, April." She introduced herself, offering to shake his enormous hand.

"I'm honoured to meet you, Ma'am. I'm Sergeant Will Bartholomew, and I've heard so much about you. Will explained awkwardly, as he gently shook her hand. "Now can we get aboard? We must get moving."

April bade Adam, and his friends a tearful goodbye, apologising for not sharing their meal with them, but promising to return whenever the opportunity allowed.

Clambering into the chopper they were soon flying towards Haiti's boarder with the Dominican Republic. Accessing her phone again April began, "Hello Charles, are you still tracking De-Mundo's movements?"

"Yes, but firstly are you okay now?"

"I'm okay Charles, thank you. Now, what's happening?" April asked impatiently. "We haven't the time to have a cosy little chat right now."

"I know, but we all worry about you here. Anyway, he's not heading towards Santo Domingo as you'd thought he would do. That's unless he's circling round to get to it. He's headed northeast towards the Sierra De Bahoruco, National Park. They stopped briefly at Aqua Negra, presumably for something to eat or drink, and now they're about half way to the national park,"

"How long did they stop for, Charles?"

"Just a moment and I'll find out." There was a short silence while he checked.

"We're nearing the boarder April, and I'll have to notify them," Will told her, as he picked up the radio's handset.

"Just a few minutes April, three to be exact," Charles confirmed.

"THREE FUCKING MINUTES isn't long enough to have a piss. What are they up to?" she struggled to find a logical explanation.

"I'm just relaying the pictures to the helicopter's console. Can you see it now?"

"Yes, I can see it. Can you run it through slowly?" April asked him, watching very intently. "They just mingled then got back into their vehicles, but why? Ask somebody to run it through extremely slowly, and see exactly what De-Mundo did."

"We're trying to do that but De-Mundo did pick his spot. The rain forest and fading light is making it difficult to enhance the images without distorting them. Where are you now?"

"Tell him the guards are insisting that we land," interrupted Will, as he negotiated a landing spot on the Haiti side of the boarder. "I'm sorry about this. I'll try to find out what exactly is the problem."

"Did you hear that, Charles? We need the clearance like yesterday. Hurry and I'll leave this line open and on speakerphone." April had barely finished when two gun-wielding guards signalled for her to get out, pulling at her roughly. Will had already alighted, and April could see him laughing and joking with the guards through the office window. They asked her at gunpoint to raise her hands, as she tried in vain to protest.

As the guards spoke in their native Kreyol Ayisyen, it left April feeling vulnerable and intimidated. She could still see Will, who seemed to be drinking beer while he joked with them.

Drinking from a beer bottle he sauntered slowly over towards her. "Hello, doll." He began. The alcohol had obviously transformed the shy retiring man into an obnoxious, brash, and forthright, person. "I'm afraid this is as far as you go," he smirked. Then he spoke to the men guarding April in their native Kreyol Ayisyen. They all nodded their heads as they laughed. "I've just suggested a little treat for them," he sneered, "I think we should strip search you when we're all together, just so that we can each check in turn to see if you have anything concealed in that pretty little pussy of yours." He rubbed his hand across April's breasts.

Seething because of his audacity, April gripped the top of the helicopter door with both hands. "First, we should make it a bit more interesting by playing a sexy game of two balls."

The dull witless Will wore a puzzled expression on his face as he became curious, "Okay. So how do we play this sexy two ball game?"

"I'm dead if this goes wrong," she thought to herself. She explained, "Like this, you close your eyes and I'll try to guide your hands to finding two balls," she suggested, as she smiled enigmatically

"Where are you going to find balls out here, are you a magician or something?" he smirked. "Okay, I'll humour you and play along," Will agree. The bemused guards looked on. "Now where are the balls?" He asked, shutting his eyes as he held out his hands.

"Here," April shouted as she kicked him in the testicles as hard as she could.

Will grabbed at his testicles as he doubled over with pain, his eyes widening and crossed. Then April poked him in them with two straight fingers. The guards froze momentarily, so April was able to wrench the gun from the nearest one shooting them both dead, and then placing a well-aimed bullet between Will's eyes.

Holding and firing the rifle in one hand she clambered aboard the helicopter, mowing down the remaining guards as they aimlessly emerged from their hut.

Bringing the engine whirled into life she lifted off she banked to avoid a hail of bullets. Flying the helicopter low she brushed over the treetops until she was well out of sight.

"Are you there, April. What the hell is going on?" she could hear a concerned Charles calling.

"That overgrown baboon you sent was in De-Mundo's pocket too. You can tell the Yanks that's why I had to shoot him." April hastily explained as she started to climb. "I'm in his helicopter so you can also deny all prior knowledge of this if you need to. Now where are the other sewer Rats?"

"They've just entered the national park, April. And they've just once again stopped."

"Good. It'll give me time to catch them up."

"They're on the move again. BLAST IT," Charles snapped angrily.

"What now, has your coffee gone cold," April asked sarcastically, pressing on towards the national park.

"Can't we at least be civil to each other instead of all this constant sniping at every conceivable opportunity?" Charles suggested. "The convoy has divided, and the truck is heading east. But Carlos's car is continuing to travel northeast."

"Well, who do you suggest I follow, Boss?" continued April, whilst gnawing away at his conscience.

"There you go again. I see you are getting the bitchiness befitting your adopted gender. Maybe we'll have to review your position when this is all over. Now the school of thought here is that Carlo De-Mundo will still be in the land cruiser, so if you follow that Northeast," he explained with exasperation. "We'll keep trying to confirm about Carlos's status, and also keep tracking the other vehicle just in case you need to go after that. So I'll update you as, and when, I can," he told April as he rang off abruptly.

April knew that her jealousy was uncalled for, but she was feeling so hurt. She tried to suppress these feelings as she continued to search for them amid the fading light. "Where are you, scum bag?" she said to herself, waving the search light from side to side. "Eureka!" She shouted with glee when she saw his Land cruiser. "I have them in my sight now," she told Charles. "They seem to be heading up to, Santiago. Shall I take them out now?"

He reminded her, "Not just yet, we still need to know exactly where they're headed for."

"I hope you know what you're doing, they –,"

"What's happening?" Charles shouted with concern.

After a short silence, April told him, "I'm coming under fire. That was close it put a hole through my door. OH NO!"

"WHAT IS IT?" He shouted again.

"They've got a hand held rocket launcher now that they've stopped and got out of their car. They've just fired a tracer bullet that's hit my tail fin."

"Get out of there, April. Our ground troops are moving in on them now.

GO," he urged.

Not needing telling twice, April banked and headed away from the shooting. "Okay! I'm out of here," she confirmed. April picked up speed while still skimming the treetops. "OH, SHIT!" She yelled, weaving from side to side.

A panicking Charles asked again. "Speak to me. What's wrong, April?"

"I thought you were tracking me. Can't you see that thing in my heat stream?" she said to him, while trying in vain to take evasive action. She turned back towards the gunfire.

"I'm sorry, Carlos. But you'll have to walk home." April muttered to herself, sweeping low over the Land cruiser. "The soft bastards have left their engine running, Charles. Hopefully the heat will attract the missile as it passes over them."

"It should do. But be careful, April. They're still firing at you remember."

"I'll take my chances there, Charles." April said as she flew over the car, spraying it with bullets. A bullet pierced the fuel tank causing it to erupt in flames, and a second explosion quickly ensued enlarging the fire, as the heat-seeking missile was drawn in the conflagration.

"The troops have them surrounded now, so you can get out of—." The link went dead when the helicopter received a salvo of bullets into the control panel. As simultaneously the engines spluttered, then fell silent. Struggling with the controls, April flicked the rotors into feather, and spiralled down, crash-landing into a shrubbery. She bolted from the helicopter with her sparse belongings, diving into a deep hollow, as the helicopter quickly erupted into flames. This added to the mayhem that was rapidly developing in the park.

April heard the sliding of the bolt of a rifle. Then a voice ordered, "Stand up, and hold your hands in the air, Miss."

Cautiously April obeyed and slowly turned to face her adversary. The man was wearing Carlos's white tuxedo, causing April to burst into a fit of uncontrollable laughter, which acted as a distraction while she activated the radio devise in her ring.

The man demanded, "Stop that. What's so funny, woman?"

April regained her composure. "You're wearing your boss's jacket. I've been following the wrong vehicle."

Hearing sporadic gunfire, April realised that the troops were engaging the remainder of Carlos's men.

The man gave a smug smile knowing that they'd outwitted her. "Yes. So you're not so smart after all. Are you, Miss?" He told her patronisingly.

"I'm afraid I can't take all the credit for that error. It was all down to some half-witted idiots in London making that mistake." April corrected him, hoping that the radio was working. She sauntered slowly towards the gun-wielding mercenary. "Well, I must give you credit for outwitting my dimwit of a boss, and his associates." She continued with the insults, thinking that a large number in the department would be witnessing Charles' acute embarrassment.

"Now where are your troops?" April asked, trying unsuccessfully to climb from the pit. Then she asked meekly, "Could you please help me, soldier?"

The man became compassionate as he watched April's useless attempts to climb out of the hole. "Here, pass me your things first, Miss?" he then pulled her from the ditch.

"I hope you don't mind, but I'm afraid I must frisk you," he apologised. "That's okay. You're only doing what you must do. Most of your friends wouldn't even have had decency to asked, or to apologise." April told him, holding up her hands voluntarily so he could give her a brief body search. To April's surprise, the soldier missed the gun that she had in the lining of her dress.

"Okay. You seem to be clean. You can put your hands down now, Miss." He then rummaged through her belongings. "They're fine too. I'm letting you fetch those so that you'll have something to change into." He explained as he pointed with his rifle, gesturing for April to walk in front of him.

"Where are you taking me?"

"Mr. De-Mundo wants you delivered directly to him, Miss."

"You know he's going to kill me, don't you?" April said sadly, trying to provoke his pity. Then she suddenly became aware that the shooting had stopped.

"I'm sorry about that. But I'm afraid I have my orders, Miss." He apologised. They reached the burning vehicles as a soldier was executing the final Marine.

April protested, "You bastard savages. Why did you have to kill them? Wasn't capturing them enough for you? Are you also going to murder me now?"

"We have are orders to keep you alive until we deliver you to Mr. De-Mundo." The soldier explained sincerely.

"And then HE'LL kill me," snapped April. She was counting the remaining men in her head. 'Only six men,' she thought. 'I should be able to surprise them and take some of them out. I'll just need a little distraction of some sort. She watched as they surrounded the dead Marines, laughing at their lifeless bodies.

"ENOUGH!" the man guarding her shouted. "Do we have to behave like savages?" His voice now was extremely stern, "are you all that's left alive?"

Charles was listening to everything as he tracked April's movements via a satellite link up. "I know she's, insubordinate and annoyed at me personally, and she cannot resist having a pop at me whenever she can. But don't lose her. We need to get her some more help to her, and as quickly as possible," he insisted.

"But Sir, we only have thirty minutes left before we lose the satellite link up," the computer operator explained. "Then it'll be at least an hour before we can get it back."

A disconsolate Charles insisted, "Just do the best you can, AND MORE." Seeing the anguish that Charles was experiencing, the operator promised,

"We'll do all that we know how, Sir. If I might presume to ask a personnel question, is this agent somebody that's special to you?"

"Yes. She is my prodigy. As well as being the finest agent that this department, and the country, has ever produced. Or will ever have in the foreseeable future. She's a remarkable and a caring person, as well as being a formidable adversary."

"We'll make sure that we don't lose her then." The man vowed as he picked up the telephone. "I'll call a friend of mine in Brazil and ask her to lone me her computer."

"We don't have the time for you to go to Brazil, man," Charles snapped at the startled operative.

"No sir," the man smiled. "I need to link up my computer via hers. So that when the satellite is out of range for my PC I can access it via a link through her computer. Hello. Is that you, Cassandra?"

Charles took a whiskey from the drinks cabinet to settle his nerves, while waiting for his computer operator to conclude his business.

"We have our link up, and Cassandra is keeping herself available to give us any assistance we need," the man confirmed. He then added, "It seems that the lady's involved in some sort of fracas."

Charles rushed over to the computer. "That's my girl, go on give them hell." A jubilant Charles called out, as he witnessed April's retaliatory actions.

She'd quickly grasped the butt of a gun and the shocked man still had his finger on the trigger. In one single swift movement, April pulled at the gun and aimed it towards the remaining marauding guards, who were occupied rifling through the burnt out helicopter. In the same movement she gave the gun a sharp tug away from the surprised man, causing his finger to activate the trigger and kill two of his associates. Instantly regaining his composure he snatched the gun from her grip as he swung it round, striking her on the head with the butt.

Unconscious, April's body slumped to the floor, as a man hastily tethered her so that she couldn't create any further havoc. As her head slowly cleared she could see two gun wielding men perched on the tail gate of the pickup truck as it trundled along, jerking and weaving on the dusty uneven track.

She attempted to struggle free when she realised the predicament that she was in, lying flat on her back with her tethered feet pointing towards the rear of the truck.

The two men were leering down at her menacingly.

"WHAT THE FUCKING HELL ARE YOU TWO UGLY FREAKS LOOKING AT?" She yelled at them, as her bruised back took another pounding from the pot-holed track. When trying to alter the position that she was lying in, April noticed the tailgate wasn't properly fastened. One of the clasps had become unattached. This gave her inspiration. 'If only I could shuffle closer, then maybe I would be able to kick the tailgate off. That would wipe the smug smile of their ugly mugs,' she thought, as she fidgeted, constantly drawing closer to the back of the truck. Finally, she'd got within reaching distance of them. Concentrating all of her energy she released a two-footed kick at the tailgate. The shocked men dropped their weapons, as they made a vain attempt to save themselves from falling by gripping the loose tailgate as they fell into the path of a following vehicle, and were instantly killed.

April bent her knees up to her chest, and pushed her arms down, feeding her feet through the ropes and bringing her arms to the front. Quickly grabbing for one of the guns that they'd dropped, she shot through the rope to free her legs. Hurriedly she flicked off her shoe which allowed her to use her big toe on the trigger. Engaging a single shot mode, April mumbled, "I'd better be bloody accurate," as she pointed the muzzle at the rope tying her wrists together. Pushing down on the trigger with her toe, she shot through the rope freeing her hands. The driver, who realised the fate that had befallen his compatriots, was slowing down.

April rolled onto her stomach and released another single shot through the rear window of the cab, and into the back of his head. April leaned over the side of the swerving truck and opened the driver's door to pull the dead body out. Then she swung into the cab, keeping the gun pointed at the man wearing Carlos's coat.

"So we meet again my friend. Now where are we heading for?" she asked, as she took over the controls, swerving to avoid the vehicle crashing off the mountainous road.

"We're not friends." The man stuttered, as he reached for his pistol.

"I'll take that, thank you. Now I'll ask you only once more, where are you going to meet up with, De-Mundo?" April insisted, in a very stern voice.

"Go and fuck yourself," he said adamantly. "You've done enough damage for me. Mr. De-Mundo will kill me when he finds out that I'm the sole survivor."

"You can wallow in your pity if you like, BUT YOU WILL tell me where your rendezvous point is going to be." She threatened, struggling to drive one handed on the rough terrain. "I'll count to three, One… Two… Three," bang. April shot him in the leg.

"OUCH! You mad fucking bitch," he yelled as he clutched his leg. "I hope you rot in hell for that."

"That's as maybe. Now where are you going to meeting, Carlos?"

"GET FUCKING KNOTTED. You're just a heartless fucking cow."

April released another shot into his other leg. "Ouch! You merciless bastard," he cried out as the blood started flowing profusely.

"Don't be a fool man. Tell me what I want to know," April asked, drawing the truck to a halt. "Then I'll get you to a doctor."

"No. You've done your fucking worst to me. Haven't you, bitch?"

April was feeling exasperated, but she admired the man's misplaced sense of loyalty. "Have I?" she warned, thrusting the gun into his groin. "I'll not kill you but you'll certainly wish I had."

"NO. Don't shoot my prick, he pleaded. "One… Two…," she started coldly.

"STOP, Angelina airport, we've arranged to meet at Angelina airport," he volunteered as he sobbed like a baby.

"Good. That wasn't too hard, was it? I'll keep my promise now and get you to a doctor," agreed April as she started the truck. As she drove fast down the hazardous mountain road, she asked, "Where is Angelina airport?"

"Go and find it by your fucking self," he told her as he flung open the door and rolled out headfirst. He left a small round casket behind before he fell headlong into the tree which killed him instantly.

"Ouch. I felt that," April said, screwing her face up as if she had experienced the pain personally. "But what have you dropped this for, is it a pressy for me?" April stopped as she reached down to pick up the casket, a move that April was about to regret as she gingerly unscrewed the top.

Nearing the final thread the top sprung off, bursting into a multicoloured stardust. Then it transformed into dark smoke as it filled the cab with a pungent odour. A smell worse than she'd ever experienced before. It was accompanied by a loud and ghostly deafening laughter. April instantly recognised it as the laughter of the dead witchdoctors.

She tried frantically to escape, but found that she was trapped, and unable to open the doors. Paralysis rapidly crept over her body as she drifted quickly into an eerie semiconscious state. Her eyes stared fixedly as if their lids had been pinned open. She'd been frozen within a restless semi-coma, hovering between life, and the supernatural deathly underworld.

Whilst compelled to keep her eyes open, she felt her inner self, her very life giving soul floating from her body, as it passed through the windscreen as if it were not a solid matter. Then April found herself lying horizontally on the mountain track, her soul was now a subservient to another almighty power.

April then was subject to the experience of seeing, and feeling, the truck being driven over her very slowly. It was being driven by her own earthly body as it laughed uncontrollably at her souls suffering.

———

The snarling of a wild beast could be heard drawing closer, as the vehicle passed over and stopped. The tailgate dropped open as a rampant tiger leapt from the truck as April sensed being lifted out of its path, as the tiger's claw started to tear into the flesh of her legs. She felt now that she was wrapped and lifted to safety, by the trunk of an elephant. Then it placed her safely high up in the branches of a tall tree.

Now the low purring of a lion was heard as it drew nearer. April saw its face as it looked down at her, drooling on her as it licked her face. Lying gentle at her side, it plucked a vulture from the sky as it swooped down to pick out her eyes. 'My protector,' she thought. There was then the sense of feeling slowly sliding off the branch.

With a sinking feeling, April's soul floated down toward the firm and solid ground below, as the lion and the tree evaporated in a puff of white smoke.

Once again the scene was transformed. April now found herself standing in the centre of a busy motorway. The witchdoctors mocking laughter gave way to the incessant honking of car horns, as the cars passed through her matter-less body. April now had the feeling of being hoisted above, but this time she was within the talons of a gigantic bird as it took her soaring up into the night sky. It carried her across the open sea, releasing her from within the clouds. She plummeted down towards the watery depths far below.

Still unable to move a solitary muscle, April experienced the sensation of plummeting down to watery grave below, which was waiting ominously to receive her. As her feet entered into the water April's eyes closed, as if in death, killed by the impact of entering into the cold and treacherous waters of a tempestuous ocean.

Suddenly April became aware of a tapping noise as her eyes started to slowly focus. Again there was a tapping. "Are you all right Miss?" a voice was heard anxiously asking. A torch shone through the window and into the cab, piecing the deathly darkness. "Your truck seems undamaged, Miss. Are you Okay?" The voice continued to ask.

Looking round, April found that she'd driven into a tree. "It was an hallucination, or was it a dream?" April thought with relief.

Convincing herself, "I must have knocked my head and dreamt it all," as she wound open the window.

"What's that thing?" The man asked as he shrunk back in total horror. "Is it—."

"It was left here by him," April pointed to where the body had fallen. She then gazed open mouthed at the empty space, "It's gone. The bloody body's gone. That's unless I've dreamt that as well," She wondered, wearing a very puzzled expression. Then looking at her watch she added, "Damn it, it's stopped at five thirty."

"You are Miss who?"

"Oh I'm sorry. I'm, Miss April Darling, and you are Dr. Watson, I presume."

The man laughed. "A fellow Lancastrian it seems by your accent. I'm, Alan. It's my pleasure to meet you, Miss April Darling." He told her, as he shook her hand enthusiastically. "Blood, your hand covered in blood. Where are you hurt?"

For the first time she became aware that she was injured. As April began to get out of the car, she saw that her skirt was torn and soaked in blood. On closer examination, she could see three deep gashes down her leg that were bleeding profusely.

"Let me fetch my medical bag out of the car?" The doctor said to her, disappearing into the darkness to collect it. Returning he told her, "I'm a doctor, and as luck would have it I'm out here in this early hour because I've just delivered a beautiful baby. Now sit and hold still while I clean your wounds." Opening his bag he removed some swabs, and a bottle of saline solution. He questioned, "Are you going to tell me what happened, April?"

"I don't really know. I was just driving with a man towards Angelina airport, and then he jumped out and left that trinket box. I must have knocked my head trying to retrieve it. Now I find that his body has just disappeared. Vamoosed as they say."

Alan stopped when he saw the extent of the injuries to her leg. He asked, "How did you say you sustained these injuries?"

"I didn't, because I don't really know that either. Maybe I scratched it on the gear lever or something like that?"

While continuing to clean up the wounds, he explained to her. "I've only ever seen this type of injury once before, and that was when I was working in India. It looks like the results of being mauled by a Tiger, but as there are no Tigers in the Dominican, perhaps you'd better start from the very beginning, April?" He suggested, while he gave her a penicillin injection.

April looked into the kindly eyes of the young doctor before deciding to confide in him, or at least partially.

"Well Alan," began April taking a deep breath, "I'm out here in pursuit of an obnoxious drugs baron."

"That scum bag De-Mundo, I suppose. Why are you after him on your own, April? You'll just get yourself killed."

"Got him in one, Carlo De-Mundo the slimy maggot, he's a heartless death-dealing bastard who's killing thousands of people worldwide every day. So he has got to be stopped," she explained. April noticed that it was becoming lighter. "The last thing I remember it was becoming dusk, now it seems to be sunrise," she muttered thoughtfully. "Anyway, I digress. I intend to try to stop him, or at least I will if I can get to the airport in time."

"What time is he flying, and where is he flying too?" Alan asked her, as he finished dressing her wounds. "Much as I would like to see him brought to justice, I don't wish to see a pretty little thing like you, getting yourself hurt in the process."

"Well I thank you kindly for your concern. However, I can assure you that I'm more than capable of eradicating that trash," April mocked, in a fake American drawl.

"You sound as though you're a trained government agent," he ventured to ask.

April thought for a moment before confirming, "Yes I am, but don't tell anyone, will you. Now are you finished?" she asked, delving into her handbag for her mobile phone.

"I used to work for the cloak and dagger mob myself. It was when I returned from India. They recruited me because of a thesis I'd written on mental gender transference, and they wanted me to assist in forcibly helping a man to become a woman, mentally. Anyway, as I would not be a party to their deviously ghoulish experiments because I found it to be totally immoral, I quit, and came out here. But that still doesn't explain the Tiger scratches to your leg?" The doctor continued to press, as he sat in the passenger seat beside her.

April asked him, "Was it a Sir Charles Hyde-Smith who recruited you?" trying to avoid his question.

"No, it was a Robert somebody."

"Montgomery?" she suggested.

He asked, "Yes. That's the man, Robert Montgomery. Why, do you know him?" April nodded.

"I was then introduced to Sir Charles, who in turn introduced me to his gruesome team of boffins, and their equally gruesome plans. That's when I decided it was not for me. Forcing somebody to mentally transfer to the opposite gender against their will, I find it utterly and totally immoral. So I quit, and escaped out here to obscurity. I doubt if they can even remember me now."

"Well thank you very much." April said indignantly, squeezing his hand gently.

"Why. Do you —," then he stopped in mid-sentence. "You're not," he stopped again.

"Yes, I'm now Mrs. Freakish fucking Frankenstein. There's no way you can ever stop that lot, not if they are determined to do something. And yes, they'll still have you on file. They're probably observing your every move." She assured him. "But unfortunately I have now been told that I can't have a successful reversal operation, after this is all over of course."

"Physically you probably could. Just how successfully it would be, well that's entirely dependent on the medical team performing the operation. The danger would be whether you could cope with the mental trauma for the second time. And remain sane of course. The best consultant in this field is a Doctor David Urhart, of the University of Leningrad. He's the finest surgeon in this field, and I can say this because I've followed his career with interest. Would you like me to make some tentative enquiries for you? Although I must say, you are a beautiful and desirable lady, and you appear to be accepting your new persona much better than I'd ever have anticipated anybody could. Are you sure that you need to go through all that hell again, April?"

"Yes, for the sake of my wife Mandy, and my two lovely children, Pamela and Andrew. So if you'd sound the doctor out for me, I'd be eternally grateful to you. But be very careful. If the powers that be ever get wind that you're trying to help me return to my former self, well it could become extremely dangerous for you. Now about the scratches," April started to describe the events that had happened over the last twenty-four hours. She finished with the nightmare that had resulted in her injuries. April concluded, "But my strong Christian faith won't let me believe in such hocus-pocus."

While giving some thought to April's description of her latest escapades, the doctor sat back to pondered the situation. "Well, although I have very strong Christian beliefs too, I can't have lived out here and refuted the existence of voodooism. As I firmly believe in the awesome power of my God, as it seems you do. We must also accept the terrifying, and equally awesome power of evil, Satan. As the glory of my God can be manifested so in many shapes and forms, so I must accept also that the powers of Satan, Beelzebub, and their evil ways, can manifest themselves in many different forms of the occult too. One of them being the power of witchcraft, black magic, voodooism, you can call it what you like. So what you thought you dreamt, hallucinated, whatever you want to call it. You could have been actually experiencing it totally, and not just dreaming it. You possibly did actually see your soul being sucked from your body, and the damage it suffered would also have to have manifested itself onto your physical being." Sinking into profound silence, whilst digesting what she had just heard.

Eventually, April turned on her mobile phone. She asked Alan. "Do you wish me to continue to keep your identity, and your involvement here with me, a clandestine one?"

"It does not matter now, April. I'm no threat to them anymore."

"You would be if you contacted your Doctor friend, so perhaps you'd better keep well out of it all." She said with genuine concern. "I wouldn't like to see you get hurt."

"I've told you it doesn't matter, April. I'm due to attend a conference in Prague where he'll be speaking, so I'll just sound him out and then ring you. That's, if that's acceptable to you of course, and if you give me your private mobile phone number."

"I'll ring you. Or, I'll return here for a holiday when this is all over," April told him. "But now I must speak to the boss. Hello Charles, what is De-Mundo's status?"

"Where the hell have you been? We have all been frantic here, worrying about whether you were still alive or not," he greeted her.

"It's a long, long, story Charles. But to put it briefly, I got caught up with this islands black magic. A very nice young doctor, who I believe you might already be acquainted with, has just been addressing my wounds," she explained.

Charles interrupted with, "Dr. Alan Williamson I believe, April."

"Yes. So you do remember him, as I've told him you would. He's stopped the bleeding, and helped to calm my nerves. He thought that you would have long since forgotten him, but I set him straight about that one."

"Put him on would you, just so I can thank him personally." April readily obliged, handing Doctor Williamson the phone.

They had a lengthy exchange of words, during which Alan explained to Charles at some length, the onerous experience she thought she'd endured.

"Well thank you again. If there's anything I can do for you do not hesitate to contact me personally. Now would you be kind enough to hand the telephone back to, Miss Darling. Please, Alan?"

After putting the phone back to her ear, April started. "Right Charles, I owe Alan big time, so I would be very, VERY upset, if anything untoward ever were to happen to him."

"Don't you worry he poses us no threat now. Now Carlos De-Mundo and his remaining henchmen boarded a privately chartered plane. It seems that they may be headed for Tallinn Estonia. There's still no sign of McDougal here though, are you sure this is where they were heading."

"Yes, I'm positive. For some unknown reason they're in need of those planes. Make sure that you keep them well protected, Charles.

Better still, move them to a safer place as I've already suggested. Now I suppose I must get to Estonia somehow. Can you advise me of a good travel agency out here? Bye for now, Charles." She turned off the phone and put it down, while standing sideways to avoid the strong early morning sun.

April asked Alan, "I'll need to find a hotel to rest before I fall down. Can you recommend one to me?"

"Yes April, the doctors retreat. It can be very tranquil there."

"And where will I find—, how slow of me, you mean your place. Don't you, Alan?"

He smiled broadly, "You'll be most welcome even-." The ringing of April's mobile interrupted.

"Yes, Charles. I was just trying to organise somewhere to rest when you butted in. I hope you've a very good reason."

"I'm sorry, April. I've given some more thought as to our little problems. First, it will be forty-eight hours before a plane can take you to Estonia. Even then you'll need to change at Berlin. Now one of our scientists is hoping to fly to Puerto Plata tomorrow, he'll be travelling by private jet. I'll be able to tell you the exact details of the flights when I have it. So of course you can use the private Jet if you so wish. Now tell me, where are you going to stay?"

"Alan has proposed that I use his spare bedroom, so I might as well take up his kind offer, because, well I'm just too knackered to go any further right now."

"That's perfect. Can you let me speak to Alan again?"

She handed the phone to the doctor, resting her head on her arms on the steering wheel. "The boss wants to talk to you again, so you can wake me up when you've both finished nattering."

"Okay April. Just rest yourself for a moment." The doctor suggested, before turning his attention to the telephone. "Yes, Sir Charles. You want to talk to me I believe?"

These were the last words that April heard Alan say before slipping into a deep, but restless, sleep.

"Hold on for a second would you, Sir Charles. There's something weird happening out here." Alan urged him, as an eerie darkness rapidly descended and masked out the early morning sunlight, as the whole area became drowned into total blackness. A strong wind began to blow as forked lightening criss-crossed the sky, being the sole source of illumination.

The doctor sidled towards his car, only having the brief flashes from the lightning to light his path as he struggled against the strong wind, which had now developed to hurricane force.

"What do you mean? What is happening? Is everything alright?" Charles questioned with a genuine panic. "Speak to me somebody. Are you still there, Alan?" He called in vain because Doctor Williamson had put the phone into his pocket.

"APRIL," Alan called frantically, moving back towards her truck and stumbling in the black mist that was thickening, filling the area with its odorous stench.

Ignoring Charles, Alan was trying to lift April into his arms so he could carry her quickly to his own car, but without any success. It was a struggle to stay on his feet.

The ground began to tremble now, and the doctor could only watch in sheer horror as a shiny black stone wall broke through the ground, and grew into epic proportions. It towered high up towards the heavens, reaching far beyond the blackened skies. Gargoyles started appearing as they encrusted the wall, as the blood of tormented souls began to flow profusely from their sneering mouths, as the air was now filled with the vile and stench of burning flesh.

A deathly laughter could be heard, as the three faces of the witchdoctors, started appearing and covered the wall like graffiti. Mischievous sprites formed two lines ready to act as escorts, as they waited for the sinister event to unfold totally.

Alan now stood transfixed, as he stared at the enormous black wall. The centrally placed witchdoctor's mouth started to open, and grew into a huge aperture, which formed the ominously threatening entrance.

Then there appeared a flight of descending steps, which was illuminated from within the depths by the flickering flames of a large conflagration. The sinister laughter became ever louder, as a voice started to boom from the deep bowels of the pit. "Come to me my precious one. Come to your master. Come to me now. COME, **COME**," it called, in an ever increasing crescendo.

The doctor managed to break the trance that was transfixing him, as he yelled out. "NO, NO, YOU'LL NEVER HAVE HER, OUR GOD WILL PROTECT HER." He struggled to reach where April was still sitting comatose.

He reached for her but then was forced to watch in horror, as her spirit and flesh started to separate. Her soul floated from her body and was hovering, slowly being drawn towards the threatening aperture. April's arms were out stretched, with her long hair blowing in the cold and icy winds that had developed.

Alan tried desperately to find any semblance of a pulse on her earthly body, but without success. Was he too late he thought, as she was being drawn down into the very depth of Hades' self.

All seemed to be in vain, so Alan again turned to his faith and started to pray, asking for divine intervention. Suddenly, he was inspired as he rushed passed the hovering apparition. Pulling April's body from the vehicle, he hastily fumbled to release the steering lock of the truck and spark its engine into life. He engaged the gearshift into first gear, and reached for the jack handle in the same movement. Jamming the accelerator pedal hard against the floor with the jack handle, he released the clutch as the truck leapt forward and toward the hell bound steps, as he rolled out just in time.

"No, she's mine. SHE'S MINE. She has been pledge to me because she killed my loyal servants. Stop, STOP," a voice called from the grave. The truck raced beyond her soul and crashed through the nefarious apparition. Causing it all to implode, and descend back to where it had originally risen. As it screwed down into the ground in a strong and vicious whirlwind, it left no evidence that the macabre and sinister manifestation, had ever taken place.

Alan slumped back against his car totally exhausted. He could hear Charles' panicking voice. It was asking, "Hello. Can somebody tell me what the bloody hell's happening?"

"Hello, Charles," an exhausted Alan eventually replied. "I think it's all over now," he gasped to him. He felt April's feeble pulse, as it slowly returning to normality.

"Luckily the video camera was still running or I'd have found it totally unbelievable. What was that incredulous sight I could see? It looked like sheer hell for you guys?" he inadvertently commented.

"Well you have certainly got that one spot on, Sir Charles. Can I call you later? I need to get April back to my home so she can rest."

"Of course you can, Alan. How selfish of me. But can you keep me posted as to April's progress?" requested a humbled, Sir Charles.

"Yes, I will do that," he promised, as he warily started his car and drove steadily back towards the sanctuary of his Santiago home.

CHAPTER 23

April's eyes flickered as they adjusted to the strong midday sun that streamed through the open window.

Alan greeting her with, "Good morning April, well it still is morning but only just. I hope you're feeling better now? You must have been totally exhausted."

"Why? What's happened? What time is it?" she asked anxiously.

"It's just before noon. You've slept for over twenty-four hours. Here's a cup of coffee while my housekeeper prepares you some lunch," Alan explained, as he prepared to leave the bedroom.

Starting to throw off the bed-sheet, April stopping abruptly when she realised she was totally naked.

She asked him, feeling awkwardly embarrassed. "Did you put me to bed, and where are my clothes?"

"No. I'm afraid my housekeeper come nurse had that pleasure," Alan told her, smiling when he noticed her reddening from embarrassment. "She's laid a robe out for you on the chair," he told her, pointing towards the bedside chair. "Now shall I send your lunch through here, or do you feel strong enough to join me on the veranda?"

"I'll join you as soon as I've taken a shower to liven myself up, Alan. So where are my clothes?"

"All your belongings are hung up in the wardrobe, or have been put in the drawers. Sanchez, she's my housekeeper, has washed and pressed them for you."

After taking a shower April dressed and applied her makeup, before joining the good doctor on the veranda.

The doctor abruptly ended a call he was making as April appeared.

"Now perhaps you'd be kind enough to explain to me what's happened, and why I've slept for so long. Did I have an accident or something?" Suddenly, she added thoughtfully, "Do you know Alan, I had the wildest dream last night, and I don't usually dream. Why's that I wonder. And why have I got a wound dressing on my leg?"

"Firstly, tell me about the dream that you think you had?" Alan asked, as his Dominican housekeeper served coffee.

"Good morning, Madam. I hope that you are feeling much better this morning," Said the stout middle-aged woman, "I'm Sanchez, and I'm very pleased to meet with you."

"I'm, April. I'm very pleased to meet with you too, Sanchez," April replied warmly.

"Are you ready for me to start serving lunch, Doctor?" she asked dutifully. "Yes, Sanny, I imagine April must be famished," he told her as he looked towards April.

"Yes. I am, Alan. Do you know, I can't remember when I last ate, I guess I just went passed having any hunger pains."

While they ate lunch, attended by the faithful Sanchez, April described all she could recollect about what she thought was a dream. Sanchez and the doctor listened intently as April graphically described her dream, when she was encountering overwhelming evil. Then as Sanchez served dessert, April finished. "And then I woke up here, and completely starker's at that I might add, except for the dressing on my leg."

"And what do you conclude about your little reverie? Was it really a dream?" Alan suggested.

"What else could it have bloody been? A nightmare or hallucinating, or have I suffered a bang on the head and imagined I was experiencing it all? You found me, so what do you think it was?"

"What would you say if I told you that I had witnessed and undergone the entire experience as you?"

"And when was that?" she asked him, getting more and more confused.

"At the same time as you did, would it still be a nightmare or a dream? Or would you think that I'd been hallucinating too?"

"Well it sure would inject a large helping of doubt, Alan. And it would explain what the leg injury is. Perhaps I should revisit the area in the cold light of day."

Sanchez, who had listened silently up until now, interrupted, "No, Miss April. Leave it well alone. There's some things that are best left unexplained," she beseeched her nervously. "So just avoid the area while you remain on the Island. It's for your own safety, Miss April." she implored her, her eyes filled with fear.

"Why not? What's wrong? What are you not telling me?" April asked anxiously.

"I'm just saying that sometimes it's better not to know the real truth. There are customs and beliefs out here that the western world, your world, does not, and will not, ever understand. Please, just accept what you think has happened, that it was all just a horrible nightmare," a fearful Sanchez finished.

The ringing of the phone interrupted. "Good morning, Charles," April started. Then she just listened silently to what he had to say. Holding her hand over the mouthpiece, she told them. "It's Sir Charles. I bet they've lost De-Mundo. Yes, I'm okay. Now tell me the real reason why you've rung me. What is it that you're building up to? Has De-Mundo given you, and your collection of experts, and your advanced electronics, the slip again?"

"Yes we have lost them temporarily. Most of his remaining men have now dispersed, and are scattered round the island. De-Mundo and half a dozen of his men took off in a private jet towards Estonia as we predicted before, but after taking off they seem to head back to Columbia. At least we think that it was Carlos De-Mundo, because they just disappeared on us. They flew right under our Radar.

"So much for don't kill him we want him kept alive. We want to perfect losing him ourselves. Well, what now?" she asked with frustration.

"You may as well come back here after you've rested. At least until Carlos raises his—. Just a moment April, there's something happening here. I'll have to call you back."

After explaining to Alan what has happened, they both sat and relaxed by his pool. An hour passed before her phone rang again. "You've got some good news for me, Charles. At least I can hope that you have?"

"I'm afraid not, April. Such incompetence must be dealt with severely, but after this is all over with of course. And of that, I can assure you. Now I've further bad news to tell you, the planes have been stolen," he waited silently for April's reaction.

"And are you going to tell me just how that happened. Did you just advertise them in the local paper, Or something like that? You know, the first to come can have a special offer, two for one? I thought you were going to tell security to move them?"

"Bloody bureaucracy, we have lost our planes because of our own bloody bureaucracy. I implored them to have the planes moved ASAP, but apparently they were waiting on the appropriate documentation. Just so that they could sanction the aircraft to be redeployed elseware, as they put it,"

While he had stopped to regain his composure, April finished it for him. "And somebody that didn't need the appropriate paperwork, well, they just moved them for you I suppose?" she said sarcastically.

"If you want to put it that bluntly, well yes, that's exactly what's happened. It's a very serious breach of our security, and the minister is absolutely furious about it. But when he was assured that you would be assigned to retrieving the planes, well he requested that we put any and all of our resources at your disposal. You can have whatever resources and personnel you think you will need, April?"

"Well thank him for me. I'm glad he has faith in me at least. And I'm sorry about my bitchiness and lack of respect to you, Charles. I don't really know why I keep feeling like this. Of course you have the right to live your life how, and with whom, you so desire. So I hope Mandy and you, will be ecstatically happy, as I once was." she apologised meekly.

"Just forget it ever happened. Maybe it's some form of delayed post-operative depression. It may be possible that Alan could help you with it while you're there. So do you think I could explain things to him? I do have something important to ask him at the same time."

While pacing to and fro, April grew impatient. Alan seemed to be remonstrating with Charles, until eventually he reluctantly conceding to whatever Charles was asking him to do.

Ringing off, and handing the phone back to April, he went straight to the drink cabinet to pour himself a large whiskey. Swallowing it straight down, he then refilled his glass before sitting back down. April watched him nervously moving about, wondering why his behaviour had changed so dramatically, and what Charles could have said that has upset this mild mannered doctor so much.

"You seem agitated after your conversation with, Sir Charles?" April said cautiously. "Wasn't he grateful to you for saving my life?"

"Yes, he's too bloody grateful," began Alan, as he poured yet another large Scotch. "He reminded me that I'm still covered by the official secrets act, as apparently I always will be. So I've not to repeat what has happened here to anybody. He has also suggests, and very forcibly, that to all intent and purpose I must treat the whole experience as if it were just an apparition."

"So why are you so upset?" April asked, looking very confused.

"He again has forcibly insisted that I return to old Blighty with you, just for a debriefing apparently. He also reminded me that I would always be affiliated to his elite little bloody group, even though I've been allowed to become dormant over these past couple of years. As he so forcefully puts it, I can always be recalled into service at any time he so chooses. But you've already told me that much. So here's to the dirty tricks fucking cloak and dagger, brigade. One that I thought, no, I was led to believe I had well and truly finished with."

April got up and crossed to where the doctor was forlornly sitting. Placing her hand onto his shoulder she tried to console him. "Never mind Alan it probably is only for a debriefing, then you will be able to return here. Lucky you, I wish I could reside here permanently." She attempted to cheer him up.

The doctor put his hand onto his shoulder and cupped April's hand in his.

And he gently guided her round until she was sitting on the arm of his chair. "The point is I thought I was well and truly finished with all that shit. After all, I didn't even get started with them. When I realised what they were about I instantly resigned and thought that would be it. Finito as it were. God, you are a very beautiful woman." Alan digressed. He had changed the subject abruptly as the alcohol started to take a hold on him.

"And I think you're a very nice, but slightly inebriated, man." April said, as she removed the glass from his unsteady hand. "So I suggest that you have a nice little siesta, to sleep off the whiskey you've just consumed."

Nodding his agreement, Alan reluctantly teetered off unsteadily, but unaided, towards his bedroom. His head had hardly touched the pillow before he'd fallen into a sound asleep and was snoring merrily. April smiled to herself as she listened to Alan snoring, thinking how relaxed and laid back his life had now become. She could fully understand the resentment he must be feeling at this time, due to the intrusion she was causing into his peaceful island life.

During the following days April totally relaxed, as she enjoyed Alan's very pleasant company. All too soon the peace and tranquillity was to be brought to an abrupt ending by the ringing of her telephone.

"Hello, Charles. I knew that you'd be the one to eventually penetrate into my private nirvaniadic state."

"I'm sorry about that. However, there's one of the new super planes heading there, it's leaving Gatwick at 1430 hrs tomorrow. I've booked two tickets for Alan and yourself to be on the return journey. The tickets are to be collected from the customer services desk."

"First class I hope, Charles?"

"Of course they are. I'll let you tell Doctor Williamson about the flight, he was rather annoyed with me when I asked him to return here temporarily. Now I'll arrange to have somebody meet you both at the airport when you arrive here. So have a pleasant flight my dear." Charles finished as he rang off.

April explained to Alan in as much detail as she felt she was allowed to, just how, and why, she'd come to be in the Dominican Republic in the first place. Finishing with, "And I'm afraid Carlos De-Mundo still has to be found and stopped. But no matter what Charles says, the next time I have him in my sights I will kill the bastard."

"Yes, well that's as maybe, but tell me where I fit in to all of this? After all, I'm not a fighting man," Alan queried. "I deplore violence in any shape or form."

"Don't worry. You need only be there to escort me. You shouldn't have any need to be further involved than that," she assured him. April added, "I'll personally ensure that Charles fully comprehends just how you feel about violence. Now shall we have a little drink before we retire for the night?" she suggested, an invitation he readily accepted.

The morning of the flight April rose early. After showering she dressed in a casual outfit, thinking it would be more suitable for the long flight home. Then she joined Alan on the porch while they ate breakfast. April asked, "How long has it been since you last visited the homeland, Alan?"

"Let me think now. I haven't been home since moving here, it must be all of four years ago now. I didn't feel the need to return. There's nothing back in England for me now, anyway."

"Four years! Is that how long I was in the planning stages?"

"Longer, I was originally approached about, now let me think?" Alan went into deep thought, then eventually explaining, "It was eight years ago. I should imagine the plan would have been hatched some years before that again."

"Knowing them devious bastards it's a wonder they waited for that long," joked April. After they had finished eating, she offered, "May I help you with the dishes before we go, Sanchez?"

"No thank you, Missy April. That's my job. You and Doctor Alan just relax on the porch," Sanchez insisted. So April took a glass of fresh orange juice with her out onto the porch.

Soon after a taxi arrived and they found themselves travelling along the bumpy road, that led to Puerto Plata Airport.

An hour passed before they heard the announcement telling them to board.

Soon after that the plane was winging its way eastbound towards the UK.

They consumed a number of drinks before settling down and drifting into a very blissful sleep. A terrified hostess abruptly woke April after only a few hours.

"Miss Darling, Miss Darling," she whispered frantically. "You're wanted urgently on the flight deck. Please hurry, Miss Darling?"

Leaving the doctor asleep, the hostess led April down the forward steps that led directly onto the flight deck.

"And what's so urgent may I ask?"

"I have been asked to leave the explanations to the Captain, Miss?" the hostess answered nervously as she tapped on the cabin door. Hearing a call to enter she opened the door. "This is Miss Darling, sir," she introduced them as she left.

"Ah, Miss Darling I believe. We find we have a serious situation here. A Sir Charles Hyde-Smith has requested that you speak to him, so he will explain it to you personally. You can use that handset over there." The Captain told her, as he pointed towards a telephone. Suggesting, "If you sit in the observer seat it will be more comfortable for you."

"Thank you," April said to them gratefully. She dialled Charles' phone. "This had better be good, Charles. I was just enjoying a very well deserved sleep," she started sternly.

"You have a suicide bomber on board. There are three protagonists that have been recruited, or coerced, by Carlos De-Mundo. There's one male, and two female. The ladies are dressed in black from head to toe, and will probably be wearing Niqab's. The man is smallish, and he is sporting a false beard, so as to resemble a Mr. Bashier. The women booked tickets legitimately as husband, wife and daughter, under their own surname of Bashier. But this man has assumed the identity of their husband whose body we found dumped in a ditch at the airport, but we don't yet know if the women are willing participants on not. What we do know is that the man is an absolute bloody fanatic. He's swapped identities with Mr. Bashier and taken his place on the plane."

"It was that easy. Is he a twin brother or a look alike? How the fuck has he got through the security checks, Charles?"

"You know the security there's not as high tech as ours. We have looked through the tapes of the surveillance cameras and it seems that the Bashier's booked in as normal. Then, as they stepped onto the tarmac to board the plane Mr. Bushier is seen answering his mobile telephone, and was then escorted by an official looking gentleman towards a hanger. A man looking a bit like him, you know the type, greying receding hair and a long greying beard. He was approximately the same height and build. He then left with the women and boarded the plane. The camera inside the hanger shows Mr. Bashier being brutally bludgeoned to death after they'd left, and then two men carried his body through a rear door where they were detained, but only after they'd dumped the body. Also, we've arrested a baggage handler and an official. They were seen emptying one of the suitcases and inserting a smaller case inside it. That's probably so that it will retain all of the original booking information."

What information Charles had was text to a stunned April. "Well, have you managed to make anybody talk, yet? And what the bloody hell's going to happen now?" she anxiously asked.

"Well, sort of. But it's not a lot of help to you, I'm afraid. Apparently, the man is a human bomb, and the smaller suitcase he inserted into the luggage is packed with explosives too. We know that it's primed and set to explode at 2230 hrs, which would put you directly over London. Well it would have done if we hadn't discovered their hideous little plan in time. It has also been booby-trapped with tamper proof switches, so extreme caution must be taken when handling it," Charles fell silent while he waited for her response.

"Well what the hell do I do now, Charles?" she snapped impatiently.

"Well firstly you must tell the pilot to alter his course to avoid passing over any land, or shipping lanes. I suggest you put this call onto speaker phone so he can join in with this conversation?"

"Okay. Now say what you really mean. You think that there's nothing I can do about this. Don't you? Except to wait to be blown out of the fucking sky by some lunatic of course," was April's shocked reaction, "Do you know why it's this plane?"

"I'm most sincerely sorry my love. Apparently, Carlos had a man watching the passenger lists. When they found that you'd be flying on one of the new super planes, well he then ordered his men to act," started Charles.

April interrupted, "It was you who booked me under my own name, and this new plane is carrying 1000 passengers and 35 crew, so why this plane?" April became more frustrated.

"It's probably just a terrorist target to them to make a political point. It would have left a doubt as to whether it was Carlos De-Mundo, or possibly some other right wing fascist splinter group from somewhere else. Anyway, as I've said before, I'm so very, very sorry, but it seems that you're in nowhere land now, there isn't anywhere we can divert you to in time. Again, I'm so deeply sorry," he apologised profusely again.

The bleary-eyed doctor appeared at the cockpit door, "Is this just a private party, or is anybody allowed to join in?" he said sleepily.

She explained to him the dire situation that they found themselves in. She watched as the blood draining from his face, and his legs began to buckle.

"Do you mean that you've brought me from my island paradise, just to be blow up at forty five thousand feet?"

"I'm afraid that's precisely what's happened," Charles confirmed.

April interrupted. "Not while I've any breath left in my body it won't happen," she began. Then turning to the shocked flight crew April apologised to them. "I'm sorry you've been caught up in all this, but there must be a way out of it. And if there is one, well then I'll find it I can promise you that," she tried to reassure them. "Firstly, could you slowly wander to a vacant flight path? One where there aren't any shipping lanes. We don't want to give anyone an indication as to our altitude. Then, very gently commence descending to round about ten thousand feet. But do it very gradually because we don't want to alert the passengers, PARTICULARLY that fucking walking bomb. Now can your most senior cabin crew keep a very attentive eye on the terrorists for me, but take care not to alarm them."

"What are you going to do?" a curious Charles asked. "And Captain, tell your crew to follow Miss Darlings orders to the letter. She's the most qualified anti-terrorist operative that there is in these situations. And she's so successful because she's completely unorthodox."

"I don't know yet, Charles. One thing I definitely can assure you of is that I do not intend to just sit here and wait for that bastard to blow me out of the sky. Now where is his luggage stowed, do we at least know that much?" April asked anxious, as the chief steward appeared at the flight deck door. April explained to him all he needed to know, and asked him to get her a spare stewardess uniform for her. "Preferably one with trousers, then tell the other stewardess' to change into the same outfit as me so I won't look out of place." She finished, as the man left to follow the instructions.

"We think that the bomb will be in the second quarter from the front as that's the planes most vulnerable point. But that's only pure speculation," Charles told her.

"You think. There are at least seven hundred passengers with luggage.

Surely you can be a little bit more precise than that?"

"I'm afraid we can't. The case was taken from its original slot to insert the bomb in, then put back wherever they decided to put it."

"Well I'll have to hurry. I DON'T just intend to just sit here on my arse twiddling my thumbs waiting to enter through those pearly gates. So only call me if you've any new developments, Charles." April turned her attention to the traumatised Doctor, "I'll need your expertise, Alan. Try to put your fear to the back of your mind and pull yourself together. Well for the time being, at least."

April beckoned the steward, "Do you see the gentleman in the black hat. He's over on the port side of the plane and he's with the two

Muslim ladies. I need to know what he's drinking. My guess is they'll all be drinking water because of their faith?"

"That's true of the ladies Miss, but the gentleman is drinking double Vodkas neat, and he's drinking quite a lot of it. I was wondering if we should refuse to serve him any more drinks."

"Does he knock them back in one straight gulp?"

"Yes. That's why he's getting through so much. Should we stop serving him?" the concerned steward asked again.

"No. Well not just yet anyway. It could all work to our advantage eventually. Tell me, when will you be taking the drinks trolley round again?"

"We should be starting the rounds in a few moments."

"Well ring the service bell when you're nearing their row." April instructed him, as she began to change into the stewardess uniform. "I'm sorry if I embarrass anybody, but this is no time for me to be modest. I don't usually get the luxury for such niceties as privacy anyway. Now to work," April asked Alan, "how do you feel now? Are you any stronger now?"

"Yes thank you, April. I'm sorry I went queasy on you. I'm more used to helping other people to face their deaths, but when the tables turned on oneself, well that's not an easy pill to swallow. And it's not covered by the manuals either." He explained tentatively. "Now what can I do to help, at least it'll help to occupy my mind. Well at least while I wait for the foreboding event that must inevitably unfold."

"Funny that because I never pictured you as a defeatist before now. Pull yourself together man, because we're fast running out of time here. I for one don't accept that those brainless misguided fools have the right to decide when I should die. THAT! I believe, is my Gods privilege. Now have a good stiff drink, then you have some work to do for me."

Taking a large whiskey from the steward the doctor gulped it down in one swallow, asking April, "Now what do you need me to do to help?"

"That's better. Can you arrange sedatives that will work instantly, but will remain completely undetectable by smell or taste?" April asked, while taking the pistol from the lining of her dress and concealing it in the back of her belt. "How did you smuggle that through the security checks?" a curious co-pilot asked.

"I'll tell you that later," April promised, turning her attention back to the doctor.

"I've got a few sedatives in my bag, but which one depends on how long you need to keep whoever unconscious for. Also, it'll depend on their body weight, etcetera?"

"Long enough to restrain him and try to disarm the bomb, then I'll have to find the bloody suitcase and disarm that. Now the man looks to be around sixteen stone to me."

"But are you qualified to do all of this, Miss Darling?" the Captain interrupted.

"I've told you to just call me, April. And I'm the only hope that you're likely to find up here. Now if you all follow my instructions, I promise I'll find a way to deal with this imposing threat." She reassured them, as a stewardess entered the flight deck.

"We're getting closer to serving them, what do you want us to do?"

"How many rows are there before you serve them?"

"Six or seven, shall I count them for you?"

"No. I'm ready to come now. If you get some fresh glasses and keep the top three to use for them, then place them inside the trolley with the spare glasses. The doctor will lace the three with the sedative, but it won't kill them. When you start serving them, knock all the glasses off the top of your trolley as if by accident. Then you'll need to get the fresh glasses from the trolley to serve with." explained April as she handed her the plastic glasses that the doctor had prepared, "Ring for a brush to clean up the mess, and that's when I will take over from you. Now will you be okay with that?"

"Yes, I will be able to do it," the stewardess confirmed. Heading nervously back through into the cabin.

"Is there anything we can do to assist you, April?" asked the Captain.

"I could use a little extra muscle to restrain him, particularly if he tries to activate that bloody bomb. Also, can you detail somebody to start searching for that suitcase; it will save me some time later. But make sure you stress to them, if they do find it they must tell me. They must on no account try to handle it, or they'll trigger of the explosive," she warned firmly.

"Perhaps we should hand pick somebody to help to do the search," the Captain suggested. "The less people that's aware of our predicament, the less chance there will be of mass hysteria."

"Maybe I could help with the search?" volunteered Alan, "There isn't much else I can do here, and I'll take the chief steward to help me."

April agreed, "Yes, that's a great idea. Now this is what you'll be looking for." Showing them the photograph that Charles had downloaded to her mobile. April then forwarded it to their personal phones. "On the ticket will be the name of Mr. Bashier. I suggest you pick a spot in the centre of the hold and work outwards. You can also put my mobile number into your phone, so you can ring me when you've located it."

"Don't you mean IF, we locate it?" The disconsolate steward asked.

"No! I distinctly said when. What's our altitude now, Captain?" April asked, as the two volunteers descended through the trap door in the floor of the flight deck, taking them directly down into the luggage hold.

"We're at twenty thousand feet. You did say to descend very gradually," the Captain reminded her as he got out of his seat. "Now, isn't it time we went into the lion's den, so to speak? The co-pilot can take over the controls," he confirmed, as they heard the stewardess ringing for assistance.

"Nice timing. Now if you work down the opposite side to me. Act as if you're just stretching your legs or something like that. Say hello to passengers, as you pass, etc., you know to look casual. Then just work round behind him as if you're coming to tell me something. Let me go first, then after a minute or two you follow." April instructed the Captain as she left with a brush and shovel.

Walking swiftly towards the trolley, she nodded to the stewardess as she began to sweep up the mess. The young girl moved the trolley forward to the next row, after serving the spiked drinks to the protagonists.

April started to clean up, while continually aware of the small party's movements. Again the man swiftly swallowed his drink. It seemed clear that he was obviously trying to calm his fragmented nerves, and mask his true innermost fear.

Suddenly his eyes widened as he fought desperately against the urgent feeling to render himself unconscious, as his hand started to move down towards his midriff. Presumably, to detonate the devise he was wearing.

April dropped the brush and threw herself across the unconscious ladies lap, and griped at the man's wrists.

Moving with the agility of a cat, she twisted herself until her feet were against the back of the seat in front, so she could use it for extra leverage. April then pushed with her legs while holding his wrists to pin the man back firmly into his seat, making sure that he was unable to reach the detonator. She found the man to be surprisingly strong, as she concentrated the whole of her body strength into holding him firmly.

"Don't just stand there like a dummy, help me Captain. It seems the sedative was not strong enough."

But the Captain was riveted to the spot with fear. "I, I can't move my legs."

"Pull yourself together man and help me," April ordered the Captain. The suicide bomber was now slowly slipping from her grip.

A pair of strong arms appeared over the seat pinning the terrorist back into it. Asking, "Can I help you, April?" in a very familiar voice.

"JAMES!" She shouted thankfully, looking into the smiling face of Lieutenant James Edwards. "Were the fucking hell did you spring from? I thought you were," she stopped.

James finished it, "Dead."

"Well yes. Well after you were reported missing. Anyway, you can tell me all about that later. Now can you hold his arms for a sec, James?"

"I'll try," he confirmed as April reached for the brush. He explained, "I've been following this bastard undercover to catch who he's working for."

April then fed it through his sleeves. "Can you hold the arms straight so I can feed the brush handle straight across, making him cruciform?" she asked him hopefully as the terrorist yelled Christian profanities towards her.

"No, he's far too strong. I thought he'd been drugged?" Asked James as he struggled to straighten the man's arms?

April reached for a can of coke from the drink trolley and smashed it against the man's lower jaw, momentarily knocking him unconscious.

Because of the surprise of the attack the man relaxed his arms, allowing April to feed the brush pole straight through his sleeves. She asked the surprised stewardess, "Have you any rope, cord, or strong string. Or at a last resort, three or four pairs of tights would do."

She promised as she hurried away, "I'll see what I can find you."

A soft moaning alerted April that the two ladies were starting to regain consciousness. "Quickly," she told the Captain, who by now had begun to help. "Help me move the woman away from this bomber, so that they can't detonate it for him. Can you watch the man while we do it, James?"

James confirmed that he could.

Hastily the Captain assisted in transferring the women into the business class cabin, as the stewardess handed over some handcuffs, and an assortment of cord.

She asked hopefully, "Will this lot help you?"

"They'll do very nicely. Thank you." April then proceeded to cuff the two women's together, looping the cuffs through the armrest.

"That should keep them out of trouble for now. Now let's sort out that bloody stupid man?" she said to the Captain, while returning to where the man and James where.

She tethered the man to the seat, with the help of James, and the Captain, tying his outstretched arms to the headrests of the seats adjacent to him. After thanking the Captain for his assistance, April asked him if he would be good enough to explain to the shocked passengers what was happening, but omitting about there being another bomb in the hold. And would he do it before there was widespread panic to add to the problems. This, the much relieved Captain, agreed to do.

The terrorist began to moan as he started to revive and sober up.

"We must hurry," April urged, rummaging through the lengths of cords. "Blast! There isn't any long enough." she said to herself in exasperation, as she started to join the longest cords together. "There, now that should be long enough."

"For what?" asked a perplexed James, who had been patiently watching as she joined each of the ropes?

"I need him to keep perfectly still while I try to defuse his lethal vest." She explained, tying the suspects feet firmly together. Then she threaded the ends of the rope under his seat. Moving round to behind the seat, April then pulled his legs through as far as they would go; feeding the rope up behind the seat and securing it firmly round the man's neck. Finishing just as he regained his full consciousness.

Tethering the man so firmly that he was unable to move a muscle, she said proudly while admiring her handiwork. "There, you're trussed up just like a turkey cock as they say, and now for the tricky bit, James."

The man started to struggle, but was only successful in restricting his own air supply.

"It's futile to struggle mate, you'll just end up strangling yourself," April told him. Hearing this, an evil smile grew across the terrorist's face, "Before you get any bright ideas about strangling yourself to detonate the explosive. You must remember that you'll first lose consciousness, and then you'll eventually revive. So it doesn't seem worth going through all of the pain. Now does it?" April smiled cynically at him.

Slowly and carefully April cut his clothes off, one garment as a time. "Don't worry folks. I'll stop before he's in his birthday suit." April laughingly shouted, trying to ease the tension that was visibly growing on the face of the passengers.

"Should I move the passengers to the rear of the plane?" James whispered. "Why. What good would that do?" she whispered back to him. "If it does go off there won't be a safe area anywhere on this plane. So we'll just let the passengers stay in the comfort of their own seats for now."

"INFIDELS, YOU ARE ALL IN—," the terrorist began to shout.

April stopped him with a well-directed knee into his groin. Taking a piece of his own clothing that she'd cut off, April stuffed it in to his mouth. "Find some tape for his big fucking mouth. Will you please, James?"

James obliged and got some sticky tape off a stewardess; then he securely covered the mouth of the man. Suddenly an irate misguided passenger appeared to protest at the treatment of the prisoner.

"It's inhumane how you're treating this man. What about the poor man's civil rights?"

April saw red. "Do you want to do this?" she snapped, pointing to the bomb.

"You can just restrain him until we land." The passenger shouted at her, as he tried to release the prisoner.

"If you're not away from here in two fucking seconds I'll personally restrain you as well. Now, FUCK OFF," she shouted at him, getting more and more exasperated.

James attempted to lead the passenger back toward his seat.

The passenger was a broad and muscular man, so he easily fended James off. He shoved him and sent him sprawling down the aisle.

With this April exploded with rage as she confronted the man. "I'll tell you only once more to get back to your bloody seat NOW, before I lose what's left of my fraying temper." Then she noticed that when he'd pushed James, James had struck his head on a seat as he fell, knocking him unconscious with blood streaming out of a gash he'd sustained to his head.

Defiantly the passenger attempted to shove April aside. He reached for the prisoner once again, insisting, "Very well. I'll free the man myself."

Instantly April's brain switched to emergency mode as she grabbed at the man. Gripping his coat she pulled him towards her and tripped him, thrusting his head against the back of one of the seats. Before he could regain his senses, she spun him round and fell backwards to deliver a two-footed throw. She used the man's own body weight, and propelled him headfirst into the drink trolley. Taking a spare pair of handcuffs, she dragged the man towards his seat and cuffed him to it.

———

Apologising to the passengers shocked wife, April reminded her. "Standing up to bullies is very commendable, but standing up for that scumbag terrorist is just ludicrous." While she was telling her, the husband began to regain consciousness. "Anyway, he'll have a headache. That's if that thick head of his has any feelings. You had better ask the stewardess for two painkillers for him? But more importantly, ask her to see to James over there for me, he still hasn't regained unconscious?" Insisted April firmly as she returned to the task in hand.

Working fastidiously April stripped off the man's remaining outer garments, so as to enable her to start disarming the bomb.

"That's it. Now I can see what I'm doing," she muttered carefully as she examined the devise.

A steward volunteered, "Can I help you at all?"

"Maybe in a second you can. And thank you for offering," said a grateful April. "While you're waiting I suggest that you tell the staff to serve everybody a complimentary drink. They've stayed pretty calm considering, which makes my job a lot easier."

"I'll do that, Miss." The lad agreed as he headed towards the galley. A few seconds later he returned, "They're going to start serving the free drinks to the passengers now."

April dialled Charles' number and put it on hands free. Telling the steward, "Now don't talk to me while I concentrate. Just hold the phone steady will you? Hello, Charles. Can you get the bomb disposal unit on the line for me?"

She slipped her hand between the bombers vest and his chest.

"I've anticipated you will need them, so one of them is standing by for you right now, April. I'll just set us up on a three way hands free conversation." Charles went quiet while he made the necessary adjustments. "Now can we all hear each other?"

They all confirmed that they could. "Okay April. Now this is Albert. I'll let you take over now and talk directly with him."

"Hello, Albert. I'm, April. Now can you see the set up on your phone's video?"

He confirmed, "Yes. It all seems pretty standard to me though. Is there a reason that's stopping you from just disconnecting the detonator?"

"Yes. There's a bloody tamper proof sensor. And there's another sensor that's registering his heart beat."

"I obviously can't see them. Can you describe them to me, April?"

After taking a deep breath April began, "I think the tamper proof sensor I can deal with. I should be able to just disconnect it carefully from the detonator. Now there are four wires here. There are two reds, a blue, and a black one. The trick probably is in which order I should cut them." April then asked the steward to fetch something to cut the wires with.

"I've brought you a tool kit, April," he told her on his return.

She thanked him. April returned her attention to Albert, and asked, "Now which wire do you suggest I cut first?

With obvious panic in his voice, he answered, "I don't really know, April. There should only be three wires for this type of devise. But there's an extra red wire on yours."

Putting her head closer, April tried to trace the sources of the wire terminals. "The wires are connected to a small printed circuit," she described to Albert. Then she painstakingly followed each circuit. Eventually she shouted, "EUREKA! This red wire's connected to a dead end on the circuit board." April snipped the spare wire off. "Now, the other red wire goes to a green L.E.D, so I'll cut that too, shall I?"

"NO! Did you say it's connected to a green L.E.D, April?"

"Yes. Why, Albert?"

"If you cut that wire you'll trigger off the bomb. The crafty buggers have switched the wires round. Now just relax and tell me which colour goes to a black thing with a lot of little brass legs on it."

"Do you mean a processor?"

A surprised Albert answered, "Yes. I'm sorry. I didn't expect you to know what a processor was. Can you follow it?"

"I think so. The blue wire goes to the processor, and the black wire goes to a diode."

"Where did you learn about electronics, April? Now they have switched all the colours round so we need the cut the black wire first. Then the blue wire, and lastly cut the red wire." Albert explained, as he waited for confirmation that she'd disarmed it.

After what seemed like an eternity, April finished, "And finally the red wire." A click could be heard as she snipped through the final wire. "Right, that's disarmed now. Now for the other sensor, have you got any ideas on that, Albert?"

"I'm afraid not, except for maybe moving the man into the hold." Alan came to tell April that they'd located the suitcase.

"Good. Just don't let anybody touch it," April told him. She asked the steward helping her to hold the lethal harness firmly over the man's heart. "I'll try to unfasten the harness, but don't let it slip off his chest. If you do it will detonate the bomb thinking that his heart has stopped beating."

Tentatively April released each strap until reaching the final one. "Now I will take over alone thank you." She told the steward. "So can you move away a little and give me some elbow room, please. Are you still with us, Albert?"

"We are all here waiting with baited breath. What can we do now?"

"Give me a brief breakdown of how this sensor works. And make it very brief, and very simple. You know I'm only a simple female," April attempted to jest as she wiped the perspiration from her brow.

"Oh yes. You certainly sound it. Well to put it in layman's terms, every time the heart beats it emits a very small electrical pulse. The sensor picks this up and resets itself to the rhythm of the pulse. If it were to stop for a set period of time, let's say ten to twenty seconds, then it will detonate the bomb automatically."

"How can I substitute these pulses?"

"If we were dealing with it here, then we would probably use what is called an oscilloscope, which-."

April interrupted, "I know what an oscilloscope does. How strong does the pulse have to be?"

"That's unimportant as long as it's regular, that is the important thing."

"Now what can I use?" she muttered to herself, looking round for inspiration. April noticed the steward's mobile phone hooked to his belt. It had a green light on the side of it flashing on and off periodically.

"The flashing light of a mobile phone, does that emit an electrical pulse too? And will it be strong enough, Albert?" April asked hopefully, crossing her fingers while she waited for the reply.

"It should be its regular. I'll just do some rough calculations for you very quickly. Just to make sure," Albert explained, as the phone went quiet for a brief few moments. "Are you still there?"

"No. I've gone to Blackpool for the weekend. Now I ask you, where am I likely to be?"

"And funny with it, I like her, Charles. Can she join my team?" He asked Charles before continuing. "The flash of a mobile phones L.E.D should do the trick. You would need to remove the coloured plastic cover that's over it though, and without damaging the L.E.D. So that it would ensure maximum voltage from the electronic pulse. Do you think you can do that? Oh, and you'll need to fasten the phone directly onto the sensor."

"Do I have a choice?" April added jokingly. "Perhaps you can send a team up here to do the job for me."

"Are you getting any trouble with the passengers?" Charles interrupted. "No, thank God. They're all surprisingly calm. They are either comatose with fear, or they trust me implicitly. Anyway, enough of this procrastinating, I must press on." She asked if anybody had a spare mobile phone. "You owe the chief steward, Dave his name is, a new mobile phone, Charles. Now if I bar all incoming calls, just so it won't ring and stop the diode from flashing, and now for the plastic covering it."

April tried with various implements to remove the small cover, but without any success.

"Blast it! I can't get this small cover off." she noticed a small soldering iron among the tools. Then she told the steward to hold the vest in place, "Don't go away. I'll be back in a jiffy." Taking the soldering iron and mobile phone into the galley April heated up the iron. She then carefully burnt through the plastic cover. "Now that should do the trick," muttering to herself proud that her idea had worked. Returning with it quickly, April explaining to Albert how she'd burnt through the small cover.

"As I've said, you're not just a pretty face. Are you, April?"

April ignored everything while she concentrated on what she was doing. Very gingerly, she held the phone close to the sensor. Then April tried to tease up the edge of the sucker on the man's chest, only to find that it had been super-glued to him.

Telling the terrorist, "This would hurt you if you were to remain awake," as she punched the man on the chin knocking him out cold. "But I'm not as evil as you lot are," she continued telling the unconscious man. Then April peeled the sensor off, sliding it onto the phone diode and pressing them tightly together. She secured them firmly using sticky tape.

"Put loads of tape round it will you, so that it can't detach itself," April asked the steward. She then informed Albert with relief, "It's working. The sensor's off him now."

James appeared besides her holding a swab against his wound. "Are you feeling better after your little nap then?" She joked.

"I'm sorry I—," James began to apologise, but April stopped him.

"I'm only joking, James. Where's your sense of humour gone?" she asked, as she carried the explosive vest carefully towards the plane's lift.

"Ask one of the stewardesses to treat your wound then follow me down into the cargo hold. But that's only if you feel well enough to do so, James. While you're at it, ask them to dress this man's wound, the one I caused when I pulled the skin off his chest to remove the sensor," she finished, closing the lift door and descending into the cargo hold.

Arriving in the hold, April quickly moved to where the suitcase had been located and secured the lethal harness to it. "Thank you. Now I want you both to return topside and resume your normal duties. I'll need some solitude to deal with this stupid threat alone."

The steward asked, "Is they're nothing that we can do to help you, Ms. Darling?"

"Yes. You can tell me where the nearest in-flight intercom is located before you leave?"

"There's one on that pillar besides you."

"Now that's what I call convenient. Isn't it? Thank you again for what you've both done for me. Now get to fuck out of here," she insisted firmly, as James rejoined her sporting a large head dressing on his wound.

"That's very trendy, James. It's just your colour so it suits you," she joked, trying to cheer him up while she waited for the others to leave the hold.

"Oh very droll, now what is your plan of action?" he asked. He was still looking extremely sombre.

"Are you feeling okay?"

"It's just my headache, April. The pain is getting gradually worse. But I'll manage until we're finished."

Reaching up April held up his upper eyelid to check his pupils. "I'm afraid you seem to be suffering from the early stages of concussion. Get yourself back up to the cabin and rest. I'll manage here."

"No way, the only time I'll return to the cabin is with you."

Knowing how stubborn James could be, April decided that the best thing to do was complete the job as quickly as possible. Then she could see that James got the treatment he needed.

Pressing the intercom she asked the pilot. "How are we doing for altitude, Captain?"

"We are at ten thousand feet and circling in a twenty mile radius. It's the best we can do, I'm afraid. What would you like me to do now?"

"Just keep it steady at that, and try to avoid any turbulence will you? Now are you able to drop the landing gear independently of each other?" Turning to James, April asked him if he could collect any spare luggage straps that are not being used, and knot them together to form a one long rope.

"We can only drop the rear nose wheel independently of the others. The second one is only for when we have more than a seventy-five percent payload. It's a bit like the spare axles on a juggernaut. Why? Which one do you want dropping?" The bemused Captain asked.

"None yet, I'll need the rear of the two opened to drop the bomb through. Make doubly sure that we're not above any shipping lanes when we do though." April then helped James to finish knotting the straps together.

"That should reach that nose wheel. Now secure your end firmly round the post that the intercom's on." She told him, tying the other end firmly round her waist. "Don't look so worried, James. I'm only doing this purely as a precautionary measure?"

"I'm not sure of what you intend doing, April. But I know I'm not going to like it." James reluctantly admitted, as he finished securing the rope.

"Now you stay on that intercom, and make sure you keep a firm grip on that post as well. She said, as she gingerly moved the explosives forwards. Slowly and laboriously April edged onwards. Inch by inch she tentatively drew nearer to the landing gear. "Can I help?"

"I'm afraid not, James. They're not really heavy; it's just that I'm trying to avoid any sudden jolts." April stopped momentarily to wipe the sweat from her face.

"Another six feet should do it." she mumbled to herself as she slowly continued. "I can't be sure that they haven't booby-trapped the outer case, otherwise I'd remove the bomb and defuse it." She told James. Then she asked, as she reached the doors, "Will you get the Captain on the intercom again for me? Right Captain, are you ready to drop the rear nose wheels for me?"

The Captain asked tentatively, "Are you sure about this? You don't sound it to me."

"What's the alternative? It will definitely explode before we land, and we haven't got a scanner on board so that I can check for any hidden devices that would allow me to defuse it. So any other suggestions would be most welcome at this moment, Captain."

"Sorry Miss Darling. It's just that I meant."

"I know what you meant, and thank you. Now are we ready to open the bomb doors?"

"What bomb—?" he suddenly realised that April was joking. "How slow of me, so that we can drop the bomb out of it. I haven't done this before at this height so I contacted Sir Charles and his boffins. They said, even though I have descended to ten thousand feet, and have slowed down as much as it's safe to do so. After the doors open to drop the wheels at this speed and height, the air currant passing along the under belly will create a very powerful down draft. In other words, you're in real danger of being sucked out of the plane."

"Well thank you. You certainly know how to cheer a girl up." She told him intransigently. "Well I have a rope holding me to a pillar, so let's hope that it'll still hold me when you drop the wheels. Now can we get on with it before I change my mind, April asked cautiously, taking a firm grip on a securing rail as the plane hit turbulence. She told the Captain, "That, I most certainly didn't need."

"I'm sorry, Miss. I'll try to avoid any further sudden movements. Now if you're ready I'll lower the rear nose wheel?"

"Ready when you are?" she confirmed as she braced herself.

A low whirling of the motors started as April took a firmer grip on the rail, while steeling her-self in preparation for the doors opening. A loud cracking noise could be heard as the door seal parted and the doors started to slowly open. The wheels began to slowly descend, amid the deafening sound of the wind-rushing past the underbelly, as April felt herself being drawn towards the open doors by the strong downdraft.

Falling to the floor as the rope snapped. Desperately she tried to find another grip on the rail. She felt herself sliding towards the doors and her most certain death. Struggling to maintain a grip, April used her feet to push the explosives through the undercarriage.

The devices exploded as it cleared the hold, causing the plane to rock violently. The crew struggled to stabilise the aircraft. April's grip slipped from the rail. She fought frantically to gain a new hold with which she could anchor herself, then her hand rubbed against a luggage cage as she managed to grab a firm hold of another rail, and cling to it as tight as she possibly could.

Suddenly, April became aware that an unconscious James was sliding towards her. She frantically tried to get a firmer grip, wrapping her arm around the rail while gabbing for James with her free arm.

"CLOSE THEM BLOODY DOORS," she shouted in desperation. As she felt James slowly slip from her grip. The thought suddenly occurred to her, 'What if James hasn't left the intercom on transmit.' But with relief, April heard the motors starting, and eventually after what seemed like an eternity, the doors sealed closed.

Feeling as though her arms had been ripped from their sockets, April lay flat on the floor of the cargo hold. She was far too exhausted to move.

"Are you okay?" she asked James. She was met with a stony silence. In blind panic April tried in vain to summon the strength to get up. "James, can you hear me, JAMES?" Again silence was her sombre reply. April was grateful to heard the sound of the lift arriving.

"April. Are you okay, April?" a panicking Alan called.

"I will keep. Quickly, you must see to James. I think he's concussed from hitting his head against that bloody seat."

After a few anxious moments, Alan confirmed, "I think he's having a brain haemorrhage that's spreading rapidly. I'm afraid that if he doesn't get to a hospital soon, he'll die."

"Surely there's something you can do to stop, or at least slow down, the haemorrhaging," April questioned with deep concern as she rose to her feet. "Maybe ice packs or something like that."

"I'll need to get him upstairs first. I believe they have a small medical unit in the tail section on the plane. Maybe I can try to stem the haemorrhaging in there, at least until we land. However, I will need a stretcher or a wheelchair to move him with?" Alan told her as he tried in vain to lift the patient.

"I'll have one sent down to you," April said as she moved towards the in-flight intercom on the pillar. "Captain, we need a stretcher or a wheelchair down here like yesterday, and two or three accomplished stretcher-bearers. So they can help the doctor to carry Lieutenant Edwards to your medical unit. Oh! And all the ice the stewards can find, or generate. I'll come to the flight deck to report to London as soon as Lieutenant Edwards is stable."

After double-checking that the doctor had everything under control, and insisting that she be kept fully aware of James' progress, or lack of it. April proceeded to the flight deck to give her report to, Charles.

"Just before you issue your report we have realised another dire situation has occurred," the Captain interrupted, "due to the time that we've spent in circling, plus having to reduce our altitude and speed, we'll not have sufficient fuel left to reach London."

"Did you hear that, Charles? We need clearance to land and refuel at the nearest airport, ASAP." She asked the Captain how much fuel do we have left.

"Lisbon has a runway long enough for you to land that plane. Can you get there, Captain?" Charles asked anxiously.

"If we maintain a high enough altitude and we get clearance to go straight in to land, then we might just be able to make it. But we will be landing on just the fumes, so set up for an emergency landing, Sir Charles." Explained the flight engineer, as he added, "We're diverting to Lisbon now."

"I'm setting up for an emergency landing there for you. Just go straight in on runway three," Charles instructed the Captain. He then asked for April's report on what has been happening.

"Go and get some rest now. Try not to worry I'll have an ambulance standing by to take Lieutenant Edwards directly to a neurological unit, immediately when you land." He assured her, as April prepared to leave the flight deck.

After frisking and releasing the terrorist, April left him handcuffed in his seat, so that he'd be much more comfortable. She then asked the hostess to feed him. April then returned to the first class cabin to catch up on some well-earned rest.

CHAPTER 24

The first class lounge was empty except for a small party of passengers that were sitting at the bar chatting. Before April could drift into a well-earned sleep, the Captain made an appearance in the lounge.

"Excuse me, Miss Darling."

"I've told you to call me, April. Miss Darling is far too formal it makes me feel like an old spinster. I hope that you are the bearer of good tidings this time."

"I'm afraid not. We have just re-calculated our remaining fuel, and because we're flying into bad weather, and a strong head wind, we'll have a shortfall of a considerable number of miles. We're all reasonably inexperienced with this aircraft, and it seems that nobody has felt the need to imagine such a scenario would ever occur, not in this day and age. So we are unsure of what exactly we could do about it. The control tower wondered if you might be able to suggest anything that we can do to solve the fuel shortage, and Portugal is refusing to let us enter their airspace unless we can guarantee that we have sufficient fuel with which to land safely."

"You say your manual doesn't cover such a scenario, Captain?"

"I'm afraid not. We always carry a little extra fuel should we ever have the need to deviate a little, or if we encounter bad weather, etc., but not enough to cover such a lengthy diversion as we've had to make."

April went into deep thought whilst staring out of the window. She said to the Captain, "Surely the solution should be patently obvious to you, this plane has got four engines? You must be able to shut two engines down at this altitude, and still be able to stay quite safely in the sky, and that would conserve enough fuel, would it not?" she suggested to the Captain quietly, so that she would not alarm any other passengers.

"Yes, but a plane this heavy and size needs the extra boost for takeoff. And for landing purposes in the event we should find the need to pull out and climb, if an emergency arose," he explained to her.

"Yes, I know that. But do we need all four engines during flight?"

"I see where you're coming from. It's totally irregular but it just might work. We should have thought of it ourselves, as you've said it's patently obvious. I'll have to contact the company for their approval first though, but I'll only get back to you should I need to. Thank you, Miss. Sorry, I mean, April." he said, as he rushed back towards the flight deck.

"Are you okay, Miss Darling?" asked the concerned stewardess. "Only you seem to be in some sort of distress, or discomfort."

"Yes I'm okay, and my name's April as I've told your Captain. I've just got severe stomach cramps, but I don't really know why. It must be something that I've eaten?"

"Maybe it's your time of the month?"

"I don't think so. I don't have periods." Realising the carelessness of her flippant remark, April added quickly. "They've stopped for some reason since I had my op."

"Lucky you, so maybe you've over exerted yourself restraining that terrorist. Anyway, can I get you some painkillers, April?"

"I'll rest to see if that helps first, and thank you for your concern." She told her, tensing her body once again as she felt another sharp pain.

The hostess began to panic, "What's wrong. Let me help you?"

Starting to get up, April said, "I need to go to the toilet. I'm very sorry, but I seem be too late." She said to her in panic, "Oh no!" When she saw the blood stained seat. "I don't have a change of clothing. They're all in the case in the hold."

"Now don't you worry about it April, I'll see to you first, and then I'll clean up the seat. I told you they seemed to be period pains, didn't I? They must have started again." The stewardess suggested, as she helped April to the toilet. "While you wash yourself, I'll get you a change of clothes. We always carry a spare set of clothing for emergency purposes, and you seem to be about the same size as me."

When the stewardess went away April began removing the blood stained clothing, and washing herself. A short time passed before there was a soft tapping on the door.

"Are you okay, April? I have a change of clothing for you," the hostess called in.

April opened the door to let the stewardess enter, "I hope these fit you okay. My name is Camellia, but everybody just calls me Cam."

"Okay Cam," April said as she dressed. "But somebody is going to pay for this mess," she threatened through clenched teeth. There was a sudden jerking of the plane before it stabilised. April realised that this was because the pilot had just shut down two of its engines.

"There's no charge," Cam explained, misunderstanding what April had meant.

Cam told her that she'd fetch a hot sweet coffee while April finished getting ready, handing April a sanitary towel as she left. Barely had April returned to her seat than Alan re-appeared.

A concerned Alan asked, "Are you okay, April? I was told you were hurt."

"Sit down so that I don't need to let all and sundry know what's just happened," she insisted Alan sat beside her. "I've just started to have bloody periods."

"How's that happened? You're a transsexual really so you shouldn't be having periods," the surprised Alan tried to reason. "You know what this will mean don't you? You have just made medical history.

Now it will make it even harder, no, nigh on impossible for you to prove what you once were."

"I've worked most of that out for myself, thank you, I'll now be lucky to persuade any doctor to consider me for a reversal. That's what you mean. But it'll still not be impossible though. Will it?"

"It's not just that, if they're not convinced of who you once were, and of the trauma that your body has already experienced, well they wouldn't be prepared for the secondary shock or much worse. Plus the secondary rejection your body will be exposed to. In other words, it would probably be fatal for you."

She turned on her phone to contact Charles. But before she was able to make the call, the Captain came back into the lounge.

"April, our calculations confirm that now we've shut down two of our engines; we now have more than sufficient fuel to reach our destination. So we will be okay. Thank you for all your help."

She watched him descend to the flight deck before she dialled Charles' number. After a few rings Charles answered.

"YOU BASTARDS, YOU'RE ALL A BUNCH OF FUCKING BASTARDS," April shouted tearfully.

"What's wrong now, April? The Captain tells me that you're going to land safely, and it's all thanks to you," started a bewildered Charles who was mystified at what could be upsetting April.

"IT'S NOT THAT YOU BLOODY FOOL, I'M NOW MENSTRUATING. I HAVE NOW STARTED TO HAVE BLOODY PERIODS," April shouted at him down the phone. She was oblivious that she was being overheard by the other startled passengers. Realising that she'd spoken to loud April blushed profusely with embarrassment, so she rang off abruptly.

"Don't be too hard on yourself, April. You know that you're still a very beautiful lady. Regarding the funny handshake brigade, well, don't be too hasty to judge them either, they're only doing what they thought was best for our country. After all, it's what they're trained to do," Dabbing the tears from her cheek with a tissue. Alan finished, "You know how thick they can be at times. They're just like robots really. They can't see further than their handbook, and have lost all the ability to think for themselves."

Smiling at what he'd said, April confirmed, "You've got that one spot on, Alan. They are zombies really. But some of them were aware of the consequences that I might remember. They just thought of me as an expendable experiment. I probably still am to all intent and purpose. Anyway, how's James? Shouldn't you be getting back to him?"

"He's sleeping like a baby so there's not a lot more that I can do until we land. I've asked one of the passengers, who just happens to be a trained SRN, if she'd watch over him for me, and tell me if there's any sign of a change in his condition. No matter how slight it is."

The next hour passed uneventfully with Alan chatting merrily, trying to lift her spirits. Eventually, he returned to prepare his patient for transfer to a Portuguese hospital immediately upon landing. Gazing through the window, April felt the two idle engines kicking in, as the pilot began the slow descent into Lisbon airport.

Quickly after landing, James and Alan, as per Charles's instructions, were transferred to an awaiting ambulance. Then two heavily armed policemen boarded the plane to escort the male prisoner off, as April just sat patiently while they refuelled the plane.

When the plane had taken on sufficient fuel to continue, they were soon continuing their journey towards London. After landing in London, April supervised the handing over of the female terror suspects, briefed the security forces, and asking them to thank the Portuguese police officially for their invaluable help. Then April travelled on to Chelsea, and her London apartment.

Unplugging the main telephone, she then turned her mobile off to allow for some privacy and solitude, so that she could attempt to come to terms with the final step of her enforced femininity. She was unsure of what to do, so April decided to soak in the bath, and at least temporarily escape from the realities of her arduous profession.

Removing her clothes while filling the bath, April also removed the soiled towel. Just standing holding the sanitary towel she was fought back tears, realising only too clearly that she was totally unprepared for what had just happened. April realised that she had not had the advantage of growing up in the knowledge that this would eventually happen one day. She had also not experienced the years of puberty leading up to this very moment either. There was no mother, aunt, or even big sister to help and support her. Or to help her through the deep depression that was fast setting in. The only possibility of help was from Mandy, her former wife. But April felt reluctant to ask her, because of her association with Charles.

Instinctively feeling that her body had gone into total shock, she questioned how she would ever learn to cope with this, particularly while she was still having to carrying out the stressful tasks that had now befallen her. Tussling with the problems mentally and the severe stomach cramp that she was getting periodically, she tried hard to relax. She tried to let them all gently drift from her, carried away on the steam from the warm aromatic waters she was submersed in. There was no way of escaping her new persona at the present time, or the profession that she'd been coerced into. So April dismissed it all as she started relaxing.

Closing her eyes and trying to switch her thoughts to much happier times, April turned her attention to her two beloved children. How now could she still be involved with them growing up? After all, she could not always be there for them. Should she out of kindness keep at a distance from them?

Mentally tussling with these thoughts that were clouding her mind, this was also added to the sheer mental exhaustion from the last twenty-four hours, so April soon drifted into an uneasy sleep.

Waking with an abrupt shock she became aware that night had now descended, and the bath water had become cold. Quickly stepping from the bath and wrapping herself in a towelling robe, April switched on the light. 'Eleven p.m. I've slept for six hours,' she thought while making a hot drink to warm her up. She then carried it through into the bedroom and got into bed.

April didn't remember falling asleep, but a fierce knocking at her door woke her. Looking at the clock next to the half drank coffee, she could see that it was ten thirty in the morning.

"Okay I'm coming," she shouted, "there's no need to knock the ruddy door off its hinges." She opened the door to a distraught looking Charles. Asking him casually, "Where's the fire?"

"You're not answering your phone, April."

"That's because I've unplugged it, and turned off my mobile."

"But why did you? I've been frantic worrying that something may have happened to you?" Charles questioned, as he sat down to catch his breath.

"I've already explained that I've started to menstruate. So I needed some quality time to try to come to terms with that. Besides, I WAS very tired. Now as that's not the real reason you've called. What is the reason?" she asked, sipping a fresh orange juice.

"Well no. It isn't. I need to go to Portugal to assist with the interrogating the terrorist. I was wondering if you'd like to accompany me?" he waited patiently for an answer as April paced up and down the lounge, pondering whether to go.

Finally, she said to him. "I feel a bit out of sorts with woman's troubles. You know what I mean, don't you?" April pretended to whisper. "So if there's somebody else you could take I'd very much appreciate the time to rest. After all, my body's got to adjust to all of the shit you've imposed on me."

"I suppose you're right. Us men don't understand you women and your mood swings," he teased. "I just thought you'd welcome the opportunity to visit James?" he casually remarked then waited for April's response.

"How is James doing?" April asked him with profound concern.

"He's out of surgery and recovering well I'm led to believe." A hopeful Charles added, "He's been asking about you. Well between drifting in and out of consciousness that is."

"What time do we leave?" April hastily asked Charles, "I will need to buy some towels, and to see the doctor to get something for these bloody stomach cramps. Also, I want to see if he can give me something to stem the heavy blood flow while he's at it."

"We'll call to see the doctor en-route. Now while you get ready I'll make you an appointment." A much-relieved Charles told her, as she walked through into the bedroom. After a couple of minutes he called to her, "The appointment's set for whenever you're ready, April." He added purposefully, "I suppose this will scotch all your aspirations of returning to your male persona again?" bracing himself in readiness for her catty retort.

Angrily April shouted back to him, "I might have known it would get back to your bat ears. I won't waste my time asking you who told you, but he still is working for you, isn't he. And I imagine what's happened to me will make your bloody day."

"I must admit that you did have me worried for a while. You're disrespectful, ante authoritarian, and insubordinate. That is what makes you peerless in your field. Besides, it would be such a criminal waste. Just you take a look at yourself in the mirror, and then tell me that you wouldn't have drooled over a woman with your assets. When you were a man, that is?"

"That's as maybe, but I didn't have any choice in the matter. Did I? That's, what really bugs me. I'm sure you could have found a more willing participant. One who would willingly join in your devious little game?" April re-emerging from the bedroom, "Right, I'm ready. Shall we go, Charlie boy?" she asked, putting on a long leather coat.

He opened the door and asked, "Have you got your keys?"

She waved them at him, and locked the security lock before standing with him at the closed front door, waiting for him to open it. "Thank you, Charles. You can be such a gentleman when you really try." She said gratefully, as they passed through the door.

A bullet ricocheted off the masonry besides her head. She pushed Charles back inside and fell onto one knee, all in the same instinctive movement. Within the twinkling of an eye a pistol was in her hand, as she carefully took aim at the car speeding away from the scene. Squeezing the trigger, April released a shot through the driver's window and in to his head. His dead body slumped forwards making the car career into a line of parked vehicles. She carefully took aim and shot again, hitting the gunman in his left shoulder as the car came to an abrupt stop. The wounded gunman rolled from the back door firing his Chubb nosed machine gun. Again April aimed, and then she shot again, killing the man.

Charles was calling for back up as April began to examine the two bodies for any sign of a heartbeat.

"Forget the backup, just ask them to bring the body bags," she told him, frisking the bodies for any signs of identity. "They are professional hit men, Charles. Carrying no ID, and having no distinguishing marks on them. But they look as though they could be South American to me, so my guess would be De-Mundo's behind this."

Within five minutes the coroners van, and a car carrying four security men, screeched to a halt. After informing them of the urgency to identify the dead assailants, Charles and April continued on to the airport. They enjoyed an uneventful flight to Portugal, and after disembarking the aircraft at Lisbon airport, a police car took them directly to the main police headquarters in Lisbon.

A lengthy meeting followed. Sir Charles gave a detailed description of the events to date, telling them what had led to the risk of the lives of the passengers, and caused the enforced emergency landing at Lisbon some twenty-four hours earlier. Eventually, April asked if she could be excused to visit an injured colleague, and leaving Charles there to assist in the interrogation of the male terrorist.

"But before I leave gentlemen I would just like to reiterate something. What you tell me about the two ladies protesting their innocence is probably true. I could sense at the time their reluctance to participate in the attempted mass slaughter. So yes, maybe what they're claiming is quite right, that they believed their husband was still alive and being held hostage. That would explain their reluctant participation in the attempted hijacking, and their willingness to risk their own lives to save the life of their husband, and father, Mr. Bashier," April reminded them.

After asking the desk Sergeant to call her a taxi, April proceeded to the hospital where James was, and a porter showed her to the private ward where she found Alan busily attending to him. After explaining how they'd had to operate again to release the pressure from James's brain, he gave April a layman's report on James's progress.

April interrupted, and asked, "When do you think he'll wake up again?"

"His pulse is still pretty weak, but it's getting stronger by the hour. I expect he should wake again very soon. Definitely during the next twenty-four hours, but much sooner than that I should think. And how are you, April?"

"I'm okay. I'm just feeling jet lagged, Alan. How do you feel?"

"Tired like you. I'm just going to lunch if you'd care to join me?"

"It'll be my pleasure, but I insist on paying. It will be my way of thanking you for helping James, and probably saving his life. Although I hear you've been feeding Charles with more information than he needed to know."

Alan's face reddened as he tried to ignore April's last remark. "Well I never argue with a beautiful lady if she wants to pay. I'll just collect my coat," He said, smiling awkwardly. When he returned to the private ward, April was just finishing praying. He asked, "Are you okay?"

"Yes. I was just talking to the ultimate physician, and asking him to help you," April explained as she linked Alan's arm and they walked sprightly out into the warm autumn sunshine.

"Charles is with me as you know, so I suppose I should ring and ask if he'd like to join us." she suggested as she dialled Charles' number.

After a short conversation April confirmed, "He does want to meet up for lunch, so he's asked me if we would wait for him here. He says that he's on his way."

While they waited Alan explained to her James' present condition, and how they'd used laser surgery to disperse the blood clot. Then he added cautiously, "We'll not know until he wakes whether there has been any long-term brain damage. He could recover fully, or," he hesitated for a moment.

"Or he could now become a cabbage," Charles suggested through the open window of the car that had just pulled up beside them. "Is that what you were trying to say, Doctor Williamson?"

"Good to see you again, Sir Charles," Alan greeted him warmly as he approached the car offering to shake Charles' hand.

Charles willingly accepted, as they cordially exchanged greetings. "It's been a long time. How are you keeping, Doctor?" began Charles

April butted in, "You know how he is. I told Alan that you wouldn't have lost touch with him, EVEN if he thinks you have," she corrected him. "And it was through him that you got your information, wasn't it? Now stop playing mind games with me you two, or else!"

Charles laughed nervously out of embarrassment, he asked, "Shall we go and dine now?" While he held open the door for them both to enter the Limo. "I've taken the liberty of inviting the Chief of Police to join us," he told them as they entered the car. The chauffeur drove the short distance to the restaurant, as Charles introduced Alan and April, to Manuel.

"London tells us that the captives have talked willingly," began Charles. "Apparently, although they are devout Muslims they were unwilling participants in all of this. It seems they were willing to give up their lives to save the life of their loved one, as you have already suggested, April. The two ladies are inconsolable, knowing that Mr. Bashier has been so savagely beaten to death. We have also dispatched a small detachment to search for their children. It was all part of the deal if they co-operated with us. However, the man we are unsure about. He's given his name as, Ali Cohen, but we suspect that, that's just an alias. He also told us that they are holding his wife, and his baby hostage. We're checking that story out too, and the address that he's given us in Gaza. Ah! We're here now," said Charles, as the limousine drew to a halt. "I've booked a private function room so we can talk more freely." he explained, as he again held the door open for April.

Placing their coats across a chair the men left to visit the lavatory, while April stayed in the waiting area. She seized the opportunity to remove the bullets furtively from Charles gun, replacing it just in time as the three men returned.

The manager was patiently waited for their arrival, and he bowed respectfully as they entered the waiting area.

"This way, please," he invited, as they collected their coats. He led them into a small function room. Informing them, "I will attend to you personally. My name is Juan Carlos Mandessa, but just call me Carlos." he told them as he courteously held back April's chair.

"That's Spanish for John Charles," April explained to Charles.

After choosing their drinks and selecting from the menu, they gave their orders to Carlos, who left the room and headed to the kitchen.

"Alone at last," Manuel said with relief. "Although everything in my country is mañana, there are times when even we find things should be a little more pressing. It's a pleasure to meet you in person, Miss Darling. Your reputation precedes you, and the description Charles gave of you could never have done you true justice," Manuel complimented as he respectfully kissed the back of her hand.

"Just call me April, and it's a pleasure to meet you too, Manuel. And may I thank your country for attending to the needs of Lieutenant Edwards."

"Yes. He's doing fine, I believe. However, they'll need to keep him partly sedated for at least another twenty four hours." Manuel explained as the first course was being served. "They'll then wait a further seven days before testing for any long term damage. Is he a close friend of yours, April?"

"Not in the way that you are implying, but we have been through hell and all together, so we have become very close friends. Now Charles, about Carlos De-Mundo, do we know of his whereabouts, YET?"

"We're not sure. There has been some unusual activity off the Northwest coast of Siberia, a little known island called Novaya Zemlya. Anyway, we're monitoring the situation very closely." Then Charles turned his attention to Alan, "I have some good news for you too, Doctor Williamson."

"Call me Alan, Sir Charles."

"Okay, Alan. We have no need of your services any longer at this present time, so you're free to return to your beloved Dominican if you so wish. However, would you remain prepared for us recall you? That is if we should need your invaluable services in the future?" he asked, using an insistent tone to his voice.

"So Sir Charles, it seems it was an unnecessary upheaval for me?" Alan snapped indignantly, trying to sound very annoyed.

"Well, yes and no. But it was very fortuitous as it so happened. If you hadn't been on that plane James would most certainly not be alive today."

"That was one saving grace I suppose. Having the very pleasant company of April was also a priceless bonus." Then, with afterthought, Alan added, "But I was hoping for a further abundance of her extremely pleasant company, Sir Charles."

Smiling, April advised him, "Well thank you, Alan. But it may be wiser for you to return home. Agents that accompany me on assignments usually end up getting shot at." Then correcting any misunderstanding, she bumbled, "Not by me I might add. Those being shot at I mean. I didn't shoot them." They all laughed as April fumbled her words. "As I've said Alan you are still an active agent anyway, aren't you? Despite you're pretence, and playing those silly little mind games with me."

This accusation they tried to ignore, again.

Charles quickly came to Alan's aid, suggesting, "Perhaps you should stop there. Before you say something that can be misinterpreted, April," as they all joined in the laughter.

"Okay. So I've explained it all wrong," April continued to try making excuses as their laughter became infectious. Continuing to blush, she told them, "But you all know what I meant. Now can we please change the subject?"

"Charles, what are your plans now? Do we go after that Colombian bastard, and pronto? Or do we again wait for verification, just so that he has the time to get a head start on us, and escape us yet again?"

"No, April. As soon as we're sure it's De-Mundo we'll act immediately. But until then I suggest that we all use the time we have to relax, and soak up this warm relaxing Portuguese sunshine. At least while we can," he suggested, as they continued with their meal. "There are a few things that have been happening while you've been away though, April. The most important one being that all of the more influential nations have come to realise at long last, that if we are to defeat the constant threats of global terrorism we must pool our resources, and all pull together. It's a course of action as you already know, that I've been trying to advocate for some considerable time."

"Well Charles, I wish you luck. Although it would work in theory, and make it much harder for these fanatics to find refuge in which to hide, there are and always will be, the countries that will work with you as a shield, diverting any suspicion away from them of what they are actually doing," April reminded him.

"We do of course realise that fact. However, there's been a series of secret exploratory meeting with our European counterparts, and the other major nations, American, Russian, and China, etcetera." Charles paused while Carlos served the sweet course before continuing, "They've all agreed that the first priority must be to set up a truly international task force. They will be fully equipped, prepared, and ready to strike at a moment's notice. It will be fully self-supportive and mobile, and they will co-operate fully on matters of national, or global, security."

"Well as I keep saying, I wish you luck. Not wishing to appear pessimistic, or pour oil onto already troubled waters, I can already see it as a weapon for disaster. The fanatical insurgents will use it to propagate their cancerous fanaticism, AND as a way of concealing their true beliefs and aims," April finished as Carlos began to clear the table.

Charles, who realised that their privacy would always be invaded in such a situation, suggested that he settled the bill and continue the conversation alfresco. As they walked, April linked Charles' arm. She could sense that he was feeling uncomfortable with this.

"I'm sure Mandy won't mind. In fact, I'm positive she won't," she reassured him, as she felt his arm beginning to relax. "That's better, relax and take your pants off."

He pulled away with shock, "What did you just say, April?" Charles said with shocked disbelief as he turned towards her.

Seeing April laughing uncontrollable, he realised that she was only jesting. "That's better. Loosen up Charles. I know that we're finished in that way, so I'm just trying to be all womanly and friendly. After all, that was part of your master plan, wasn't it?"

Charles gave a nervous cough as he blushed and nodded uncomfortably.

Then he said, "You always seem to do it, don't you, April? Take the Mickey out of me, that is. And I always seem to fall for it, don't I?" he asked, as he took her arm willingly. Then he noticed Alan and Manuel were following closely behind, bemused at April's mickey taking. "But we're neglecting our other guests," he tried to change the subject.

"She can certainly wind you up, Charles. She knows exactly which buttons to press. Doesn't she?" Alan remarked.

"Yes, it's her twisted scouse sense of humour I'm afraid. We tend forget where she hails from, she can be so witty and mentally agile. That's what makes her so unpredictable, and such a formidable adversary. Now can we return to the matter in hand?" he insisted firmly.

"Only if sir doesn't mind this poor under-trodden wench listening in on the big gentlemen's conversations," she continued.

Charles smiled, "See what I mean. There's no stopping her once she gets in this kind of a mood. However, let's get down to the matter in hand," Suggested Charles again. "We're fully aware of the countries that'll try to join us and use us to their advantage. That's why the Russians have tabled a motion that we all agreed on."

Charles stopped speaking to take in a deep breath before continuing. "The motion is that any task force ought to be spearheaded by you."

He waited patiently for her reply.

Sauntering silently whilst mulling over the idea, Charles waited anxiously for her to agree, or voice any objections she had. Then to lay down her own criteria and preconditions, that would make the offer more acceptable to her.

"I do find these adult games you all play totally puerile, and completely unacceptable to me. This you already know, Charles. You use the title of "SECRET AGENT" for me, then in the next breath tell me that I've developed a global reputation. How do you expect me to ever plan a future with that hanging over my head? The department knows that it's most likely that my adversaries will recognise me on sight, and long before I'll ever know of their existence. So I'm very sorry, Charles. You know I always work better alone and without the added pressure of looking out for a partner, or partners, or being restricted by this international team that you are advocating."

While Alan and Manuel meandered aimlessly in their wake, Charles continued to remonstrate with April. He was trying desperately to make her change her mind.

"It was a unanimous decision to elect you to pioneer this task force. You have proven yourself to be peerless in this field of expertise. So tell me what the problem is?"

"Charles, I would be a marked man. I mean, woman. There'll already probably be a price on my head. That will almost certainly be increased as time goes on. You may as well just paint a target on my back. I'll be the target of every misguided dissident that's able to con you, and infiltrate their way into any newly formed organisation."

"The vetting criteria would be extremely stringent, I can promise you that. Now what can I say to convince you?"

"Nothing, Charles. You know I don't like having the responsibility of working with other people," sobbed April. "Look what's happened to Winston, and James. They're amongst a long list of other good people that have worked with me, but have ended up paying the ultimate price for doing so."

"But this is a very dirty cold war, April. The dirtiest there possibly has ever been. But we must always believe that these tragedies will pave the way to a better world. So please reconsider the offer. I've the power to grant you whatever you ask for." Then he realised that April would ask for the one thing that he was powerless to grant. He hastily corrected himself, "With the exception of a reversal that is. You can have whatever else you ask for."

Thinking long and hard April silently prayed for guidance, while patiently, Charles, Alan and Miguel, walked quietly besides her. She mentally tussled with the dilemma, until eventually, as they walked past a bar April stood at a table.

"Buy a girl a drink while we discuss it?" she suggested. He gladly pulled back a seat for her to sit on.

"Before we start can I order four beers?" April asked, as the waiter approached.

"Yes, please." They all readily agreed. "Hola Señors, Senorita," he greeted them.

"Hola Señor. Do you speak English?" she asked. "No comprenda," the man replied.

"Si. Cuatro cervezas agragan, por favor?" April asked. The man then left to fulfil their order.

"I've ordered four beers as the man does not understand any English. So we should be safe enough to talk freely here. Now, I find it very hard to believe that you are willing to promise me anything that I ask you for, Charles."

"I can assure you that whatever it is you'd like you only have to ask for it," Charles tried to re-assure her. "But as I've already said though, there is only one request I'm not empowered to fulfil. You already know what that is."

Taking a deep breath, she asked, "Okay. Now where have you put the implants?"

"What implants?" a shocked Charles asked.

"Now don't you try to become the innocent with me, you're only wasting my time. And it's an insult to my intelligence. So I suggest that you either answer my question, or I stick with an emphatic, NO!"

"Well how do you know that there are any implants," a puzzled Charles asked.

"Come on, it's not too hard to work it out, even one of those blithering idiot that work for you could have worked it out. You're able to trace me and my every movement. And, just in case I fuck up and become an embarrassment to you or the department, if I haven't already, you'll need a way of terminating me. After all, it's not as if you usually sack your agents, is it?" April relaxed back and waited for some sort of response.

Alan, and Miguel, began to feel uncomfortable by the tension that was rapidly developing.

"I'll need to return to my office, I've a mound of paperwork to deal with. Will you all please excuse me? You have my number Charles, so if I can be of any further assistance please do not hesitate to call me on my direct number," Manuel said as he respectfully kissed April on the cheek before leaving.

Alan stood up as Miguel left, "I think I'll stroll back to our hotel, so I can enjoy the warm sunshine and fresh air," he started. But he was abruptly interrupted by April.

"You just sit there," She shouted, pointing to his seat. "I may need your expertise here, and very soon."

"I'll need to contact the minister for verification," Charles began, and started to dial the number.

Snatching the phone from his hand, April reminded him, "I thought you had the full authority to grant me whatever I wished for Carte Blanche. So you should not need to contact the Minister. Should you, Charles? If you do, then your promises are empty and worthless, and my answer must be a no way, José," she warned him. Then she ordered three more beers.

Charles sat pondering his predicament, while April ruthlessly insisted that he and he alone, should supply the information that she needed. And not allowing London to suggest any stalling tactics. More importantly, she was aware that if Charles contacted London they would most likely insist that they removed the tags. Then hatch a devious plan to replace them with a modified, more deeply implanted, version.

"Well who do you have in mind to remove them? It would need to be a skilled neurological surgeon, and a skilled gynaecologist."

"Let me worry about who, the how when, and wherefore, Charles. The less you know about it the less you will be tempted to spill the beans, or to use your influence to further interfere. Another thing you should know about, I've written down a description of the whole sordid incident. Starting with my abduction, and going on to describing how I was press ganged into this stinking service of yours."

"Nobody would ever believe you. Where is your proof, April?" he asked smugly.

"You can wipe that smug smile off your face; I have used my idle time in London to gather my proof. There are copies of tapes from your office, and duplicates of photographs that you had taken step by step of my transformation, JUST for my records, of course."

Charles laughed nervously; "You're bluffing me."

She reached into her purse and took out a photograph of them removing the penis. Flicking it towards him, April asked him, "Am I? Well that's an extra copy of one stage I've printed. You must remember you've created me, so I'm now the devious fucking bitch that you've turned me into. Also, I've left orders, and money, to have you assassinated if I die in unforeseen circumstances," April said cockily. Settling back into the seat she asked casually, "Doe's anybody want another beer? Or maybe you'd like something a little stronger, Charles?"

April noticed the expression of shock on Alan's face. This disturbed her as she had originally thought of him as being her stalwart. But the sad reality was rapidly looming that her suspicions were right, he's still an active agent after all. Maybe what she'd thought of as a fortuitous meeting was actually part of a deviously elaborate plot. And maybe they were planning to terminate her at some point in the very near future.

"What's wrong, Alan. Are you finding it hard to keep up your pretence as well? We know that you actually aren't a reluctant participant in all of this, DON'T WE? And you Charles, don't waste your time searching for my insurance, it would only be a fruitless exercise on your part. Not to mention the criminal waste of public money that would be involved. I advise you not to tell the minister about my insurance, they may just hang you out to dry, and then deny all knowledge of all of this." April ended as she ordered more drinks.

Charles phoned the ministry after April had returned his phone too him. He remonstrated with him as he argued the case for complying with April's wishes, and to the letter. Finally, he rang off telling April that he could grant her wishes. He added slyly, "You know April, you should be very careful about who you threaten. What's to stop me from shooting you with the gun that I have pointed at you under the table?"

"Go ahead, Charles. Just pull the trigger and see what happens?"

"No, certainly not," he said sharply. "I was just showing you how easy it would be to end all of this."

"It's not as easy as you think," April enlightened him. She snatched the gun from his grip and pulled the trigger. Click, click, the hammer sounded as it struck the empty chambers. "See, you would need these," April reached into her pocket and produced the bullets. Finally insisting, "Now can we stop playing these puerile bloody games? I'm finding them extremely tiresome now."

———

"Okay you win April. But firstly, tell me when you neutralise my weapon? And more to the point, why did you?" A bewildered Charles asked, as a shocked Dr. Alan Williamson still was sitting dumbstruck.

"The when doesn't really matter, but the why? I've been suspicious as to why you have distanced yourself from me. It's not just because you and Mandy are to be married. How shall I put it, you have become completely apathetic towards me, and it's as if you expect me not to return from each assignment I've been sent on?" April started sobbing bitterly, "Sometimes it's so lonely being me. I don't need the added pressure of having to watch my back from my own fucking lot."

Alan placed a compassionate arm round her. "Don't cry. We're all just doing a very dirty job. Let's face it; somebody has to do it. Don't they?"

Brushing his arm away, April quickly composed herself. "I hereby give you both fair warning. Anybody that tries to eradicate me, I'll personally send home in a bloody body bag. Then I'll disappear where nobody will EVER, find me. Now about those damn implants, or did you think that I'd forget all about them?"

"No. It's the least I can do for you my dear." Charles began, as his heart softened towards her. "When we pierced your ears we inserted a soft minute transparent sleeve into the holes. It's made of a new and revolutionary material we call 'polyplasmatic,' a circuitry medium for want of a better name. Using a small sample of the patient's blood plasma, we then put it through a sophisticated process we have perfected, and then it's transformed and developed into a highly durable microprocessor. It was then transformed into a transparent circuitry, moulding it into a minute tubular insert to fit into the pierced lobes. Because it has been developed using you own blood plasma, then there would be no adverse reactions to it."

"So there's one in either ear for tracking me?"

"Amongst other things, we are also able to eaves drop, and send out small signals to tap into other local electronic devices. Now are you happy?" he asked.

April insisted, "The others, Charles. Where are they?"

"What others?" He tried to play dumb again while April glared at him. "Oh you mean those ones; one is just under the rear of your cranium, which is what you'd need a neuro surgeon for."

"And," April interrupted, "the rest. What about the rest?"

After a long silence, Charles reluctantly explained. "It's in one of your ovaries. When we transplanted the womb, well we substituted the right ovary with a hollow man made one containing the implant. Now that's all there is. Would you like Dr. Williamson to supervise their removal?"

She gave a loud sarcastic laugh, "Do I look fucking stupid, or have I got dumbo tattooed on my forehead, or something like that. Maybe I've got half my brain missing. Originally I intended to ask Alan, but now that I'm sure that he's in your pocket you can forget it." Then changing the subject she said, "James should be regaining consciousness about now, so shall we go and visit him."

After calling for a taxi to take them to the hospital, April led the way to the second floor and proceeded to James's room. James was sitting up, and April was pleased to see that he was enjoying a drink.

"Hello," he welcomed them. Then to April's shocked horror he asked, "And who might you all be?"

Fighting back the urge to cry, April was the first to speak. She asked, "How are you feeling today? Do you remember anything about the accident yet, James?"

"No, Madam. Do you know anything about the accident? Can you have me moved to a different room; they speak some foreign language in this one, Miss."

"We'll see what we can do for you. Meanwhile you must try to get some rest," she tried to pacify him.

When they were outside the ward April broke down and cried bitterly. "Will he ever regain his memory and remember me?"

"It's not unusual after a brain operation to suffer temporary loss of memory. Give him a little more time, April," Alan tried to comfort her.

Leaving a short note for James just in case he regained his memory, the three of them returned to the hotel. They then showered before meeting up for the evening meal.

"I have a big favour to ask you, Charles."

"Anything my dear, you know you only have to ask. Now what is the favour?"

She could sense a definite softening of attitude in his tone of voice, so April exploited it. "I'm all dried out. I need some quality time out alone to relax and charge my batteries, and to contemplate your offer of course. So, I thought now might be a good time, just while we wait to clarify De-Mundo's intentions and whereabouts. I'll keep my mobile with me at all times, so I'll be able to return at a moment's notice. You can even book me the hotel room so you know exactly where I am, Charles."

After giving it some lengthy consideration Charles agreed, "But I expect you to keep your word and stay in contact with me. Now where would you like to go?"

"I don't really know so maybe round here somewhere, or alternatively North Africa. As long as it's only three or four hours from home would fit the bill very nicely. That's if you know of a good hotel round here? Otherwise whatever you can find for me, I'm not bothered. I just need to relax and do some shopping, sunbathe etcetera."

"Right, well I'll organise something for you so get packing and I'll see to it tomorrow," Promised Charles, as the three of them spent the remainder of the evening at the bar chatting idly, and attempting to bury the hatchet.

CHAPTER 25

"I think I'll take a stroll to help me sleep," April told Charles and Alan as she draped her coat across her shoulders. "I'll see you both in the morning at breakfast. Oh, you'll remember to tell Mandy and the children. Won't you, Charles. I mean, that I'll ring them soon. But I just need a little more time to adjust to the news of your forthcoming wedding."

Leaving the hotel, April ambled apparently aimlessly through the maze of brightly-lit shops and markets stalls. While she was giving the appearance of pointless meandering and window shopping, April was in actual fact being deliberate. She kept alert to anybody who might be following her. Each time she stopped, she noticed the same Portuguese couple would stop to window shop too. Needing to lose them, she noticed a taxi rank ahead of her where a solitary vacant cab was waiting for a fare. 'Now let's see how clever you two are,' she thought, ambling casually towards the rank.

As she got near to the rank another cab was just parking behind it. 'Blast it, now there are two cabs there,' she said to herself, looking for a suitable diversion. 'This café might give me the answer I want,' she thought as she entered it, closely followed by the obvious two plain clothes officers from the local police department.

"A hot black coffee with no sugar, please," April asked, taking half a step back to be nearer to the couple. After paying the assistant, she purposely spun round quickly and collided with them, but trying to make it seem to be an accident. Her hot coffee drenched them both as she'd intended, causing them to run screaming to their respective toilets.

"Will you tell them that I'm very sorry when they return?" April asked the assistant. She then rushed from the cafeteria toward the taxi rank, where the two drivers where idly talking to each other. "Can you take me to the harbour please, and as quick as you can?" she said loud enough for them both to hear. When they'd driven a short distance, April asked the driver to stop at a shopping arcade. Before paying the driver, she asked him, "Will you continue to the harbour? When your friend gets there with two people in his cab, a man and a woman in their early thirties fetch them here to meet me in twenty minutes."

"Thank you, lady. It will be my pleasure. Are they friends of yours?"

"Not really, more business associates really," she thanked the driver, paying him extra to cover his time, and then she walked into the Mall.

Meandering between the maze of small stalls and shops until eventually April found a small jewellers shop. She entered it after seeing that the jeweller was alone.

"Buenos Dais," the man welcomed her, switching to English when he realised his mistake, "Can I help you?"

"Buenos Dais, Señor. I would like to purchase a jewellers eye glass if I may."

"You'll need to contact an optical wholesalers, Miss. I only carry two, and one is my spare glass in case of an accident," he explained politely.

"Couldn't I purchase your spare glass then, and then and you can order another one. Please, it's very urgent?" she begged him. "I would pay you double, or even treble its value. It's for a dire emergency."

"Well," he started thoughtfully, "I'll be placing an order tomorrow so I might be able to accommodate you. Shall we call it just three hundred Euro's, Miss?"

"Thank you very much, you're a life saver," she told him gratefully. After paying him in cash, April started back towards her suggested rendezvous point.

On the way April purchased sewing needles, a cigarette lighter, some lint dressings, tweezers, small plastic cash bags, and a new mobile phone and sim card. Then after meeting up with the two embarrassed surveillance officers, April returned to the hotel.

Before retiring to bed she set about trying to remove two of the tracking devices. Taking her earrings out and putting the jeweller's eye glass on, April pressed the clear minute plastic sleeves outwards with her thumb, holding the lob back with the middle and index fingers. Sterilising one of the sharp sewing needles with the lighter, she scraped the needle point continually round between the sleeves and her ear lobe. Eventually, with the ear bloodied and swollen April was able to remove the clear sleeve with the tweezers. Then April firmly held her lob with some lint until the bleeding had stopped.

Repeating the procedure on the other ear, April put the small devices into one of the small plastic bags and placed them inside her purse. She then showered to remove all traces of blood from her hair and body before retiring to bed.

April rose early the next morning and was busy packing her sparse belongings when a knock at the door interrupted. Opening it, she saw the stern faced Charles standing there.

"Why are you looking so glum, Charles. Have you come to tell me that I can't have my short break?"

"It's James; he started haemorrhaging during the early hours. They've had to carry out emergency surgery to relieve the pressure again, and to cauterise the blood vessel."

Plonking down heavily on the settee, April asked, "I thought he was on the mend, Charles. What has gone wrong now?"

"We're going to have him transferred by air ambulance to England, the neurological unit at either Liverpool, or Manchester I believe, they're not too sure which one yet. I'll keep you fully informed of his progress," he promised. "I believe it's not unusual for this to happen, but at least he was in the right place this time."

"Yes, I suppose you're right. But I can't go and relax while I'm worried about him," April insisted as she started to unpack.

"No, April. On the contrary you must go because you need the rest. Anyway, I'll keep you fully informed of any new developments with James. And remember, you're only a stone's throw away from here. So you go. I've booked you on the noon flight to Tangiers," he told her as he waited patiently for her agreement.

Charles had booked a short break in Tangiers on a complex, as he'd suspected she may have had an ulterior motive for wanting the holiday to be on the Algarve. After the short uneventful flight April found herself landing at Boukhalef airport, Tangier. Then she took the eleven kilometre taxi journey to the beach hotel, and was shown to her room by the porter.

Noticing that the hotel was one of three on a holiday-designed complex, April decided to remain booked in where Charles had booked her, but to transfer with all her belongings to a neighbouring apartment that had a vacancy. So as to try to foil any attempts Charles made to have her followed.

She left the tracking devises under the pillow and telephoned Charles, to inform him of her safe arrival, and promising to contact him further in a couple of days after she had rested. Then April turned off her cell phone and removed the battery, so that it could not be tracked. She then moved into the alternative apartment in the adjoining hotel.

After eating her new phone had sufficiently charged for her to be able to use it, she dialled the number for Rebecca.

When Rebecca answered April greeted her with. "Hello, Becky. Do you remember me, April?"

"April, my darling, how could I ever forget about you. Where are you?"

"I'm in Boukhalef, Tangiers. Where are you?"

"Oran Algeria on holiday, it's about a hundred kilometres away from you, I think. Can we meet up maybe? Just for old time sake," she asked excitedly.

"How fortuitous that is. Yes, I'd like that very much. In fact I have a big favour to ask you. There are some electronic tags that I need to have removed furtively, very furtively. So do you know a surgeon who can do it?" she asked, keeping her fingers crossed.

"I think you're in luck, sweetheart. Correction, I know you're in luck. My new partner's a first class surgeon."

"Don't tell me you've gone heterosexual, now!" April exclaimed with surprise.

Rebecca started laughing, "And don't you tell me you've become chauvinistic in your assessments. No, she's a very, very nice feminist. You'll like her, April. But remember she's all mine."

"Don't worry," giggled April, "I've got enough problems at the moment. I do need a big favour though. Is she a good surgeon, Becky?"

"Yes. She's one of the best. But it's a pity you're not interested though, I'd have enjoyed a threesome with you," reflected Rebecca dolefully. "I'll see you sometime tomorrow, and I'll ring you again when we're nearly there. So good night April my darling, I love you and I can't wait to see you again," she said excitedly as she rang off.

After familiarising herself with the area, and then having a few of drinks at the bar, April felt fatigued because of the travelling and the lack of sleep, so decided to have an early night.

Rising at seven thirty a.m. she showered and dressed then took breakfast. After that she took a solitary stroll along the esplanade, tacking the tracking devises with her.

Eventually her mobile rang. "We're just heading towards the sea front now love. If you head for the tourist information centre we'll meet you in about five minutes." Rebecca then added, "I can't wait to see you. I love you so much."

Seeing the kiosk, April sat on the seat beside it anxiously waiting for Rebecca's arrival. She hadn't long to wait when an open top jeep screeched to a halt in front of her.

Nearly tripping over the seat belt with excitement, Rebecca sprang from the jeep and raced over to where April was patiently waiting, hugging her zealously. April could hardly breathe under Rebecca's enthusiastic welcome.

Pushing her away gently so that she could breathe, April confirmed, "And I'm very pleased to see you again too, Becks. But I still need to breathe you know," she laughed. "And this is?" April asked, pointing to a slim sultry lady in her early forties.

"I'm so sorry for not introducing you too this lovely lady. She's Dr. Sasha Patel. She's my regular partner and my dearest friend. But she's not jealous of you, April. I've told her all about you, and how you've saved my life on many an occasion. Anyway, how are you? You look absolutely fabulous."

"Thank you and you look very well too. Now shall we have a drink? And now that I can speak, I'm very pleased to meet you too, Sasha," said April, giving Sasha a hug. She then asked, "Can we drive into town and find a quiet little bar so we can talk?"

As Sasha drove, Rebecca talked incessantly. Asking April constant questions about where she'd been, and what she'd done.

But April was preoccupied in constantly turning to look behind them. "You're not listening to me. What's wrong, April?"

"Oh sorry, you know me Becks, old habits die hard. I was just double checking that nobody was following us, but we seem to be in the clear. Now what were you saying?"

"Nothing important, so where is there a little quiet bar? I could kill for a drink."

"Take the next left, and the first left again. Then you can park wherever you can find a space, Sasha." April directed her as she relaxed in the knowledge that they were not being followed.

Sasha soon found a place and was parking up. She and Rebecca walked either side of April, linking her as they walked to the bar.

April ordered a round of drinks as Sasha started with, "Becky tells me you're in need of a Doctor? Are you ill, April?"

April waited until the waitress had placed the drinks on the table and returned to the bar. She then showed Sasha her still swollen earlobes, "I should imagine Rebecca's already explained to you about what's happened to me. Anyway, during the transformation the bastards fitted a few little extras. I've managed to remove these two satellite tracking devices from my ear lobes." She showed the inserts to Sasha. "But I still have two minute capsules implanted inside of me, which obviously I can't get at. They were put there so that they could terminate me whenever they wished to press their little button. So as you can imagine, I'll need a little helping hand in removing them."

As Sasha examined the small ear inserts, she remarked, "I bet it hurt removing these. How the hell did you do it, April?"

"It was extremely difficult and very painful. But I'll need to keep them together to make them think that they're still in place." April explained, replacing them back into the little plastic bag. "Now Sasha, what's your field of expertise?"

"I'm a doctor in Africa remember, so I need to be able to deal with whatever comes along, and when or where it comes."

April asked hesitantly, "How about surgery?"

"What type of surgery is it that you're asking about?" Sasha questioned, as Rebecca asked the barmaid to fetch another round of drinks.

"Neurological and Gynaecological it would need to be."

Sasha sat back, an expression of shock and confusion had replaced her infectious smile. "Well you don't want much, April. Where exactly are these implants?"

She explained how they'd fitted a false ovary containing one of the implants, April then explained that the second implant was located just below the back of the cranium. Sitting back she waited patiently while Sasha contemplated her problem.

She eventually explained, "I'm not qualified to deal with all of this myself, but I'm owed a couple of favours that I might be able to call in. But first I will need to give you a CAT scan to locate the foreign bodies. Now I can get you a private room in the main clinic here so we can identify the problem precisely. Then, and only then, will I be able to make a final assessment and advise you further. You know April: if Rebecca hadn't told me about your enforced transformation I'd think you had a screw loose or something." Sasha remarked, as she took her mobile from her purse to make some preliminary inquiries.

While Rebecca and April chatted, Sasha interrupted, "April, will tomorrow morning be soon enough for you?"

"The sooner the better for me Sasha, before the boss finds out that I've gone AWOL. And if you can deal with it at the same time I'd be eternally in your debt. I'll of course pay whatever you ask for."

Confirming the hospital reservation, Sasha then turned her attention back to April. "I'll not charge such a good friend of Rebecca. But if you would like to pay the hospital expenses and make a donation to the clinic, I'm sure they would be most grateful to you. They are extremely short of funds, as you can well imagine."

"I'll do that gladly. Now, shall we say £250.000 in cash, but nobody must know where it came from. Now who wants another drink'?" April finished, as the three girls continued to chat incessantly. Rebecca and April recalled their past exploits together, laughing at the funny moments, and reflecting sadly at the tragic events and loss of dear friends that they'd shared. Rebecca was extremely sad at hearing the news about Winston, and James Edwards

April visited a bank on the way back to withdraw the cash, then that evening she retired early to bed. Rising at the crack of dawn the following morning, she showered and dressed in a sombre trouser suit, refraining from any oral intake. She then sat patiently waiting to be picked up by the two girls. She didn't have to wait long before hearing the tooting of their car horn. "Good morning girls. Let us get this over with, shall we?" she greeted them cheerily.

"Are you nervous? That isn't like you, darling," Rebecca remarked, kissing her on both cheeks.

"No. Well not nervous exactly it's more anxious, knowing finally that I'll be getting this over with at long last. Just so that I can have some freedom away from they're constantly prying eyes and onerous threats." April explained, as she fidgeted in the back seat. "Just knowing these time bombs won't be in me to malfunction will be an enormous weight off my mind too."

"Well, here we are," Sasha told her, bringing the jeep to a halt outside a modern new clinic. "So as you say, let's get this show on the road."

Rebecca and April followed in silence as Sasha led them through a maze of corridors. Eventually, they reached a lavishly appointed modern operating theatre and X-ray department.

"Step behind that screen and undress then put on this gown?" Sasha asked, as she handed over a gown. "We'll then be able to give you the scan."

Willingly complying, April was soon changed and was then shown into the room to be scanned. As the radiographer prepared, she asked April to remain as still as possible. Then she asked, "Where in your head am I—" Sasha entering the room and interrupted to explain exactly what she wanted doing. April passed slowly through the scanner, and when it had ended they asked her to wait with Rebecca in an anti-room.

Soon after Sasha called April into the consulting room. "Let me introduce you to Dr Sharha, Dr. Ruben Sharha. He's a very well respected neurological Surgeon," she started, "Now we've located the foreign bodies as you've said. I must say April, if you hadn't told us where to look then we could have quite easily have missed them. The ovary we can remove easily by using keyhole surgery under epidural conditions. But Dr. Sharha here's not happy about removing the cranial bug without anaesthetising you completely. You see, April," she pointed to the X-ray, "it's tucked away neatly just inside the cranium and very close to the lower lobs of the brain. Ruben says that if he fed a micro tube in just below your hairline, he thinks he can extract it using a low suction pump." Sasha waited while April digested what she was explaining before continuing. "Now here is the problem love. If you were to move even a millimetre, it could kill you. So you see why you need to be totally anaesthetised. Don't you agree?"

Taking her time April thought long and hard before answering. "I'm afraid the answer is still a no. I still must insist on it being done under epidural conditions. You see, with all due respect I have been brainwashed into fully trusting nobody at all, not even my ex-partner." April deliberately chose to use the words partner rather than ex-wife, not wishing to delay the operation while she explained about her sordid past. "So can we get on with, please? I promise I will remain perfectly still, and I'll sign a disclaimer form to absolve you of any blame."

Dr. Sharha reluctantly nodded to Sasha, and so they began to sterilise their equipment, while April was laid on the operating table for the nurses to sterilise and shave the areas to be treated.

After administering the anaesthetic, Rubin said, "I can see that you're a very determined young lady who knows exactly what she wants, so we'll all get along just fine. Now, Sasha, which one shall we address first? Maybe we should remove the ovary first."

As they worked together steadily and methodically, the two doctors talked light heatedly with the theatre staff. Eventually, after what seemed like an age, but was only in fact about fifteen minutes, Sasha announced. "That's that part finished. What shall I do with it, April? Bin it?"

"I need the bug out of it Sasha, and then you can bin the shell." April watched while Sasha sliced the artificial ovary open and removed the offending part, and then she placed it in a small plastic sachet.

"Now, you must remain perfectly still, April." Sasha urged, as they turned April into the prone position. "We're hoping if we open a very tiny aperture at the base of the hair line we'll be able to feed a microscopic tube up to the, whatever it is. And using only a light suction we should be able to withdraw the little bugger out." Ruben explained, as the nurses were securing April's head in a specially constructed cranium clamp. They then shaved a small area of hair to allow for the incision.

"I know it isn't very comfortable which is why we prefer our patients to be asleep," he explained as he switched on the monitors.

"Now with the aid of these I can guide the tube with pin point accuracy," he explained to Sasha, commencing the task. Working fastidiously he withdrew the foreign body and completed the operation within a surprisingly short period of time, although in such an uncomfortable position it felt like an eternity to April.

As she began to sit up she was surprised to hear Rubin saying, "You know Ms. Darling, if my eyes weren't beholding such a beautiful example of the fairer sex, as you are, I would swear that you were a man in drag, or a transsexual."

Startled, by his remark, she asked him, "Why? I mean what makes you say that?"

"I'm sorry if that offends you at all, because outwardly nobody could ever dispute your sexuality. No, it's just that in my field of expertise we recognise subtle differences between the male and female brain. Yours, I would have said was definitely male dominant. Again,

I'm sorry if you find that offensive, because I didn't mean it to be, or to hurt your feelings in any way," he finished, as the nurse helped April from the table.

"Not at all Rubin, that's the best news that I've had in years. Can I quote you on that?"

"Yes, but why?" A confused Rubin asked.

Explaining briefly about the enforced transformation, the shocked doctor agreed to supply any help, or documentation, that was needed.

For this news April thanked him sincerely, promising to get back to him when her present assignment was completed.

After a short period of recovery she handed them the promised donation, and covered the expenses. Again they attempted unsuccessfully to persuade April to remain at the clinic for forty-eight hours to recuperate.

April thanked them, and left for her resort hotel with the removed implants safely in her handbag.

She put the tracking devices in her original room, and then she spent the next seven days relaxing while the scars healed, before preparing to return to her sordid existence.

Cases packed, the three girls bid each other a tearful farewell. April then boarded the airport bound taxi and switched on her original mobile phone to ring Charles.

CHAPTER 26

"Where the hell have you been, and why has your phone been switched off? You did promise me that you'd stay in touch at all times," Charles raged. "I've turned my phone on now. Haven't I? I told you that I needed a complete rest, REMEMBER?" April yelled back at him.

"You're so disrespectful and insubordinate. Remember I'm your superior. We sent our men out there to find you but they found your room hadn't even been slept in," he continued with annoyance. "Now where the hell have you been, April?"

April was still remonstrating with him as the taxi drew to a halt outside the departure terminal. "Remember you fucking lot are the ones who taught me to play dirty. I needed the time on my own that YOU had promised me, so I took steps to insured that I got it. Now what's so fucking urgent?"

"Erm, nothing, I was just worried that something might have happened to you. Are you okay and rested now? I los—" he stopped abruptly.

"You did what? You were about to say that you lost track of me. Weren't you, you a slime ball? Haven't you realised that you can trust me implicitly yet. Perhaps the next time I should disappear for good,"

April said through clenched teeth. "You lot make me sick. Now I'm going to check in so you can meet me when I land at Lisbon."

"Wait a minute! There has been a change to the flight arrangement. If you go to the customer service desk they have your new tickets for a London bound flight in three hours. I'm sorry we checked up on you but old habits do die-hard, you know. It's your unpredictability that makes you the best in your field, but it's also our biggest area of concern about you. By the way, why couldn't our men find you? Where were you hiding from them?"

"Behind the bloody curtains, where do you think? Now I'll see you in your office tomorrow morning," she finished, leaving Charles bewildered. April complied with the regulations and switched her mobile phone off, leaving him puzzled as to why she was not were the tracking signal came from, and how she was able to mislead them. He was totally unaware that April had now removed the devices, and that she had hidden them under the pillow of the hotel room that he'd booked her into.

After having a few drinks at the bar they eventually announced the flight, and soon after that April was homeward bound.

It was late in the evening when April landed at London and took the long taxi ride to her apartment. After showering, April retired to bed for what remained of the night.

Rising early the following morning she breakfasted, while checking her answer machine and post. Only then did she proceed to headquarters, and Sir Charles's office.

"Good morning, Charles." April said as she breezed into his office. "How's, James?"

"He's going to be okay. His memory's returning but very gradually. We will have to give him early retirement though because he seems to have lost all of his confidence now. Now the reason I've brought you straight to London is because things appear to be happening off the north coast of Russia, Novaya Zemlya to be exact. So if you go to the Prof's office I believe he has all that you'll need for the trip. I have booked you on the 1830 flight to Arkhangelsk where a Russian agent will meet you. As it's very cold there you'll need warm clothing, and take your thermals with you, April."

She felt as though Charles was distancing himself further and further from her, as he gave her the instructions so curtly. It was as if she was not expected to return.

Shelving these thoughts, April collected advice and a variety of gadgetry from the professor, before returning home to pack. Dining out whilst doing some last minute shopping, it was then soon time for her to head once more to the airport.

Travelling with Charles's in his Limousine, they arrived at the airport in plenty of time for the flight. "Here are your tickets, Madam. Have a nice flight," said the man at the checking-in desk, as April thanked him.

"You take special care of yourself, April," Charles told her as he kissed her on the cheek. "And remember there's only one of you."

"Yes, and to make another me will cost you far too much money," April answered sarcastically. She was becoming more and more confused by Charles's varying changes of attitude.

"I didn't mean it that way, April," flustered Charles, as he stopped at the passport control gate. "You're a very special lady too me. Now keep in regular contact, and look after yourself," he told her as he wished her, "Bon Voyage."

"Don't worry, I intend too. But as far as I'm concerned, there's nobody here that gives a rat's arse about me, just as long as the job gets done," she responded bitterly. Then she walked through the passport control without glancing back towards him.

As the plane landed at Arkhangelsk the snowstorm was worsening. Just as April was about to remove the suitcases from the carousel, an arm reached past her to lift it off for her.

"I will carry your baggage, Miss Darling," a soft and gentle voice with a heavy Russian accent, offered. Taking her arm, he explained, "I have my car waiting for us. I'm Conrad Lewinsky, and I'm very pleased to meet you. If I may be so bold, the description of you could never have done you full justification. You're a very beautiful lady."

There was a fierce icy wind blowing as they walked to his car in the early hours of the dark and dismal morning. The wind chilled April to her bone, as they trudged through the thick layer of snow. She was glad when they reached the four by fore as she took her place in the passenger seat.

"Thank you, Conrad. I can call you, Conrad. Can't I?" To which the man nodded as he clicked his heels together.

"It would be my pleasure," he agreed, climbing into the driving seat. April realised from these actions that Conrad must be, or has been, a military man. The car engine sluggishly turned before it sparked into life. Conrad explained, "I've had snow chains fitted to our wheels to increase our traction. I'm sorry; you won't understand what I'm talking about will you?"

"Yes I do, I," stopping herself April corrected. "My brother used to use them. Is it always this cold here, Conrad?" April asked him as she began to thaw out.

"Yes. I'm afraid it is. But it is winter remember. Just wait until we reach Novaya Zemlya, now there it's so much colder at this time of year. I have brought you a warmer coat; it's on the back seat. It has a thermal lining in it so it'll keep you very warm. And I have got you a fur hat gloves and leg warmers. There are also a set of clip on spikes for your boots, should we need them." Conrad told April, as she gratefully changed into them.

"Thank you again, Conrad. You are so kind and thoughtful, and these are much warmer than my own clothes. Now I look like a real Russian леди," she joked as she nestled into the seat.

"Russian lady, so you speak Russian?" Conrad said with surprise.

"Only a little, so don't try testing me on it, will you?" April lied. As she spoke Russian fluently, but decided it could give her an edge if she kept that fact a secret, or at least temporarily. The snow again began to fall and quickly built into a blizzard again, as the car ploughed on through the white wall that confronted them.

Conrad said as he skilfully negotiated the treacherously icy roads, "It'll take us at least six to eight hours to reach Krasnoje in this weather. Normally we could fly there by helicopter, but sadly the weather has grounded all of our aircraft. If you'd been any later you would have been diverted to St Petersburg. I'm sorry, I talk too much and you must be very tired. Try to get some sleep, April."

"No it's okay, I slept on the plane. What do we do when we reach Krasnoje?" She asked, keeping the conversation going to keep Conrad alert.

"We'll need to stop for fuel and to get some warm coffee, but here's some Vodka to warm you in the meantime." He handed over a hip flask as they continued trundling across the vast snow covered tundra. After crossing into Imeni Molotova, they headed north until reaching Krasnyj Poselok.

Conrad drew the car to a halt in front of a small general store that had a refreshment area, and a solitary petrol/diesel pump. "Аполните это с бензином пожалуйста," Conrad told the man. Then he explained to April, "I have asked the man to fill the car up with diesel. Now shall we get a hot breakfast, April?" He suggested, as he held the door open for her to enter into the warm little café.

"It's warmer in here; and a hot breakfast would be most welcome. I've never felt so cold in my life before. It must be twenty degrees below outside?" she suggested as she removed her gloves. She pretended to search in her purse for something, but instead she carefully removed a transparent surveillance sticker. Then April dropped her keys so that she'd have to reach down for them, allowing her the opportunity to secure the tiny transmitter under the wooden table, but without anybody seeing her.

"Would you order while I freshen up, please Conrad?" she asked him, and then she headed towards the toilets. Once inside April quickly took her phone from her handbag and turned it on. Entering the predetermined code to convert it into a receiver, so she could eavesdrop on any conversations Conrad, had. April used the barely adequate toilet facilities and began to wash and freshen up when she heard a man speaking to Conrad in English.

"What can I get you, Sir?"

"What are you serving for breakfast that is hot and nutritious, and taking into account that my companion is an English lady?"

"So I'd noticed, Sir. And if I may be so bold, she's a beautiful lady. Now we serve mainly fish here, as you can well imagine. However, I do have some tinned bacon I've kept for such a visitor, would you like me to cook her a typically English breakfast?" he asked, as his wife served piping hot coffees.

"If you could, I imagine she would find that very welcoming. Has there been any strangers passing through here lately, or any unusual activity round this area?"

"No, Sir. We haven't seen a stranger here since last summer. That's at least six months ago, now. You're the first to pass through here since then. Why? And are you from the KGB, sir?" The owner asked nervously.

"Relax. I'm just an ordinary policeman nowadays who's on a special assignment. Now where's my companion, Miss Darling?" Conrad asked, as he looked towards the cloakrooms.

Being satisfied after hearing the conversation that Conrad was having, that he was who he had said he was, April hastily switched the phone back onto normal mode and dialled Charles's number.

She was leaving the toilet to return to their table when Charles answered. April told him, "We've stopped in a place called Krasnyj Poselok for our breakfast, and to refuel, Charles. It's so bloody cold here that I can't imagine why anybody would choose it for a self-imposed exile."

"It's because it's a god-forsaken land that Carlos has chosen it apparently. He probably thinks that we'll not waste our time, and resources, observing the baron wastelands. How about Captain Conrad Lewinsky? Have you checked him out yet?" a concerned Charles asked.

"Everything seems kosher there. Have you any further news about what De-Mundo is up to here?" April asked, as the owner proudly placed an English breakfast in front of her. "Thank you. That looks, and smells, absolutely delicious." April then turned her attention back to Charles. "The nice gentleman's just served me with bacon, eggs, tomatoes, and fried bread, so I'll ring you back later when we're on the road again." April rang off abruptly to eat the breakfast while it was still hot.

After enjoying the hospitality of the owners, Conrad paid the bill and they prepared to leave. "We must go in the cold car, but it'll soon warm up," Conrad assured her. But to their delight the owner's son had warmed the engine in anticipation of their leaving.

Conrad gratefully left an extra-large tip, as they bade the good people goodbye, thanking them for their most welcome hospitality. They promised to endeavour to call on their return journey if it was possible. As they in return presented Conrad and April with a large flask of hot coffee for their onward journey.

Rested and nourished, they were soon continuing on the long trek towards the crossing point at Konvejer. April took a turn driving, as Conrad told her, "The consolation is that this De-Mundo character won't be expecting us to come after him overland. He probably thinks we've all given up on him by now."

"That bastard knows that I'll come after him, and that it won't end until one of us is dead," growled April through clenched teeth.

"It sounds as though you've a personnel vendetta too settle with him. Do you, April? Have you met him before?"

"Oh yes. And I do have a score to settle with him, Conrad. Just make sure that you don't get caught up in the crossfire won't you? Anyway, let's forget about him for the time being, at least until we get closer."

"That's much better; you look so beautiful when you're not angry. Ah we have arrived at the bridge," Conrad told her, as April dropped down a gear to slow towards the barrier. "Would you like me to drive from here, April?"

"It's okay, I'm fine to drive on from here for a little longer," she assured Conrad. They showed their respective I, D cards to the guards.

"I'm sorry sir. I didn't recognise you. You can drive straight on through, Madam." The guard apologised as April accelerated away.

They chatted idly as April skilfully negotiated the icy covered road. The brief sunlight sank rapidly back over the horizon, engulfing the landscape in an eerie darkness once again. Only the headlights on the snow covered land lit their path, and the occasional rays of moonlight shining through the broken clouds.

Trundling onwards as the snow started to fall again, April avoided unnecessary chattering, needing to keep all her concentration on negotiating the rapidly disappearing road. Thankful that they'd fitted a satellite navigation system to aid the progress, and kept them on the snow-hidden route.

"It'll be during the early hours when we reach Krasnoje, so we'll need somewhere warm to shelter and rest while we wait. Otherwise we'll most certainly freeze to death." April reminded him.

"It's all in hand, April. If we head straight on and into the harbour area, we'll get on a fishing boat when it sets sail at dawn. That way we can use the cover of the fishing fleet. When we're out of sight of land we'll part from the fleet and head on towards the, Matochkin Shar Straits. There we will be put ashore and a local guide will meet up with us and guide us on our onwards journey."

"How much further till we reach the meeting point, Conrad? This snow's getting heavier," April told him, struggling to maintain traction on the winding track of a road.

"I'd say about two hours in this weather. If you pull over, then I'll drive again, if you'd like me too," Conrad suggested. "I keep offering, but I must say you're handling these road conditions very well, for a lady."

"Don't be so chauvinistic, Conrad. I can match anything you can do and more, as I'm sure you'll find out in due course. I have one small confession to make though, well more of an apology really. I wasn't one hundred per cent convinced that I could trust you, so I pretended that I couldn't speak your native tongue," she admitted with a sheepish grin.

"И вы понимаете мой красивейший язык, April?" he asked, (which translates to, 'and you do understand most of my beautiful language,')

"Почти так же, как вы сделайте, огорченно о обмане но мне знать я могло доверить вам," April replied, which is, (Almost as well as you do, sorry about the deception but I needed to know that I was able to trust you.)

"I'm very impressed. Do you speak any other languages?" he asked, as they idled away the time.

"Besides English and Russian, I speak five other languages. Spanish, French, German, Italian, and gibberish," April boasted.

"All as fluently as you do Russian?"

"With the exception of English, that can get a little colourful at times," she told him with a cheeky giggle.

His phone started to ring, "Здравствулте," (Hello) he answered in Russian. "Ah, Petra. Do you have news for us?" He switched to English as April smiled at him. He asked her, "What do you find so funny?"

"You. You greeted him in Russian, and then spoke to him in English."

"Well I didn't know it was, Petra. Did I? He can speak perfect English like you can. Now where were we, Petra?" Conrad asked, as he returned his attention back to his old friend and comrade. He had a lengthy conversation, which April mostly ignored while needing to focus on the driving.

It was becoming dawn as she guided the four by four onto the quayside. Alighting from the vehicle Conrad gave the keys to the harbourmaster, to enable the vehicle to be retrieved by one of his comrades. Passing along the line of fishing vessels, they soon located the motley crew of their ship.

"Come aboard, Miss. Don't let my crew's appearances frighten you off, they're really a kind hearted bunch of lads," the Captain explained cheerfully, as Conrad helped her aboard. "Now we must set sail while we still can as the weather's worsening by the second. If we wait much longer we won't be able to even clear the harbour. Now this young lad here will show you to your respective cabins."

April chose to remain in the wheelhouse, while the grey-faced Conrad began to be sea sick, even before they'd left the partly sheltered harbour. Conrad spent the entire voyage in his cabin, but April chatted, apparently unconcernedly to the crewmembers.

Using the cover of the fishing fleet to clear the harbour, as they had anticipated, they were then shrouded by the freezing fog that had descended as he headed north east, and on towards the harbour of Smidovich, Novaya Zemlya.

The small vessel sailed across the stormy Barents Sea, as it was tossed from side to side by the swirling winds, and raging tempestuous waters.

"No need for you to feel afraid, Miss Darling. This old tub will not let us down, I can assure you of that. We've sailed in worse weather than this." The Captain explained as he tried to reassure her.

"I'm not. Forgive me Captain, but my trust is in my maker upstairs. I'll either arrive in Smidovich, or in heaven, the choice is entirely his," she said tentatively, as a wave washed over the boat.

"You've got that correct, April. We're all in his hands. It's a pity Captain Lewinsky doesn't have our faith though. Anyway, the weather's becoming far worse than usual, so although it makes it harder for anyone to follow us, it will make the journey two or three hours longer than anticipated. Most of the time the screws are above the water line, so they aren't able to propel us."

Eventually, after the long and hazardous journey, April watched the crew skilfully guiding the small boat into the sheltered harbour. Captain Conrad Lewinsky finally emerged from below deck, looking decidedly worse for the sea trip.

"Quick, let me get ashore. I never want to ride in your boat again, Captain." He insisted, as he brushed past and alighted onto firmer ground. "How is it you weren't sick, April?" Conrad asked her, as she followed him ashore.

"Maybe I'm more used to sea travel than you," she started to explain, as two men interrupted.

"You're Miss Darling, and Mr. Lewinsky, I believe?" the man asked.

"At your service, sir," responded Conrad. Saluting and snapping his heels together.

Exchanging cordial greetings, the strangers explained that we'd still a daunting journey ahead of us. "De-Mundo and his men are in an underground camp, midway between here and Archangel Skaya. It's a couple of mile inland from the coast. Now, the weather has abated a little at the moment, so I suggest that we take full advantage of that. We should make as much headway as we possibly can before the light fades."

As she climbed into the back seat of the four-by-four half-tracks, April was glad that she was not driving so that she could catch up on some of her rest.

One of the guides passed Conrad and April, a flask of hot coffee, and a half a bottle of Vodka, each. "Here's something that'll warm you both up," as the driver revved the engine until it found its traction, and the jeep slowly moved forward. They began to gradually inch their way on their journey. "Here we go. Why don't you just relax and try to catch up on some of your sleep," the driver suggested.

Folding her coat to make an impromptu pillow, April placed it against the side window and rested her head on it. Soon she'd drifted into a deep, but restless sleep. She began dreaming about her distant past, the happy family outings, and the friends that she had been forced to abandon. Soon she was dreaming about the happiness that flowed from the faces of her beloved wife and children. Her sleep was abruptly interrupted by the jeep rocking violently as it started to ascend a steep glacier.

"I'm sorry we've disturbed your sleep, Miss Darling. Have you enjoyed your little nap?"

"Yes. And I needed it. And my name is, April. Miss Darling makes me sound old. Where are we now?"

"About ten miles to go, but it'll take us at least an hour in this hail storm."

Trying unsuccessfully to get a signal on her cell phone, April explained, "I was going to see if there have been any new developments, but I can't get a signal in this weather."

"One thing about this weather is that we should catch them off guard. They won't expect anybody in this horrible weather," Conrad predicted.

"I've told you not to bank on that, Conrad. I know Carlo De-Mundo of old. You can't predict what a madman like that might, or might not, be thinking."

The jeep eventually drew to a halt below a snow-covered ridge.

"They are just beyond that ridge in an underground complex. We'll need to wait for the hail storm to relent a bit first, at least." The driver explained, "During the cold war we used Novaya Zemlya to bury our own nuclear waste. We did it by drilling miles down beyond the frozen sub soil. What this De-Mundo has done is that he's found one that hadn't been used, and then set it up as his headquarters."

April interrupted, "He'll still need light, heat, and a convenient way in and out of it."

"He's installed nuclear powered generators, and an escape capsule shoot for dire emergencies, which terminates at his submarine base just below the glacier." The guide continued, "It's like a mini city underneath there, they even grow their own food. When you peer over the ridge you'll see a large dome covering. What is it that you call it? Oh yes, the Adit I believe, which acts as a heat barrier and keeps his subterranean world separate from ours. Once inside it, there is a series of lift shafts down to his world. But, beware! There are cameras everywhere. Plus, it's regularly patrolled by his foot soldiers. It does seem to be rather impregnable, April."

"Yes, well I'll try to alter that fact. Now the weather is starting to abate so we should soon know if De-Mundo is here or not. Won't we?"

"Yes, he'll still be here. He never leaves there now. Be very careful, and keep your goggles on or your eyelids will freeze to your eyeballs," warned the guide. "How long shall we wait for you, April?"

"You can go straight back. And Conrad, it's not too late for you to go with them. Carlos and I have an old score to settle."

"No. I'll stay with you, April. It has stopped snowing so shall we take a look?" the guide asked, as Conrad and April put on their warm thermal snowsuits, balaclava's, goggles, and snow boots. Dressed all in white, so as to give them some camouflage, they were now ready to leave. They deployed their weapons round their bodies, and the specially designed multi task rifles were slung over their shoulder in a white sling.

Finally, April got the tracking devices that she'd had removed, and put them furtively into the cups of her bra.

"Lead the way, Conrad," she said, as she alighted from the jeep.

CHAPTER 27

As they stepped out into the icy howling wind, Conrad moved quickly to support April, as she was finding it difficult to prevent her light frame from being blown off the slippery glacier.

"Here, let me help you?" he insisted, through the intercom built into their snowsuit. Taking hold of her arm, he joked, "See, sometimes being heavy is an asset," as he helped April up the icy slope, and onto the ridge.

"Thank you for your timely intervention, it was very welcome, Conrad," she said gratefully, as the two of them eventually reached a point from where they could catch their breath, and observe their objective. Also, where they would be able to take the time to consider how best it was possible to gain access to the shaft. One where they hoped they wouldn't alert them of their impending presence. From the ridge April could see the two stolen stealth planes in a small clearing, fifty metres from the entrance. They were concealed under white-sheeting, camouflaging them from any surveillance. April noticed that one of the cockpits had been left very slightly ajar, as if it was being prepared for use.

"Good," she thought to herself. "Now if I could just reach them, then I might be able to hide a rifle inside it."

Glancing behind April saw the half-track disappearing back down the track. Suddenly, a missile from the dock area screeched overhead careering towards the vehicle. It hit the jeep with pinpoint accuracy, blowing it into smithereens, and killing the two guides inside it.

"I guess they now know that we're here then. Those poor sods didn't stand a chance," she said sadly, "so let's dispense some retribution for them."

Carlos' voice could be heard booming from the loud speakers. "Ah! Miss April Darling I presume. So we meet again. I have been half expecting you of course, so you wish to meet your end in this God forsaken hole do you, April? You know I'm anxious to grant your every wish, PERSONALLY. So step this way, your coffin, I mean your lift, awaits your presence my pretty little minx."

Turning to Conrad April whispered to him, "Carlos is preoccupied with catching me, so just dig into the snow and keep well hidden. When you find it's safe to do so, sidle along this ridge and down off the glacier, and just keep going until you reach the coast. From there you can call, Field Marshal Sir Charles Hythe-Smith, using this number? Tell him where I am. Say he must do nothing yet, just be ready and waiting for my signal, okay?" she insisted, passing him a slip of paper with Charles's number on it.

"But," Conrad protested, "what about you? And he must know that I'm here with you?"

"Don't worry about that I'll create a diversion. Carlos will be so preoccupied with seeing me again that he'll forget all about you being here, so it will give you time to make good your escape. Now when that helicopter explodes," she pointed towards a helicopter that was starting up. "You head that way for about a hundred metres, and then you will need to dig yourself into the snow so that you are well and truly hidden. No matter what happens to me, you must stay silent and hidden. Just remember, Carlos will want to exact his revenge on me personally. Now are you ready?"

Conrad reluctantly nodded, as April switched her multi task rifle onto rocket mode.

"Right, now go. And keep your head down," she told him, as she took careful aim and fired. The shot was precise and hit the helicopter as it was just lifting off, causing it to explode and set off a chain reaction, demolishing the fleet of half-tracks and the remaining copters. "That should keep your attention while Conrad hides," she thought.

A troop of De-Mundo's armed guards poured from the domed shaft, as they moved slowly and carefully, towards the spot from where April had fired from. Keeping low she crept in the opposite direction to Conrad, edging closer towards the stolen planes. Switching the gun to tamper-proof mode, April moved between the aircraft and dropped the gun into the slightly open cockpit as she passed.

"That'll give them a nasty surprise if they find it and try to use it," she thought smugly, walking from the shelter of the planes. Holding up her arms, April shouted to them, "Hey gumbos, I'm over here you bloody daft half-witted baboons."

Quickly they encircled her with two of them grasping an arm each, whilst a third guard seized her from behind, and hold her in a headlock. Then the fourth man frisked her, removing her pistol.

"Don't move a muscle," ordered the man in charge, "I've been warned about you."

Struggling to speak under the vice like grip round her throat, April eventually managed to say, "I'm too busy, I think the ugly clown behind me wants to dance." The insulted guard tightened his gripe, leaving April gasping harder for her breath. "I've had enough of this," warned April, bringing her leg up behind to deliver a ferocious mule kick into his groin. The men either side released their grips, so April began to walk towards the entrance. The guard in charge prodded her in the back with his rifle, ordering, "Walk straight ahead, and don't try any tricks."

This amused her after what she'd just done. So keeping a straight face, April warned him, "Prod me again with that rifle and I'll use it on you as a suppository."

"I'm sorry, Miss," he apologised profusely. Then he asked, "Where is the other person?"

"What other person? You idiot, you blew everybody else away you soft bastards. Now take me to your leader, Adolph?"

"Pardon," a confused guard asked, as they reached the entrance.

"Oh never mind. Ah! It's warmer in here, isn't it?" she commented, removing the goggles, hood, and balaclava. April then shook her head to allow her golden tresses to rest softly on her shoulders.

Staring at April's unparalleled beauty and slender stature, the guard eventually managed to splutter, "It's right what they say about you, Miss. You're an extremely beautiful lady, extremely dangerous by all accounts, but a very beautiful lady." He smiled when he removed his hood and revealed his handsome face. "Now are you going to still resist, or will you come quietly, please, Miss Darling?"

"Oh, I'll come quietly, seeing that you've asked so nicely and said please. I can't wait to see that old farts face though, just so I can wipe the smarmy smile off it, PERMANENTLY." April said in a loud enough voice, as they reached the next level. She knew that it would definitely get back to Carlos De-Mundo.

Changing lifts three times, they eventually emerged into a vast concrete lined bunker, within the deep bowels of the earth. "Will you come this way, Miss Darling? Please?" the guard courteously invited. "Mr. De-Mundo wants to see you in his office."

"Lead the way into the lion's den. You know he intends to kill me, don't you?" April asked, trying in vain to invoke the guards' pity as they continued through the long maze of corridors.

"You'll do well not to provoke, Mr. De-Mundo. He's a very volatile, violent, and vindictive man, when he wants to be. There's nobody that can help you down here. So try to please him by conforming to his demands, whatever they might be. That will buy you some time at least. Ah! Here we are. This is Mr. De-Mundo's office." He knocked on the door.

A tall-armed guard opened the door and ordered April inside, as the other escorts were dismissed. Once she was inside the large room a further three heavily armed men confronted her.

"Sit down there," the man ordered, pointing to a chair in the middle of the room. "Mr. De-Mundo will see you when, HE is ready."

As April looked round the lavishly carpeted room, she could see a leather settee, computer, television, and a desk. There were also a number of doors, which she presumed led to various anterooms. One of the guards stood close brandishing their rifle ominously. April also noticed the obvious leader smirking at her.

"What're you smirking at, you fucking ugly monkey? I'll make it very painfully for you to smile in a moment if you don't stop it," warned April. The other men found the threats hollow and amusing, as they looked at each other and laughed. April was tiring of their childishness and tried to ignore them.

Her thoughts quickly turned to Conrad. Did he manage to escape the area, and will he reach safety to alert Charles in time?

Unbeknown to April, Conrad had waited until dark before he searched for a means of escaping. He was high up in the Ural Mountain range, and the only obvious route down he could find, was a precipitous and icy face. Remembering his youth, when he had been an Olympic athlete, and a member of the Russian bob sleigh team, he remembered how he rode down such a course frequently for practise. This thought inspired him, so he searched for a make shift sled.

As he wandered towards what remained of the half-tracks, he stumbled across a bonnet that had been blown off one of the trucks.

"That will fit the bill very nicely. Now if I can devise a way of steering it," he told himself as he searched the remainder of the wreckage. Stumbling across a piece of the wiring harness, he ripped it out. "And this will help too," he thought, as he attached either end of the wire to the hinge anchor points, forming a reign type steering devise.

"Here goes nothing," he said tentatively, as he crossed himself before lying flat on his back on the home-made sled. Pushing himself off, he started careering down the steep slope, digging his heels into the ice to reduce his speed when he needed to. Eventually, three-quarters of the way down the mountain, Conrad could see he was fast approaching the cliff's edge, and a sheer drop. He frantically dug in his heels trying to reduce his speed as much as he could, it slowed down but Conrad realised that he wasn't going to stop in the distance that was left, as he pulled at one side of the reign trying in vain to steer it away from the edge. Conrad rolled off onto the frozen snow, sliding headlong into a convenient boulder, and knocking himself out.

His eyes slowly focused and his head started to clear, as he became aware that the rock had prevented him from going over the cliff. "April's right, her God is truly watching over us," he said gratefully as he cross himself before rising to his feet. To reach the harbour he would still need to descend the remaining two hundred metres down the sheer face, so he searched for a way with which he could do that.

Wandering along the wide ledge, he fortuitously happened upon an abandoned trapper's log cabin, hidden among the tall pines trees. Forcing open the door, Conrad was grateful for the temporary shelter from the piercing winds, while he rummaged in the cabin for any aids to assist his descent.

"Good, our trapper was well equipped," he told himself, as he found an array of mountaineering equipment.

Conrad clamped the spikes onto his boots, and clipped a well-equipped belt round his waist. Slinging a rope over each shoulder and picking up an ice pick, he strode confidently towards the edge. Skilfully, Conrad used all of his considerable experience to descend the icy face, being grateful for the clear moonlit skies that illuminate his path. Although Conrad was a KGB trained skilled mountaineer, his descent was slow and laborious. But eventually he reached the safety of the quayside.

He rested for a short while to regain his breath before he called Sir Charles, and relay April's message to him. "She insisted that I descend the glassier and contact you sir, she needs you to tell the American navy to destroy the submarine docked in the harbour. You'll need to hurry though they seem to be preparing to set sail very soon," he urged, as the phone lost the connection. Conrad waited, and then he watched helplessly as he saw the submarine set sail and head slowly towards the open sea. The American Destroyer appeared and was sailing at full speed towards it, as the sub's sirens began to signal dive. The men of the sub feverishly disappeared below the decks, and the submarine quickly sank below the turbulent water.

Trying in vain, the destroyer discharged round after round of depth charges to the place that they presumed the sub to be, until it became obvious that it had evaded them once more.

A launch was then dispatched to ferry Conrad onto the Destroyer, so that they could commence his debriefing.

Meanwhile, while waiting for Carlos to make his appearance April toyed with the guards. "I'm tired of having to look at your ugly, smirking, faces. So I'm warning you for the very last time," April yawned out of fatigue.

"And what are you warning us about, woman?" one of the men asked, his supercilious grin growing even larger.

She'd had enough of their attitude so April fell backwards onto the floor and delivered a well-placed kick into the abdomen of the leader, causing him to crumble to the floor. She rolled into a crouch position and launched herself towards him, grabbing his sub machine gun as she went into a forward roll across his stomach, wrenching the gun from his grasp as she went, ending up crouching with the gun in her hands.

"Now, you can all drop your weapons gentlemen, including your pistols, your knives, etcetera." April ordered, pointing the gun at them menacingly. They immediately complied with her demand nervously, but readily. "Now strip down to your undies and kneel facing that wall, NOW!" she shouted, spraying the wall above their heads with bullets as the men rushed to obey her. "That's good little boys. I'll teach you not to smirk at me. Now put your hands behind your heads and interlock your fingers." Again they tried in vain to protest, but April was enjoying this far too much and ignored their feeble protests. "Now, or I'll make you greet Carlos with your dicks in each other's hands." To this last threat they readily did what she was asking, clasping their hands behind their heads. "Good. Now just stay like that, and keep on reciting I must not smirk at Miss April Darling. Come on, LOUDER!" April shouted, releasing a warning shot into the ceiling.

Rummaging quickly through the men's belonging, April salvaged a mobile phone from the pocket of one of the tunic jackets. She turned it on, and was able to check the address book. "Bingo!" She muttered, finding Carlos' mobile number. "I'll feed the address book into my phone just in case I need it." She then replaced the phone back into the tunic pocket.

The hapless guards were unaware that she'd placed the gun onto the desk and was now unarmed. As the near naked men continued to recite the door opened, and Carlos De-Mundo entered the room with an armed escorts. Faced with the pathetic scene of his humiliated men, he burst into laughter.

"Get up, you fucking idiots. Miss Darling's unarmed," he spluttered, amid his hysterical laughter.

The humiliated men hastily gathered their belongings and weapons before they scuttled from the room.

"So we meet again, April," he eventually greeted her. "You're in remarkably good spirits. Well, considering I don't intend to let you ever leave here alive."

"I'm looking on it from the brighter side, Carlos."

"Oh, so your demise has a bright side to it. What may I ask is the bright side of your dying? Except for the fact that the world and I will be rid of you forever," he asked smugly, as he reclined back in his chair.

"Well, let me see now," April began cheerfully. "Not only will I be going to rejoice with my maker, but I'll have the added satisfaction of taking you with me. To be judged of course."

His nervous smile was replaced by a worried frown, "Not if I shoot you now, then how would you take me with you?"

"Look under your desk," she told him, having the pistol that she'd taken from one of the humiliated guards pointed towards him.

After checking he dropped his gun. "Okay, okay, let's call a truce. Well at least for now," he conceded, as he offered to shake her hand. This April declined. He remarked to his men, "Didn't I tell you that she was dangerous, but also so very beautiful?"

"You know as well as I do that it's purely a tentative truce. But this time when I destroy all of this, YOU, will be going with it," she warned him sternly.

This made Carlos nervous as he fidgeted with his shirt collar, trying to sound secure in his fortified domain. "And how, with all of my guards in here, do you intend to accomplish that, my dear little vixen?"

To this she just gave a knowing smile. Carlos was well aware that if anybody could accomplish this, it would be April.

Reclined back in her seat, April watched Carlos walk towards his drink cabinet.

"How inhospitable of me not to offer you a drink, what would you like, April?"

"A coffee would be nice, Carlos," she surprised him, as he poured himself a whiskey.

"You heard the lady, get her a drink of coffee," he instructed his guard, "I'll be okay alone with her. Won't I, April?"

Just nodding, she was occupied trying constantly to search for an escape route. She was trying to form a plan of how to reduce the sanctuary Carlos had created, and return it to the uninhabitable heap of rubble it originally was. Whilst sipping her coffee, April remained oblivious to Carlos De-Mundo's constant nervous chatter. She realised that she would need to work fast in formulating, and implementing, Carlos's downfall. If she was to avoid being subject to a repeat of the depravities she had suffered at his hands when they last met.

Carefully April assessed the situation. She knew that they were deep below ground level and that it was a large concrete lined complex of bunkers. But knowing Carlos as she did, she was aware that there must be an alternative exit. Where was his transport? How did he come and go undetected? She would need to tour the place before making any plans. But how could she bring that about? Perhaps appealing to his over inflated ego, she thought. April suddenly became aware that Carlos had stopped talking.

"Sorry. What were you saying, Carlos?"

"Nothing important, I can see that you're finding my conversation somewhat boring. Maybe a spell locked away on your own while I contemplate your fate will make you wish that you'd paid me more attention," said an infuriated Carlos De-Mundo. He instructed the guards, "Take her away."

Thinking fast for inspiration, April decided to appeal to his ego again. "I was just marvelling in awe at what you've created here. How clever you must be to have organised fitting it all out. It's so warm and cosy in here, you would never think we were under a glassier. Would you?"

It worked as Carlos took the bait. He started to explain how he'd transported most of the equipment here by sea. "The ships papers needed to have it down as mining equipment to avoid suspicion of course," he explained. Then he went into the most intricate details of how he'd foiled the authorities.

"You don't keep any dope here though, do you Carlos?"

"Only for personnel use, I've learnt how easy it is to lose it all. You taught me that lesson."

"But of course you still have the two legged variety of dope I see." April couldn't resist having a swipe at his manpower.

"They are all good men. They would give their lives for me," boasted Carlos.

"As I've said, they are dopes in trousers," she continued to wind him up. "Anyway, where's your hospitality? You haven't shown me round all you have achieved here. By the way, don't the Russians object to your presence?"

"I've bought this northern half of the island. I had my lawyers prepare the paper work to declare this a principality, with me as the crown prince," he boasted, as he became even more supercilious.

Seeing the insanity returning to his eyes, April decided to continue appealing to his ego. "Well show me round your realm, O Lord and Master. I'm intrigued at your plans for the future."

Carlos couldn't resist the invitation to show off his newly acquired property. April linked his arm to lull him into a false sense of security, as they ambled round whilst chattering generally. Carlos was boasting about the underground domain he'd created, while April carefully assessing the complex, looking for all the possible escape routes.

Finally, she asked, "If one of the lifts was to fail for any reason, then you'd be trapped down here. Wouldn't you?" April questioned, as they continued to tour the complex. "You'll need to install yourself an emergency exit of some sort."

"You think you know everything, don't you. Well that's where you're wrong. I have had an emergency shaft erected, it was built insides the air vent ducting, as it was being reconstructed," he told her, he seemed to forget momentarily that she was his prisoner, and archenemy. "And besides, just you look at this?" he invited, as he proudly opened large double doors, and revealed a large cavernous dock housing a submarine. "This is my very own private dock."

The scene that met her was of a large cavern and a large body of water. A second sub was moored at a purpose built quayside with armed men protecting it. As April looked beyond the sub and into the obviously deep expanse of water, she noticed a number of sharks swimming idly to and fro, and a portcullis covering the entrance and preventing them from escaping into the open sea. There were periodically along the dock, stacks of drums of shark repellent, and looking up she saw sweeping searchlights suspended from the roof, which glinted off the ripples caused by the passing sharks.

April shuddered due to a mixture of the cold, and her ominous thoughts of the foreboding scene. Thinking quickly she rummaged through her pocket for an explosive sticker, while Carlos was engrossed in a conversation with his personnel guard. April meandered toward the open hatch of the submarine, and leant over to peer down inside it. Stretching down, she pretended to steady herself placing a hand against what looked like the exhaust manifold, and air conditioning ducts. She attached the transparent sticker and set it on a seventy two-hour fuse.

"Watch you don't fall in, Miss." A man warned, as he helped her to stand up. "You could've slipped headlong onto the steel decking."

April thanked the man; satisfied that the real reason she'd stooped down had gone unnoticed as she again shuddered with the cold.

"Are you cold, or afraid?" Carlos, asked her.

"Cold," she snapped sharply. "You'd freeze to death before the sharks ate you, so there's nothing to fear from them. Is there?"

"I'm glad you think that way. You'll probably get the chance to put that theory to the test later. Now, shall we finish our tour?"

"Yes, okay," agreed April anxiously. They continued ambling slowly as April linked Carlos's arm tight, hoping she could buy some time to plan a way out of this mess. Carlos showed her the men's quarters, the quarters for the married men and their families, the woman's quarters, and the communal lounge and dining hall. The tour then ended near his private quarters. "There, your tour is now complete," Carlos proudly told her.

"Oh! I see. So I'm not allowed near the nerve centre of your little Empire."

"Not at this precise time, no," he insisted as they entered his private lounge. "Now, would you do me the honour of dining with me tonight?"

"Yes I'd like that, Carlos. But I'm afraid I have nothing clean to wear."

"You may use this bathroom, and you will find that wardrobe is full of ladies clothing. They belonged to my ex-partner, Sarah. I'm afraid she won't be in need of them anymore."

"Why, Carlos. Has she left you?"

This enraged him, "Nobody leaves me. I'm the king down here, and don't you ever forget it. No, I caught her with one of the men."

"So you sent her home did you?"

"You know better than that too, I had her and the man stripped of their clothes, then I told them to walk home," he laughed.

"And what happened to them?" April asked, with a worried frown.

"What do you think happened to them out there? Now get yourself cleaned up. You need a shower I can smell you from here," he snapped, as he left the room.

While April was showering and dressing, she tried to think up a mental plan of how to deal with Carlos De-Mundo, once and for all, and to hopefully escape from it with her life. "I must find the emergency lift shaft. Also, I need to find out where he keeps his arsenal of weapons." A knock at the door interrupted her thoughts.

Calling out, "Come in, I'm decent." As the door swung open, a fresh faced young man was stood there.

"Mr. De-Mundo wants to know if you're ready to join him for lunch, madam?" he requested courteously.

"I'll just put my shoes on and you can escort me to show me the way. That's if you don't mind." She asked the young man, as his face lit up with obvious delight.

"It will be my pleasure, madam."

"Can we dispense with the madam title? It only reminds me of how old I'm getting."

"You're not old, madam. I mean Miss April. You truly are the most beautiful lady I've ever seen," he ventured to say, as he walked proudly by her side. "I'll be the envy of every man down here walking with you."

"Oh well, in that case let's make them even more jealous," suggested April, linking his arm to draw him closer. "How's, that?"

"It is the nearest thing I know to heaven, but won't Mr. De-Mundo be annoyed with me?" the lad asked nervously.

"Why? He doesn't own me. And I'm only a temporary guest here. Anyway, I won't tell him if you don't. What's your name? I mean, what shall I call you?" The lad didn't realise but April was trying to gain his confidence. She needed information from somebody, so why not this star struck young man, who obviously fancied her something rotten.

"Joseph, I'm named after the great Russian leader. Now this is Mr. De-Mundo's private dining room," he told April as he freed himself from her arm. He then held open the door for her to enter.

"Thank you Joseph for showing me the way, I'd definitely have got lost," she told him, leaning towards him and kissing him on his cheek. Joseph blushed profusely as he closed the door.

"Good evening, Carlos. Are you well? And what's for dinner? I'm starving."

"You sound in a good mood, April. What's brought that about?"

"I've had a shower, put on clean clothes, and applied fresh war paint. I feel like a new woman. So shall we eat now?"

As they dinned, April chatted generally, not allowing Carlos to express his plans for any future that he thought they might have, if she wished to stay alive.

"Don't you ever shut up?" he finally managed to say. "I keep trying to approach the subject of us, but you just keep evading it."

"I know Carlos, but could I have a little more time to adjust and think about us. After all, it's not every day a girl gets the opportunity to become a real live princess. It's not as if I can go anywhere in the meantime, now is it? And it has all been such an exhausting day."

"Very well, I'm not altogether without a heart as you might think. I'll give you twenty-four more hours. But I warn you, April, over dinner tomorrow evening I will want your final answer. Be assured of one thing if you do reject my offer, I'll let my men take turns with you, and then feed what's left to the sharks, piece by tiny piece. IS THAT CLEAR?" he warned sternly.

"Clear as crystal. Anyway, you know I'll eventually succumb to your irresistible charm," she smiled. "Oh, and by the way, I noticed that up at the top you have two very unique aircraft. I haven't seen anything like them before, did you design them too?" she asked, continuing to appeal to his ego.

"No, I borrowed them. There seems no reason why I can't explain to you now. They were specially designed, and built, for long-range missions, so I borrowed them. Remember McDougal? Well he brought them from Scotland. He was the one sleeping with my wife and is now walking her home."

"But what do you need them for?" she continued to probe, "you have your subs. You've only alerted the special services to try to find them."

"Let them fucking look, they'll be long gone before they find them. I'm going to infect the drinking water of strategic reservoirs round the world by using special bombs. I have filled them with a new, but highly addictive and concentrated drug. One that I've had developed especially. Starting with England and America, they will then fan out over Canada and the Far East with one plane, while the other one starts sweeping Europe, then down through Australasia.

You see, the shit I've developed is so concentrated it will only need a small amount to make everybody that drinks the water, addicts."

"And I suppose you'll be ready to supply their every need, Carlos. But at a very high price of course. When do you intend to execute this devilish master plan and make us both rich?"

"We, and who said that you were to be included. No, I have set up a Cartel to take charge with me as their grand supremo, so soon I really will rule the whole world, and the poor fools will all be dependent on me." Carlos bragged, as he sat back smugly.

"Ah! But when are you thinking of implementing these dastardly plans of yours? They may find the planes first, have you ever thought of that, Carlos?" April persisted, as she saw the madness returning to his eyes.

"I don't think so, we'll start loading the stuff within twenty four hours," then an angry look covered his face. "Anyway, why are you so bloody interested, bitch?"

"Because I'm tired of England using me, so I just maybe, if the offer's still open of course, consent to become, Mrs. Grand Supremo?"

This news gave Carlos an impish grin. "I've told you enough for now," he finished as he left the room.

Knowing she'd need to work fast, April was thinking profoundly as she returned to her quarters, considering what all her alternatives were. As she did, she noticed that the doors to the ventilation shaft had been left slightly ajar so she peered furtively inside. There was a very large communal area, which also gave access to a number of doors leading presumably to a variety of anti-rooms. In the centre of the area was a flimsily built vertical lift shaft stretching high up towards a distant glimmer of moonlight at the outer surface of the glassier. Glancing round at the open doors, April could see the weapons and ammunition store. There was also a boiler room and a food store, both adjacent to a large kitchen. Before April could finish the mental examination of the area, the noise of approaching footsteps interrupted her thoughts. She quickly blocked the door lock with a loose piece of wood that she'd found lying round, then continued towards her designated quarters.

April used her time praying while waiting for the early hours of the morning to arrive; this was when it was hoped that the guards would be at their least alert. When three a.m. approached, she rummaged through the wardrobe in search of something more suitable to wear. "That should do me very nicely," she told herself, selecting a black leather trouser suit, dark blue blouse and black boots. "Now I need to cover my blond hair or they'll spot me a mile away." April looked through the drawers until eventually she found a packet of black stockings. Rolling a stocking up, she pulled it over her head and tucked in her blond hair.

"That's, as ready as I'll ever be so here goes," April tried to convince herself as she crept from her room. Reaching the ventilation shaft, she was grateful that the door was still open. She thought as she slipped silently inside, "Serves them right, they were just too lazy to clear the lock." The kitchen doors had also been left wide open, and she could hear the staff snoring merrily while waiting for the early breakfast call. April moved stealthily into the kitchen and turned on the gas taps, removing the control knobs. Closing the doors quietly, she jammed it with a handy metal rod through the handles.

Moving into the ammunition room and rummaging about searching for some inspiration, she gathered up plastic explosives, detonators', timers, and an assortment of guns. April then found some sticky tape and remote detonators. Carefully and silently, she sealed the kitchen doors using the tape. Next she tied bundles of plastic explosive together, attaching them as high up on the framework of the lift shaft she could reach, and placing a parcel of plastic explosive against the kitchen door so it would ignite the gas, finishing by placing a bundle of plastic explosive in the centre of the armoury.

Cutting equal lengths of cable, April fitted the detonators to the gelignite, and attached a cable to each one, feeding it through into an empty side room. She finished by twisting each of them together and coupling them to the remote detonator.

'All done,' April thought, as she heard feeble calls for help from the kitchen. Ignoring the urge to relent and release them, April locked most of the rooms before throwing the keys into the armoury.

———

Thinking, "Now find them," She then quickly changed into her all-weather thermal suit in preparation for the trip outside.

As she left April walked into an unsuspecting guard, she delivered him a high kick to his chest, grabbing him from behind as he slumped to the floor. Twisting his head sharply, a cracking sound confirmed that she'd broken his neck. Slinging the bag of assorted weapons across her shoulder and tucking a knife and pistol into her belt, April picked up the remote control and remaining parcels of explosive, she ran swiftly but silently towards the unguarded lift shaft.

As she took the lifts to each of the levels she left a small parcel of explosives on top of each lift. Entering the final lift, April could hear a hive of activity below, as the body of the dead guard had been discovered, and the alarm had been raised.

"She's nearly at the top. Quick, cut the power to that lift?" April could hear somebody shouting as the bottom lift started to ascend.

"It's that April Darling bitch. I want her alive," Carlos De-Mundo was heard ordering the men frantically

When the lift came to an abrupt halt, April climbed onto its roof through the maintenance hatch. Placing a parcel of explosives and a timer in the lift, April set it to detonate in five minutes. She then started to ascend the framework towards the surface. Nearing the top a man began firing down at her, as she desperately clung on to the cold metal. Removing the snub nosed Sten gun from her shoulder bag, April took careful aim and released a single shot, sending the injured guard plummeting down to his death. She now saw that the penultimate lift was fast approaching as she replaced the gun into the bag. Taking out two grenades, she dropped them onto the ascending lift, and as it exploded it brought the lift to an abrupt halt.

As fast as it was possible April climbed the remaining distance to the surface, hearing the pursuing party getting ever nearer to her.

Rolling exhausted from the lift shaft she looked down and could see the men were only thirty yards behind her, and closing in fast. April left the warm dome and walked out onto the glassier, jamming the chute doors closed behind her. She used the butt of her gun as a hammer, and smashed the electronic locks that operated the doors, leaving the last remote device against the doors. Then she dashed towards the makeshift hanger.

After removing the chocks from the wheels of one of the aircraft, April coupled up the motorised sled and towed the plane clear of the makeshift hanger.

She heard the men frantically trying to smash the doors open to exit the dome.

"Throwing her bags, guns, and detonator, into the cockpit, April climbed in sealing down the canopy and brought the engines to life. Familiarising herself with the controls as fast as she possibly could, April engaged vertical lift, and the plane started to slowly rise above the ground.

Removing the remote control from the bag as the plane cleared the site, April pressed the button to start a chain of explosions in the subterranean complex. Flames and dust clouds billowed from the shaft, causing a landslide of ice, as the glassier slipped into the shaft and sealed the fate of the poor misguided fools that lived so far below the surface.

Manoeuvring the plane round to allow her to discharge a missile, April destroyed the remaining jet before heading towards the port. But as she crossed the icy peaks of the Ural Mountains, April could see Carlos' submarine as it disappeared below the turbulent waves.

The American Destroyer now re-emerged, heading into the bay.

Frantically searching the radio for the destroyers' wavelength, April eventually heard the Captains voice. "Where the fucking hell have you been, SUNBATHING?" April yelled at him, as she continued sarcastically, "Didn't you see the submarine escaping from the bay?"

"Sorry, Miss Darling, we were waiting on our orders. What do you want us to do now?" he asked nonchalantly.

London broke into the conversation as April soared high into the clouds, setting a course for England

"Did you get, De-Mundo?" Charles asked.

"No, Sir. He escaped us," the Captain started to explain.

April interrupted, "Charles! These incompetent baboons watched Carlos De-Mundo sail from the bay. They just sat on their fat arses whilst waiting for further orders. Can't anybody show a bit of initiative for once? Before I'm tempted to make them all swim after him by blowing their stupid little boat from under them, I'm heading for Brize Norton. Can you arrange for somebody to meet me there? Because I'm far too knackered to drive myself home in a hired car. Also, get armed guards ready to protect this plane when I land it, until you decide where to put it for safety. I might venture to suggest that you ask the Prof if he can convert a Denver boot to fit the nose wheels. But please, don't let anybody else borrow it, or I swear I'll personally show somebody where to put it for safe keeping, Charles."

I will do that for you, April. You just head for home while I speak to my American counterpart. Do you happen to know where De-Mundo is heading?" Charles asked hopefully.

"I'm not too sure. My guess will be Columbia because that is where he feels safest. Anyway, we'll talk about it tomorrow, I'm far too exhausted tonight to try to predict what that mad scum bag might, or might not do," she told Charles, before disconnecting the link.

CHAPTER 28

During the long flight home, April was unable to use the autopilot so she could rest because the adverse weather conditions, which caused the small jet to buffet in the violent turbulence. She was relieved when she saw the Scottish coastline coming into view, as the clouds gradually cleared to reveal a clearer dawn sky above the UK. She then headed south, and towards the county of Berkshire.

The towers of the city of Oxford appear below her port wing, as April commenced the final descent into the R.A.F airfield. Landing the plane, she taxied towards the heavily armed squadron of men and armoured vehicles, which were assembled at the northern perimeter of the airfield, in readiness of her impending arrival.

Clambering laboriously from the cockpit April dropped heavily to the ground, she could see the men were already fitting clamps to all three of the wheel clusters.

"That's right lads, you make sure that it can't go anywhere without authority this time," April told them. She advised the man in charge, "And don't keep the keys to the clamps here for added security. Will you, Sergeant?"

Getting into the chauffeur driven car she was driven to her London apartment, with the certain knowledge that the security of the plane would be quite adequate this time.

The following couple of days past without incident as April relaxed, she refraining from making any unnecessary contact with Sir Charles, or Mandy and her beloved children. They in turn respected April's request for solitude, as she patiently waited for news about a sighting of Carlos De-Mundo. Using the time to tone up her shapely figure in her private gymnasium with her personal trainer, the remainder of the time was spent relaxing, shopping, and generally pampering herself at every conceivable opportunity.

Finally, the inevitable happened and Carlos De-Mundo was sighted. His submarine was seen slowly limping through the windward strait on the Ocean surface; it was on a heading leading towards one of the small bays on the Colombian/Panama border.

The tranquillity was now interrupted by April's phone ringing. Charles briefed her on the intelligence that they'd managed to gather, telling her to report to base. And to be prepared to leave for South America, immediately after the formal briefing was over.

"Well let's hope this madman is finally put to rest this time," April finished. Then, after packing a case, she headed to the nerve centre of the British Intelligence Agency.

Passing through the various security checks, which included thumb and eye prints, April was finally escorted into the operations centre where Charles was impatiently waiting for her arrival, as he paced up and down the corridor nervously.

"My dear, it's so good to see you at last, and you look radiant as ever. But why haven't you responded to our dinner invitations?" he asked, as he held the door open for April to enter the briefing room.

"I needed to remain focused on the assignment in hand. Besides, I could have been followed by one of Carlos's henchmen like I was before remember, then I would have put you all in danger. Anyway, it'll give Mandy and the children, time to adjust to you and their new lifestyle. Have you named the day yet, Charles?" April asked, as she sat in the vacant chair, acting as if it was no longer of any importance to her.

"No. Mandy insists that you must be there as her matron of honour, and she'll not consider anybody else in your place. Now I think you know most of the people gathered here, except maybe for that crack team newly assembled to assist you," he explained, as he pointed out a dozen men sitting at the rear of the room. "There's at least one representative from each of the major countries involved, and each one has a small detachment of men under their command."

A large burly Sergeant protested, "You never told us that we'd have to take orders from a mere woman, and a civilian one at that."

Charles stood to answer but April prevented him from doing so. Ambling slowly towards the Sergeant she mumbled quietly, "I'm getting sick of this." Then she challenged the Sergeant, "My, you are a big strong hunk of a man. Aren't you? I suggest we set you a little task. If you can evict me from this room Charles will replace me with a man. If not. Well I stay here and no more arguing about it. Now is that a fair challenge for you, Sergeant?"

The man smiled smugly at what he thought was to be a single sided contest, which with any other lady would have been understandable. He then strutted towards her, egged on by the other men under his command.

"I'm sorry to have to do this to you, Miss," he told her, as he reached for April's arm. This was watched with deep concern by the assembly of dignitaries gathered there, most of whom remembered her show of temper when she was first awakened after her transformation operation.

Springing into action, April seized the Sergeants' hand and pulled him towards her. Spinning a hundred and eighty degrees April deliver a mule kick high up into the man's throat, and in the same movement she jumped and extended both her legs to the side, executing a series of rapid kicks to each side of his head. Landing as nimbly as a cat, April fell into a handstand and kicked her legs upward below the Sergeants' chin, causing him to collapse into an unconscious heap.

"Any more brave men want to challenger me?" she offered, as the remaining men tried to melt into the obscurity of the wall. "I thought not, so get a bucket of water to wake sleeping beauty here. Then perhaps we can proceed without any more of this stupidity."

After the Sergeant had recovered consciousness he approached her, and offered to shake her hand. "No man has ever managed to put me down like that, let alone knock me out cold. You have more than earned your stripes with me, lady. Can we now are friends? I'm Sergeant Bass Maloney."

"I'm pleased to meet you, Bass. I'm April, and yes I hope we can be friends. Now can you return to your seat and let's proceed," she nodded towards Sir Charles, who was fidgeting impatiently.

"Thank you, Miss Darling. Now we believe the situation in Columbia to have become dire. Miss Darling here, or as she prefers to be known as, April, has been pursuing Carlos De-Mundo, for some time now, as most of you here know. Every time she destroys his new location, he eludes her, and manages to escape to safety. She has now undoubtedly become not only our finest agent, but probably the finest agent on this, God's green planet, so you can well appreciate just how slippery Mr. De-Mundo has now become."

Sir Charles took a sip of water to moisten his parched lips before continuing. "I've gathered you all together to try to formulate a plan of action to enable us to capture or destroy this man, once and for all. Now, as April is more familiar with his movements and unpredictability than anybody else in this room, I strongly suggest that she take charge of the ground troops. And, I also propose that she be given carte blanche authority to make any and all, decisions in the field. We'll of course supply the backup to all of her requests from here, and make this office the crux of the entire operation. Now De-Mundo's submarine has just been sighted on the surface sailing through the Windward Passage. It seems to be limping home with what looks to be smoke billowing from the open hatch."

April began to giggle as she explained, "I'm afraid that's my doing. I attached a small explosive device to the exhaust manifold, and I timed it to detonate after seventy-two hours, when I hoped it would be still submerged. That was, in case the despicable shit bag manage to elude me again?"

"And what was your reasoning behind that action?" asked a distinguished looking gentleman.

"So it would leave him without any option but to sail on the surface. Unless of course they wanted to sleep themselves to death on the bed of the Atlantic Ocean," April smiled as she visualised the sub sailing on blindly with a ghost crew.

"Well, thank God you did, otherwise we may not have found him for some time. You see gentlemen why she's our finest agent, she has such tremendous foresight. But now we must push, time remember is of the essence. We believe Carlos De-Mundo to be heading to a small cove just north of Colón, Panama. It's just across the border from Colombia. The assumption we arrived at is based on information supplied by our American friends here. Apparently they have intercepted a telephone conversation giving them an ETA of noon tomorrow. Of course thanks to April here, that will be delayed somewhat."

A tea trolley was wheeled into the room, "I thought you'd all welcome some light refreshment, gentlemen. So I requested it be served while we speak. Now where was I? Oh yes. The United Nations have supplied the multi-national task force, and it goes without saying that there'll be a detachment of our American cousin with us. All of us can work with one goal in mind, to stop this madman once and for all. April, here will take sole charge, and co-ordinate the operation on the ground. And we'll supply from here whatever backup she asks for, so that we can insure a successful conclusion to the operation," Charles ended.

"Right," April started, "I guess as time is of the essence we'd better make a start. Now this is a list that we shall probably require," she requested, passing Charles a piece of paper. "I've scribbled it out as we've all been talking, but I'll probably have to add to the list as we go along. I suggest that we wait till after they've docked the sub, then we send a team of frog men in after dark to disable the props and render the sub useless. Maybe if they did something simple like entwining a steel cable in the screws, to snap the shafts. As long as it's put it out of action permanently, I don't care how it's done. Also, we'll have to close the airports temporarily to prevent De-Mundo using that as a means of escaping, or as a diversion like he did in the Dominican Republic. Now we'll initiate the attack from all sides in small groups, the special boat squad will advancing from the west up the Panama Canal, and east from the Atlantic. While the ground troop's close in from the north and south, this will complete a pincer movement. In the meantime, I expect you Charles to track every move De-Mundo makes, using your satellite thermal imaging, so that we'll be aware at all times of exactly where the bastard is. Then there should be no unforeseen surprises for us, as we must try to avoid any innocent civilians getting caught up in this."

"We have our people working on that as we speak," Charles confirmed. "Good! Well let's get this show on the road, gentlemen. We will leave in exactly two hours from now." April insisted, as the assembled dignitaries nodded their individual consents. "There's just one small problem I can see, Charles. The Panamanian government need to be kept aware of exactly what's happening, but you'll need to ensure it can't be leaked to De-Mundo."

"I represent the Central American states, so I'll handle that personally. I do know a man in Panama that I can trust implicitly," offered a man of Mexican origin.

"Thank you, Alphonso. We'll leave that in your very capable hands then," Charles agreed as he left the room, closely followed by, April.

"I'll meet you in your office. I just need to confirm that they're monitoring Carlos' movements, Charles."

Entering the operations room, April asked perkily, "Hello you lot, which of you has the task of following Mr. Carlos De-Mundo for me?"

"Me Miss Darling, can I help you?" Asked a young lady, "or, John here, as we're the team that's been assigned to it."

"Good. Now where are you up to?" she asked, walking over to their workstation.

"We've pinpointed that the most likely place he'll come ashore is at, Coco Solo. There's a large fleet of fishing vessels working that area from its small bay, and the inlet between Colón and Coco Solo is the only one with a deep enough channel to accommodate the draft of the submarine. So that does seem to be the most obvious point of entry. But from our angle it makes the job a much more difficult one."

"And why's that, John?"

"Look at the hive of activity of the fishing fleet, also the number of people working on the quayside. We're going to find it near impossible to follow them without being able to tag them first."

"Can't you track them through one of their mobile phones, John?"

"Yes, Miss Darling. If I had a number we could do just that, but without a number?" John told her as he shrugged his shoulders.

"Well, tell me how many numbers you need, or will just, De-Mundo's, suffice," April boasted, as she showed him the address book she'd downloaded to her phone. "I thought these numbers might come in handy one day."

"You little beauty," he yelled, as he wrapped his arms round her. Hugging April tight, and repeatedly kissing her cheek with excitement.

"Okay, Okay, I get the message, John," she said, gently prized away from his zealous grip. "I guess that will help you then. Just download the address book then let me have my phone back?"

"Of course, I'm—," John started to explain.

April cut him off in mid-sentence, "No need to explain John, I understand that you fancy me and just needed the excuse," she teased.

"Who wouldn't," John muttered, thinking that she couldn't hear him, "but Sir Charles will probably fire me when he finds out what I did."

"And why should he do that?"

"Why Miss, everybody knows of his deep affection for you, and how he sees you as his very own personnel property."

"Then let it just be our little secret. And the rest of you, don't mention this show of John's exuberance or you'll answer to me, personally. Now we'll not mention it again, but it was nice," April assured him as she left. Leaving John flushed with embarrassment.

Calling briefly at Charles's office to inform him what was happening, she carried on to the operations room to finalise the plans for the forthcoming trip.

"We'll land at San José, Costa Rica, and make the onward journey by helicopters. I believe the choppers are en-route from Belize as we speak. Now we must all assemble at Colón ready for the final assault in exactly twenty hours from now. SO LET'S MOVE IT," April shouted. She started to collect the kit that had just been delivered, "Come on gang, we'll meet the rest of this motley crew at the airbase before take-off," she continued to spur them as they started to kit up.

"Are you sure you wouldn't rather direct operations from here, April?" Bass suggested, showing genuine concern.

"And miss all the fun of seeing De-Mundo's end? Don't you worry about me soldier; it's your men's and your own arse, you should be concerning yourself with saving. Now can I leave you in charge here to ensure that everybody is fully kited up, and wearing body armour?"

"Yes Ma'am. You certainly can." Turning to the men, he ordered, "Right you bloody lot, fall in for a full kit inspection, AND ON THE DOUBLE?" he barked out, as April left the room to walk to Charles' office.

Knocking on his door, April was invited in to find Sir Charles in conversation with three other gentlemen. She confirmed, "We're nearly ready to leave now, Sir Charles."

"A slender Lady, you're putting a slender woman in charge of ground ops. Perhaps you should reconsider putting, Sergeant Bass Maloney in charge?" One of the men suggested with alarm, in an American accent.

"Not again," April said in exasperation.

"Gentlemen, let me assure you that Miss Darling here is more capable, and qualified, than any other man on this team," Charles explained.

"Miss Darling. Do you mean, Miss April Darling?" The man asked.

"It's me in the flesh gentlemen. Well so to speak that is. Now in answer to your suggestion, I'd be more than happy to change places with any one of you lot. I can sit in your cosy little office scratching my little arse, and you can go after this madman yourselves. And possibly get, your bloody heads blown off instead of little old me." April reminded them as she sat in a vacant seat.

"I humbly apologise, Miss Darling. I wasn't aware that it was you. Your peerless reputation precedes you," he apologised meekly, blushing profusely as he fumbled and grovelled to excuse his rash request. "I know we're all in the safest hands with you spear heading this operation. If there's anybody that can stop De-Mundo, it has to be you, Miss Darling," he continued to grovel as he sat back in his seat.

"Ah well. I see it's all down to little old me again. Nobody's willing to exchange places with little old me. Oh! What a surprise," April said, as she pretended to cry.

"Okay, April. You've had your bit of fun now. So can we get down to business, please?" interrupted an impatient Sir Charles.

"I'm sorry, Sir. I just couldn't resist it. Now gentlemen, can we get to the more serious business of, Carlos De-Mundo. We believe that he's enlisted the help of some of the most powerful drug lords that we know of. And if the information that we've gathered is correct, and we have no reason to doubt it, they have all assembled in the Colón area at the head of the inlet, waiting for De-Mundo. We have of course to be careful not to spook them, so we must not make any premature move before he's disembarked. Preferably it will be best when he, and the other barons are all in conference and their guard is down. Now there's no offence gentleman, but that's as far as I intend to enlighten you of the plans, so it will protect the safety of the men," she finished, as the ministry men attempted to bombard her with questions.

Sir Charles asked, "Surely you don't think there's a leak here, April?"

"No sir. But I don't intend to jeopardise the mission if I'm wrong. I hope you can all understand that, gentlemen. Anyway, sometimes the less you actually know officially, the better it is for you in the long run." She reminded them, standing to leave. "Now if you gentlemen will please excuse me, I've got a plane to catch?"

Re-joining the rest of the task force, April found them all kited up and ready to leave. Charles joined them in the briefing room as April was preparing them for their highly dangerous mission.

"May I sit in on your briefing, April?"

"Of course you can, Sir Charles. We're relying on you to give us the backup we need from this end. And to keep track of Houdini, of course, just in case he decides to do another vanishing trick.

Now gentlemen, let's get down to business. The mission is a highly dangerous one, as I'm sure you're already aware of. As surprise is to be our best form of defence, then we do not wish to advertise our impending arrival. So follow the orders of Sergeant Bass Maloney and myself, and to the letter without question, SAVVY?" Insisted April, as the assembled men signalled their agreement. "Good," she continued, "It seems that Carlos De-Mundo will—," April stopped when she noticed one of the Colombian men sniffling and shaking.

"What's wrong with you, soldier?" April asked abruptly, as his shaking became more violent.

Brandishing his machine gun he backed towards the wall. "You idiots will never stop that, bastard," he started, mopping his feverish brow. "He'll wipe you all out if you're stupid enough to try to stop him."

"Now stay calm so we can work this out, soldier," April tried to reason with him in a very calm, relaxed voice, as she slowly edged towards him.

"Stop right there. Mr. De-Mundo said that you're the worst one, Miss Darling. Just stop there," he repeated, as he became obviously more distressed.

"What's up soldier? Do you need a fix?" she suggested in a matronly manner.

"No. I don't use that shit."

"Then what's wrong with you? Why are you sweating up so much?" April continued, as she slowly edged closer, and closer to him.

"Stop there I said. I don't want to shoot you, but I will," he threatened, as he wiped the sweat away again.

Seizing her opportunity while he'd removed a hand from his weapon to wipe his brow, April lunged at him and wrestled the gun from his grasp. The distraught man fell to his knees and sobbed bitterly. "Don't. He'll kill them," he pleaded between the sobs.

"There now, sit down and tell me who'll kill who?" April calmly asked gently, using a sympathetic tone of voice. This seemed to reassure the man as he told his pitiful story. He told how Carlos De-Mundo was holding his entire family hostage, and how he threatened he would kill them all if the man didn't comply with his unsavoury demands. "He's threatened to kill them all by injecting them with dirty needles from his HIV clients. He will do it if I don't stop you, but I don't want to kill anybody."

"And how are you supposed to stop me, soldier?"

"By killing you, but you are such a kind lady, but he holds my family hostage. What can I do?"

"We must hurry," Sir Charles intervened.

"We need to know all the facts, and this may be an important one, Charles.

Now do you know where he's holding your family?"

"In the mountains about twenty miles north of Bogotá, they're in an isolated shack," volunteered the troubled man. Asking hopefully, "Will you be able to save them?"

"I'm positive we can. That shit bag won't expect our company there. Now can you pinpoint the whereabouts of the shack on this map?" she led him to a wall chart.

"Yes I can, it's my old family farmhouse so I know exactly where it is."

Calling John at the control room to join them, April explained briefly about the Colombian problem. Adding, "If he tells you where they are, and how many of his family are in there, then you should be able to discern just how many men have been left there to guard them. But do it like yesterday, John." He handed her back her phone, saying, "It shouldn't take very long. By the way, I was told to tell you that the next couple of days will see heavy cloud cover over central and southern parts of Central America, but it won't affect me being able to do this for you now. It'll take me about five minutes," John assured her, as he took the Colombian man to his office.

"We can't allow this to distract or delay us in anyway, April," Charles reminded her, as the remainder of the assembled men sat quietly, patiently waiting for her to resume the briefing.

"It could work to our advantage. If we aim to release the hostages first, and we ensure that Carlos is made aware of that fact, it could cause sufficient distraction for us to move in. Well at least on paper it could work that way. Although you can never be absolutely certain what a madman like De-Mundo's going to do next. I suggest a small task force clad in black combat suits be dropped at dusk using black chutes. They'll need to be dropped close enough to launch a surprise attack, but just out of their earshot. Remember in that terrain you can hear a pin drop from a mile away. If they take out his men, and then using the guard's own mobile phones they can ring Carlos De-Mundo, and inform him that the hostages have all been released. Co-ordinate this with us attacking him if possible, it might just force him into panic mode momentarily. And that would give us a small advantage in which to work."

John returned to give them the exact location of the shack.

"There's a small detachment of Americans that are preparing to go and liberate the hostages, so you can leave for Panama immediately," urged Charles. "We have loaded a truck with the heavier artillery, and some gadgetry that you might need. It's on its way now to the RAF base to be loaded, and should all be ready and loaded, by the time you all get there. We've of course also transported the remainder of your personnel; they will also be loaded and waiting for you to arrive. All that's left for me to do is to wish you all bon voyage, gentlemen, and God speed."

April returned from changing into her battle dress. Charles said to her, "And you my dear little lady, you take extra special care and return here safely. Remember, you have a wedding to officiate at?" He reminded her, as he kissed April on both cheeks.

The trip to the air base took longer than expected; this was due to the heavy rush hour traffic congestion on the motorway. April sat at the rear alone, spending her time in silent prayer.

"Are you okay, April?" Sergeant Bass Maloney interrupted her thoughts. "Only you seem to be preoccupied. Is it just because of this particular mission? If you're worried about it, don't be, we'll all watch out for you."

"No, it's not just this mission, Carlos De-Mundo and I are old adversaries, and have locked horns on many an occasion. No, I was just having a quiet word with my God while I still had the time, and the solitude, to do so." April explained, as they neared the base.

"Well April, I must admit that I always pray before going into battle. There's no greater comfort than knowing that your God's with you when you go into a hostile situation, like this one. It seems we're at the base now, so let us all ask our respective Gods to protect us?" Bass suggested, as they passed silently through the gates and headed towards the waiting planes.

Mounting the steps to board the plane, April couldn't help wondering if when this mission was finally complete she would be allowed to retire, and to live as near a normal existence as she could. Also, whether her future would remain as a woman, or if the chance meeting with Dr. Sasha Patel would bear fruit, and allow her to return to her previous existence as a husband, and as a father.

Laying her head back against the side of the plane April closed her eyes. She could feel the rhythmic throbbing of the engines as they gently vibrated through the body of the plane. Being so preoccupied with the current events, April was not aware of how fatigued she'd become, and before very long into the flight she'd drifted into a light sleep.

Eventually the ringing of her phone disturbed her, "Yes Charles?" She answered warily, "I was just having a catnap, and a wonderful dream that I was back to whom I once was. You know, before you fucked me up. So I hope there's a good reason for disturbing me."

"We've freed the family of hostages, April."

She snapped, "I thought I asked you to wait till we were all in position first."

"That was the plan, but a ministry man that I'd asked to be put under house arrest escaped. He told Carlos De-Mundo that we were preparing to attack and free the hostages. So as we were already in position, we had to attack before he killed them."

"What's happened to the Minister? Have you located him? And does he know that we're mobilised?"

"No, thank God. He was shot before he could finish warning, De-Mundo. Do we proceed as normal? Or do we need to call it all off until we've revise the battle plans and re-grouped, April?"

"No, Charles, we need to get on with it now, so let's hope he won't be expecting us yet. Make sure you keep me informed if there's any further development, will you? Otherwise, we go ahead as planned." April rang off.

"Right lads, listen up. We've left Cuban air space and are about an hour or so out from our objective. I'm afraid De-Mundo was alerted about our plan to free the hostages, but we think that the source of the leak was plugged before he was warned of our impending arrival. BUT! We can't afford to leave anything to chance. We'll fly over Belize, and head south to pass over Colón. The first detachment will jump five miles out from the inlet, and the other detachment five miles beyond it. We will then march in double quick time to the village. Hopefully the boat squads can time their arrival to co-ordinate with ours. We should be able to launch a surprise attack from all sides, and so cut down the risk of any undue casualties. Bass, you'll jump and command the second group, while I of course will assume temporary command over the first group. When I've received verification we've all reached our designated vantage-point I'll release a distress flare to signal the order to attack. I hope, that if we strike just before dawn and make a lot of noise, yelling, firing into the air, banging on doors, breaking windows etcetera, you're all familiar with the drill. Then those drugged up hapless fools of De-Mundo's will give themselves up without a fight, and so reduce anymore unnecessary bloodshed. That's if things go according to plan gentlemen. But, as we all know, it's not normally the case. So I wish you all good luck, and don't take any unnecessary risks. AND DON'T, forget to wear your body armour at all times. Now all carry out your last minute checks on your equipment, and then buckle up your chutes. The first drop is in," April checked her watch. "Fifteen minutes from now."

Proceeding to carry out her own checks, Bass came over and wished April good luck, "I'll see you when this is all over. Won't I?"

"As long as we get De-Mundo, otherwise I must go after him immediately. I need to finish it this time, once and for all." She told him as she dialled Charles's number.

"We should make the first jump around five, ten minutes from now. Now have there been any late developments in that area?"

"There's a hive of activity in the area. John is busy comparing it to other days, and he's trying to ascertain if today's anything different from them. There's a flotilla of boats leaving the area heading south. But as the fishing is exceptionally good in the Gulf of Darien at this time of year, then that's no surprise. So it's probably just a normal fishing fleet. Ah! Here's, John. I'll hand him the phone."

"Hello, Miss Darling. It seems from my comparisons that there may be a five per cent increase in traffic out of the bay, but it's no more than that. Also, there are the usual activities going on in the village," he explained, as he returned the phone to Charles.

"Is that of any help to you, April? It seems to us that it may only be a normal adjustment. Recovery from illness, repairs to boats and nets, etc. We'll of course continue to monitor the area for you. How are you bearing up?"

April warned, "Don't you worry about me, worry about that toe rag when I finally catch up with him, again."

"Be careful. Remember he always seems to hold the ace cards in his hands. Now you must keep me informed," Charles insisted, "I'll stay at the office until this is all over."

"To tell you the truth, Charles, I'm getting a very bad feeling about this one, and I don't really know why." She explained, as Sergeant Maloney came within earshot.

"Don't worry April, just stay in the back ground and let my men take care of business for you."

"Why don't you take that offer up? You can direct ops from a safe distance, April?" suggested, Charles.

"No, I'll see this through to the bitter end, whatever happens. But just watch my back everybody, remember it's me that he'll be targeting. Anyway, I'm sure I'll be okay. Now we're a couple of minutes from the first drop zone, Charles, so I must go and prepare myself."

"Can I have a quick word with Sergeant Maloney before you go? And as I've said, please be careful. And good luck,"

April didn't answer and just handed her mobile phone to Bass. Telling him, "Here, Sir Charles wants a quick word with you. I'll be at the jump zone preparing when you're finished."

As she prepared her squad for the jump, Charles was busily telling Sergeant Maloney how concerned he was becoming about April. "She's not normally this sombre or nervous, so watch out for her?"

"That I would do anyway, she's some special lady though, isn't she? But I must return her mobile before she jumps. I'll speak with you when this is all over, Sir Charles."

Returning the phone to April he bent forwards and kissed her on one cheek, "That's for good luck, April. I'll kiss you on the opposite cheek when we get back," he attempted to joke. But she still maintained a serious expression, as the plane dipped below the cloud cover.

"One minutes to our first objective," a voice announced over the tannoy. "Right men; try to keep in close formation. We'll free fall until we reach the last three thousand feet before pulling the cord. That way we should further avoid detection," April reminded them as the light turned to green. "HERE WE GO, JERONIMOOOOOOO," she shouted, as they began jumping out from the plane in close formation.

CHAPTER 29

Hurtling towards the ground, April looked to see if the rest of the men had all ejected safely from the plane, as she saw the plane was already climbing back behind the heavy cover of the clouds.

Watching the altimeter, April was all too soon approaching the point at which she needed to open the chute. Pulling on her ripcord her descent slowed with a jerk, as she began floating safely towards terra firma. As she looked round to check if all the men were safe, April noticed one man had been blown off course. 'He's heading towards that clump of trees,' April thought as she landed safely, followed by the remainder of the squad.

"One man has gone astray and landed over there," April told the Corporal.

Ordering him, "Send two men to help retrieve him, and hurry."

"Yes, Ma'am," he obeyed, as he detailed two of his men to carry out the order.

Fifteen minutes pasted before they returned without him. "I'm afraid he got hung up sir and broke his neck. I've checked him and there's no sign on life, so I removed his dog tag and hid the body until after the mission is over, sir."

"We haven't got any more time to lose, so we must press on," April intervened. "But you must retrieve his body after the mission is over as you say, and then return it for a military funeral. But now let's move out," April ordered with authority, as the remaining men formed an orderly line two abreast, and began to move out.

April instructed as they broke into a trot, "We'll alternate it, jog a mile and quick march for a mile alternatively, until we reach our intended objective."

Under the cover of darkness they were able to make excellent progress, reaching the position early and giving the men time in which to rest up. April took up a point where she could observe the village.

The Corporal joined her just as there was a bleep on her mobile. It was to signal that the second squad had taken up its position.

The Corporal asked her, "Is there any sign of activity in the village?"

"No, and I don't like it," she whispered, continuing to search for some activity.

"It's early morning, Miss Darling. They may be all asleep still."

"It's a fishing village, the villagers should be out tending to, or repairing the nets by now, and preparing for the fleet to return," she pointed out.

"I see what you mean, Miss. It's as if they're expecting us?"

"Yes, and De-Mundo is using the villagers as his human shield, the bastard," April explained, as her mobile signalled another squad was taking up its position. "One more squad to take up its position and then we'll know if he's expecting us or not. But I do hope not, there's too many civilians involved so I would need to rethink this." April conceded as the last squad took up its position. April told the soldier as she set up a four-man conference on her mobile, "I must check with each of the other platoon commanders, to see how, and if, we can devise a way to minimise civilian casualties."

Conversing with them it soon became apparently clear that they couldn't come up with an alternative plan, one that would minimise harm to innocent villagers who had been inadvertently caught up in this dire situation. "Hold your positions while I contact HQ," April ordered, using the secure number that Charles had given her to speak to him directly.

She asked, "Are you monitoring our movements?"

When he had confirmed that they were, April hastily outlined her concerns for the lives of the innocent people, saying it was her belief that De-Mundo was expecting them and was using them as his human shield.

"It may be unfortunately unavoidably, April. But if De-Mundo isn't stopped this time, he'll continue to make dependent drug addicts of more people in high places. That's until such time that he can penetrate and control all of the governments of the important financial and strategic countries. Then all global security will be breached, and security as we know it will become non-existent," Charles reminded her.

"I'm still not happy about risking the lives of these innocent civilians, Charles. I must reduce the risk to them somehow. Could you use the thermal imaging to try to locate the most congested building, and then download it to my mobile, so I'll have a good idea where they're congregating?"

"Yes, but we are losing time, April. It'll soon be daylight, and then we will lose the advantage of the night-time attack we were relying on."

"As I've said, it seems that the shit bag is expecting us now anyway, but it may still work to our advantage and make De-Mundo complacent, thinking that we've withdrawn because of his human shield, I mean. But I can't be altogether sure of that. But either way I'm sure he's expecting us now Charles."

"I don't think he'll fall for that old trick will he, thinking we have withdrawn?" Charles asked, with an air of hesitancy.

"You don't know him as well as I do; he isn't the sharpest knife in the drawer you know. What brains he might have had originally he sits on, or he's destroyed them by taking his own concoction of drugs. His entourage isn't any brighter either; he makes them act as human guinea pigs for any new drugs he develops. Anyway, that's also why they're so volatile and dangerous. Now how are we doing with the tracking images?"

"We're downloading it to you now," he told her as her phone bleeped, notifying April that she was receiving a picture message. "As you'll see, the largest gathering is in the village store. We are still unsure whether it's all the innocent local people, or just Carlos De-Mundo's men. That's something we're still trying to ascertain for you. But we do know that De-Mundo's there by tracking the mobile number you gave us."

"We'll get in touch later when you've more news," April said, ringing off and reconnecting to the four-man conference.

Starting, "Right gentlemen, this is our problem." She proceeded to explain the fuller picture to them. "I don't want to use one of our missiles and find that I have only wiped out innocent fishermen and their entire families, so has anybody got any ideas?"

"We've been trained in such conditions, Ma'am. Let me and my men use what's left of the night cover to do a reiki of the village," the boat squad Commander suggested.

"Okay, but we must maintain radio silence. If you need to inform us on anything at all, just send me a very brief text. Be very, very careful; remember he seems to be aware that we're here." Agreed April reluctantly, seeming to have no other alternatives open to her.

Waiting impatiently as the short time past like an eternity. April used the night vision on her field glasses to follow the painstakingly slow advancement of the small, but elite squad. Eventually the whirling of engines broke April's concentration.

Somebody was attempting to start the engines of the sub. A loud snapping noise was heard as the steel ropes tightened and stopped the screws from turning. Breaking the drive shaft, and rendering the sub completely inoperable.

Good, the divers have done the job in binding the screws together, she thought, while watching the crew spilling out from the sub and scrambling for cover. Sporadic gunfire quickly drew her attention back to the scene below. The squads of special service personnel were seen scrambling for cover amid a barrage of bullets from the storehouse, as April's mobile phone rang.

"Return fire. Return fire," the boat squad Commander shouted frantically down the phone. April ordered the remaining troops to open fire. They rained down a hail of bullets to give the special boat squad covering fire, and allowing them to withdraw safely, but only after they had planted a devise, which would allow London to observe the inside of the shacks more accurately.

April needed again to discuss the situation with Charles and the Commanders.

"It seems most of the hostages are assembled in the centre of the storehouse. But it looks as though they are all knelt on the floor and huddled together. But De-Mundo and his men have placed some of them up against the windows and door as a human shield." Charles explained, "We've now lost the element of surprise, so some civilian casualties are unavoidable I'm afraid, you must go ahead and attack them now?"

"Hold your horses a minute while I think," she insisted, scouring the village from her position and looking for divine inspiration. She asked, "What's that smoke from the smoke stack?"

"It's probably the grill that they use to smoke the morning catch. It looks like they may be making the shop keeper cook them some breakfast," the boat commander suggested.

April asked, "Does anybody know a way that we can cap that smoke stack off?"

"The choppers are standing by to airlift us out of here if need be, they could be here within minutes," Sergeant Maloney interrupted. "If it flew over from the east, they could use those hills for cover until the last moment."

"And what happens then?" April invited him to finish.

"Oh I'm sorry, I didn't finish. The choppers could drop a wet tarpaulin over the roof to cover the smoke stack."

"Brilliant. It's so simple and yet so brilliant. Get on it Bass, but while we wait let us edge as close as possible to be ready to pick off the rebels as they spill out," she advised. Edging her small group forward, April thought to herself, *I'm getting so sick of innocent people getting caught up in De-Mundo's evil web, perhaps this time nobody innocent needs to get hurt. Please God help me to avoid unnecessary bloodshed?*

The sound of the helicopter grew ever closer until it could be seen over the hilltop; it was dangling a wet tarpaulin from the open door. Hovering above the shack it dropped the sheet covering the shack roof; then turned and disappeared back over the top of the hill.

After a short time smoke began to billow out from the doors and windows, as violent coughing could be heard from within the store.

"Okay, we're coming out so don't shoot," a voice was heard to shout, as the occupants began to stumble out into the early morning sunrise.

"Drop your weapons and interlock your fingers behind your heads, then kneel down on the ground," Sergeant Maloney ordered, as they cautiously approached the rebels. He repeated to them, "INTERLOCK YOUR FUCKING FINGERS BEHIND YOUR FUCKING HEADS, AND KNEEL ON THE FUCKING FLOOR, NOW."

One of the rebels reached for his side arm as a burst of automatic gunfire rang out, and a marine riddled him with bullets. His lifeless body slumped onto the floor.

April demanded, "Who's in charge here?" The confused men complied by kneeling and clasping their hands behind their heads, as she repeated the question more forcefully. "WHO THE FUCKING HELL IS IN CHARGE, I ASKED YOU?"

A young fresh face boy nervously stood up, his trousers became soaked as he urinated himself with fear. Then he volunteered, "I, I, I am, Mr. De-Mundo left me in charge, Miss."

"WHERE'S THAT COWARDLY BASTARD NOW?"

The young lad hung his head with embarrassment at having urinated himself, as he mumbled; "He's gone."

April was filled with pity as the youth began to shake violently. He asked her, "Are you going to kill us all, Miss?"

"Not if you tell us what we need to know. So tell me, where's that bastard De-Mundo?"

"He's gone over that hill to the next cove," the young lad willingly volunteered, as he pointed to the hills behind them. "He was to be met there by his private launch."

Hastily April contacted London. "Charles, De-Mundo had his launch pick him up from the next cove. How did you miss that one? Now can you have somebody there track him while we follow him on foot? Also, the rabble he's left here need questioning and sending home. They're not rebels, they're just poor misguided young fools," explained April. She instructed a marine to escort the lad to change out of his urine soaked trousers.

"Come on you piss head, move it," the marine ordered. As he prodded him forcefully with his rifle, making the young boy call out with pain. The marine took aim to shoot the lad as April delivered a drop kick to his arm, forcing him to drop his rifle.

Sergeant Bass Maloney rushed to his rescue before realising who had inflicted the damage. He demanded, "What's the problem, Miss Darling?"

"I just asked one of your baboons here to accompany this young lad to change out of his wet trousers. But not for them to intimidate and abuse him, so I suggest you instruct your men to follow my orders to the letter, or you can get them to hell out of my sight," she insisted. She then turned her attention back to her mobile and told Charles, "I'll ring you back shortly Charles. I have a Yankee problem here."

"We have our orders, as I think you know, and they are to stem the threat of Carlos De-Mundo by any means that we deem necessary. And to let nobody, BUT NOBODY, get in our way," threatened Maloney, as April drew her pistol.

"You trigger happy fucking Yanks make me sick, I'll shoot WHOEVER tries to countermand my orders. Now who's the brainless fucker that's going to make the first move?" she threatened them through clenched teeth.

A marine moved towards her and she shot him in his leg. "Call that a warning shot soldier, but the next one will be fatal for the idiot who wants to act like a tin pot hero. Come with me, I'll stand outside the door and protect you while you change into dry clothing," April promised the terrified boy. Leaving Maloney lost for words.

After collecting dry clothing from the store, April made good her promise and guarded the door. Eventually the lad emerged, "Thank you, Miss."

"April, just call me April, everybody else does. Now would you answer me some more questions?" she asked him politely as they walked back to where the multi task force stood silently. Shocked at April's reaction, but still dutifully guarding the remaining prisoners.

"Yes, because you've been so kind to me it's the least I can do for you, Miss,"

"Right, Sergeant Maloney will you come with me. The rest of you try to act civil towards the prisoners or else." April threatened again as they walked the lad towards a clear area, and out of earshot of the remaining insurgents. Sergeant Maloney tried to intervene but April stopped him. "You know Sergeant, I'm sure you're a highly trained and competent soldier for dear old Uncle Sam, but do you know the one thing that you lack that you cannot be taught? That's the good old British finesse that separates you from me. Now I suggest. No, I insist, that you just act as an observer whilst I inte… question our young friend here. Otherwise you can get your men together now and all FUCK OFF."

The Sergeant went meekly quiet as April continued, "Now just relax and we'll dispense with all the formalities, so as to keep this on a purely friendly footing. As you know my name is. April, and this is, Sergeant Bass Maloney, so you can just call him Bass. Now what should we call you?"

"José Miss, I mean April, José Martinez," he volunteered willingly. "Okay José, now who's in charge here? Is it just you?"

"Yes, the soldier shot the other one. As Mr. De-Mundo left he put him and me in charge before he went. I didn't want the responsibility," the lad continued nervously, "but he said if I didn't accept the honour he was bestowing on me, well he threatened he would rape and kill my wife and baby when he returned to Colombia." The boy started to cry.

"Don't cry, when we've finished I'll send your wife's address to London, so they can instruct a platoon of soldiers to guard them for you. Well at least until I can deal with De-Mundo and neutralise any more threats to you and your family. Or anybody else's for that matter," April assured the boy.

"Thank you, Miss April. I know I can trust what you promise, so what else is it that you need to know?" The boy continued willingly.

"Good, I'll leave Bass to take down the information from you. Now do you know where Carlos De-Mundo is heading for? And how many men are there still with him? Also, what does he intends to do next etc. Of course your address so that we can protect your wife and child too?" April promised, as she walked into a clearing to again speak with Sir Charles.

"Charles, I have had to threaten the bloody American marines yet again. They're getting far too heavy handed out here. The poor bastards here are petrified enough, and at least one of them has pissed his trousers. I need you to tell your American counterpart to instruct their men to follow my orders, and if not they can all piss off. They either ease up on their attitude, or sod off as far as I'm concerned. Otherwise I'll not be responsible for what I do to them. I've already had to shoot one of them in the leg for threateningly countermanding my orders."

"Okay I'll sort it out, they're very grateful that you are in charge so I shouldn't have any problem with them. Now we're tracking De-Mundo's launch across the Gulf of Darien, but we'll lose the satellite link very soon. We predict that he's probably headed for the Gulf of Venezuela, and then we think he'll probably go over land to Bogotá. The trouble is that we only have five minutes of the satellite link left open. It'll then be ninety minutes before we can pick up the signal again. And by then they could well be ashore."

"Why don't you try to contact that girl in, was it Brazil Charles? So you can set up a satellite link like you did once before?"

"That's a very good idea, April. I'd clean forgotten about her with all that's going on. Will you just hold for a second?" He eventually returned, saying, "I'm back, I've instructed Bert to contact her and set up the link with her post-haste, you remember Bert don't you?"

"Yes, say hello to him for me will you. Now Sergeant Maloney will handle debriefing the prisoners, then can you see that they're all repatriated home safely. Oh, and will you get a detachment of men to José Martinez's home to protect his family, just until I've dealt with De-Mundo. I've promised him that in return for his co-operation. Now I need transport out of here to catch up with that Colombian shit head, Charles?"

Sergeant Maloney approached having finished questioning José, so April handed him her mobile-phone to enable him to tell Charles what he'd managed to ascertain. He told Sir Charles all the relevant information he'd managed to extract from the young lad, and the address of his wife. After he had finished Charles gave him instructions on how he was to repatriate the prisoners humanely, then he asked him to return the mobile to April.

"I've given him his instructions to delegate the repatriation of the men. But he and a small but crack troop are to escort you in the more urgent pursuit of, Carlos De-Mundo. I've also put one of the helicopters at your disposal, while the others will be occupied in returning the young men to their respective homes safely," confirmed Charles.

"How's that satellite link-up coming along, Charles?" April asked, watching the remaining dejected rebel's being loaded aboard the choppers.

"We've got the link enabled and Cassandra says, 'Hi'. Do you want it linked up to your mobile?"

"Not at this precise moment, Charles, you can let Bert monitor Carlos's progress while we make a start towards Bogotá. Just keep me informed if anything changes, will you?" she finished, as Bass waved for her to get aboard the waiting copter.

The helicopter rose quickly into the air and was soon winging its way across the water. Keeping low to avoid detection by radar, they headed towards the Colombian coastline. All too soon they'd crossed the water and were skimming across the grasslands.

Keeping drifting in and out of sleep, April tried to doze, trying desperately to alleviate her fatigue. She watched the workers tending their crops as the flatlands gave way to the sparsely grassed slopes of the hillside. Then the helicopter started ascending yet again as it approached the Andes Mountains.

"You've been very quiet," Sergeant Maloney remarked, "is there anything wrong with you, April?"

"No, I'm just taking the opportunity to rest while I can. I mustn't let De-Mundo elude me again this time so I need to keep alert," April explained to him. "Besides, why would I want to join in with your men's talk?" she asked, returning to watching the rugged scenery passing below them.

The helicopter veered south following the rocky spine of the Andes Mountain range, until eventually it banked heading in towards southeast Bogotá. As it slowly descended onto an open meadow southwest of the Capital, where a group of canvas shelters had been erected by advanced troops, in readiness of their impending arrival.

After she'd been directed to her quarters, April collapsed onto the make shift bunk, and soon fell into a much needed sleep. The ringing of her phone disturbed her as she looked at the time on her watch.

"Shit," April snapped, as she realised she had only slept for thirty minutes. "Yes Charles? Your timing's impeccable you know? You've just disturbed a much needed sleep, yet again. So what's so important this time?"

"Sorry about that but I thought you'd like to know that Carlos De-Mundo's party has just crossed the Venezuelan border, and it's now en-route for Bogotá. He should reach there at about noon, April."

"Do you know where he's headed for yet, Charles?"

"Not exactly, but he owns a number of farms and properties in that area apparently, so we'll need to wait until he actually stops at one of them. Anyway, I'm sorry I disturbed your sleep, so if you'd like to get back to your slumber I won't disturb you again. At least, not unless something very important arises that is."

"There's no need to apologise, Charles, it's just me being cranky. I needed to know that, so feel free to ring me if you find out anything else."

"Might I ask what's wrong, April? Only you aren't your usual bubbly self."

"I keep getting a foreboding feeling about this assignment now, and I'm sick to the stomach with what I've now become, Charles."

"Do you mean your gender?"

"No, Charles. I'm getting used to that now. I mean the foul mouthed sadistic killing bitch that you've turned me into. I still struggle trying to justify it within my faith."

"I think we need to get you some help with that one, when you come home that is. But what do you mean by foreboding?"

"I don't really know that is the problem. Knowing first-hand how cunning and devious De-Mundo can be, well the situation has become very volatile out here now. It seems every time I think I've cornered him; he gives me the slip again. Only for the possible consequences I would now like to shoot him on sight, Charles. Well at least that's what I feel like doing."

"You do whatever your instincts tell you to do this time; you know I'll always keep you protected. Besides, none of the Major Counties would hold you accountable for eradicating that vermin. While Carlos De-Mundo is alive, and the major drug barons that are with him, there's not a single country's security that is safe. So stop your worrying and try to rest, let me do all the worrying for you," Charles insisted, as he tried to reassure her.

"Don't worry, I'll always do what I get paid to do and exterminate the vermin. But I will have to be at my most vigilant, so I'll speak to you later, Charles. And thank you," April said sincerely as she rang off.

After a sleep, then eating with the men, April excused herself before taking a stroll through the wild countryside.

"Can you use some companionship, April?" Sergeant Maloney offered. Adding, "Only you seem so lonely and nervous about this mission, and I'm sorry about our attitude towards you earlier."

Linking his friendly arm April confided, "It's just this assignment Bass. I've been within a gnat's whisker of obliterating this bastard, and each time he's eluded me. He's abused, insulted, belittled, threatened, and tried to kill me. I've been fortunate more than once to escape with my life. Now does that go anywhere near to giving you an explanation as to why I am feeling so apprehensive? And why I'm not confident about apprehending him, this or any other time, or of escaping it with my life."

The Sergeant tried to comfort her, "This time you have and me my men to watch over you, and we won't let anything happen to you. I promise."

"I'm afraid knowing him as well as I do, well it'll take more than just words to convince me. I'll only be convinced when he's in custody, or when I see his bloody dead body. I'm sorry about the dressing down I gave you and your men, Bass. But you have to admit that you can be unnecessarily trigger-happy at times."

"Well, we'll follow your lead from now on, and to the letter. And I'll instruct the men to make watching your back their number one priority," he was interrupted by the ringing of her phone.

"It's the boss again, Bass," April explained, putting the phone to her ear. "Hello Charles, what news is there?" she asked in a calmer tone of voice.

"Carlos's convoy of trucks has divided into three and they're all heading for different locations," he started to explain. "But the trouble is we don't know which party Carlos De-Mundo is in. It seems that he's more clued up than we first gave him credit for."

"And what conclusions have the brains come up with?" she asked sarcastically.

"The best guess we can make is that he's aware that we're tracking him so he's toying with us. I wondered if you had any ideas that might help us. After all, you know the man better than any one of us do."

"Not really Charles, is Cassandra giving you the satellite link up so that there aren't any blank areas?"

"Yes, but her p.c. seems to be playing up, her screen keeps on flashing to a split of two identical screens. Our computer buffs aren't sure what can be causing it."

"Have you thought she might be doing it on purpose to warn you about something?"

"For what reason would she do that? Just a moment, the convoy has changed direction and is headed straight towards you," said Charles, with an air of urgency in his voice. "He seems to know exactly where you are."

"Are we on a secure hook up, Charles?"

"Yes. Why?" A puzzled Charles asked.

"With what you're saying I think Cassandra is trying to warn us," April started. "The flashing to a twin screen could mean somebody else is tapping in to her p.c."

"But who, and more importantly, why," a thoughtful Charles asked. "And why doesn't she just break the link?"

"I'm not certain, but if I was to hazard a guess I'd say she keeps flashing to split screens to let you know that she's not alone, probably one of De-Mundo's men is there with her. He's probably making her give him information about our whereabouts and movements. Can you feed her false information until an agent is able to check up on her? Meanwhile, we'll move leaving the tents here to try to fool them. Also you should give some thought as to how they've found out about Cassandra."

"Unless you know who the traitor could be, then we'll have to conduct the witch hunt at a later date," suggested Charles. "It'll take far too long for us to do it now."

"I have a suggestion to speed it up Charles. If you implement an impromptu fire drill immediately, then while they're outside get somebody not connected to us to check the stations, and access the history of each computer station, that way you will find out who's had access to Cassandra's address, and who is contacting De-Mundo from their station. You will then quickly narrow it down to who it was. Remember Charles, whoever it is will have needed to be given the security code to operate that station in the first place."

"I'm setting off the fire alarm as we speak, there's maintenance engineer here doing some repairs, but what shall we do about Cassandra? There's a task force doing exercises in the River Plate, so we could dispatch a small squad of American navy Seals I suppose; they could reach Cassandra's apartment within the hour. But we'll still need to keep up the charade until then so as not to arouse their suspicions. Just a moment, they've started with Bert's station and it seems he's our mole. He seemed to be so loyal; I wonder how they've got to him." Charles reflected thoughtfully, as Sergeant Maloney interrupted.

"We're all set to break camp, April," he began. "And I've left a few surprises for our friend too."

"Did you hear that, Charles? We're ready to pull out to an observation point to see if Bass's surprise's work. Have you mobilised any back up for us yet?"

"Yes April, but they won't reach you in time now."

"Well when they do, will you ask them to eliminate De-Mundo's other convoys? I'm sure that they will be carrying the other drugs barons. Now we must get moving, so I'll ring you later, Charles."

"You'd better hurry because Carlos's convoy is only five minutes away now, and they've divided again. It looks like they plan to surround you, but I'll keep you informed."

Barely had they finished than there was a loud explosion, as a missile exploded in the middle of the camp, injuring two men.

"Take cover here they come," April shouted, running for cover and diving into the gorse thickets, followed very closely by Sergeant Bass Maloney.

"Can you use some company?" He asked, as they watched his remaining men frantically diving for cover, amidst relentless machine gun fire which was systematically mowing them down. "The poor bastards don't stand a chance," Bass screamed, as he watched his men dying, one by one.

April demanded in a whisper, "Give me that rifle," as tears filled her eyes. Then her voice became louder as she realised, "They're dying out there because of me, so give me that bloody gun." This attracted the attention of the marauding troops. April whispered, "Stay down out of sight. It's me they want, and if you show your face you're dead. Then you're of no further use to Uncle Sam, or me. Besides, Carlos will want me alive," April convinced him, as she slowly began to sidle away from him.

When there was sufficient distance between Sergeant Maloney and April, she emerged from the undergrowth firing her weapon at a rebel as he executed one of the marines.

"DIE YOU FUCKING BASTARD," she yelled, as the shocked rebels watched their compatriot collapse into a lifeless heap. The remaining dishevelled group trained their guns on April, and then Carlos's familiar voice called out.

"I said I want that bitch alive, you'll get your chance to exact revenge when I'm through with her," he promised in a sinister voice.

Saying as he emerged through the silenced group, "Hello again my little minx, this time there will be no escaping your demise." He threatened, as her hands and feet were tightly bound. After taping across her mouth, Carlos told his men, "Throw her up onto the back of the truck, and you don't have to be too careful with her either." One man held April through her arms, while another took hold of her legs and started to swing her as they counted.

"Uno, dos, tres," then they threw her onto the truck and she landed with a heavy bang, as April's head and back landed hard on the metal floor of the wagon.

The distant sound of helicopters started to grow louder and louder, as Carlos urged his men to hurry. Then they disappeared over the brow of the hill, and onto the busy dusty road leading into the Capital.

Chapter 30

As the convoy divided to allow them to intermingle under the cover of innocent motorists, they intertwined the convoy to give Carlos the security of an impromptu, human shield. It also made it difficult, if not impossible, for the computer experts to keep track of them, as the trucks trundled on towards the overcrowded outskirts of the city.

After breaking from the cover of the traffic, the trucks weaved their way through the narrow uneven back streets. April's head was continually being thrown from side to side, as it constantly and violently, crashed against the metal decking with every bump. Carlos's men sat either side of the truck using her body as a footrest. This time she was grateful they did, because it prevented her back from taking an even worse pounding, as the weight of their heavy muddy boots held her body down. She was relieved as she sensed the convoy starting to reduce speed and eventually it turned into a narrow alley and ground to a halt.

"Everybody out, and bring that bloody whoring bitch with you," Carlos ordered, as he strode into a disused garage.

One of the men dragged her off the truck by the feet, causing her head to crash onto the stony road surface and knocking her unconscious.

April started to slowly regain her senses as she became aware that she was suspended in the air. She glanced round the empty garage and realised she was alone. Her wrists had been bound together and she was suspended by them from a block and tackle, her feet barely able to reach the floor.

Lost for inspiration because her head still pounded from the blow she'd received when she was hauled from the truck, April could feel the blood still running profusely from the wound on the back of her head, as it ran slowly down to her legs, forming a gory puddle at her feet. April was trying unsuccessfully to take her body weight on tiptoes: so that she would be able to flick the rope off the hook that was supporting her.

Hanging like a piece of meat in an abattoir, helpless and totally exhausted, April was sore and weakened by her pounding headache. So once again she was left with her only tool of comfort, praying to Almighty God.

April concentrated her every ounce of energy in silent prayer, as she asked the Lord for divine guidance to aid her through this, and beyond the evil darkness that she was now in. The prayers were soon interrupted as the doors swung noisily open.

"Ah you're awake now? So now my men can start having a little fun with you at last." Boomed Carlos, as his henchmen leered menacingly beside him. "I've promised them that they can let off a little steam on you, just as a reward for their undying loyalty."

Forced to keep silent because her mouth was taped, April was left wondering what exactly he meant. If it was to be sexual, then they'd need to release her from the hoist, and that might give April the opportunity with which to aid her escape.

Carlos interrupted her thoughts as he answered April's silent question. "They won't rape you. I have told them not to contaminate they're dicks with a slut like you are. No, instead we intend to let you die a slow and painful death, very slow, and very painful. After all, you've cost me dear over these last couple of months with your interference, and the damage you have caused to my property. So now it is, PAYBACK TIME," he warned ominously, as he punched April full in the face bloodying her nose.

Laughing loudly they all left, letting April ponder her demise. Instinctively April knew that he'd broken her nose, but she was powerless to stem the bleeding being tethered as she was. Dazed from the blow, April rotated slowly as she searched desperately for a means of escaping this hellhole that she found herself in. But it was all to no avail, she seemed doomed to suffer the fate that Carlos De-Mundo, and his misguided army of fools, were planning for her.

Drifting in and out of consciousness, she was abruptly awakened by cold water from a fire hose: as a bearded little man laughingly hosed her down. The force of the water pushed her back until April's feet could no longer reached the floor, and it also increased the strain on her already aching limbs; as the water soaked clothes added extra weight onto them, the pain in her arms now reach an unbearable point.

Turning the water off, the little man said laughingly in a broken Mexican accent. "There, now you should smell a little better you shitty English bitch," he and his friends continued mocking, as they laughed uncontrollably.

One of them walked up to April and stood within inches of her face as he spat on her. As it mingled with the blood he said to his friend, "See Pedro, you have missed a little bit on her face." They all jeered as Pedro again started to hose April down, aiming the full force of the water onto her face. This made it impossible for her to breathe, so she was forced to hold her breadth until again reaching the verge of unconsciousness.

After they'd turning off the water again, she was left gasped desperately for breath.

Pedro suggested, "I think we should let her drip dry now," amid there uncontrollable laughter.

She had now lost all her feeling in her arms and legs as the wet ropes tightened. Her breathing was returning slowly to normality, as again she tried desperately looking round for inspiration. "If only I could take my body weight on my legs, then I might then be able to free my arms off the hook. But I will need something to stand on," she thought to herself, shivering from the drenching that she'd just received. But there was nothing that could be reached with her legs.

Her attention again returned to unhooking herself from the hoist so she tried desperately to gain a firm hold on the chain so she could raise herself up, but she was again forced into dismissing the idea.

April could hear approaching footsteps then the door swung open and two more men entering.

"Now you fucking cow, just how much real pain can you take?" the smaller man asked. But April was unable to answer due to the tape that was still covering her mouth.

"Don't answer us then," the taller man said, as he delivered a punch into her kidneys. Her body swung away from him and towards his friend under the force of the blow, as the smaller man then swung a club hitting April in the stomach.

April was now feeling nauseous from the pain as he ripped off the tape to hear her beg for mercy, but she only started to vomit from the sheer pain that she felt. As she swayed back towards the leering taller man April felt another sickening pain, when he hit her across the small of her back with a wooden plank.

Struggling to fight the urge to scream out in pain, April withstood the next punch to the point of the jaw and blackness engulfed her once again. Her swollen eyes slowly opened as April saw that night had now descended. The excruciating pain in April's shoulders had now reached the point where it was unbearable. She could hear the laughter from the drunken rabble, as she struggled unsuccessfully to try to shift her body weight to ease her pain.

Carlo De-Mundo suddenly appeared seemingly out of nowhere, he was flanked by two of his burly inept minders, "You don't look so beautiful now. Do you, Miss April fucking Darling? No, you look more like the dirty scruffy little English slut that you are," he jeered with the escorting men joined in. "Take her down but leave her tied up and gagged, we'll resume operations in the morning. After all, we don't want her to die too quickly do we? It will spoil our little bit of fun."

She was released from the hook as Carlos' piercing laughter rang in her ears, then she fell heavily onto the oily concrete floor.

Before trying desperately to sleep and build up her strength, April wrestled with the bindings, attempting to stretch them and free herself and escape from this living hell. But it was all too no avail.

487

Two drunken men then emerged from the office and staggered towards her. "Let's shag the arse off the bitch, I just feel like a good shag," one of the men suggested.

"No, you know what our orders are, and what Mr. De-Mundo said he'd do to us if we disobeyed him," explained his friend.

"Well it might just be worth it. Just look at that tight arse and those big tits that she's got. I know, let's get her tits out and play with them a little bit first," said the little man as he groped her.

April knew she would be unable to prevent them.

"Over her clothes then, so that Mr. De-Mundo won't know," advised his friend.

Carlos boomed from the door, "What won't I know?" The frightened man hastily withdrew his hands from April. "I, I, I was just checking that she was still alive, Mr. De-Mundo."

"LIAR, look at your prick. You were going to shag her. Weren't you? Go on, be a man and admit it. You wanted to shag her didn't you?" Carlos demanded.

The little man shook violently with fear as he urinated himself. "No Mr. De-Mundo, you told us not too so I—."

"Hold his arms," Carlos instructed his minders.

They obeyed without questioning him, being too afraid not to, as the guilty man protested frantically.

Carlos then ordered his friend to cut off his trousers.

"Please, Mr. De-Mundo. My friend didn't mean any harm he is drunk. Let him go, please?" he pleaded.

"I said cut off his pants," Carlos insisted, as the man reluctantly obeyed. He apologising profusely to his friend through floods of tears.

"Your prick isn't so big now, is it?" Carlos asked, as he poked it menacingly with his pistol. The man nodded his head with agreement, as Carlos grasped for the hook of the hoist and thrust it up between the terrified man's legs. He thrust it through his skin just behind his scrotum, as the minders and his friend could only watch in sheer horror, but Carlos only laughed at him as he hoisted him up.

He screamed unmercifully begging him for mercy, as the man tried desperately to grasp at the chain and ease the weight of his body on the hook. Still laughing like the sadistic madman that he'd become, Carlos De-Mundo then shot the man's left arm, forcing him to hang on desperately with only one hand.

"You'll never disobey me again you bastard," he told him, as he shot his other arm and walked from the garage, laughing sadistically.

April closed her eyes as the screaming hit fever pitch as the hook began to tear up through his abdomen. It then slowly disembowelled the man, until eventually mercifully he died, but it was a slow and agonising death.

His friend was only able to watch in sheer horror at the sadistic actions of this madman. Regaining his composure, he told April how sorry he was he could not release her, but he removed the tape from her mouth before he disappeared through the open door. Escaping, before Carlos made him suffer the same fate as his dead friend.

Able now to breathe more freely, April tried to loosen the knots securing her wrists with her teeth. But they had become too tight due to the drenching she'd undergone, but she continued in vain to struggle with the knots.

It was late morning when De-Mundo returned with four of his minders to find her alone, "That spineless little bastard's gone has he, well never mind, we still have you to play with. Don't we my fucking little vixen? I can see you've got the tape off your mouth? Good, I'll be able to hear you beg for mercy before you eventually die."

"GO TO HELL, YOU'VE FINALLY LOST YOUR MARBLES COMPLETELY. YOU'RE JUST AN INSANE FUCKING BASTARD,"

April shouted. She was trying to provoke him into finishing her off quickly, instead of her needing to suffer the slow and painful death that he'd planned for her.

April was again hauled to her feet as they made her shuffle across to the hoist. She slipped in a pool of blood and narrowly missed the disembowelled corpse, which was lying beneath the hoist.

The building was now becoming a scene of evil carnage and butchery, and bore little resemblance to the garage that it once was.

Again she searched with difficulty for a means of escaping, but April's pain and fatigue hampered her. The rope restricting her feet allowed April to shuffle, in steps on only one and a half to two feet. If maybe I could use that to snare one of the guards?" she thought, as Carlos and his half-crazed drunken slobs enjoyed watching her struggling.

After hooking the rope between her tethered wrists onto the hoist, and without any warning, one of the guards delivered a karate kick into April's abdomen. This caused April to vomit up blood as they hoisted her up, again with only her tiptoes able to reach the floor.

"Do you want a little drink?" Carlos asked, as he turned on the fire hose, aiming it full into April's face.

This April was partially glad of; because now she started to develop sores inside her parched mouth, due to my lack of liquid intake. But as soon as the flow of water had stopped, she received another blow from a fist, full into her face.

"I warned you that you would pay for the way that you've treated me, and still you refuse to cry out for mercy. But you will before you die, THAT, you fucking English bitch I promise you, you will plead with me, Carlos De-Mundo, for clemency." He warned, as he pistol wiped her. Again April drifted was knocked unconscious amid their mocking laughter, as they walked from the shack like building.

Regaining her senses, April became aware of the increasing stench that the rotting corpses, and dried blood, gave out. Her stomach heaved as she tried unsuccessfully to vomit, but she found her stomach was far too empty.

Carlos emerged through the doors brandishing a bullwhip. "Ah my little toy, are you ready to play again?" He asked, as he menacingly cracked the whip.

"Go to hell you fat ugly bastard, you've finally lost it," April told him in a waspishly croaky voice.

"You're a mouthy bitch, but I'll teach you to respect me," He shouted at April, as he ripped open her suit to bare her back. He stepped back and started to lash April wildly with his whip, as April flinched with pain. "You disrespectful British bloody whore, don't you realise who I am? I'm the great Carlos De-Mundo, the most powerful of all the drug lords." He finished, leaving her back a criss-cross of bloody lesions.

April passed out with the pain as blood continued to ooze from her open lesions. This was slowly sapping what was left of her fading energy. Regaining consciousness as night was descending; April found a solitary guard had been left to watch over her.

"If he comes close enough I could maybe snare him with my legs," April thought to herself. The man sat ogling her near naked body, as he swigged whisky from his bottle. Her clothes now were becoming just a shredded mess of blood soaked rags,

As if he knew of April's intentions, the guard lowered the hoist to allow her to fall to the floor. "You just lie there and rest, I'll just sit here and watch over you like, Mr. De-Mundo's ordered me too."

As April fell hard onto the floor, she said to him, "You know he's finally snapped. Don't you?"

"It's just the drugs, Miss. You see he's been taking a lot of them just lately. It's because he's under a lot of pressure, but he'll be okay," the man tried to convince himself. He asked, "But you seem to have pissed him off real bad. What did you do to him that was so bad?"

"Just my job, like you are. You know you'll all be killed eventually," she tried to bluff him. "The security services are closing in as we speak, and they'll be here very soon now." Her voice now was very weak.

"Are you okay, Miss? Well, as well as you can be under the circumstances that you're in." The man asked with genuine concern.

"I haven't eaten or drank for two days now as you well know. I wonder what Carlos would do to you if you let me die of hunger and spoilt his fun?"

"What do you mean? He hasn't told me to feed you," the dim witless man said, wearing an extremely worried frown.

"It's your dilemma then, but you know how vicious and volatile he can be. So YOU must decide for yourself I'm afraid," April commented. But then she added thoughtfully, "But I wouldn't like to take that chance if I were you?"

It worked as the man became frightened and passed over some sandwiches and a glass of water to her, saying, "I'm not untying you though, so you will just have to manage the best that you can."

He watched as April struggled to hold the drink of water between her bound hands, gulping it down without stopping. She asked, "Could I have some more water please?" as she gobbled up the sandwiches. "Thank you, you're a very kind man. Why don't you save yourself while you still can? After all, most of De-Mundo's men have already deserted him by now. Haven't they?"

"We're just waiting here for re-enforcement's to join us from Ecuador. About fifty men are coming soon, and we'll be able to move on and crush the imperialistic pigs."

"Can't you see that Carlos has finally flipped completely, all he's got left is his vivid imagination and dreams of grandeur? You get out of here while you still can and I'll help you," she urged. "The only plans Carlos has left are in his vivid imagination. They're probably aren't any re-enforcement's joining you from Ecuador, or anywhere else for that matter. So go on, save yourself."

"Oh yes there is, and Mr. De-Mundo's friend's going to help us too."

"And which friend is that supposed to be? The imaginary fairy godmother, or some other figment of his imagination I suppose," she continued to press.

"He's a very important man at the pentagon, because he's a military attaché to the assistant head of staff. He's just waiting for Mr. De-Mundo's command," the man was opening up and volunteering information readily, as the large amount of whisky he was drinking was lowering his guard.

"Command, what command, and who's it too? No, it's all over now, he's conning you with his dreams. The actual truth is you'll all be killed along with him if you stay."

The worried guard nervously tried to regain the upper hand by delivering a bombshell, "It's a stroke of genius really," laughed the man nervously, "they've altered the sceptre. When it strikes the doors to open your parliament it will send a signal to our contact at the pentagon and then the Semtex filled orb will explode. It will set off a chain reaction that we've had planted and destroy your Parliament, and kill all of your M. P.'s."

"And what makes you think you can get away with that stupid plan? Remember Guy Fawkes, he tried it once. Anyway, why the signal to the man at the Pentagon?" she continued with concern. Realising that with his money Carlos will always find a vulnerable fool that he can buy, as long as the right amount of money was put on offer.

"Well Mr. De-Mundo's not so stupid, the Vice Commanders secretary, I mean the contact at the Pentagon; he'll do a similar thing and set off a string of explosions to destroy the Pentagon, and the White House. But when the signals that started the devastation are finally traced, well, they will just blame each other."

She realised that the madman's harebrained scheme was so bizarre that it could possibly succeed, as relations between the two countries were already at straining point. This was all due to a threatened oil embargo by the United Arab oil States.

April questioned, "When is this master plan supposed to be implemented then?"

"Next week, it's when your Parliament opens. That's why we're waiting here, so that we'll not seem to be implicated," the man finished, as a shot rang out and sent his body crashing to the floor.

Unable to help him in his dying moments, April could only beg unsuccessfully to Carlos for clemency for the man. The man himself also pleaded with Carlos for mercy before being shot through the back of his head.

"It's right what they say about you, you are the biggest bastard on God's green planet," April yelled at him, as one of his men kicked her full in the face.

"Show Mr. De-Mundo some respect, you fucking cow."

"Don't do it like that, do it like this," Carlos suggested to him, as he kicked her in the stomach then in the head, sending her head sharply back and momentarily stunning her. Their evil laughter continued too ring in her ears as she was being hoisted half-conscious back onto the lifting gear, with punch's raining mercilessly into her body and face.

"She makes a good punch bag, doesn't she?" April heard someone saying, before slipping back into a state of semi consciousness.

As blood ran from April's mouth and nose her eyes opened, only to see the menacing grin of one of Carlos' brainless men.

"Boss, she's waking up again," he grinned. April could see Carlos was talking on his phone. "She's a tough little cookie. Isn't she Boss?"

"Be patient. I've told you I'm on the phone," he snapped, swinging a wild kick towards the man and narrowly missed him.

After he'd finished he assured April, "You'll die eventually. But hey, what's the hurry. Didn't I tell you that you'd pay your debt to me in full one day? But while we're waiting for my men to arrive," he delivered a left and right swinging punch into April's face, knocking her head one way then the other. Carlos then remarked, "And still you refuse to scream out."

The silence was frustrating him, but it was more due to being unable to speak rather than out of a brave sense of stubbornness. The constant punching to her face and throat was taking its toll now, and her swollen damaged mouth and face were now covered in blood, making it impossible for her to speak, and increasingly difficult for April to breath or see.

The sick laughter of them were still ringing in her ears as she felt the bullwhip lash at her abdomen, and the tail of the whip wrapping round her body. April was barely able to open her swollen eyes, but she could just see Carlos snatching at the whip as it sent her body spinning like a whipping top, whipping at her wildly as she spun round.

After she'd again regained full consciousness, April found herself suspended upside down by the rope tethering her feet, causing the blood to rush to her head. They had also placed a sack over April's head that had been soaked in urine.

Spinning her as they lashed and punched at April, they continuously derided her. Suddenly they were disturbed by the sound of approaching vehicles interrupting their sick games. She now was becoming deranged and confused, due to the urine soaked sack over her head.

"The troops have arrived, so let's proceed without the interference of this fucking bitch," Carlos could be heard saying.

"Shall we finish her off, boss?" somebody asked him.

"No. She's barely alive now, so let her suffer while she dies slowly. But this will help her," he said as she felt a sharp blade slashing open her stomach as he tore the bag from her head.

The sound of helicopter rotors awakened her as they passed overhead, while April forced open her swollen eyes. She looked round in vain for any signs of life.

After attempting to free herself from the hoist, she found that she was too exhausted and needed to rest a while. A few minutes passed before April had regained sufficient of her senses and became aware that time was definitely not on her side. Her life was slowly passing away with every drop of blood that was dripping from her half naked and mutilated body. Concentrating all of her senses and strength, April made one last ditch attempt to push with her hands against the floor whilst straightening her body into a full handstand to allow her to use her legs to flick the rope off the hook. It worked, as she went crashing heavily onto the blood splattered concrete floor of the derelict building, sending an empty oil drum rolling into the deserted back street as she landed against a decaying corpse.

Winded, April lay motionless trying to catch her breath again, using the time to assess the gory area for any tools that could help her to free herself. Rolling and crawling alternatively, eventually she reached one of the dead bodies.

Trying not to inhale the stench from the rotting corpses, April searched without success for a mobile phone. Taking a large knife from his belt she used her weight on the hilt to pin it against the floor, thus allowing April to rub the rope up and down the blade, until eventually freeing her hands. Releasing her feet she was at last able to sit up and allow her circulation to slowly return.

"What's that ticking?" April wondered to herself, as she looked for the source of the noise. "Good, it's not a ticking bomb but a dripping tap." She muttered, laboriously climbing to her feet and slowly moving towards it. Tripping and falling through sheer weakness, April doggedly made her way onward towards the life-saving water.

Eventually reaching the water she removed what was left of the torn blouse, and with the help of the knife she'd taken off a dead corpse, she tore it into separate pieces. Using one of the pieces to wash the congealing blood from across her stomach, she then made a compress for her stomach wound, binding it tightly with another shred of her torn clothing. Cupping her hands and filling them with water, April sipped small amounts of water into her injured bloody mouth, cooling the inflammation, so slowly the movement could return to her jaw. Bathing the remaining wounds she was able to reach, she washed away all the dried blood, but found that she'd insufficient material with which to dress all of her countless injuries. So she pressed a cold compress against her swollen eyes to try to reduce the swelling, so her blurred vision could gradually start to return.

After sipping some more water, April sat back and closed her eyes, leaning against a convenient wall. Very gradually the feelings started returning to her entire body, as the blood again flowed unrestrictedly through her arteries and veins, bringing back movement and feelings too all of her extremities.

As she closed her eyes she tried to put the events of recent days into their right prospective. But she was disturbed by the sense that there was another live presence in this building.

Keeping her eyes closed April listened intensely, trying to identify the cause of the ominous feeling. She braced herself ready to defend against any attack, while still feigned to be unconscious. After a few moments she decided to open her eyes quickly, startling two young children that were standing in the doorway, as they jumped back into the shadows abruptly out of fear.

"Don't be frightened. Do either of you understand English?" April managed to ask.

The two children, a fourteen-year-old boy, and a much younger girl, both nodded in unison.

"Yes, we both do," the boy eventually answered.

"You don't have to be afraid of me. Now my name is, April. Do you live far from here?"

"We live just down there," the little girl volunteered. "Why did those men do this to you?"

"Because they are just very bad and evil men, that's why. Now will you go and fetch your mummy or daddy for me, as quickly as you can please?"

Waiting patiently for what seemed like an eternity to pass, the children finally returned with their parents.

"Are you all right? Who did this terrible thing to you? And why did they? Do you want us to call the police for you?" The young Colombian lady questioned, as she raced to April's side.

"This was all done by your number one drugs lord," April started to explain.

The man interrupted, "Carlos De-Mundo. I might have known?"

"Do you know him then?"

"Everybody round here knows of that evil man, he's killed at least one person from each of our families one way or another," explained the man angrily, as his wife gently sponged the wounds on April's back that she couldn't reach.

She asked hopefully, "Can you bandage my wounds and let me borrow some clean clothes?"

"Firstly you need a Doctor to stitch up your wounds before you bleed to death. My son will fetch one while we try to help you to our home," the lady said with genuine concern. "Then I'll be pleased to lend you some clothing. Now my name's Gloria, and my husband here's called David. And you are?"

"April, April Darling, I'll arrange for you to be paid for helping me, but first I must find a mobile phone to call my boss." April told her as she searched in vain for a working mobile phone, until she eventually found one on a corpse, Saying to herself while keying in Charles's number, "Just my luck, the batteries are nearly dead, but it'll have to do for now,"

After a few agonising moments, she heard Mandy's voice answering, "Hello. Can I help you at all?"

"Hello sweetheart, it's me. Can you put Charles on the phone quickly, my batteries are nearly gone?"

"He won't be a second he's in the bathroom. But more importantly, how are you? We've all been worrying about you here. We thought you were de—."

"I'm okay I've just been too busy to call you. I should be home soon now, so don't you worry about me." April tried to reassure her as Charles took the phone from Mandy.

"April, are you okay?"

"No, but as far as Mandy and the children are concerned I am. Now just listen, the batteries are nearly dead. Firstly, track this phone to pinpoint my whereabouts, and secondly, there's a family here saving my life as we speak, so make sure that you take care of them. Their names are, Gloria and David, they have sent their son to get some medical help for me. I'm waiting for the doctor to come and stitch me up and clean and dress my many wounds before I bleed to death."

"Where are you hurt, April?"

"Where aren't I hurt would be more to the point. Carlos and his goons have bullwhipped, punched and kicked me all over, and then they sliced my stomach open. I've lost a lot of blood. Carlos and about fifty of his goons have left here about two hours ago I think, so can you and your team of experts find him, and PRONTO?"

"We'll get right on with it. Now about you, how can we contact you?"

"The Doctor's just arrived, so I'll put Gloria on to tell you how to contact her."

Gloria was furnishing Charles with the information he needed, as the Doctor started to address April's injuries. "Somebody certainly wanted you to tell them something the way that they've tortured you," he remarked, as he examined her. "They must have needed to know something pretty damn important."

"No, they were just pure evil sadistic bastards that enjoy inflicting pain on people."

"Well I'll need to move you to a hospital because you need so many stitches, and you also could need a blood transfusion because you've lost so much blood. You know, you're very lucky to still be alive," the ageing Doctor observed sadly.

"Well Doctor, what shall I call you by the way?"

"Call me, Joe. That's what everybody else does; it's much easier than trying to pronounce my birth name."

"I'm April, April Darling. Well Joe, you'll have to do the best you can, I don't have the luxury of time to attend the hospital right now. I urgently need to get this bastard before he inflicts damage on other innocent people."

"I'm afraid he must wait: whoever he is. Does he live in Colombia?" Joe asked, as he asked David to assist him in moving April into the clean fresh air, and away from the stench of death and rotting corpses.

Wincing with pain as she was hauled to her feet, they then acted as human crutches, supporting her on either side.

"Oh yes, he's the number one on the all-time bastards list," April started, as the doctor finished with.

"CARLOS DE-MUNDO. I might have known it was him. You'll need a lot of help to catch him, or better still to kill him. But first we have to get you well, April."

April again writhed with the pain as they struggled to take her outside. "Sorry, but we're being as gentle as we can be. Was that your superior you were talking to just then?" the doctor asked her, as they passed through the door and into the clean air of the early evening.

"Yes, I've said that I'll give him an update after you've finished, providing that there's enough life in the bloody battery, that is."

"I've sorted that out for you, April. As it's the same charger connection as I have, I've sent my son to put your phone on charge for you," interrupted Gloria.

"Thank you. You're all ever so kind. It was very fortuitous having the same connections though. Isn't it?"

The Doctor interrupted. "We really should get you to a hospital, but as you've refused to go the next best thing has to be my home. I haven't brought enough medical supplies to treat this many wounds out here, so if you let me speak to your superior I'll explain the extent of your injuries to him. Now what's his number and I'll use my phone?"

"Okay, give me your phone it'll be quicker if I dial." April hastily keying in Charles's number, then when he answered she gave him the doctors' number. "So call back on that number now, the doctor wants to speak to you," she insisted as she fainted.

When she woke April found herself in a large double bed. She glanced round the room that was lined with bookshelves crammed wall to wall with medical books, and various types of classical literature.

Attempting to get up, she threw over the covers to find that she was completely naked. Desperately she looked for some clothes, but the search was without any success. The turning of the door handle interrupted as she quickly returned to the bed, covering up just in time as the door swung widely open, and the doctor entered.

"Ah, I thought I heard you moving about April, I've brought you a drink of coffee."

"Where are my clothes, doc?"

"Gloria is fetching you some of hers, she said that you asked her to lone you some. Sir Charles Hythe-Smith has asked me to make some decisions, like whether you are capable of fulfilling your duties at present, or when you'll be fit enough to resume them, etcetera," Joe explained to her. "I hope you don't mind, but I took his number from your phones address book."

"No, I don't mind, Joe. Did Charles stress to you how imperative it was for me to mobilise myself immediately, because I must go after De-Mundo post-haste. Now, how soon can I have some clothing?"

"All in good time, April, as I've said, you do need to be strong enough to pursue vermin like that. So just try to relax while I check your blood count, pulse, and all that usual stuff." Joe said kindly, as he held her wrist to take her pulse.

Keeping silent while the doctor made his checks, then April held the bedclothes to cover her modesty as she sat up. "Right doc, will you pass me that coffee, I'm spitting feathers here," she said to him, trying to sound chirpy as he passed her the drink. "Well Doctor, you can tell me the truth. Now, how long have I got left?"

"Pardon," the puzzled doctor asked. "You know, to live that is?" joked April.

"Oh, I see," he smiled. "I just can't understand it, after seeing you so close too deaths door not twelve hours ago, and now all of your vital signs are nearly back to normal again. God knows, I laughed at Sir Charles when he said how remarkable your powers of recovery were, but I've never seen anybody recover so quickly before in my life. The physical signs will take a little longer to heal of course, but I've used soluble sutures on your wounds so that you'll not need to have them removed. Now, Sir Charles wants to speak to you as soon as you're well enough, so use the extension the other side of the bed," Joe explained, indicating towards the telephone on the bedside table.

Lying resting and sipping her coffee, Gloria opened the door, "Are you decent April?" she called in.

"Of course I'm not. Anyway, I don't have anything you haven't got, have I?"

As Gloria entered carrying a small suitcase, she greeted her with, "My April, don't you look well now. David sends his best wishes but he had to go to work. Now I've brought you an assortment of clothing for you to choose from, so I hope that they'll be to your liking."

"I'm sure they will be. Would you be kind enough to help me dress, I am still very, very sore? But don't tell Joe that, will you?" she asked, as Gloria agreed.

Helping April into the loose fitting clothes, she explained, "I didn't think you'd want anything that was too tight fitting April, except for underclothing of course."

"You've got that one right, Gloria. My body feels like it's covered from head to toe in pain, but these clothes are very soft and loose, so thank you." she said gratefully, kissing her on the cheek. Then she added reluctantly, "Now I suppose I must ring Charles," as she picked up the phone and dialled his number.

"Charles, tell me you haven't lost, De-Mundo again?" she began. "We need to eradicate that venomous slime ball this time, ONCE AND FOR ALL."

"No my dear, we know exactly where he is. He hasn't moved too far because he thinks that you're dead. He's on a plantation south of where you are now; I'll hazard a guess that it's one that he owns. So don't you fret about it, just you rest and recuperate? We have dispatched a body of elite troops as re-enforcement's, just to ensure that we do get Carlos De-Mundo. Oh, and by the way April, Sergeant Maloney will be part of the task force."

"Good, Charles. I was wondering if he made it or not. But I'll rest much easier when we've put an end to this Carlos De-Mundo threat though. We've got him cornered now, so we need to put an end to all of his unearthly plans.

So let's go finish him now, before he can use his money to form himself another private army."

"Not so fast April, we need to be absolutely sure this time, so let us step back and review and re-plan the situation. Now as I've said, firstly we'll get the task force in position to support you before doing anything. So you use the time left to relax and recharge your batteries, and I'll check, and double-check every minute detail. And then, and only then, will I get back to you. Just remember, April, Carlos De-Mundo thinks that he's killed you, and that might be his Achilles' heel. Now I'll speak to you later love," Charles told her as he rang off.

Whiling away the next couple of days enjoying the warm South American sunshine, mixed with the blend of friendliness of the naturally geniality of the local people. April pleasured herself sauntering through the wild and untamed countryside, enthralled by the sights of wild parrots, and the large variety of bird types soaring freely overhead. Stray dogs followed as she dropped morsels of food for them, wagging their tails with the pleasure of knowing that somebody had actually bothered to notice them.

The humid evenings were spent in the pleasant company of the doctor, and Gloria and her family They chatted generally, but enthusiastically, telling April all about the natural flora and fauna in that area.

"You seem to have a keen interest in our wildlife, April," the doctor observed.

"I love animals, particularly parrots and dogs. But I like all animals."

"Well you are witnessing a rapidly diminishing pleasure then, because the greedy developers see our beautiful landscape differently than we do. The only thing that this all represents to them is financial gain, they seem to have no interest at all in God's wonderful creation," explained David. "But Gloria and I pray that it will all change again one day, so that our grandchildren and their grandchildren after them, will be able to enjoy the natural beauty that God has created freely for us all to enjoy, and for all our future descendants too."

"Amen to that," confirmed the doctor, who up until now had listened silently to David's concerns. "Money is so insignificant compared to the glory that God has given freely to us. Here the manifestation couldn't give us a clearer picture, that we are destroying our own natural environment."

April offered, "Well, when this is all over I'm hoping to have some time to myself, I would certainly love to try to help you in some way?"

"In what way could you help?" Gloria asked, enthusiastically. "Do you have any influential contacts at all?"

"Well although I'm supposed to be a nonentity really, no past, no present, and a very uncertain future. There are no records of my existence anywhere, officially that is. And yet every government agency, agent, and low life criminal, recognises me on sight. So yes, I can open doors, and whisper into the most influential ears for you."

"Oh good," Gloria screamed excitedly, "you're the answer to all of our prayers and dreams. There's a mini summit planned for tomorrow, it will be in Florida and the American government is our strongest opposition."

"I'll speak to Charles I believe the American President feels some affection towards me. He keeps asking our P.M. to introduce me to him. When this is all over I will plead your, no, our case with him."

"Thank you, you are what we have been praying for, darling," said an ecstatic Gloria, as she hugged April who cringed with pain. "I'm sorry, I'm so sorry, I forgot about your injuries," Gloria apologised profusely.

"Don't give it another thought, it's only a little bit tender now," April lied, whilst trying to hide the true pain. She promised, "Now you just leave it with me and I'll see what I can do for you."

As the days passed, Gloria and David visited at every conceivable opportune moment. Enthusiastically, they shared with April their dreams and visions for a green and more pleasant future. The doctor continually remarked on April's remarkable powers of healing, as the wounds healed rapidly, leaving only temporary superficial scaring. Then eventually the ringing of the phone interrupted April's private Nirvana.

"Yes, Charles. I knew you'd eventually be the proverbial bad penny that would burst my bubble of bliss."

"What do you mean, April?" a perplexed Charles asked.

"Like the proverbial bad penny, I knew that you'd eventually turn up," she explained with a chuckled.

"Oh how slow of me. But you do have such a sharp and fast wit at times. Perhaps you've missed your true vocation, April. Anyway, the reason I'm ringing is that our planning has now been finalised, so it is now time to exact some retribution. A detachment of troops is en-route to you as we speak, and they have been instructed to follow your orders to the letter. As you know, Sergeant Brad Maloney is leading the task force."

"He is okay, isn't he, and he didn't get injured?" April interrupted anxiously.

"He's fine. But he regrets not staying to defend you."

"That would have been suicidal for him. I tried to explain to him that it was me De-Mundo wanted. Now, I hope that will be the ace up my sleeve." A puzzled Charles asked, "How do you mean?"

"Well when he finds out that I'm still alive and I'm leading a task force to eradicate him. To put it bluntly Charles, he'll literally shit himself."

"Very ladylike," he laughed.

"Well you know my past, so you must know THAT, that's not very ladylike either. You have seen too that. Now to change the subject, when will the troops arrive? And more importantly, when do we finally move in on De-Mundo?"

"They should meet up with you about noon tomorrow. Taking into account the terrain to and around Carlos De-Mundo's plantation, it will be the following evening before you reach there. Is there anything else that you think you might need, April?"

"What type of building is he holed up in? Do we at least know that?"

"Yes, apparently it's an old bungalow type manor house that's fallen into disrepair. Why do you ask?"

"Firstly, Charles, is there any chance you can prepare and deliver me a fully armed and combat ready, stealth helicopter?"

"Well yes. I think we can. The USS Free America is standing off shore to evacuate you if necessary. I'm sure they could accommodate you. What do you have in mind?"

"Oh, it's just that the stealth mode would keep my arrival a secret until the last moment, if it was necessary."

"I see April, but exactly what are you planning to do then?"

"I just thought maybe I should drop in on him. Just for old time sake. Will you make the arrangements and get back to me?"

"I must say, April, I don't like the sound of that at all."

"Well then the less you know, the less you'll need to worry about it. Okay Charles. So if you just let me know when you've made the arrangements for the helicopter."

April lazed round for the remainder of the day, as the doctor dressed and redressed her wounds. He thoroughly checked that there were no signs of any delayed infection developing.

After wishing Gloria and David a tearful farewell, April pledged that she'd return, and help them in their endeavours to make the superpowers listen to their concerns.

"Well don't you do anything silly like getting yourself killed then, will you?" David said as he hugged her.

"Don't you worry about me David, I've got the man upstairs to watch over me, and I know he won't ever leave me," she assured him. Then turning to Gloria, she said between sobs, "And as for you, take very good care of yourself and you're wonderful family until I return."

Sitting on the porch in the warmth of the evening, the ageing doctor and April exchanged pleasantries over drinks. April, was becoming slightly inebriated as she started to reminisce about her beloved children.

"You have children, April!" The doctor said with surprise. "I wouldn't have thought you were ever married."

"I'm not anymore, my bloody boss put an end to all of that," was April's forlorn reply.

"Oh! I'm sorry. Where are the children now, with your ex?"

"They're with Mandy, my wi-." April suddenly stopped, realising that the alcohol had gone to her head and made her drop her guard.

"I hope you don't mind my saying so, April, but you were about to say wife. Are you, how shall I put it, attracted to your own sex? If you were, then that would be entirely your own business."

Realising that she'd gotten herself into a tight spot that was purely of her own making, April thought about what she should do. Eventually, she decided to take Joe into her confidence. She thought, after all that's the least she could do to repay his kindness and hospitality.

"What I am about to tell you is highly confidential, top secret and all that. But I know as a doctor you won't repeat it to anybody else. Normally I wouldn't tell you, or tell anybody for that matter. But as the saying goes, I've started so I'll finish." April explained as she began to sober up.

"You know I'm bound by the Hippocratic Oath, April, and anything that you do tell me I'll treat in the strictest of confidence. But as you've now sobered up somewhat, then you needn't tell me anything if you don't wish to."

"Well once upon a time, long, long ago, our story started somewhere in the south Lancashire. They're, there lived a happily married man, his beautiful young wife, and they had two adorable children, a boy, and a girl. One day the men from bad Uncle Charles' secret society invaded their peaceful little haven, and turning their private little Utopia into a living hell. The man was changed beyond all recognition, and he was to set out on a quest that was to turn out to be a fruitless undertaking. But the desire to return to the life that he once knew was all that was left to impel him on relentlessly."

"Do I sense a hint of bitterness for some reason, April?"

"I'm glad you find it so funny, Joe. But would you if you were the victim?"

The doctor face suddenly became serious, "Do you mean," he started pointing at her, "Do you mean that you are the wife in your little story?"

"Close Joe, but no cigar. Try again?" she invited. "Well are you the daughter gown up then?"

"Nope, and I'm not the son either," she pre-empted him. "Then what's the point of your little story then?" he asked.

April pointed out, "Well you've deliberately left one piece of the puzzle out doc, haven't you?"

"You mean, you're not, I mean, you mean you where the husband?" he struggled to say, to which April nodded apathetically. "But I've seen you undressed, and you are every inch a woman," he became more and more intrigued by the story.

"As they used to say in the six million dollar man, they have the technology and so can rebuild him, or her, or whatever they are." the alcohol started to retake its hold on her.

"Well you certainly have my attention now, April, I'm so intrigued. So tell me as much as you're allowed to tell me."

"Well if you are sitting comfortable, Joe, I'll begin. But first I must have a top up," she said as she poured herself another tumbler of scotch. "Well one day in what seems to be a century ago, somewhere in a sleepy little hamlet up in Lancashire, I was happily married to a lovely lady, and the happy father of two young children. On one crazy evening there was a party at the local village pub, so, as a family we decided unwisely to join in the spirit of things at the evening's fancy dress. Unaware as we were of the presence of stranger and his dastardly intentions, that just happened to be passing through our village at that precise moment in time. If it had been a week earlier, or a week later, then I'd still be a happily married man. So anyway, unaware of this, we thought we'd throw caution to the wind and enjoyed the evening's festivities to the full."

She poured herself another drink as she continued to become drunker. "Unbeknown to me and my unsuspecting family, the man was maintaining a constant live video link directly to bad Uncle Charles's office. To allow bad Uncle Charles, and his handpicked motley crew to pass their judgment as to my, or should I say the head of the family at that times, suitability to be coerced, transformed, and totally fucked up."

"Do you mean that they forced you into becoming a transsexual?" the interested Joe asked, as he became more concerned, but at the same time totally enthralled by the mysteriously true story.

"Although I may use many descriptions of how the saga unfolded, coerced is by far too nice a word for their devilish deeds. My close friends and then next door neighbours, was suddenly given no option but to move away. It was supposed to be with a promotion and financial inducement to do so, or they could have stayed and become unemployable. Then I find that he and his wife were to die in a horrific fireball. So when I attended his funeral, accompanied by the local Mr. Plod, he drugged me on the return journey. He then delivered me to a very top-secret underground hospital, it was somewhere in the Cotswolds. After the preparations and surgery, most of which consisted of transplanting female organs rather than adapting them, I was subjected to a uniquely new intense course of personality transfer while still heavily sedated. However, the clever bastards hadn't reckoned on my being a very strong willed northerner, and born under the sign of the bull, so when I finally awoke from my drug induced slumber, guess what? The personality transfer had failed. So you see, Joe, why I've been searching for a medical team to return me to what I think of as normality, back to being good old boring, George." she sighed mournfully.

The doctor had listened with interest and intrigue to April's rancorous description of events. He then searched deep within himself for some words of comfort that he could offer. So after much soul searching, he finally admitted, "You have every right to feel the profound anger that wells deep within you, April. But I must add that in spite of all your injuries, you are every inch a very beautiful and extremely classy lady. I've examined you thoroughly, only because your injuries were so extensive, and I must say that you seem to be without any question, a woman in every possible sense."

"I've heard that answer before, Joe. In fact, every time I told a doctor about my past life. I sometime wonder if I'll ever find a surgeon willing, or capable, of performing a successful reversal operation," reflected April in a sad pathetic voice.

Joe interrupted, "I must say that I come from the old school of medicine, and so I have no specialties. What I do have is a good sound all round medical knowledge, one that covers across the whole spectrum of medicine, but without a specialty. That's why I must urge you, both as your doctor, and I hope now your good friend, to tread carefully, very carefully. To have undergone such a skilful operation as you have, which included transplants and neurological surgery I believe, combine this with specially designed psychological gender enhancement and memory transferring techniques. They have all combined in making you into the perfect lady that you've now become. As well as it being such a criminal waste, God knows there is little enough beauty in this evil twisted world of ours that it could afford to lose such a vision of beauty as the one that is facing me now. Also, there's an even bigger problem that you should be concerned with."

"And what's that?"

"The danger to you and your sanity," he urged, "there's a high level of risk to your life. Let me explain to you in the simplest of layman's terms. For your body to have suffered the trauma and stress involved in such an operation was very difficult indeed, I bet it was shear hell going through the initial adjustment period?"

"That must be the world's biggest understatement, and it was all because it wasn't my choice in the first place. Or a growing gnawing feeling I had, that I was a freak of nature as a man, and that I ought to have been born a woman. I was totally unprepared to wake up with tits," she told him crudely, as her words started to slur.

"Your breasts grew that quickly, or we're they implanted?"

"Neither, they were transplants that were grafted onto me. I'll explain as best I can understand it myself. Apparently a beautiful young lady died in tragic circumstances, but her will stated that she wished to donate her body to medical science. That was where bad Uncle Charles and Co where able to implement their dastardly plan, one that had been ten, fifteen, who knows how many years in the planning. Don't ask me if they had any part in the ladies death, because that's something we can only speculate about. However, to continue with this travesty, they transplanted all of her sexual organs, womb, ovaries, fallopian tubes, clitoris, etcetera, I have even started to menstruate. Then they grafted onto me the woman's breasts, they even removed my lower ribs to slim down my waistline. They removed from me anything that could give the slightest of hints of what, or who, I once was, and replaced it with body parts from our unfortunate victim. All apparently except for my brain, which I believe is still very much male dominant."

"Well, April. I am aghast. I've never known of such transplants being as successful as yours seem to have been. Singularly, let alone in totally.

They're has never been even a rumour in the medical journals, or even in the corridors of the medical conferences that I've attended in the past. But that does explain your rancour towards your employer, and your quest to return to your former self of course. As I've stressed before I knew all that you've just told me, swapping genders itself isn't the problem, but being forced into it, is. And with such an extensive operation, well, it's in itself hard to undo. But the real danger is to you, both mentally and physically. It could be disastrous, and the worst scenario is that it could prove to be fatal. You see, it would not only test your mental and physical strengths again, but would have far more reaching effects too. It could affect your skin structure, causing it to lose its elasticity, and it could even make it transparent as it accelerates your ageing process. Giving you back genitals would probably just make you impotent, so with everything else you would probably lose your sanity."

"But Joe, often transsexuals have been known to go through a reversal?"

"Yes, but they've only had what I would call superficial surgery, just enough to perform as a woman, or a man. But they have not had what you've been forced to undergo. As you've already said, you can possibly conceive and give birth." Then the doctor stressed as he sat forwards and cupped her hands in his, "I can't instil in you enough the dangers in your pursuing this fruitless goal my dear. Perhaps if you were to try to except it and relax a bit, you might even start to enjoy your new persona."

April bent forward and kissed the doctor on the forehead. "And what did I do to earn such a high reward?"

"You are a wily old fox on the quiet, aren't you? You have been the first doctor that I've been able to confide in with confidence, knowing that they're not contaminated, controlled, call it what you like, by bad Uncle Charles. So yes, I will try to follow your invaluable advice."

"Good girl, April. And who knows, given time you might even learn to forgive your transgressors, especially, Sir Charles?"

"He, Joe, the slimy toad, will take a lot longer. He led me to believe that we had a future together, and even that we'd marry and start a family together one-day. THEN the bastard renegade."

"I presume he took advantage of you to have his wicked way, as men are prone to doing I might add. Well bring the woman out in you and mark it down to experience."

"I know I was naive, and I could accept that. But that's not quite all that there is to this little saga. The slimy old bullfrog has also been bedding my wife, well my ex-wife, AND NOW I learn that THEY are to be married instead of me and him, and that Mandy and my children are to become his, so to speak."

"How ironic a twist in the tail, still, at least you have the peace of mind of knowing that they're to be well looked after. Let's face it, April, you can see them whenever you so desire I presume."

"Well yes, but it sticks in my claw to know that he has engineered all of this, and now he's reaping such high rewards." April gave a little chuckle to herself as she added. "I suppose it is funny, looking at it as an outsider."

"That's my girl, don't you let them bastard grind you down," Joe said as he glanced at his watch. "We've talked the whole night through, its four thirty. You'd better get what sleep you can too prepare you for tomorrow, April."

"Yes, and thank you so very much, Joe. As the saying goes, tomorrow is the first day of the rest of my life. So I bid you good night my dear and wise old friend," she teetered off unsteadily towards the bedroom.

CHAPTER 32

Despite retiring to her bed during the early hours of the previous evening, April rose at six thirty as was usual time. Hurriedly, she scribbling a note to explain to Joe where she had gone, then she set out on a ten-mile run to confirm her fitness. After completing the run, although she was feeling more fatigued than usual, she felt content in the knowledge that she'd healed sufficiently to fulfil the exercise.

"Good morning, April. You woke early. Couldn't you sleep?" he asked kindly, as he started to prepare the breakfast.

"No, I just thought I'd better see exactly how fit I was before leaving here today."

"Well breakfast will be about fifteen minutes if you intend to shower first," he suggested, passing over a cup of coffee.

"Yes, I must shower, I can't sit at the table smelling like this, now can I?" April laughed, as she took the coffee with her into the shower room.

"Don't underestimate yourself, April. You're a breath of fresh air to me. I'll miss you after you've gone. You will come back to see me soon, won't you? You weren't just saying that you would?"

April shouted over the noise of the running water, "No, Joe. I will come back I promise."

Joe smiled to himself at this answer as he'd grown quite fond of April and enjoyed her company immensely, and spending the pleasant evenings chatting with her. He was beginning to look on April as the daughter that he'd never had.

Walking from the shower brushing her long flowing hair, April told him, "You know Joe, you've not only been my most excellent physician, but you have become like a father figure to me here. So for that I thank you," she kissed him on the cheek before sitting at the table. "So how could I not come back here to visit you?"

"And you have become like the long lost daughter that I've never had, and for that you have made this, what was it you called me? Ah yes, this wily old fox very happy," he smiled smugly as he served breakfast.

After they'd eaten April dried the dishes as Joe washed them, while they chatted, laughed, and joked, about her gender dilemma.

"You don't appear to be so angry about it all now, April?"

"No, not since our little chat last night, I'm going to take your most invaluable advice and accept things as they are now, not as they were. And do you know what Joe, I feel really good about myself for the first time since this all happened."

The ringing of her mobile interrupted, "And a very good morning to you, Charles. How do we find you on this fine and beautiful morning?"

"Good morning, April. You sound very chirpy this morning. What's brought all this about?"

"Joe. He has helped me to see things in a different perspective, so for the first time since you fu, messed me up, I feel good about myself again. So I hope you'll reward him for his very timely intervention." Then she asked, Charles, "Now how are we progressing with our Colombian headache?"

"Do you realise that you even stopped yourself from swearing that time, and that's much more ladylike so keep up the good work. Now unfortunately it's fast approaching the time when you must resume business, so how are you feeling now?"

"Thanks to, Joe, I'm feeling very well. I'm still a little sore, but other than that surprisingly well and happy with my lot."

"Good, April, because you had us all very worried here for quite some time."

"It had me very worried too, Charles. Now when can I expect Sergeant Maloney to manifest himself?"

"He should be with you within the next two to three hours, and he's fetching you a camouflage suit and some body armour. Now De-Mundo's holed up on his ranch and training camp, as I've told you. It's not easily accessible though, so you'll need to get your head together with Sergeant Maloney and work out your best strategy. He has a map of the terrain, so until he arrives I suggest that you use the remaining time to just relax. Now could I speak with the good doctor please, I would like to thank him personally for all that he's done for you?" asked Charles politely, as she handed Joe the phone.

After a short conversation the doctor thanked, Charles. Then he handed her back the phone and explained that Charles would ring her later.

"Good, now how about you and I taking a stroll together, Joe, so I can walk off that wonderful breakfast I've just eaten?"

"Now that's an offer that I can't refuse, a chance to further enjoy your delightful company," he willingly accepted.

As they ambled arm in arm through what's left of the very pleasant, but mostly untamed countryside, which was round the vicinity of Joe's home, April chatted incessantly about the abundance of fauna, and of the natural beauty of nature when it's allowed to develop as God had intended it too. All too soon they were walking back up the garden path, and towards Joe's door.

It's so lovely to enjoy your company without interruptions," he remarked. "It will all seem so lonely after you've gone."

"I've promised you that I'll return. Haven't I? Anyway, you will have your work here till then, which come to think of it must be mounting up quite a lot because of me." She reminded him, trying to bring him some words of comfort.

"No. It's not, I'm semi-retired so I have little to do except my voluntary work at the hospital. Charles say's the British government will donate a large sum of money to a good cause that I name because I won't take any payment off them personally. I think I should suggest that they replant many trees and try to replace some of the rain forest. Ah it sounds as though your friends are coming," he said, as the sound of vehicles grew ever louder, intruded on their intimacy.

"Yes, I can hear them," sighed April. "The tranquillity is about to be rudely interrupted. Oh, will you say goodbye to Gloria, David and the children for me?"

"They said that they'd be here to see you off, so if you all have some lunch with me maybe they'll get here before you leave." Joe suggested, as a convoy of vehicles drew to a halt outside the garden gate.

"April, you're looking exceptionally well," Bass greeted her, as he kissed her on the cheek.

"It's all thanks to Joe here, otherwise you would have been seeing me in a wooden suit," jested April as she introduced them. "Joe, this is Sergeant Bass Maloney. Bass, this is Doctor Joe, who's my very own personal physician, and my very special friend."

The two men shook hands warmly as Joe suggested that they all ate lunch together before proceeding on the mission.

"A nice idea, Joe, but as you can see, I have ten men with me. But I wasn't planning to move on until it became dusk," Bass explained.

"That's not a problem, we can all have a picnic styled lunch on the lawn here while you all relax and recharge your batteries. Ah good, here comes Gloria and David," the doctor finished, as he went towards the kitchen to begin to prepare the food, with Gloria and David volunteering to help him. This left Bass free to discuss a plan of action with April, in readiness for the forthcoming very dangerous assignment.

After organising his troops so that they could also relax, Bass gently cupped April's small hands in his large and callused ones. He asked affectionately, "How are you really feeling? And tell me the truth now."

"I'm feeling fine now thanks to Joe."

"You know your body cannot keep taking such violent punishment as this. Anybody would think that you had a death wish, OR IS THAT THE BIG IDEA? Only Sir Charles Hythe-Smith has expressed deep concern about your recklessness too, and I for one must say that he's got a very good point."

April went quiet as she thought deeply, 'If I'm to try to accept who I am and start over again, then I can't keep referring to my past as an excuse. So I must now move on as I am, that's until I manage to find a way to become again what I once was.' April relaxed back before asking him tentatively, "What exactly have you been told about me, Bass?"

"Well not a great deal really. You are still a bit of an enigma to me. Field Marshal Sir Charles Hythe-Smith," he started.

April interrupted, "Just call him Charles while he's not listening. Field Marshal Sir Charles Hythe-Smith is such a mouthful. It's practically a full sentence all of its own, so we'll be here all day at that rate."

"You are so right," he chuckled, "you lose your breath just giving him his full title. Now all I've been able to ascertain about you is that you're a highly trained field operative. Apparently, you're the finest that there is and that you're to be given overall control at all times. The rest I can work out for myself, I think," he commented, as he undressed her with his eyes.

"Oh, like what?" she teased.

Bass blushed when he realised what he'd started, then he continued coyly. "Well you are a very beautiful, and an extremely exciting and desirable lady. Any sane man would give his right arm for a date with you, let alone a permanent relationship."

"You don't know me well enough, Bass. Under this soft and gentle exterior beats a swinging slab of concrete."

"No, I can't believe that, you're not as tough as you try to make out. Ah, here comes our picnic now lads." He called to the other men with relief at Gloria's timely intervention, alleviated his awkward embarrassment.

"May we join you?" she asked, as David and Joe sat with her. "Have you concluded your plans yet?"

"No. Well not yet. Bass here was discussing something quite different. Weren't you Bass?" she continued to tease, making him blush profusely again.

"I was just idling away time, Gloria," he explained, as we all started to eat the appetising picnic whilst chattering generally.

With the meal over, April offered to help Gloria to clear away the dishes. Joe interrupted, "No. We'll do that while you two conclude your business."

As he, Gloria and David started towards the house. Bass and April strolled he explained their predicament.

"We are aware of Carlos' whereabouts, but we remain unsure as to the best way of approaching it. He and the dishevelled remains of his men are holed up in an old dilapidated villa at the centre of his estate, which is adjacent to a small village that his employees have erected while working for him. We've formed various plans, but then we've had to dismiss them for fear of the possible heavy rate of civilian casualties. Here let me show you?" he explained as he drew a crude map in the soil. "You can see that if we approach it from the south or east: the villagers would be caught up in the cross fire. The west is far too close to the cliff edge, so that only leaves us with the northern option which would take us across an expanse of open flat grassland, and without any cover whatsoever."

"I see the problem," April agreed. She used her foot to erase the map, explaining to Bass, "We can't be too careful, anybody here could be working for Carlos De-Mundo. Now is there no way at all of approaching the village without being detected?"

"For the most part yes, but the last two hundred meters would be open countryside, and we believe it to be booby trapped, April. We think that the traps will be crude homemade devises, and if so they'll be extremely volatile. The trouble is we don't really know how crude, or how volatile they really are, or whether they exist at all."

"And dropping in at night, is that a viable option?"

"Not really, we are still trying to ascertain whether he's got innocent women and children in his villa to act as a human shield for him again. It's becoming quite a nightmare, knowing how to take Carlos out without some innocent people getting hurt. So if you have any suggestions at all they would be most welcome. I've been told that if there's anybody who can find an answer, then it will be you, April, because you will look at it from an unorthodox angle?"

"The powers that be keep on saying that, but there's only one difference between you and me. While you are highly trained by the rules of the manual, I'm completely untrained. I rely on my wit, quick thinking, and the will to survive against all the odds. Your hands are tied by tried and tested methods. Were as mine, well I always do the unexpected. The best weapon we have is in the fact that Carlos De-Mundo thinks that I'm dead."

"Well how do you think we could use that? And without you getting hurt anymore?" a puzzled Bass Maloney asked.

"I'm not sure yet, I still have his number so perhaps I should give him a ring, but not until we're in position to finish the bas-, him off. I personally think that capturing him is not a tenable option anymore. Remember with his power and wealth he would eventually buy his freedom, or some do goodies will always plead his case out of some misguided idea of fair play. No, this time we must go for his jugular as they say, and exterminate the rat permanently. But I'll need to give it some careful thought so we can minimise the risk to the innocent villagers."

"Ah, you're back," David greeted, "Gloria and Joe are preparing some cool refreshment for you. Have you now concluded your business?"

"Sort of, but until we're on site as it were, we can't finalise any plans," she told them as Gloria started to pass round some cool drinks.

After passing the next few hours in idle gossip the light began to fade, signalling it was time for them to start the trek south, and deeper into Columbia, and on until they reached Carlos De-Mundo's estate.

They drove overland under the guise of a medical team, to try to avoid drawing unnecessary suspicion to the convoy. Keeping off the main highways the journey was laborious on the almost non-existent tracks. Despite this, they made excellent progress, and arrived at their destination later the following afternoon, and ahead of schedule. Stopping at a safe distance a temporary camp was soon erected to allow them to rest, while they waited for the cover of darkness to descend. All too soon the time came when they were to break camp, and finally advance on their target.

"We have to cover the last few miles on foot, because on these still nights out here the sound of an engine would carry for miles, and we don't want to announce our imminent arrival too soon. Do we? Even the sound of the snapping of a twig will carry to warn them, if the wind's happened to be from the wrong direction. So tread carefully, won't you? Unfortunately the wind directions south, so it will carry any sounds we make directly towards the house."

"Then I should contact Sir Charles now and ask for a blanket radio silence, Bass."

"A good idea, maybe we should call the other squads and tell them that as well."

While she rang Charles on his secure number, Bass was busy setting up a mini conference ready to make any final plans. "On the south side of his shack is a shear drop to the river Charles, but I'll bet that slimy bastard has some way of escaping via there."

"You can count on that, April, but we're not sure what or how. But whatever it is, it will be well camouflaged. The Yankee navy seals are scaling the face as we speak, so they should be able to spoil any of De-Mundo's little plans. Now is there anything we can do from this end?"

"Yes, Charles. When we start the attack can the stealth choppers start bombarding the cliff-face, so to effectively seal off any back door escape routes that De-Mundo has planned? Providing the American seals will have reached their target by then."

"Okay, but we'll need to set up a code name so that we know when you are in position, or should you feel the need to abort. Maybe we should use, 'the parties on when you're ready, and 'landslide' if we need to abort the mission."

"That'll do nicely Charles. Let's just keep it simple," April agreed. She continued, "The conference has been set up now for the final briefing, it's just buzzed in my ear to let me know that they're ready. Right gentlemen, Sir Charles is joining in with the conference now, he has the code names for our mission," she started. "As we're speaking can we advance steadily on our target? We need to be in position and prepared to strike by daybreak. Now I'll hand over to Sir Charles who will tell you what they have been able to ascertain to date. It's over to you, Sir Charles."

"Thank you, Miss Darling. Gentlemen, if you compose a text saying the shops are closed into the send later folder, when you reach the predetermined positions send me that text. After you have all reached your designated positions I'll text you all, the party's on, then you need to follow Miss Darling's instructions, and to the letter gentlemen. If in the unlikely event we need to abort, the text should read, 'landslide.' If this should happen, and I sincerely hope that it doesn't, you will all head north to the spot marked B on your maps. A fleet of helicopters is standing by there to evacuate you at a moment's notice. Now Gentlemen, are there any unanswered questions?"

"Yes Sir," A soldier interrupted, "what will happen to the seals if we abort, they will all be butchered by this maniac."

"They are setting up ropes in readiness of any emergency evacuation, so they will be able to abseil down the cliff face. This way hopefully any casualties will be kept to a bare minimum. Now if there are no more questions, then all that's left for me to say to you is good luck gentlemen, we are all praying for you here." Charles finished as he ended his call.

"Right lads," began April, "we're approximately at the halfway point now. You are all aware of just how dangerous a wild animal is when it is cornered: well let me tell you that Carlos De-Mundo is the wildest of them all. So be very careful out there. Although those that are left seem to be only a rabble, remember they are armed to the teeth with nothing to lose. The drugs and cheap plonk that they keep taking have incensed them, and so they will be completely fearless to any possible danger. They are not like your normal adversaries, logical and predictable, these are untrained and unpredictable. And always remember that innocent civilians are possibly being held in there, so you must keep that important fact uppermost in your mind at all times. Although I admit that some civilian casualties may be unavoidable this time, because the annihilation of the De-Mundo's Empire must always take precedence over everything else. We'll soon break cover when we reach open land for the last mile or so, so wait at the end of the undergrowth for my signal to advance before you emerge."

As they neared the clearing lights could be seen reflecting in the clear moonlit sky.

"What are those lights, Bass?"

"It looks like lights from the villa, so maybe they're having a party, April."

"Let's hope so, but I can't hear any sounds, music, singing etc. So I'm not sure if you're right."

"Well April, we'll know in the next five minutes as we are nearing the edge of the clearing now. You're very fit too have kept up with us."

"Don't be so chauvinistic; let's just say that I work out a lot. We must press on now," April urged, as a shot rang out.

"Come out, come out, whoever you are," Carlos was heard calling over a megaphone.

"You were right about the noise travelling, Bass. It looks as if we are expected," April admitted, as they reached the edge of the clearing. Lying flat on the ground as they observed the villa through the field glasses, they looked in horror at the spectacle that confronted them.

Carlos had captured the squad of navy seals and was using them to strengthen his human shield. He'd forced them to strip to their underclothes and they were kneeling with their hands clasped behind their neck.

"If you don't show yourselves before I count to ten, well then I'll start executing these stupid bastards. One, two-"

"Bass, I'll show myself alone and hope the surprise it'll give him will buy you a little more time. At least that's what I hope it will do. Tell the choppers to start firing at the cliff face in five minutes from now? And then all of you edge to the flanks and advance on the villa from each side, while I hold his attention. It's my guess he'll pepper this area of undergrowth with indiscriminate automatic gunfire. So now let's go."

"Six, seven, I mean it you cowards. I'll shoot them," De-Mundo threatened again.

Ignoring Bass's objections, April tucked a small pistol into one of her boots, and a knife into the other. Wearing dark glasses she stepped into the open as Carlos's count reached nine. "Okay," she shouted, as Carlos stopped his count, "I'm coming out now so don't shoot."

Carlos didn't recognise her as he said to his men, "See, they can't find any more men too fight, so they're using women instead now." April got within twenty yards of them when he ordered his men to fire into the undergrowth, as she'd anticipated he'd do. They concentrated their fire on where she had just emerged from. "And you lady will be a welcome source of pleasure for me and my loyal troops. Now drop your weapons, and that includes your backup. But do it very slowly."

April greeted him with, "Nice to see you haven't changed much, Carlos. You're still the sick bastard I remember you to be." As she tossed the AKA rifle to the right, followed by her pistol from the back of her belt. By now April was standing within a few feet of him.

Looking extremely perplexed, Carlos asked, "Do I know you? When did we meet?"

"My, you have got a short memory. Your own dope must have killed off what was left of your tiny little brain cell. Now let those poor soldiers get dressed while I remind you?"

"You're in no position to give me orders lady it seems you were a fool to come here alone. Take off her glasses," he ordered a guard, as he became even more intrigued, "I need to see the bitch's face."

She had calculated that most of his men had emerged to the front of the villa by now. This would leave only a handful, if any, to guard the innocent civilians.

As a leering guard reached for her glasses, April warned him, "Touch them and I'll break your fucking arm soldier."

Carlos stood up and nervously approached, "There's only one person with that much gall, and I killed her. So who are you?" Standing within inches of April's face he tried hard to identify her, while still holding a gun pointed at her head. "For the last time, who the fucking hell are you, bitch."

"I've told you before not to call me a bitch, I don't like it. I'm not a dog, and your breath hasn't sweetened up any either I see," she continued to goad him.

Knowing that it was now near to the time for the attack to start, April removed her glasses. She stared into the face of Carlos De-Mundo and watched the blood draining from him as his legs started to buckle.

"Hello, Carlos. Remember me?" April said with a menacing tone to her voice as she wrestled the gun from his hands.

"Y, you are de, dead," Carlos stuttered, as one of his men kicked the pistol from April's hand. "I'll make sure you die this time. I'll cut your fucking heart out, you obnoxious fucking bitch." Carlos threatened, as he pulled his knife from its sheath and lunged towards her.

As she dodged his attack he accidentally plunged the knife into one of his unsuspecting guards. Carlos, seething with anger made an attempt to grab April by the throat, only to trip over the dying man that he'd just stabbed.

Amid the noise and mayhem, the half-naked seals grabbed their clothes and freed the civilian hostages, leading them to the safety of the bush. The troops now were able to advance and close in on the villa, as April tried to avoid the bullets of the oncoming troops. Carlos knocked April to the floor with a blow to the back of her head, and grabbed for her.

"If I'm going to die then you're coming with me, you bitch," he yelled as he reached for a machete and swung wildly at April head.

Trying to avoid the wild swinging of the machete, she rolled to the left and right. She felt a searing pain as the machete cut into her body. Unable to reach the gun in her boot because of her injuries, April struggled. She pulled the knife from the other boot with her uninjured arm.

She could barely manage to push Carlos away due to her injured with the blood flowing profusely down her, as he hacked a deep cut into April's only uninjured limb.

"DIE YOU FUCKING ENGLISH BITCH. DIE," Carlos yelled like the mad man that he was, as he dived on top of April delivering a glancing blow from the machete to her head.

April tried unsuccessfully to move and avoid it.

But luckily for her, Carlos had fallen onto her knife and pierced his heart, and his evil life slowly oozed from his body.

"Are you alright, April? Medic, get over here quickly?" She could hear the concerned voice of Sergeant Bass Maloney calling as the gunfire ceased, and the remaining bedraggled men of the fallen drugs Baron surrendered willingly. Or they committed suicide by jumping from the cliff.

The amount of blood that April was losing carried her quickly into a state of shock, as she fell quickly into unconsciousness.

CHAPTER 33

S he awoke abruptly as the nurse disturbed her to administer treatment. She realised that her life from that fateful day when she was innocently having a quiet drink with her wife and friends, until the present day when she was recovering from her injuries, had just flashed through her in a dream, which made April pine even more to return to her past existence.

Continuing to recover quickly, she relished the opportunity she now had to relax and recuperate in peace. When affairs of state would allow, April had long flirtatious telephone conversations with Walter, the American President. Then after only three weeks had elapsed the doctor revisited her room.

"Sir Charles was right about your healing powers being quite remarkable. In fact, if I'd not witnessed it for myself I would never have believed it. Anyway Miss Darling, you're well enough to leave us I'm sorry to say, because we've all enjoyed your so pleasant company. The President has insisted on sending his personal helicopter to collect you."

After dressing and packing her remaining sparse belongings, April sat patiently waiting for her transport to arrive. She didn't wait for long before the helicopter was landing, and April was bidding the entire medical staff a final farewell.

Enjoying the ride without incident, April watched as the helicopter eventually descended on the grounds of the White House. Walter was there to meet her personally, and with his security staff flanked them, he ushered April through and into the oval office.

Chatting like old friends as they took coffee, April eventually reminded him that she needed to visit some costumiers. To buy more suitable attire to attend the planned banquet that evening.

The President insisted on a member of his security staff escorts her, and suggested that April took his personnel assistant with her as a guide, and as somebody who could advise her of which shops she should visit.

She confidently entered the Grand Hall that evening dressed in a long gold figure hugging dress, with a plunging neckline. April adorned herself in equally extravagantly matching accessories, and a broad black belt to accentuate her trim figure. Walter stood and his guests followed his lead when April's impending arrival was finally announced.

"You're simply breathtaking, April. Simply breathtaking," Walter complemented her. Adding as he broke with protocol and sat her besides him, "I wish you could be by my side permanently as my first lady, April."

"Well I don't think even you would get that idea through congress. Remember I'm not an American citizen. Plus, they'll never be able to research my past, so I'm not of the right breeding stock for those fuddy-duddies who you need to support you. So you'll have to be content with just this dinner date I'm afraid, Mr. President."

"I'm the President of the United States of America, so I can do anything I so wish too. I can even change the criteria for selecting a first lady." The President whispered as they were served the sweet course.

"Don't you realise Mr. President that you're ignoring all of your other more influential guests?"

"What other guests," he jested, as they began to giggle.

The elderly gentleman sitting opposite interrupted. "If I may be so bold as to butt into you're enthralling conversation, Mr. President?" He paused while he waited for permission to continue. After Walter nodded his consent, he continued, "Miss Darling, as an old fuddy-duddy as you called us, I agree that you are a breathtaking vision of peerless beauty. There's not a man, or woman, at this very table this evening, who does not keep giving you furtive admiring glances because of your very presence. And we know that Mr. President has never ever looked as happy as he does tonight. As we're all very influential people at this table, then you would most certainly get our backing."

As April glanced towards Walter he smiled and raised his eyebrows, inviting her to respond.

"I'll need to return to England in the next couple of days, so that I can finish off my report, and to officiate at a dear friend's wedding. You know what I've just been through, Mr. President, so I need a little more time to come to terms with that also. So can I take a rain check, and then we can just take things one step at a time, please everybody?"

"Of course we can, April, but we must keep in touch at all times though. Promise me that much at least?" The President insisted. "And in the mean time I'll push ahead with my new criteria for selecting a, First Lady."

"I promise to keep in contact with you, Mr. President," April vowed, as they all withdrew to the ballroom for the remainder of the evening's entertainment.

All too soon the time was reached when April was to bid Walter, and America, a fond farewell, and return to England. She busied herself submitting her report and avoided any contact with Mandy and Charles as much as she possibly could.

As April shopped in preparation for the wedding her phone rang. "Hello Charles, to what do I owe this unexpected pleasure?"

"The President has been on the phone constantly to me, he's been asking me when we'll be able to allow you to return to the States."

"I've already told him that I need to attend your wedding before I can go anywhere."

"He's admitted that, but he's growing impatient waiting for you. I know that he's completely enthralled by you."

"Well, throw a bucket of cold water over him, Charles. You know he's got designs on me that could never possibly be allowed to happen. And you know I could never get closely involved with anybody, let alone a man in such an influential position."

"You've lost me now, April. Why can't you?"

"Charles, have YOU forgotten who I really am. My past, or lack of it, makes me the most unacceptable woman on this planet, particularly when it comes to any future planning that is, which would include me and any third party on a permanent basis."

"I know what you mean, but nobody outside of this department needs to ever know about any of that. Can't we let it just be our little secret, April. I promise you that I'll never let it ever leak out."

"No, well I think it's already out. Remember our trip up to Rivulet, Charles? Besides, I could never take the chance of somebody else finding out. You've really fucked my life up good and proper, haven't you?"

"You're making a mountain out of a molehill, but as that's how you feel I will have to give it some more thought and get back to you about it." He promised, as he rang off.

The day eventually arrived, but it felt far too soon, when April's precious Mandy was to begin her new life that would leave no room for April in it. Passing without a hitch, April was pleased when the proceedings were drawing to a close. She had purposely tried to avoid Mandy or Charles.

Mandy eventually came and sought her out, "Have you been avoiding me darling? You know I want some photographs with you, and, with you and Charles, and with the children too?"

"So where are you going for your honeymoon, Mandy. Who will be taking care of the children while you're away?" April asked, trying to look unconcerned and to change the subject.

"We're going to Kenya for a month and taking the children with us, April my darling. You don't mind do you?"

"Why should I mind, though I must say it's very unusual taking the children on honeymoon with you, but I guess it's a novel thing to do, so have a nice time and say goodbye to Charles and the children, for me." April asked, kissing her on the cheek and trying to avoid the photographic session. "I'll see you after you all return home," April said hastily, trying to beat a speedy retreat and ignore Mandy's request to stay for longer. "This is your day Mandy, so I must go now and let you enjoy it."

"Oh please, April. Don't be like that. This will all mean nothing without your blessing."

"Okay pet, but after the photographs I must leave. This all brings back such painful memories for me, as you must well be able to imagine?"

Mandy hurriedly assembled Charles, the children and the photographer, together.

The photographer took an assortment of photos, which included Mandy and April, the children and April, and one with Charles and April, plus a family group which included them all.

Again April tried to leave but Charles took her to one side, saying, "Firstly my dear, I promise I'll stop the department and anybody else, from ever trying to retrieve any money from you ever again. You have more than earned what you have been given. Secondly, I've given your dilemma a lot of thought, and I hope you don't mind but I got the Prime Ministers permission to take the American President into our confidence. I have explained to him about your lack of history and about why, and that it was not your choice. I explained to him that it had all been forced upon you, and the reasons why it had been. I've also explained that you felt that there could never be a future for you with him, or anybody else because of this. He was very surprised, as you can well imagine, but very sympathetic towards you as well. He said that he would contact you as soon as he can get the time, so let's just see how it goes from here on?"

"That sounds more like a Dear John to me, Charles. Anyway it doesn't matter anymore, I'm getting used to being alone. I need to get away on my own to ponder my problems, so that I can decide what I really want to do next. So Charles, you enjoy your honeymoon and don't worry about me. I'll be okay. You have made me into the ultimate survivor, remember?"

"I know that. But I still can't help feeling responsible for you being so sad. Remember you're a very special lady to me, and to all of us for that matter. So wherever you go you must promise me you'll always keep in touch with us."

"You should feel responsible because it was you who fucked me up in the first place. Anyway, I'm sure you'll be able to find me if you ever really need too. Otherwise, I'll be back here after I've rested." April said sadly as she reached her car. "So good bye and good luck, Charles, and take extra special care of Mandy and the children for me. If you don't, you'll forever regret what you've created in me. And that is a threat." April warned him, pushing the accelerator to the floor and speeding off towards her apartment.

After receiving Mandy's text telling her that they were about to board the Kenya bound flight, she said that she would contact April immediately on her return to England. April now felt a profound sadness, knowing that even if she could find a way of returning to her original gender, any dreams April had of returning to her original family life as it was, had just been shattered beyond all redemption.

A few days later April was soaking in a warm bath as she tried to take stock of her life. It seemed any chance of becoming George again was extremely unlikely, and that any close friendships with Walter was also out of the question. He had not even contacted her since Charles explained to him about her lack of history, and the reason for it. So April must prepare herself now for a life full to the brim with solitude and disappointments.

After restocking her wardrobe, she put her affairs in order with a visit to the accountant, and then April visited her solicitor to alter her Will, so it would now only favour her beloved children.

She then made a conscious decision to pamper herself before visiting Haiti and Columbia. Booking the flights before packed her suitcase and heading to the airport, so she could take a much-earned holiday amongst her few genuine friends.

April approached the checking-in desk to book in, her mobile phone rang. It was Walter, "Hello, Mr. President," she started cautiously, "how are you keeping these days?"

"I'm fine, April. I'm sorry that I've taken so long in contacting you again my love, but I needed to get the Senates on our side, so we can start planning for a future, hopefully one in which we can be together. Now we need to meet again as soon as possible to discuss it. There is so much we need to talk about."

"I'm at the airport now en-route to Haiti and Columbia, just so that I can fulfil a promise and visit some very dear friends of mine. They saved my life you know? I thought there was to be a no us. Well not after Charles spoke to you and you never rang me," she explained through floods of tears.

"You're the most beautiful, sensitive, genuine and caring person I've ever known, so how could you ever think that I would think any less of you? I thought you knew me better than that. From what Sir Charles has said I believe that you have not been changed, well not as a normal transsexual would have been changed. You have actually been transformed using original female organs transplanted into you. Sort of rebuilt so to speak, which is what made it much easier for me to plead my, no, our, case and to win over the Senators. So please don't cry. Now I'm planning to visit the depleted rain forest in Columbia next week to see it for myself, so can I meet you there, April?"

"Oh yes please, Walter. I would like that very much. When you've made the final arrangements please ring me back with all the details. I must go now the plane is boarding. I do miss you so very much my love." April finished, as she complied with the regulations and turned off her mobile phone.

With a lighter more hopeful heart, April preceded on her way to board the Haiti bound plane. She was silently praying, and thanking God for His kind blessings, and asking Him for a safe and relaxing flight and vacation.

Although she still knew that she had a very uncertain future ahead. She now carried a heart full of hope that she'd be able to start to rebuild a new life, not the one that had been so viciously forced upon her.

She hoped that the meeting with the American President could prove to be the final missing link that she'd been missing in her new persona's jigsaw, and also hoped and prayed that it would finalise the completion in her transition into, Miss April Darling. At least April would hope that it would. And so she looked forward to a new chapter in her life, but left to wonder what it would now hold.

www.ingramcontent.com/pod-product-compliance
Lightning Source LLC
Chambersburg PA
CBHW020239120726
47904CB00001B/20